WOMEN CRIME WRITERS

FOUR SUSPENSE
NOVELS OF THE 1940s

WOMEN CRIME WRITERS

FOUR SUSPENSE NOVELS OF THE 1940s

Laura • Vera Caspary
The Horizontal Man • Helen Eustis
In a Lonely Place • Dorothy B. Hughes
The Blank Wall • Elisabeth Sanxay Holding

Sarah Weinman, *editor*

THE LIBRARY OF AMERICA

Visit our website at www.loa.org.

This paper meets the requirements of
ANSI/NISO Z39.48–1992 (Permanence of Paper).

Distributed to the trade in the United States
by Penguin Random House Inc.
and in Canada by Penguin Random House Canada Ltd.

Library of Congress Control Number: 2014959884
ISBN 978–1–59853–430–6

Second Printing
The Library of America—268

Manufactured in the United States of America

Contents

For an online companion to this volume visit womencrime.loa.org.

LAURA

Vera Caspary

PART ONE

I

THE CITY that Sunday morning was quiet. Those millions of New Yorkers who, by need or preference, remain in town over a summer week-end had been crushed spiritless by humidity. Over the island hung a fog that smelled and felt like water in which too many soda-water glasses have been washed. Sitting at my desk, pen in hand, I treasured the sense that, among those millions, only I, Waldo Lydecker, was up and doing. The day just past, devoted to shock and misery, had stripped me of sorrow. Now I had gathered strength for the writing of Laura's epitaph. My grief at her sudden and violent death found consolation in the thought that my friend, had she lived to a ripe old age, would have passed into oblivion, whereas the violence of her passing and the genius of her admirer gave her a fair chance at immortality.

My doorbell rang. Its electric vibrations had barely ceased when Roberto, my Filipino manservant, came to tell me that Mr. McPherson had asked to see me.

"Mark McPherson!" I exclaimed, and then, assuming the air of one who might meet Mussolini without trepidation, I bade Roberto ask Mr. McPherson to wait. Mahomet had not rushed out to meet the mountain.

This visit of a not unimportant member of the Police Department—although I am still uncertain of his title or office—conferred a certain honor. Lesser folk are unceremoniously questioned at Headquarters. But what had young McPherson to do with the murder? His triumphs were concerned with political rather than civil crime. In the case of The People of New York vs. Associated Dairymen his findings had been responsible—or so the editorial writers said—for bringing down the price of milk a penny a quart. A senatorial committee had borrowed him for an investigation of labor rackets, and only recently his name had been offered by a group of progressives as leader of a national inquiry into defense profits.

Screened by the half-open door of my study, I watched him move restlessly about my drawing-room. He was the sort of man, I saw at once, who affects to scorn affectation; a veritable

Cassius who emphasized the lean and hungry look by clothing himself darkly in blue, double-breasted worsted, unadorned white shirt and dull tie. His hands were long and tense, his face slender, his eyes watchful, his nose a direct inheritance from those dour ancestors who had sniffed sin with such constancy that their very nostrils had become aggressive. He carried his shoulders high and walked with a taut erectness as if he were careful of being watched. My drawing-room irritated him; to a man of his fiercely virile temperament, the delicate perfection must be cloying. It was audacious, I admit, to expect appreciation. Was it not slightly optimistic of me to imagine that good taste was responsible for the concentration with which he studied my not unworthy collection of British and American glassware?

I noted that his scowl was fixed upon a shining object, one of my peculiar treasures. Habit, then, had made him alert to detail. On the mantel of Laura's living-room he had, no doubt, observed the partner to my globe-and-pedestal vase of mercury glass. He stretched his hand toward the shelf.

I leaped like a mother leopard.

"Careful, young man. That stuff's priceless."

He turned so sharply that the small rug slid along the polished floor. As he steadied himself against the cabinet, porcelain and glass danced upon the shelves.

"A bull in a china shop," I remarked. The pun restored my humor. I extended my hand.

He smiled mechanically. "I'm here to talk about the Laura Hunt case, Mr. Lydecker."

"Naturally. Have a seat."

He settled his long frame carefully upon a frail chair. I offered cigarettes from a Haviland casket, but he pulled out a pipe.

"You're supposed to be quite an authority on crime yourself, Mr. Lydecker. What do you think about this business?"

I warmed. No writer, however popular, disdains a reader, however humble. "I am honored to know that you read *And More Anon*."

"Only when my paper happens to open to the page."

The affront was not displeasing. In the world I frequent,

where personality is generously exposed and friendship offered without reticence, his aloofness struck an uncommon note. I offered my charm. "You may not be a Lydecker fan, Mr. McPherson, but I confess that I've followed your career with breathless excitement."

"You ought to know enough not to believe everything you read in the papers," he said dryly.

I was not to be discouraged. "Isn't criminal investigation a bit out of your line? A trifle unimportant for a man of your achievements?"

"I've been assigned to the case."

"Office politics?"

Except for the purp-purp of his pipe, the room was silent.

"The month is August," I mused. "The Commissioner is off on his holiday, the Deputy Commissioner has always been resentful of your success, and since retail murder is somewhat out of fashion these days and usually, after the first sensation, relegated to Page Two or worse, he has found a convenient way of diminishing your importance."

"The plain truth, if you want to know it"—he was obviously annoyed with himself for bothering to give an excuse—"is that he knew I wanted to see the Dodgers play Boston yesterday afternoon."

I was enchanted. "From trifling enmities do great adventures grow."

"Great adventures! A two-timing dame gets murdered in her flat. So what? A man did it. Find the man. Believe me, Mr. Lydecker, I'm seeing the game this afternoon. The killer himself couldn't stop me."

Pained by his vulgar estimate of my beloved Laura, I spoke mockingly. "Baseball, eh? No wonder your profession has fallen upon evil days. The Great Detectives neither rested nor relaxed until they had relentlessly tracked down their quarry."

"I'm a workingman, I've got hours like everyone else. And if you expect me to work overtime on this third-class mystery, you're thinking of a couple of other fellows."

"Crime doesn't stop because it's Sunday."

"From what I've seen of your late girl friend, Mr. Lydecker, I'd bet my bottom dollar that whoever did that job takes his

Sunday off like the rest of us. Probably sleeping until noon and waking himself up with three brandies. Besides, I've got a couple of men working on detail."

"To a man of your achievement, Mr. McPherson, the investigation of a simple murder is probably as interesting as a column of figures to a public accountant who started as a bookkeeper."

This time he laughed. The shell of toughness was wearing thin. He shifted in his chair.

"The sofa," I urged gently, "might be easier on that leg."

He scowled. "Observant, aren't you?"

"You walk carefully, McPherson. Most members of your profession tread like elephants. But since you're sensitive, let me assure you that it's not conspicuous. Extreme astigmatism gives me greater power in the observation of other people's handicaps."

"It's no handicap," he retorted.

"Souvenir of service?" I inquired.

He nodded. "Babylon."

I bounced out of my chair. "The Siege of Babylon, Long Island! Have you read my piece? Wait a minute . . . don't tell me you're the one with the silver fibula."

"Tibia."

"How magnificently exciting! Mattie Grayson! There was a man. Killers aren't what they used to be."

"That's okay with me."

"How many detectives did he get?"

"Three of us with the machine-gun at his mother-in-law's house. Then a couple of us went after him down the alley. Three died and another guy—he got it in the lungs—is still up in Saranac."

"Honorable wounds. You shouldn't be sensitive. How brave it was of you to go back!"

"I was lucky to get back. There was a time, Mr. Lydecker, when I saw a great future as a night watchman. Bravery's got nothing to do with it. A job's a job. Hell, I'm as gun-shy as a traveling salesman that's known too many farmers' daughters."

I laughed aloud. "For a few minutes there, McPherson, I was afraid you had all the Scotch virtues except humor and a taste for good whiskey. How about the whiskey, man?"

"Don't care if I do."

I poured him a stiff one. He took it like the pure waters of Loch Lomond and returned the empty glass for another.

"I hope you don't mind the crack I made about your column, Mr. Lydecker. To tell the truth, I do read it once in a while."

"Why don't you like it?"

Without hesitancy he answered, "You're smooth all right, but you've got nothing to say."

"McPherson, you're a snob. And what's worse, a Scotch snob, than which—as no less an authority than Thackeray has remarked—the world contains no more offensive creature."

He poured his own whiskey this time.

"What is your idea of good literature, Mr. McPherson?"

When he laughed he looked like a Scotch boy who has just learned to accept pleasure without fear of sin. "Yesterday morning, after the body was discovered and we learned that Laura Hunt had stood you up for dinner on Friday night, Sergeant Schultz was sent up here to question you. So he asks you what you did all evening . . ."

"And I told him," I interrupted, "that I had eaten a lonely dinner, reviling the woman for her desertion, and read Gibbon in a tepid tub."

"Yeh, and you know what Schultz says? He says this writer guy, Gibbon, must be pretty hot for you to have to read him in a cold bath." After a brief pause, he continued, "I've read Gibbon myself, the whole set, and Prescott and Motley and Josephus' *History of the Jews.*" There was exuberance in the confession.

"At college or *pour le sport*?" I asked.

"When does a dick get a chance to go to college? But being laid up in the hospital fourteen months, what can you do but read books?"

"That, I take it, is when you became interested in the social backgrounds of crime."

"Up to that time I was a cluck," he confessed modestly.

"Mattie Grayson's machine-gun wasn't such a tragedy, then. You'd probably still be a cluck on the Homicide Squad."

"You like a man better if he's not hundred per cent, don't you, Mr. Lydecker?"

"I've always doubted the sensibilities of Apollo Belvedere."

Roberto announced breakfast. With his natural good manners, he had set a second place at the table. Mark protested at my invitation since he had come here, not as a guest, but in the pursuit of duty which must be as onerous to me as to himself.

I laughed away his embarrassment. "This is in the line of duty. We haven't even started talking about the murder and I don't propose to starve while we do."

Twenty-four hours earlier a cynical but not unkindly police officer had come into my dining-room with the news that Laura's body had been discovered in her apartment. No morsel of food had passed my lips since that moment when Sergeant Schultz had interrupted a peaceful breakfast with the news that Laura Hunt, after failing to keep her dinner engagement with me, had been shot and killed. Now, in the attempt to restore my failing appetite, Roberto had stewed kidneys and mushrooms in claret. While we ate, Mark described the scene at the morgue where Laura's body had been identified by Bessie, her maid, and her aunt, Susan Treadwell.

In spite of deep suffering, I could not but enjoy the contrast between the young man's appreciation of the meal and the morbid quality of his talk. "When they were shown the body"—he paused to lift a morsel on his fork—"both women collapsed. It was hard to take even if you didn't know her. A lot of blood"—he soaked a bit of toast in the sauce. "With BB shot . . . You can imagine . . ."

I closed my eyes as if she lay there on the Aubusson rug, as Bessie had discovered her, naked except for a blue silk taffeta robe and a pair of silver slippers.

"Fired at close range"—he spooned relish on his plate. "Mrs. Treadwell passed out, but the servant took it like a veteran. She's a queer duck, that Bessie."

"She's been more than maid to Laura. Guide, philosopher, and worst enemy of all of Laura's best friends. Cooks like an angel, but serves bitter herbs with the choicest roasts. No man that entered the apartment was, in Bessie's opinion, good enough for Laura."

"She was cool as a cucumber when the boys got there. Opened the door and pointed to the body so calmly you'd have thought it was an everyday thing for her to find her boss murdered."

"That's Bessie," I commented. "But wait till you get her roused."

Roberto brought in the coffee. Eighteen stories below a motorist blew his siren. Through open windows we heard the rhythms of a Sunday morning radio concert.

"No! No! No!" I cried as Roberto handed Mark my Napoleon cup. I reached across the table and took it myself, leaving the Empress Josephine for my guest.

He drank his coffee in silent disapproval, watching as I unscrewed the carnelian cap of the silver box in which I keep my saccharine tablets. Although I spread butter lavishly on my brioches, I cling religiously to the belief that the substitution of saccharine for sugar in coffee will make me slender and fascinating. His scorn robbed my attitudes of character.

"I must say you go about your work in a leisurely way," I remarked petulantly. "Why don't you go out and take some fingerprints?"

"There are times in the investigation of a crime when it's more important to look at faces."

I turned to the mirror. "How singularly innocent I seem this morning! Tell me, McPherson, have you ever seen such candid eyes?" I took off my glasses and presented my face, round and pink as a cherub's. "But speaking of faces, McPherson, have you met the bridegroom?"

"Shelby Carpenter. I'm seeing him at twelve. He's staying with Mrs. Treadwell."

I seized the fact avidly. "Shelby staying there! Wouldn't he just?"

"He finds the Hotel Framingham too public. Crowds wait in the lobby to see the fellow who was going to marry a murder victim."

"What do you think of Shelby's alibi?"

"What do I think of yours?" he retorted.

"But you've agreed that it's quite normal for a man to spend an evening at home with Gibbon."

"What's wrong about a man going to a Stadium concert?" Puritan nostrils quivered. "Among a lot of music-lovers and art collectors, that seems a pretty natural way to spend an evening."

"If you knew the bridegroom, you'd not think a twenty-five-

cent seat normal. But he finds it a convenient way of not having
been seen by any of his friends."

"I'm always grateful for information, Mr. Lydecker, but I
prefer forming my own opinions."

"Neat, McPherson. Very neat."

"How long had you known her, Mr. Lydecker?"

"Seven, eight—yes, it was eight years," I told him. "We met
in '34. Shall I tell you about it?"

Mark puffed at his pipe, the room was filled with its rancid
sweet odor. Roberto entered noiselessly to refill the coffee-
cups. The radio orchestra played a rhumba.

"She rang my doorbell, McPherson, much as you rang it
this morning. I was working at my desk, writing, as I remember, a birthday piece about a certain eminent American, the
Father of Our Country. I should never have committed such a
cliché, but, as my editor had asked for it and as we were in the
midst of some rather delicate financial rearrangements, I had
decided that I could not but gain by appeasement. Just as I
was about to throw away a substantial increase in earning
power as indulgence for my boredom, this lovely child entered
my life."

I should have been an actor. Had I been physically better
suited to the narcissistic profession, I should probably have
been among the greatest of my time. Now, as Mark let the
second cup of coffee grow cold, he saw me as I had been eight
years before, wrapped in the same style of Persian dressing-
gown, pad on loose Japanese clogs to answer the doorbell.

"Carlo, who was Roberto's predecessor, had gone out to do
the daily marketing. I think she was surprised to see that I answered my own doorbell. She was a slender thing, timid as a
fawn and fawn-like, too, in her young uncertain grace. She had
a tiny head, delicate for even that thin body, and the tilt of it
along with the bright shyness of her slightly oblique dark eyes
further contributed to the sense that Bambi—or Bambi's
doe—had escaped from the forest and galloped up the eighteen flights to this apartment.

"When I asked why she had come, she gave a little clucking
sound. Fear had taken her voice. I was certain that she had
walked around and around the building before daring to enter,

and that she had stood in the corridor hearing her own heart pound before she dared touch a frightened finger to my door-bell.

"'Well, out with it!' Unwilling to acknowledge that I had been touched by her pretty shyness, I spoke harshly. My temper was more choleric in those days, Mr. McPherson.

"She spoke softly and very rapidly. I remember it as all one sentence, beginning with a plea that I forgive her for disturbing me and then promising that I should receive huge publicity for reward if I would endorse a fountain pen her employers were advertising. It was called the Byron.

"I exploded. 'Give *me* publicity, my good girl! Your reasoning is sadly distorted. It's my name that will give distinction to your cheap fountain pen. And how dared you take the sacred name of Byron? Who gave you the right? I've a good mind to write the manufacturers a stiff letter.'

"I tried not to notice the brightness of her eyes, McPherson. I was not aware at this time that she had named the fountain pen herself and that she was proud of its literary sound. She persisted bravely, telling me about a fifty-thousand-dollar advertising campaign which could not fail to glorify my name.

"I felt it my duty to become apoplectic. 'Do you know how many dollars' worth of white space my syndicated columns now occupy? And do you realize that manufacturers of typewriters, toothpaste, and razors with fifty-thousand-dollar checks in their pockets are turned away from this door daily? You talk of giving me publicity!'

"Her embarrassment was painful. I asked if she would stay and have a glass of sherry. Doubtless she would have preferred flight, but she was too shy to refuse. While we drank the sherry, I made her tell me about herself. This was her first job and it represented the apex of her ambitions at the time. She had visited sixty-eight advertising agencies before she got the job. Buried beneath that air of timidity was a magnificent will. Laura knew she was clever, and she was willing to suffer endless rebuffs in order to prove her talents. When she had finished, I said, 'I suppose you think I'm moved by your story and that I'm going to break down and give you that endorsement.'"

"Did you?" Mark inquired.

"McPherson, I am the most mercenary man in America. I never take any action without computing the profit."

"You gave her the endorsement."

I bowed my head in shame. "For seven years Waldo Lydecker has enthusiastically acclaimed the Byron Pen. Without it, I am sure that my collected essays would never sell one hundred thousand copies."

"She must have been a terrific kid," he remarked.

"Only mildly terrific at that period. I recognized her possibilities, however. The next week I entertained her at dinner. That was the beginning. Under my tutelage she developed from a gauche child to a gracious New Yorker. After a year no one would have suspected that she came from Colorado Springs. And she remained loyal and appreciative, McPherson. Of all my friends she is the only one with whom I was willing to share my prestige. She became as well known at opening nights as Waldo Lydecker's graying Van Dyke or his gold-banded stick."

My guest offered no comment. The saturnine mood had returned. Scotch piety and Brooklyn poverty had developed his resistance to chic women. "Was she ever in love with you?"

I recoiled. My answer came in a thick voice. "Laura was always fond of me. She rejected suitor after suitor during those eight years of loyalty."

The contradiction was named Shelby Carpenter. But explanation would come later. Mark knew the value of silence in dealing with such a voluble creature as myself.

"My *love* for Laura," I explained, "was not merely the desire of a mature man for a pretty young thing. There was a deeper basis of affection. Laura had made me a generous man. It's quite fallacious to believe that we grow fond of those whom we've hurt. Remorse cannot compensate. It's more human to shun those whose presence reminds us of a shoddy past. Generosity, not evil, flourishes like the green bay tree. Laura considered me the kindest man in the universe, hence I had to grow to that stature. For her I was always Jovian, in humanity as well as intelligence."

I suspected doubt behind his swift glance of appraisal. He rose. "It's getting late. I've got a date with Carpenter."

"Behold, the bridegroom waits!" As we walked to the door, I added, "I wonder how you're going to like Shelby."

"It's not my business to like or dislike anyone. I'm only interested in her friends . . ."

"As suspects?" I teased.

"For information. I shall probably call on you again, Mr. Lydecker."

"Whenever you like. I do indeed hope to aid, if I can, in the apprehension of the vile being—we can't call him human, can we?—who could have performed such a villainous and uselessly tragic deed. But in the meantime I shall be curious to know your opinion of Shelby."

"You don't think much of him yourself, do you?"

"Shelby was Laura's other life." I stood with my hand on the doorknob. "To my prejudiced way of thinking, the more commonplace and less distinguished side of her existence. But judge for yourself, young man."

We shook hands.

"To solve the puzzle of her death, you must first resolve the mystery of Laura's life. This is no simple task. She had no secret fortune, no hidden rubies. But, I warn you, McPherson, the activities of crooks and racketeers will seem simple in comparison with the motives of a modern woman."

He showed impatience.

"A complicated, cultivated modern woman. 'Concealment, like a worm i' the bud, fed on her damask cheek.' I shall be at your command whenever you call, McPherson. Au revoir."

I stood at the door until he had got into the elevator.

II

WHILE A not inconsiderable share of my work has been devoted to the study of murder, I have never stooped to the narration of a mystery story. At the risk of seeming somewhat less than modest, I shall quote from my own works. The sentence, so often reprinted, that opens my essay "Of Sound and Fury,"[1] is pertinent here:

"When, during the 1936 campaign, I learned that the President was a devotee of mystery stories, I voted a straight Republican ticket."

My prejudices have not been shed. I still consider the conventional mystery story an excess of sound and fury, signifying, far worse than nothing, a barbaric need for violence and revenge in that timid horde known as the reading public. The literature of murder investigation bores me as profoundly as its practice irritated Mark McPherson. Yet I am bound to tell this story, just as he was obliged to continue his searches, out of a deep emotional involvement in the case of Laura Hunt. I offer the narrative, not so much as a detective yarn as a love story.

I wish I were its hero. I fancy myself a pensive figure drawn, without conscious will, into a love that was born of violence and destined for tragedy. I am given to thinking of myself in the third person. Many a time, when I have suffered some clumsy misadventure, I am saved from remorse by the substitution for unsavory memory of another captivating installment in *The Life and Times of Waldo Lydecker*. Rare are the nights when I fail to lull myself to sleep without the sedative of some such heroic statement as "Waldo Lydecker stood, untroubled, at the edge of a cliff beneath which ten thousand angry lions roared."

I make this confession at the risk of exhibiting absurdity. My proportions are, if anything, too heroic. While I measure three inches above six feet, the magnificence of my skeleton is hidden by the weight of my flesh. My dreams dwindle in contrast. Yet I dare say that if the dreams of any so-called normal man

[1] In the volume *Time, You Thief*, by Waldo Lydecker, 1938.

were exposed, like Dalí drawings, to the vulgar eyes of the
masses, there would be no more gravity and dignity left for
mankind. At certain times in history, flesh was considered a
sign of good disposition, but we live in a tiresome era wherein
exercise is held sacred and heroes are always slender. I have
more than once endured the ordeal of reducing, but I always
give it up when I reflect that no philosophy or fantasy dare
enter a mind as usurious as Shylock's over each pound of flesh.
So I have learned, at the age of fifty-two, to accept this burden
with the same philosophical calm with which I endure such
indecencies as hot weather and war news.

But it will not be possible to write of myself heroically in
those chapters wherein Mark McPherson moves the story. I
have long learned to uphold my ego in a world that also contains Shelby Carpenter, but the young detective is a more potent man. There is no wax in Mark; he is hard coin metal who
impresses his own definite stamp upon those who seek to
mould him.

He is definite but not simple. His complexities trouble him.
Contemptuous of luxury, he is also charmed by it. He resents
my collection of glass and porcelain, my Biedermeier and my
library, but envies the culture which has developed appreciation of surface lustres. His remarking upon my preference for
men who are less than hundred per cent exposed his own sensitivity. Reared in a world that honors only hundred per cents,
he has learned in maturity what I knew as a miserable, obese
adolescent, that the lame, the halt, and the blind have more
malice in their souls, therefore more acumen. Cherishing secret hurt, they probe for the pains and weaknesses of others.
And probing is the secret of finding. Through telescopic lenses
I discerned in Mark the weakness that normal eyesight might
never discover.

The hard coin metal of his character fails to arouse my envy.
I am jealous of severed bone, of tortured muscle, of scars
whose existence demands such firmness of footstep, such stern,
military erectness. My own failings, obesity, astigmatism, the
softness of pale flesh, can find no such heroic apology. But a
silver shinbone, the legacy of a dying desperado! There is romance in the very anatomy of the man.

For an hour after he had gone, I sat upon the sofa, listless, toying with my envy. That hour exhausted me. I turned for solace to Laura's epitaph. Rhythms failed, words eluded me. Mark had observed that I wrote smoothly but said nothing. I have sometimes suspected this flaw in my talent, but have never faced myself with the admission of failure. Upon that Sunday noon I saw myself as a fat, fussy, and useless male of middle age and doubtful charm. By all that is logical I should have despised Mark McPherson. I could not. For all of his rough edges, he was the man I should have been, the hero of the story.

The hero, but not the interpreter. That is my omniscient rôle. As narrator and interpreter, I shall describe scenes which I never saw and record dialogues which I did not hear. For this impudence I offer no excuse. I am an artist, and it is my business to re-create movement precisely as I create mood. I know these people, their voices ring in my ears, and I need only close my eyes and see characteristic gestures. My written dialogue will have more clarity, compactness, and essence of character than their spoken lines, for I am able to edit while I write, whereas they carried on their conversations in a loose and pointless fashion with no sense of form or crisis in the building of their scenes. And when I write of myself as a character in the story, I shall endeavor to record my flaws with the same objectivity as if I were no more important than any other figure in this macabre romance.

III

LAURA'S AUNT SUSAN once sang in musical comedy. Then she became a widow. The period between—the hyphen of marriage—is best forgotten. Never in the years I have known her have I heard her lament the late Horace Q. Treadwell. The news of Laura's death had brought her hastily from her summer place on Long Island to the mausoleum on upper Fifth Avenue. One servant, a grim Finn, had accompanied her. It was Helga who opened the door for Mark and led him through a maze of dark canals into a vast uncarpeted chamber in which every piece of furniture, every picture and ornament, wore a shroud of pale, striped linen.

This was Mark's first visit to a private home on Fifth Avenue. As he waited, he paced the long room, accosting and retreating from his lean, dark-clad image in a full-length gold-framed mirror. His thoughts dwelt upon the meeting with the bereaved bridegroom. Laura was to have married Shelby Carpenter on the following Thursday. They had passed their blood tests and answered the questions on the application for a marriage license.

Mark knew these facts thoroughly. Shelby had been disarmingly frank with the police sergeant who asked the first questions. Folded in Mark's coat-pocket was a carbon record of the lovers' last meeting. The facts were commonplace but not conventional.

Laura had been infected with the week-end sickness. From the first of May until the last of September, she joined the fanatic mob in week-end pilgrimages to Connecticut. The mouldy house described in "The Fermenting of New England,"[1] was Laura's converted barn. Her garden suffered pernicious anaemia and the sums she spent to fertilize that rocky soil would have provided a purple orchid every day of the year with a corsage of *Odontoglossum grande* for Sundays. But she persisted in the belief that she saved a vast fortune because, for five months of the year, she had only to buy flowers once a week.

After my first visit, no amount of persuasion could induce

[1] In the volume *Time, You Thief*, by Waldo Lydecker, 1938.

me to step foot upon the Wilton train. Shelby, however, was a not unwilling victim. And sometimes she took the maid, Bessie, and thus relieved herself of household duties which she pretended to enjoy. On this Friday, she had decided to leave them both in town. She needed four or five days of loneliness, she told Shelby, to bridge the gap between a Lady Lilith Face Cream campaign and her honeymoon. It would never do to start as a nervous bride. This reasoning satisfied Shelby. It never occurred to him that she might have other plans. Nor did he question her farewell dinner with me. She had arranged, or so she told Shelby, to leave my house in time to catch the ten-twenty train.

She and Shelby had worked for the same advertising agency. At five o'clock on Friday afternoon, he went into her office. She gave her secretary a few final instructions, powdered her nose, reddened her lips, and rode down in the elevator with him. They stopped for Martinis at the Tropicale, a bar frequented by advertising and radio writers. Laura spoke of her plans for the week. She was not certain as to the hour of her return, but she did not expect Shelby to meet her train. The trip to and from Wilton was no more to her than a subway ride. She set Wednesday as the day of her return and promised to telephone him immediately upon her arrival.

As Mark pondered these facts, his eyes on the checkerboard of light and dark woods set into Mrs. Treadwell's floor, he became aware that his restlessness was the subject of nervous scrutiny. The long mirror framed his first impression of Shelby Carpenter. Against the shrouded furniture, Shelby was like a brightly lithographed figure on the gaudy motion-picture poster decorating the sombre granite of an ancient opera house. The dark suit chosen for this day of mourning could not dull his vivid grandeur. Male energy shone in his tanned skin, gleamed from his clear gray eyes, swelled powerful biceps. Later, as Mark told me of the meeting, he confessed that he was puzzled by an almost overwhelming sense of familiarity. Shelby spoke with the voice of a stranger but with lips whose considered smile seemed as familiar as Mark's own reflection. All through the interview and in several later meetings, Mark sought vainly to recall some earlier association. The enigma enraged him. Failure seemed to indicate a softening process within himself. Encounters with Shelby diminished his self-confidence.

They chose chairs at opposite ends of the long room. Shelby had offered, Mark accepted, a Turkish cigarette. Oppressed by Fifth Avenue magnificence, he had barely the courage to ask for an ashtray. And this a man who had faced machine-guns.

Shelby had borne up bravely during the ordeal at Headquarters. As his gentle Southern voice repeated the details of that tragic farewell, he showed clearly that he wished to spare his visitor the effort of sympathy.

"So I put her in the taxi and gave the driver Waldo Lydecker's address. Laura said, 'Good-bye until Wednesday,' and leaned out to kiss me. The next morning the police came to tell me that Bessie had found her body in the apartment. I wouldn't believe it. Laura was in the country. That's what she'd told me, and Laura had not lied to me before."

"We found the taxi-driver and checked with him," Mark informed him. "As soon as they'd turned the corner, she said that he was not to go to Mr. Lydecker's address, but to take her to Grand Central. She'd telephoned Mr. Lydecker earlier in the afternoon to break the dinner date. Have you any idea why she should have lied to you?"

Cigarette smoke curled in flawless circles from Shelby's flawless lips. "I don't like to believe she lied to me. Why should she tell me she was dining with Waldo if she wasn't?"

"She lied twice, first in regard to dining with Mr. Lydecker, and second about leaving town that night."

"I can't believe it. We were always so honest with each other."

Mark accepted the statement without comment. "We've interviewed the porters on duty Friday night at Grand Central and a couple remember her face."

"She always took the Friday night train."

"That's the catch. The only porter who swears to a definite recollection of Laura on this particular night also asked if he'd have his picture in the newspapers. So we strike a dead-end there. She might have taken another taxi from the Forty-Second or Lexington Avenue exits."

"Why?" Shelby sighed. "Why should she have done such a ridiculous thing?"

"If we knew, we might have a reasonable clue. Now as to your alibi, Mr. Carpenter . . ."

Shelby groaned.

"I won't make you go through it again. I've got the details. You had dinner at the Myrtle Cafeteria on Forty-Second Street, you walked to Fifth Avenue, took a bus to a Hundred and Forty-Sixth Street, bought a twenty-five-cent seat for the concert . . ."

Shelby pouted like a hurt child. "I've had some bad times, you know. When I'm alone I try to save money. I'm just getting on my feet again."

"There's no shame in saving money," Mark reminded him. "That's the only reasonable explanation anyone's given for anything so far. You walked home after the concert, eh? Quite a distance."

"The poor man's exercise." Shelby grinned feebly.

Mark dropped the alibi, and with one of those characteristic swift thrusts, asked: "Why didn't you get married before this? Why did the engagement last so long?"

Shelby cleared his throat.

"Money, wasn't it?"

A schoolboy flush ripened Shelby's skin. He spoke bitterly. "When I went to work for Rose, Rowe and Sanders, I made thirty-five dollars a week. She was getting a hundred and seventy-five." He hesitated, the color of his cheeks brightened to the tones of an over-ripe peach. "Not that I resented her success. She was so clever that I was awed and respectful. And I wanted her to make as much as she could; believe that, Mr. McPherson. But it's hard on a man's pride. I was brought up to think of women . . . differently."

"And what made you decide to marry?"

Shelby brightened. "I've had a little success myself."

"But she was still holding a better job. What made you change your mind?"

"There wasn't so much discrepancy. My salary, if not munificent, was respectable. And I felt that I was advancing. Besides, I'd been catching up with my debts. A man doesn't like to get married, you know, while he owes money."

"Except to the woman he's marrying," a shrill voice added.

In the mirror's gilt frame Mark saw the reflection of an advancing figure. She was small, robed in deepest mourning and carrying under her right arm a Pomeranian whose auburn coat matched her own bright hair. As she paused in the door with the marble statues and bronze figurines behind her, the gold frame giving margins to the portrait, she was like a picture done by one of Sargent's imitators who had failed to carry over to the twentieth century the dignity of the nineteenth. Mark had seen her briefly at the inquest and had thought her young to be Laura's aunt. Now he saw that she was well over fifty. The rigid perfection of her face was almost artificial, as if flesh-pink velvet were drawn over an iron frame.

Shelby leaped. "Darling! You remarkable creature! How you've recovered! How can you be so beautiful, darling, when you've gone through such intolerable agonies?" He led her to the room's most important chair.

"I hope you find the fiend"—she addressed Mark but gave attention to her chiffon. "I hope you find him and scrouge his eyes out and drive hot nails through his body and boil him in oil." Her vehemence spent, she tossed Mark her most enchanting smile.

"Comfortable, darling?" Shelby inquired. "How about your fan? Would you like a cool drink?"

Had the dog's affection begun to bore her, she might have dismissed it with the same pretty indifference. To Mark she said: "Has Shelby told you the story of his romantic courtship? I hope he's not left out any of the thrilling episodes."

"Now, darling, what would Laura have said if she could hear you?"

"She'd say I was a jealous bitch. And she'd be right. Except that I'm not jealous. I wouldn't have you on a gold platter, darling."

"You mustn't mind Auntie Sue, Mr. McPherson. She's prejudiced because I'm poor."

"Isn't he cute?" cooed Auntie Sue, petting the dog.

"I never asked Laura for money"—Shelby might have been taking an oath at an altar. "If she were here, she'd swear it, too. I never asked. She knew I was having a hard time and insisted, simply insisted upon lending it to me. She always made money so easily, she said."

"She worked like a dog!" cried Laura's aunt.

The Pomeranian sniffed. Aunt Sue pressed its small nose to her cheek, then settled it upon her lap. Having achieved this enviable position, the Pomeranian looked upon the men smugly.

"Do you know, Mrs. Treadwell, if your niece had any"— Mark produced the word uneasily—"enemies?"

"Enemies!" the good lady shrieked. "Everyone adored her. Didn't everyone adore her, Shelby? She had more friends than money."

"That," Shelby added gravely, "was one of the finest things about her."

"Anyone who had troubles came to her," Aunt Sue declaimed, quite in the manner of the immortal Bernhardt. "I warned her more than once. It's when you put yourself out for people that you find yourself in trouble. Don't you think that's true, Mr. McPherson?"

"I don't know. I've probably not put myself out for enough people." The posturing offended him; he had become curt.

His annoyance failed to check the lady's histrionic aspirations. "'The evil that men do lives after them; the good is oft buried with their bones,'" she misquoted, and giggling lightly, added, "although her poor bones aren't buried yet. But we must be truthful, even about the dead. It wasn't money principally with Laura, it was people, if you know what I mean. She was always running around, doing favors, wasting her time and strength on people she scarcely knew. Remember that model, Shelby, the girl with the fancy name? Laura got me to give her my leopard coat. It wasn't half worn out either. I could have got another winter out of it and spared my mink. Don't you remember, Shelby?"

Shelby had become infatuated with a bronze Diana who had been threatening for years to leap, with dog and stag, from her pedestal.

Auntie Sue continued naughtily: "And Shelby's job! Do you know how he got it, Mr. McPherson? He'd been selling washing machines—or was it casings for frankfurters, darling? Or was that the time when you earned thirty dollars a week writing letters for a school that taught people to be successful business executives?"

Shelby turned defiantly from Diana. "What's that to be

ashamed of? When I met Laura, Mr. McPherson, I happened to be working as correspondent for the University of the Science of Finance. Laura saw some of my copy, realized that I was wasting a certain gift or flair, and with her usual generosity . . ."

"Generosity wasn't the half of it," Auntie Sue interrupted.

"She spoke to Mr. Rowe about me and a few months later, when there was a vacancy, he called me in. You can't say I've been ungrateful"—he forgave Mrs. Treadwell with his gentle smile. "It was she, not I, who suggested that you forget it."

"There were a number of other things, darling, that Laura asked me to forget."

"Mustn't be vicious, dear. You'll be giving Mr. McPherson a lot of misleading ideas." With the tenderness of a nurse Shelby rearranged Auntie Sue's cushions, smiling and treating her malice like some secret malady.

The scene took on a theatric quality. Mark saw Shelby through the woman's eyes, clothed in the charm he had donned, like a bright domino, for the woman's pleasure. The ripe color, the chiseled features, the clear, long-lashed eyes had been created, his manner said, for her particular enjoyment. Through it all Mark felt that this was not a new exhibition. He had seen it somewhere before. So irritated by faltering memory that he had to strain harshness from his voice, he told them he was through with them for the day, and rose to go.

Shelby rose, too. "I'll go out for a bit of air. If you think you can get along without me for a while."

"Of course, darling. It's been wicked of me to take up so much of your time." Shelby's feeble sarcasm had softened the lady. White, faded, ruby-tipped hands rested on his dark sleeve. "I'll never forget how kind you've been."

Shelby forgave magnanimously. He put himself at her disposal as if he were already Laura's husband, the man of the family whose duty it was to serve a sorrowing woman in this hour of grief.

Like a penitent mistress returning to her lover, she cooed at Shelby. "With all your faults, you've got manners, darling. That's more than most men have nowadays. I'm sorry I've been so bad-tempered."

He kissed her forehead.

As they left the house, Shelby turned to Mark. "Don't take Mrs. Treadwell too seriously. Her bark is worse than her bite. It's only that she'd disapproved of my marrying her niece, and now she's got to stand by her opinions."

"What she disapproved of," Mark observed, "was Laura's marrying you."

Shelby smiled ruefully. "We ought all to be a little more decent now, oughtn't we? After all! Probably Auntie Sue is sorry she hurt poor Laura by constantly criticizing me, and now she's too proud to say so. That's why she had to take it out on me this morning."

They stood in the burning sunlight. Both were anxious to get away, yet both hesitated. The scene was unfinished. Mark had not learned enough, Shelby had not told all he wanted Mark to know.

When, after a brief pause devoted to a final struggle with his limping memory, Mark cleared his throat, Shelby started as if he had been roused from the remoteness of a dream. Both smiled mechanically.

"Tell me," Mark commanded, "where have I seen you before?"

Shelby couldn't imagine. "But I've been around. Parties and all that. One sees people at bars and restaurants. Sometimes a stranger's face is more familiar than your best friend's."

Mark shook his head. "Cocktail bars aren't in my line."

"You'll remember when you're thinking of something else. That's how it always is." Then, without changing his tone, Shelby added, "You know, Mr. McPherson, that I was beneficiary of Laura's insurance, don't you?"

Mark nodded.

"I wanted to tell you myself. Otherwise you might think . . . well . . . it's only natural in your work to"—Shelby chose the word tactfully—"suspect every motive. Laura carried an annuity, you know, and there was a twenty-five-thousand-dollar death benefit. She'd had it in her sister's name, but after we decided to get married she insisted upon making it out to me."

"I'll remember that you told me," Mark promised.

Shelby offered his hand. Mark took it. They hesitated while the sun smote their uncovered heads.

"I hope you don't think I'm completely a heel, Mr. McPherson," Shelby said ruefully. "I never liked borrowing from a woman."

IV

WHEN, AT precisely twelve minutes past four by the ormolu clock on my mantel, the telephone interrupted, I was deep in the Sunday papers. Laura had become a Manhattan legend. Scarlet-minded headline artists had named her tragedy "THE BACHELOR GIRL MURDER" and one example of Sunday edition belles-lettres was tantalizingly titled "SEEK ROMEO IN EAST SIDE LOVE-KILLING." By the necromancy of modern journalism, a gracious young woman had been transformed into a dangerous siren who practiced her wiles in that fascinating neighborhood where Park Avenue meets Bohemia. Her generous way of life had become an uninterrupted orgy of drunkenness, lust, and deceit, as titivating to the masses as it was profitable to the publishers. At this very hour, I reflected as I lumbered to the telephone, men were bandying her name in pool parlors and women shouting her secrets from tenement windows.

I heard Mark McPherson's voice on the wire. "Mr. Lydecker, I was just wondering if you could help me. There are several questions I'd like to ask you."

"And what of the baseball game?" I inquired.

Self-conscious laughter vibrated the diaphragm and tickled my ear. "It was too late. I'd have missed the first couple of innings. Can you come over?"

"Where?"

"The apartment. Miss Hunt's place."

"I don't want to come up there. It's cruel of you to ask me."

"Sorry," he said after a moment of cold silence. "Perhaps Shelby Carpenter can help me. I'll try to get in touch with him."

"Never mind. I'll come."

Ten minutes later I stood beside him in the bay window of Laura's living-room. East Sixty-Second Street had yielded to the spirit of carnival. Popcorn vendors and pushcart peddlers, sensing the profit in disaster, offered ice-cream sandwiches, pickles, and nickel franks to buzzards who battened on excitement. Sunday's sweethearts had deserted the green pastures of

Central Park to stroll arm-in-arm past her house, gaping at daisies which had been watered by the hands of a murder victim. Fathers pushed perambulators and mothers scolded the brats who tortured the cops who guarded the door of a house in which a bachelor girl had been slain.

"Coney Island moved to the Platinum Belt," I observed.

Mark nodded. "Murder is the city's best free entertainment. I hope it doesn't bother you, Mr. Lydecker."

"Quite the contrary. It's the odor of tuberoses and the timbre of organ music that depress me. Public festivity gives death a classic importance. No one would have enjoyed the spectacle more than Laura."

He sighed.

"If she were here now, she'd open the windows, pluck daisies out of her window-boxes and strew the sidewalks. Then she'd send me down the stairs for a penny pickle."

Mark plucked a daisy and tore off the petals.

"Laura loved dancing in the streets. She gave dollar bills to organ-grinders."

He shook his head. "You'd never think it, judging from the neighborhood."

"She also had a taste for privacy."

The house was one of a row of converted mansions, preserved in such fashion that Victorian architecture sacrificed none of its substantial elegance to twentieth-century chic. High stoops had given way to lacquered doors three steps down; scrofulous daisies and rachitic geraniums bloomed in extraordinarily bright blue and green window-boxes; rents were exorbitant. Laura had lived here, she told me, because she enjoyed snubbing Park Avenue's pretentious foyers. After a trying day in the office, she could neither face a superman in gilt braid nor discuss the weather with politely indifferent elevator boys. She had enjoyed opening the street door with a key and climbing the stairs to her remodeled third floor. It was this taste for privacy that led to her death, for there had been no one to ask at the door if Miss Hunt expected a visitor on the night the murderer came.

"The doorbell rang," Mark announced suddenly.

"What?"

"That's how it must have happened. The doorbell rang. She

was in the bedroom without clothes on. By the time she'd put
on that silk thing and her slippers, he'd probably rung a second
time. She went to the door and as she opened it, the shot was
fired!"

"How do you know all this?" I demanded.

"She fell backward. The body lay there."

We both stared at the bare, polished floor. He had seen the
body, the pale blue garment blood-stained and the blood
running in rivulets to the edge of the green carpet.

"The door downstairs had evidently been left unlocked. It
was unlocked when Bessie came to work yesterday morning.
Before she came upstairs, Bessie looked for the superintendent
to bawl him out for his carelessness, but he'd taken his family
down to Manhattan Beach for the week-end. The tenants of
the first and second floors are away for the summer and there
was no one else in the house. The houses on both sides are
empty, too, at this time of year."

"Probably the murderer thought of that," I observed.

"The door might have been left open for him. She might
have been expecting a caller."

"Do you think so?"

"You knew her, Mr. Lydecker. Tell me, what kind of a dame
was she anyway?"

"She was not the sort of woman you call a dame," I retorted.

"Okay. But what was she like?"

"Look at this room. Does it reveal nothing of the person
who planned and decorated it? Does it contain, for your eyes,
the vulgar memories of a bachelor girl? Does it seem to you
the home of a young woman who would lie to her fiancé, deceive her oldest friend, and sneak off to a rendezvous with a
murderer?"

I awaited his answer like a touchy Jehovah. If he failed to
appreciate the quality of the woman who had adorned this
room, I should know that his interest in literature was but the
priggish aspiration of a seeker after self-improvement, his sensitivity no more than proletarian prudery. For me the room
still shone with Laura's lustre. Perhaps it was in the crowding
memories of firelit conversations, of laughing dinners at the
candle-bright refectory table, of midnight confidences fattened
by spicy snacks and endless cups of steaming coffee. But even

as it stood for him, mysterious and bare of memory, it must have represented, in the deepest sense of the words, a *living room*.

For answer he chose the long green chair, stretched his legs on the ottoman, and pulled out his pipe. His eyes traveled from the black marble fireplace in which the logs were piled, ready for the first cool evening, to softly faded chintz whose deep folds shut out the glare of the hot twilight.

After a time he burst out: "I wish to Christ my sister could see this place. Since she married and went to live in Kew Gardens, she won't have kitchen matches in the parlor. This place has"—he hesitated—"it's very comfortable."

I think the word in his mind had been *class*, but he kept it from me, knowing that intellectual snobbism is nourished by such trivial crudities. His attention wandered to the book-shelves.

"She had a lot of books. Did she ever read them?"

"What do you think?"

He shrugged. "You never know about women."

"Don't tell me you're a misogynist."

He clamped his teeth hard upon his pipestem and glanced at me with an air of urchin defiance.

"Come, now, what of the girl friend?" I pleaded.

He answered dryly: "I've had plenty in my life. I'm no angel."

"Ever loved one?"

"A doll in Washington Heights got a fox fur out of me. And I'm a Scotchman, Mr. Lydecker. So make what you want of it."

"Ever know one who wasn't a doll? Or a dame?"

He went to the bookshelves. While he talked, his hands and eyes were concerned with a certain small volume bound in red morocco. "Sometimes I used to take my sisters' girl friends out. They never talked about anything except going steady and getting married. Always wanted to take you past furniture stores to show you the parlor suites. One of them almost hooked me."

"And what saved you?"

"Mattie Grayson's machine-gun. You were right. It was no tragedy."

"Didn't she wait?"

"Hell, yes. The day they discharged me, there she was at the hospital door. Full of love and plans; her old man had plenty of dough, owned a fish store, and was ready to furnish the flat, first payment down. I was still using crutches so I told her I wouldn't let her sacrifice herself." He laughed aloud. "After the months I'd put in reading and thinking, I couldn't go for a parlor suite. She's married now, got a couple of kids, lives in Jersey."

"Never read any books, eh?"

"Oh, she's probably bought a couple of sets for the bookcase. Keeps them dusted and never reads them."

He snapped the cover on the red morocco volume. The shrill blast of the popcorn whistle insulted our ears and the voices of children rose to remind us of the carnival of death in the street below. Bessie Clary, Laura's maid, had told the police that her first glimpse of the body had been a distorted reflection in the mercury-glass globe on Laura's mantel. That tarnished bubble caught and held our eyes, and we saw in it fleetingly, as in a crystal ball, a vision of the inert body in the blue robe, dark blood matted in the dark hair.

"What did you want to ask me, McPherson? Why did you bring me up here?"

His face had the watchfulness that comes after generations to a conquered people. The Avenger, when he comes, will wear that proud, guarded look. For a moment I glimpsed enmity. My fingers beat a tattoo on the arm of my chair. Strangely, the padded rhythms seemed to reach him, for he turned, staring as if my face were a memory from some fugitive reverie. Another thirty seconds had passed, I dare say, before he took from her desk a spherical object covered in soiled leather.

"What's this, Mr. Lydecker?"

"Surely a man of your sporting tastes is familiar with that ecstatic toy, McPherson."

"But why did *she* keep a baseball on her desk?" He emphasized the pronoun. *She* had begun to live. Then, examining the tattered leather and loosened bindings, he asked, "Has she had it since '38?"

"I'm sure I didn't notice the precise date when this *objet d'art* was introduced into the household."

"It's autographed by Cookie Lavagetto. That was his big year. Was she a Dodgers fan?"

"There were many facets to her character."

"Was Shelby a fan, too?"

"Will the answer to that question help you solve the murder, my dear fellow?"

He set the baseball down so that it should lie precisely where Laura had left it. "I just wanted to know. If it bothers you to answer the question, Mr. Lydecker . . ."

"There's no reason to get sullen about it," I snapped. "As a matter of fact, Shelby wasn't a fan. He preferred . . . why do I speak of him in the past tense? He prefers the more aristocratic sports, tennis, riding, hunting, you know."

"Yep," he said.

Near the door, a few feet from the spot where the body had fallen, hung Stuart Jacoby's portrait of Laura. Jacoby, one of the imitators of Eugene Speicher, had produced a flattened version of a face that was anything but flat. The best feature of the painting, as they had been her best feature, were the eyes. The oblique tendency, emphasized by the sharp tilt of dark brows, gave her face that shy, fawn-like quality which had so enchanted me the day I opened the door to a slender child who had asked me to endorse a fountain pen. Jacoby had caught the fluid sense of restlessness in the position of her body, perched on the arm of a chair, a pair of yellow gloves in one hand, a green hunter's hat in the other. The portrait was a trifle unreal, however, a trifle studied, too much Jacoby and not enough Laura.

"She wasn't a bad-looking da——" He hesitated, smiled ruefully, "—girl, was she, Mr. Lydecker?"

"That's a sentimental portrait. Jacoby was in love with her at the time."

"She had a lot of men in love with her, didn't she?"

"She was a very kind woman. Kind and generous."

"That's not what men fall for."

"She had delicacy. If she was aware of a man's shortcomings, she never showed it."

"Full of bull?"

"No, extremely honest. Her flattery was never shallow. She

found the real qualities and made them important. Surface faults and affectations fell away like false friends at the approach of adversity."

He studied the portrait. "Why didn't she get married, then? Earlier, I mean?"

"She was disappointed when she was very young."

"Most people are disappointed when they're young. That doesn't keep them from finding someone else. Particularly women."

"She wasn't like your erstwhile fiancée, McPherson. Laura had no need for a parlor suite. Marriage wasn't her career. She had her career, she made plenty of money, and there were always men to squire and admire her. Marriage could give her only one sort of completion, and she was keeping herself for that."

"Keeping herself busy," he added dryly.

"Would you have prescribed a nunnery for a woman of her temperament? She had a man's job and a man's worries. Knitting wasn't one of her talents. Who are you to judge her?"

"Keep your shirt on," Mark said. "I didn't make any comments."

I had gone to the bookshelves and removed the volume to which he had given such careful scrutiny. He gave no sign that he had noticed, but fixed his fury upon an enlarged snapshot of Shelby looking uncommonly handsome in tennis flannels.

Dusk had descended. I switched on the lamp. In that swift transition from dusk to illumination, I caught a glimpse of darker, more impenetrable mystery. Here was no simple Police Department investigation. In such inconsistent trifles as an ancient baseball, a worn *Gulliver*, a treasured snapshot, he sought clues, not to the passing riddle of a murder, but to the eternally enigmatic nature of woman. This was a search no man could make with his eyes alone; the heart must also be engaged. He, stern fellow, would have been the first to deny such implication, but I, through these prognostic lenses, perceived the true cause of his resentment against Shelby. His private enigma, so much deeper than the professional solution of the crime, concerned the answer to a question which has ever baffled the lover, "What did she see in that other fellow?" As he glowered at the snapshot I knew that he was pondering on the quality of Laura's affection for Shelby, wondering whether a woman of her sensitivity and intelligence could be satisfied merely with the perfect mould of a man.

"Too late, my friend," I said jocosely. "The final suitor has rung her doorbell."

With a gesture whose fierceness betrayed the zeal with which his heart was guarded, he snatched up some odds and ends piled on Laura's desk, her address and engagement book, letters and bills bound by a rubber band, unopened bank statements, checkbooks, an old diary, and a photograph album.

"Come on," he snapped. "I'm hungry. Let's get out of this dump."

V

"WE'VE DISCOVERED certain clues, but we are not ready to make a statement."

The reporters found McPherson dignified, formal, and somewhat aloof that Monday morning. He felt a new importance in himself as if his life had taken on new meaning. The pursuit of individual crime had ceased to be trivial. A girl reporter, using female tricks to win information denied her trousered competitors, exclaimed, "I shouldn't mind being murdered half so much, Mr. McPherson, if you were the detective seeking clues to my private life."

His mouth twisted. The flattery was not delicate.

Her address and engagement books, bank statements, bills, check stubs, and correspondence filled his desk and his mind. Through them he had discovered the richness of her life, but also the profligacy. Too many guests and too many dinners, too many letters assuring her of undying devotion, too much of herself spent on the casual and petty, the transitory, the undeserving. Thus his Presbyterian virtue rejected the danger of covetousness. He had discovered the best of life in a gray-walled hospital room and had spent the years that followed asking himself timorously whether loneliness must be the inevitable companion of appreciation. This summing-up of Laura's life answered his question, but the answer failed to satisfy the demands of his stern upbringing. He learned, as he read her letters, balanced her unbalanced accounts, added the sums of unpaid bills, that while the connoisseur of living is not lonely, the price is high. To support the richness of life she had worked until she was too tired to approach her wedding day with joy or freedom.

The snapshot album was filled with portraits of Shelby Carpenter. In a single summer, Laura had fallen victim to his charms and the candid camera. She had caught him full face and profile, closeup and bust, on the tennis court, at the wheel of her roadster, in swimming trunks, in overalls, in hip boots with a basket slung over his shoulder, a fishing reel in his hand.

Mark paused at the portrait of Shelby, the hunter, surrounded by dead ducks.

Surely the reader must, by this time, be questioning the impertinence of a reporter who records unseen actions as nonchalantly as if he had been hiding in Mark's office behind a framed photograph of the New York Police Department Baseball Team, 1912. But I would take oath, and in that very room where they keep the sphygmomanometer, that a good third of this was told me and a richer two-thirds intimated on that very Monday afternoon when, returning from a short journey to the barber's, I found Mark waiting in my apartment. And I would further swear, although I am sure the sensitive hand of the lie-detector would record an Alpine sweep at the statement, that he had yielded to the charm of old porcelain. For the second time I discovered him in my drawing-room, his hands stretched toward my favorite shelf. I cleared my throat before entering. He turned with a rueful smile.

"Don't look so sheepish," I admonished. "I'll never tell them at the Police Department that you're acquiring taste."

His eyes shot red sparks. "Do you know what Doctor Sigmund Freud said about collectors?"

"I know what Doctor Waldo Lydecker thinks of people who quote Freud." We sat down. "To what kind whim of Fate do I owe this unexpected visit?"

"I happened to be passing by."

My spirits rose. This casual visit was not without a certain warm note of flattery. Yesterday's disapproval had melted like an ice-cube surprised by a shower of hot coffee. But even as I hastened to fetch whiskey for my guest, I cautioned myself against an injudicious display of enthusiasm. Whereas a detective may be a unique and even trustworthy friend, one must always remember that he has made a profession of curiosity.

"I've been with Shelby Carpenter," he announced as we drank a small toast to the solution of the mystery.

"Indeed," said I, assuming the air of a cool but not ungracious citizen who cherishes a modicum of privacy.

"Does he know anything about music?"

"He talks a music-lover's patter, but his information is shallow. You'll probably find him raising ecstatic eyes to heaven at the name of Beethoven and shuddering piously if someone should be so indiscreet as to mention Ethelbert Nevin."

"Would he know the difference"—Mark consulted his notebook—"between 'Finlandia' by Si-bee-lee-us and 'Toccata and Fugue' by Johann Sebastian Bach?"

"Anyone who can't distinguish between Sibelius and Bach, my dear fellow, is fit for treason, stratagem, and spoils."

"I'm a cluck when it comes to music. Duke Ellington's my soup." He offered a sheet from his notebook. "This is what Carpenter told me they were playing on Friday night. He didn't bother to check on the program. This is what they played."

I drew a sharp breath.

"It shoots his alibi as full of holes as a mosquito net. But it still doesn't prove he murdered her," Mark reminded me with righteous sharpness.

I poured him another drink. "Come, now, you haven't told me what you think of Shelby Carpenter."

"It's a shame he isn't a cop."

I cast discretion to the wind. Clapping him on the shoulder, I cried zestfully: "My dear lad, you are precious! A cop! The flower of old Kentucky! Mah deah suh, the ghosts of a legion of Confederate Colonels rise up to haunt you. Old Missy is whirling in her grave. Come, another drink on that, my astute young Hawkshaw. Properly we should be drinking mint juleps, but unfortunately Uncle Tom of Manila has lost the secret." And I went off into roars of unrestrained appreciation.

He regarded my mirth with some skepticism. "He's got all the physical requirements. And you wouldn't have to teach him to be polite."

"And fancy him in a uniform," I added, my imagination rollicking. "I can see him on the corner of Fifth Avenue where Art meets Bergdorf-Goodman. What a tangle of traffic at the hour when the cars roll in from Westchester to meet the husbands! There would be no less rioting in Wall Street, I can tell you, than on a certain historic day in '29."

"There are a lot of people who haven't got the brains for their college educations." The comment, while uttered honestly, was tinged faintly with the verdigris of envy. "The trouble is that they've been brought up with ideas of class and education so they can't relax and work in common jobs. There are plenty of fellows in these fancy offices who'd be a lot happier working in filling stations."

"I've seen many of them break under the strain of intelligence," I agreed. "Hundreds have been committed for life to the cocktail bars of Madison Avenue. There ought to be a special department in Washington to handle the problem of old Princeton men. I dare say Shelby looks down with no little condescension upon your profession."

A curt nod rewarded my astuteness. Mr. McPherson did not fancy Mr. Carpenter, but, as he had sternly reminded me on a former occasion, it was his business to observe rather than to judge the people encountered in professional adventure.

"The only thing that worries me, Mr. Lydecker, is that I can't place the guy. I've seen that face before. But where and when? Usually I'm a fool for faces. I can give you names and dates and the places I've seen them." His jaw shot forward and his lips pressed themselves into the tight mould of determination.

I laughed with secret tolerance as he gave what he considered an objective picture of his visit to the offices of Rose, Rowe, and Sanders, Advertising Counsellors. In that hot-air-conditioned atmosphere he must have seemed as alien as a share-cropper in a night club. He tried hard not to show disapproval, but opinion was as natural to him as appetite. There was fine juicy prejudice in his portrait of three advertising executives pretending to be dismayed by the notoriety of a front-page murder. While they mourned her death, Laura's bosses were not unaware of the publicity value of a crime which cast no shadow upon their own respectability.

"I bet they had a conference and decided that a high-class murder wouldn't lose any business."

"And considered the titillating confidences they could whisper to prospective clients at lunch," I added.

Mark's malice was impudent. Bosses aroused no respect in his savage breast. His proletarian prejudices were as rigid as any you will find in the upper reaches of so-called Society. It pleased him more to discover sincere praise and mourning among her fellow-workers than to hear her employers' high estimate of Laura's character and talents. Anyone who was smart, he opined, could please the boss, but it took the real stuff for a girl in a high-class job to be popular with her fellow-employees.

"So you think Laura had the real stuff?"

He affected deafness. I studied his face, but caught no shadow of conflict. It was not until several hours later that I reviewed the conversation and reflected upon the fact that he was shaping Laura's character to fit his attitudes as a young man might when enamored of a living woman. My mind was clear and penetrating at the time, for it was midnight, the hour at which I am most brave and most free. Since I learned some years ago that the terrors of insomnia could be overcome by a half-hour's brisk walk, I have not once allowed lassitude, weather, nor the sorry events of a disappointing day to interfere with this nocturnal practice. By habit I chose a street which had become important to me since Laura moved into that apartment.

Naturally I was shocked to see a light burning in the house of the dead; but after a moment's reflection, I knew that a young man who had once scorned overtime had given his heart to a job.

VI

T WO RITUALS on Tuesday marked the passing of Laura
Hunt. The first, a command performance in the coroner's
office, gathered together that small and none too congenial
group who had been concerned in the activities of her last day
of life. Because she had failed me in that final moment, I was
honored with an invitation. I shall not attempt to report the
unimaginative proceedings which went to hideous lengths to
prove a fact that everyone had known from the start—that
Laura Hunt was dead; the cause, murder by the hand of an
unknown assailant.

The second ritual, her funeral, took place that afternoon in
the chapel of W. W. Heatherstone and Son. Old Heatherstone,
long experienced in the interment of movie stars, ward leaders,
and successful gangsters, supervised the arrangements so that
there might be a semblance of order among the morbid who
started their clamor at his doors at eight o'clock in the morning.

Mark had asked me to meet him on the balcony that over-
looked the chapel.

"But I don't attend funerals."

"She was your friend."

"Laura was far too considerate to demand that anyone venture out at such a barbaric hour and to exhibit emotions which,
if earnest, are far too personal for scrutiny."

"But I wanted you to help me identify some of the people
whose names are in her address book."

"Do you think the murderer will be there?"

"It's possible."

"How'd we know him? Do you think he might swoon at the
bier?"

"Will you come?"

"No," I said firmly, and added, "Let Shelby help you this
time."

"He's chief mourner. You must come. No one will see you.
Use the side entrance and tell them you're meeting me. I'll be
on the balcony."

Her friends had loved Laura and been desolate at her passing, but they would not have been human if they had failed to
enjoy the excitement. Like Mark, they hoped for some crisis of
discovery. Eyes that should have been downcast in grief and
piety were sliding this way and that in the hope of perceiving
the flushed countenance, the guilty gesture that would enable
lips, later, to boast, "I knew it the moment I saw that sly face
and noted the way he rubbed his hands together during the
Twenty-Third Psalm."

She lay in a coffin covered in white silk. Pale ringless hands
had been folded against the lavender-tinted white moiré of her
favorite evening gown. An arrangement of gardenias, draped
like a confirmation veil, covered the ruined face. The only
mourners deserving seats in the section reserved for deepest
suffering were Auntie Sue and Shelby Carpenter. Her sister,
brother-in-law, and some far-western cousins had been unwilling or unable to make the long journey for the sake of this hour
in the mortuary. After the service was read, the organ pealed
and Heatherstone attendants wheeled the casket into a private
chamber from which it was later transferred to the crematorium.

It is from the lush sentimentality of the newspaper versions
that I prune this brief account of the obsequies. I did not attend. Mark waited in vain.

As he descended from the balcony and joined the slowly
moving mass, he noted a hand, gloved in black, signalling him.
Bessie Clary pushed her way through the crowd.

"I got something to tell you, Mr. McPherson."

He took her arm. "Shall we go upstairs where it's quiet or
does this place depress you?"

"If you wouldn't mind, we could go back to the flat," Bessie
suggested. "It's up there, what I got to show you."

Mark had his car. Bessie sat beside him primly, black gloved
hands folded in the lap of her black silk dress.

"It's hot enough to kill a cat," she said by way of making
conversation.

"What have you got to tell me?"

"You needn't to yell at me. I ain't afraid of cops, or dicks either." She drew out her best handkerchief and blew such a
clarion note that her nose seemed an instrument fashioned for

the purpose of sounding defiance. "I was brought up to spit whenever I saw one."

"I was brought up to hate the Irish," Mark observed, "but I'm a grown man now. I haven't asked for love, Miss Clary. What is it you want to tell me?"

"You won't get on my good side by that Miss Clary stuff either. Bessie's my name, I'm domestic and I got nothing to be ashamed of."

They drove across the Park in silence. When they passed the policeman who stood guard at the door of Laura's house, Bessie smiled down upon him with virtuous hauteur. Once in the apartment, she assumed the airs of ownership, raised windows, adjusted curtains, emptied trays filled with ashes from Mark's pipe.

"Cops, brought up in barns," she sniffed as she drew hatpins from out of the structure that rode high on her head, "don't know how to act when they get in a decent house." When she had drawn off black gloves, folded them and stored them in her bag, settled herself on the straightest chair, and fixed a glassy stare upon his face, she asked, "What do they do to people that hide something from the cops?"

The question, so humble in contrast with her belligerence, provided him with a weapon. "So you've been trying to shield the murderer? That's dangerous, Bessie!"

Her knotted hands unfolded. "What makes you think I know the murderer?"

"By hiding evidence, you have become an accessory after the fact. What is the evidence, and what was your purpose in concealing it?"

Bessie turned her eyes ceilingward as though she expected help from heaven. "If I'd hold out on you, you'd never know nothing about it. And if they hadn't played that music at the funeral, I'd never've told you. Church music makes me soft."

"Whom were you shielding, Bessie?"

"Her."

"Miss Hunt?"

Bessie nodded grimly.

"Why, Bessie? She's dead."

"Her reputation ain't," Bessie observed righteously and

went to the corner cabinet, in which Laura had always kept a small stock of liquor. "Just look at this."

Mark leaped. "Hey, be careful. There may be fingerprints."

Bessie laughed. "Maybe there was a lot of fingerprints around here! But the cops never seen them."

"You wiped them off, Bessie? For God's sakes!"

"That ain't all I wiped off," Bessie chuckled. "I cleaned off the bed and table in there and the bathroom before the cops come."

Mark seized bony wrists. "I've a good mind to take you into custody."

She pulled her hands away. "I don't believe in fingerprints anyway. All Saturday afternoon the cops was sprinkling white powder around my clean flat. Didn't do them no good because I polished all the furniture on Friday after she'd went to the office. If they found any fingerprints, they was mine."

"If you don't believe in fingerprints, why were you so anxious to get rid of those in the bedroom?"

"Cops got dirty minds. I don't want the whole world thinking she was the kind that got drunk with a fellow in her bedroom, God rest her soul."

"Drunk in her bedroom? Bessie, what does this mean?"

"So help me," Bessie swore, "there was two glasses."

He seized her wrists again. "Why are you making up this story, Bessie? What have you to gain by it?"

Hers was the hauteur of an enraged duchess. "What right you got to yell at me? You don't believe me, huh? Say, I was the one that cared about her reputation. You never even knew her. What are you getting so mad about?"

Mark retreated, the sudden display of temper puzzling and shaming him. His fury had grown out of all proportions to its cause.

Bessie drew out a bottle. "Where do you think I found this? Right there." She pointed through the open door to the bedroom. "On the table by the bed. With two dirty glasses."

Laura's bedroom was as chaste and peaceful as the chamber of a young girl whose experience of love has been confined to sonnets, dreams, and a diary. The white Swiss spread lay smooth and starched, the pillow rounded neatly at the polished pine headboard, a white-and-blue knitted afghan folded at the foot.

"I cleaned up the room and washed the glasses before the first cop got here. Lucky I come to my senses in time," Bessie sniffed. "The bottle I put in the cabinet so's no one would notice. It wasn't her kind of liquor. I can tell you this much, Mr. McPherson, this here bottle was brought in after I left on Friday."

Mark examined the bottle. It was Three Horses Bourbon, a brand favored by frugal tipplers. "Are you sure, Bessie? How do you know? You must keep close watch on the liquor that's used in this place."

Bessie's iron jaw shot forward; cords stiffened in her bony neck. "If you don't believe me, ask Mr. Mosconi, the liquor fellow over on Third Avenue. We always got ours from Mosconi, better stuff than this, I'm telling you. She always left me the list and I ordered on the phone. This here's the brand we use." She swung the doors wider and revealed, among the neatly arranged bottles, four unopened fifths of J and D Blue Grass Bourbon, the brand which I had taught her to buy.

Such unexpected evidence, throwing unmistakable light on the last moments of the murdered, should have gladdened the detective heart. Contrarily, Mark found himself loath to accept the facts. This was not because he had reason to disbelieve Bessie's story, but because the sordid character of her revelations had disarranged the pattern of his thinking. Last night, alone in the apartment, he had made unscientific investigation of Laura's closets, chests of drawers, dressing-table, and bathroom. He knew Laura, not only with his intelligence, but with his senses. His fingers had touched fabrics that had known her body, his ears had heard the rustle of her silks, his nostrils sniffed at the varied, heady fragrances of her perfumes. Never before had the stern young Scot known a woman in this fashion. Just as her library had revealed the quality of her mind, the boudoir had yielded the secrets of feminine personality.

He did not like to think of her drinking with a man in her bedroom like a cutie in a hotel.

In his coldest, most official voice he said, "If there was someone in the bedroom with her, we have a completely new picture of the crime."

"You mean it wasn't like you said in the paper, that it must have happened when the doorbell rang and she went to open it?"

"I accepted that as the most probable explanation, considering the body's position." He crossed from the bedroom slowly, his eyes upon the arrangement of carpets on the polished floor. "If a man had been in the bedroom with her, he might have been on the point of leaving. She went to the door with him, perhaps." He stood rigid at the spot where the river of dark blood had been dammed by the thick pile of the carpet. "Perhaps they were quarreling and, just as he reached the door, he turned and shot her."

"Gosh," said Bessie, blowing her nose weakly, "it gives you the creeps, don't it?"

From the wall Stuart Jacoby's portrait smiled down.

VII

O N WEDNESDAY afternoon, twenty-four hours after the funeral, Lancaster Corey came to see me. I found him con-
templating my porcelains lustfully.

"Corey, my good fellow, to what do I owe this dispensa-
tion?"

We wrung each other's hands like long-lost brothers.

"I'll not mince words, Waldo. I've come on business."

"I smelled sulphur and brimstone. Have a drink before you
reveal your diabolical schemes."

He twisted the end of his white, crisp mustache. "I've got a
great opportunity for you, my good friend. You know Jacoby's
work. Getting more valuable every day."

I made a sound with my lips.

"It's not that I'm trying to sell you a picture. As a matter of
fact, I've already got a buyer. You know Jacoby's portrait of
Laura Hunt . . . several of the papers carried reproductions
after the murder. Tragic, wasn't it? Since you were so attached
to the lady, I thought you'd want to bid before . . ."

"I knew there was something divine about your visit, Corey.
Now I see that it's your insolence."

He shrugged off the insult. "Merely a courtesy."

"How dare you?" I shouted. "How dare you come to my
house and coolly offer me that worthless canvas? In the first
place, I consider it a bad imitation of Speicher. In the second
place, I deplore Speicher. And in the third, I loathe portraits in
oil."

"Very well. I shall feel free to sell it to my other buyer." He
snatched up his Fedora.

"Wait a minute," I commanded. "How can you offer what
you don't own? That picture is hanging on the wall of her
apartment now. She died without a will, the lawyers will have
to fight it out."

"I believe that Mrs. Treadwell, her aunt, is assuming responsibility for the family. You might communicate with her or
with Salsbury, Haskins, Warder, and Bone, her attorneys. The
landlord, I heard this morning, had released the estate from its

47

obligation to fulfill the lease on condition that the apartment is
vacated by the first of the month. They're going to make a
special effort to hurry the proceedings . . ."

His knowledge infuriated me. "The vultures gather!" I
shouted, smacking my forehead with an anguished palm. And
a moment later cried out in alarm: "Do you know what arrangements have been made for her other things? Whether
there's to be a sale?"

"This bid came through a private channel. Someone who
had seen the portrait in her apartment, no doubt, made inquiries of several dealers. He hadn't known that we were Jacoby's
agents . . ."

"His taste makes it clear that he knows very little about
painting."

Corey made a purse of his lips. "Everyone is not as prejudiced as you are, Waldo. I prophesy the day when Jacoby will
be worth real money."

"Comfort yourself, my sweet buzzard. Both you and I shall
be dead by that time. But tell me," I continued mockingly, "is
your prospective sucker some connoisseur who saw the picture
in the Sunday tabloids and wants to own the portrait of a
murder victim?"

"I do not believe that it would be strictly ethical to give my
customer's name."

"Your pardon, Corey. My question must have shocked your
delicate sensibilities of a business man. Unfortunately I shall
have to write the story without using names."

Lancaster Corey responded like a hunting dog to the smell
of rabbit. "What story?"

"You have just given me material for a magnificent piece!" I
cried, simulating creative excitement. "An ironic small story
about the struggling young painter whose genius goes unrecognized until one of his sitters is violently murdered. And
suddenly he, because he had done her portrait, becomes the
painter of the year. His name is not only on the lips of collectors, but the public, the public, Corey, know him as they know
Mickey Rooney. His prices skyrocket, fashionable women beg
to sit for him, he is reproduced in *Life, Vogue, Town and
Country* . . ."

My fantasy so titivated his greed that he could no longer

show pride. "You've got to mention Jacoby's name. The story would be meaningless without it."

"And a footnote, no doubt, explaining that his works are on view in the galleries of Lancaster Corey."

"That wouldn't hurt."

I spoke bitterly. "Your point of view is painfully commercial. Such considerations never enter my mind. Art, Corey, endures. All else passes. My piece would be as vivid and original as a Jacoby portrait."

"Just include his name. One mention of it," Corey pleaded.

"That inclusion would remove my story from the realms of literature and place it in the category of journalism. In that case, I'd have to know the facts, even if I did not include all of them. To protect my reputation for veracity, you understand."

"You've won," Corey admitted and whispered the art-lover's name.

I sank upon the Biedermeier, laughing as I had not laughed since Laura had been here to share such merry secrets of human frailty.

Along with this genial and amusing tidbit, Corey had, however, brought some distressing information. As soon as I had got rid of him, I changed my clothes, seized hat and stick, and bade Roberto summon a taxi. Hence to Laura's apartment, where I found not only Mrs. Treadwell, whom I had expected to find there, but Shelby and the Pomeranian. Laura's aunt was musing on the value of the few genuinely antique pieces, Shelby taking inventory, and the dog sniffing chair legs.

"To what do we owe this unexpected pleasure?" cried Mrs. Treadwell, who, in spite of expressing open disapproval of my friendship with her niece, had always fluttered before my fame.

"To cupidity, dear lady. I have come to share the booty."

"This is a painful task." She sank back into an upholstered chair watching, through heavily blackened lashes, my every movement and glance. "But my lawyer simply insists."

"How generous of you!" I chattered. "You spare yourself no pains. In spite of grief and sentiment, you carry on bravely. I dare say you'll account for every button in poor Laura's wardrobe."

A key turned in the lock. We assumed postures of piety as Mark entered.

"Your men let us in, Mr. McPherson," explained Mrs. Treadwell. "I called your office, but you weren't in. I hope there's nothing wrong about our . . . our attempt to bring order. Poor Laura was so careless, she never knew what she owned."

"I gave orders to let you in if you came," Mark told her. "I hope you've found everything as it should be."

"Someone has been in the closet. One of the dresses has fallen off the hook and perfume was spilled."

"The police are heavy-handed," was my innocent observation.

Mark, I thought, took extra pains to appear nonchalant.

"There's nothing of great value," Mrs. Treadwell remarked. "Laura would never put her money into things that lasted. But there are certain trinkets, souvenirs that people might appropriate for sentimental reasons." She smiled so sweetly in my direction that I knew she suspected the reason for my presence.

I took direct action. "Perhaps you know, Mrs. Treadwell, that this vase did not belong to Laura." I nodded toward the mercury glass globe upon the mantel. "I'd merely lent it to her."

"Now, Waldo, don't be naughty. I saw you bring that vase on Christmas, all tied up in red ribbons. You must remember, Shelby."

Shelby looked up as if he had not heard the argument. The rôle of innocence, he knew by experience, would protect him equally from my wit and her revenge. "Sorry, darling, I didn't hear what you were saying." He returned to his inventories.

"Not ribbons, dear lady. There was a string tied to my Christmas package. Laura wasn't to give it away. You know that Spanish prodigality of hers, handing things to anyone who admired them. This vase is part of my collection and I intend to take it now. That's quite in order, don't you think, McPherson?"

"You'd better leave it. You might find yourself in trouble," Mark said.

"How petty-official of you! You're acting like a detective."

He shrugged as if my good opinion were of no importance. I laughed and turned the talk to inquiry about the progress of his work. Had he found any clues that might lead to the murderer's house?

"Plenty," he taunted.

"Oh, do tell us," Mrs. Treadwell begged, sliding forward in her chair and clasping her hands together in a gesture of rapturous attention. Shelby had climbed upon a chair so that he might record the titles of volumes on the topmost bookshelf. From this vantage-point, he glanced down at Mark with fearless curiosity. The Pomeranian sniffed at the detective's trousers. All awaited revelation. All Mark said was, "I hope you don't mind," and took out his pipe. The snub was meant to arouse fear and bid us mind the majesty of the law.

I seized the moment for my own. "It might interest you to know that I've got a clue." My eyes were fixed on Mrs. Treadwell, but beyond her floating veil the mirror showed me Mark's guarded countenance.

"Do you know there's an art-lover connected with this case? As probable heir, Mrs. Treadwell, you might be pleased to know that this little museum piece"—I directed her attention to the Jacoby portrait—"has already been bid for."

"Really! How much?"

"I'd keep the price up if I were you. The portrait may have a sentimental value for the buyer."

"Who is it?" asked Shelby.

"Someone with money? Could we ask a thousand?" demanded Mrs. Treadwell.

Mark used the pipe as a shield for self-consciousness. Behind his cupped hand, I noted rising color. A man girding himself for the torture chamber could not have shown greater dignity.

"Someone we know?"

"Do you think there might be a clue in it?" I asked mischievously. "If this is a *crime passionnel*, the killer might be a man of sentiment. Don't you think the lead's worth following, McPherson?"

His answer was something between a grunt and a sigh.

"It's terribly exciting," said Mrs. Treadwell. "You've got to tell me, Waldo, you've just got to."

I was never a child to torture butterflies. The death agonies of small fish have never been a sight that I witnessed with pleasure. I remember blanching with terror and scurrying across the lane when, during an ill-advised visit to a farm, I was forced to watch a decapitated chicken running around and around its astonished head. Even on the stage I prefer death to follow a swift, clean stroke of a sharp blade. To spare Mark's blushes I spoke hastily and with the air of gravity: "I cannot betray the confidence of Lancaster Corey. An art dealer is, after all, somewhat in the position of a doctor or lawyer. In matters of taste, discretion is the better part of profit."

I sought his eyes, but Mark turned away. His next move, I thought, was meant to divert conversation, but I learned later that he had had a definite purpose in meeting Shelby here this afternoon.

"I've been working and could use a drink," he announced. "As chief trustee, Mrs. Treadwell, would you mind if I took some of Miss Hunt's liquor?"

"How stingy you make me sound! Shelby, darling, be useful. I wonder if the icebox is turned on."

Shelby leaped from his perch and went into the kitchen. Mark opened the corner cabinet.

"He certainly knows his way about this apartment," I observed.

He paid no attention. "What do you drink, Mrs. Treadwell? Yours is Scotch, isn't it, Lydecker?"

He waited until Shelby returned before he brought out the Bourbon. "I think I'll drink this today. What's yours, Carpenter?"

Shelby glanced at the bottle, decorated with the profiles of three noble steeds. His hands tensed, but he could not hold them steady enough to keep the glasses from rattling on the tray.

"None—for—me—thanks."

The softness had fled his voice. He was as harsh as metal, and his chiseled features, robbed of color, had the marble virtue of a statue erected to the honor of a dead Victorian.

VIII

MARK ASKED me to dine with him that night.
"But I thought you were displeased with me."

"Why?"

"I failed you at the funeral."

"I know how you felt." His hand lay for a moment upon my coat-sleeve.

"Then why didn't you help me get my vase away from that she-vulture?"

"I was being petty-official," he teased. "I'd like to take you to dinner, Mr. Lydecker. Will you come?"

He carried a book in his coat-pocket. I saw only the top inch of the binding, but unless I was mistaken, it was the work of a not unfamiliar author.

"I am flattered," I remarked with a jocular nod toward the bulging pocket.

He fingered the book, with some affection, I fancied.

"Have you read it yet, McPherson?" He nodded. "And do you still consider me smooth but trivial?"

"Sometimes you're not bad," he conceded.

"Your flattery overwhelms me," I retorted. "And where shall we dine?"

His car was open and he drove so wildly that I clung with one hand to the door, with the other to my black Homburg. I wondered why he chose the narrowest streets in the slums until I saw the red neon above Montagnino's door. Montagnino himself met us and to my surprise greeted Mark as an honored customer. I saw then that it would take little effort to guide him along the road of good taste. We passed through a corridor steamy with the odors of tomato paste, peppers, and oregano to the garden, which was, on this incredible night, only a few degrees cooler than the kitchen; with the air of a Caesar conferring honor upon pet commoners, Montagnino led us to a table beside a trellis twined with artificial lilac. Through the dusty wooden lattice and weary cotton vines we witnessed a battle between the hordes of angry clouds and a fierce copper moon. The leaves of the one living tree in the neighborhood, a skinny catalpa, hung like the black bones of skeleton hands, as dead as the cotton lilac. With the flavors of Montagnino's kitchen and the slum smells was mingled the sulphurous odor of the rising storm.

We dined on mussels cooked with mustard greens in Chianti and a chicken, fried in olive oil, laid upon a bed of yellow taglierini and garlanded with mushrooms and red peppers. At my suggestion we drank that pale still wine with the magic name, *Lacrymae Christi*. Mark had never tasted it, but once his tongue had tested and approved the golden flavor, he tossed it off like Scotch whiskey. He came of a race of drinkers who look contemptuously upon an alcoholic content of twelve per cent, unaware that the fermented grape works its enchantments more subtly than the distilled spirits of grain. I do not imply that he was drunk; let us say, rather, that the Tears of Christ opened his heart. He became less Scottish and more boyish; less the professional detective and more the youth in need of a confidant.

I remarked that I had dined here with Laura. We had eaten the same food at this very table. The same weary cotton leaves had hung above her head. The place had been one of her favorites. Had he guessed it when he planned the dinner?

He shrugged. A mechanical contrivance filled the restaurant with music and sent faint melody into the garden. Noël Coward wrote an unforgettable line (whose precise wording I have forgotten) upon the ineluctable charm of old popular songs. That is why, I venture to say, a nation sways to George Gershwin while the good works of Calvin Coolidge have become arid words in unread volumes. Old tunes had been as much a part of Laura as her laughter. Her mind had been a fulsome catalogue of musical trivia. A hearty and unashamed lowbrow, she had listened to Brahms but had heard Kern. Her one Great had been Bach, whom she learned to cherish, believe it or not, by listening to a Benny Goodman record.

When I mentioned this to Mark, he nodded gravely and said, "Yep, I know."

"What do you know and how do you know so much?" I demanded, suddenly outraged by his superior airs. "You act as though you'd been Laura's friend for years."

"I looked at her records," he said. "I even played some of them. Make what you want of that, Mr. Lydecker."

I poured him another glass of wine. His belligerency dwindled and it was not long afterward that he poured forth the revelations recorded in foregoing chapters: the scene with Bessie; his annoyance at the clumsy flattery of the girl reporter; the sudden interest in painting which had caused him to discover Lancaster Corey and ask the price of the Jacoby portrait; and finally, with the second bottle of wine, of Shelby Carpenter.

I confess that I was not without guilt in plying him with liquor and provocative questions. We discussed the insurance policy, the false alibi, and, at my subtle instigation, Shelby's familiarity with firearms.

"He's quite the sporting type, you know. Hunting, shooting, and all that. Once had a collection of guns, I believe."

Mark nodded knowingly.

"Have you checked on them? How do you go about getting all these items of information? Or did Shelby confess that, too?"

"I'm a detective. What do you think I do with my time? It was a simple matter of two and two on the guns. Photographs in her album and storage receipts in his room at the Framingham. He went up to the warehouse with me himself on Monday and we looked over the arsenal. His father used to hunt foxes in a red coat, he told me."

"Well?" I awaited revelation.

"According to the records in the warehouse, nothing had been touched for over a year. Most of the stuff showed rust and the dust was an inch thick."

"Of course a man might have guns that he didn't put into a warehouse for safekeeping."

"He's not the type to use a sawed-off shotgun."

"A sawed-off shotgun!" I exclaimed. "Do you know positively?"

"We know nothing *positively*." He underscored the adverb brusquely. "But where do you use BB shot?"

"I'm no sportsman," I confessed.

"Imagine anyone trying to carry a shotgun around the streets of this town. How could he get away with it?"

"Sawed-off shotguns are carried by gangsters," I observed. "At least according to the education I've received at that fount of popular learning, the movies."

"Did Laura know any gangsters?"

"In a way, McPherson, we're all gangsters. We all have our confederates and our sworn foes, our loyalties and our enmities. We have our pasts to shed and our futures to protect."

"In the advertising business they use different weapons," he observed.

"If a man were desperate, might he not sacrifice sportsmanship for the nonce and step out of his class? And tell me, McPherson, just how does one saw off a sawed-off shotgun?"

My plea for practical information was disregarded. Mark became guarded again. I spoke of the insurance policy.

"Shelby's eagerness to tell you about it was undoubtedly a device for disarming you with his charming frankness."

"I've thought of that."

The music changed. My hand, holding a wineglass, was stayed on its journey to my lips. My face was drained of color. In the bewildered countenance of my companion I caught a reflection of my pallor.

Yellow hands slid coffee-cups across the table. At the next table a woman laughed. The moon had lost its battle with the clouds and retreated, leaving no trace of copper brilliance in the ominous sky. The air had grown heavier. In the window of a tenement a slim girl stood, her angular dark silhouette sharpened by a naked electric bulb.

At the table on our left a woman was singing:

> So I smile and say,
> When a lovely flame dies,
> Smoke gets in your eyes.

Fixing offended eyes upon her face, I spoke in my courtliest tones. "Madame, if you would spare the eardrums of one who heard Tamara introduce that enchanting song, you will restrain your clumsy efforts at imitation."

She made a remark and gesture which, lest my readers be squeamish, I shall not describe. Mark's eyes were fixed on my face with the squinting attentiveness of a scientist at a microscope.

I laughed and said hastily: "That melody is significant.

Common as it has become, it has never lost a peculiarly individual flavor. Jerry Kern has never surpassed it, you know."

"The first time you heard it you were with Laura," Mark said.

"How astute of you!"

"I'm getting used to your ways, Mr. Lydecker."

"You shall be rewarded," I promised, "by the story of that night."

"Go on."

"It was in the fall of '33, you know, that Max Gordon put on the show, *Roberta*, book by Hammerstein Junior after a novel by Alice Duer Miller. Trivia, of course, but, as we know, there is no lack of sustenance in whipped cream. It was Laura's first opening night. She was no end excited, her eyes burning like a child's, her voice rising in adolescent squeaks as I pointed out this and that human creature who had been, until that night, magic names to the little girl from Colorado Springs. She wore a gown of champagne-colored chiffon and jade-colored slippers. Extraordinarily effective with her eyes and hair.

"'Laura, my precious babe,' I said to her, 'we shall drink to your frock in champagne.' It was her first taste of it, McPherson. Her pleasure gave me the sensation that God must know when He transforms the blasts of March into the melting winds of April.

"Add to this mood a show which is all glitter and chic, and top it with the bittersweet froth of song, throatily sung by a Russian girl with a guitar. I felt a small warmth upon my hand, and then, as the song continued, a pressure that filled me with swelling ecstasy. Do you think this a shameful confession? A man of my sort has many easy emotions—I have been known to shout with equal fervor over the Beethoven Ninth or a penny lollypop—but few great moments. But I swear to you, McPherson, in this simple sharing of melody we had attained something which few achieve in the more conventional attitudes of affection.

"Her eyes were swimming. Later she told me that she had recently been rejected in love—imagine anyone rejecting Laura. The fellow, I take it, was rather insensitive. She had, alas, a low taste in love. Through the confession I clung to her hand tightly, that small, tender hand which held such extraordinary firmness that she used to say it was slightly masculine. But the elements are so mixed in us, McPherson, that Nature must blush to quote Shakespeare when she stands and says to all the world, 'This was a man!'"

The music flowed between the white dusty boards of the trellis, through vines of artificial lilac. I had never before spoken aloud nor written of the reverie which had filled me since that night with Laura at the theatre, yet I felt certain security in entrusting it to a man whose nostalgia was concerned with a woman whose face he had never seen.

At long last the song ceased. Freed from pensive memories, I drained my glass and returned to the less oppressive topic of murder. I had by this time sufficient command of myself to speak of the scene we had witnessed in Laura's room and of Shelby's pallor at the sight of the Bourbon bottle. Mark said that the evidence gathered thus far was too circumstantial and frail to give substance to a case against the bridegroom.

"Do tell me this, McPherson. In your opinion is he guilty?"

I had given myself freely. In return I expected frankness. He answered with an insolent smile.

I set to work on his emotions. "Poor Laura," I sighed. "How ironic for her if it actually was Shelby! After having loved so generously, to discover treachery. Those last hideous moments before she died!"

"Death was almost instantaneous. Within a few seconds she was unconscious."

"You're pleased, Mark, aren't you? You're glad to know she had no time to regret the love she had given?"

He said icily, "I've expressed no such opinion."

"Don't be ashamed. Your heart's no softer than any other Scot's. Sir Walter and Sir James would have been delighted with you. A nature rocky as the hills, a tombstone and a wee bit o' heather."

"You rockbound Americans, you're sentimental like worms." Bony hands gripped the table. "Let's have another drink."

I suggested Courvoisier.

"You order. I can't pronounce it."

After a short pause, he said: "Listen, Mr. Lydecker, there's one thing I want to know. Why did she keep putting off the wedding? She was crazy about him, she had pictures of him all over the place, and still she kept postponing it. Why?"

"The familiar curse of gold."

He shook his head. "Carpenter and I have gone into that. The guy's fairly decent about it, if a man can be decent and take money from a woman. But this is what gets me. They're going together for a hell of a long time and at last they decide to break down and get married. So she plans a vacation and a honeymoon, and then has to have a week by herself before she goes through with it. What was holding her back?"

"She was tired. She wanted to rest."

"When everyone says the same thing and it's the easiest answer, you know damn well it's baloney."

"Are you suggesting that Laura might have been seeking excuses for postponing the wedding? That she wasn't awaiting the great day with the tremulous expectancy of a happy bride?"

"Could be."

"Strange," I sighed, "incredibly strange and tragic for us to be sitting here, at this very table, under these same weary lilacs, listening to her favorite tunes and stewing over our jealousy. She's dead, man, dead!"

Nervous hands toyed with the stem of the brandy snifter. Then, with his dark eyes piercing the gossamer of my defenses, he asked, "If you were so crazy about her, why didn't you do something about Shelby?"

I met this scrutiny contemptuously.

"Why?"

"Laura was a grown woman. Her freedom was dear to her and jealously guarded. She knew her own heart. Or thought she did."

"If I had known her . . ." he began in a voice of masculine omnipotence, but paused, leaving the rest unsaid.

"What a contradictory person you are, McPherson!"

"Contradictory!" He tossed the word into the very centre of the garden. Several diners stared at us. "I'm contradictory. Well, what about the rest of you? And what about her? Wherever you turn, a contradiction."

"It's the contradictions that make her seem alive to you. Life itself is contradictory. Only death is consistent."

With a great sigh he unburdened himself of another weighty question. "Did she ever talk to you about *Gulliver*?"

My mind leaped nimbly in pursuit. "It's one of your favorites, too, I take it."

"How do you know that?" he challenged.

"Your boasted powers of observation are failing sadly, my dear fellow, if you failed to notice that I took care to see what volume it was that you examined so scrupulously in her apartment on Sunday afternoon. I knew that book well. It was an old copy and I had it rebound for her in red morocco."

He smiled shyly. "I knew you were spying on me."

"You said nothing, because you wished to let me think it was a murder clue you sought among the Lilliputians. If it gives you pleasure, young man, I'll confirm the hope that she shared your literary enthusiasms."

His gratitude was charming. I counted the days that had passed since he had spoken of Laura as a two-timing dame. Had I reminded him tonight, I dare say he would have punched my face.

The genial combination of good food, wine, music, brandy, and sympathy had corrupted his defenses. He spoke with touching frankness. "We lived within half a mile of each other for over three years. Must have taken the same bus, the same subway, passed each other on the street hundreds of times. She went to Schwartz's for her drugs, too."

"Remarkable coincidence," I said.

The irony was lost. He had surrendered.

"We must have passed each other on the street often."

It was a slender morsel of consolation he had found among all the grim facts. I resolved then and there to write about this frustrated romance, so fragile and so typical of New York. It was the perfect O. Henry story. I can hear old Sydney Porter coughing himself into a fever over it.

"Wonderful ankles," he muttered, half-aloud. "The first thing I look at is the ankles. Wonderful."

They had turned off the music and most of the diners had left the garden. A couple passed our table. The girl, I noted, had remarkable ankles. Mark did not turn his head. He dwelt, for that brief moment, in the fancy of a meeting at Schwartz's drugstore. He had been buying pipe tobacco and she had put a dime into the postage-stamp machine. She might have dropped her purse. Or perhaps there had been a cinder in her eye. She had uttered but a single word, "Thanks," but for him sweet bells jangled and the harps of heaven were joined in mighty paean. A glance at her ankles, a meeting of their eyes, and it was as simple as with Charles Boyer and Margaret Sullavan.

"Have you ever read my story of Conrad?"[1] I inquired.

My question interrupted the schoolboy reverie. He regarded me with a desolate glance.

"It is a legend told over port and cigars at Philadelphia dining-tables some seventy-five years ago, and whispered in softer tones over tapestry frames and macramé work. The story has of late been attributed to me, but I take no credit. What I am telling is a tale whose only basis of truth lies in its power over stolid folk celebrated for their honesty and lack of imagination. I refer to the Amish of Pennsylvania.

"Conrad was one of these. A stalwart, earthy lad more given to the cultivation of rutabagas than to flights of superstitious fancy. One day as he worked in the field, he heard a great crash upon the road. Running, hoe in hand, he came upon the confusion attendant upon an accident. A vegetable cart had collided with a smart carriage. To his great surprise Conrad found a woman in his arms in the place of his hoe.

"Among the Amish, who boasted that they were known as *plain*, buttons were considered ungodly ornament. To this moment in his life Conrad had seen only girls in faded ginghams hooked tight across their chests and with hair stretched from their temples into wiry pigtails. He wore a blue work shirt fastened severely to the throat and upon his chin a fringe, like monkey fur, of thin whiskers affected by his people as a mark of piety.

"The injury to the lady's carriage was repaired sooner than the damage to Conrad's heart. Never could he close his eyes without beholding a vision of this creature with her powdered skin, her wanton lips, and mischievous eyes, as black as the ebony stick of her lilac-silk parasol. From that day on, Conrad

[1] "Conrad of Lebanon," in the volume, *February, Which Alone*, by Waldo Lydecker, 1936.

was no longer content with his pigtailed neighbors and his rutabagas. He must find Troy and seek Helen. He sold his farm, walked dusty roads to Philadelphia, and being canny as the pious always are, invested his small capital in a lucrative business whose proprietor was willing to teach him the trade.

"Without money, without access to the society frequented by the elegant creature, Conrad was actually no closer to her than he had been at Lebanon. Yet his faith never flagged. He believed, as he believed in evil and sin, that he would again hold her in his arms.

"And the miracle occurred. Before so many years had passed that he was too old to know the joy of fulfillment, he held her close to his breast, his heart pounding with such a savage beat that its vigor gave life to every inanimate thing around him. And once again, as on the hot noon when he first beheld her, the lids lifted like curtains over those dark eyes . . ."

"How did he make it?" Mark inquired. "How did he get to know her?"

I waved aside the interruption. "She had never seemed so lovely as now, and though he had heard her name whispered in the city and knew her reputation to be unsavory, he felt that his eyes had never met such purity as he saw in that marble brow, nor such chastity as was encased in those immobile lips. Let us forgive Conrad his confusion. At such moments a man's mind does not achieve its highest point of logic. Remember, the lady was clothed all in white from the tips of her satin slippers to the crown of blossoms in her dark hair. And the shadows, lilac-tinted, in the shroud . . ."

At the word Mark recoiled.

I fixed my eyes upon him innocently. "Shroud. In those days it was still the custom."

"Was she," he asked, biting down slowly as if each word were poisoned fruit, "dead?"

"Perhaps I neglected to mention that he had become apprenticed to an undertaker. And while the surgeon had declared her dead before Conrad was called to the dwelling, he afterward . . ."

Mark's eyes were dark holes burning through the white fabric of a mask. His lips puckered as if the poisoned fruit were bitter.

"I cannot tell if the story is true," I said, sensing his unrest and hastening the moral, "but since Conrad came of a people who never encouraged fantasy, one cannot help but pay him the respect of credence. He returned to Lebanon, but the folk around reported that women were forevermore destroyed for him. Had he known and lost a living love, he would never have been so marked as by this short excursion into necrophilia."

Thunder rumbled closer. The sky had become sulphurous. As we left the garden, I touched his arm gently.

"Tell me, McPherson, how much were you prepared to pay for the portrait?"

He turned on me a look of dark malevolence. "Tell me, Lydecker, did you walk past Laura's apartment every night before she was killed, or is it a habit you've developed since her death?"

Thunder crashed above us. The storm was coming closer.

PART TWO

I

W HEN WALDO LYDECKER learned what happened after our dinner at Montagnino's on Wednesday night, he could write no more about the Laura Hunt case. The prose style was knocked right out of him.

He had written the foregoing between ten o'clock on Wednesday night and four on Thursday afternoon with only five hours' sleep, a quart of black coffee, and three hearty meals to keep up his strength. I suppose he had intended to fit the story to one of those typical Lydecker last paragraphs where a brave smile always shows through the tears.

I am going on with the story. My writing won't have the smooth professional touch which, as he would say, distinguishes Waldo Lydecker's prose. God help any of us if we'd tried to write our reports with style. But for once in my life, since this is unofficial anyway, I am going to forget Detective Bureau shorthand and express a few personal opinions. This is my first experience with citizens who get their pictures into that part of the funny papers called the Society Section. Even professionally I've never been inside a night club with leopard-skin covers on the chairs. When these people want to insult each other, they say *darling*, and when they get affectionate they throw around words that a Jefferson Market bailiff wouldn't use to a pimp. Poor people brought up to hear their neighbors screaming filth every Saturday night are more careful of their language than well-bred smart-alecks. I know as many four-letter words as anybody in the business and use them when I feel like it. But not with ladies. Nor in writing. It takes a college education to teach a man that he can put on paper what he used to write on a fence.

I'm starting the story where Waldo ended . . . In Montagnino's back yard after the third brandy.

As we stepped out of the restaurant, the heat hit us like a blast from a furnace. The air was dead. Not a shirt-tail moved on the washlines of McDougal Street. The town smelled like rotten eggs. A thunderstorm was rolling in.

"Can I drive you home?"

"No, thanks; I feel like walking."

"I'm not drunk. I can drive," I said.

"Have I implied that you're drunk? It's my whim to walk. I'm working tonight." He started off, pounding his stick against the pavement. "Thanks for the feast," he called as I drove off.

I took it slowly because my head was still heavy. I drove past the corner where I should have turned for the Athletic Club, and then I knew that I didn't want to go home. I didn't feel like bowling or pool, my mind wasn't sharp enough for poker, and I've never sat in the lounge in the two years I've lived there. The steel furniture in my bedroom reminded me of a dentist's office. There wasn't a comfortable chair in the room, and if you lay on the couch the cover wrinkled under you. These are all the excuses I can find for going to Laura's apartment that night. Maybe I was just drunk.

Before I went upstairs, I stopped to raise the top of my car and shut the windows. Later, when the thing that happened caused me to question my sanity, I remembered that I had performed the acts of a sober man. I had the key in my pocket and I let myself in as coolly as if I'd been entering my own place. As I opened the door I saw the first streaks of lightning through the blinds. Thunder crashed. It was followed by the stillness that precedes heavy rain. I was sweating and my head ached. I got myself a drink of water from the kitchen, took off my coat, opened my collar, and stretched in the long chair. The light hurt my eyes and I turned it off. I fell asleep before the storm broke.

Thunder sounded like a squadron of bombers above the roof. Lightning did not flash away immediately. After a few seconds I saw that it was not lightning at all, but the lamp with the green shade. I had not turned it on. I had not moved from the long chair.

Thunder crashed again. Then I saw her. She held a rain-streaked hat in one hand and a pair of light gloves in the other. Her rain-spattered silk dress was moulded tight to her body. She was five-foot seven, weighed about one-thirty, dark eyes slightly slanted, dark hair, and tanned skin. Nothing wrong about her ankles either.

"What are you doing here?" she said.

I couldn't answer.

"What are you doing here?"

I remembered the wine and looked around to see if she'd brought any pink elephants.

"If you don't get out this moment," she said, and her voice trembled, "I'll call the police."

"I am the police," I said.

My voice told me that I was alive. I jerked myself out of the chair. The girl backed away. The picture of Laura Hunt was just behind her.

I had a voice. I spoke with authority. "You're dead."

My wild stare and the strange accusation convinced her that she was facing a dangerous lunatic. She edged toward the door.

"Are you . . ." But I couldn't say the name. She had spoken, she was wet with rain, she had been frightened and had tried to escape. Were these real evidences of life just another set of contradictions?

I don't know how long we stood, facing each other and awaiting revelation. For a crazy half-second I remembered what my grandmother used to tell me about meeting in heaven those whom we had lost on earth. Peal after peal of thunder shook the house. Lightning flashed past the window. The ground seemed to be trembling below us and the skies splitting overhead. This was Laura Hunt's apartment; I felt in my pocket for my pipe.

I had bought a paper. As I unfolded it, I said: "Have you seen any newspapers lately? Don't you know what's happened?" The questions made me feel sane again.

She shrank away, clinging with both hands to the table.

I said: "Please don't be frightened; there must be an explanation. If you haven't seen the papers . . ."

"I haven't. I've been in the country. My radio's broken." And then slowly, as if she were fitting the pieces together, she said: "Why? Do the papers say I'm . . ."

I nodded. She took the paper. There was nothing on Page One. A new battle on the Eastern Front and a speech by Churchill had pushed her off the front pages. I turned to Page Four. There was her picture.

Wind howled through the narrow court between the houses. Rain spattered the window-panes. The only sound inside the

house was the rhythm of her breathing. Then she looked over
the paper into my face and her eyes were filled with tears.

"The poor thing," she said, "the poor, poor kid."

"Who?"

"Diane Redfern. A girl I knew. I'd lent her the apartment."

II

WE SAT on the couch while I told her about the discovery of the body, the destruction of the face by BB shot, and the identification at the morgue by her aunt and Bessie Clary.

She said: "Yes, of course. We were about the same size and she had my robe on. We wore the same size; I'd given her a few of my dresses. Her hair was a little lighter, but if there was a lot of blood . . ."

She groped for her purse. I gave her my handkerchief.

After she had dried her eyes, she read the rest of the story in the paper. "Are you Mark McPherson?"

I nodded.

"You haven't found the murderer?"

"Nope."

"Did he want to murder her or me?"

"I don't know."

"What are you going to do now that I'm alive?"

"Find out who murdered the other girl."

She sighed and sank back against the cushions. "You'd better have a drink," I said, and went to the corner cabinet. "Scotch, gin, or Bourbon?"

There was the bottle of Three Horses. I should have asked her about it then, before she had time to think. But I was thinking less about the job than the girl, and still so dazed that I wasn't even sure that I was alive, awake and in my right mind.

"How do you know my house so well, Mr. McPherson?"

"There isn't much about you I don't know."

"Gosh," she said; and after a little while, she laughed and asked: "Do you realize that you're the only person in New York who knows I'm alive? The only one of six million people?"

Thunder and lightning had ceased, but rain beat on the windows. It made us feel separate from everyone else in the city, and important because we shared a secret.

She held up her glass. "To life!"

"To resurrection," I said.

We laughed.

"Go and change your dress," I said. "You'll catch cold."

"Oh," she said. "You're giving me orders."

"Change it. You'll catch cold."

"How masterful, Mr. McPherson!"

She went. I was too nervous to sit down. I was like a kid in a dark house on Hallowe'en; everything seemed mystic and supernatural, and I listened at the door so I should hear her moving about the bedroom, and know that she had not vanished again. My mind was filled with a miracle, life and resurrection, and I had to battle my way through clouds before I could think like a human being. Finally I managed to anchor myself to a chair and light my pipe.

There was, of course, no more Laura Hunt case. But what about the other girl? The body had been cremated. You've got to have a *corpus delicti* to prove murder.

This did not mean that my job was finished. Neither the Department nor the D. A.'s office would let a case slip through their hands so smoothly. Our job was to establish circumstantial evidence of the girl's disappearance, to discover where she had last been seen and by whom. Unless we had cogent evidence that the crime had been committed, the murderer might confess and still escape conviction.

"What do you know about this girl?" I called in to Laura. "What did you say her name was? Were you close friends?"

The bedroom door opened and there was Laura in a long, loose sort of gold-colored robe that made her look like a saint on the window of the Catholic Church. She carried the magazine that had been on the bed-table. On the back cover there was a photograph of a girl in evening clothes smiling at a fellow as he lit her cigarette. The advertisement said:

COMPANIONABLE!

THERE'S NOTHING AS COMPANIONABLE AS A LANCASTER

"Oh, she was a model?"

"Wasn't she lovely?" Laura asked.

"She looks like a model," I said.

"She was beautiful," Laura insisted.

"What else?"

"What else what?"

"What was she like? How well did you know her? Where did she live? How much did she earn? Married, single, divorced? How old? Did she have a family? Who were her friends?"

"Please, Mr. McPherson. One question at a time. What was Diane like?" She hesitated. "I don't think a woman can answer that question quite honestly. You ought to ask a man."

"Your opinion would probably be safer."

"I might be prejudiced. Women with faces like mine can't be too objective about girls like Diane."

"I see nothing wrong with your face, Miss Hunt."

"Skip it. I've never tried to get by on my beauty. And if I should tell you that I considered Diane rather unintelligent and awfully shallow and quite a negative person, you might think I was jealous."

"If you felt that way about her, why did you let her have your apartment?"

"She lived in a hot little room in a boarding-house. And since nobody would have been using this place for a few days, I gave her the key."

"Why did you keep it so secret? Even Bessie didn't know."

"There was nothing secret about it. I had lunch with Diane on Friday. She told me how beastly hot it was in her room and I said she might come up here and live in comparative comfort. If I'd have come home on Friday afternoon or seen Bessie, I'd have mentioned it, but Bessie would have found it out anyway when she came to work on Saturday."

"Have you ever lent your apartment before?"

"Of course. Why not?"

"They said you were generous. Impulsive, too, aren't you?"

She laughed again. "My Aunt Susie says I'm a sucker for a hard-luck story, but I always tell her the sucker wins in the end. You don't get neuroses worrying over people's motives and wondering whether they're trying to use you."

"Sometimes you get shot by mistake," I said. "You happened to be lucky this time."

"Go on," she laughed. "You're not so hard-boiled, McPherson. How many shirts have you given away in your life?"

"I'm a Scotchman," I said stiffly; I did not want to show too much pleasure at the way she had read my character.

She laughed again. "Scotch thrift is vastly overrated. My granny Kirkland was the most liberal and open-handed woman in the world."

"You had a Scotch grandmother?"

"From a place called Pitlochry."

"Pitlochry! I've heard of Pitlochry. My father's people came from Blair-Atholl."

We shook hands.

"Were your people very religious?" Laura asked.

"Not my father. But original sin started in my mother's family."

"Ah-hah!" she said. "Dissension in the home. Don't tell me that your father read Darwin."

"Robert Ingersoll."

She clapped her hand to her head. "What a childhood you must have had!"

"Only when my old man took a drop too much. Otherwise Robert Ingersoll never even got to the Apostles' forty-yard line."

"But the name had a sort of magic and you read him secretly as you grew older."

"How did you know?"

"And you decided to learn everything in the world so people couldn't push you around."

That started the life story. It must have sounded like a combination of Frank Merriwell and Superman in ninety-nine volumes, each worth a nickel. McPherson *vs.* Associated Dairymen. McPherson in Washington. McPherson's Big Night with the Hopheads. Down Among the Bucket Shops with Mark McPherson. Labor Spy Rackets as Seen by McPherson. Killers I Have Known. From there somehow we got back to Mark McPherson's Childhood Days. From Rags to Riches, or Barefoot Boy in Brooklyn. I guess I described every game I'd pitched for the Long Island Mohawks. And told her about the time I knocked out Rocco, the Wop Terror, and how Sparks Lampini, who had bet his paper route on Rocco, knocked me out for revenge. And about my folks, my mother, and my sister who had made up her mind to marry the boss, and what a heel she had turned out to be. I even told her about the time we all had diphtheria and Davey, the kid brother, died. It must have been ten years since I had mentioned Davey.

She sat with her hands folded against the gold-colored cloth of her dress and a look on her face as if she were hearing the Commandments read by Moses himself. That's probably what Waldo meant by delicate flattery.

She said, "You don't seem at all like a detective."

"Have you ever known any detectives?"

"In detective stories there are two kinds, the hard-boiled ones who are always drunk and talk out of the corners of their mouths and do it all by instinct; and the cold, dry, scientific kind who split hairs under a microscope."

"Which do you prefer?"

"Neither," she said. "I don't like people who make their livings out of spying and poking into people's lives. Detectives aren't heroes to me, they're detestable."

"Thanks," I said.

She smiled a little. "But you're different. The people you've gone after ought to be exposed. Your work is important. I hope you've got a million more stories to tell me."

"Sure," I said, swelling like a balloon. "I'm the Arabian Nights. Spend a thousand and one evenings with me and you won't hear the half of my daring exploits."

"You don't talk like a detective, either."

"Neither hard-boiled nor scientific?"

We laughed. A girl had died. Her body had lain on the floor of this room. That is how Laura and I met. And we couldn't stop laughing. We were like old friends, and later, at half-past three, when she said she was hungry, we went into the kitchen and opened some cans. We drank strong tea at the kitchen table like home-folks. Everything was just the way I had felt it would be with her there, alive and warm and interested in a fellow.

III

"LISTEN!" she said.

We heard the sound of rain and the crackling of wood in the fireplace and foghorns on the East River.

"We're in the midst of Manhattan and this is our private world," she said.

I liked it. I didn't want the rain to stop or the sun to rise. For once in my life I had quit being restless.

She said, "I wonder what people are going to say when they hear I'm not dead."

I thought of the people whose names were in her address book and the stuffed shirts at her office. I thought of Shelby, but what I said was, "One thing I don't want to miss is Waldo when he finds out." I laughed.

She said: "Poor darling Waldo! Did he take it hard?"

"What do you think?"

"He loves me," she said.

I put another log on the fire. My back was turned so that I could not see her face when she asked about Shelby. This was Thursday, the twenty-eighth of August; it was to have been their wedding day.

I answered without turning around. "Shelby has been okay. He's been frank and cooperative, and kind to your aunt."

"Shelby has great self-control. You liked him, didn't you?"

I kept poking at the fire until I almost succeeded in smothering it. There had been the phoney alibi and the bottle of Three Horses Bourbon, the insurance money and the collection of unused shotguns. But now I had run into a new set of contradictions. Two and two no longer added up to four. The twenty-five-thousand-dollar insurance motive was definitely out.

It was hard for me to start asking her questions. She seemed tired. And Shelby was to have been today's bridegroom. I asked only one question.

"Did Shelby know this girl?"

She answered instantly. "Why, yes, of course. She modeled

for several of the accounts in our office. All of us knew Diane."
She yawned.

"You're tired, aren't you?"

"Would you mind very much if I tried to get some sleep? In
the morning—later, I mean—I'll answer all the questions you
want to ask."

I phoned the office and told them to send a man to watch
her front door.

"Is that necessary?" she said.

"Someone tried to murder you before. I'm not going to
take any chances."

"How thoughtful of you! Detectives are all right, I suppose,
when they're on your side."

"Look here, Miss Hunt, will you promise me something?"

"You know me much too well to call me Miss Hunt, Mark."

My heart beat like the drum in a Harlem dance band.

"Laura," I said; she smiled at me. "You'll promise, Laura,
not to leave this house until I give you permission. Or answer
the phone."

"Who'd ring if everybody thinks I'm dead?"

"Promise me, just in case."

She sighed. "All right. I won't answer. And can't I phone
anyone either?"

"No," I said.

"But people would be glad to know I'm alive. There are
people I ought to tell right away."

"Look here, you're the one living person who can help solve
this crime. Laura Hunt must find the person who tried to
murder Laura Hunt. Are you game?"

She offered her hand.

The sucker took it and believed her.

IV

I T WAS almost six when I checked in at the club. I decided that I'd need a clear head for the day's work and left a call for eight. I dreamed for two hours about Laura Hunt. The dream had five or six variations, but the meaning was always the same. She was just beyond my reach. As soon as I came close, she floated off into space. Or ran away. Or locked a door. Each time I came to, I cursed myself for letting a dream hold me in such horror. As time passed and I struggled from dream to dream, the real incidents of the night became less real than my nightmares. Each time I woke, cold and sweating, I believed more firmly that I had dreamed of finding her in the apartment and that Laura was still dead.

When the desk clerk called, I jumped as if a bomb had gone off under my bed. Exhausted, my head aching, I swore never to drink Italian wine again. The return of Laura Hunt seemed so unreal that I wondered if I had ever actually considered reporting it to the Department. I stared hard at real things, the steel tubes of the chairs and writing desk, the brown curtains at the windows, the chimneys across the street. Then I saw, on the bureau with my wallet and keys, a spot of red. This brought me out of bed with a leap. It was the stain of lip rouge on my handkerchief which she had used. So I knew she was alive.

As I reached for the telephone, I remembered that I had told her not to answer it. She was probably sleeping anyway, and wouldn't have been pleased if a thoughtless mug called her at that hour.

I went down to the office, wrote out my report on the typewriter, sealed and filed all copies. Then I went in to see Deputy Commissioner Preble.

Every morning I had gone into his office to report on the Laura Hunt case and every day he had said the same thing.

"Stick to the case a little longer, my boy, and maybe you'll find that murder's big enough for your talents."

His cheeks were like purple plums. I wanted to squash them with my fists. We represented opposing interests, I being one of the Commissioner's inside men, and more active than anyone in the Department on the progressive angle. Deputy Commissioner Preble was his party's front. Now that they were out of power, his was strictly an appeasement job.

As I walked into his office, he gave me the usual razzberry. Before I could say a word he started: "Do you know what this case is costing the Department? I've had a memo sent to your office. You'd better step on it or I'll have to assign someone to the case who knows how to handle homicide."

"You might have thought of that in the beginning," I said, because I wasn't going to let him know that I hadn't been on to his tactics. He had been waiting all along to show me up by letting me work until I'd hit a dead end and then handing the case to one of his favorites.

"What have you to say? Another of those minute-and-a-half reports, huh?"

"You needn't worry about our not getting Laura Hunt's murderer," I said. "That part of the case is completed."

"What do you mean? You've got him?" He looked disappointed.

"Laura Hunt isn't dead."

His eyes popped like golf balls. "She's in her apartment now. I had Ryan on guard until eight this morning, then Behrens came on. No one knows of this yet."

He pointed at his head. "Perhaps I ought to get in touch with Bellevue, McPherson. Psychopathic Ward."

I told him briefly what had happened. Although the heat wave was over and there was a chill in the air, he fanned himself with both hands.

"Who murdered the other girl?"

"I don't know yet."

"What does Miss Hunt say about it?"

"I've reported everything that she told me."

"Do you think she knows anything she hasn't told you?"

I said: "Miss Hunt was suffering from shock after she heard that her friend had been killed. She wasn't able to talk a lot."

He snorted. "Is she pretty, McPherson?"

I said: "I'm going to question her this morning. I also intend to surprise several people who think she is dead. It would be better if this were kept out of the newspapers until I've had time to work out my plans."

It was strictly Front Page even for the *Times*, and a coast-to-coast hook-up on the news broadcasts. I could tell by his face that he was working out an angle that would immortalize the name of Preble.

He said: "This changes the case, you know. There is no *corpus delicti*. We'll have to investigate the death of the other girl. I'm wondering, McPherson . . ."

"I wondered, too," I said. "You'll find it all in my report. A sealed copy has been sent to the Commissioner's office and you'll find yours on your secretary's desk. And I don't want to be relieved. You assigned me to the case in the beginning and I'm sticking until it's finished." I shouted and pounded on the desk, knowing that a man is most easily intimidated by his own methods. "And if one word of this gets into the papers before I've given the green light, there'll be hell to pay around here on Monday when the Commissioner gets back."

I told only one other person about Laura's return. That was Jake Mooney. Jake is a tall, sad-faced Yankee from Providence, known among the boys as the Rhode Island Clam. Once a reporter wrote, "Mooney maintained a clam-like silence," and it got Jake so angry that he's lived up to the name ever since. By the time I came out of Preble's office, Jake had got a list of the photographers for whom Diane Redfern posed.

"Go and see these fellows," I said. "Get what you can on her. Look over her room. Don't tell anyone she's dead."

He nodded.

"I want all the papers and letters you find in her room. And be sure to ask the landlady what kind of men she knew. She might have picked up some boy friends who played with sawed-off shotguns."

The telephone rang. It was Mrs. Treadwell. She wanted me to come to her house right away.

"There's something I ought to tell you, Mr. McPherson. I'd intended going back to the country today; there was nothing more I could do for poor Laura, was there? My lawyers are going to take care of her things. But now something has happened . . ."

"All right, I'll be there, Mrs. Treadwell."

As I drove up Park Avenue, I decided to keep Mrs. Treadwell waiting while I saw Laura. She had promised to stay in the apartment and keep away from the telephone, and I knew there was no fresh food in the house. I drove around to Third Avenue, bought milk, cream, butter, eggs, and bread.

Behrens was on guard at the door. His eyes bulged at the sight of the groceries, but he evidently thought I'd set up housekeeping.

I had the key in my pocket. But before I entered, I called a warning.

She came out of the kitchen. "I'm glad you didn't ring the bell," she said. "Since you told me about the murder"—she shuddered and looked at the spot where the body had fallen— "I'm afraid of every stray sound.

"I'm sure you're the only detective in the world who'd think of *that*," she said when I gave her the groceries. "Have you eaten breakfast?"

"Now that you've reminded me, no."

It seemed natural for me to be carrying in the groceries and lounging in the kitchen while she cooked. I had thought of that kind of girl, with all those swell clothes and a servant to wait on her, as holding herself above housework. But not Laura.

"Should we be elegant and carry it to the other room or folksy and eat in the kitchen?"

"Until I was a grown man, I never ate in anything but a kitchen."

"Then it's the kitchen," she said. "There's no place like home."

While we were eating, I told her that I had informed the Deputy Commissioner of her return.

"Was he startled?"

"He threatened to commit me to the Psychopathic Ward. And then"—I looked straight into her eyes—"he asked if I thought you knew anything about that other girl's death."

"And what did you say?"

"Listen," I said; "there are going to be a lot of questions asked and you'll probably have to tell a lot more than you'd like about your private life. The more honest you are, the easier it will be for you in the end. I hope you don't mind my telling you this."

"Don't you trust me?"

I said, "It's my job to suspect everyone."

She looked at me over her coffee-cup. "And just what do you suspect me of?"

I tried to be impersonal. "Why did you lie to Shelby about going to Waldo Lydecker's for dinner on Friday night?"

"So that's what's bothering you?"

"You lied, Miss Hunt."

"Oh, I'm Miss Hunt to you now, Mister McPherson."

"Quit sparring," I said. "Why did you lie?"

"I'm afraid if I told you the truth, you might not understand."

"Okay," I said. "I'm dumb. I'm a detective. I don't speak English."

"I'm sorry if I've hurt your feelings, but"—she drew the knife along the checks in the red-and-white tablecloth—"it's hardly the sort of thing that one finds on a police blotter. Blotter, isn't that what you call it?"

"Go on," I said.

"You see," she said, "I've been a single woman for such a long time."

"It's as clear as mud," I said.

"Men have bachelor dinners," she said. "They get drunk. They go out for a last binge with chorus girls. That, I guess, is what freedom means to them. So they've got to make a splurge before they get married."

I laughed. "Poor Waldo! I bet he wouldn't care very much to be compared with a chorus girl."

She shook her head. "Freedom meant something quite different to me, Mark. Maybe you'll understand. It meant owning myself, possessing all my silly and useless routines, being the sole mistress of my habits. Do I make sense?"

"Is that why you kept putting off the wedding?"

She said: "Get me a cigarette, will you? They're in the living-room."

I got her the cigarettes and lit my pipe.

She went on talking. "Freedom meant my privacy. It's not that I want to lead any sort of double life, it's simply that I resent intrusion. Perhaps because Mama always used to ask where I was going and what time I'd be home and always made me feel guilty if I changed my mind. I love doing things impulsively, and I resent it to a point where my spine stiffens

and I get gooseflesh if people ask where and what and why."
She was like a child, crying to be understood.

"On Friday I had a date with Waldo for a sort of bachelor
dinner before I left for Wilton. It was to be my last night in
town before my wedding . . ."

"Didn't Shelby resent it?"

"Naturally. Wouldn't you?" She laughed and showed the tip
of her tongue between her lips. "Waldo resented Shelby. But I
couldn't help it. I never flirted or urged them on. And I'm
fond of Waldo; he's a fussy old maid, but he's been kind to me,
very kind. Besides, we've been friends for years. Shelby just
had to make the best of it. We're civilized people, we don't try
to change each other."

"And Shelby, I suppose, had habits that weren't hundred per
cent with you?"

She ignored the question. "On Friday I fully intended to
dine with Waldo and take the ten-twenty train. But in the afternoon I changed my mind."

"Why?"

"Why?" she mocked. "That's precisely why I didn't tell him.
Because he'd ask why."

I got angry. "You can have your prejudices if you like, and
God knows I don't care if you want to make your habits sacred,
but this is a murder case. Murder! There must have been some
reason why you changed your mind."

"I'm like that."

"Are you?" I asked. "They told me you were a kind woman
who thought more of an old friend than to stand him up for
the sake of a selfish whim. You're supposed to be generous and
considerate. It sounds like a lot of bull to me!"

"Why, Mr. McPherson, you are a vehement person."

"Please tell me exactly why you changed your mind about
having dinner at Waldo's."

"I had a headache."

"I know. That's what you told him."

"Don't you believe me?"

"Women always have headaches when they don't want to do
something. Why did you come back from lunch with such a
headache that you phoned Waldo before you took your hat
off?"

"My secretary told you that, I suppose. How important trifles become when something violent happens!"

She walked over to the couch and sat down. I followed. Suddenly she touched my arm with her hand and looked up into my eyes so sweetly that I smiled. We both laughed and the trifles became less important.

She said: "So help me, Mark, I've told you the truth. I felt so wretched after lunch on Friday, I just couldn't face Waldo's chatter, and I couldn't sit through dinner with Shelby either because he'd have been too pleased at my breaking the date with Waldo. I just had to get away from everybody."

"Why?"

"What a persistent man you are!"

She shivered. The day was cold. Rain beat against the window. The sky was the color of lead.

"Should I make you a fire?"

"Don't bother." Her voice was cold, too.

I got logs out of the cabinet under the bookshelves and built her a fire. She sat at the end of the couch, her knees tucked up, her arms hugging her body. She seemed defenseless.

"There," I said. "You'll be warm soon."

"Please, please, Mark, believe me. There was no more to it than that. You're not just a detective who sees nothing but surface actions. You're a sensitive man, you react to nuances. So please try to understand, please."

The attack was well-aimed. A man is no stronger than his vanity. If I doubted her, I'd show myself to be nothing more than a crude detective.

"All right," I said, "we'll skip it now. Maybe you saw a ghost at lunch. Maybe your girl friend said something that reminded you of something else. Hell, everybody gets temperamental once in a while."

She slipped off the couch and ran toward me, her hands extended. "You're a darling, really. I knew last night that I'd never have to be afraid of you."

I took her hands. They were soft to touch, but strong underneath. Sucker, I said to myself, and decided to do something about it then and there. My self-respect was involved. I was a detective, a servant of the people, a representative of law and order.

I went to the liquor cabinet. "Ever seen this before?"

It was the bottle with the Three Horses on the label.

She answered without the slightest hesitation, "Of course; it's been in the house for weeks."

"This isn't the brand you usually buy, is it? Did you get this from Mosconi's, too?"

She answered in one long unpunctuated sentence. "No no I picked it up one night we were out of Bourbon I had company for dinner and stopped on the way home from the office it was on Lexington or maybe Third Avenue I don't remember."

She lied like a goon. I had checked with Mosconi and discovered that on Friday night, between seven and eight, Shelby Carpenter had stopped at the store, bought the bottle of Three Horses, and, instead of charging it to Miss Hunt's account, had paid cash.

V

"WHAT TOOK you so long, Mr. McPherson? You should have come earlier. Maybe it's too late now, maybe he's gone forever."

In a pink bed, wearing a pink jacket with fur on the sleeves, lay Mrs. Susan Treadwell. I sat like the doctor on a straight chair.

"Shelby?"

She nodded. Her pink massaged skin looked dry and old, her eyes were swollen and the black stuff had matted under her lashes. The Pomeranian lay on the pink silk comfort, whimpering.

"Do make Wolf stop that sniffling," begged the lady. She dried her eyes with a paper handkerchief that she took from a silk box. "My nerves are completely gone. I can't bear it."

The dog went on whimpering. She sat up and spanked it feebly.

"He's gone?" I asked. "Where?"

"How do I know?" She looked at a diamond wristwatch. "He's been gone since six-thirty this morning."

I was not upset. One of our men had been following Shelby since I'd checked with Mosconi on the Bourbon bottle.

"You were awake when he left? You heard him go? Did he sneak out?"

"I lent him my car," she sniffled.

"Do you think he was trying to escape the law, Mrs. Treadwell?"

She blew her nose and dabbed at her eyes again. "Oh, I knew it was weak of me, Mr. McPherson. But you know Shelby, he has a way with him. He asks you for something and you can't resist him; and then you hate yourself for giving in. He said it was a matter of life and death, and if I ever discovered the reason, I'd always be grateful."

I let her cry for a few minutes before I asked, "Do you believe that he committed the murder . . . the murder of your niece, Mrs. Treadwell?"

"No! No! I don't, Mr. McPherson. He just hasn't got the

86

stomach. Criminals go after what they want, but Shelby's just a big kid. He's always being sorry for something. My poor, poor Laura!"

I said nothing about Laura's return.

"You don't like Shelby very much, do you, Mrs. Treadwell?"

"He's a darling boy," she said, "but not for Laura. Laura couldn't afford him."

"Oh," I said.

She was afraid I had got the wrong impression and added quickly: "Not that he's a gigolo. Shelby comes from a wonderful family. But in some ways a gigolo's cheaper. You know where you are. With a man like Shelby you can't slip the money under the table."

I decided that it was lucky that most of my cases had not involved women. Their logic confused me.

"She was always doing the most absurd things about his pride. Like the cigarette case. That was typical. And then he had to go and lose it."

By this time I'd lost the scent.

"She couldn't afford it, of course; she had to charge it on my account and pay me back by the month. A solid gold cigarette case, he had to have it, she said, so he'd feel equal to the men he lunched with at the club and the clients in their business. Does it make sense to you, Mr. McPherson?"

"No," I said honestly, "it doesn't."

"But it's just like Laura."

I could have agreed to that, too, but I controlled myself.

"And he lost it?" I asked, leading her back to the trail.

"Um-hum. In April, before she'd even finished paying for it. Can you imagine?" Suddenly, for no reason that I could understand, she took an atomizer from the bed-table and sprayed herself with perfume. Then she made up her lips and combed her hair. "I thought of the cigarette case as soon as he'd gone off with the keys to my car. Did I feel like a sucker!"

"I understand that," I said.

Her smile was a clue to the business with the perfume and lipstick. I was a man, she had to get around me.

"You're not going to blame me for giving him the car? Really, I didn't think of it at the time. He has a way with him, you know."

"You shouldn't have given it to him if you felt that way," said the stern detective.

She fell for it.

"It was weak, Mr. McPherson, I know how weak I was to have done it. I should have been more suspicious, I know I should, especially after that phone call."

"What phone call, Mrs. Treadwell?"

It was only by careful questioning that I got the story straight. If I told it her way, there would be no end to this chapter. The phone had wakened her at half-past five that morning. She lifted the receiver in time to hear Shelby, on the upstairs extension, talking to the night clerk at the Hotel Framingham. The clerk apologized for disturbing him at this hour, but said that someone wanted to get in touch with him on a life-and-death matter. That person was waiting on another wire. Should the clerk give that party Mr. Carpenter's number?

"I'll call back in ten minutes," Shelby had said. "Tell them to call you again."

He had dressed and tiptoed down the stairs.

"He was going out to phone," Mrs. Treadwell said. "He was afraid I'd listen on the extension."

At twenty minutes past six she had heard him coming up the stairs. He had knocked at her bedroom door, apologized for waking her, and asked for the use of the car.

"Does that make me an accessory or something, Mr. McPherson?" Tears rolled down her cheeks.

I phoned the office and asked if there had been any reports from the man who had been following Shelby Carpenter. Nothing had been heard since he went on duty at midnight, and the man who was to have relieved him at eight in the morning was still waiting.

As I put down the phone, the dog began to bark. Shelby walked in.

"Good morning." He went straight to the bed. "I'm glad you rested, darling. It was cruel of me to disturb you at that mad hour. But you don't show it at all. You're divine this morning." He kissed her forehead and then turned to welcome me.

"Where've you been?" she asked.

"Can't you guess, darling?"

He petted the dog. I sat back and watched. There was something familiar and unreal about Shelby. I was always uncomfortable when he was in the room, and always struggling to remember where I had seen him. The memory was like a dream, unsubstantial and baffling.

"I can't imagine where anyone would go at that wild hour, darling. You had me quite alarmed."

If Shelby guessed that the lady's alarm had caused her to summon the police, he was too tactful to mention it.

"I went up to Laura's place," he said. "I made a sentimental journey. This was to have been our wedding day, you know."

"Oh, I'd forgotten." Mrs. Treadwell caught his hand. He was sitting on the edge of the bed, comfortable and sure of himself.

"I couldn't sleep. And when that absurd phone call woke us, Auntie Sue, I was too upset to stay in my room. I felt such a longing for Laura, I wanted to be close to something she had loved. There was the garden. She'd cared for it herself, Mr. McPherson, with her own hands. It was lovely in the gray morning light."

"I don't know whether I quite believe you," Mrs. Treadwell said. "What's your opinion, Mr. McPherson?"

"You're embarrassing him, darling. Remember, he's a detective," Shelby said as if she had been talking about leprosy in front of a leper.

"Why couldn't you take that telephone call in the house?" asked Mrs. Treadwell. "Did you think I'd stoop so low as to listen on the extension?"

"If you hadn't been listening on the extension, you'd not have known that I had to go out to a phone booth," he said, laughing.

"Why were you afraid to have me hear?"

Shelby offered me a cigarette. He carried the pack in his pocket without a case.

"Was it a girl?" asked Mrs. Treadwell.

"I don't know. He . . . she . . . whoever it was . . . refused to leave a number. I called the Framingham three times, but they hadn't called back." He blew smoke rings toward the ceiling. Then, smiling at me like the King of England in a newsreel showing their majesties' visit to coal miners' huts, he said: "A yellow cab followed me all the way to the cottage and

back. On these country roads at that hour your man couldn't
very well hide himself. Don't be angry with the poor chap because I spotted him."

"He kept you covered. That was all he was told to do.
Whether you knew or not makes no difference." I got up. "I'm
going to be up at Miss Hunt's apartment at three o'clock. I
want you to meet me there, Carpenter."

"Is it necessary? I rather dislike going up there today of all
days. You know, we were to have been married . . ."

"Consider it a sentimental journey," I said.

Mrs. Treadwell barely noticed when I left. She was busy
with her face.

At the office I learned that Shelby's sentimental journey had
added a five-hour taxi bill to the cost of the Laura Hunt case.
Nothing had been discovered. Shelby had not even entered
the house, but had stood in the garden in the rain and blown
his nose vigorously. He might also, it was hinted, have been
crying.

VI

MOONEY WAS waiting in my office with his report on Diane Redfern.

She had not been seen since Friday. The landlady remembered because Diane had paid her room rent that day. She had come from work at five o'clock, stopped in the landlady's basement flat to hand her the money, gone to her room on the fourth floor, bathed, changed her clothes, and gone out again. The landlady had seen her hail a cab at the corner of Seventh Avenue and Christopher Street. She remembered because she considered taxis a sinful extravagance for girls like Diane.

The girl might have come in late on Friday night and gone out again on Saturday morning, but the landlady had not seen her. There were still boarders to be questioned, but the landlady had not known where they worked, and Mooney would have to go back at six o'clock to check with them.

"Did the landlady seem surprised that Diane hadn't been seen since Friday?"

"She says it doesn't matter to her whether the boarders use their rooms or not as long as they pay the rent. The girls that stay in places like that are often out all night."

"But it's five days," I said. "Was there nobody to bother about her disappearance?"

"You know how it is with those kind of girls, Mac. Here today, gone tomorrow. Who cares?"

"Hasn't she any friends? Didn't anyone come to see her or telephone?"

"There were some phone calls. Tuesday and Wednesday. I checked. Photographers calling her to come and work."

"Nothing personal?"

"There might have been a couple of other calls, but no messages. The landlady don't remember what she didn't write down on the pad."

I had known girls like that around New York. No home, no friends, not much money. Diane had been a beauty, but beauties are a dime a dozen on both sides of Fifth Avenue between Eighth Street and Ninety-Sixth. Mooney's report gave facts

and figures, showed an estimate of Diane's earnings according
to figures provided by the Models' Guild. She could have
supported a husband and kids on the money she earned when
she worked, but the work was unsteady. And according to
Mooney's rough estimate, the clothes in her closet had cost
plenty. Twenty pairs of shoes. There were no bills as there had
been in Laura's desk, for Diane came from the lower classes,
she paid cash. The sum of it all was a shabby and shiftless life.
Fancy perfume bottles, Kewpie dolls, and toy animals were all
she brought home from expensive dinners and suppers in
night spots. The letters from her family, plain working people
who lived in Paterson, New Jersey, were written in night-
school English and told about lay-offs and money troubles.

Her name had been Jennie Swobodo.

Mooney had taken nothing from the room but the letters.
He'd had a special lock put on the door and threatened the
landlady with the clink if she opened her face.

He gave me a duplicate key. "You might want to look in
yourself. I'll be back there at six to talk to the other tenants."

I had no time then to look into the life of Jennie Swobodo,
alias Diane Redfern. But when I got up to Laura's apartment,
I asked if there hadn't been any pocketbooks or clothes left
there by the murdered model.

Laura said: "Yes, if Bessie had examined the clothes in the
closet, she'd have found Diane's dress. And her purse was in
my dresser drawer. She had put everything away neatly."

There was a dresser drawer filled with purses. Among them
was the black silk bag that Diane had carried. There was eighteen dollars in it, the key to her room, lipstick, eyeshadow,
powder, a little tin phial of perfume, and a straw cigarette case
with a broken clasp.

Laura watched quietly while I examined Diane's belongings.
When I went back to the living-room, she followed me like a
child. She had changed into a tan dress and brown high-heeled
slippers that set off her wonderful ankles. Her earrings were
little gold bells.

"I've sent for Bessie."

"How thoughtful you are!"

I felt like a hypocrite. My reason for sending for Bessie had been purely selfish. I wanted to observe her reaction to Laura's return.

When I explained, Laura said, "But you don't suspect poor old Bessie?"

"I just want to see how a non-suspect takes it."

"As a basis for comparison?"

"Maybe."

"Then there's someone you do suspect?"

I said, "There are several lies which will have to be explained."

When she moved, the gold bells tinkled. Her face was like a mask.

"Mind a pipe?"

The bells tinkled again. I struck a match. It scraped like an emery wheel. I thought of Laura's lie and hated her because she was making a fool of herself for Shelby Carpenter. And trying to make a fool of me. I was glad when the doorbell rang. I told Laura to wait in the bedroom for my signal.

Bessie knew at once that something had happened. She looked around the room, she stared at the place where the body had fallen, she studied each ornament and every piece of furniture. I saw it with a housekeeper's eyes then, noticed that the newspaper had been folded carelessly and left on the big table, that Laura's lunch tray with an empty plate and coffee-cup remained on the coffee-table beside the couch, that a book lay open, that the fire burned behind the screen, and red-tipped cigarette stubs filled the ashtrays.

"Sit down," I told her. "Something's happened."

"What?"

"Sit down."

"I can take it standing."

"Someone has come to stay here," I said, and went to the bedroom door.

Laura came out.

I have heard women scream when their husbands beat them and mothers sobbing over dead and injured children, but I have never heard such eery shrieks as Bessie let out at the sight of Laura. She dropped her pocketbook. She crossed herself. Then, very slowly, she backed toward a chair and sat down.

"Do you see what I see, Mr. McPherson?"

"It's all right, Bessie. She's alive."

Bessie called upon God, Jesus, Mary, and her patron saint Elizabeth to witness the miracle.

"Bessie, calm yourself. I'm all right; I just went to the country. Someone else was murdered."

It was easier to believe in miracles. Bessie insisted upon telling Laura that she had herself found the body, that she had identified it as Laura Hunt's, that it had worn Laura's best negligee and silver mules. And she was just as positive about her uncle's sister-in-law's cousin who had met her dead sweetheart in an orchard in County Galway.

None of our arguments convinced her until Laura said, "Well, what are we going to have for dinner, Bessie?"

"Blessed Mary, I never thought I'd be hearing you ask that no more, Miss Laura."

"I'm asking, Bessie. How about a steak and French fried and apple pie, Bessie?"

Bessie brightened. "Would a ghost be asking for French fried and apple pie? Who was it got murdered, Miss Laura?"

"Miss Redfern, you remember . . . the girl who . . ."

"It's no more than she deserved," said Bessie, and went into the kitchen to change into her work clothes.

I told her to shop for dinner in stores where they did not know her as the servant of a murder victim, and warned her against mentioning the miracle of Laura's return.

"Evidently Bessie disapproved of Diane. Why?" I asked Laura when we were alone again.

"Bessie's opinionated," she said. "There was no particular reason."

"No?"

"No," said Laura firmly.

The doorbell rang again.

"Stay here this time," I whispered. "We'll try another kind of surprise."

She waited, sitting stiffly at the edge of the couch. I opened the door. I had expected to see Shelby, but it was Waldo Lydecker who walked in.

VII

SELF-CENTERED people see only what they want to see. Astigmatism might have been his excuse for his failure to notice her at first, but I think it was covetousness. His gaze was so concentrated upon the antique glass vase that the rest of the room might have been sky or desert.

"Your office told me I'd find you here, McPherson. I've talked to my lawyer and he advises me to take my vase and let the bitch sue."

He had to pass the sofa on the way to the mantel. Laura turned her head, the gold bells tinkled. Waldo paused as if he had heard some ghostly warning. Then, like a man afraid of his imagination and determined to show himself above fear, he stretched his hands toward the shining globe. Laura turned to see how I was taking it. Her gold bells struck such a sharp note that Waldo whirled on his heels and faced her.

He was whiter than death. He did not stagger nor fall, but stood paralyzed, his arms raised toward the vase. He was like a caricature, pitiful and funny at the same time. The Van Dyke beard, the stick crooked over his arm, the well-cut suit, the flower in his buttonhole, were like decorations on the dead.

We were quiet. The clock ticked.

"Waldo," Laura said softly.

He seemed not to have heard.

She took hold of his rigid arms and led him to the couch. He moved like a mechanical doll. She urged him to a seat, gently pushed down his arms, handed me his hat and stick. "Waldo," she whispered in the voice of a mother to a hurt child, "Waldo, darling."

His neck turned like a mechanism on springs. His glazed eyes, empty of understanding, were fastened on her face.

"It's all right, Mr. Lydecker. She's alive and well. There's been a mistake."

My voice touched him, but not in the right place. He swayed backward on the couch, then jerked forward with a mechanical rather than willful reaction. He trembled so violently that some inner force seemed to be shaking his body. Sweat rose in crystals on his forehead and upper lip.

"There's brandy in the cabinet. Get some, Mark. Quickly," Laura said.

I fetched the brandy. She lifted the glass to his lips. Most of the liquor trickled down his chin. After a while he lifted his right hand, looked at it, dropped it, and lifted the left. He seemed to be testing himself to see if he was capable of willing his muscles to action.

Laura kneeled beside him, her hands on his knees. Her voice was gentle as she explained that it was Diane Redfern who had died and been buried while Laura was staying at her little house in the country. I could not tell whether he heard or whether it was her voice that soothed him, but when she suggested that he rest on the bed, he rose obediently. Laura took him into the bedroom, helped him lie down, spread her blue-and-white cover over his legs. He let himself be led around like a child.

When she came back she asked if I thought we ought to call a doctor.

"I don't know," I said. "He's not young and he's fat. But it doesn't look like any stroke I've ever seen."

"It's happened before."

"Like this?"

She nodded. "In the theatre one night. He got angry that we'd called a doctor. Maybe we'd better let him rest."

We sat like people in a hospital corridor.

"I'm sorry," I said. "If I'd known it was Waldo, I'd have warned him."

"You're still planning to do it to Shelby, aren't you?"

"Shelby's nerves are stronger. He'll take it better."

Her eyes were narrow with anger.

I said: "Look here, you know that Shelby's lied. I'm not saying that he's committed murder, but I know he's hiding something. There are several things he's got to explain."

"He can, I'm sure he can. Shelby can explain everything."

She went into the bedroom to see how Waldo was getting on.

"He seems to be sleeping. He's breathing regularly. Maybe we'd better just leave him."

We sat without speaking until the doorbell rang again.

"You'll have to see him first and tell him," Laura said. "I'm not going to let anyone else go through that shock." She disappeared behind the swinging door that led to the kitchen.

The bell rang again. When I opened the door, Shelby pushed past.

"Where is she?" he shouted.

"Oh, you know, then?"

I heard the back door open, and I knew that he had met Bessie on the stairs.

"God damn women," I said.

Then Laura came out of the kitchen. I saw at once that Bessie wasn't the woman who deserved my curses. The lovers' meeting was too perfect. They embraced, kissed, and clung. An actor after a dozen rehearsals would have groped for his handkerchief in that same dazed way. An actor would have held her at arm's length, staring at her with that choir-boy look on his face. There was something prearranged about the whole scene. His tenderness and her joy.

I turned my back.

Laura's voice was melted syrup. "Happy, darling?"

He answered in a whisper.

My pipe had gone out. If I turned and got a match from the table, they would think I was watching. I bit on the cold stem. The whispering and muttering went on. I watched the minute hand creep around the dial of my watch. I thought of the night I had waited for Pinky Moran to come out of his sweetheart's house. It had been four above at ten o'clock and by midnight it was below zero. I had waited in the snow and thought about the gangster lying warm in the arms of his fat slut. I turned and saw Shelby's hands feeling, touching, moving along the tan material of Laura's dress.

"How infinitely touching! What inexpressible tenderness! Juliet risen from the grave! Welcome, Romeo!"

It was, of course, Waldo. He had not only recovered his strength, but his bounce.

"Forgive me," he said, "for a wee touch of epilepsy. It's an old family custom." He jerked Laura away from Shelby, kissed both cheeks, whirled around with her as if they were waltzing. "Welcome, wench! Tell us how it feels to return from the grave."

"Be yourself, Waldo."

"More truly myself you have never seen me, you beautiful zombie. I, too, am resurrected. The news of your death had me at the brink of eternity. We are both reborn, we must celebrate the miracle of life, beloved. Let's have a drink."

She started toward the liquor cabinet, but Waldo barred her way. "No, darling, no whiskey tonight. We're drinking champagne." And he bustled to the kitchen, shouting that Bessie was to hurry over to Mosconi's and bring back some wine with a name that he had to write down on a piece of paper.

VIII

LAURA SAT with three men drinking champagne. It was a familiar scene to them, Old Home Week. Even Bessie took it like a veteran. They seemed ready to take up where they had left off last week, before someone rang the bell and blew a girl's face away with a charge of BB shot. That's why I was there, the third man.

When they drank a toast to Laura, I took a sip of the wine. The rest of it stayed in my glass until the bubbles died.

"Aren't you drinking?" Waldo asked me.

"I happen to be on a job," I said.

"He's a prig," said Waldo. "A proletarian snob with a Puritan conscience."

Because I was on a job and because Laura was there, I didn't use the only words I knew for describing him. They were short words and to the point.

"Don't be cross with us," Laura said. "These are my best friends in the whole world and naturally they want to celebrate my not being dead."

I reminded them that Diane Redfern's death was still a mystery.

"But I'm sure we know nothing about it," Shelby said.

"Ah-hah!" said Waldo. "The ghost at the feast. Shall we drink a respectful toast?"

Laura put down her glass and said, "Waldo, please."

"That's in questionable taste," said Shelby.

Waldo sighed. "How pious we've all grown! It's your influence, McPherson. As walking delegate for the Union of the Dead . . ."

"Please shut up!" said Laura.

She moved closer to Shelby. He took her hand. Waldo watched like a cat with a family of mice.

"Well, McPherson, since you insist upon casting the shadow of sobriety upon our sunny reunion, tell us how you're proceeding with the investigation. Have you cleared the confusion surrounding that bottle of Bourbon?"

Laura said quietly: "It was I who bought that bottle of

Three Horses, Waldo. I know it's not as good as the stuff you taught me to buy, but one night I was in a hurry and brought it home. Don't you remember, Shelby?"

"I do indeed." Shelby pressed her hand.

They seemed to be getting closer together and shoving Waldo out into the cold. He poured himself another glass of champagne.

"Tell us, McPherson, were there any mysteries in the life of the little model? Have you discovered any evil companions? Do you know the secrets of her gay life in Greenwich Village?"

Waldo was using me as a weapon against Shelby. It was clear as water out of the old oaken bucket. Here he was, a man who had read practically all that was great in English literature, and a mug could have taught him the alphabet. I felt fine. He was shooting right up my alley.

"My assistant," I said with an official roll in my voice, "is on the trail of her enemies."

Waldo choked on his wine.

"Enemies," said Laura. "She?"

"There might have been things about her life that you didn't know," said Shelby.

"Pooh!"

"Most of those girls live very questionable lives," Shelby said firmly. "For all we know, the poor girl might have got herself mixed up with all sorts of people. Men she'd met in night clubs."

"How do you know so much about her?" Waldo asked.

"I don't know. I'm merely mentioning possibilities," Shelby said. He turned to me and asked, "These models, they're often friendly with underworld characters, aren't they?"

"Poor Diane," Laura said. "She wasn't the sort of person anyone could hate. I mean . . . she didn't have much . . . well, passion. Just beauty and vague dreams. I can't imagine anyone hating a kid like that. She was so . . . I mean . . . you wanted to help her."

"Was that Shelby's explanation?" Waldo asked. "His was a purely philanthropic interest, I take it."

Bright spots burned on Laura's cheeks. "Yes, it was!" she said hotly. "I'd asked him to be kind to her, hadn't I, Shelby?"

Shelby went to the cupboard for a log. He was glad for the excuse to move around. Laura's eyes followed his movements.

"Had you asked him to be particularly kind to her last Wednesday, darling?" Waldo pretended to ask the question innocently, but he was slanting curious glances at me.

"Wednesday?" she said with an effort to appear absent-minded.

"Last Wednesday. Or was it Tuesday? The night they did the Toccata and Fugue at the Stadium, wasn't that Wednesday?" He rolled his eyes toward the fireplace and Shelby. "When was your cocktail party, Laura?"

"Oh, that," she said. "On Wednesday."

"You should have been here, McPherson," Waldo said. "It was too, too jolly."

Laura said, "You're being silly, Waldo."

But Waldo wanted to put on a show and nothing could stop him. He got up with the champagne glass in his hand and gave an imitation of Laura as hostess to a lot of cocktail-drinkers. He did not merely speak in a falsetto voice and swing his hips the way most men do when they imitate women. He had a real talent for acting. He was the hostess, he moved from guest to guest, he introduced strangers, he saw that the glasses were filled, he carried a tray of sandwiches.

"Hello, darling, I'm so glad you could come . . . you must meet . . . I know you'll simply adore . . . Don't tell me you're not drinking . . . Not eating! . . . Come now, this tiny caviar sandwich wouldn't put weight on a sturgeon . . . You haven't met . . . but how incredible, everyone knows Waldo Lydecker, he's the heavyweight Noël Coward . . . Waldo darling, one of your most loyal admirers . . ."

It was a good show. You could see the stuffed shirts and the highbrow women, and all the time that he moved around the room, imitating Laura and carrying that imaginary tray, you knew she had been watching something that was going on at the bay window.

Now Waldo skipped to the bay window. He changed his movements and his gestures became manly. He was Shelby being gallant and cautious. And he was a girl, looking up at Shelby, blinking her eyes and tugging at his lapels. He caught

Shelby's voice perfectly, and while I had never heard her voice, I'd known plenty of dolls who talked as he had Diane talking.

"Oh, but darling, you are the best-looking man in the room . . . Can't I even say so?" "You're drunk, baby, don't talk so loud." "What harm can there be, Shelby, if I just quietly worship you?" "Quietly, for God's sakes, kid. Remember where we are." "Shelby, please, I'm not tight, I never get tight, I'm not talking loud." "Sh-sh, honey, everyone's looking at you." "Let 'em look, you think I care?" The doll-voice became shrill and angry. Drunken young girls in bars always scream like that.

Shelby had left the fire. His fists were clenched, his jaw pushed forward, his skin green.

Laura was trembling.

Waldo walked to the middle of the room, said in his own voice: "There was a terrible hush. Everyone looked at Laura. She was carrying that tray of hors d'oeuvres."

Everyone in the room must have felt sorry for Laura. Her wedding was to have taken place in a week and a day.

Waldo crossed toward the bay window with cat-like, female steps. I watched as if Diane were there with Shelby.

"Diane had taken hold of his lapels . . ."

Laura, the real one, the girl on the couch in the tan dress, said: "I'm sorry. For God's sakes, how often do I have to say I'm sorry?"

Shelby raised his clenched fists and said: "Yes, Lydecker, we've had enough. Enough of your clowning."

Waldo looked at me. "What a shame, McPherson! You've missed the best part of the scene."

"What did she do?" I asked.

"May I tell him?" said Waldo.

"You'd better," said Shelby, "or he'll imagine something far worse."

Laura began to laugh. "I conked her with a tray of hors d'oeuvres. I conked her!"

We waited until her hysteria had died down. She was crying and laughing at the same time. Shelby tried to take her hand, but she pulled away. Then she looked at me with shame on her face and said: "I'd never done anything like that before. I didn't dream I could do such a thing. I wanted to die."

"Is that all?" I asked.

"All!" said Shelby.

"In my own house," Laura said.

"What happened afterward?"

"I went into my bedroom. I wouldn't let anyone come in and talk to me. I was so ashamed. Then after a while Shelby did come in and he told me Diane had left and that I'd simply have to come out and face my guests."

"After all," said Shelby.

"Everyone was tactful, but that made me feel worse. But Shelby was darling, he insisted that we go out and get a little tight so I wouldn't think about it and keep reproaching myself."

"How kind of him!" I couldn't help saying.

"Shelby's broad-minded, he forgives easily," added Waldo.

"Shelby couldn't help it if Diane fell in love with him." Laura ignored the other two; she was explaining it to me. "He'd been kind and polite and thoughtful as he always is. Diane was a poor kid who'd come from the sort of home where they beat up women. She'd never met a . . . a gentleman before."

"Oddzooks!" Waldo said.

"She wanted something better than she'd had at home. Her life had been terribly sordid. Even her name, silly as it sounded, showed that she wanted a better sort of life."

"You're breaking my heart," Waldo said.

Laura took a cigarette. Her hands were unsteady. "I'm not so different. I came to New York, too, a poor kid without friends or money. People were kind to me"—she pointed with the cigarette at Waldo—"and I felt almost an obligation toward kids like Diane. I was the only friend she had. And Shelby."

It sounded simple and human as she stood there, so close that I could smell her perfume. I backed away.

She said, "You believe me, don't you, Mark?"

"What was this lunch on Friday? An armistice?" I asked her.

She smiled. "Yes, yes, an armistice. I went around from Wednesday evening until Friday morning feeling like a heel. And I knew if I didn't see Diane and say I was sorry my whole vacation would be ruined. Do you think I'm very silly?"

"A soft-hearted slob," said Waldo.

Shelby picked up the poker, but it was only to stoke the fire.

My nerves were on edge and I saw violence every time a cigarette was lighted. That was because I craved violence. My hands itched for a fat neck.

I took two steps forward and was close to Laura again. "Then it was at lunch that you smoked . . ."

I stopped right there. She was whiter than the white dress that Diane had been buried in.

"Smoked," she whispered the word.

"Smoked the pipe of peace," I said, "and offered her your apartment."

"Yes, the pipe of peace," Laura said. She had come to life again. Her eyes sparkled, her cheeks glowed with color. Her thin, strong fingers lay on my coat-sleeve. "You must believe me, Mark, you must believe that everything was all right when I offered her the apartment. Please, please believe me."

Shelby didn't say a word. But I think he was smiling. Waldo laughed aloud and said, "Careful, Laura, he's a detective."

Her hand slipped off my coat-sleeve.

IX

I ATE dinner again that night with Waldo. Ask me why. I asked myself as I looked at his fat face over a bowl of bird's-nest soup at the Golden Lizard. It was raining. I was lonely. I wanted to talk. I wanted to talk about Laura. She was eating steak and French fried with Shelby. I clung to Waldo. I was afraid of losing him. I despised the guy and he fascinated me. The deeper I got into this case, the less I seemed like myself and the more I felt like a greenhorn in a new world.

My mind was foggy. I was going somewhere, but I'd lost the road. I remember asking myself about clues. What were clues, what had I looked for in other cases? A smile couldn't be brought into court as evidence. You couldn't arrest a man because he had trembled. Brown eyes had stolen a peep at gray eyes, so what? The tone of a voice was something that died with a word.

The Chinese waiter brought a platter of eggroll. Waldo reached for it like a man on the breadline.

"Well," he said, "what do you think of her now that you've met her?"

I helped myself to eggroll. "It's my job . . ."

He finished for me. ". . . to look at facts and hold no opinions. Where have I heard that before?"

The waiter brought a trayful of covered dishes. Waldo had to have his plate arranged just so, pork on this side, duck over there, noodles under the chicken-almond, sweet and pungent spareribs next to the lobster, Chinese ravioli on a separate plate because there might be a conflict in the sauces. Until he had tried each dish with and without beetle juice, there was no more talk at our table.

At last he stopped for breath, and said: "I remember something you said when you first came to see me on Sunday morning. Do you remember?"

"We said a lot of things on Sunday morning. Both of us."

"You said that it wasn't fingerprints you'd want to study in this case, but faces. That was very dull of you, I thought."

"Then why did you remember it?"

"Because I was moved by the sorry spectacle of a conventional young man thinking that he had become radically unconventional."

"So what?" I said.

He snapped his fingers. Two waiters came running. It seems they had forgotten the fried rice. There was more talk than necessary, and he had to rearrange his plate. Between giving orders to the Chinese and moaning because the ritual (his word) of his dinner was upset, he talked about Elwell and Dot King and Starr Faithfull and several other well-known murder cases.

"And you think this is going to be the unsolved Diane Redfern case?" I asked.

"Not the Redfern case, my friend. In the public mind and in the newspapers, it will be the Laura Hunt case forevermore. Laura will go through life a marked woman, the living victim of unsolved murder."

He was trying to get me angry. There were no direct hits, only darts and pinpricks. I tried to avoid his face, but I could not escape that doughy smirk. If I turned around, he moved too, his fat head rolling like a ball-bearing in his starched collar.

"You'd die before you'd let that happen, my gallant Hawkshaw? You'd risk your precious hide before you'd let that poor innocent girl suffer such lifelong indignity, eh?" He laughed aloud. Two waiters poked their heads out of the kitchen.

"Your jokes aren't so funny," I said.

"Woof! Woof! How savage our bark is tonight. What's tormenting you? Is it fear of failure or the ominous competition with Apollo Belvedere?"

I could feel my face getting red. "Look here," I said.

Again he interrupted. "Look here, my dear lad, at the risk of losing your esteemed friendship . . . and the friendship of such an estimable character as yourself I do value, whether you believe me or not . . . at the risk, I say of losing . . ."

"Get to the point," I said.

"Advice to a young man. Don't lose your head. She's not for you."

"Mind your god-damned business," I said.

"Some day you will thank me for this. Unless you fail to heed my advice, of course. Didn't you hear her describing

Diane's infatuation for Shelby? A gentleman, oddzooks! Do you think that Diane has died so completely that chivalry must die, too? If you were more astute, my friend, you would see that Laura is Diane and Diane was Laura . . ."

"Her real name was Jennie Swobodo. She used to work in a mill in Jersey."

"It's like a bad novel."

"But Laura's no dope. She must have known he was a heel."

"Long after the core of gentility is gone, the husks remain. The educated woman, no less than the poor mill girl, is bound by the shackles of romance. The aristocratic tradition, my dear good friend, with its faint sweet odor of corruption. Romantics are children, they never grow up." He helped himself to another round of chicken, pork, duck, and rice. "Didn't I tell you the day we met that Shelby was Laura's softer, less distinguished side? Do you see it now, the answer to that longing for perfection? Pass the soy sauce, please."

Romance was something for crooners, for the movies. The only person I ever heard use the word in common life was my kid sister, and she'd raised herself by romance, married the boss.

"I was hopeful once that Laura'd grow up, get over Shelby. She'd have been a great woman if she had, you know. But the dream still held her, the hero she could love forever immaturely, the mould of perfection whose flawlessness made no demands upon her sympathies or her intelligence."

I was tired of his talk. "Come on, let's get out of this dump," I said. He made me feel that everything was hopeless.

While we were waiting for change, I picked up his cane.

"What do you carry this for?" I said.

"Don't you like it?"

"It's an affectation."

"You're a prig," he said.

"Just the same," I said, "I think it's a phoney."

"Everyone in New York knows Waldo Lydecker's walking-stick. It gives me importance."

I was willing to let the subject drop, but he liked to brag about his possessions. "I picked it up in Dublin. The dealer told me that it had been carried by an Irish baronet whose lofty and furious temper became a legend in the country."

"Probably used it for beating up the poor devils who dug

peat on his lands," I said, not being very sympathetic to hot-blooded noblemen, my grandmother's stories having given me the other side of the picture. The cane was one of the heaviest I have ever handled, weighing at least one pound, twelve ounces. Below the crook, the stick was encircled by two gold bands set about three inches apart.

He snatched it out of my hands. "Give it back to me."

"What's eating you? Nobody wants your damn cane."

The Chinese brought change. Waldo watched out of the corner of his eye, and I added a quarter to the tip, hating myself but too weak to give him a reason to sneer.

"Don't sulk," he said. "If you need a cane, I'll buy you one. With a rubber tip."

I felt like picking up that big hunk of blubber and bouncing him like a ball. But I couldn't take any chances of losing his friendship. Not now. He asked where I was going, and when I said downtown, asked me to drop him at the Lafayette.

"Don't be so ungracious," he said. "I should think you'd be glad for an extra quarter-hour of my admirable discourse."

While we were driving along Fourth Avenue, he grabbed my arm. The car almost skidded.

"What's the idea?" I said.

"You must stop! Please, you must. Be generous for once in your life."

I was curious to know the cause of his excitement, so I stopped the car. He hurried back along the block to Mr. Claudius' antique shop.

Mr. Claudius' last name was Cohen. He was more like a Yankee than a Jew. He was about five-foot eleven, weighed no more than a hundred and fifty, had light eyes and a bald head that rose to a point like a pear. I knew him because he had once had a partner who was a fence. Claudius was an innocent guy, absent-minded and so crazy about antiques that he had no idea of his partner's double-crossing. I had been able to keep him out of court, and in gratitude he had given me a set of the Encyclopaedia Britannica.

It was natural that he and Waldo should know each other. They could both go into a trance over an old teapot.

What Waldo had seen in Claudius' window was a duplicate of the vase he had given Laura. It was made like a globe set upon a pedestal. To me it looked like one of those silver balls that hang on Christmas trees, strictly Woolworth. And I understand that it is not so rare and costly as many of the pieces that cause collectors to swoon. Waldo valued it because he had started the craze for mercury glass among certain high-class antique snobs. In his piece, "Distortion and Refraction,"[1] he had written:

> Glass, blown bubble thin, is coated on the inner surface with a layer of quicksilver so that it shines like a mirror. And just as the mercury in a thermometer reveals the body's temperature, so do the refractions in that discerning globe discover the fevers of temperament in those unfortunate visitors who, upon entering my drawing-room, are first glimpsed in its globular surfaces as deformed dwarfs.

"Claudius, you dolt, why in the sacred name of Josiah Wedgwood have you been keeping this from me?"

Claudius took it out of the window. While Waldo made love to the vase, I looked at some old pistols. The conversation went on behind my back.

"Where did you get it?" Waldo asked.

"From a house in Beacon."

"How much are you going to soak me for it, you old horsethief?"

"It's not for sale."

"Not for sale! But my good man . . ."

"It's sold," Claudius said.

Waldo pounded his stick against the skinny legs of an old table. "What right have you to sell it without offering it to me first? You know my needs."

"I found it for a customer. He'd commissioned me to buy any mercury glass I found at any price I thought was right."

"You had it in your window. That means you're offering it for sale."

"It don't mean that at all. It means I like to show the public something nice. I got a right to put things in my window, Mr. Lydecker."

[1] In the volume, *February, Which Alone*, by Waldo Lydecker, 1936.

"Did you buy it for Philip Anthony?"

There was a silence. Then Waldo shouted: "You knew I'd be interested in anything he'd want. You had no right not to offer it to me."

His voice was like an old woman's. I turned around and saw that his face had grown beet-red.

Claudius said: "The piece belongs to Anthony, there's nothing I can do about it now. If you want it, submit an offer to him."

"You know he won't sell it to me."

The argument went on like that. I was looking at an old muzzle-loader that must have been a relic when Abe Lincoln was a boy. I heard a crash. I looked around. Silver splinters shone on the floor.

Claudius was pale. Something human might have been killed.

"It was an accident, I assure you," Waldo said.

Claudius moaned.

"Your shop is badly lighted, the aisles are crowded, I tripped," Waldo said.

"Poor Mr. Anthony."

"Don't make such a fuss. I'll pay whatever you ask."

From where I stood, the shop looked like a dark cavern. The antique furniture, the old clocks, vases, dishes, drinking-glasses, China dogs, and tarnished candlesticks were like a scavenger's storehouse. The two men whispered. Waldo, with his thick body, his black hat and heavy stick, Claudius with his pear-shaped head, reminded me of old women like witches on Hallowe'en. I walked out.

Waldo joined me at the car. He had his wallet in his hand. But his mood had improved. He stood in the rain, looking back at Claudius' shop and smiling. Almost as if he'd got the vase anyway.

X

MOONEY'S REPORT on the murdered model hadn't satisfied me. I wanted to investigate for myself.

By the time I got to Christopher Street he had already interviewed the other tenants. No one had seen Miss Redfern since Friday.

The house was one of a row of shabby old places that carried signs: Vacancy, Persian Cats, Dressmaking, Occult Science, French Home Cooking. As I stood in the drizzle, I understood why a girl would hesitate to spend a hot week-end here.

The landlady was like an old flour-sack, bleached white and tied in the middle. She said that she was tired of cops and that if you asked her opinion, Diane was staying with a man somewhere. There were so many girls in the city and they were such loose creatures that it didn't make any difference whether one of them got misplaced once in a while. She wouldn't be a bit surprised if Diane turned up in the morning.

I left her chattering in the vestibule and climbed three flights of mouldy stairs. I knew the smells. Sleep, dried soap, and shoe leather. After I left home I'd lived in several of these houses. I felt sorry for the kid, being young and expecting something of her beauty, and coming home to this suicide staircase. And I thought of Laura, offering her apartment because she had probably lived in these dumps, too, and remembered the smells on a summer night.

Even the wallpaper, brown and mustard yellow, was familiar. There was a single bed, a second-hand dresser, a sagging armchair, and a wardrobe with an oval glass set in the door. Diane had made enough to live in a better place, but she had been sending money to the family. And the upkeep of her beauty had evidently cost plenty. She'd been crazy about clothes; there were hats and gloves and shoes of every color.

There were stacks of movie magazines in the room. Pages had been turned down and paragraphs marked. You could tell that Diane had dreamed of Hollywood. Less beautiful girls had become stars, married stars, and owned swimming pools. There were some of those confession magazines, too, the sort

that told stories of girls who had sinned, suffered, and been reclaimed by the love of good men. Poor Jennie Swobodo.

Her consolation must have been the photographs which she had thumb-tacked upon the ugly wallpaper. They were proofs and glossy prints showing her at work; Diane Redfern in Fifth Avenue furs; Diane at the opera; Diane pouring coffee from a silver pot; Diane in a satin nightgown with a satin quilt falling off the chaise-longue in a way that showed a pretty leg.

It was hard to think of those legs dead and gone forever.

I sat on the edge of her bed and thought about the poor kid's life. Perhaps those photographs represented a real world to the young girl. All day while she worked, she lived in their expensive settings. And at night she came home to this cell. She must have been hurt by the contrast between those sleek studio interiors and the second-hand furniture of the boarding-house; between the silky models who posed with her and the poor slobs she met on the mouldy staircase.

Laura's apartment must have seemed like a studio setting to Jennie Swobodo, who hadn't been so long away from Paterson and the silk mills. Laura's Upper East Side friends must have been posing all the time in her eyes, like models before a camera. And Shelby . . .

I saw it all then.

I knew why Shelby was so familiar.

I'd never met him while I was pursuing crooks. He'd never mixed with the gents I'd encountered in my professional life. I'd seen him in the advertisements.

Maybe it wasn't Shelby himself. There was no record of his ever actually having been a photographer's model. But the young men who drove Packards and wore Arrow shirts, smoked Chesterfields, and paid their insurance premiums and clipped coupons were Shelby. What had Waldo said? *The hero she could love forever immaturely, the mould of perfection whose flawlessness made no demands upon her sympathies or her intelligence.*

I was sore. First, at myself for having believed that I'd find a real clue in a man who wasn't real. I'd been thinking of Shelby as I had always thought of common killers, shysters, finks, goons, and hopheads. The king of the artichoke racket had been real; the pinball gang had been flesh-and-blood men with hands that could pull triggers; even the Associated Dairymen had been living profiteers. But Shelby was a dream walking. He was God's gift to women. I hated him for it and I hated the women for falling for the romance racket. I didn't stop to think that men aren't much different, that I had wasted a lot of adult time on the strictly twelve-year-old dream of getting back to the old neighborhood with the world's championship and Hedy Lamarr beside me on the seat of a five-grand roadster.

But I had expected Laura to be above that sort of nonsense. I thought I had found a woman who would know a real man when she saw one; a woman whose bright eyes would go right through the mask and tell her that the man underneath was Lincoln and Columbus and Thomas A. Edison. And Tarzan, too.

I felt cheated.

There was still a job to be done. Sitting on a bed and figuring out the philosophy of love was not solving a murder. I had discovered the dream world of Jennie-Swobodo-Diane-Redfern, and so what? Not a shred of evidence that she might also have been playing around with the kind of pals who used sawed-off shotguns.

The trail led back to Laura's apartment and Shelby. I found evidence in Diane's green pocketbook.

Before I left the house, I checked with the landlady, who told me that Diane had carried the green pocketbook on Friday. But I knew without being told. She had respected her clothes; she had put her dresses on hangers and stuffed shoetrees into twenty pairs of slippers. Even at Laura's, she had hung her dress away and put her hat on the shelf and her pocketbook in the drawer. So I knew she had dressed in a hurry for her date on Friday night. Green hat, gloves, and pocketbook had been left on the bed. Her shoes had been kicked under a chair. I had seen the same thing happen at home. When my sister used to get ready for a date with her boss, she always left stockings curled over the backs of chairs and pink step-ins on the bathroom floor.

I picked up the green pocketbook. It was heavy. I knew it should have been empty because Laura had showed me the black purse she had found in her drawer, the purse into which

Diane had put her compact, her lipstick, her keys, her money, and a torn straw cigarette case.

There was a cigarette case in the green pocketbook. It was made of gold and it was initialed with the letters S.J.C.

XI

TWENTY MINUTES later I was sitting in Laura's living-room. The cigarette case was in my pocket.

Laura and Shelby were together on the couch. She had been crying. They had been together since Waldo and I left them at five o'clock. It was about ten. Bessie had gone home.

I wondered what they had been talking about for five hours.

I was business-like. I was crisp and efficient. I sounded like a detective in a detective story. "I am going to be direct," I said. "There are several facts in this case which need explaining. If you two will help me clear away these contradictions, I'll know you're as anxious as I am to solve this murder. Otherwise I'll be forced to believe you have some private reason for not wanting the murderer to be found."

Laura sat with her hands folded in her lap like a schoolgirl in the principal's office. I was the principal. She was afraid of me. Shelby wore a death mask. The clock ticked like a man's heart beating. I took out the gold cigarette case.

The muscles tightened around Shelby's eyes. Nobody spoke.

I held it toward Laura. "You knew where this was, didn't you? She had the green pocketbook with her at lunch Friday, didn't she? Tell me, Laura, did you invite her to use your apartment before or after you discovered the cigarette case?"

The tears began to roll down Laura's cheeks.

Shelby said: "Why don't you tell him what you just told me, Laura. It was *before!*"

She nodded like a Sunday-School kid. "Yes, it was before."

They didn't look at each other, but I felt a swift interchange of some sort. Shelby had begun to whistle out of tune. Laura took off her gold earrings and rested her head against the back of the couch.

I said: "Laura was feeling bad because she had been rude to Diane on Wednesday. So she invited her to lunch, and then, because Diane complained about her uncomfortable room, Laura offered her the use of this apartment. Later, probably when they were having coffee, Diane pulled out this cigarette case. Forgetting who she was with, maybe . . ."

Laura said, "How did you know?"

"Isn't that what you want me to know?" I asked her. "Isn't that the easiest way to explain the situation?"

"But it's true," she said. "It's . . ."

Shelby interrupted. "See here, McPherson, I won't have you talking to her like that." He didn't wear the death mask any longer. The plaster had cracked. His eyes were narrow and mean, his mouth a tight line.

"Shelby," said Laura; "Please, Shelby."

He stood in front of her. His legs were apart, his fists clenched as if I had been threatening her. "I refuse to let this go on, McPherson. These insinuations . . ."

"Shelby, Shelby darling," Laura said. She pulled at his hands.

"I don't know what you assume that I'm insinuating, Carpenter," I said. "I asked Miss Hunt a question. Then I reconstructed a scene which she tells me is accurate. What's making you so nervous?"

The scene was unreal again. I was talking detective-story language. Shelby made it impossible for a person to be himself.

"You see, darling," Laura said, "you're only making it worse by getting so excited."

They sat down again, her hand resting on his coat-sleeve. You could see that he didn't want her to control him. He squirmed. He looked at her bitterly. Then he pulled his arm away and moved to the end of the couch.

He spoke like a man who wants to show authority. "Look here, if you insult Miss Hunt again, I'll have to lodge a complaint against you."

"Have I been insulting you, Miss Hunt?"

She started to speak but he interrupted. "If she has anything to tell, her lawyer will make a statement."

Laura said: "You're making it worse, dear. There's no need to be so nervous."

It seemed to me that words were printed on a page or rolling off a sound-track. A gallant hero protecting a helpless female against a crude minion of the law. I lit my pipe, giving him time to recover from the attack of gallantry. Laura reached for a cigarette. He sprang to light it. She looked in the other direction.

"All I'm asking from you at this moment," I told him, "is

the low-down on that bottle of Bourbon. Why have you told one story and Mosconi another?"

She slanted a look in his direction. Shelby gave no sign that he had noticed, but he could see her without moving his eyes. It struck me that these two were clinging together, not so much out of love as in desperation. But I couldn't trust my own judgment. Personal feelings were involved. I had got beyond the point where I cared to look at faces. Fact was all that I wanted now. It had to be black or white, direct question, simple answer. Yes or no, Mr. Carpenter, were you in the apartment with Diane Redfern on Wednesday night? Yes or no, Miss Hunt, did you know he was going to meet her in your house?

Laura began to speak. Shelby coughed. She glanced frankly in his direction, but she might have looked at a worm that way. "I'm going to tell the truth, Shelby."

He seized her hands. "Laura, you're crazy. Don't you see that he's trying to get a confession? Anything we say . . . will be . . . they'll misinterpret . . . don't talk unless you've consulted a lawyer . . . you can't hope . . ."

She said: "Don't be so frightened, Shelby. Since you didn't do it, you have nothing to fear." She looked up at me and said: "Shelby thinks I killed Diane. That's why he told those lies. He's been trying to protect me."

She might have been talking about the rain or a dress or a book she had read. Frankness was her rôle now. She put it on like a coat. "Mark," she said, in a gentle voice—"do you believe I killed her, Mark?"

There it lay in the lamplight, solid gold, fourteen-karat evidence of Shelby's treachery. Laura had bought it for him at Christmas, a gift she had to charge to her aunt's account. He had told her he lost it, and on Friday, when she was trying to make up for her rudeness to Diane, she had seen it in the green pocketbook.

She had got a sudden headache at lunch that day. She hadn't waited to take off her hat to telephone Waldo and tell him she couldn't keep her dinner date. She hadn't mentioned her change of plans because she hated having people ask her questions.

It was still Thursday. Thursday, ten-fourteen P.M. They were to have been married by this time and on their way to Nova Scotia. This was the bridal night.

The lamp shone on her face. Her voice was gentle. "Do you believe I killed her, Mark? Do you believe it, too?"

PART THREE

A STENOGRAPHIC report of the statement made by Shelby J. Carpenter to Lieutenant McPherson on Friday at 3.45 P.M., August 27, 1941.

Present: Shelby J. Carpenter, Lieutenant McPherson, N. T. Salsbury, Jr.

Mr. Carpenter: I, Shelby John Carpenter, do hereby swear that the following is a true statement of the facts known to me concerning the death of Diane Redfern. At times this will contradict certain statements I've made before, but . . .

Mr. Salsbury: You are to take into consideration, Lieutenant McPherson, that any conflict between this and previous statements made by my client is due to the fact that he felt it his moral duty to protect another person.

Lieutenant McPherson: We've promised your client immunity.

Mr. Salsbury: Go on, tell me what happened, Carpenter.

Mr. Carpenter: As you know, Miss Hunt wished a few days' rest before the wedding. She had worked exceedingly hard on a campaign for the Lady Lilith cosmetic account, and I did not blame her for requesting that we postpone the wedding until she had time to recover from the strain. I have often protested at her arduous and unflagging devotion to her career, since I believe that women are highly strung and delicate, so that the burden of her position, in addition to her social duties and personal obligations, had a definite effect upon her nerves. For this reason I have always tried to understand and sympathize with her temperamental vagaries.

On that Friday morning, just a week ago, I went into her office to consult her about a piece of copy which I had written the day before. Although I had come into the business several years after she was established as an important copy-writer, she had great respect for my judgment. More than anyone knew, we depended upon each other. It was as usual for her to come to me for help in planning and presenting a campaign or merchandising idea as it was for me to seek her advice about the wording of a piece of copy. Since I was to take over the Lady Lilith account, I naturally asked her criticism. She was enthusiastic about my headline, which read, as I remember, "Is yours just another face in a crowd? Or is it the radiant, magnetic countenance that men admire and women envy?" She suggested the word "magnetic."

Lieutenant McPherson: Let's get down to facts. You can explain the advertising business later.

Mr. Carpenter: I just wanted you to understand our relationship.

Lieutenant McPherson: Did she tell you she was going to have lunch with Diane?

Mr. Carpenter: That was a subject we had agreed not to discuss.

Lieutenant McPherson: Lunch?

Mr. Carpenter: Diane Redfern. As a matter of fact, I did ask her if she'd lunch with me, but she told me she had some errands. Naturally I asked no questions. I went out with some men in the office, and later our chief, Mr. Rose, joined us for coffee. At about two-fifteen, we went back to the office and I worked steadily until about three-thirty, when the telephone rang. It was Diane.

Lieutenant McPherson: Did she tell you she'd had lunch with Laura?

Mr. Carpenter: The poor child was quite distraught. You didn't know her, McPherson, but she was one of the most feminine creatures I have ever met. Like my own mother, although she was a girl of very different background and breeding. Yet she always felt the need of turning to a man when anything distressed her. It was unfortunate that I happened to be the man of her choice. Women—I hope you don't mind my saying this, McPherson, but I'm trying to be as frank as possible—have more than once attached themselves to me quite without encouragement. As Miss Hunt herself remarked, Diane had not been bred among gentlefolk. What we considered merely good manners she took as evidence of . . . shall we call it love? Her emotions were wild and undisciplined. Although she knew that I was engaged to marry Miss Hunt, she declared herself madly in love with me and, I must say, often embarrassed me with her declarations. Perhaps you've known young girls like this, McPherson, who love so violently that nothing exists for them except their passion and the man upon whom it is fixed.

Lieutenant McPherson: You didn't exactly discourage her, did you?

Mr. Salsbury: The question is irrelevant. You needn't answer it, Mr. Carpenter.

Mr. Carpenter: I tried not to be unkind. She was young and very sensitive.

Lieutenant McPherson: Did she say anything to you about having had lunch with Laura?

Mr. Carpenter: She told me she was desperate. At first I thought her fears were nothing more than hysteria. "Don't dramatize yourself," I told her, but there was something about her voice, a wild, frightened tone, that distressed me. I knew her to be both impulsive and courageous. I was afraid she might . . . you know what I mean, McPherson. So I said I'd take her to dinner, as a sort of farewell, you understand. I meant to talk some sense into her. We agreed to meet at Montagnino's.

Lieutenant McPherson: Montagnino's.

Mr. Carpenter: I felt that Diane's morale needed a stimulant. And since Miss Hunt had often mentioned Montagnino's as a favorite restaurant, Diane considered the place quite glamorous. You have no idea of the child's devotion to Miss Hunt.

Lieutenant McPherson: You didn't mention this to Laura, did you?

Mr. Carpenter: It would only have distressed her. She had been quite unhappy about having been so rude to Diane, you know. Although I did intend to tell her about it later. And besides she was dining with Waldo Lydecker . . . or at least that's what I thought.

Lieutenant McPherson: When you had cocktails with Miss Hunt at the Tropicale Bar, what did you talk about?

Mr. Carpenter: What did we talk about? Oh . . . well . . . our plans, of course. She seemed cold and rather listless, but I attributed this to her nervous condition. I begged her to have a good rest and not to worry. Miss Hunt, you know, is a very intelligent young woman, but sometimes her emotions get the better of her, and she becomes almost hysterical about world conditions. She suffers a sort of guilt complex, and sometimes declares that we, innocent people of our sort, share the responsibility for the horror and suffering that one reads about in the newspapers. This, added to a certain cynicism about the work she does, gives her an emotional instability which, I thought, I might help to correct. And so I begged her not to read newspapers or listen to news broadcasts during this week of rest, and she was rather charming about it, unusually submissive and quiet. When we parted, she allowed me to kiss her, but there was little warmth in her response. I gave the taxi-driver Waldo Lydecker's address, since she had said nothing to me of a change in her plans. Then I went back to the hotel, changed my clothes, and went on down to Montagnino's. I must tell you that I was disappointed in the place.

Lieutenant McPherson: You'd never been there before?

Mr. Carpenter: Mr. Lydecker had always taken Miss Hunt there. They were quite exclusive about it. We'd only known it by hearsay.

Lieutenant McPherson: Did Diane tell you about having had lunch with Laura and bringing out the cigarette case?

Mr. Carpenter: Yes, she did. And I was most unhappy.

Lieutenant McPherson: I suppose you and she tried to think of some excuse which you could give Laura.

Mr. Carpenter: I decided to tell my fiancée the truth.

Lieutenant McPherson: Before or after the wedding?

Mr. Salsbury: You needn't answer that, Mr. Carpenter.

Mr. Carpenter: You seem to think, McPherson, that there was something clandestine in my relationship with Diane.

Lieutenant McPherson: There were only two ways for her to have got hold of that cigarette case. Either she stole it or you gave it to her.

Mr. Carpenter: I admit that the incident looks very shabby, but if you knew the circumstances that brought about this . . . this . . . this gesture, I'm sure you'd understand.

Lieutenant McPherson: Diane was desperate, I suppose.

Mr. Carpenter: I don't like your tone, McPherson. What you imply was not the situation.

Lieutenant McPherson: I didn't imply anything except that you had to be a big shot for Diane. Bigger than Laura. But if you want me to imply anything else, I can think of a couple of reasons why you might have given her that gold cigarette case.

Mr. Salsbury: Personal and irrelevant detail, Lieutenant.

Mr. Carpenter: Thank you, Mr. Salsbury.

Lieutenant McPherson: Okay, go on.

Mr. Carpenter: At about ten o'clock we left the restaurant. I had expected her to have recovered by that time, but she was more nervous and upset than before. She seemed to be suffering some nameless terror, almost as if she were afraid of violence. Although she would not definitely name her fear, I could see that this hysteria was not entirely groundless. In the circumstances I couldn't leave her alone, and so I promised to come up with her for a little while.

Lieutenant McPherson: To Laura's apartment?

Mr. Carpenter: I confess that I didn't quite enjoy the prospect, but in the circumstances I couldn't talk to her in a public place. And since she obviously couldn't come to my room in a hotel for men, and male guests were not allowed upstairs in her boarding-house, it seemed the only practical arrangement. So we drove uptown to the apartment . . .

Lieutenant McPherson: Where was she when you stopped in at Mosconi's to buy the Bourbon?

Mr. Carpenter: I ought to explain that, oughtn't I?

Lieutenant McPherson: It'd help.

Mr. Carpenter: Diane was distressed and needed a stimulant. We felt a little queer about taking Miss Hunt's liquor, and so I stopped at Mosconi's . . .

Lieutenant McPherson: Leaving Diane outside because Mosconi knew you as Laura's friend.

Mr. Carpenter: Not at all. Diane had to stop in the drug-store . . .

Mr. Salsbury: You went right on to Miss Hunt's apartment, didn't you?

Lieutenant McPherson: Where Diane took off her clothes and put on Laura's silk robe.

Mr. Carpenter: It was a very hot night, as you'll remember.

Lieutenant McPherson: There was a breeze in the bedroom, I suppose.

Mr. Carpenter: We talked for three hours. Then the doorbell rang and . . .

Lieutenant McPherson: Tell us exactly what happened. Don't skip anything.

Mr. Carpenter: We were both surprised, and Diane was frightened. But knowing Miss Hunt as I've known her, I've learned to be shocked at nothing. When her friends are upset about their marriages or love affairs or careers, they think nothing of disturbing her with their troubles. I told Diane to go to the door and explain that she was using the apartment while Laura was away.

Lieutenant McPherson: You stayed in the bedroom, huh?

Mr. Carpenter: Suppose one of Laura's friends had found me there? Better to avoid gossip, wasn't it?

Lieutenant McPherson: Go on.

Mr. Carpenter: The bell rang again. I heard Diane's mules clattering on the bare boards between the rugs. Then there was a moment of silence, and the shot. You can imagine how I felt. By the time I reached her, the door had closed and she lay there on the floor. The room was dark, I saw only a vague light shape, her silk robe. I asked if she had been hurt. There was no answer. Then I stooped down to feel her heart.

Lieutenant McPherson: Go on.

Mr. Carpenter: It's too hideous to talk about.

Lieutenant McPherson: And then what did you do?

Mr. Carpenter: My first instinct was to call the police.

Lieutenant McPherson: Why didn't you?

Mr. Carpenter: Just as I was about to lift the receiver, I was struck by a paralyzing thought. My hand fell at my side. I just stood there. You must remember, McPherson, that I loved Laura dearly.

Lieutenant McPherson: It wasn't Laura who was shot.

Mr. Carpenter: I owed her a certain loyalty. And in a way I felt some responsibility for this affair. I knew at once why Diane had been so terrified, after that display of bad manners Wednesday afternoon. As soon as I had put two and two together, I realized that I had one duty in regard to this tragedy. No matter how difficult it might be for me to control myself, I must keep out of it. My presence in this apartment would not only be extremely awkward, but would indubitably cast suspicion upon that one person whom I must protect. I can see now that it was extremely foolish for me to have acted upon this impulse, but there are times when a man is moved by something deeper than rational emotion.

Lieutenant McPherson: Did it occur to you that, by leaving

the apartment and withholding the truth, you were obstructing the processes of law?

Mr. Carpenter: I had only one thought in mind: the safety of a person whose life was dearer to me than my own.

Lieutenant McPherson: On Saturday morning, when our men came to the Framingham to tell you that Laura was dead, you seemed sincerely shocked.

Mr. Carpenter: I must admit that I was not prepared for that interpretation.

Lieutenant McPherson: But you had your alibi ready, and no matter who was dead, you stuck to your story.

Mr. Carpenter: If I had become involved in the case, someone else would eventually have been suspected. This is what I hoped to avoid. But you must realize that my grief was real, both for Diane and the other person. I don't believe I've slept a full two hours since this thing happened. It's not like me to lie. I'm happiest when I can be completely frank with myself and the world.

Lieutenant McPherson: Although you knew Laura was not dead, you evidently made no effort to get in touch with her. Why not?

Mr. Carpenter: Wasn't it better to let her pursue her own course? I felt that if she wanted me, she'd call upon me, knowing that I'd stand by her to the bitter end.

Lieutenant McPherson: Why did you go and stay with Laura's aunt?

Mr. Carpenter: Since I was almost a member of the family, it was more or less my duty to attend to the unpleasant details. Mrs. Treadwell was very gracious, I must say, in suggesting that public curiosity made it uncomfortable for me at the hotel. After all, I was in mourning.

Lieutenant McPherson: And you allowed Diane to be buried —or cremated—as Laura Hunt.

Mr. Carpenter: I can't tell you what I suffered during those terrible four days.

Lieutenant McPherson: On the night that Laura came back, she phoned you at the Framingham, didn't she? And you'd given instructions that they weren't to give out your number . . .

Mr. Carpenter: The reporters were making me quite uncomfortable, McPherson. I thought it best anyway not to have her telephoning her aunt's house. When they phoned me on Wednesday night—or Thursday morning, it was—I knew at once. And although I don't wish to seem ungrateful to my hostess, I knew Mrs. Treadwell to be an inquisitive woman. And since it would have been a shock for her to hear the voice of a person whose funeral she had just attended, I went out to a pay booth to telephone Miss Hunt.

Lieutenant McPherson: Repeat that conversation as fully as you remember it.

Mr. Carpenter: She said, "Shelby?" and I said, "Hello, my darling," and she said, "Did you think I was dead, Shelby?" I asked her if she was all right.

Lieutenant McPherson: Did you say you thought she had died?

Mr. Carpenter: I asked if she was all right. She said that she felt terribly about poor Diane, and asked if I knew anyone who might have wished her to die. I knew then that Miss Hunt did not intend to give me her full confidence. Nor could I talk to her frankly on the telephone. But I knew there was one detail which might prove embarrassing—or downright dangerous—and I made up my mind to save her, if I could.

Lieutenant McPherson: What was that detail?

Mr. Carpenter: It's right there, on your desk, McPherson.

Lieutenant McPherson: You knew she had the shotgun?

Mr. Carpenter: I had given it to her. She frequently stayed alone in her country house. Those initials are my mother's—Delilah Shelby Carpenter.

Lieutenant McPherson: And that's why you borrowed Mrs. Treadwell's car and drove up to Wilton?

Mr. Carpenter: Yes, that's right. But when your man followed me in the cab, I didn't dare go into the house. I stood in the garden for a while and I was considerably overcome because I couldn't help remembering what that little cottage and garden had meant to us. When I returned to town and found you with Mrs. Treadwell, I was not completely untruthful in saying that it had been a sentimental pilgrimage. Later in the day you asked me to come up to the apartment. I was to be surprised at finding Miss Hunt alive and as you were going to study my reactions, McPherson, I decided to give you the show that you expected, for I still believed that there was a chance to save the situation.

Lieutenant McPherson: But after I left, you talked it over with Laura. You told her exactly what you thought.

Mr. Carpenter: Miss Hunt has admitted nothing.

Mr. Salsbury: Lieutenant McPherson, my client has gone to considerable trouble and risked his personal safety in order to protect another person. He is not obliged to answer any question which might incriminate that person.

Lieutenant McPherson: Okay, I've got it straight. I'll get in touch with you if I need you, Carpenter. But don't leave the city.

Mr. Carpenter: Thank you so much for your understanding attitude, McPherson.

PART FOUR

I

L AST WEEK, when I thought I was to be married, I burned
my girlhood behind me. And vowed never to keep another
diary. The other night, when I came home and found Mark
McPherson in my apartment, more intimate than my oldest
friend, my first thought was gratitude for the destruction of
those shameful pages. How inconsistent he would have thought
me if he had read them! I can never keep a proper diary, simmer
my life down to a line a day, nor make breakfast on the sixteenth
of the month as important as falling in love on the seventeenth.
It's always when I start on a long journey or meet an exciting
man or take a new job that I must sit for hours in a frenzy of
recapitulation. The idea that I am an intelligent woman is pure
myth. I can never grasp an abstraction except through emotion,
and before I can begin to think with my head about any fact, I
must see it as a solid thing on paper.

At work, when I plan a campaign for Lady Lilith Face
Powder or Jix Soap Flakes, my mind is orderly. I write dramatic
headlines and follow them with sales arguments that have
unity, coherence, and emphasis. But when I think about myself, my mind whirls like a merry-go-round. All the horses, the
bright and the drab, dance around a shining, mirrored centre
whose dazzling rays and frivolous music make concentration
impossible. I am trying to think clearly of all that has happened
in the last few days, to remember the facts and set them upon
the horses and send them out in neat parade like sales arguments for Jix or Lady Lilith. They disobey, they whirl and
dance to the music, and all I remember is that a man who had
heard me accused of murder was concerned about my getting
enough sleep.

"Sleep," he said to me, "get some sleep." As if sleep were
something you could buy at the Five-and-Ten. After he'd been
gone for a little while, he came back with a package from
Schwartz's drugstore. They were pills to make me sleep, but he
would only leave me two because he knew how sick I was with
fear and worry.

"Do you believe I killed Diane?" I asked him again.

"It doesn't matter what I think." His voice grated. "It isn't my business to think; it's only facts I want, facts."

Shelby watched. He looked more than ever like a beautiful tomcat, ready to leap. Shelby said: "Be careful, Laura. Don't trust him."

"Yes," he said, "I'm a cop, you mustn't trust me. Anything you say might be used against you." His lips were drawn hard over his teeth, he spoke without opening his mouth.

"Are you going to arrest me?" I said.

Shelby became very man-of-the-house, protector of frail womanhood. It was all pretense, his courage was as thin as tissue paper, he trembled inwardly. Shelby used phrases like false arrest and circumstantial evidence; you could tell he was proud of displaying technical knowledge like when he could explain to people about the rules of fencing or backgammon. Auntie Sue once told me I'd grow tired of a six-foot child. Auntie Sue said that when a woman feels the need for a man that way, she ought to have a baby. I kept thinking of Auntie Sue's remarks while Shelby talked about circumstantial evidence and Mark walked around and around the room, looking at things, at my autographed baseball and my Mexican tray and the shelf where I keep my very favorite books.

"She'll get in touch with her lawyer," Shelby said. "That's what she'll do."

Mark came back to me. "You mustn't try to leave here, Laura."

"No, I won't leave."

"He's got a man outside. You couldn't leave anyway," Shelby said. "He's having you watched."

Mark left without another word, without telling me to sleep again or good-bye.

"I don't like that fellow. He's a sly one," Shelby said as soon as the door had closed.

"You said that before."

"You're gullible, Laura. You trust people too easily."

I stood with my back to Shelby, looking at the shelf with all my favorite books. "He's been very kind," I said—"considering. I think he's nice. You'd never think of a detective being like that."

I felt Shelby's hands stretching toward me and I moved

away. He was quiet. I knew, without turning, how his face would look.

He picked up the two pills that Mark had left on the table. "Do you think you ought to take these, Laura?"

I whirled around. "Great God, you don't think he's trying to give me poison!"

"He ought to be hard-boiled. You'd expect him to be tougher. I don't like his trying to act like a gentleman."

"Oh, pooh!" I said.

"You don't see it. The man's trying to make you like him so you'll break down and confess. That's what he's been working for all along, a confession. Damned caddish, I'd say."

I sat down on the sofa and pounded my fists against a pillow. "I hate that word. Caddish! I've begged you a million times to quit using it."

Shelby said, "It's a good English word."

"It's old-fashioned. It's out of date. People don't talk about cads any more. It's Victorian."

"A cad is a cad, whether the word is obsolete or not."

"Quit being so Southern. Quit being so righteous. You and your damn gallantry." I was crying. The tears ran down my cheeks and dripped off my jaws. My tan dress was all wet with tears.

"You're nervous, sweet," Shelby said. "That damned cad has been working on you subtly, he's been trying to wear you down."

"I told you," I screamed, "that I wish you'd stop using that word."

"It's a perfectly good English word," he said.

"You said that before. You've said it a million times."

"You'll find it in Webster," he said. "And in Funk and Wagnalls."

"I'm so tired," I said. I rubbed my eyes with my fists because I'm never able to find a handkerchief in a crisis.

"It's a perfectly good English word," Shelby said again.

I jumped up, the pillow in my arms like a shield against him. "A fine one you are to talk about cads, Shelby Carpenter."

"I've been trying to protect you!"

When he spoke like that, his voice deep with reproach, I felt as if I had hurt a helpless child. Shelby knew how his voice

worked on me; he could color his voice with the precise shade
of reproach so that I would hate that heartless bitch, Laura
Hunt, and forgive his faults. He remembered as well as I the
day we went duck hunting and he bragged and I said I despised him, and he won me again with the tones of his voice;
he remembered the fight we had at the office party and the
time he kept me waiting two hours in the Paramount lobby,
and our terrible quarrel the night he gave me the gun. All of
those quarrels rose in our minds now; there were almost two
years of quarrels and reproach between us, and two years of
love and forgiveness and the little jokes that neither could forget. I hated his voice for reminding me, and I was afraid because I had always been weak with a thirty-two-year-old baby.

"I've been trying to protect you," Shelby said.

"Great God, Shelby, we're right back where we started from.
We've been saying the same thing over and over again since
five o'clock this afternoon."

"You're getting bitter," he said, "terribly bitter, Laura. Of
course, after what's happened, one can't completely blame
you."

"Oh, go away," I said. "Go home and let me sleep."

I took the two white pills and went into the bedroom. I
slammed the door hard. After a while I heard Shelby leave. I
went to the window. There were two men on the steps. After
Shelby had gone a little way, one followed him. The other lit a
cigarette. I saw the match flame and die in the misty darkness.
The houses opposite mine are rich people's private houses.
Not one of my neighbors stays in town during the summer.
There was only a cat, the thin yellow homeless cat that nuzzles
against my legs when I come from work at night. The cat
crossed the street daintily, pointing his feet like a ballet dancer,
lifting them high as if his feet were too good for the pavement.
On Friday night when Diane was killed, the street was quiet,
too.

II

SLEEP HE had said, try to get some sleep. Two pills weren't enough. When I turned out the lights, the darkness whined around me. The old dead tenants came creeping up the stairs, their footsteps cautious on the tired boards. They sighed and whispered behind doors, they rattled the old latches, they plotted conspiracies. I saw Diane, too, in my aquamarine house coat; I saw her with dark hair flowing about her shoulders, running to answer the doorbell.

The doorbell had rung, Shelby told me, and he stayed in the bedroom while she ran to answer it. As soon as she had opened the front door, he heard the shot. Then the door snapped shut. After a time that might have been thirty seconds or thirty years, Shelby said, he had left the bedroom. He tried to speak to her, his lips framed her name, but his voice was dead. The room was dark, the light came in from the street lamp in stripes through the Venetian blinds. He saw the pale silk of my robe spread about her on the floor, but he could not see her face. It seemed gone. When his blood had thawed, Shelby said, he had stooped to feel for the place where her heart should have been. His hand was paralyzed, he felt nothing, he knew she was dead. He went to the telephone, meaning to call the police. When Shelby told me about that part of it, he stretched out his hand as he had stretched it toward the telephone, and then he pulled his hand back quickly just as he had done that night. If the police had known he was there in my apartment with Diane, they would have known, too, who had killed her, Shelby said.

"That was your guilty conscience," I told him. "Guilty because you were here. In my own house with her. You wanted to believe *that*, because you were ashamed."

"I was trying to protect you," Shelby said.

This was early in the evening, after Mark had gone off for dinner with Waldo, and before Mark came back with the cigarette case.

Auntie Sue told me I was a fool when I bought that cigarette case. I am so gullible that I trust a detective, but Auntie Sue didn't even trust Uncle Horace to make his will; she sat behind

the curtains while he and the lawyer figured out the bequests.
Auntie Sue said I'd always regret the cigarette case. I gave it to
Shelby because he needed grandeur when he talked to prospective clients or had drinks with men he'd known at college.
Shelby had his airs and graces, manner and a name that made
him feel superior, but these were things that mattered in
Covington, Kentucky, not in New York. Ten years in and out
of precarious jobs hadn't taught him that gestures and phrases
were of less importance in our world than aggressiveness and
self-interest; and that the gentlemanly arts were not nearly so
useful as proficiency in double-dealing, bootlicking, and pushing yourself ahead of the other fellow.

The tea was pale, pale green with one dark leaf curled in it,
when I saw the cigarette case in Diane's hand. I saw Diane's
pointed magenta nails curving over the edge of the gold case,
but I could not look at her face. The tea had a delicate Chinese
smell. I did not feel pain or anger, I felt giddy. I said to Diane,
"Please, dear, I have a headache, do you mind if I leave now?"
It was not like me to be calm. I tell the truth shrilly and then I
am sorry. But this was deeper, so deep that I could only watch
the leaf floating in the teacup.

Shelby had given her the cigarette case so that he might feel
rich and generous, too. Like a gigolo seeking revenge against a
fat old dowager with a jet band binding the wattles under her
chin. It was all clear then, as if the tea leaf had been my fortune
in the cup, for I knew why Shelby and I had quarreled so that
we could go on pretending to love. He was not sure of himself;
he still needed the help I could give him; but he hated himself
for clinging to me, and hated me because I let him cling.

They had been lovers since April eighteenth. I remember
the date because it was Paul Revere's ride and Auntie Sue's
birthday. The date smells of cleaning fluid. We were in a taxi
on the way to the Coq d'Or where Auntie Sue was having her
birthday party. I wore my sixteen-button fawn gloves; they had
just come from the cleaner and the smell was stronger than the
odor of taxi-leather and tobacco and the Tabu with which I
had scented my handkerchief and my hair. That was when
Shelby told me about losing the cigarette case. He used the
hurt voice and his remorse was so real that I begged him not

to feel it too deeply. Shelby said I was a wonderful woman, tolerant and forgiving. Damned patronizing bitch, he must have been thinking as we sat in the taxi, holding hands.

Lovers since April eighteenth. And this was almost the end of August. Diane and Shelby had been holding hands, too, and laughing behind my back.

When I walked through the office after lunch, I wondered if all the faces knew and were hiding themselves from my humiliation. My friends said they could understand my having fallen in love impulsively with Shelby, but they did not see how I could go on caring. This would make me angry; I would say they judged unfairly because Shelby was too handsome. It was almost as if Shelby's looks were a handicap, a sort of deformity that had to be protected.

Usually I anger quickly. I flame and burn with shrill vehemence and suffer remorse at the spectacle of my petty female spleen. This time my fury had a new pattern. I can feel that frigid fury now as I remember how I counted the months, the weeks, the days since the eighteenth of April. I tried to remember when I had seen Diane alone and what she had said to me; and I thought of the three of us together with Diane humbly acknowledging Shelby my lover; and I tried to count the evenings that I had spent alone or with other friends, giving Shelby to her on those evenings. How tolerant we were, how modern, how ridiculous and pitiful! But I had always told Shelby about dining with Waldo and he had never told me that he was seeing Diane.

Desperate, my mother used to say, I'm desperate, when she locked herself in her bedroom with a sick headache. I always envied her; I wanted to grow up and be desperate too. On Friday afternoon, as I walked up and down my office, I whispered it over and over. Desperate, desperate, at last I'm desperate, I said, as if the word were consummation. I can see the office now, the desk and filing-case and a proof of a Lady Lilith color ad with Diane lying backward on a couch, head thrown back, breasts pointed upward like small hills. I feel, rather than smell, the arid, air-conditioned atmosphere, and I tense my right hand as if the letter-opener were still cutting a ridge across my palm. I was sick, I was desperate, I was afraid. I hid my face in my hands, my forehead against the wood of my desk.

I telephoned Waldo and told him I had a headache.

"Don't be difficult, wench," Waldo said. "Roberto has scoured the markets for our bachelor dinner."

"I'm desperate," I said.

Waldo laughed. "Put your headache off until tomorrow. The country is a good place for headaches, that's all it's fit for; have your headache among the beetles. What time shall I expect you, angel?"

I knew that if I dined with Waldo, I should tell him about the cigarette case. He would have been glad to hear that I was done with Shelby, but he would have wrapped his satisfaction elegantly in sympathy. Waldo would never have said, I told you so, Laura, I told you at the start. Not Waldo. He would have opened his best champagne and, holding up his glass, would have said, "And now, Laura, you've grown up, let us drink to your coming of age."

No, thank you, no urbanity for me tonight, Waldo. I am drunk already.

When Shelby came to my office at five o'clock, I rode down in the elevator with him, I drank two dry Martinis with him, I let him put me into the cab and give Waldo's address to the driver just as if I had never seen the cigarette case.

III

O N SATURDAY I thinned my sedum, transplanted primroses, and started a new iris bed near the brook. On Sunday I moved the peony plants. They were heavy, the roots so long that I had to dig deep holes in the ground. I had to keep myself occupied with hard physical work; the work soothed me and emptied my mind of Friday's terror.

When the gardener came on Monday, he said that I had moved the peonies too early, they would surely die now. Twenty times that day I went to look at them. I watered them gently with thin streams of tepid water, but they drooped, and I felt ashamed before the victims of my impatience.

Before the gardener left on Monday, I told him not to tell Shelby that I had killed the peony plants by moving them too early. Shelby would never have mourned the peonies, but he would have had cause to reproach me for doing a man's work in the garden instead of waiting until he came. It was curious that I should say this to the gardener because I knew that Shelby would never dig and mow and water my garden again. I was still defiant of Shelby; I was trying to irritate him by absent treatment, and provoke imaginary argument so that I could hurt him with sharp answers. Challenging Shelby, I worked in my house, washing and polishing and scrubbing on my hands and knees. He always said that I shouldn't do menial work, I could afford to hire servants; he could never know the fulfillment of working with your hands in your own house. My people were plain folk; the women went West with their men and none of them found gold; but Shelby came from "gentle" people; they had slaves to comb their hair and put on their shoes. A gentleman cannot see a lady work like a nigger; a gentleman opens the door and pulls out a lady's chair and brings a whore into her bedroom.

I saw then, working on my knees, the pattern our marriage would have taken, shoddy and deceitful, taut emotion woven with slack threads of pretense.

The fault was mine more than Shelby's. I had used him as women use men to complete the design of a full life, playing at love for the gratification of my vanity, wearing him proudly as a successful prostitute wears her silver foxes to tell the world she owns a man. Going on thirty and unmarried, I had become alarmed. Pretending to love him and playing the mother game, I bought him an extravagant cigarette case, fourteen-karat gold, as a man might buy his wife an orchid or a diamond to expiate infidelity.

And now that tragedy has wiped away all the glib excuses, I see that our love was as bare of real passion as the mating of two choice vegetables which are to be combined for the purpose of producing a profitable new item for the markets. It was like love in the movies, contrived and opportune. And now it was over.

Two strangers sat at opposite ends of the couch. We tried to find words that had the same meaning for both of us. It was still Thursday evening, before dinner, after Mark and Waldo had left. We spoke softly because Bessie was in the kitchen.

"This will all blow over in a few days," Shelby said. "If we sit tight and match our stories properly. Who'll know? That detective is an ass."

"Why must you keep on calling him *that detective?* You know his name."

"Let's not be bitter," Shelby said. "It'll only make it more difficult for us to go on."

"What makes you think I want to go on? I don't hate you and I'm not bitter, but I couldn't go on. Not now."

"I tell you, Laura, I only came because she begged me so. She begged me to come and say good-bye to her. She was in love with me; I didn't care two hoots about her, honestly, but she threatened to do something desperate unless I came up here on Friday night."

I turned my head away.

"We've got to stick together now, Laura. We're in this thing too deeply to fight each other. And I know you love me. If you hadn't loved me, you couldn't have come back here on Friday night and . . ."

"Shut up! Shut up!" I said.

"If you weren't here on Friday night, if you are innocent, then how could you have known about the Bourbon bottle, how could you have responded so instinctively to the need to protect me?"

"Must we go over it all again, Shelby? Again and again and again?"

"You lied to protect me just as I lied to protect you."

It was all so dreary and so useless. Three Horses had been Shelby's brand of Bourbon, he had been buying it for himself when he started coming to my house, and then I began buying it so he'd always find a drink when he came. But one day Waldo laughed because I kept such cheap whiskey on my shelves and named a better brand, and I tried to please Shelby with expensive Bourbon. His buying the bottle of Three Horses that night, like his giving Diane the cigarette case, was defiance, Shelby's defiance of my patronage.

Bessie announced dinner. We washed our hands, we sat at the table, we spread napkins in our laps, we touched water to our lips, we held knives and forks in our hands for Bessie's sake. With her coming and going, we couldn't talk. We sat behind steak and French fried, we dipped our spoons ceremoniously into the rum pudding which Bessie had made, good soul, to celebrate my return from death. After she had brought the coffee to the table before the fire and we had the length of the room between us and the kitchen door, Shelby asked where I had hidden the gun.

"Gun!"

"Don't talk so loud!" He nodded toward the kitchen door. "My mother's gun; why do you suppose I drove up there last night?"

"Your mother's gun is in the walnut chest, just where you saw me put it, Shelby, after we had the fight."

The fight had started because I refused the gun. I was not nearly so afraid of staying alone in my little house as of having a gun there. But Shelby had called me a coward and insisted upon my keeping it for protection, had laughed me into learning to use it.

"The first fight or the second fight?" he asked.

The second fight had been about his shooting rabbits. I had complained about their eating the iris bulbs and the gladiolus corms, and Shelby had shot a couple of them.

"Why do you lie to me, darling? You know that I'll stick with you to the end."

I picked up a cigarette. He hurried to light it. "Don't do that," I said.

"Why not?"

"You can't call me a murderer and light my cigarette."

Now that I had said the word aloud, I felt freer. I stood up, stretched my legs, blew smoke at the ceiling. I felt that I belonged to myself and could fight my own battles.

"Don't be so childish," Shelby said. "Can't you see that you're in a tight spot and that I'm trying to help you? Don't you realize the chances I've taken, the lies I've told to protect you, and last night, driving up there? That makes me an accomplice; I'm in a rather bad spot myself, and for your sake."

"I wish I hadn't phoned you last night," I said.

"Don't be petty, Laura. Your instinct was sound. You knew as well as I that they'd go up and search your place as soon as they discovered that you were back."

"That's not why I called you."

Bessie came in to say good night and tell me again that she was happy that I had not died. Tears burned the edges of my eyes.

When the door had closed behind her, Shelby said: "I'd rest easier if I had that gun in my possession now. But how can we get it with detectives on our trail? I tried to shake the fellow, I took the back road, but the cab followed me all the way. If I'd as much as searched the place, I'd have given it away instantly. So I kept up the pretense of sorrow; I stood in the garden and wept for you; I called it a sentimental journey when that detective . . ."

"His name is McPherson," I said.

"You're so bitter," Shelby said. "You'll have to get over that bitterness, Laura, or you'll never be able to fight it out. Now, if we stand together, my sweet . . ."

Mark returned. I gave Shelby my hand and we sat on the couch, side by side, like lovers. Mark turned on the light; he looked into my face; he said he was going to speak the truth directly. That was when he brought out the cigarette case and Shelby lost his nerve and Mark's face became the face of a stranger. It's hard to deceive Mark; he looks at you as if he wants you to be honest. Shelby was afraid of honesty; he kept losing his temper like a schoolboy, and it was, in the end, Shelby's fear that told Mark that Shelby believed me guilty.

"Are you going to arrest me?" I asked Mark. But he went to Schwartz's and got me the sleeping pills, and when he left, although I did not say so to Shelby, I knew he was going to Wilton to search my house.

IV

SALSBURY, HASKINS, Warder, and Bone. Every little move-ment has a meaning all its own, Salsbury, Haskins, Warder, and Bone. A small black mustache parted in the middle, a voice, the smell of mint, and all of this an enigma, a rush of words and sense memories as I woke after a hard sleep and two small white pills. Salsbury, Haskins, Warder, and Bone . . . I attached the words to a melody . . . I heard music beyond my door and the words were Salsbury, Haskins, Warder, and Bone.

The music was the vacuum cleaner outside my bedroom door. Bessie brought coffee and orange juice. The glass was beaded with ice, and as my hand chilled, grasping it, I remem-bered a dewy silvered vessel, the smell of mint, and the small black mustache crowning a toothpaste smile. It was on the lawn of Auntie Sue's place at Sands Point; the black mustache had asked if I liked mint juleps and explained that he was young Salsbury of Salsbury, Haskins, Warder, and Bone.

Bessie breathed heavily, adjusted her jaw, asked if I would eat a nice poached egg.

"A lawyer," I said, aloud. "He told me that if I ever needed a lawyer, they're a very old firm."

Having worried enough over my failure to settle the poached-egg question, Bessie sighed and departed while I, re-membering Shelby's advice, heard myself telling it all to the black mustache.

"And your alibi, Laura? What is your alibi for Friday night, August twentieth?" young Salsbury would ask, tweaking the end, which might or might not be waxed. Then I should have to repeat for the mustache what I had told Mark about Friday night after I left Shelby waving after my taxi on Lexington Avenue.

Mark had asked me while we were having breakfast together —it seems a thousand breakfasts ago—to tell him precisely how I had spent every minute of that Friday night. He had known, of course, that I had let Shelby give the taxi-driver Waldo's address and that I had then instructed the man to take me to Grand Central.

"And after that?" Mark had said.

"I took the train."

"It was crowded?"

"Terribly."

"Did you see anyone you know? Or anyone who might be able to identify you?"

"Why do you ask me these questions?"

"Routine," he said, and handed me his empty cup. "You make excellent coffee, Laura."

"You ought to come up sometime when I bake a cake."

We laughed. The kitchen was cozy with the checked cloth and my blue Danish cups. I poured cream and put two lumps of sugar into his coffee.

"How did you know?" he said.

"I watched you before. Now when you come here, you will get so much cream and two lumps."

"I'll come often," he said.

He asked about my arrival in Wilton, and I told him about getting off the train at South Norwalk and of walking quickly alone down that deserted street to the garage back of Andrew Frost's house for my car. Mark wanted to know if there weren't any public garages near the station, and I said I saved two dollars a month this way. That made him laugh again. "So you do have some thrift in you." There was little of the detective in him and much of the admiring male, so that I laughed, throwing back my head and searching his eyes. He asked if Andrew Frost or any of his family had seen me, and when I told him that Mr. Frost is a misogynist of seventy-four who sees me only the first Saturday of the month when I give him two dollars, Mark laughed uproariously and said, "That's a hell of an alibi."

I told him about driving to Norwalk on Saturday for my groceries, and he asked if anyone there would remember. But I told him I had saved money again, going to the Super-Market and trundling a basket through aisles filled with the working people of Norwalk and the summer crowd from the surrounding countryside. I could not remember whether it had been the red-headed cashier who took my money or the man with the cast in his eye. After I left the market, I told him, I had driven home, worked in the garden again, cooked myself a light dinner, and read until bedtime.

He said, "Is that all, Laura?"

Safe and friendly in my warm kitchen, I shuddered. Mark's
eyes were fixed on my face. I seized the coffee-pot and ran with
it to the stove, turning my back to him and chattering swiftly
of irrelevant things, wanting to cleanse my mind. There, at the
stove, the coffee-pot in my hand, I felt his eyes burning
through me, piercing flesh and bone, seeing me as he had seen
Diane's face, with all the paint and prettiness gone and only
blood and membrane and hideous shattered bone.

He said: "And you stayed alone for the rest of the time you
were there, Laura? You didn't see anyone who might have
heard the radio or read the newspaper and come to tell you
that you were dead?"

I repeated what I had told him the night before, that my
radio was broken, and that the only people I had seen were the
gardener and the Polish farmer from whom I had bought
some corn and lettuce and fresh eggs.

Mark shook his head.

"You don't believe me," I said.

"It doesn't sound like . . . like your sort of woman."

"What do you mean, my sort of woman?"

"You have so many friends, your life is so full, you're always
surrounded by people."

"It's when you have friends that you can afford to be lonely.
When you know a lot of people, loneliness becomes a luxury.
It's only when you're forced to be lonely that it's bad," I said.

Thin fingers drummed the table. I set the coffee-pot upon
the blue tile and my hand ached to stretch out and touch the
wrist that protruded bonily from his white cuff. Mark's loneliness had not been luxury. He did not say this aloud, for he was
a strong man and would never be wistful.

As I thought about this, lying in bed with the breakfast tray
balanced on my legs, I knew I could never speak so easily to
the black mustache of young Salsbury. A hell of an alibi, he
would say, too, but it would be without the humor or tolerance that were in Mark's eyes and his voice.

Bessie brought the poached egg. "He's a man," Bessie said
abruptly. Bessie's attitudes are high Tenth Avenue; she is off the
sidewalks of New York and as unrelenting as any snob that came
out of Murray Hill's stone mansions. I had met her brothers,

outspoken and opinionated workingmen whose black-and-white rules of virtue my intellectuals and advertising executives could never satisfy.

"A man," Bessie said. "Most of them that comes here are big babies or old women. For once, even if he's a dick, you've met a man." And then, completely in the groove of man-worship, added, "Guess I'll bake a chocolate cake."

I bathed and dressed slowly, and said to Bessie, "I'll wear my new suit on account of claustrophobia." In spite of the rain, I had decided to leave the house, looking so calmly adjusted to my own importance—like a model in *Vogue*—that the officer at the door would never dare question my leaving. I pulled on my best gloves and tucked my alligator bag under my arm. At the door, my courage failed. So long as I made no move that showed the desire to leave, this was my home; but it needed only a word from the man at the door to make it a prison.

This is a fear which has always lived in me. I leave my doors open because I am not so frightened of intruders as of being locked in. I thought of a movie I had once seen with Sylvia Sidney's pale, frightened face behind bars. "Bessie," I said, "I'd better stay home today. After all, the world still thinks I am dead."

My name was at that moment being shouted by hundreds of newsboys. When Bessie came from the market, she brought the papers. LAURA HUNT ALIVE! streamed across all the front pages. On one tabloid my face was blown up to page proportions and looked like a relief map of Asia Minor. What, I asked myself, would tomorrow's pages scream?

LAURA HUNT GUILTY?

I read that I was staying at an unnamed hotel. This was to fool the newspapermen and my friends and keep me safe from intrusion, Aunt Sue said when she came with red roses in her hands. She had not learned about me from the newspapers, but from Mark, who had awakened her that morning to bring the news.

"How thoughtful he is!" said Aunt Sue.

She had brought the roses to show that she was glad that I had not died, but she could do nothing except condemn me for having lent Diane my apartment. "I always said you'd get into trouble, being so easy with people."

Mark had not told her of the later developments. She knew nothing of the cigarette case nor of Shelby's suspicions. Shelby, who had been staying at her house, had not come home last night.

We talked about my funeral. "It was lovely," Aunt Sue said. "You couldn't expect a great attendance at this time of the year, too many people out of town, but most of them wired flowers. I was just about to write the thank-you notes. Now you can do it yourself."

"I wish I had seen the flowers," I said.

"You'll have to outlive them all. Nobody could take a second funeral seriously."

Bessie said there were people coming to the door in spite of the fact that I was supposed to be hidden in an unnamed hotel. But there were now two detectives on my doorstep and the bell did not ring. I kept looking at the clock, wondering why I had not heard from Mark.

"I'm sure he can't make more than eighteen hundred a year, two thousand at the most," Auntie Sue said suddenly.

I laughed. It was psychic, like Bessie's suddenly saying, "He's a man."

"Some men," said Auntie Sue, "are bigger than their incomes. It's not often that you find one like that."

"From you, Auntie Sue, that's heresy."

"Once I was crazy about a grip," she said. "Of course it was impossible. I had become a star and I was young. How would it have looked to the chorus girls? Natural selection is the bunk, darling, except in jungles."

Auntie Sue is always nicer when there are no men around. She is one of those women who must flirt with every taxi-driver and waiter. And then she is horrid because she must punish men for not desiring her. I love Auntie Sue, but when I am with her I am glad that I was never a famous beauty.

She said, "Are you in love with him, Laura?"

"Don't be silly," I said. "I've only known him . . ."

I couldn't count the hours.

She said: "You've been watching the clock and cocking your ear toward the door ever since I came. You don't hear half that I say . . ."

"There may be other things on my mind, Auntie Sue.

Certain things about this murder," I said, knowing I should have asked about Salsbury, Haskins, Warder, and Bone.

"You're preoccupied, Laura. Your mind is filled with the man." She came across the room; she touched me with her soft, boneless hand. Through the varnish, I saw a young girl's face. "Don't fight yourself too hard, Laura. Not this time. I've seen you give yourself too easily to all the wrong people; don't hold out against the right one."

That was strange advice from Auntie Sue, but in it I saw the design of her discontent. After she had gone, I sat for a long time uncomfortably on the arm of a chair, thinking.

I thought of my mother and how she had talked of a girl's giving herself too easily. Never give yourself, Laura, she'd say, never give yourself to a man. I must have been very young when she first said it to me, for the phrase had become deeply part of my nature, like rhymes and songs I heard when I was too small to fasten my own buttons. That is why I have given so much of everything else; myself I have always withheld. A woman may yield without giving, as Auntie Sue had yielded to Uncle Horace when she had wanted to give herself to a grip in the theatre.

I was ashamed; I kept thinking of my own life that had seemed so honest; I hid my face from daylight; I thought of the way we proud moderns have twisted and perverted love, making arguments for this and that substitute, just as I make arguments for Jix and Lady Lilith when I write advertisements. Natural selection, Auntie Sue had said, was the bunk, except in jungles.

Someone had passed the detectives at the threshold. Feet ascended to my door. I hurried to open it.

And there was Waldo.

V

"MILLIONS OF people in the city and environs," Waldo said, with envy in his voice, "are talking about Laura Hunt. Your name, witch, is sizzling on all the wires in the country."

"Do stop being childish, Waldo. I need help. You're the only person in the world I can talk to. Will you be serious?"

His eyes were small islands beyond rippling light on thick lenses. "What of Shelby?" His voice rang richly with triumph. "Isn't it his place to be at your side in the hour of travail?"

"Waldo, darling, this is a terrible and serious moment. You mustn't torture me now with your jealousy."

"Jealousy!" He hurled the word like a weapon. "Oughtn't you to be more tolerant of jealousy, my sweet?"

We were strangers. A wall had risen between us. Waldo's jealousy had been there long before Shelby's time; Waldo had been clever and cruel at the expense of other attractive men. I had been wickedly amused and proud that my charms had roused passion in this curiously unimpassioned creature. What a siren I had thought myself, Laura Hunt, to have won the love of a man born without the capacity for loving! People used to remark, to tease, to raise questioning eyebrows when they spoke of Waldo's devotion, but I had smugly enjoyed my position as companion and protégée of a distinguished man. The solid quality of our friendship had been, from my side, founded on respect for his learning and joy in the gay acrobatics of his mind. He had always insisted on the gestures of courtship; wooing had gone on for seven years with flattery and flowers, expensive gifts and oaths of undying affection. The lover rôle had been too unwavering for honesty, but Waldo would never relax it, never for a moment let either of us forget that he wore trousers and I skirts. But there had been a certain delicacy in our avoiding any implication that the wooing might have purpose beyond its charm. Auntie Sue had often said that she would shiver if Waldo kissed her; he had kissed me often; it was his habit to kiss when we met and when we parted, and often affectionately over some compliment. I felt nothing, neither shivering repulsion nor answering flame.

A kitten nuzzled against my legs, a dog licked my hands, a child's moist lips touched my cheeks: these were like Waldo's kisses.

He caught my two hands, sought my eyes, said: "I love your jealousy, Laura. You were magnificent when you assaulted her."

I jerked my hands free. "Waldo, what would you think if I were accused of the murder?"

"My dear child!"

"I have no alibi, Waldo, and there's a gun up at my place in the country. He went there last night, I'm sure. I'm frightened, Waldo."

The color had left his face. He was waxen.

"What are you trying to tell me, Laura?"

I told him about the cigarette case, the Bourbon bottle, about my lies and Shelby's lies, and of Shelby's saying before Mark that he had lied to protect me. "Shelby was here with Diane that night, you know. He says he knew when the gun was fired that I had come back."

Sweat shone on Waldo's upper lip and on his forehead. He had taken off his glasses and was staring at me through pale, naked eyes.

"There is one thing you haven't told me, Laura."

"But Waldo, you don't believe . . ."

"Did you, Laura?"

Newsboys filled the streets with gutturals whose syllable formed my name. The colors of the day were fading. A phosphorescent green streaked the sky. The rain was thin and chill like summer sleet.

"Laura!"

His naked eyes, conical in shape and gleaming with white light, were hard upon my face. I shrank from that strained scrutiny, but his eyes hypnotized me so that I could neither turn away nor lower my eyelids.

A far-off church clock struck five. This is the way one waits, I thought, for the doctor when he is coming to say that the sickness is fatal.

"You're thinking of that detective, you're waiting for him to come and arrest you! You want him to come, don't you?"

I was caught by his hands, pinioned by his eyes.

"You're in love with him, Laura. I saw it yesterday. You looked away from us, you shrank from your old friends, Shelby and I, we had ceased to matter. Your eyes were on him all the time; you fluttered like a moth; you rolled your eyes and smirked like a schoolgirl before a matinée idol."

His damp hands increased their cold pressure.

My voice, small and weak, denied his charges. He laughed.

"Don't lie, woman. I've got the eye of a fluoroscope. I perceive now the strange quiverings of the female heart. How romantic!" He shouted the word hideously. "The detective and the lady. Have you given yourself yet; has he won your confession?"

I pulled away. "Please don't talk like that, Waldo. We've only known each other since Wednesday night."

"He works fast."

"Do, do be serious, Waldo. I need help so badly."

"This, my pet, is the most serious and important help that I can give you. To put you on your guard against the most dangerous man you've ever known."

"That's ridiculous. Mark's done nothing."

"Nothing, darling, except seduce you. Nothing but win your heart, my girl. He's engaged your warm and ready affection for the honor and glory of the Detective Bureau."

"That's what Shelby said. He said that Mark was trying to make me confess."

"For once Shelby and I agree."

I went to the couch and sat on the edge, hugging a pillow. Rough linen scratched my cheek. Waldo came toward me gently and offered his scented handkerchief. Then I giggled and said, "When there's a crisis, I can never find my handkerchief."

"Depend upon me, child, I shan't desert you. Let them accuse you; we'll fight them." He stood above me, his legs spread apart, his head high, his hand thrust in his coat like Napoleon in the picture. "I've every weapon, money, connections, prestige, my column, Laura. From this day forth, every day, eighty syndicated essays will be devoted to the cause of Laura Hunt."

"Please, Waldo," I begged. "Please tell me. Do you believe me guilty, too?"

He held my hand between cold, perspiring palms. Softly, as

if I were a sick, fractious child, Waldo said, "Why should I care whether you're guilty or not guilty as long as I love you, my dear?"

It was unreal; it was a scene from a Victorian novel. I sat with my hand locked in his hands, a frail creature, possessed, like a gentle, fading, troubled woman of long ago. And he, by contrast, had become strong and masterful, the protector.

"Do you think I'd condemn you for it, Laura? Or even blame you? On the contrary"—he pressed my hand—"on the contrary, I adore you as I've never adored you before. You shall be my heroine, Laura, my greatest creation; millions will read about you, will love you. I'll make you greater"—the words rolled on his tongue—"than Lizzie Borden."

He said it mischievously as if he had been asked in some parlor game, "What would you do if Laura were accused of murder?"

"Please," I begged him, "please be serious."

"Serious!" He caught my word and tossed it back, mocking me. "You've read enough of Waldo Lydecker to know how seriously I regard murder. It is," he said, "my favorite crime."

I leaped up, jerked my hand away; I put the room between us.

"Come back, my precious. You must rest. You're very nervous. And no wonder, darling, with those vultures feeding on you. Shelby, with his precious gallantry; the other one, that detective fellow scheming to raise himself to front-page glory; they would destroy your self-esteem and corrupt the courage of your passion."

"Then you do believe me guilty."

Phosphorescent light gave green tints to Waldo's skin. I felt that my face, too, must reflect the sickly tint of fear. With an almost surreptitious movement, I pulled the cord of the lamp. Out of shadows my room grew real. I saw familiar shapes and the solidity of furniture. On the table, red against the pale wall, were Auntie Sue's roses. I pulled one from the vase, touched the cool petal to my cheek.

"Say it, Waldo. You believe me guilty."

"I adore you for it. I see before me a great woman. We live in an unreal, a castrate world, you and I. Among us, there are few souls strong enough for violence. Violence"—he spoke it

like a love-word, his voice was the voice of a lover on a pillow—
"violence gives conviction to passion, my loveliest love. You
are not dead, Laura; you are a violent, living, bloodthirsty
woman."

Red petals lay scattered at my feet on the figured rug. My
hands, cold and nervous, pulled the last petal from the rose.

VI

THIS IS no way to write the story. I should be simple and coherent, listing fact after fact, giving order to the chaos of my mind. When they ask me, "Did you return on Friday night to kill her, Laura?" I shall answer, "He hasn't the face of a man who would lie and flirt to get a confession"; and when they ask me about ringing the bell and waiting at the door for her to come and be killed, I shall tell them that I wish, more than anything in the world, that I had met him before this happened.

That's how my mind is now. For two hours I've been shivering in my slip, unable to go through the movements of undressing. Once, long ago, when I was twenty and my heart was broken, I used to sit like this at night on the edge of the bed in a room with stained walls. I'd think of the novel I was writing about a young girl and a man. The novel was bad; I never finished it; but the writing cleansed all my dusty emotional corners. But tonight writing thickens the dust. Now that Shelby has turned against me and Mark shown the nature of his trickery, I am afraid of facts in orderly sequence.

Shelby's treachery was served to us with dinner, accompanied by the raspings and groanings of rainy-weather static. I could not pretend to eat; my leaden hands refused to lift the fork; but Waldo ate as greedily as he listened to every morsel of news.

Shelby had gone to the police and sworn to the truth of his having been in the apartment with Diane on Friday night. He had told them, as he told me, how the doorbell rang and how Diane had clattered across the room in my silver mules, and how she had been shot when she opened my front door. Shelby said that Diane had summoned him to the apartment because she was afraid of violence. Diane had been threatened, Shelby said, and although he had not liked the idea of seeing her in Laura's house, she had begged so pitifully that he could not deny her.

Shelby's attorney was N. T. Salsbury, Jr. He explained that Shelby had not confessed earlier because he was shielding someone. The name of the suspect was not included in the broadcasts. Deputy Commissioner Preble had refused to tell reporters whether or not the police knew whom Shelby was shielding. Shelby's confession had turned him into a witness for the State.

In every broadcast Deputy Commissioner Preble's name was mentioned three times a minute. Mark's name was not used at all.

"Poor McPherson," Waldo said as he dropped two saccharine pills into his coffee-cup; "between Shelby and the Deputy Commissioner, he's been crowded out of the limelight."

I left the table.

Waldo followed me to the couch again, the coffee-cup in his hands.

"He's not that sort at all," I said. "Mark isn't like that, he'd never sacrifice anyone . . . anyone for the sake of notoriety and his own career."

"You poor dear child," Waldo said. The coffee-cup rang against the wood of the table, and Waldo's free hands reached again for my hand.

"He's playing a game, Laura; the fellow's devilishly clever. Preble is enjoying his little victory now, but the plum in this pudding will be pulled out by our own little Jack Horner. Heed my warning, sweet, before you're lost. He's after you; he'll be here soon enough with some scheme to worm that confession out of you."

The shadow of hysteria returned. I pulled my hand away, stretched on the couch, closed my eyes and shivered.

"You're cold," Waldo said, and went into the bedroom to fetch my afghan. He spread it over my legs, smoothing out the wrinkled surface, tucking it under my feet, and then standing above the couch again, content and possessive.

"I must protect my sweet child."

"I can't believe he's only been trying to get a confession. Mark liked me. And he's sincere," I said.

"I know him better than you do, Laura."

"That's what you think," I said.

"I've dined with the fellow practically every night since this affair began, Laura. He's courted me strangely, why I cannot say, but I've had a rare chance to observe his nature and his methods."

"Then he must be interesting," I said. "In all the years I've known you, I've never seen you dine with a dull person."

"My dear babe, you must always justify your bad taste, mustn't you?" Waldo laughed. "I spend a few hours with the fellow; *ergo*, he becomes a man of wit and profundity."

"He's a lot more intelligent than a lot of people who go around calling themselves intellectuals."

"What a die-hard you are, once you're interested in a man! Very well, if it will please you I'll plead guilty to a certain shabby interest in the fellow. I must confess, though, that my curiosity was roused by observation of the blossoming of his love for you."

"For me!"

"Don't sing so high, sweet canary. You were dead. There was dignity in that frustrate passion. He could make no use of you, he could destroy you no further, you were unattainable and thus desirable beyond all desire."

"How you twist things, Waldo! You don't understand Mark. There's something about him," I insisted, "something that's alive. If he'd been wallowing in frustrated romance, he'd never have been so glad when I came back."

"Trickery."

"You and your words," I said. "You always have words, but they don't always tell meanings."

"The man's a Scot, child, as parsimonious with emotion as with shillings. Have you ever analyzed that particular form of romanticism which burgeons on the dead, the lost, the doomed? Mary of the Wild Moor and Sweet Alice With Hair So Brown, their heroines are always dead or tubercular, death is the leit-motif of all their love-songs. A most convenient rationale for the thriftiness of their passion toward living females. Mark's future unrolls as upon a screen." Waldo's plump hand unrolled the future. "I see him now, romanticizing frustration, asking poor cheated females to sigh with him over the dead love."

"But he was glad, glad when I came alive. There was a special quality about his gladness as if"—I flung the words bravely—"as if he'd been waiting for me."

"Ah!" said Waldo. "When you came alive!" His voice bubbled. "When Laura became reality within his grasp, the other side of sentiment was revealed. The basic parsimony, the need to make profit of the living Laura."

"You mean that all of his kindness and sincerity were tricks to get a confession? That's silly," I said.

"Had he merely been trying to get a confession, the thing would have been simple. But consider the contradiction in the case. Compensation as well as confession, Laura. You had become reality, you came within the man's reach, a woman of your sort, cultivated, fastidious, clearly his superior; he was seized with the need to possess you. Possess and revenge and destroy."

He had seated himself on the couch, balancing his fat buttocks on the edge, holding my hand for support!

"Do you know Mark's words for women? Dolls. Dames." His tongue clicked out the words like a telegraph instrument clattering out the dots and dashes of a code. "What further evidence do you need of a man's vulgarity and insolence? There's a doll in Washington Heights who got a fox fur out of him—got it out, my dear, his very words. And a dame in Long Island whom he boasted of deserting after she'd waited faithfully for years."

"I don't believe a word."

"Remember the catalogue of your suitors, darling. Consider the past," Waldo said. "Your defense is always so earnest, you blush in that same delightful way and rebuke me for intolerance."

I saw shadows on the carpet. A procession passed through my mind of those friends and lovers whose manliness had dwindled as Waldo's critical sense showed me their weaknesses. I remembered his laughter, fatherly and indulgent, the first time he had taken me to the theatre and I had admired a handsome actor's bad performance.

"I hope it's not too tactless of me to mention the name of Shelby Carpenter. How much abuse I've endured because I failed to discern the manliness, the integrity, the hidden strength of that gallant poop! I humored you, I allowed you to enjoy self-deceit because I knew you'd ultimately find out for yourself. And look, today." He spread his hands in a gesture that included the rueful present.

"Mark's a man," I said.

Waldo's pale eyes took color; on his forehead the veins rose fat and blue; the waxen color of the skin deepened to an umber flush. He tried to laugh. Each note was separate and painful. "Always the same pattern, isn't it? A lean, lithe body is the measure of masculinity. A chiseled profile indicates a delicate nature. Let a man be hard and spare and you clothe him in the garments of Romeo, Superman, and Jupiter disguised as a bull.

"To say nothing," he added after a moment's dreadful silence, "of the Marquis de Sade. That need is in your nature, too."

"You can't hurt me," I said. "No man's ever going to hurt me again."

"I'm not speaking of myself," Waldo said reproachfully. "We were discussing your frustrated friend."

"But you're mad," I said. "He's not frustrated. He's a strong man; he's not afraid."

Waldo smiled as if he were bestowing some rare confidence. "That incurable female optimism has, I dare say, blinded you to the fellow's most distinguishing defect. He guards it zealously, my dear, but watch the next time you see him. When you observe that wary, tortured gait, you'll remember Waldo's warnings."

"I don't understand you," I said. "You're making things up." I heard my voice as something outside of me, shrill and ugly, the voice of a sullen schoolgirl. Auntie Sue's red roses threw purple shadows on the green wall. There were calla lilies and water lilies in the design of the chintz curtains. I thought of colors and fabrics and names because I was trying to turn my mind from Waldo and his warnings.

"A man who distrusts his body, my love, seeks weakness and impotence in every other living creature. Beware, my dear. He'll find your weakness and there plant his seeds of destruction."

I felt sorry for myself; I had become disappointed in people and in living. I closed my eyes, I sought darkness; I felt my blood chill and my bones soften.

"You'll be hurt, Laura, because the need for pain is part of your nature. You'll be hurt because you're a woman who's attracted by a man's strength and held by his weakness."

Whether he knew it or not, this was the very history of our relationship, mine and Waldo's. In the beginning it had been the steely strength of his mind, but the ripeness of my affection had grown with my knowledge of his childlike, uncertain heart. It was not a lover that Waldo needed, but love itself. With this great fat man I had learned to be patient and careful as a woman is patient and careful with a sickly, sensitive child.

"The mother," Waldo said slowly, "the mother is always destroyed by her young."

I pulled my hand away quickly. I rose, I put the room between us; I retreated from lamplight and stood shivering in shadows.

Waldo spoke softly, a man speaking to shadows. "A clean blow," Waldo said, "a clean blow destroys quickly and without pain." His hands, it seems as I grope for clear recollection, were showing the precise shape of destruction.

He came toward me and I shrank deeper into the corner. This was strange. I had never felt anything but respect and tenderness for this brilliant, unhappy friend. And I made myself think of Waldo dutifully; I thought of the years we had known each other and of his kindness. I felt sick within myself, ashamed of hysteria and weak shrinking. I made myself stand firm; I did not pull away; I accepted the embrace as women accept the caresses of men they dare not hurt. I did not yield, I submitted. I did not soften, I endured.

"You are mine," he said. "My love and my own."

Dimly, beyond his murmuring, I heard footsteps. Waldo's lips were pressed against my hair, his voice buzzed in my ears. Then there were three raps at the door, the grating of the key in the lock, and his embrace relaxed.

Mark had climbed the stairs slowly, he was slow to open the door. I backed away from Waldo, I straightened my dress, pulled at my sleeves, and as I sat down, jerked my skirt over my knees.

"He enters with a latchkey," Waldo said.

"The doorbell was the murderer's signal," Mark said. "I don't like to remind her."

"The manners of the executioner are known to be excellent," Waldo said. "It was thoughtful of you to knock."

Waldo's warning had posted signals in my mind. Seeing

Mark with his eyes, I became aware of the taut, vigilant erectness of his shoulders, the careful balance, the wary gait. It was
not so much the quality of movement as the look on his face
that told me Waldo had been right in saying that Mark guarded
himself. He caught my curiosity and threw back a challenge as
if he were saying that he could match scrutiny with scrutiny
and, as mercilessly, expose my most cherished weakness.

Seating himself in the long chair, his thin hands gripping the
arms, he seemed to relax watchfulness. Tired, I thought, and
noticed the hint of purple in the shadows of the deep-set eyes,
the tension of flesh across narrow cheekbones. Then, quickly,
hailing into my mind the scarlet caution signal, I banished
quick and foolish tenderness. Dolls and dames, I said to myself; we're all dolls and dames to him.

He said, "I want to talk to you, Laura," and looked at Waldo
as if to say that I must get rid of the intruder.

Waldo had grown roots in the couch. Mark settled himself
in the long chair, took out his pipe, gave notice of endurance.

Bessie slammed the kitchen door and shouted good night.
One of them in Washington Heights had got a fox fur out of
him, I told myself, and I wondered how much it had cost him
in pride and effort. Then I faced him boldly and asked, "Have
you come to arrest me?"

Waldo swayed toward me. "Careful, Laura; anything you say
to him can be used against you."

"How gallantly your friends protect you!" Mark said.
"Didn't Shelby warn you of the same thing last night?"

I stiffened at the sound of Shelby's name. Mark might be
laughing at me, too, for having trusted a weak man. I said
boldly: "Well, what did you come here for? Have you been to
Wilton? What did you find at my place?"

"Sh-sh," cautioned Waldo.

"I don't see how it can hurt if I ask where he's been."

"You told me that you knew nothing of the murder, that
you bought no newspapers and that the radio at your cottage
was out of order. Isn't that what you told me, Laura?"

"Yes," I said.

"The first thing I discovered is that your radio works perfectly."

My cheeks burned. "But it didn't work then. Honestly. They

must have fixed it. I told the boys at the electric shop near the railroad station in Norwalk to go up there and fix it. Before I caught my train I stopped and told them. They've got my key, that will prove it."

I had become so nervous that I ached to tear, to break, to scream aloud. Mark's deliberate hesitancy was aimed, I felt, at torturing the scene to hysterical climax. He told of checking on my actions since my alleged (that was his word) arrival in Wilton on Friday night, and of finding nothing better than the flimsy alibi I had given.

I started to speak, but Waldo signaled with a finger on his lips.

"Nothing I discovered up there," Mark said, "mitigates the case against you."

Waldo said, "How pious! Quite as if he had gone to seek evidence of your innocence rather than proof of your guilt. Amazingly charitable for a member of the Detective Bureau, don't you think?"

"It's my job to uncover all evidence, whether it proves guilt or innocence," Mark said.

"Come, now, don't tell me that guilt isn't preferable. We're realists, McPherson. We know that notoriety will inevitably accompany your triumph in a case as startling as this. Don't tell me, my dear fellow, that you're going to let Preble take all the bows."

Mark's face darkened. His embarrassment pleased Waldo. "Why deny it, McPherson? Your career is nourished by notoriety. Laura and I were discussing it at dinner; quite interesting, wasn't it, pet?" He smiled toward me as if we shared opinions. "She's as well aware as you or I, McPherson, of the celebrity this case could give your name. Consider the mutations of this murder case, the fascinating facets of this contradictory crime. A murder victim arises from the grave and becomes the murderer! Every large daily will send its ace reporters, all the syndicates will fill the courtroom with lady novelists and psychic analysts. Radio networks will fight for the right to establish broadcast studios within the court building. War will be relegated to Page Two. Here, my little dears, is what the public wants, twopenny lust, Sunday supplement passion, sin in the Park Avenue sector. Hour by hour, minute by minute, a nation will wait for dollar-a-word coverage on the trial of the decade. And the murderess"—he rolled his eyes. "You, yourself, McPherson paid tribute to her ankles."

The muscles tightened on Mark's cheeks.

"Who emerges as the hero of this plushy crime?" Waldo went on, enjoying his eloquence. "The hero of it all, that dauntless fellow who uncovers the secrets of a modern Lucretia is none other"—Waldo rose, bowed low—"none other than our gallant McPherson, the limping Hawkshaw."

Mark's hand, curved around his pipe, showed white at the knuckles.

The quiet and the dignity irked Waldo. He had expected his victim to squirm. "All right, go ahead with it. Arrest her if you think you've got sufficient proof. Bring her to trial on your flimsy evidence; it will be a triumph, I assure you."

"Waldo," I said, "let's quit this. I'm quite prepared for anything that may happen."

"Our hero," Waldo said, with swelling pride and power. "But wait, Laura, until he hears a nation's laughter. Let him try to prove you guilty, my love, let him swagger on the witness stand with his few poor shreds of evidence. What a jackanapes he'll be after I get through with him! Millions of Lydecker fans will roll with mirth at the crude antics of the silver-shinned bumpkin."

Waldo had taken hold of my hand again, displaying possession triumphantly.

Mark said, "You speak, Lydecker, as if you wanted to see her tried for this murder."

"We are not afraid," Waldo said. "Laura knows that I will use all of my power to help her."

Mark became official. "Very well, then, since you're assuming responsibility for Miss Hunt's welfare, there's no reason why you shouldn't know that the gun has been discovered. It was in the chest under the window of her bedroom in her cottage. It's a lady's hunting gun marked with the initials D.S.C. and was once owned by Mrs. John Carpenter. It is still in good condition, has been cleaned, oiled, and discharged recently. Shelby has identified it as the gun he gave Miss Hunt . . ."

It had been like waiting for the doctor and being relieved when the final word killed all hope.

I pulled away from Waldo and stood before Mark. "All right," I said. "All right, I've been expecting it. My attorneys are Salsbury, Haskins, Warder, and Bone. Do I get in touch with them now, or do you arrest me first?"

"Careful, Laura."

That was Waldo. I paid no attention. Mark had risen, too; Mark stood with his hands on my shoulders, his eyes looking into mine. The air shivered between us. Mark looked sorry. I was glad, I wanted Mark to be sorry; I was less afraid because there was a sorry look in Mark's eyes. It is hard to be coherent, to set this all down in words; I can't always remember the right words. I know that I was crying and that Mark's coat-sleeve was rough.

Waldo watched us. I was looking at Mark's face, but I felt Waldo watching as if his eyes were shooting arrows into my back.

Waldo's voice said, "Is this an act, Laura?" Mark's arm tightened.

Waldo said: "A classic precedent, you know; you're not the first woman who's given herself to the jailer. But you'll never buy your freedom that way, Laura . . ."

Mark had deserted me, he stood beside Waldo, fists aimed at Waldo's waxen face. Waldo's eyes bulged behind his glasses, but he stood straight, his arms folded on his breast.

I ran to Mark, I pulled at his arms. I said: "Mark, please. It won't do any good to get angry. If you've got to arrest me, it's all right. I'm not afraid."

Waldo was laughing at us. "You see, my noble lad, she spurns your gallantry."

"I'm not afraid," I said to Waldo's laughter.

"You ought to have learned by now, my dear, that gallantry is the last refuge of a scoundrel."

I was looking at Mark's face. He had gone without sleep, he'd spent the night driving to Wilton, he was a tired man. But a man, as Bessie had said, and Auntie Sue, when she had contradicted her whole way of life to tell me that some men were bigger than their incomes. I had been gay enough, I'd had plenty of fun, enjoyed men's companionship, but there had been too many fussy old maids and grown-up babies. I took hold of Mark's arm again, I looked at him, I smiled to give myself courage. Mark wasn't listening to Waldo either, he was looking at my face and smiling delicately. I was tired, too, longing to cling and feel his strength, to rest my head against his shoulder.

"Tough, Hawkshaw, to have to pull in a doll? Before you've had the chance to make the grade with her, eh, Hawkshaw?"

Waldo's voice was shrill, his words crude and out of character. The voice and words came between Mark and me, our moment was gone, and I was holding air in my closed fingers.

Waldo had taken off his glasses. He looked at me with naked eyes. "Laura, I'm an old friend. What I'm saying may be distasteful, but I beg you to remember that you've known this man for only forty-eight hours . . ."

"I don't care," I said. "I don't care about time. Time doesn't mean anything."

"He's a detective."

"I don't care, Waldo. Maybe he could scheme and lay traps for crooks and racketeers, but he couldn't be anything but honest with me, could you, Mark?"

For all Mark saw of me, I might have lived in another world. He was staring at the mercury-glass vase on my mantel, the gift Waldo had given me at Christmas. I looked at Waldo, then; I saw the working of his thick, sensitive lips and the creeping mist that rose over his pale conical eyeballs.

Waldo's voice taunted and tore at me. "It's always the same, isn't it, Laura. The same pattern over and over, the same trap, the same eagerness and defeat. The lean, the lithe, the obvious and muscular, and you fail to sense the sickness and decay and corruption underneath. Do you remember a man named Shelby Carpenter? He used you, too . . ."

"Shut up! Shut up! Shut up!" I shouted at Waldo's swollen eyes. "You're right, Waldo, it's the same pattern, the same sickness and decay and corruption, only they're in you. You! You, Waldo. It's your malice; you've mocked and ridiculed and ruined every hope I've ever had, Waldo. You hate the men I like, you find their weak places, you make them weaker, you've teased and shamed them before my eyes until they've hated me!"

Bloodthirsty, Waldo had called me, and bloodthirsty I had become in the sudden fever of hating him. I had not seen it clearly with Shelby or the others, I had never smelled the malice until he tried to shame Mark before me. I shouted bravely; I spoke as if I had known before, but I had been too blind and obstinate to see how his sharp little knife-thrusts had hurt my friends and destroyed love for me. I saw it clearly now, as if I were a god upon a mountain, looking down at humans through a clear light. And I was glad for my anger; I exulted in hatred; I screamed for revenge; I was bloodthirsty.

"You're trying to destroy him, too. You hate him. You're jealous. He's a man. Mark's a man. That's why you've got to destroy him."

"Mark needs no help," Waldo said. "Mark seems quite capable of self-destruction."

Waldo could always do that to me, always diminish me in an argument, turning my just anger into a fishwife's cheap frenzy. My face felt its ugliness and I turned so that Mark should not see me. But Mark was untouched, he held himself scornful. As I turned, Mark's arm caught me, pulled me close, and I stood beside Mark.

"So you've chosen?" Waldo said, his voice an echo of mockery. There was no more strength in the poison. Mark's hard, straight, unwavering gaze met Waldo's oblique, taunting glance and Waldo was left without defenses, except for the small shrill weapon of petulance.

"Blessings upon your self-destruction, my children," Waldo said, and settled his glasses on his nose.

He had lost the fight. He was trying to make a dignified retreat. I felt sorry. The anger was all drained out of me, and now that Mark had taken my fear, I had no wish to punish Waldo. We had quarreled, we had unclothed all the naked venom of our disappointments, we were finished with friendship; but I could not forget his kindness and generosity, the years behind us, the jokes and opinions we had shared. Christmas and birthdays, the intimacy of our little quarrels.

"Waldo," I said, and took a half-step toward him. Mark's arm tightened, he caught me, held me, and I forgot the old friend standing with his hat in his hand at my door. I forgot everything; I melted shamelessly, my mind clouded; I let go of all my taut fear; I lay back in his arms, a jade. I did not see Waldo leave nor hear the door close nor recollect the situation.

What room was there in me for any sense of danger, any hint of trickery, any memory of warning? My mother had said, never give yourself, and I was giving myself with wayward delight, spending myself with such abandon that his lips must have known and his heart and muscles that he possessed me.

He let go so suddenly that I felt as if I'd been flung against a wall. He let go as if he had tried to conquer and had won, and were eager to be finished.

"Mark!" I cried. "Mark!"

He was gone.

That was three hours ago, three hours and eighteen minutes. I am still sitting on the edge of the bed, half-undressed. The night is damp and there is a dampness like dew on my flesh. I feel dull and dead; my hands are so cold that I can barely hold the pencil. But I must write; I have to keep on writing it down so I can clear my mind of confusion and think clearly. I have tried to remember every scene and incident and every word he said to me.

Waldo had warned me; and Shelby. He's a detective. But if he believed me guilty, why are there no more guards outside? Or had he grown fond of me and, believing me guilty, given me this chance to escape? Every excuse and every solace are crowded out of my mind by Waldo's warnings. I had tried to believe that these warnings were born of Waldo's jealousy; that Waldo had contrived with cruel cunning to equip Mark with a set of faults and sins that were Waldo's own disguised weaknesses.

The doorbell is ringing. Perhaps he has come back to arrest me. He will find me like a slut in a pink slip with a pink strap falling over my shoulder, my hair unfastened. Like a doll, like a dame, a woman to be used by a man and thrown aside.

The bell is still ringing. It's very late. The street has grown quiet. It must have been like this the night Diane opened the door for the murderer.

PART FIVE

I

IN THE files of the Department you will find full reports on the Laura Hunt case. As officially recorded the case seems like hundreds of other successful investigations: Report of Lieutenant McPherson; Report of Sergeant Mooney; Report of Lieutenant McPherson; case closed, August 28th.

The most interesting developments of the case never got into the Department files. My report on that scene in Laura's living-room, for instance, read like this:

> At 8.15 found Lydecker in Hunt apartment with Laura. He was doing some fast talking to prove that I was plotting to get her to confess. Stayed until 9.40 (approx.), when he left; sent Behrens and Muzzio, who had been stationed at door, to trail him. I proceeded to Claudius Cohen's place . . .

The story deserves more human treatment than police records allow.

I want to confess, before I write any more, that Waldo's unfinished story and Laura's manuscript were in my hands before I put a word on paper. In writing that section which comes between his document and Laura's, I have tried to tell what happened as it happened, without too much of my own opinion or prejudice. But I am human. I had seen what Waldo wrote about me and had read Laura's flattering comments. My opinions were naturally influenced.

I can't help wondering what would have happened if the Deputy Commissioner hadn't pulled the snide trick of assigning me to the case when he knew I was counting on a Saturday afternoon at Ebbetts Field. The murder might never have been uncovered. I say this without trying to take any bows for solving the mystery. I fell for a woman and she happened to like me. That circumstance furnished the key that unlocked the main door.

I knew from the start that Waldo was hiding something. I cannot honestly say that I suspected him of love or murder.

That Sunday morning when he looked in the mirror and talked about his innocent face, I knew I was playing with a screwball. But it was not unpleasant; he was always good company. He had told me plainly that he had loved Laura, but I thought that he had become adjusted to the rôle of faithful friend.

I had to know what he was hiding, although I suspected the sort of game that would make an amateur feel superior to a professional detective. Waldo imagined himself a great authority on crime.

I played my own game. I flattered him, I sought his company, I laughed at his jokes; while I asked questions about Laura's habits, I studied his. What made a man collect old glassware and china? Why did he carry a stick and wear a beard? What caused him to scream when someone tried to drink out of his pet coffee-cup? Clues to character are the only clues that add up to the solution of any but the crudest crime.

Before that night in Montagnino's back yard when he told me about the song, Waldo's talk had made his *love* for Laura sound like a paternal and unromantic relationship. It was then that I began to see his midnight walks as something besides the affectation of a man who considered himself an heir to the literary tradition. Perhaps he had not spent all of Friday night reading Gibbon in a tepid bath.

Then Laura returned. When I discovered that it was Diane Redfern who had been murdered, I went completely off the track. There were so many crossed wires; Shelby, three unexplained lies, a gold cigarette case. During that stage of the investigation, I couldn't help looking in the mirror and asking myself if I looked like the kind of sucker who trusts a woman.

Shelby honestly believed that his fatal beauty had led Laura to murder. To relieve his two-timing conscience, Shelby protected her. If I ever saw gallantry in the reverse, that was it.

But Shelby was no coward. He risked his neck that night he went up to her cottage to get the gun. He failed because a yellow taxi was on his trail, and even Shelby was smart enough to know the Department wasn't spending money just to give one of its men a joy ride. When Shelby saw that shotgun for the first time after the murder, it lay on my desk.

The gun was a clue to Shelby. It was marked with his mother's initials. C stood for Carpenter, S for Shelby, and D for

Delilah. I could see him as a kid in knee-pants and a Buster Brown collar reciting pieces for a mother named Delilah.

He told me the gun had been used a month before. He had shot a rabbit.

I said: "Look here, Carpenter, you can relax. If you tell the truth now, we might be able to overlook a few dozen lies that make you an accessory after the fact. Tomorrow may be too late."

He looked at me as though I'd said out loud what I thought about Delilah. He would never turn State's evidence, no suh, not a descendant of the Shelbys of Kentucky. That was an underworld trick which no gentleman could sanction.

It took three hours for me to make him understand the difference between a gentleman and an ordinary heel. Then he broke down and asked if he might send for his lawyer.

I let Preble give out the news of Shelby's confession because I was playing a game with him, too. In world politics it's called appeasement. From Preble's point of view, the gun and Shelby's confession clinched the evidence against Laura. She looked as guilty as Ruth Snyder. We could have booked her then and there on suspicion of murder. A quick arrest, Preble thought, would bring a juicy confession. And orchids for the Department under the efficient administration of Deputy Commissioner Preble.

I could see his hand as clearly as though he'd shown me the cards. This was Friday, and on Monday the Commissioner would be back from his vacation. Preble had little time to garner his share of personal publicity. And this case, since Laura had come back alive, was strictly Front Page, and coast to coast on the networks. Preble's wife and kids were waiting at a summer hotel in the Thousand Islands to hear over the air waves that Papa had solved the murder mystery of the decade.

We had a knock-down and drag-out argument. I wanted time, he wanted action. I called him the worn-out wheelhorse of a political party that should have been buried years ago under a load of cow manure. He told the world that I was hanging on to the bandwagon of the party in power, a bunch of filthy Reds who'd sell the country short for thirty pieces of Moscow gold. I said he belonged back with the Indian chiefs who'd given their name to his stinking loyalties, and he said I'd send my old mother out on the Bowery if I thought it would further my career. I am not reporting our actual language because, as I mentioned before, I haven't had a college education and I keep my writing clean.

It ended in a draw.

"If you don't bring in the murderer, dead or alive, by tomorrow morning . . ."

"You're damned tooting," I said. "I'll have him stuffed and trussed and ready for your breakfast."

"Her," he said.

"Wait," I bluffed.

I hadn't a shred of evidence that wasn't against Laura. But even though my own hands had dragged that gun from the chest in her bedroom, I couldn't believe her guilty. She might conk a rival with a trayful of hors d'oeuvres, but she could no more plan a murder than I could go in for collecting antique glassware.

It was around eight o'clock. I had about twelve hours to clear Laura and prove that I wasn't one hundred per cent sucker.

I drove up to Sixty-Second Street. When I opened the door, I knew that I had burst in on a love-scene. It was the fat man's field day. Shelby had betrayed her and I seemed to be threatening her with arrest. He was the man in possession, and the deeper the spot she was in, the greater her need for him, the surer his hold. It would have been to his advantage in more ways than one to have her tried for murder.

My presence was poison to him. His face took on the color of cabbage and his fat flesh shook like cafeteria jello. He tried his best to make me look cheap, a cheap dick who'd try to make a woman fall for me so that I could advance myself. It was something like Preble's remark about my sending my mother out on the Bowery to help my career. Remarks like this are not so much accusations as revelations. Frightened people try to defend themselves by accusing others of their own motives. This was never so clear as when Waldo began to make cracks about my bad leg. When a man goes so far below the belt, you can be sure he's hiding his own weakness.

At that moment I quit thinking of Waldo as the faithful old friend. I understood why his manner toward me had changed after Laura came back. He had made a great romance of my interest in the dead girl; it gave him a companion in frustration. But with Laura alive, I had become a rival.

I sat back and listened while he called me names. The shabbier he tried to make me look, the more clearly I saw his motives. For eight years he had kept her for himself by the destruction of her suitors. Only Shelby had survived. Shelby might have been a weak man, but he was too stubborn to let himself be ousted. He had allowed Waldo to insult him again and again, but he had stuck, finding solace in playing big shot for Diane.

The pattern had straightened out, but evidence was lacking. I saw myself as the Deputy Commissioner might see me, a stubborn jackass working on instinct against known fact. Training and experience had taught me that instinct had no value in the courtroom. Your Honor, I know this man to have been bitterly jealous. Try that on the witness stand and see how far you get.

Under ordinary circumstances I do my love-making in private. But I had to turn the screws on Waldo's jealousy. When I took Laura in my arms, I was playing a scene. Her response almost ended my usefulness in the case. I knew she liked me, but I hadn't asked for heaven.

She believed that I was embracing her because she had been hurt and I, loving her, offered comfort and protection. That was the deeper truth. But I had Waldo on my mind, too. The love-scene was too strong for his sensitive nerves, and he slipped out.

I had no time to explain anything. It wasn't easy to break away, leaving Laura to think that Waldo had been right in accusing me of using her sincerity as a trap. But he was gone and I could take no chance of losing him.

I lost him.

Behrens and Muzzio let him pass. By my own instructions Waldo Lydecker had been allowed to come and go as he chose. The two cops had been lounging on the stoop, bragging about their kids probably, and not paying the slightest attention to his movements. It was my fault, not theirs.

There was no trace of his great bulk, his decorated chin, his thick cane, on Sixty-Second Street. Either he had turned the corner or he was hiding in some dark areaway. I sent Behrens toward Third Avenue and Muzzio to Lexington and ordered them to find and trail him. I jumped into my car.

It was just eighteen minutes of ten when I found Claudius putting up his shutters.

"Claudius," I said, "tell me something. Are people who collect antiques always screwy?"

He laughed.

"Claudius, when a man who's crazy about this old glassware finds a beautiful piece that he can't own, do you think he'd deliberately smash it so that no other man could ever enjoy it?"

Claudius licked his lips. "Guess I know what you're talking about, Mr. McPherson."

"Was it an accident last night?"

"I couldn't say yes and I couldn't say no. Mr. Lydecker was willing to pay and I took the money, but it could've been an accident. You see, I hadn't put any shot in . . ."

"Shot? What do you mean, shot?"

"Shot. We use it to weight down stuff when it's light and breakable."

"Not BB shot," I said.

"Yes," he said, "BB shot."

I had looked over Waldo's antiques once while I was waiting for him. There had been no BB shot weighing the old cups and vases down, but he was not such a cluck as to leave unmistakable evidence around for the first detective. I wanted to make a thorough examination this time, but I had no time to get a warrant. I entered the building through the basement and climbed eighteen flights to his apartment. This was to avoid the elevator man, who had begun to welcome me as Mr. Lydecker's best pal. If Waldo came home, he was not to have any suspicions that would cause him to leave hastily.

I let myself in with a passkey. The place was silent and dark.

There had been a murder. There had to be a gun. It wasn't a shotgun, whole or sawed-off. Waldo wasn't the type. If he owned a gun, it would look like another museum piece among the China dogs and shepherdesses and old bottles.

I made a search of cabinets and shelves in the living-room, then went into the bedroom and started on the dresser drawers. Everything he owned was special and rare. His favorite

books had been bound in selected leathers, he kept his mono-
grammed handkerchiefs and shorts and pajamas in silk cases
embroidered with his initials. Even his mouthwash and toothpaste had been made up from special prescriptions.

I heard the snap of the light switch in the next room. My
hand went automatically to my hip pocket. But I had no gun.
As I had once told Waldo, I carry weapons when I go out to
look for trouble. I hadn't figured on violence as part of this
evening's entertainment.

I turned quickly, put myself behind a chair, and saw Roberto
in a black silk dressing-gown that looked as if he was paying
the rent for this high-class apartment.

Before he had time to ask questions, I said: "What are you
doing here? Don't you usually go home nights?"

"Mr. Lydecker need me tonight," he said.

"Why?"

"He not feel himself."

"Oh," I said, and took the cue. "That's why I'm here,
Roberto. Mr. Lydecker didn't feel himself at dinner, so he gave
me the key and asked me to come up and wait for him."

Roberto smiled.

"I was just going to the bathroom," I said. That seemed the
simplest explanation of my being in the bedroom. I went to
the bathroom. When I came out, Roberto was waiting in the
parlor. He asked if I'd like a drink or a cup of coffee.

"No, thanks," I said. "You run along to bed. I'll see that Mr.
Lydecker's okay." He started to leave, but I called him back.
"What do you think's the matter with Mr. Lydecker, Roberto?
He seems nervous, doesn't he?"

Roberto smiled.

I said, "It's this murder; it's been getting on his nerves,
don't you think?"

His smile got me nervous. Even the Rhode Island clam was
a big talker compared with this Filipino oyster.

I said, "Did you ever know Quentin Waco?"

That woke him up. There are only a few Filipinos in New
York and they stick together like brothers. All the houseboys
used to put their money on Quentin Waco, who was top lightweight until he got mixed up with the girls around the Sixty-
Sixth Street dance-halls. He spent more than he made, and

when young Kardansky knocked him out, they accused him of pulling the fight. One of Quentin's pals met him at the door of the Shamrock Ballroom one night and pulled a knife. For the honor of the Islands, he told the judge. A little later it came out that Quentin hadn't pulled the fight, and the boys made a martyr of him. The religious ones kept candles burning in a church on Ninth Avenue.

I happened to have been the man who got hold of the evidence that cleared Quentin's name and, without knowing it, restored the honor of the Islands. When I told this to Roberto, he stopped smiling and became human.

We talked about Mr. Lydecker's health. We talked about the murder and about Laura's return. Roberto's point of view was strictly out of the tabloids. Miss Hunt was a nice lady, always friendly to Roberto, but her treatment of Mr. Lydecker showed her to have been no better than a dance-hall hostess. According to Roberto all women were the same. They'd turn down a steady fellow every time for a big sport guy who knew all the latest steps.

I jerked the talk around to the dinner he had cooked on the night of the murder. It wasn't hard to get him going on that subject. He wanted to give me a mushroom by mushroom description of the menu. Every half-hour during the afternoon, Roberto said, Mr. Lydecker had quit his writing and come into the kitchen to taste, smell, and ask questions.

"We have champagne; six dollars a bottle," Roberto bragged.

"Oh, boy!" I said.

Roberto told me there had been more than food and wine prepared for that evening. Waldo had arranged the records on his automatic phonograph so that Laura should enjoy her favorite music with the meal.

"He certainly prepared. What a disappointment when Miss Hunt changed her mind!" I said. "What did he do, Roberto?"

"Not eat."

Waldo told us he had eaten a solitary meal and spent the evening reading Gibbon in the bathtub.

"He didn't eat, huh? Wouldn't go near the table?"

"He go table," Roberto said. "He have me bring food, he put on plate, not eat."

"I don't expect he played the phonograph either."

"No," said Roberto.

"He hasn't played it since, I suppose."

The phonograph was big and expensive. It played ten records, then turned them over and played the other side. I looked at them to see if any of the tunes checked with the music they had talked about. There was none of this Toccata and Fugue stuff, but a lot of old songs from shows. The last was "Smoke Gets in Your Eyes."

"Roberto," I said, "maybe I'll have a whiskey anyway."

I thought of that hot night in Montagnino's back yard. A storm had been rolling in and the lady at the next table sang with the music. Waldo had talked about hearing that song with Laura as if there had been a lot more to it than just listening to music with a woman.

"I think I'll have another, Roberto."

I needed Scotch less than I needed time to think it out. The pieces were beginning to fit together. The last dinner before her marriage. Champagne and her favorite songs. Memories of shows they had seen together, talk of the past. Old stories retold. And when the meal was over and they were drinking brandy, the last record would fall into place, the needle fit into the groove.

Roberto waited with a glass in his hand. I drank. I was cold and sweating.

Since that Sunday when I'd first walked into his apartment, I'd been reading the complete works of Waldo Lydecker. There is no better key to a man's character than his use of the written word. Read enough of any man's writing and you'll have his Number One Secret. There was a line that I remembered from one of his essays: "The high crisis of frustration."

He had planned so carefully that even the music was timed for it. And that night Laura had failed to show up.

I said: "Go to bed, Roberto. I'll wait up for Mr. Lydecker."

Roberto disappeared like a shadow.

I was alone in the room. Around me were his things, spindly overdecorated furniture, striped silks, books and music and antiques. There had to be a gun somewhere. When murder and suicide are planned like a seduction, a man must have his weapon handy.

II

WHILE I waited in his parlor, Waldo was pounding his stick along the pavements. He dared not look backward. His pursuers might see him turn his head and know that he was frightened.

Muzzio caught sight of him almost a block ahead on Lexington. Waldo gave no sign that he observed Muzzio, but walked on quickly, turning east at Sixty-Fourth. At the end of the block, he saw Behrens, who had turned north on Third Avenue.

Waldo disappeared. The two men searched every areaway and vestibule on the block, but Waldo had evidently used the service tunnel of a big apartment house, gone through the basement to the rear of the building, and found another basement and service entrance on Seventy-Second.

He walked for three hours. He passed a lot of people on their way home from theatres and picture shows and bars. He met them in the light of arc lamps and under the lighted marquees of picture shows. We learned about it later the way we always do when an important case is finished and people phone in to make themselves important. Mary Lou Simmons, fifteen, of East Seventy-Sixth, had been frightened by a man who darted out of the vestibule as she came home from an evening at a girl chum's house. Gregory Finch and Enid Murphy thought it was Enid's father leaning over the banister in the dark hall where they were kissing. Mrs. Lea Kantor saw a giant ghost behind her newsstand. Several taxi-drivers had stopped in the hope of picking up a passenger. A couple of drivers had recognized Waldo Lydecker.

He walked until the streets were quiet. There were few taxis and hardly any pedestrians. He chose the darkest streets, hid in doorways, crouched on subway steps. It was almost two o'clock when he came back to Sixty-Second Street.

There was only one lighted window on the block. According to Shelby, that light had been burning on Friday night, too.

Her door was not guarded. Muzzio was still waiting on

Sixty-Fourth Street and Behrens had gone off duty. I had given
no instructions for a man to replace him, for I had no idea,
when I left Laura alone and sent the men to follow him, that
he was carrying his weapon.

He climbed the steps and rang her doorbell.

She thought I had come back to arrest her. That seemed
more reasonable than a return of the murderer. For a moment
she thought of Shelby's description of Diane's death. Then she
wrapped herself in a white bathrobe and went to the door.

By that time I knew Waldo's secret. I found no gun in his
apartment; he was carrying the gun concealed on his person,
loaded with the rest of the BB shot. What I found was a pile of
unfinished and unpublished manuscript. I read it because I was
planning to wait in the apartment, confront him, make the
accusation, and see what happened. I found the following
sentence in a piece called "The Porches of Thy Father's Ear."

In the cultivated individual, malice, a weapon darkly
concealed, wears the garments of usefulness, flashes the
disguise of wit or flaunts the ornaments of beauty.

The piece was about poisons hidden in antique rings, of
swords in sticks, of firearms concealed in old prayerbooks.

It took me about three minutes to realize that he was carrying a muzzle-loader. Last night, when we were leaving the
Golden Lizard, I had tried to look at his stick. He had snatched
it away with a crack about getting me a rubber-tipped cane.
That crack was loaded. Resentment kept me from asking any
more questions. Possessions were like people with Waldo. He
wanted to protect his precious stick from my profane hands, so
he brought out his malice without the garments of wit or
beauty. I had thought that he was showing off another of his
whims, like drinking his coffee from the Napoleon cup.

Now I knew why he had wanted to keep me from examining
his cane. He carried it, he had told me, to give himself importance. There was the man's hidden power. He probably smiled
as he stood before Laura's door, preparing to use his secret
weapon. The second time was like the first. In his failing and
disordered mind there was no original crime, no repetition.

When the doorknob turned, he aimed. He knew Laura's height and the place where her face would appear like an oval in the dark. As the door opened, he fired.

There was a shivering crash. Turning, Laura saw a thousand slivers of light. The shot, missing her by the fraction of an inch, had shattered the glass bowl. Its fragments shone on the dark carpet.

He had missed his aim because, as he fired, his legs were jerked out from under him. I had left his apartment as soon as I realized where the gun was hidden and remembered that I had deliberately put on a scene to stir up his jealousy. He was on the third-floor landing, his finger on the bell, when I opened the door downstairs.

The old-fashioned hall was dimly lighted. On the landings pale bulbs glowed. Waldo was struggling for his life with an enemy whose face he couldn't see. I am a younger man, in better condition, and know how to handle myself in a fight. But he had the strength of desperation. And a gun in his hand.

When I jerked his legs out from under him, he rolled over on top of me. Laura came out of her door, looked down at us, straining to see our dark struggle on the staircase. We rolled down the steps.

Under the bulb of the second-floor landing I saw his face. He had lost his glasses, but his pale eyes seemed to see into the distance. He said, "While a whole city pursued the killer, Waldo Lydecker, with his usual urbanity, pursued the law."

He laughed. My spine chilled. I was fighting a madman. His face contorted, his lips writhed, pointed eyeballs seemed to jerk out of their sockets. He wrenched his arm loose, raised the gun, waved it like a baton.

"Get back! Get out of the way!" I shouted up at Laura.

His flesh had seemed flabby, but there were over two hundred and fifty pounds of it, and when I jerked his arm back, he rolled over on me. The light flashed in his eyes, he recognized me, sanity returned, and with it, hatred. White streaks of foam soaped his lips. Laura called out, warning me, but his groans were closer to my ears. I managed to shove my knees up under his fat belly and push him back toward the post of the banister. He waved his gun, then shot wild, firing without aim. Laura screamed.

With the firing of that shot, his strength was gone. His eyes froze, his limbs became rigid. But I was taking no chances. I knocked his head against the banister post. On the third-floor landing, Laura heard bone crack against wood.

In the ambulance and at the hospital he kept on talking. Always about himself, always in the third person. Waldo Lydecker was someone far away from the dying fat man on the stretcher, he was like a hero a boy has always worshiped. It was the same thing over and over again, never straight and connected, but telling as much as a sworn confession.

> *Ever the connoisseur who cunningly mates flavor with occasion, Waldo Lydecker selected the vintage of the year '14 . . .*
>
> *As might Cesare Borgia have diverted himself on an afternoon pregnant with the infant of new infamy, so Waldo Lydecker passed the nervous hours in civilized diversion, reading and writing . . .*
>
> *A man might sit thus, erect as a tombstone, while composing his will; so sat Waldo Lydecker at his rosewood desk writing the essay that was to have been his legacy . . .*
>
> *The woman had failed him. Secret and alone, Waldo Lydecker celebrated death's impotence. Bitter herbs mingled their savor with the mushrooms. The soup was rue-scented . . .*
>
> *Habit led Waldo Lydecker that night past windows illumined by her treachery . . .*
>
> *Calm and untroubled, Waldo Lydecker stood, pressing an imperious finger against her doorbell . . .*

When he died, the doctor had to unclasp the fingers that gripped Laura's hand.

"Poor, poor Waldo," she said.

"He tried to kill you twice," I reminded her.

"He wanted so desperately to believe I loved him."

I looked at her face. She was honestly mourning the death of an old friend. The malice had died with him and Laura remembered that he had been kind. It is generosity, Waldo said, not evil, that flourishes like the green bay tree.

He is dead now. Let him have the last word. Among the

papers on his desk I found the unfinished piece, that final legacy which he had written while the records were waiting on
the phonograph, the wine being chilled in the icebox, Roberto
cooking the mushrooms.

He had written:

> *Then, as the final contradiction, there remains the truth
> that she made a man of him as fully as man could be made
> of that stubborn clay. And when that frail manhood is
> threatened, when her own womanliness demands more
> than he can give, his malice seeks her destruction. But she is
> carved from Adam's rib, indestructible as legend, and no
> man will ever aim his malice with sufficient accuracy to
> destroy her.*

THE HORIZONTAL MAN

Helen Eustis

Let us honor if we can
The vertical man
Though we value none
But the horizontal one.
　　　　　—W. H. AUDEN

TO JONAH

THE FIRELIGHT played over all the decent, familiar objects of his everyday life; he viewed them desperately, looking for some symbol of succor. The firelight played on his rolling eyeballs, the careless tendrils of his black hair. "Oh now," he said, "Oh now, I say, look here . . ." trying to summon a tone of commonplace to breast the tide of nightmare that was rising in that room. But his voice came out of his throat breathy and piping with fear. Outside, the college clock tolled the half hour, measured, reassuring. He blessed the bells. After all, it was not nightmare. The telephone could ring, a knock could sound at the door, and the terror would be broken. He cleared his throat and began again. "I say," he said, almost tenderly, "you're not well, you know. Do let me take you home."

But it was no use. "No!" she cried, loud and harsh—and it gave him hope that someone might hear that voice—"I'm not sick! At last I am well, at last I can tell you, Kevin! My God, do you know that it is like water running down my dry throat to say that I love you?"

His hand gripped the mantel; slowly, and—he hoped—imperceptibly, he began to edge toward the door. But her eye saw everything; she took a step toward him. "You can't stop me!" she triumphed. "*He* can't stop me! I'm free at last for once and all, and I tell you I will have you, Kevin, we can be together at last, rid of him!"

He was beginning to shake; another moment and he would be weeping with terror, he thought. No man was meant to witness this and live; it was a scene from hell; it was, of course, complete madness. It is madness, he said to himself, gripping the mantel to keep his hand from shaking, it is simply madness and insanity; it is foolish to fear it; you're behaving with the superstition of the Middle Ages. Be calm. Humor it. Outwit it. He took another cautious step toward the door. "Look, my dear," he said, trying firmness, essaying a smile which only, he was afraid, writhed on his face, "truly you must go home and lie down. I'm going to run out and get you a cab now—there's sure to be one at the corner—and I'm going to take you home and put you to bed."

But then he could bear it no longer, he turned his face from that figure, that indecent obscenity, he turned with the intention of walking calmly toward the door, but instead, met his death when the poker crashed, with a lightning upward blow, against the base of his skull.

THE DUSK was coming down; the yellow lights filling the square windows around the quadrangle of dormitories. All day long she had knelt here on the window seat, her door locked, weeping, shaking, falling asleep of exhaustion, weeping again. Had a knock sounded on her door? It seemed many had, and many footsteps passed. How they would love to tear back the walls, expose her misery, point at her, stare at her wounds, secure in their smugness! She would let no one in. This was the moment of most terrible isolation of her life—to share it with anyone would be sacrilege. To whom could she speak here, to whom could she mourn? Only himself, and he was dead, her beautiful darling gone.

"Oh my dear!" she said, "My darling!" and laying her head down on her forearms, wept again.

The quadrangle dripped and glistened under the sodden sky, the weeping, mourning sky. The trees shone wetly, the pavements reflected. There on the asphalt, four stories below, lay death—the short moment of terror, then peace. If only she had the courage to die! I hate you, Molly Morrison, she cried to herself, sobbing, I hate you!

If she had had courage—yesterday, the day before, last month—she would have run to him saying, I love you! I will black your boots, mend your clothes—anything! I love you! If yesterday were back again, how she would run to him, throw herself upon him, thrust herself between him and that bloody, importunate death! But there is no turning time; inexorably it moves from under you—what you were yesterday is fixed for always, making its mark on what you are today, what you will be tomorrow. What you are is a coward, Molly Morrison, she told herself in the deepest contempt of despair.

Good for words and weeping, that was all. How do you expect to be an artist, to speak your dearest thoughts in paint and line when you cannot even tell your love? Only the scribblings and scratchings, the horrible papers and note-books full of . . . what could only disgust her now. Thank God it was gone and out of her sight, could no longer stare her in the face and confront her with that unbelievably infamous part of herself. The treachery of the written word!

All day, in spite of her grieving and moaning, a terrible dreary sanity, like the dreary light of the November day, had held her in its grip; now, gratefully, she felt a gentle madness descending with the dusk. "Do you remember," she said conversationally, lifting her head from her arms, "do you remember yesterday?"

"Yes, Molly," he answered, in his sweet judicious voice, almost there before her, almost sitting in her own wicker chair with his long legs crossed before him. "I remember."

The black curls clenched on his forehead by the dampness, the pipe gripped in the corner of his mouth, he had sat in a booth in The Coffee Shoppe, a cup of cooling coffee before him, talking to Mrs. Cramm. After its first leap at the sight of him, her heart had sunk to see those broad yet somehow ultimately female shoulders, that flaming, smoothly coiffed head in its molten braids, blocking him off from the rest of the world, precluding the possibility of herself, only a student, invading his grown-up faculty life; preventing her from approaching, asking breathlessly, Is this seat taken? May I sit there? The seat was taken—taken like a besieged city, to be sure, by Mrs. Cramm's broad possessive buttocks. "Darling!" said Mrs. Cramm in her loud theatrical voice, meaning nothing by the endearment but her assertion of possession. Molly had sat in an empty booth where she could watch them, and had sunk her head over her books. "Darling!" Mrs. Cramm's voice rang out over the bleating of the juke box, over the chatter of the girls, turning the word like a knife in Molly's heart.

Bending her head over her *Outline of Modern European History*, she had envisioned a conversation with him. "Do you think," she would be saying to him, in a frank, curious sort of way (revealing nothing) "do you think Mrs. Cramm is—" not beautiful. Other people did not use that word as she had heard it used at home. Attractive. That was what they said—and perhaps it was more expressive after all. "Do you think Mrs. Cramm is *attractive*?" He cocked his head, maybe, and thought. "I find her," Molly pursued (but only in cowardice, only in imagination) "rather *overwhelming*." And then his head tipped back, he laughed and laughed, for overwhelming was surely the thing that Mrs. Cramm was. She was like something blown up to twice its size. Like a child as big as an adult. Like a black cherry the size of an apple. Overwhelming. "Darling!"

rang out again, disrupting Molly's dream. How little that word must mean to her that she threw it out so lightly!

Then it was ten minutes of three, as she had known it must be at last, and time to leave the warm noisy coffee shop to go to her class. Sighing, she rose, gathered her books in her arm, and took her check to the cash register. But, like a miracle, suddenly he was beside her. "Where are you going, Molly?" he said, laying his coin down beside hers. The cash register bell rang dizzily in her ears. "To Raleigh," she said faintly. "Then I'll walk along with you," he said, and held the door open for her, while Mrs. Cramm sat deserted in the booth, swilling coffee.

He was a beautiful, sloppy, gaunt figure, standing up hatless in the mizzling rain, his lean black Modigliani head at the one end, his long, lean, shambling legs sticking too far out of his raincoat at the other. And she beside him, feeling half his size, clasping her books like their new baby to her breast, flushing and perspiring a little in the dampness. In silence they paced the walk beside the row of shops; when they came to the cross walk he looked down at her suddenly. "Molly," he said, "you look pretty. What is it—a new sweater?"

She smiled at him, and blushed too, yet inside her spread a certain sadness. If he had thought of her as a woman he would never have spoken this way. It was only because he felt immune to her, because she was a student and no more, that he could speak so personally, with such ease. She shook her head no, still smiling, still blushing.

"No?" he said in mock surprise. "Then where have my eyes been when you've worn it before? What color would you say it was—a sort of octomaroon?"

Please don't talk baby talk to me, she wanted to say, it is positively insulting. For I am not a baby, I am very young, I am awkward, I know, but still I am a woman—don't you understand? What I want is to be your wife, your mistress, for all that I wear socks and sweaters like the rest of them; for all I talk of nothing but my midterm paper. Don't you see how it makes me feel to appear before you in this guise? It makes me feel like Cinderella, long, long before the ball. If I could say Darling as easily as Mrs. Cramm . . . But all she could say was, "Well, some sort of a maroon, I guess."

It was the hour when classes were changing, when students on foot and on bicycles streamed over the asphalt walks of the campus, and girls passing them spoke to him, said, "Hello, Mr. Boyle," from time to time. They passed Mr. Hungerford, who taught Shakespeare, wearing his white grieved face. "Boyle," he said, raising his hand in salute. "See you later," and walked on. Yet suddenly he turned to her as if they were in utter privacy, with his brows knitted, and said, "Molly, have you a family?"

"Oh," she said, surprised, "why, yes."

"Well," he went on, "do you like them?"

And all inside her, warm and good, she flushed, because this was a truly personal question, the kind you asked of someone you cared for. This meant—she must think it over in private, but already she could be almost sure—it meant he cared for her; even if never in the world could he be her lover, already he was her friend. "No," she said honestly, "I can't say that I do. My father is a great man, but—"

"But you don't get along with your mother?" he laughed at her.

She frowned, wanting to say more, but it was he who spoke as they passed under the bare dripping elms. "Molly, I'm sorry to say that you're going to fail my course if something doesn't happen soon."

She bowed her head; she should have known it would be this. Half the papers missing, and in the ones he had, only half what she meant said. How was she ever to say what she meant, when all she seemed to mean was, I love you, Kevin Boyle— meaning no disrespect, but it would sound so silly to say, I love you, Mr. Boyle. And what she meant he must never see in any case, what she meant was to be secretly disposed of, reams and heaps of it, scribbled and scratched to her grinding shame, thrust from her sight lest it meet her eyes by accident, that evidence of her own madness. . . .

"I'm sorry," she mumbled. "I don't seem to be very bright."

"That's nonsense," he said sharply, "and you know it, Molly. I don't know what's wrong with you, but I suspect you're upset about something."

"Oh," she said chokingly, lying in her teeth, "oh, no!"

"Don't tell me no, like the little liar that you are," he said, stopping by the walk that turned off to the Library. "Come and see me one day and let us talk over the papers and what-ever it is that's making you unhappy. When could you come? Tomorrow at four?"

Dumbly she nodded her head over and over until she could regain her voice; standing in the rain nodding and nodding like a foolish little Shetland pony with her bang falling into her eyes. "Oh yes," she said finally, "that would be fine, Mr. Boyle."

"Good," he said, "then tomorrow at four in my office. Goodbye, Molly." He raised his hand and was off toward the Library, while she stumbled on toward Raleigh Hall where her next class was. "Goodbye, my darling!" she said, whispering it under her breath. If she had shouted it! If she had cried it to the housetops! Could it be that he might have turned, might have taken some different crossroad of his destiny which would have led him away from brutal, violent death? "Goodbye, my darling," she said now, aloud, to the blue November dusk, and flowed away on another torrent of tears.

Slowly, louder and louder in her ears, a sound made itself known beyond the sound of her own crying. Someone was knocking at the door. "Molly," a voice called, "Molly, dear, please open the door! It's Miss Sanders."

She did not, could not answer, but she held back her sobs and listened. Outside the door she could hear a colloquy carried on in low murmurs. She heard the words, ". . . all day . . ." and ". . . door's locked . . ." and ". . . doctor. . . ."

At this she caught her breath and went to her bureau. Feeling about in the darkness, she found a clean handkerchief, wiped her eyes and nose. "Miss Sanders," she called out in a harsh voice that did not sound like her own, "I'll open the door for you if you'll make the rest of them go away."

"Yes, dear, of course," Miss Sanders' voice came back ea-gerly. More colloquy; the sound of diminishing footsteps. "Let me in, Molly. Everyone's gone."

She turned the key in the lock and opened the door. Miss Sanders stood in the bleak light of the corridor, twisting her hands and looking worried. "Come in," said Molly, in her new rough voice, and snapped on the overhead bulb. Miss Sanders stepped over the threshold, peering at Molly with her head cocked like a terribly worried hen's. She thrust her hand out toward Molly's face; Molly tossed her head and backed away.

"I only wanted to see if you were feverish," said Miss Sanders meekly.

Molly laid her hand on her own cheek. "No," she said after a moment, as if she were a consulting doctor at her own case, "I'm not. It's only," she spoke very evenly, "that I've been upset about the murder."

As with a tremendous roll of tympani, the sky seemed to thunder, the room reeled, Miss Sanders swelled and diminished before her lightning-struck eyes. The body, the paper had said, was found lying on the hearth. If Mr. Marks had not discovered it at 7 P.M., a severe fire might have resulted, as the dead man's coat was about to catch flame. The back of the head. . . . The back of the head was clotted with black curls and blood. Like a sleeping child he lay, his pale face pillowed peacefully on the bricks, his curved arm lying too close to the coals, so that the sleeve of his jacket was sending up a curl of smoke when they found him. Without so much as a Now-I-lay-me Kevin Boyle lay dead among his books and his private matters, the back of his head bashed in with a blunt instrument. Bashed—like an eggshell. Could the paper have said that? It sounded too graphic for a newspaper style. She must have made that up herself. The newspaper was here somewhere. She turned aside, forgetting Miss Sanders, to look for it.

"Why, Molly," said Miss Sanders, calling her back—to the land of the living, you might say, "did you *know* Mr. Boyle?" Her round black chicken's eyes rolled in their rings of bare flesh.

"I had a class with him," said Molly faintly.

"But Molly—" said Miss Sanders, working her hands, "it's shocking, my dear, quite unreal and completely upsetting, but Molly dear, you must pull yourself together! You haven't eaten all day. It isn't as if—I don't mean to sound heartless, but after all, you didn't know him *well*?" It began as a statement and ended as a question. Miss Sanders' pale henlike face hung on her bones under the glare of the ceiling light, filled with a kind of inhuman birdlike kindness, but curious, too, wondering.

Now what shall I say, she thought, as she stood there facing it out with Miss Sanders. Oh no, I didn't know him; he was only my lover—I didn't know him—he was only my husband, I only thought about him every minute of my waking life. . . .

Miss Sanders still stood before her, but dimmer, now; over her plump shoulder his saturnine, pipe-biting face grinned: Molly, my girl. . . . "It was not," she said vaguely, "that he was my lover, that he was not . . ." and burst into a long low wail of anguish, her face hidden in her thin white hands.

Then Miss Sanders wheeled and flew down like an old rolling-eyed vulture, scenting scandal, scenting carrion, wheeling down on weeping Molly through layers of air, clutching her to her bosom, patting, half strangling. "There, there, my dear," she comforted hungrily, "I'll tell you what we'll do—I'll just call a taxi and we'll go right over to the Infirmary. Dr. Abby will give you a sedative and you'll have a good night's sleep. You'll see—everything will look quite different in the morning."

Once she had been drunk, and it had been, in a way, like this. There had been a central theme—sometimes you lost the melody of it, then it returned again. You lost it because around it swirled mists and diffusions of sound, sometimes lulling, sometimes brazen. Like the putting on of the coat, the walking down the stairs, like the faces, eager, prying, looking up the stairs at her from where they clustered round the mail desk, and Miss Sanders bustling her back to the housemother's apartment while she put on her outdoor things; like the taxi, the steps . . .

In the hall of the Infirmary, the theme came back. There it was quiet and dark. She was glad she had come. One small lamp burned on a desk where a nurse sat writing, only her hand and the paper encircled in light. In the arches of darkness overhead the melody swelled out clear and purposeful, beautiful as a cadenza on a cello: Kevin Boyle is dead, was the theme; he was murdered yesterday, a bare three hours after you parted from him. Kevin Boyle is dead. You will never say to him, I love you, my darling.

Miss Sanders was murmuring to the nurse, leaving Molly standing swaying and alone in the vaults of darkness where the theme echoed. "I love you, my darling," Molly said, rather loudly and experimentally, as if she were drunk. In a bustle the nurse rose from her desk, making cooing, rustling noises like a flock of white pigeons.

"Come along, dear," she said, "we'll tuck you up in bed and give you a nice sleeping pill."

MANY A time he had sat here with Kevin Boyle, slouched comfortably in the worn old armchairs, looking into the fire and talking of this and that—though mostly of that, mostly of Kevin. Oh, sometimes he would try to make a bold beginning, saying, Kevin, do you know what it is I want? I want to get married. But before the words were out of his mouth, Kevin would be roaring and shouting with laughter, slapping his knees and pulling his own hair. "What in the name of God and the Devil does a man want to get married for?" he would say. "Why, boy, you've nothing to gain but your chains!" Then it would be another tale of conquest—the shy, sly glance she had thrown at him, the note slipped under the door, the sweet warm wrestling in the strange bed. . . . Was ever a man so pursued of women? Could it be true that any man was so pursued? Or was it all a beautiful Irish fiction, invented half to please that broth of a Kevin, half to torture poor, weak-chinned, bespectacled Leonard? Sometimes, after Kevin had crossed the hall to his own rooms and Leonard had brushed his teeth, put on his neat striped pajamas, and folded himself between the tight-pulled sheets, he would lie there in a passion (for even a weak-chinned man with his glasses off is sometimes capable of passion) cursing the Irish who were born to outshine, with their wild romanticism, all the other, soberer, steadier, less noticeable races of mankind.

Yet if Kevin had been lying with his tales of conquest (not to say rape) it was his lies, at last, which had done him in. For last evening Leonard, sitting by the fire over his books, had heard Kevin's voice cry out "No!" in protest, sounding through the two closed doors, had heard the thud, the slam, the footsteps, yet had never gone to investigate till more than an hour later, thinking this was one of *them*, the ladies who could not resist the melancholy Hibernian charm of him, who threw themselves upon him in the extremity of their passion (or so he had related it—many times) so that he had to disengage their clasping arms gently and let them know that no single woman would ever possess him for her own. It had been a long time before Leonard had got back to his books after that "No," that thud, that clacking latch. He had stared into the coals long and profitlessly, gritting his teeth, upper against lower, and cursing

198

the Irish, without whom the rest of the world might have gone along its quiet way, flirting gently with librarians, and not wishing for what was beyond its means.

But two hours later, his notes prepared for the next day's classes, when he had knocked at Kevin's door to see if he was ready for supper, opened without waiting for an answer, Kevin had been lying dead, the back of his head smashed in with the poker.

What does a man think of when first he sees a corpse, and one done violently to death, at that? For Leonard had seen not so much as a dead grandmother, not so much as a dead dog that he could remember in all the days of his life, so that now . . . now . . . He was not sick at his stomach, although he would have expected himself to be. He stood there looking at Kevin's unmistakably dead body with a strange kind of excitement swelling inside him. Kevin is dead, he thought, somebody has murdered him. That is Kevin Boyle. He was alive and now he is dead. The thing to do is not to touch anything. The thing to do is call the police. Yet he stood there for minutes more, looking at the dead Kevin, lying there so peaceful (except for the bloody hole in his skull), peaceful as if in sleep, with his mouth a little open, and the smoke curling up from one sleeve that lay too close to the coals. The thing to do was not touch anything, but if he did not move that sleeve the corpse would catch fire. And at this thought the terrible thing had come over him that he was not shut of yet: he kept wanting to laugh. The corpse will catch fire, he thought, and giggled right out loud, nervously. Then he knew he would have to keep rein on himself for a long time to come, or every time he had to speak Kevin Boyle's name and tell how it was he had found him, he would begin to snicker helplessly, like a schoolboy who had perpetrated a hoax.

He had taken three cautious steps to the fireplace, leaned down and gingerly pinched up a piece of Kevin's coat sleeve in his fingers. The fabric was hot; the arm within it moved with a curious acquiescent limpness. Again he felt the horrible, shocking impulse to laugh. You would have to listen if I talked to you now, my boy! he crowed inwardly. And was deeply shocked at himself, and began to feel queasy, at last, at the sight and the faint smell of the blood.

He had gone through it all admirably; had shut the door carefully behind him, had called Miss Stone, the landlady, and broken the news, had telephoned the police, answered their questions, run to the corner for spirits of ammonia for Miss Stone, spoken to the reporter from the West Lyman *Star*—but cautiously, giving only the barest outline, avoiding all question of Kevin's character, his habits. He had not gone to bed until long after midnight, yet had risen as usual for an eight-thirty class. He had conducted himself well, and here was his reward. Across the hearth from him, in the worn leather chair where Kevin had so often lolled—indeed, he had had almost no callers *but* Kevin—the great George Hungerford now sat, hunched forward over his knees, prodding the coals with the short iron poker. It was not, Leonard observed in some wild and uncontrollable part of his mind, the day to be poking about with a poker, and he swallowed a nervous giggle as painfully as if it had been a retch. What was to become of him with this awful compulsion to laugh at the wrong moments? The charitable view of himself would be that he was simply hysterical with the events of the last day, but if he burst out laughing in George Hungerford's infinitely melancholy face, no such charitable view was likely to be taken. And what he felt at the sight of Hungerford, sitting there in his own chair, was far from laughter. Call it reverence. Call it incredulity. Call it a prayer of gratitude.

Suddenly Hungerford raised his head. "Mix me a drink, will you, Marks?" he said, his face pale even in the firelight, and terribly worn. With a nervous jerk of eagerness Leonard was out of his chair and half across the room before the words had died on the quiet air. He pulled the light chain in the little closet where his refrigerator and sink stood. He took out an ice tray, letting water run over it. "Marks!" Hungerford's voice came to him suddenly, sounding over the flowing water with a tortured, pleading note. "Marks, who could have killed him? Why should *he*, of any of us, have to die?"

It was strange to Leonard that a man of Hungerford's intellect, Hungerford's sensitivity, his—why not say it?—genius, should question so naïvely a fate which, in the last analysis, Leonard could only feel as appropriate. Carefully he measured out the jiggers of whisky in each glass, trying how to answer this innocence without sounding impertinent.

"He was," he called at last, forcing open the soda bottle so that the warm effervescence ran down over his hand, "a passionate man."

"Passionate," he heard Hungerford mumble, and the sound of a log breaking in two, with a snapping of sparks. He set the glasses on a tray, pulled the light chain again, and bore the drinks out into the dimly lighted room. He was gnawed by an enormous curiosity which he dared not indulge. Hungerford had visited Kevin two and three times a week. Leonard, coming home from the Library, or crossing the hall to see if Kevin were free, would hear their voices behind the thin door, talking and talking. He did not dare to knock, Hungerford being Hungerford, and Kevin being Kevin. But he had often wondered on what paths such conversation could have wandered. For himself, he had heard Kevin enlarge on only one subject— sex. Could it be that with Hungerford he had skirted the topic entirely?

He had just sat down with his drink when Hungerford said abruptly, as if clairvoyant, "What makes you say that, Marks— that he was passionate? Was it something specific that led you to conclude . . . Not to say, of course, that it wasn't plain without any direct instance, but if there might be a clue—"

"Why," said Leonard, giggling his nervous treble laugh, "to tell you the truth, sir, we generally talked about women—that is to say, he did."

Hungerford was afflicted by a severe tic which drew up the whole side of his face from time to time, like one of those rubber faces children play with and distort. Now the muscles of the left side of his serenely tragic mask drew together spasmodically, as if in agony. "That was a side of him I never knew," he said, leaning back in the chair and letting the poker drop. "Our conversations were generally literary or professional. Possibly," he added, his mouth sardonic, "he regarded me as a creature whose passion was spent . . . Did you know he was collecting poems for a book?"

Leonard shook his head, and a stab of bitter jealousy, the first since Kevin's murder, attacked him once more. So it was *not* done—his brutal eminence, their impossible, unequal rivalry. Ah, well . . .

"But that's hardly relevant," Hungerford frowned. "As to

women. It seemed to me he acted with utmost discretion with regard to the students."

"Absolutely, he stayed absolutely clear of anything of that sort," Leonard said quickly. He hesitated a moment, then risked it, with another snigger. "To tell the truth, I often wondered how he avoided it so completely with the sort of—the sort of history he professed."

Hungerford frowned deeper and chewed the inside of his cheek. "Well," he said, "let us be open about it, Marks. What do you know of his relations with women?"

Have I, thought Leonard, in cautious anxiety, pushed too far? He made his face very serious and earnest. "He was always most discreet and indirect, Mr. Hungerford, in the sense that I never heard him mention a woman's name, and I was often puzzled as to whether a specific incident had occurred last week in West Lyman or ten years ago in Dublin. I even suspected sometimes that he was only indulging an aptitude for Rabelaisian invention. But as far as women coming to his rooms here, the only ones I have ever seen were Miss Stone and Mrs. Cramm."

"Oh, Freda . . ." said Hungerford, and waved his hand in dismissal with a kind of exhausted humor. Inside Leonard flared a wave of rage; he knew he was about to say something unwise, unpolitic, but he could not help himself.

"Mrs. Cramm," he said carefully, "was in and out a good deal. At all hours."

"Freda has too much bark to be much of a biter," said Hungerford, and stared into the fire.

Hah! cried Leonard silently, if you only knew! The bite of her tongue! The bite of her indifference! The way she reduced a man to the place of poor relative with a glance and the ignoring of his joke. If he had a scar for every one of his sentences she had interrupted in English Department meetings, for the tête-à-têtes between himself and Kevin on which she had broken, sending him off to his rooms like a child who has outstayed his bedtime. . . . She was the living negation of all that he counted his manhood. "She always struck me as a rather violent woman," he said quietly, "but perhaps—"

"That's exactly it," said Hungerford irritably, as if tired of the subject, "if Freda had murdered Kevin she would now be enjoying her confession like an old courtesan writing her memoirs."

"Of course, I don't know her," Leonard mumbled. "I've only seen her for minutes at Kevin's, and about the campus. . . ." He was desperately afraid he had said too much. He wanted so to remember this as perfect, to recollect in privacy that he had, for once, on this great occasion, said the right thing . . .

Suddenly Hungerford took up his glass and drained off the whole drink at a gulp. He sat up in the chair, and it was plain that he was about to leave. Don't go, don't go! Leonard wanted to beg him. There are so many things we could have said . . . "I suppose there's no use indulging in amateur detection; the police will do what they can, and what they can't, we can't. I have no faith in the use of the academic intellect for practical purposes. We shall have to see. We shall simply have to see," said Hungerford.

He set his hands on the arms of the chair, raised his elbows in the air preparatory to pushing himself to his feet. Suddenly the tic seized hold of his face; he sat frozen in the awkward position, staring into the fire, and to Leonard's horror, two tears slipped over his eyelids, ran down his cheeks. Oh, Mr. Hungerford! he wanted to cry, wanted to kneel at his feet, offering service. Oh Master! he would have cried, had he dared. But Hungerford's lips moved, drew together several times soundlessly before his voice issued. "I loved that boy," he said brokenly. "With all the worn-out mechanics of my lost emotions I felt it in him for the first time in—how long?—Life," he said finally, and rose like an old, old man. "Life."

Mutely, Leonard rose too; took Hungerford's coat and hat from the closet, helped him into the sleeves. "Goodnight, Marks," said Hungerford, the great Hungerford—almost pitifully, looking into Leonard's eyes as they stood at the door.

It is over, mourned Leonard silently. He will never come again. I have lost my only, only opportunity. If only I could say something to hold him. But when he looked into Hungerford's ravaged face, the great wells of his mourning eyes, he was unable to speak in his own interest; the real emotion of his homage overcame him. Clumsily, he took hold of Hungerford's elbow and shook it a little. "Get some sleep, sir," he said rather chokingly. And that was the end.

THE BRICK faces of the neo-Gothic buildings showed bleakly in the night, illuminated by the cheerless street lamps. Hungerford walked slowly, draggingly, leaning on the crook of his umbrella, oblivious to the rain. The architecture of despair, he thought. The blood and bones of hopelessness. He hardly knew what he meant. Was he awake or asleep? Was this the landscape of some dream? Surely it was too awful to be real. The darkened Library, the buildings full of empty classrooms, the threatening olive-green shape of the mailbox under the lamp at the center of the campus . . . And then behind him, footsteps. Brisk, intended, rubber shod, and dull, yet plainly distinguishable. I know who that is, said his mind. That is Death. That is the old Reaper, gumshoeing behind you. He thought he would turn and shake Death's hand when Death came abreast of him. Hello, Death, said his mind, playing tricks, suddenly dancing foolishly in his head. The footsteps drew closer, gaining on him. Death would take his arm and they would would walk together like the good friends they were. I have been your good friend for a long time, his mind said to Death, but you have turned your face away from me. Are we to be reunited now? Will you take me where you took Kevin Boyle, leave me safe from the pryings of hope and life? . . . Death was at his side now. "Good evening, Mr. Hungerford," said Death.

"Hullo, Tom," said George Hungerford wearily, leaning like a sick man on his umbrella.

"Wet night," said the campus policeman.

"Very wet," said George Hungerford, and hurrying his pace, passed on.

"Goodnight, Mr. Hungerford."

"Goodnight, Tom."

Death, you bloody cheat, you humbug! The bare white bones of the auditorium grinned at him like a skull, white columned, barren. It was as if his whole life was a trial by torture to prove himself worthy of death. Ever since the grey morning when they waked him somehow, retching and vomiting, from the overdose of nembutal. Ever since then it had been one torture added to another, to last God knew how long, testing his readiness for death. The torture of breathing. The torture of doctors. The torture of the sanitarium, of learning to be quiet . . . The torture of the notebooks . . . The torture of Kevin Boyle's murder. Yet since his attempted suicide he was aware that something had changed in him, grown hardier, more impervious to blows. When he held the razor to his wrist, debating whether he should cut the arteries, some new voice spoke in his head, small and far away, but indomitably authoritative, saying No! By its command he was compelled to go on and on, through the trials and agonies devised for him, never able to pass the examination which was to prove him ready to be graduated from life.

He walked through the iron gates of the college to the main street of the town. Across from the auditorium stood the house where he rented rooms, tall and Victorian, set back on its lawn behind its iron Saint Bernard. A lamp gleamed ruby, amber, and sapphire through the colored panes of the hall door. He liked his tall old house. It had a bitter friendly ugliness, like a hideous spinster who has learned the grim humor of the disappointments of life. He unlocked the door and climbed the stairs to his apartment. He was almost smiling at the friendly ugliness of the chocolate wallpaper, the dreary brown landscapes in their gilt frames that hung over the stairs. He thought he might sleep tonight. It was good for him to talk when it touched at all on what was in his mind—even to so colorless a figure as Leonard Marks. It was good to lay aside however small a portion of the burden of silence in something other than the addlepated chattering of the faculty tearoom. He turned on the light in his living room, and inside his head, the voice began to laugh, faint and distant and vicious. For there on his desk lay the notebook, opened wide; across the room the huge mad handwriting screamed at him, commanding him to read, commanding him to taste again the depths of human vileness and despise . . .

THE BIG hall filled slowly; the floor and then the balcony. Finally the organ sounded out, the students rose, hymn-books in hand.

Oh God, our help in ages past,
Our hope for years to come,
Our shelter from the stormy blast
And our eternal home.

They sat down again; from offstage President Bainbridge suddenly appeared, his face red, his gown billowing, puffing onto the scene like a belated bridegroom. Behind him the faculty sat in two rows, mute and blinking. A whisper passed over the rows of girls, audible as the visibility of a little wind silvering a field of grass. The president shuffled a handful of notes. "The Athletic Association will hold trials for . . ." he read. "Tryouts for *Antigone* will be held on . . ." At last he stopped, laid down the notes, and looked out at the field of faces upturned to him. Visibly he paused, braced himself, began.

"I believe all of you are aware of the subject on which I must speak this morning. Mr. Kevin Boyle, a member of the English Department, was found murdered in his rooms on Monday evening. I find it purposeless to mention the horror and shock which has come to all of us in hearing this news. You may find it petty in me that I am going to speak of the matters of which I must speak this morning in the face of this kind of a catastrophe. Yet it is the unfortunate fate of a college president—" there was the briefest murmur of amusement at the assumption that the fate of a college president might be conceived as unfortunate—"always to be considering the matter of the reputation of the college. And it is of this I must speak this morning, philistine or even brutal as you may find it at the time of this tragedy."

"To be brief: we are beginning to be, and may expect to be even more in the future, besieged by newspapermen. Their business is to make of this event a story which will be as sensational as possible. Any one of you may be asked questions which by their very nature can elicit answers to be twisted to the damage of the college." There was a pause for a presidential twinkle, then a parenthesis. "I am talking to you like a trustees' meeting—I hope you will listen to me in kind." A gentle shout of laughter went up. His round face drooped again to seriousness. "I do not mean to imply that any of you will deliberately give out false or irresponsible information, or information which might more suitably be given to the police or myself. My only point is that newspapermen have a way with them—" giggles—"a way of putting matters in their most lurid light. I want to make a personal plea to every student in this college to abstain from conversation with any stranger who seems inclined to draw her out on the subject of Mr. Boyle. I ask you this selfishly, because your behavior will reflect on my position, and less selfishly, because in loyalty to this college which offers you so much, you must use your foresight and discretion to safeguard its reputation."

The president withdrew to his armchair, the organist, observing him in her rear-view mirror, struck up once more; the audience rose for the closing hymn.

> *Once more the liberal year laughs out*
> *With richer stores than gems or gold . . .*

When it was over, the organist began a recessional, the faculty filed off the stage in orderly fashion, the audience of girls rose and began struggling into their coats, pushing in a sluggish stream out the aisles.

"I think it's *silly*," a clear voice rose out of an eddy of talk. "You'd think we were children . . ."

"He's thinking about that time those girls in Fairish House talked to the *Journal-American* reporter about drinking . . ."

"God, what do you suppose *happened* to him, though? Do you suppose it's a *maniac* or something?"

"Miss Austen is going to take his classes . . ."

"Oh, be honest and admit it's simply too fruity having a murder on the campus!"

They spilled out the doors and flowed between the white pillars of the Greek Revival front, like sand flowing between the fingers of a hand. Outside was a brilliant blue Indian summer day, glorifying the bare November trees, the dingy grass. Around the steps of the auditorium there raged the usual

pandemonium of chatter and movement, of disengaging bicycles from racks, of shouting across heads to distant friends.

"A girl in our house had such a mad crush on him that she
went completely off her rocker. They sent her up to the
Infirmary simply screaming with hysterics."

"No! who?"

"Nobody you'd know. Some little creep of a freshman
named Morrison. Very drippy."

"Suppose *she* did it?"

"My dear, she doesn't have what it *takes*."

Freda Cramm, looking enormous and golden in a very
expensive russet tweed topcoat, wedged her way through the
mass of girls and caught Miss Sanders by the elbow as she
was turning down the brick walk toward the quadrangle.
"Maude!" she said commandingly. Miss Sanders turned and
blinked her lashless eyes. "Hello, Freda dear," she said. "Isn't
it too horrible?"

"My dear," said Freda ominously, "you don't know *how*
horrible!"

Miss Sanders simply blinked more violently, a mottling of
nervous blotches beginning to discolor her neck.

"I want you to come to my house for coffee now," said
Freda. "I have to talk to you. It's very important."

"Now?" said Miss Sanders weakly. "There's all the day's
planning—"

"No, you must come," Freda ordered, and steered her to
the sleek black convertible, its top put back, which waited
glossily at the curb.

Freda drove abominably. Miss Sanders sat in clenched anxiety, pressing her feet against imaginary brakes as the car wound
through the streets of the town. Twenty years ago Freda had
been a pet student in Miss Sanders' house. Now that she was a
member of the faculty (heaven knew why, for she had all the
money she wanted and a good many opportunities for glamorous living) Miss Sanders found herself relegated (or elevated)
to a position in Freda's life like that of a superannuated nanny
in a noble English household, who, having dandled the young
lady of the family in her infancy, now bends a deferential ear to
her debutante confidences.

Freda lived on a hilltop back of the campus in a remodeled mansion of the eighties, equipped with the most modern plumbing, the most baroque furniture. She extracted Miss Sanders rather forcibly from her wraps, ordered the maid to bring coffee, and led the way to the anachronistic solarium, where the Indian summer sun poured its splendor onto the comfortable bamboo furniture. She would allow no questions until the coffee was poured, the sugar and cream measured, the maid retired to the bowels of the house. Then she sighed deep, and reclined in her chair. "Maude darling," she said, "I talk too much."

Miss Sanders, sitting up toward the edge of her seat, holding her cup and saucer in mid-air, blinked her eyes and didn't know what to say. This was incontrovertibly true.

Freda sighed again and closed her eyes a moment. Since her divorce, she had become quite stout; it always startled Miss Sanders to recall the picture of her as a long gawky girl in the chemise dresses of the 1920's. Her small, delicate, deceptively gentle features were strangely imbedded in the new flesh, yet they had managed to retain much of the force of their old seductiveness. "I've been seeing too much of Kevin Boyle," Freda went on. "It's bound to come out."

For a moment a little smile flickered in the corner of Miss Sanders' lips. She was certainly having her share of Kevin Boyle's "girl friends," as they said. The little Morrison girl—well, think of that later. "Come on, Freda," she said in a timidly teasing way, "out with it!"

Freda opened her heavy-lidded eyes and stared through the plate glass down to the valley below the house, where the river meandered through the flat, frost-burnt meadows. Was she going to be practical or dramatic, Miss Sanders wondered. "Darling, it isn't that I've been sleeping with him," Freda said practically. "It's just that I've been talking too much again."

Somewhere, buried deep under Maude Sanders' henlike exterior, her fluttering manner, her kindly ineffectuality, was a little spear of ridicule which responded irresistibly to the stimulus of Freda's flamboyant egocentricity. "After all these years," she essayed, "how could that make any difference?"

"Well," said Freda, "it could make a lot of difference, it

seems to me, if he had been loose-mouthed about some of the things we talked about. Because if some of the things I said in perfect innocence and frankness—the fact is he had a letter that belonged to me. We had a quarrel about it."

"What sort of letter?"

Freda stamped out her cigarette and rose to pace the brick floor like an overfed cat. "Oh, it's too maddening!" she said. Miss Sanders sat blinking, waiting for her to go on. "It was just an ordinary begging letter," said Freda overprotestingly, at last.

"Then I can't see—"

"Oh, you don't understand!" cried Freda. "We had this horrible fight about it. Kevin was perfectly brutal. And I went off in a rage, leaving the thing behind, and I can't be sure he destroyed it."

"Suppose he didn't? If it was just an ordinary sort of begging letter, how could it reflect on you, Freda?"

Freda stood in front of the windows with her hands clasped behind her back. "Well, it wasn't *just* an ordinary begging letter. It was rather horrible. Oh, Maude, you don't know how utterly nasty people can be!"

"Who was it from?"

"Oh, one of my lame-duck relatives."

Miss Sanders went on quietly blinking, but an internal smile illuminated her eyes. The story was growing plainer to her with each scrap that Freda tossed out. A poor relative had asked her (with signal lack of insight) for money. Freda had refused, but had felt uncomfortable about it, so she had gone to Mr. Boyle with the story, hoping for outside justification of her behavior. Mr. Boyle, a young man with a good deal of charm, but little tact, from what Maude Sanders had been able to observe of him at faculty dinners, had told Freda she had been wrong in refusing. And Freda, who could bear to be wrong almost less than she could bear to give away money, had got in a fight with him in order to discredit his opinion. It was not difficult to piece this together from her remembrance of Freda's impoverished college days, when she had cultivated the wealthier girls on the campus, choosing her friends as carefully and by the same standards as a bond salesman chooses his customers, and when politic or possible, borrowing their fur coats, their ready cash, their young men. She had acquired Michael Cramm by this means—borrowing him from a drab little heiress—who, as she later justly pointed out, had much less need for him than she. She had parted from him later only under the pressure of his willingness to settle a large piece of property on her in return for being freed to marry the show-girl of his choice. Freda had many public vices; parsimony was the one she tried to keep secret, even from herself. "It does seem to me," Miss Sanders said finally, "that you're making something out of nothing. Suppose a letter belonging to you is found in Mr. Boyle's effects. Even suppose that the police question you about it. I hardly see—"

"Maude," said Freda, sitting down and clasping her hands in her lap, "you know how I *yell*?"

In silence, Miss Sanders agreed that in moments of emotional stress, Freda had been known to raise her voice.

"Well, there I was in this rattletrap house Kevin lives in—lived in—screaming like a banshee because he practically accused me of stealing bread out of starving mouths—I mean, Maude, he was practically a *Communist*, you know—and when I was finally leaving in a rage, there was that slimy Leonard Marks, just putting his key in the lock across the hall. Now goodness knows how long he had been listening."

"Mr. Marks?" said Miss Sanders. "Oh, Freda, I hardly think—I mean, he's such a—"

"Pipsqueak," supplied Freda. "That's just the point. I can't stand the man; I've been abominably rude to him, and he's just the one to hate me like poison and make a point of bringing it up that I was heard behaving like a fishwife in Kevin's apartment last week. Furthermore, Kevin may have talked to him."

"About you? Oh, Freda, I *do* have the impression that Mr. Boyle was above all things a *gentleman*!"

Freda snorted. "I did a lot of talking to Kevin because—well, he was one of the few people around here you *could* talk to without having him blanch at your language. But I never labored under the impression that he was a sealed vault. A man like Kevin Boyle needs a man like Leonard Marks to show off to. He needed the good opinion of the world—otherwise why would he have been an assistant professor in an expensive women's college instead of a wild Irish poet in a Greenwich Village attic? Leonard Marks would have provided an excellent listener—a man with no life of his own would drink up Kevin's tales of roistering and hobnobbing with the great, without competing or condemning, or even doubting the veraciousness."

Miss Sanders, who was not always the fool she made herself out to be, thought, Yes, Freda dear, like you and me, while remarking aloud, "I doubt that Mr. Marks could feel that anything Mr. Boyle might have repeated would have bearing on the murder."

"The point is, he might put odds and ends together and motivate them with his own dislike for me. I was in and out of Kevin's place a good deal. Everybody in the neighborhood must know it from seeing the car outside."

Miss Sanders frowned and tapped her finger on her imitation alligator bag. "Couldn't you go to Mr. Marks?" she wondered.

Freda sighed and poured more coffee for both of them. "I've positively antagonized him," she said. "Couldn't stand the sight of him. I've insulted him several times. Now how will it look if after the murder I go to him and say, Look here, Marks, don't repeat anything Kevin may have said I said to the police?"

Miss Sanders knit her brows. The cook at Birnham House had already threatened to leave several times. Miss Sanders had been expected back a half hour ago to do the ordering and plan tomorrow's meals. An immediate conclusion of some kind must be made, but she allowed a silence to elapse while she tried to think of one that would be foolproof. Finally she began tentatively, "What if . . . what if you gave a large party—quite large. Asked all the members of the English Department, say, so that it would seem natural to have Mr. Marks. Then, rather unostentatiously, pay him a good deal of attention—win him over to your side?"

Freda frowned, pinched her lower lip between her fingers. "Not bad," she muttered. "Not bad at all. In fact very good. Could I make it some sort of memorial thing for Kevin—otherwise wouldn't it look funny to be giving a party? I'll think about it. I really think that's very good. If it's a memorial, I can have it soon, too, so that I can get to Marks before . . . unless he's already . . ."

Miss Sanders gathered up her bag decisively. "Freda, I positively *must*. . . ." Freda rose abruptly. "Oh, darling, I've been keeping you! You're an angel, Maude, and I love you dearly!"

Making small murmurs of deprecation, Miss Sanders made her way to the door, retrieved her coat and hat. "I'll drive you back to the house," said Freda. "I have to go to my office anyway."

Back in the autumn sunlight, the spicy air, Miss Sanders felt a sudden surge of gaiety and liberation, such as a visit with Freda was always likely to give her. "Freda," she said in a spurt of indiscretion, "the most appalling thing has happened at Birnham. A little freshman has collapsed over the murder. She's a neurotic little thing in any case and seems to have had one of those violent crushes on Mr. Boyle. It looks like a nervous breakdown to me. I think we'll have to send her home."

"*Really?*" cried Freda, turning her attention dangerously from the road in her ever-ready prurience. "You don't suppose she *did* it?"

"Oh, pooh," said Miss Sanders, laughing as they recklessly rounded the corner into the quadrangle, "she didn't do it any more than you did!"

"I GOTTA get an angle," crooned the young man, rocking his face between his hands. "I simply gotta get an angle."

The bartender slammed his beer down in front of him unsympathetically, and began mixing an Alexander for an order from the back room.

"Who drinks that stuff?" said the young man, looking nauseated.

"College girls," said the bartender, pouring the liquid into a glass.

"Makes me want to puke to think of it," said the young man. The bartender said nothing, but signaled to a waitress who carried the glass away.

"Listen, Joe, whattaya know?" the young man pursued. "Honestly, somebody's gotta know something. Haven't you heard anybody talking? Can't you even make something up? I'm supposed to get a story."

A pleased look came over the bartender's craggy embittered face. "See no evil, hear no evil, speak no evil," he said. It was a joke.

"Listen, Joe," the young man pleaded, "didn't the guy ever come in here?"

"Name's Stanislas," said the bartender, relapsing into moroseness.

"Oh, all *right*!" said the young man, "but look, didn't you ever see the fellow?"

"Yep," said the bartender.

"Well, what kind of guy was he? Did he come here with women?"

"Nope," said Stanislas, swiping the bar with a damp cloth.

"Did he flirt with the waitresses? Was he mixed up with the local strong-arm boys? Was he a pansy? A lot of these college professors are."

Stanislas went on wiping the bar, his eyes lowered. "Used to come here about every other night," he said at last. "Always some bunch of girls—students—would ask him to come sit at their booth in the back room. He'd go and sit with 'em. Ten o'clock they'd leave—have to be back at the college at ten-fifteen. Then he'd come out here and have another beer. Maybe he'd meet Mr. Marks. Maybe he'd meet Mr.

Hungerford. Him and Mr. Hungerford would talk poetry like. Him and Mr. Marks'd talk about women. He'd tell some mighty hot stories all right about all the dames couldn't stay away from him, but the truth of it is, I never seen him with no woman. Used to go down to one of the local houses and get himself laid once in a while, that I know for a fact. Used to go down to New York ever' so often. Tell you the truth," said Stanislas, warming at last and leaning on the bar with the cloth in his hand, "I think he was a kind of timid fellow, for all his big talk."

"Oh hell," said the reporter disgustedly, "that's no story."

Stanislas' brow lowered. "If you don't like it you know what you can do with it. Now you know as much as I do."

"Gimme another beer," said the reporter.

"Listen, Mister," said the bartender, "why'n't you go in the back room and strike up a conversation with some of them students. They're always full of a pack of lies."

"Try anything," muttered the young man, climbing down from his stool, his beer in his hand.

The back room had two rows of fumed-oak booths running the length of the walls. The reporter carried his beer to an empty booth opposite one where two girls sat. He could have passed for a college boy, with his crew cut and his horn-rimmed glasses, his sloppy tweeds. He sat down discreetly, not giving the girls any kind of obvious eye. One of them was quite a tomato—what is referred to as a long-stemmed American beauty. This was going to be what you call mixing business with pleasure. The other was on the dumpy side, with a frowsy feather cut and horn-rimmed glasses like the young man's own. She was wearing dungarees and a sweatshirt; the first had on a pale-pink sweater and skirt—good enough to eat. The reporter sat regarding them out of the corner of his eye as he sipped his beer, thinking about the best approach. Casing the joint, you might say. The pink one was not so bright—she was the one to work on. The fat cookie looked like an intellectual. She was the one to watch out for at first, but if you get her on your side, she could help you more. O.K., now he had it straight. He raised his head and looked straight into the fat one's eyes. "Can I sit with you?"

Fatty looked him up and down very coolly and turned to

the beauty. "Do we want to talk to him?" she said in a cold voice. "I think he's a reporter."

She was smart and no mistake. In a way it made things easier.

The one in the pink sweater ran her hand under the fine blond hair that fell to her shoulders like gentle plumes. She giggled. "I think reporters are *cute*," she said in a severe southern accent.

He had crossed the aisle and sat down beside the pink sweater before any discussion could go on. "My name is Jack Donelly," he said, pursuing the frank line.

"Mine is Kate Innes," said Fatty, "and this is Honey Sacheveral."

"Well, you have to have a drink with me now," he said, "now that I'm *in*," and laughed. "What'll it be?"

"Scotch and soda," said Kate promptly.

"Alexayunduh," said Honey, and giggled.

He beckoned to the waitress and ordered, changing to Scotch himself.

"Well," said Kate, leaning against the back of the booth and folding her short arms across her sweatshirt, "the president told us not to talk to reporters this morning. Naturally we have to try it. Like sticking beans up your nose."

"*What?*" said Donelly, slightly alarmed.

"Skip it," said Kate. "What do you want to worm out of us?"

He did not look at her, but brought out a handful of change from his pocket and selected some nickels. "I'm tired of worming things out of people," he said. "All day I go around worming, and what do I get—not even an early bird. What'll I play on the juke machine?"

"Stah-dust," said Honey immediately, and giggled.

"Let's see how *your* taste runs," said Kate, rather menacingly.

While he was gone the waitress brought the drinks and mixed the highballs.

Sometimes I WON-der why I spend my lonely ni-i-ights— whined the record. Honey hummed and leaned back against the seat. A delicate line of cream collected on her upper lip; she ran out her tongue and removed it neatly, leaving the fuchsia lipstick intact.

"What paper are you on?" said Kate.

"*Messenger*," he said glumly.

"Scandal sheet," said Kate.

"A person has to eat," said Donelly. "Anyway, I'm a good Guild member."

"*Mah* daddy says," Honey remarked suddenly, speaking from what seemed to be a trance, "don't quarrel with your bread and butter."

"Practical puss, aren't you?" said Donelly, in some surprise.

"Will you buy me another Alexayunduh, Mistuh Donelly?" she said, looking at him slant-eyed.

"A pleasure, my dear," he replied benignly, summoning the waitress.

"Don't act so regal," said Kate. "You should know I know it's on the expense account."

"You should remember what Honey's daddy says," cracked Donelly, and drew a grin for the first time.

"So what have you picked up about the murder?" Kate said, looking down at her drink.

"Isn't it just aw-ful?" said Honey dreamily. "Isn't it just simply terrible? He was so dar-lin'."

"He was darlin' as all get out," said Kate, and finished off the last of her Scotch. Jack ordered her another without asking.

"I haven't found out a damn thing," he said disgustedly. "All I know is what I read in the papers. Not a single soul who has ever been to his rooms has an alibi for the time of the murder, and nobody seems to care. Leonard Marks was sitting across the hall in his room—could have come over and slugged him as easy as not. George Hungerford was sleeping off a sick headache. That's a fine alibi. A dame named Freda Cramm was out for a drive to see the hunter's moon rise. Nobody remembers seeing her. The landlady in the place where he lives was at the movies—nobody saw her there. Nobody saw anybody. I personally think that either the guy slipped and fell on the poker, thereby busting in his own head, or else everybody in town bumped him off in a group. No out-of-town connections known. A showgirl named Bubbles Merryweather has turned up in New York with a poem which he dedicated to her after a warm evening in the local bistros, but that was the only time she ever saw him, and could be her press agent wrote the thing anyhow—for my money it stinks. It's what you call a mystery."

"There's a girl at our house," said Honey dreamily, "who had an aw-ful crush on him."

Kate set her drink down abruptly and glared at her. "Shut up!" she snapped. "Nobody asked you anything!"

Honey ran her hand under her hair, unmoved. "It doesn't make any difference," she said. "She's an awful drip."

"She's a nice enough kid," said Kate fiercely. "She's just miserable. Keep your trap shut when you don't know what you're talking about, which is usually."

"Ah-ah-ah!" said Donelly. "Birds in their little nests agree! What drew you two turtle doves together is something I've been asking myself all evening."

"I'm making a study of remnants of feudalism in the United States for a sociology course," said Kate coldly.

"Are you ready for another Alexander, honey-chile?" said the reporter tenderly, and she was.

He thought he wouldn't push it just now; he put some more nickels in the machine and came back to the table. "Dance?" he said to Kate. She turned scarlet. "In these?" she said, looking down at her dungarees. Then she tightened her mouth. "Sure." Honey sipped indifferently at her Alexander, mildly surprised at this turn of events, but, as he had predicted to himself, not unduly disturbed. If he had danced with Honey, Kate would have sulked the rest of the evening. Surprisingly, she was not a bad dancer. She floated along like a firm little balloon in her dirty tennis shoes. When it seemed a possible moment, he said, "Did Honey have a crush on this guy?"

"That narcissist?" said Kate scornfully. "Two loves has she and both of them are herself."

"Then what's she got against the kid that had the crush on Boyle?"

"You wouldn't try to pump me, would you, Mister?" said Kate. "Ask her."

"O.K., I will," he said, getting a little sore.

They danced for a while in silence, and when the record was over, went back to the table. Honey's drink was gone again; she was beginning to look glassy eyed.

"What about the kid that had the crush on Boyle?" said Donelly abruptly, sitting down beside her.

"Huh?" she said, coming out of her fog. "I beg your pardon? Oh—Mister—I forget your name. She has an awful crush on him. Juss tanawfulcrush. *She* got so hys-*ter*-ical *they* had to send her to the In-*fir*-mary. Mr. I-forgetchername, will you buy me another Alexayunduh?"

"You mean so you can go to the Infirmary too?" said Kate. "You're plastered, Sacheveral."

Honey raised her hand in a gracious but too sweeping gesture, then ran it under her hair. "The Sacheverals *always* hold their liquor like gentlemen. I mean, ladies too. I mean."

"Pull yourself together, chum," said Kate, rising abruptly. "It's five of ten and I'm going to walk you home."

Jack rose too. "Look, I've got a car, let me drive you."

"Nuh-uh," Kate refused, thrusting Honey's limp arms into the sleeves of her polo coat. "Not that I think you're wolf enough for the two of us, but she needs the walk if she's going to face Miss Sanders."

She was propelling the giggling Honey out into the bar when he caught at her elbow desperately. "Look," he said, "give me a break. What's the name of the cookie with the crush?"

"Morrison," said Honey, before Kate could stop her, "Molly Morrison. And is she a *goon*!"

Kate let go of Honey who reeled slightly, then sat down on a bar stool, smiling amiably. "I think you're a heel," she said to Donelly fiercely. "You leave that kid alone! If this sees the light of print I'll—I'll rend you limb from limb! I'll bash *your* head with a poker!"

Donelly smirked. "Business is business," he said, "but I do love spirit in a woman. Tell you what, Chubby, if I thought you could look other than as if you'd just crawled out from under a car, I'd ask you to take in a flick with me Friday night."

"You!" spluttered Kate. "You yellow journalist!" But he saw the rush of pink come into her face as she grabbed Honey roughly and hauled her out of the bar.

THE LIGHT in the room was a pale diffused whiteness coming through the neat sterile curtains. The blankets were white, the iron bed was white, the absurd nightshirt they had put her into was white. Her brain too, was white—she saw it lying inside her skull like some strange, beautiful, convoluted white coral. She thought what a fine painting her brain would make. She began composing a letter to her father. Dear Daddy, she would say, I would like you to paint a picture of my brain. It is to be very white and pure, with pure grey-white shadows in the crevices. It is to be lying on a thick white plate, which is decorated with an olive-green band . . . Then, as she imagined this, she suddenly saw that in the center of the white, white brain, which had somehow, magically, been cleft, a little red heart lay, like the Sacred Heart in the engraving on the wall of her Catholic nurse's room when she was a little girl. "Oh, this is very silly!" she said out loud, and giggled, and the tears ran down her cheeks onto the pillow.

She was just dropping off to sleep again when Miss Justin stuck her white-capped head around the door. "Molly," she said in a blasting whisper, "are you awake?"

She opened her eyes wide and tried to keep the room from tilting. They kept giving her pills—sedatives. "Yes," she said thickly, "I'm awake—I think."

"Your brother is here," Miss Justin said, and withdrew her head before Molly could answer.

Now this is really very strange, she thought. Because, *surely* I have no brother. I *couldn't* be as mixed up as *that*. But Miss Justin had said so. "Lord have mercy, can this be I?" Molly said aloud, giggling, the tears running out of her eyes once more.

She heard their voices outside her door—Miss Justin's and a man's. In a moment Miss Justin stuck her head round again. "Here he is!" she cried. Then a young tweedy-looking man with a crew cut and horn-rimmed glasses edged through the door. "Molly!" he said, in what sounded to her like a very loud voice. He shut the door behind him.

"Why," she said, "I don't know you at all." And began to cry.

"Sh-sh-sh!" he said nervously, tiptoeing to her bedside, "There's nothing to cry about."

"Nothing to cry about!" she repeated in bitter hopelessness, the tears pouring and pouring out from under her closed eyelids. She felt something being pushed into her hand; she opened her eyes and saw it was the young man's handkerchief. She was grateful, but could not speak. She blew her nose.

"Molly," he said, "I want to help you."

"Help me?" she said violently. "Help me? No one can help me. They all hate me, and now he is dead."

"Why," he said, "I'm sure nobody hates you, Molly. Who do you think could hate you?"

"They all do," she said. "All of them. I sit at the tables with them, looking at their cold faces, and I think that if by magic I disappeared, no one would know the difference. And if I say, Pass the butter, Pass the cream, nobody hears me until I say it too loud. Then they all look at me and laugh at me and hate me. They laugh at my clothes and my . . ." Now she was sobbing uncontrollably in great compulsive hiccoughs.

"Molly!" he tried to stop her. "Molly!"

Gradually the sobbing slowed. "Molly, do you know what happened to Mr. Boyle?"

"Oh," she moaned, twisting away on the pillow, "he was murdered, most cruelly murdered. Do you think it was my fault he was murdered?"

"Your fault—how could it have been your fault, Molly?"

"Do you think I could have turned him from it if I'd been brave? Suppose I had said to him, I love you. That would have changed his whole life, you know, however much or little, for better or for worse. If I had said to him, I love you, my darling, I will black your boots, mend your clothes . . . Kevin Boyle!"

"Did you ever go to his house, Molly?"

"Go to his house? It's as if I had lain in his bed by his heart every night that I lay down to sleep. You close your eyes, and there you are, nestled and cradled in warmth . . ."

"Molly," the voice broke in, "where were you when the murder took place?"

Her hands were over her upturned face, hiding it, her words came out muffled from under her palms. "I feel sometimes that it might have been myself that killed him, that broke his darling head. For if I had had the courage . . ."

"Was he in love with you, Molly?"

At that she laughed out loud between her hands, in the midst of her tears. "In love with me? Why he hardly knew I was on the earth, and yet . . ."

Miss Justin's bright voice broke in as she opened the door. "Time's up, Mr. Morrison!" she cried. "Can't have our little girl all tired out!"

"Goodbye, Molly," said the man's voice. "I'll be back."

She was broken and sunk with the disappointment of not being able to finish what she had to say . . . "Why?" she almost shouted at him. "Why should you?"

"Oh, Molly," soothed Miss Justin, "your brother wants to see you cheer up, just as we all do!"

"My brother!" said Molly sardonically, and began to sob again as the door closed.

SCHOOLGIRL CRUSH KEY TO CAMPUS MURDER?
"MY FAULT HE DIED," MOLLY MORRISON TELLS
MESSENGER REPORTER

Newsman Discovers New Suspect in Boyle Killing
November 17th, West Lyman, Conn. Messenger
Exclusive.

"Was it my fault he was murdered?" moaned Molly
Morrison, prostrate in her shaded room at the vine-clad
Infirmary of exclusive Hollymount College. When queried, she lapsed into one of the fits of weeping which
have characterized her state since she has been a patient
in the Hollymount Infirmary where she was taken last
Tuesday when she collapsed after the murder of Kevin
Boyle. Molly, a wan but pretty girl of eighteen, described
Boyle as her lover and spoke of frequent visits to his
home. Her whereabouts at the time of the murder are as
yet undetermined, but fellow students knew of her
"crush" on the handsome young professor of English,
and described her frequent walks in the direction of the
house where he lodged.

Boyle, a twenty-nine-year-old professor of English literature and author of some published verse, was killed last
Monday, November 13, in his rooms at 145 West Street,
West Lyman, Connecticut. Police have as yet made no
arrests in connection with the murder.

Miss Morrison, a student at Hollymount, in her freshman year, is a native of Cincinnati, Ohio, and daughter
of the well-known portrait and landscape painter, Miles
Morrison, and Mrs. Dorothea Morrison.

The bleak light came through the long windows and re-
fracted pallidly from Bainbridge's bald head. He sat at his large
desk between large studio portraits of his large wife and three
children, and looked down at the newspaper, slowly shaking his
head. "Just what I was afraid of," he said with mournful finality.

His secretary was pacing up and down the room, her face
scarlet. It was one of her numerous (always well-performed)

duties to get angry for Mr. Bainbridge. "It's—it's unconscionable!" she sputtered. "It's yellow journalism! Why, Mr. Bainbridge, it isn't even a Hearst paper!"

The president laughed shortly. He laid the paper down and began tapping it with his forefinger. "What's to be done, what's to be done . . ."

"Make them retract!" said Miss Seltzer fiercely.

"How do I know it isn't true?"

"Oh dear," she moaned, "I should have called the Infirmary at *once*. How they could have let him *in* . . ."

"Good," said Bainbridge, rising from his chair and slapping his hand down on the paper. "Call Miss Wellaby or Dr. Abby or somebody. I'll call Alex Brill. He'll have some suggestion."

Miss Seltzer disappeared to the reception desk to use her phone; Bainbridge took up the instrument on his desk to call Alexander Brill, the consulting lawyer for the college. Miss Seltzer was back by the time he was finished; they looked at each other hopelessly.

"What are lawyers for, anyhow, Seltz?" said the president miserably. "When it isn't in the law books they're no more use than anybody else."

"You pays your money and they makes your choice," said Miss Seltzer. "What did he say?"

"Oh, he was sensible, but no more than you or I could have been. The real point is that the milk is spilt, as we both knew, I suppose. He suggested that I inform myself as thoroughly as possible as to the facts about the girl so that I would be able to meet the questions that are bound to come up. Damn it, Seltz, when I talked to Hungerford, he told me he had it on good authority that Boyle was pretty careful about students."

"Oh, Mr. Bainbridge, you know how Mr. Hungerford is! He wouldn't know about a thing like that. Even before his breakdown last year he was a regular as—ascetic—or do I mean aesthetic?" said Miss Seltzer, who affected malapropisms as a contrast to her academic surroundings.

"What about the Infirmary?"

"I talked to Miss Justin. She says the only person who has been to see the girl is her brother. He asked to see her alone."

"That doesn't make sense. Probably—oh, I'll have to go up there and have a talk with them." He was rising from his swivel

chair when the phone rang. He started to lift it out of its cradle, then motioned to Miss Seltzer. "I don't want to talk to
anybody until I've got just what has been going on straight in
my mind."

She picked up the phone. "Hello? Who's calling? Oh . . .
Will you hold the wire a moment?" She pressed her palm over
the speaking end of the phone. "The Chief of Police," she said,
with a half-comical look of woe.

"Oh God," said Bainbridge. "Damn, damn . . . Yes, I
guess I'd better speak to him." He took the phone. "Hello,
Captain Flaherty. Yes, yes, I have. Yes, I just did. I can't imagine . . . You WHAT? . . . Oh, look here, Flaherty! The least
you could have done was to call me first. . . . Town and
gown be damned, there's a lot of taxpayers in this town
wouldn't have property to tax if it weren't for the business they
do with this college . . ." Miss Seltzer was nodding her head
and clapping her hands in silent approval.

"Give him what-for!" she mouthed without sound.

"Don't apologize; I see no excuse for it. Look here,
Flaherty—" Bainbridge was passing his free hand rapidly over
his bald spot and looking at the ceiling. "Why do you suppose
we have that girl in the Infirmary? Because the college doctors
suspect and have suspected that she is seriously mentally unbalanced . . . You didn't give me a chance. If you'd called me first
. . . I certainly did . . . We've called in a psychiatrist who is
to see her today . . . Dr. Julian Forstmann from Springfield.
We should have a report tomorrow. He's coming to examine
her . . . If you let out a word of that confession . . ."

Miss Seltzer's jaw dropped, her eyes grew round as the
lenses of her Oxford glasses, and she clasped her hands in
pantomimed prayer.

"I should think so . . ." said Bainbridge. "Hold everything
until you hear from him. All right. I'll call you. Goodbye."

He hung up the phone and immediately gestured wildly to
Miss Seltzer. "Get Forstmann on the phone! Get him right
away!"

She ran to the outer office, got her special address book, and
rang Dr. Forstmann. She had to wait while Dr. Forstmann
finished on another wire. Bainbridge looked up at her rather
helplessly, sunk in his tilted chair. "My God, Seltz," he said

softly, "how do I know I'm not aiding and abetting a criminal? What do I know about the girl? The old save-the-surface instinct . . ."

"Now, Mr. Bainbridge," she soothed, the telephone still at her ear, "there's a ninety-nine and forty-four hundredths per cent chance . . . Hello? Dr. Forstmann? Here's Mr. Bainbridge to speak to you."

"Julian?" said Bainbridge, and relaxed visibly at the sound of the professional voice at his ear. "You saw it? How soon can you look her over? My dear man, *I* don't know why you weren't called before . . . I wish to God you had been . . . I know, I know . . . How soon could you look her over? I have to talk to you, too—she's signed a confession. Yes . . . God, I don't know . . . If you could see her first . . . Can you make it in three-quarters of an hour? . . . Not till one-thirty? . . . Oh, all right. I'll meet you at my office at one-thirty . . . Yes, of course I am. What did you expect, a state of coma? . . . Don't tell me to be calm, you—you psychoanalyst!" He hung up and sighed. To Miss Seltzer's raised eyebrows he replied, "Be here at one-thirty." Once more he raised himself from his chair, this time somewhat wearily. "Well, I'm going to the Infirmary to find out what they have on the girl. Have the Registrar's office send up her records. Put off all engagements for today, and phone Mrs. Bainbridge that I won't be home to lunch. I'll be back in about an hour, I guess. Try to hold everything at arm's length until then."

"You said—" breathed Miss Seltzer, "you said—*confession*?"

"I did," said Bainbridge, taking his coat and hat from the old-fashioned hat tree in the corner. "Signed confession that she killed him."

D R. JULIAN FORSTMANN arrived at one-thirty sharp. "Hello, Seltz," he said to Miss Seltzer hurriedly, and knocked on the president's door. Bainbridge opened it with his hat and coat in hand. "Don't come in and sit down," he said. "I'll tell you what I know on the way to the Infirmary. I want to be able to tell the police as soon as I can that you've examined her."

Forstmann nodded his Lincoln-like forelock into his eyes, and the two men left the building together. "Take my car," said Forstmann.

"All right."

Indian summer was holding. The bare vaults of the trees spread black against the brilliant sky. Dr. Forstmann drove in silence, and for a few moments, Bainbridge said nothing either. "How's Hungerford?" said Dr. Forstmann suddenly.

The president turned. "Hungerford? Oh, he seems very well. Doesn't go out much, but handles his classes all right."

Forstmann grunted and turned the car down a side street. "Tell me about the girl," he said. "We're almost there."

"It's hard," said Bainbridge. "When I come right down to it, I don't know very much. I know nothing at all of the child personally. I didn't try to see her."

"What about her family?" said Forstmann. They drew up in front of the white clapboard Infirmary—vine-clad, as the *Messenger* had described it. "How about her academic record and so forth?"

"I looked up what we had on her," said Bainbridge, settling back in his corner of the seat. Forstmann pulled the brake and switched off the ignition. "Comes from Cincinnati, father is an artist, mother is a—housewife. Went to public school, showed a marked talent for drawing. Fair enough marks in high school, passed her college boards easily. Won a small scholarship, in fact. Since she's been here she's been failing four out of five courses, the fifth being an art course—drawing. I am told by the housemother in her dormitory that she has been rather unpopular and antisocial. Since she's been in the Infirmary, some of the girls have told Miss Sanders—that's the housemother—that she was always writing in journals, or something of the sort, but frankly, I haven't felt justified in having the girl's room searched for private papers as yet. I'm probably overdelicate."

"Yes," said Forstmann gravely. "It would probably be best to have such matters in a safe place, in any case."

"Good," said Bainbridge, "I'll have Miss Sanders look through her things. Then there has been this so-called crush on Boyle. She's been pretty obviously in love with him, I gather, and when he was killed, she went completely haywire. Miss Sanders thought it best to send her to the Infirmary. She wrote to the girl's mother, but hasn't had an answer. Let me see. Am I telling you anything you want to know?"

"Go ahead," Forstmann nodded.

"Yesterday, a young man turned up who announced himself at the Infirmary as her brother. The head nurse had no reason to suspect he was anything else, and let him in to see her. That, apparently, was the *Messenger* reporter," said Bainbridge, pulling his ear.

"So?" said the doctor, raising his eyebrows and hooking his long arm over the steering wheel.

"The next thing was that Flaherty, the chief of police, got hold of the *Messenger* story first thing this morning, and came hightailing it up here, blustered his way into the girl's room, and got a confession from her—by what means I don't like to think, knowing Flaherty's attitude about his duty to the taxpayers."

"Have you seen—or have you got the confession?"

"Oh Lord," groaned Bainbridge, "What a fool. Of course you would want to see that first of all. I had so little inclination to see Flaherty that I never even thought of it."

"Never mind. I'll see it later. What else?"

"I guess that's about all. No, I can't think of anything. Shall we go in, then?"

They got out of the car and hurried up the brick walk, looking like Mutt and Jeff, the psychiatrist tall and lanky, the president short and rotund. "Will you see the girl at once?" said Bainbridge.

"First the nurse and the charts," said Forstmann. "I thought that if it was at all possible I'd give her a Rorschach test today."

"That's the ink-blot thing?"

Forstmann nodded.

"You witch doctors!" said Bainbridge, and rang the door-bell. A nurse opened the door, a red-headed, hatchet-faced woman who had been weeping. "Oh, Miss—ah—"

"Justin, Mr. Bainbridge," said the nurse, and looked as if she were going to begin to cry again.

"Miss Justin is putting herself through the torments of the damned for having let the reporter in," said Bainbridge wearily to his companion. "It is with difficulty that I have restrained her from turning in her uniform. Maybe you can convince her, Dr. Forstmann, that it could, as they say, have happened to anyone."

"Are you Molly Morrison's nurse?" asked Forstmann. "Have you her charts?"

"Oh, yes, Dr. Forstmann," cried Miss Justin in relief, and disappeared starchily down the hall. Bainbridge shook his head in admiration. "All morning she wept on my shoulder. *You* present her with a tidbit of occupational therapy and she's off as happily as a beagle after a rabbit. It's as my wife used to say when the children were in nursery school—child psychology doesn't work for parents."

"I think you'd better go away, Lucien," said Forstmann amiably. "You communicate your state of nerves to everyone but me."

"What's the matter with you?" said Bainbridge. "I've always meant to ask."

"Psychiatrists are meant to be nonconductors—that's all. Now go away and balance the budget or something."

"Oh, Julian, be charitable and let me wait! You know I'll want to have the verdict as soon as you've seen her."

"You won't have anything like a *verdict*, Lucien," said Dr. Forstmann. "You'll have my opinion, which in this case is as fallible as yours or Flaherty's. The girl is undoubtedly neurotic from what has been said of her, but so are most of the people you know; I can probably tell you whether or not she is psychotic, but that still won't prove her a murderess. As for the Rorschach test, there isn't nearly enough statistical material to support its absolute validity—I use it because I have found it helpful as a short cut to diagnosis. In any case, I can't have the test scored before tomorrow at the earliest, assuming that I find the girl in a state to take it. My advice to you—which I render gratis—is to go and take a long walk in the country, come home and take a nap, wake up and have a drink ready for me at five o'clock."

"Five o'clock!" said Bainbridge reproachfully. "Oh, Julian!"

"I may have to go back to town," said the doctor, "and in any case I want some time to think how I can best advise you. Now go on, go on home, get out before you send Miss Justin into her act again—go on, I hear her coming."

Woebegone, the president let himself out the door as Dr. Forstmann took off his coat and hat and set down his brief case just as Miss Justin arrived with the charts in her hand. She gave them to him and stood sniffing as he looked them over. "Had a good deal of seconal, hasn't she?"

"Oh, Dr. Forstmann," Miss Justin exploded, "Dr. Abby gave me permission to give it to her at my discretion because the girl just never would have slept—just lay there crying and crying to herself."

"I'm surprised I haven't heard about her from Dr. Abby before now."

"Oh," said Miss Justin, making her red-rimmed eyes wide, "she's not what you'd call crazy, you know. That is, you would never have thought so until—oh, Dr. Forstmann," cried Miss Justin, an incipient howl in her voice, "I'll just never forgive myself! I mean, even if she did it! I mean—"

"Suppose you let me see her now," said Forstmann quickly.

"Oh, yes, Doctor!" sniffed Miss Justin, and led him off toward the end of the hall. She opened the last door and said through it in a bright voice, "Here's Dr. Forstmann to see you, Molly!" She led him into a dim white room. Through the curious sterile light he made out a white bloated face on the pillow, a pointed face under an auburn bang, distorted by weeping—almost like the face of a drowned girl. "How do you do?" the face said faintly, politely.

"How's our girl, now?" said Miss Justin, half to the doctor.

"Suppose you let me speak with Molly alone for a few moments," said the psychiatrist.

"Of course, of course," agreed Miss Justin, and disappeared in a rustle.

Forstmann pulled the low wicker chair up to the bedside, sat down and crossed his long legs, then rose again. "Mind if I raise the shade?" he said.

"Oh, no," said the face, and something came over it which was almost recognizable as a smile, "I feel just like a corpse all laid out here." But immediately the tears began to pour from the swollen slits of eyes, down the temples to the pillow.

Forstmann raised the shade and sat down again. "That better?" he said, but the face only rolled away from him.

"Why like a corpse, Molly?" he said. "What makes you say that?"

"Oh, I don't know," she said, so faintly that he could hardly hear her. "It's like white flowers—waxy—and white skin, and—everything is so white. I keep thinking about my brain."

"What about your brain?"

"I keep thinking what a fine painting it would make. I couldn't paint it, but my father could."

"Why couldn't you paint it yourself? You thought of it."

The face turned back to him now, he thought he could see something like indignation on it. "Oh, this is a really *fine* painting that I have in mind."

"Is your father Miles Morrison?"

"Yes," she said, almost eagerly, "do you know his work?"

"There's a painting—a landscape—in the Springfield museum."

"Yes!" she said excitedly, "I know it, I know it! You're the first one who's known about it!"

"Molly," he said, "I'm a psychiatrist. I'm here to find out why it is you're so unhappy." At this she sobbed out loud, once, then caught her breath. "And to see if you can't find the source of your unhappiness and be rid of it."

"That's impossible," she said flatly.

"I don't think so," he said.

"It is incontrovertible," she said with dignity. "He is dead. I killed him."

Forstmann sat forward in his chair. "How did you kill him, Molly?"

"I killed him because I had no courage. I killed him."

"Why did you kill him, Molly?"

She opened her swollen eyes a little wider and stared at him. "Why? Why, because I had no courage."

"Listen, Molly," he said, "do you mean literally that you killed Kevin Boyle, or do you mean that you feel you are responsible for his death?"

She began to sob aloud and roll her head back and forth on the pillow. "I killed him!" she said. "I killed him, I killed him! I murdered him! He is dead, murdered, and I killed him! He was all I had in the world and I killed him!"

"If you killed him, Molly, you must have had a great deal of hostility against him—you must have wanted to do him an injury," said Forstmann deliberately.

Suddenly she propped herself up on her elbows, her head rolling weakly on her neck. "If you think that," she whispered, "you are very wrong, and I will never speak to you again." She fell back on the pillow and tears welled up in her eyes again. "And I should be sorry for that," she went on, whispering, "because you look like him."

"Like Kevin Boyle, Molly?"

"Of course," she whispered harshly, "of course, like him."

WHEN BAINBRIDGE returned to his office in spite of Dr. Forstmann's advice, sneaking in at the back door of College Hall in order to avoid possible lurking reporters, he found Miss Seltzer alone in the outer office except for a bedraggled figure sitting in a pose of utter dejection on one of the straight chairs. When he walked in, Miss Seltzer raised her head from her typing, and her eyebrows flew up her forehead as she indicated the visitor.

"I managed to stall everybody except Miss Innes here," she said. "She says she must speak to you about the story in the *Messenger.*"

Bainbridge removed his hat. "Very well, very well," he said, in weary irritation. "Come inside, Miss—whatever you said your name was."

"Innes," said Kate drearily. "Kate Innes." She followed Bainbridge into his office.

"Sit down," he said, as he removed his coat and hat, hung them on the hat tree. She obeyed. Then he sat down behind his desk and looked at her pointedly. "Well?"

"Mr. Bainbridge," she said, "I feel terrible."

The president looked her over from top to toe. She was clad in a smudgy polo coat, blue jeans and sweatshirt, and a pair of elderly tennis shoes. Her short hair bent weakly upward from her face. Her horn-rimmed glasses were sliding down her gleaming nose. For once in a way he let himself go. "You *look* terrible," he snapped back at her. "You girls are a blot on the institution of womanhood. I sometimes feel that the students at Hollymount have created a third sex—and please don't misunderstand me—which bears little resemblance to the male and none to the female."

"It's just an affectation," said Kate meekly.

"For God's sake, when are you going to grow out of it?" said Bainbridge, his temper almost spent. "Well, get on with it. You didn't come here for a lecture on apparel. I'll save that for a general assembly. What's on your mind?"

"Mr. Bainbridge," said Kate miserably, "that story in the *Messenger* is all my fault, in a way."

"It doesn't matter whose fault it is any more," Bainbridge said resignedly. "The damage is done now. But I suppose you

want to make your confession and that's what I'm here for.
You seem to have good sense, girl. What in the world possessed you to talk to a reporter instead of coming to me or to
the police if you had some kind of information you felt to be
important?"

"I *didn't* have anything at all—I—we—it was all my damned
curiosity. Like sticking beans up your nose," said Kate. "I don't
know what good it will do, really, but if I tell you how it was,
I'm pretty sure we can get hold of the reporter who wrote the
piece, and when we do—" her brows drew together, "if nothing else comes of it, *you* can put a scare into him, and I know *I*
can make him feel so low he'll be able to sit on a dime and
swing his feet. He is," she added more complacently, "a rather
malleable young man, I should judge."

"Oh you should, should you?" said Bainbridge, and rose
from behind his desk. "If I don't eat now, I'm not going to get
any lunch today. Have you had yours, Miss—don't tell me
now—Innes?"

Kate shook her head No.

"Then you'll join me, otherwise I'll have to eat while you
watch me with your mouth watering." Bainbridge stuck his
head out the door and said to Miss Seltzer, "Have The Coffee
Shoppe send me a liverwurst sandwich on rye bread and a
black coffee. What'll you have, Miss Innes?"

"The same," said Kate.

He went back to his desk and sat down again. "Now, what's
the story?"

Kate looked down at her lap for a moment, then pushed her
glasses up her nose. "Mr. Bainbridge, there is another person
involved in this story, but I am morally responsible. If I bring
this other person in just to keep myself from getting involved
in a pack of little white lies, will you believe me when I say I'm
the one who really deserves the blame? I mean, are you willing
to assume that I have better than average intelligence and this
other person is a high-grade moron—which is no insult, Mr.
Bainbridge—she's just an average student."

"I don't know," said Bainbridge. "I'll have to see."

Kate looked at him suspiciously for a moment. "Well, I'll
just not mention the other person's name, then. Here's how it
happened: I was sitting in the Harlow Taproom with this other

person when a young man came in whom I spotted at once for a reporter."

"How?" said Bainbridge.

"Well, he looked like a Harvard boy except for the rings around his eyes and a certain indefinable something."

"I guess I'll have to take your word for it."

"I *deliberately lured* him to come and sit with us, Mr. Bainbridge, because you had asked us not to talk to reporters!"

"Oh fine, fine!" snorted Bainbridge. "This leads me to regard my position of mentor in an entirely new light."

"I can't help it, Mr. Bainbridge," said Kate solemnly, "when anybody talks to me as if I hadn't good sense, I'm immediately tempted to act as if I hadn't. Like sticking beans up your nose."

"That's a very suggestive phrase; would you elucidate its meaning?"

"Why, you know the story about the mother who said to her children the last thing before she went out, Now be sure not to stick beans up your nose? Naturally, they would never have thought of it if she hadn't put the idea into their heads."

Bainbridge nodded sadly, and at that moment Miss Seltzer appeared with the paper bag of lunch. Bainbridge removed the sandwiches and cartons from the bag to his blotter, Kate wrestled out of her coat, and for a moment they were silent while they arranged themselves to eat.

"Well," said Kate, around a partially consumed mouthful, "I guess my motivations are sort of irrelevant. The point is, he came and sat with us, and we had a couple of drinks, and one thing led to another until this person I was with got a little tight." She laid down her sandwich on the paper napkin that lay on the arm of her chair and gazed at him steadfastly over the rims of her glasses. "If I were noble, Mr. Bainbridge, I'd say I was the one who let the cat out of the bag, but anybody can see I'm not the kind of a girl a man gets drunk and worms things out of."

"Anybody," said Bainbridge, as drily as he could with his mouth full.

"So this person began responding to his little insinuations about what did we know about the murder by talking about Molly Morrison, because her crush on Mr. Boyle had gotten to be the house joke, only when she went to the Infirmary after he was killed, it was more the house scandal."

"What do you think of Molly Morrison?" said Bainbridge, with sudden sharpness.

"What do I think of her?"

"I mean, how do you size her up? How did she seem among the other girls? I've talked to Miss Sanders, but I'm glad to have a chance to hear how she appeared to other students."

Kate paused a moment and pushed her glasses up. "Well," she began slowly, "I didn't see an awful lot of her because I'm a Senior and she's a Freshman, and besides we're on different floors. But I noticed her, because I could see she was miserable, only I'm not the type to be helpful with lame-ducks, even when I want to—I just go crashing in where angels fear to tread. Nobody liked her much, because she was too quiet and scared and obviously a misfit. She was a little too intellectual for her own good, too."

"She was failing four out of five subjects, although I don't know why I should be telling you," said Bainbridge.

"You know that doesn't mean a thing as well as I do," said Kate, who was warming up with the coffee. "My guess is that she came from some sort of artistic or intellectual family where she heard real adults talking most of the time."

"Her father is a painter—Miles Morrison."

"Gee, I'm getting good!"

"Don't let it go to your head," said Bainbridge, who had been forgetting he was a college president under the stresses of the day. "What were the girls saying about her—ah—attachment to Mr. Boyle?"

"Well, it was very obvious that she had a terrible crush on him—she was always seeing to it that she sat in his booth at The Coffee Shoppe and when she couldn't, she would moon at him from near by. She was in his section of freshman English, and the girls in the class with her said she would always have something cooked up to talk to him about after class. Then there were some of us in the house who were kind of nauseated by the girlish response to all the wild Irish charm he passed around. Not Molly's—she had a kind of dignity about it, in a way I couldn't explain—maybe just because she was so hard hit. But the ones who didn't really care about him but who were always shooting off their mouths about wasn't he *darling*. One day she spoke up at the table—which was unusual in itself—and gave me the devil after I'd taken a crack at Our Kevin, and after that she got a certain amount of attention and riding about her great love. It always made me squirm when they went after her—it seemed to mean so much more to her than an ordinary crush—as if it were the only thing she had in her life."

"Miss Innes," said Bainbridge, who had been staring gravely into his carton of coffee while Kate talked, "What would you say if I told you that Molly Morrison signed a confession of having murdered Kevin Boyle for the police this morning?"

Kate went white, then flushed bright red. "Oh, no!" she said, wadding her paper napkin in her hand. "That's impossible! It's all that *Messenger* thing—that damned distorted—"

Bainbridge was watching her steadily. "You mean you think she is incapable of such an act?"

"As murder? Absolutely! I'll—I'll stake my reputation on it!"

Bainbridge raised his eyebrows. "Well, I hope you're right. We're going to have a professional opinion on it this afternoon—Dr. Forstmann, our consulting psychiatrist, is examining the girl. But I would like to know how you, knowing Molly Morrison, would explain that confession."

Without hesitation Kate said, "Pure hysteria. She's thought about the murder until somehow she's twisted it around so she thinks she could have saved him, or something. And probably when the police questioned her, she took some kind of pleasure in accusing herself."

Bainbridge pulled his ear and shook his head. "The things you children say!" he remarked insultingly. "Where do you borrow your wisdom?"

But now that she had confessed and eaten, Kate refused to be baited. "I'm a psychology major," she said composedly. "A little Freud and a little Horney combined with a certain amount of common sense go a long way. Have you ever read a book called *The Criminal, the Judge and the Public* by Alexander and Staub, Mr. Bainbridge? It suffers from a strictly Freudian viewpoint, but it makes certain sound conclusions about the desire for love and the fear of punishment which seem relevant to the case at hand. The authors say—"

Bainbridge raised his hand and cried, "Please, Miss Innes, I'm having a hard enough day; don't begin educating me! What I wanted to say was that if you honestly feel that it's impossible for Molly Morrison to have committed this murder, you won't feel you're acting as my—ah—stooge if I ask you to make a definite effort to scotch some of the wild rumors that are bound to crop up—probably have already. So far we've been able to keep this thing relatively quiet and to restrain conjecture. With the *Messenger* article, I imagine that all hell—if you'll pardon the expression—will break loose."

Kate began working her way into her coat as if ready for immediate action. "What about the reporter, Mr. Bainbridge? Do you want to level him? Sa-ay! I'll bet you that between us we could enlist him in an *anti*-smear campaign! I mean," she said, blushing, "he seemed a *relatively* decent guy."

"I don't imagine we could persuade him to focus attention away from the college, which is my objective at the moment, so I can't see much point in bothering with him."

"No, wait a minute," said Kate, excitedly flapping the empty end of her coat sleeve. "It never does to antagonize the press. I'll bet that if you talked to him and scared him witless first— threatened a libel suit or something—and then relented, you could get yourself some publicity of the kind you'd really like to have."

"The only kind of publicity I want at this juncture is an honorable obituary some forty years hence," said Bainbridge, "although . . ."

"See him, Mr. Bainbridge!" pleaded Kate. "I'm *sure* there'd be something in it—besides my seeing him beaten down to his socks—and if I could just feel I'd done something to vindicate myself for being such a ninny—"

"All right," said Bainbridge doubtfully, "I suppose I'm going to have to see some reporter some time. When can you bring him round?"

"Well," said Kate, "he said something about a movie to-night . . ."

Bainbridge cocked an eyebrow, but said nothing except, "Very well, you can bring him round to my house, if you like, between eight and nine."

"Good," cried Kate, rising and pulling her coat all the way

on. "If I have to manacle him." She paused in the half-open door with a worried look. "Mr. Bainbridge, don't you think you ought to give me a demerit or something? I kind of defamed the good name of the college, you know."

"A demerit won't help me," said the president. "From now on you're a public relations woman working for me behind the lines of the student body. Just keep that in mind and we'll neglect the demerit."

"A very sound disciplinary measure," said Kate nodding approvingly until her glasses slid to the end of her nose. Bainbridge could hear her rubber soles thudding helter-skelter down the staircase outside the office door.

HUNGERFORD LAY on the day bed, clutching the mattress as if the couch were rocking and he feared to fall off. His eyes were strained open in self-torture, focused on the row of volumes on the top shelf of his bookcase. *The Round Earth's Corners*, by George Hungerford. *The Psychology of Chance*, by George Hungerford. *Where No Man Pursueth*, by George Hungerford. *Henry James, an Anatomy of Anxiety*, by George Hungerford. *Edgar Allan Poe, the Great Neurotic*, by George Hungerford.

"Where there is no vision the people perish," he said aloud. The room was blue with early winter twilight. Outside, the bare branches rattled against the windowpanes, the windows rattled in their frames. He began to shiver, although the apartment was overheated—the steam was knocking and sizzling in the radiator.

He had perished, for he had lost his vision. In his mind the corpse of his imagination lay dead and rotting, poisoning his being with its remains. He could no more set pen to paper with words of his own creating than he could . . . give birth to a child . . . No . . . Fly . . . Than he could . . . Sometimes he looked in the mirror and thought it was the face of his own corpse he saw there. His vision had perished. On the table, within reach of his hand, lay the single capsule, resplendent on a saucer, and a tumbler of water, jewelled with bubbles all around the sides. The thing to do now was clutch the mattress until it became quite unbearable, until strange things began to happen in your brain and you were terrified, you sat up with a jerk, you swallowed the capsule and gratefully found unconsciousness, as one day, one sweet day, you would find death.

Twilight was the worst hour, because it was the hour of indecision. The day had its own tone: gray, or resplendent with sun, full of the grinding efforts of talking to students, chattering with imbecile colleagues, lecturing to classes; the more private burdens of shaving one's face, keeping one's shoes shined, paring one's fingernails, preventing one's flesh from stinking of putrefaction. (Too bitter. These things he should not think for a half hour or so. It was the poem had done it. Kevin Boyle's poem. No. Not Kevin. Get on with the train of the thought.)

The nights too had their tone. Sometimes a student asked him to a dormitory to a faculty dinner, and when he could bear it at all, he went. More often he called at the last minute, saying he was ill. But when the shades were drawn, the lamps lighted, one could write one's letters, move about among one's books, mark one's papers. And if the crippled mind found itself capable of moving from the house after the efforts of the day, one could—once—have gone to call on Kevin Boyle. Why Kevin? (He was asking this coolly—he had not allowed his emotions to outstrip his time schedule—truly he had not.) For Kevin understood so little the agonies which had become his daily fare, and in general he found it more and more his custom to keep clear of those in whom he could not detect the symptoms of infection by his own disease. Perhaps it was that Kevin was his only hold on health; Kevin was youth and strength; might become the poet and the man George Hungerford had once hoped to be. Now his mind threw up Kevin Boyle's poem, complete, intact, on an uncontrollable wave of nausea:

He who has eaten ambition, accepted it into his person
Cannot un-eat or reject it: it is now part of his essence.
Once a man has devoured hope and desire for power
He must accept his exclusion out of the ranks of humility.
He must declare for devotion, renouncing renunciation,
Abstaining from his abstentions, asserting against denial.
For he is as much committed to commission and to deed
As to Pluto, Persephone, who ate pomegranate seed.

"You must get away from here," Hungerford had said to him in most deadly earnestness. "If you want to be a poet, you must not stay. You will be wrung dry—and I know how foolish it sounds to you that I should assume one place more than another could injure a writer—but because human nature is flawed, and cracks under certain pressures, I know this to be *true*!"

But Kevin had laughed his high awkward laugh, the only crevice in his smooth Irish exterior through which you might detect a little core of uncertainty in him, even in him. "I'll stay yet a while," he had said overconfidently, in a way which made

Hungerford know that he doubted himself. "I've nothing to lose, and three square meals a day plus a pleasant life to gain."

"You've a great, great deal to lose," Hungerford had said to him sadly. Though he had not meant that Kevin would lose his life. No, not that. In life, in strife, without friend, without wife. . . .

His mind was getting ahead of the schedule. There were many ways he could tell, and this was one of them—the rhymes. He could not take the capsule until the hand had reached six o'clock. Then he could sleep like death for an hour, and be able to go down to his supper. Now he must check, backtrack a bit, for the hand said only ten minutes of the hour. Like a woman in labor, he gripped the mattress, pulling hard at the muscles of his neck, gritting his teeth.

Last year at this time the lot of them would have been collected in the sitting room for tomato juice or some other bland apéritif. Among them the doctors, the nurses, would be wandering like policemen through a crowd of strikers, dispensing cheerful little warnings of normality. Perhaps if he had gone to one of the really expensive sanitaria instead of to the obscure establishment he had found within his means, he would have despised it less. Yet he doubted it . . . He had hated those doctors and nurses with the blind rage of a wise man in minority for the fools in power. The sickening good sense of them! Keep yourself occupied, keep your body fit, learn to mouth the proper clichés and you will solve all problems. They were one step removed, one short step only, from the self-improvement quacks, the philistine executioners of the spirit who said kindly but firmly, Pull yourself together, man, it's all in your mind, as if the mind were the most dispensable part of the man.

Bainbridge had sent him there when he began to crack. The quarrel with Freda Cramm when he had told her at last what a bloody bitch he thought she was; the attempted suicide (the bitterness of failing even at your own death!) and the foul, unutterable kindness of them all, hovering over him, sucking the beautiful gossip from his wounds. "You'll be much happier . . ." they said. "You're worn out . . . It's an occupational disease. You need a rest." Bainbridge was more sensible, cooler than the others. He had made the arrangements and sent him

off to the sanitarium, had given him a year's leave of absence.
And when he came back, having learned to dissemble—
something—he found himself honorary chairman of the
English Department, smothered in kindness, in understanding. Sometimes he would close his eyes and devise tortures for
the kindest of them. It was doing battle with smoke . . . In
smoke, my head broke; I thought you spoke, but I awoke . . .
The room was almost completely dark; he could see the illuminated hand on the clock. Still five minutes to six. He drew up
his knees and twisted on the bed. All was not kindness. All was
not understanding. There was malice and torture and brutality
too. Someone hated him, deeply and bitterly. Someone wished
to drive him mad. And, not impossibly, it was the same someone who had murdered Kevin Boyle . . .

He had sometimes thought it was a college girl, perpetrating
a diabolical hoax. Yet he could not imagine what warped mind
could have chosen such a means, or him for an object. It had
begun last month, just as college was getting into its yearly
rhythm. He had returned from supper one evening to find an
open notebook lying on his desk. It was a common sort of
notebook—he had a number of the same sort himself—brown
cardboard covers which turned back on a spiral spring so that
the pages lay flat when you opened it. He had gone to examine
it, and found the pages covered with enormous, backhand, yet
somehow warped schoolgirl writing. There was a date at the
top; what followed was an entry in a journal, an entry devoted
to a description of himself. It was in part obscene, in part exag-
geratedly cruel, in part brutally true. Most of all there was the
impression of a mind which was cunning, sensitive to evil only,
and brutal beyond words. All that George Hungerford had
feared in another human being in his life—the ferreting out of
another's doubts of self, the use of them to flay the other's spirit
with a merciless hand. It was of such a devilishness that he
could not remember a word of it, only the terrible shock of first
reading, the impact of the hatred someone bore for him.
Carefully, he had laid the tablet away, meaning to examine it at
some time when the shock of its vileness had diminished, but
he had never found the courage, until one day it lay open again
on his desk, a new entry, a new page of vitriolic animosity and
obscenity. There had been several now—five or six. They came

when he was at his weakest, his most vulnerable, his weariest. He would have stumbled out to dinner, bleary from his drugged sleep; when he returned, almost revived with food and lights and the companionship of the restaurant, it would be there waiting to destroy him; the white pages, the lunatic calligraphy. It was diabolical—obviously the work of a madwoman (for it became plain that the writer was a woman or girl). And he did not know where to turn for a solution, now that Kevin Boyle was dead. For in the last entry it had become clear that the creature was someone known to both of them—or at least someone who knew them both—someone, in fact, who had been in love with Kevin.

The hand of the clock reached the top; it was six. He closed his eyes. Could he—was it possible that he could sleep without the capsule? For a moment his muscles relaxed. Then suddenly his entire body contracted in a spasm; the telephone bell drilled mercilessly; Hungerford started like a man pierced by a bullet. Shaking all over, he rose unsteadily and lifted the phone from its cradle. "Hello," he said tremulously.

"George," said the miniature voice at his ear, "it's Freda Cramm."

"He-hello," he stammered, trying to keep his jaws from clacking together, "Hello, Freda."

"George, I want to ask a favor of you."

He closed his eyes wearily, swaying as he stood. "Yes."

"I want to get the English Department together for some sort of memorial gathering for Kevin Boyle."

"The funeral baked meats," said Hungerford, almost inaudibly.

"What?"

"Nothing."

"It was something nasty, I can tell."

"Quite innocent, I assure you."

"Kevin told me you had the manuscript of his book of poems," said Freda. "Have you it still?"

"Yes, I have."

"I wondered if you would be willing to read a group of them to us on Friday evening, and maybe say something about them? What do you think?"

I think it is a maudlin, disgusting, self-advertising notion, and quite typical of your very vulgar mind, he thought. "Very well; at what time?"

"Oh, George, that's wonderful! You see Philip Frisbee, one of the editors from Cornish House is passing through, and I thought there might be a possibility of their doing the book."

"What difference does it make," said Hungerford, "now he's dead?" But he knew he was being unreasonable—he only wanted to end the conversation and sleep; he must not bicker this way.

"Why," Freda bridled audibly, "I should think you'd be glad . . ." Then, just as audibly, he could hear her recollecting that he had had a nervous breakdown, that he had been in a sanitarium last year, that she must humor him . . . "If you won't mind doing it, I think it will be a fine memorial for Kevin," she said. "If you come at eight on Saturday, and plan on reading at eight-thirty."

"Very well," he said shortly, and hung up.

The room was quite dark now, the furniture looming in black blotches. His hands were shaking; suddenly the side of his face drew together in the distorting tic, and the thing in his mind began to happen. He flung himself on the table by the day bed, but he upset the water. No matter; he took the capsule and swallowed it dry, the gelatinous sides melting and sticking in his throat. He lay down and clutched the mattress again. Now he was safe from it, sleep would come; he could even think of it, because it could not happen to him now. It was that a terrible thing happened in his head. There was a mountain—that was his brain. He was on the plain, looking up at it. Suddenly he saw a crevice begin to open down its side, a terrible wound from which the bowels of the earth in all their foulness came spilling out . . . the mountain was splitting apart, and at the same time something was happening to him. His face contorted into the tic because it was changing, slowly, slowly changing, his hands were changing, his feet were changing—but it was never really accomplished, thank God. He would, when it happened, get up, turn on the light, pace the floor, recite poems, have a drink, run out into the street to where the lights of town shone, or, as today, take the capsule and sleep.

A GIRL came through the swinging doors and stood in the middle of the corridor. "Kate In-nes! Tel-e-phone!" she shouted. Down the corridor a door burst open and a grotesque figure scuttled out. The hair was pinned in flat snails over the head, the face was white with grease, a red flannel bathrobe partly covered complete nudity, and one foot was in a white-fur scuff while the other was bare.

"Innes!" gasped the girl as the figure dashed around her as if she were second base. "Are you sick?"

"Don't bother me!" muttered Kate. "Is it an outside call?"

"Yes," said the girl weakly. "Yes it is. A man, come to think of it."

But Kate was gone. "My God!" screamed the girl faintly. "Bring my smelling salts, Maude—Innes has a man!"

In the phone booth at the head of the stairs Kate shut the door carefully and tried to find an ungreased portion of her cheek against which to lay the receiver.

"Hello," she said silkily.

"Hello, gorgeous," said the voice at her ear, "still the cutest tomato on the vine?"

"Just a little love apple waiting to be plucked," she said, blushed, stuck out her tongue at the telephone, and drew her brows together.

"Think you can get out of your overalls long enough to take in a flicker tonight?"

"Why, Mr. Donelly," she said, like honey out of a comb, "at least I assume from the southern Bronx accent that it *is* Mr. Donelly, I think that would be *lovely*." She scowled horribly and stuck out her tongue again, as if to reassure herself.

"Hey, are you sick or something?" said the voice. "You don't sound like yourself."

"Oh, Mr. Donelly," she breathed, this time crossing her eyes at the telephone because she couldn't talk and stick her tongue out at the same time, "since the other night I don't *feel* like myself."

"Hey, cut that stuff out, baby! I don't trust you."

"I have my moods," said Kate, crossing her legs as well as she could in the limited space. "You remember me as—ah—crustier?"

246

"It was the crust that got me. Could you get a little of it back before tonight?"

"I'll work on it, Mr. Donelly, I sho'ly will work on it."

"I'll pick you up at seven-thirty or so. I'd ask you for dinner, but I have to see a man."

"That's so kind of you, so terribly kind. Make it eight," said Kate, and hung up. "That rat," she whispered to herself fiercely, "That snake in the grass! That—that traitor to his class!"

She swept out of the phone booth and back down the hall, exposing wide reaches of her ample anatomy as she walked.

At eight o'clock she sat resplendent in the smoking room of Birnham House, kibitzing on a bridge game. Her hair was clean and curled, she had foregone her glasses and had, as she put it, painted herself like a Third Avenue harlot, although the effect was not so glaring as she pretended. A black dress did its best for her girdled curves; she wore sheer stockings and black pumps. At five minutes after eight the maid came to the door and said, "Miss Innes, you have a caller." Gathering up her purse and squinting in order to avoid the furniture, she made her way into the foyer where Donelly stood, digging his hands into the pockets of his reversible and reading a post card that lay writing-side-up on the mail desk. Observing his activity she forgot herself for the moment and remarked savagely, "Once a bloodhound, always a son of a bitch."

He winced and put his hand up as if to ward off a blow. "Crusty is the word, all right," he said in a hurt voice. "Say, you look just as cute as a little red wagon!"

"I please you? Good. You may help me with my coat." In a queenly manner she picked up her borrowed Persian lamb and held it out to him. He helped her into it and they set off. In the doorway she paused and looked up at him through the mascara. "I forgot to tell you, I have to stop at a friend's house to pick up a book. Will you go by Eden Street?"

"Sure, sure," he said innocently. They got into an elderly Plymouth coupe with labels stuck on the windshield saying *Press* and *Messenger*.

At Kate's direction they wound through the dark streets of the town and in a few moments pulled up in front of Bainbridge's house.

"Quite a little shack your friend has," Donelly remarked, pulling on the brake.

"Just a fourteen-room bungalow," Kate answered abstractedly. "Come on in, I won't be a minute."

"Hey," said Donelly suspiciously, "What gives here?"

She turned on him viciously. "I'm a white slaver—didn't you know? What have you got to lose?"

"O.K., O.K.," he pacified meekly, and piled out of the car.

Kate rang the bell and Bainbridge himself opened the door. "Hello, Mr. Bainbridge," she said, "may I present that Galahad of the newspaper world, Mr. Jack Donelly?"

"Oh-oh," said Donelly, and regarded the tips of his shoes.

"How do you do, Mr. Donelly?" said the president. "Will you permit me to observe that it is a somewhat mixed pleasure to meet you?"

"I'll permit you," said Donelly resignedly.

"Won't you come in?"

"As Miss Innes so aptly puts it, what have I got to lose?"

Bainbridge ushered them into the living room where a fire crackled and the lamps shone dimly against the dark cherry paneling. When they were out of their coats and seated, a silence fell. Finally Bainbridge, staring into the fire with his plump hands resting on his knees, spoke, "So you're in the newspaper business, Mr. Donelly."

"Racket is what they generally say," said Jack.

"I suppose it was in the line of business that you misrepresented yourself to gain admission to a sick girl's room and led her to say things which you might twist into an admission of having committed murder?"

"I was sent here to get a story; I got one."

"Oh, you did, you did indeed," said Bainbridge. Kate snorted. Another silence fell in which the fire popped, and someone walked across the floor of the room overhead.

Suddenly Bainbridge looked up. "Is it your impression that Molly Morrison murdered Kevin Boyle?" he said to Donelly.

The reporter raised his head and stared back at him a moment. "How should I know?" he said defensively. "I'm sent here to find out what I can—I take what I found out and make it into a story to help raise circulation. That's what I'm paid for—not to have an expert opinion on who murdered who."

"*Whom*," muttered Kate.

"I didn't ask you what you knew," Bainbridge pointed out gently, "I asked you for your impression. I asked if it was your impression that Molly Morrison murdered Boyle. I'm not baiting you, Donelly. I'll leave that to Miss Innes. Frankly, I'm scared of your paper—it's known as a scandal sheet, and I'd much prefer to have you working with me than to have you against me."

"I don't see just how that will work out," said Jack sulkily.

"Neither do I, neither do I," said Bainbridge. "But I thought we might talk it over. Will you answer my question?"

"No," said Jack finally, "it is not my impression that that kid murdered Boyle—whatever good my impression is to anybody; but it is also my impression that any district attorney who had nobody better to pick on could work up a pretty enough case against her. Nobody knows where she was at the time of the murder—somebody thought she saw her in the Library, but she wasn't sure, somebody thought she might have been at The Coffee Shoppe; another person was positive she saw her at the movies. So much for her alibi. As for her own account of herself, it's my opinion that the kid is a little off her rocker—as you might gather from the story. And I'm not too proud of it, if you're waiting for me to say so."

Kate sniffed.

Bainbridge shook his head. "Then she has too many alibis, and every other person at all personally connected with Boyle has none at all." He paused, beating his knees with his fingers. "Mr. Donelly, the police have cooperated with me in hushing up the fact that Molly Morrison signed a confession for them this morning—"

"Holy smoke!" breathed Jack.

"Since then," Bainbridge continued, "I have had her examined by Dr. Forstmann, our consulting psychiatrist. Unfortunately, he gave me just the same answer that you did a moment ago—that he could give an impression, but not a verdict. That was before he saw the girl. Since he has seen her, he won't even give his impression as to whether she could possibly have been the killer—says she was too much disturbed when he saw her and he can't surmise as to what she could or could not have committed in the way of violence. Her perturbation, he

says, may actually result from the emotional expenditure of
committing the murder, or may be pure reaction to the news of
Boyle's violent death, since she seems to have placed an importance on Boyle far beyond any actual relation she had with him.
Unless she had some secret connection with him of which we
know nothing . . . Oh, Lord," Bainbridge groaned finally,
"it's such a mess."

"It certainly is," said Jack, scratching his crew cut impolitely,
"and I don't get it. Why are you spilling all this to me?"

"I don't exactly know," said Bainbridge frankly. "Mainly, I
think, because I'm getting tired of regarding the press as a
large party of ambushed Indians whom I have to look for behind every tree. One always fears the known less than the unknown. I haven't much hope of your cooperation, but I
thought I could have a look at you at least."

"What's *your* impression?" said Donelly sniffily.

"You *seem* human," said the president.

"Yeah, but what's the angle—what's in it for you?" said Jack.
"What do you want me to do?"

"Oh," said Bainbridge, "I guess I had something in mind of
this sort—I give you first call on what information I get—and
I've already given you the confession story ahead of the other
papers—if you'll help me tone down the *Messenger*'s view of
the lurid side of college life a bit. After all, I'm a sort of duenna
to five hundred young women, Mr. Donelly. Put yourself in
my place and have a heart."

"Unfortunately my paper has a policy to the effect that if a
story stinks, we make it stink worse."

"I somehow felt I was speaking to you rather than to your
paper, Mr. Donelly."

"Oh, that line," said Jack, hunching his shoulders and staring into the fire.

"I rather imagined that Miss Innes might help me to enforce
my persuasion—she gave me what may have been an overopti-
mistic view of your conscience."

Donelly got up and thrust his hands in his pockets as he
glared at Kate over Bainbridge's head. "What do you want me
to do? Play detective?"

"Oh, that's a great deal more than I expect! I somehow have
a profound conviction that this murder will be traced to some

simple person with simple motivations, if it is traced at all—someone who entered the house with the intention of robbery, was frightened by Boyle, or something of the sort. More than anything now, I should like to prevent this Morrison child's reputation from being ruined, until it seems there is a good deal more evidence against her than now exists."

"More than a confession?" said Jack.

Bainbridge stood up suddenly and faced him. "Yes," he said hotly, "more than a confession obtained by as big a moron of a police chief as one could hope to find, from a drugged and hysterical girl, who has already had her words twisted into lies—in effect if not in fact—in a scurrilous newspaper piece written by you, Mr. Donelly. Molly Morrison may be a murderess, but you doubt it, I doubt it, Miss Innes doubts it. Does it make you happy to think of the kind of scandal that will surround her after this thing, even if she comes out legally clear?"

"Honestly, Mr. Bainbridge," said Jack, "I can't drop that story, big a heel as I may be. I'm not in the business for my health, and the story's too hot. It's the only hot lead of the murder."

"How about this—ah—Bubbles Merryweather?"

"She's been cleared and double-checked," said Jack impatiently, "don't you read the papers?"

Kate rose too. "I guess I'll have to work on him, Mr. Bainbridge. I still have faith in the re-education of criminals, but there's no use wasting more of *your* time. I'll have to dream up something to enforce his motivation toward reform."

Jack glanced at her unresponsively, Bainbridge forced a smile. "Thanks, Miss Innes."

"Goodnight, sir," said Jack uncomfortably.

They moved from the living room to the hall.

"Goodnight, Mr. Bainbridge; I'm sorry," said Kate.

"Goodnight."

Outside a wind had sprung up and was whipping dry leaves down the sidewalks and across the lawns. In silence Kate and Jack got into the car. Jack stepped on the starter. "It's too late for the movies," he said expressionlessly, "want a drink?"

"You can take me home," said Kate.

"I thought you wanted to reform me."

"You can take me home."

"All right," said Jack, and swung the car angrily in a U-turn. They drove in silence for five minutes.

"This isn't the way to the quad," Kate said indignantly at last.

"Oh hell," said Jack, "I just wasn't paying attention. I'm driving past the scene of the crime out of sheer habit. You'll get home all right, picklepuss. What's the matter—want to be a virgin all your life?"

"There's a difference between abstention and discrimination," said Kate huffily, and turned her gaze out the window. Suddenly she sat forward in the seat and yelled, "Hey, stop!"

"Want to neck?" said her companion acidly.

"Oh, Donelly, you bore me," she brushed him off. "There's a light in Kevin Boyle's apartment!"

"No doubt the murderer has come back to check on clues," said Jack with fatigued sarcasm. He stopped in front of an ugly, rambling, gray frame house. Across the front of it ran a series of small-paned windows, behind which a light was flickering, though uncertainly. "Like a flashlight!" said Kate breathlessly.

"All right, all right, I'll go look," said Jack. "You stay there."

"The hell I'll stay here!" whispered Kate, opening the door.

"If you make those steps creak," hissed Jack irately, "I'll make you sign a pledge to lose ten pounds before I take you out again."

She glared at him in silence as they mounted the porch steps with exaggerated stealth. The light was out on the porch; the corner of the house covered them in shadow. They crossed on tiptoe to where a single window of Kevin Boyle's apartment looked out on the porch. "Can't see a damn thing," whispered Jack.

"Shut up," said Kate. They made cups of their hands and peered through the glass. Behind them the house door opened quietly, a step sounded on the porch, and a woman gave a short scream. They whirled around and found themselves confronted by the massive figure of Freda Cramm.

"Mrs. Cramm!" said Kate quaveringly.

For a long moment Freda glared at them, then Jack recovered himself and went into his spiel, like a barker at a side show: "Hello, Mrs. Cramm, care to make a statement for the

Messenger as to why you were visiting the apartment of the deceased at—ah—" he looked at his watch—"9:14 on the evening of the seventeenth?"

"I wasn't—" began Freda Cramm.

"Ah-ah-ah! Mrs. Cramm!" cautioned Jack. "We've been peeking."

"Oh, Jack, we didn't—" mumbled Kate, who had suddenly lost her *savoir faire*.

"*I* did," growled Jack.

Freda was looking at Kate with a threatening eye. "This is Miss Innes, editor of *The Holly*, I believe," she remarked in a voice of doom.

"Yes," blithered Kate, "I mean—"

"I assume, Miss Innes, that since Wednesday morning chapel was required, you heard Mr. Bainbridge's remarks about students associating with reporters?"

"Yes, Mrs. Cramm, we just came from Mr. Bainbridge's house, as you can easily find out if you call him," put in Jack smoothly. "If you don't care to make a statement, I'm wondering just how to word this. 'Leaving the house of the murdered man, flashlight in hand, Mrs. Cramm refuses to—'"

"My dear man," said Freda, suddenly urbane, "it's quite simple. It's just that it irritates me to be jumped at from dark corners. Certainly I was in Kevin Boyle's apartment. I'm getting a collection of Mr. Boyle's poems together to show to a publisher—Philip Frisbee at Cornish House, to make it *quite* authentic. I have most of the manuscripts from Mr. Boyle's book, but one of my favorite poems was missing, I found, so I went to look for it."

"Did you find it?" said Jack.

"As a matter of fact, I didn't."

"Maybe it would have been easier if you'd turned on the light."

Freda threw back her head and suddenly laughed her full, stagy laugh. It rang out startlingly, making them all aware that they had been talking in hushed tones. "I *love* it!" she cried. "Oh, I *love* it! Oh, *do* suspect me of the murder—nothing so gay has happened to me in years! If you'll notice, my dear, darling *Messenger* reporter, this porch light is out?"

Jack nodded dubiously.

"It's quite as simple as a blown fuse—evidently Kevin's apartment is on the same circuit. Run in and try it—I do assure you you'll find every lamp in the place dead!"

"Lucky you had a flashlight," said Jack sourly.

"Isn't it?" agreed Freda brightly. "Why don't you children run me up to my house and I'll give you some cocoa or something. The reason I have a flashlight is that I happened to walk. My driveway is always black as the ace of spades. Do come along and have something hot."

"Miss Innes here is on a diet," said Jack, "but get in and I'll drive you home."

"Now in that case, I can see I mustn't spoil your twosome," said Freda with elephantine coyness. "And if it comes to diets, of course I'd *much* better walk."

"Just as you please," said Jack. Together they descended the porch steps.

"Goodni-eet!" cried Freda, waving to them as she turned down the sidewalk.

"Goodnight," said Kate and Jack in unison.

They got into the car before she was out of sight.

"Short circuit!" snorted Jack.

"Diet!" snarled Kate. "Aren't you even going to check on whether there *was* one?"

"I'll give dollars for doughnuts there was one all right. They aren't hard to produce, and she must have known I'd check."

"Which you aren't doing."

"Oh, *all right*." He climbed out of the car again and back up the porch steps. Kate left her door open to watch him. Just as he reached the front door, the porch light winked on, the front door opened, and a tall gaunt woman was silhouetted in it. "Yes," she said to Jack nervously, "did you want something?"

"Oh," said Jack "—ah—Miss Stone, isn't it? Have you—I mean *had* you a blown fuse?"

"Yes," said Miss Stone, with her nervously interrogative inflection, "yes, we had. I just put a new one in."

"Well, I'm from the electric shop. Mrs. Cramm phoned for me."

"Phoned for you? There's no Mrs. Cramm here. You must have the wrong house, young man."

"Oh no," said Jack easily. "She said she was phoning from Mr. Boyle's apartment. I just met her on the way out. She said she'd been looking for a manuscript in his place. Didn't you let her in?"

Miss Stone's hands flew to her topknot and fluttered there like two distracted birds, playing with her hairpins. "Oh, dear me!" she cried. "Oh dear me, no! And how could she have got in otherwise, for the door was tight locked!"

H E LAID his tuxedo tenderly on the bed. It was new—the first he had ever owned. His black oxfords, carefully polished, were set beneath it, and a pair of black silk socks. The shirt, collar, studs, and tie. His hands trembled a little as he assembled them all on the bed. He had bought them, all at once, except the shoes, in a medium-priced New York haberdashery, where they had cost just a bit more than he could afford. They represented his homage to himself after the letter had come assuring him the job. He had the habit of giving himself presents on special occasions, because no one else did. His father was dead, he supported his mother, and there was no other soul in the world who sufficiently cared for him to make such gestures. Suddenly, in the midst of arranging his shaving things in careful preparation, he stopped and stared at himself in the paint-flecked bathroom mirror. That was a thing that he and Kevin had in common. He remembered a night last month when Boyle had burst into his room without knocking, a bottle of Scotch under his arm. "Let's get drunk, Leonard, old boy," he had cried, "for it's the day of my coming into the world, and not a soul to present me with a gift but my own sweet self. Get out the mixings, lad, and let's become roaring boys!" . . . Then he shook his head and went on arranging his shaving implements, taking old-maidish care, selecting a new blade, screwing it into the razor. Not comparable, really. Probably it was only that no one had known it was Kevin's birthday. If Freda Cramm, for instance . . .

Suddenly Leonard set up a tuneless little hum, wet his shaving brush, and swiped it round the jar of soap. Briskly he lathered his face, avoiding with care the tuft of moustache on his upper lip, and began to shave. When he had cleared the suds off one side of his face, he stopped shaving, leaned his hands on the bowl, looked his reflection straight in the eye, and, for once in a way, laughed out loud his odd womanish cackle. He had not yet recovered from the strange ailment that had overtaken him after the murder—he was still likely to giggle at the name of Kevin Boyle, and he thought it best to get the laughter as thoroughly out of his system as possible before tonight, since tonight the name of Kevin Boyle was likely to be bandied about a good deal.

It is, he remarked to himself, an ill wind that blows nobody good. Best to face it finally and frankly, perhaps: he, Leonard Marks, had gained a good deal by Kevin's death, and he could not, for the life of him, be anything but glad. And why not? he argued with his middlewestern, churchly background. Shall I pretend overwhelming grief at the death of a man whom I knew for two months? Shall I ignore the fact that for me his murder has become an invaluable social and professional asset? Yet he gasped a little, and cut his cheek with the razor as he thought this, for he had been brought up in a stuffy world of piety and hypocrisy; to mourn the dead was the convention, and the convention was the law. What would Freda Cramm make of such shilly-shallyings with the past? Tonight he was invited to Freda Cramm's house; now was the time to let the past bury its dead, and look bravely to the future.

He had come to Hollymount as an instructor in English with high hopes, as the saying went. With a brand new Ph.D. from Columbia, a reputation as a serious scholar among his fellow graduate students, and a number of A's and other encomiums from his professors, he came prepared to sweep all before him, to rise from honor to honor. But already, in November of his first year, it had been made plain that it was not to be that way—not that way at all.

Nothing in New York had prepared him for the reception he had received here. His meager room on 114th Street had often been a center for scholarly debates on the Elizabethan poets. His professors had not taken him to their bosoms socially, to be sure, but they had loaded him with academic praise. Yet from the moment he had taken lodging in West Lyman, settled his few belongings and set about his work, nothing had been as he had hoped. Had he dreamed of scholarly discussions of the varying editions of *Hamlet* with George Hungerford, the great scholar, critic, and novelist? He remembered his first conversation often and bitterly. He had approached him in the faculty tea room, brightly, intelligently, with a question on his lips. "Do you think, sir—" Leonard had begun. But Hungerford, who had been staring out the window with his strange fixed gaze, whirled about suddenly and said, "Young man, I make it a practice never to think these days unless I am paid for it," and had walked away, leaving Leonard almost weeping with humiliation.

Yet he had forgiven Hungerford. Afterwards he had learned of
his nervous breakdown and his consequent eccentricities, and
even if there had been no such excuse, his love of the man's
work would have forced him to overlook the rudeness. No, it
was the ones like Freda Cramm, the big, overbearing, husband-
less women who peopled the faculty of Hollymount, who
peered at him, leered at him, and set him running off with his
tail between his legs after their acid thrusts, who rankled. The
same who purred and fawned on Kevin Boyle—they had convinced him at last that whatever his successes in the past, here
he was regarded as—what? Not even on trial. Already con-
demned as something they thought of as a hopeless bore. The
students too—whispering and muttering through his lectures;
giggling at him before his back was turned. He was invited nowhere but to the most general gatherings—the President's
reception—only once to a faculty dinner in a dormitory. If he
had said that he knew Kevin little, he must also say that it was
only Kevin whom he had known at all here. The only talk he
had, finally, were the hours of Kevin's boasting by the fire, the
recitals of Kevin's successes ground like salt in his wounds. He
had spent two months of miserable loneliness with the sense of
being not disliked, but un-liked. In the last week he had had
more attention than in the eight that preceded it, and all because Kevin Boyle, who had lived across the hall from him, was
murdered, and with his own ears he had heard the footsteps of
the murderer outside his door. He had talked to the president
of the college privately three or four times, George Hungerford
had called on him, the ladies in the tea room had condescended
to ply him with questions, and now he had been specifically invited to the house of Freda Cramm for a memorial reading of
the poems of Kevin Boyle.

He dusted his face with talcum and dampening a nail-white
pencil drew it meticulously under each of his fingernails. Then
he put away his toilet articles and cleaned the bowl, whistling
softly through his teeth. He looked at his watch. Seven-fifteen.
He had allowed himself a little too much time. He sat down on
the bed, drew on his socks, and clasped the garters around his
skinny, heavily furred legs. Suddenly, thrillingly, his telephone—
that symbol of unfulfilled hope, since no one ever called him—
rang loudly. In his shorts, oblivious of neighbors in his

excitement, he strode into the unshaded living room. "Hullo?" he said anxiously.

"Mr. Marks?" said a commanding, female voice at his ear.

"Ye-yes?"

"Oh, Mr. Marks, I'm in a devil of a hole, and I'm counting on you to help me out. It's Freda Cramm."

Of course, of course it was Freda Cramm! "Of course, of course, Mrs. Cramm, anything I can—"

"George Hungerford was to read Kevin's poems and now he's begged off with some excuse about being sick. You knew Kevin's work—Mr. Marks, *could* you read them instead?"

"Re-read Kevin's poems?" he quavered.

"Yes, I mean, I thought you could dash over a bit early and look through them—I'll show you the ones George had se-lected."

"Oh, Mrs. Cramm, I—" Suddenly the picture of all their hostile faces rose before him, and himself the child who has forgotten his piece at the recital, the eight-year-old orator uri-nating in his trouser leg. "Oh, Mrs. Cramm—"

"Oh, now, dear, darling Mr. Marks, there simply isn't any-thing you can say but yes, so say it! Really, I *will* be in such a devil of a hole, and frankly, it will be awfully good for you, as you should see yourself."

"For me?"

"Of course, with all the English Department and Bainbridge there, and you really have an awfully good voice—I know you'll read them well—I mean people will *remember* you."

It was as if she had noticed, and cared. Even though she had taken part in harrying him, she still had noticed that he was in the predicament of rabbit pursued by hounds. Could it be—could it be that everything *would* change. "Well, if you think—" he faltered.

"I do, I do really think! Now get your trousers on—" he started, as if she could see through the telephone—"and come right over. You *are* being an angel and saving my life, Mr. Marks."

She had hung up. "Goodbye," he said to the air. His hands were trembling and sweating. He ran back to the bedroom, jerked on his clothes clumsily, brushed his hair, polished his glasses. His tie would not tie. It simply would not tie.

"Oh blast!" he whispered, "Oh damn and blast!" At last he got it straight. At the last moment he called a taxi, regally, and was wafted off to Freda Cramm's house, as if he were Lohengrin, being transported to Elsa by special swan.

THEY HAD parted rather gruffly, and she wasn't sure whether they were supposed to be sore or not. She supposed that according to Hoyle she should have waited until he called her, but this was business—anyway, that was what her conscious mind had to say about it. She regarded herself in the mirror with some dissatisfaction. "You are not what they call a man's woman, toots," she remarked, and fishing a nickel out of her dungarees pocket, went to the phone booth. It was five-thirty, when people should be taking baths or getting ready to have a drink, or should be home for some reason; it seemed the most likely time to catch him. She got the Harlow, and they rang his room for her. "Hello," he said, hard and fast. He sounded cross, and she blushed. "Hello," she said, trying to sound cross too, "this is Kate Innes."

"Why, cookie!" he said in a pleased voice, and she relaxed.

"Listen, my erring Lincoln Steffens," she sneered, "I have for you what is known in the Grade B's as a hot tip."

"Gee," he said irresponsibly, "isn't this cute—you calling me."

"It is solely in the interests of justice," she snarled, "so don't get overheated about it."

"Well, shoot the snoop to me, droop," he requested amiably.

"Did you know Freda Cramm is throwing a memorial gathering for Kevin Boyle this evening?"

"No. Is that the customary gesture when a colleague gets bumped off? Me, I never had an education."

"For my money," said Kate seriously, "something smells. I don't know what, exactly—maybe I'm just turning melodramatic in my old age, but first we meet the lady coming out of his apartment; now she's giving a memorial party or something—in my right mind I'd say that was just typical of her; give that woman a chance to exhibit herself and right away she starts a strip tease—only I keep wondering if it's more. How well did she know Boyle—she certainly admitted she went to his place a lot. Could she have been in love with him or vice versa?"

"Not vice versa, unless my unfailing eye for femininity is dimmed, but go on."

"Well, stop me if I sound like Hercule Poirot, but I do find murders rather heady for my blood, and I have the feeling you ought to take a look-in at this gathering."

"You mean put on my blue lace and go as Elsa Maxwell?"

"You can find a way to get in, stupid. After all, you're supposed to be a yellow journalist from a pink tabloid."

"Oh sure, I can get in all right. But you have before you a man in whom duty wars with inclination. I had dreams of getting out my pipe and slippers and pulling up to a big open bar with you tonight."

"Not with me will you be bending the elbow, friend—I have a lab report due Monday."

"All right, honey," he said wistfully. "Where's the dame's house?"

"It's behind the campus, way the hell and gone out Eden Street. Could you find Bainbridge's house again?"

"Yeah, I think so."

"Well, just keep going to the top of the hill," she directed. "As a matter of fact, I seem to remember there is some sort of sun porch on the house you might get in. She was talking about it at a faculty dinner here once—about how the architect had designed it to be warm even in the dead of winter if the sun was shining, but you couldn't use it if it wasn't."

"What if I catch a cold?" he said plaintively.

"Drink a hot lemonade."

"You're as hard boiled as a city editor, but I love it," he sighed. "All right. Can I call you tonight and let you know how it comes out?"

"No outside calls to the dormitories after ten-fifteen," she said, "and you'll be there later than that if you have any luck. Call me tomorrow." She blushed.

"O.K., honey. Goodbye, now."

She left the booth, noting her pulse rate scientifically. Out of some compulsion which she did not examine, she changed from dungarees to a sweater and skirt, and devoted some time to brushing her hair. At supper she sat abstractedly, chewing a hangnail instead of eating. There was chocolate pudding for dessert, and when she gave hers away to the girl sitting next to her, her table mates made gestures of fainting. "Innes," said the girl who had taken Jack's call yesterday, "is irrefutably in love."

"I am not!" she said hotly, coming out of a brown study with all her armor down, and then blushed radiantly. A great hoot went up so that the other girls in the dining room turned to look at their table. She pulled herself together and organized a strong defense of attack which kept them in line until the end of the meal. Then, making noises about her lab report, she ran upstairs immediately, and locked herself in her room, first tacking a DO NOT DISTURB sign to the door.

From 7:15 to 8:15 she typed diligently. From 8:15 to 8:34 she made graphs. From 8:34 to 8:50 she chewed the hangnail. At 8:50 she got her nail scissors and cut it off. At 9:03 she said to herself, aloud, and in a very reasonable tone, "O.K., so suppose I am?" got her coat from the closet, put it on, started out the door, came back, rooted in a dresser drawer and found a lipstick, which she used. Then she hurtled down the stairs and out into the night.

ALL THE lamps in the room were lighted, illuminating the turquoise walls with a gentle yet festive brilliance. The doorbell rang at odd intervals, the maid would open the door, Freda would make a little rush toward the hall, and the volume of the talk would rise a bit, though always restrained, memorial in tone. Faces shimmered with two emotions: embarrassment and excitement. It was embarrassing to feel excited at a gathering in honor of the dead—practically a funeral service, in fact, since Kevin Boyle had left directions in a will that his body be cremated without ceremony—yet such a lovely party: all the English Department in evening dress (however variant the vintage), the chrysanthemums radiant as van Gogh suns in the lamplight, the excellent whisky . . . The doorbell sounded a final peal, and Bainbridge entered after a moment, his wife on his arm, chatting with Freda. Some crossed the room to greet him, some merely eyed him and returned to their talk. When the two of them were seated, Freda raised her hands and her voice and commanded the room to silence. "Will you all sit down and make yourselves comfortable?" she said. There was a rustle, a redistribution of guests. When everyone had found places, Freda went on, "George Hungerford was to read Kevin Boyle's poems to us this evening, but he has phoned to say he is ill and unable to do so. Mr. Marks has very kindly consented to read in his place." There was a tiny murmur and turning of heads in the room whether at the absence of Hungerford or the presence of Marks it would have been difficult to say. Freda nodded to Leonard, who sat in the farthest corner of the room, shuffling and reshuffling typescript, moistening his lips with his tongue, and whispering the poems over to himself. "Will you?" she said.

Leonard cleared his throat, and hunched his chair out around the end of the table behind which he had hidden. But he was not to be let off. "Sit over here by the fireplace, Mr. Marks," Freda commanded. So he had to rise, to pick his way among them, to plant himself at the side of Bainbridge himself. When he was resettled, an expectant hush fell. "I thought—" he began desperately, but his voice came out a dry squeak. He cleared his throat and began over. "I thought I would say something about Kevin Boyle's poems, but then I decided that

I might better let them speak for themselves." His face turned bright scarlet, and he ducked his head agonizedly, once more reshuffling the sheets. "Mrs. Cramm and Mr. Hungerford have made this selection in chronological order. The first poem is called—" he looked at it, drew out his handkerchief and loosed into a strangled cough—"*Timor Mortis Conturbat Me*." . . . He began to read, sounding as if invisible hands were at his throat. The room was tense with response to his tension. But the words and meaning took hold at last; even Leonard seemed to forget that it was he who was on exhibit in listening to the sense of Kevin Boyle's poems.

Halfway through the reading, a slight disturbance sounded from the closed door to the sun porch, and a few heads turned momentarily. Jack Donelly, lying shivering on the brick solarium floor, somewhat camouflaged by the bamboo coffee table under which he reclined, rose to his knees as abruptly as he dared and whirled round on all fours like an angry Newfoundland, the coffee table dangling like a saddle from his back. "What the hell!" he said in an enraged whisper.

"Down Fido!" came a whisper in return, and the sound of the latch being half closed. In a moment Kate joined him in his prone indignity and they lay regarding each other blinkingly, their faces dimly lit by the glow that shone through the thin curtains on the glass-paned door to the living room.

"You're a damned nuisance," hissed Jack. "Go away!"

For answer, Kate propped her chin on her hands and waved her feet airily behind her.

"Listen, baby, chivalry is as dead as an old T. S. Eliot geranium as far as I'm concerned, and if we get sent up for housebreaking, we'll split the sentence evenly, believe me."

"I can take care of myself," said Kate, looking at him rather absently, "What's been going on?"

"Not a damn thing except that I'm getting a severe sinus attack," Jack whispered back disgustedly, "and Marks has been spouting that *merde* for the last three hours, at a rough guess."

"Your judgment is fair but your time discrimination is poor," said Kate, edging forward a little on her stomach. "Where's la Cramm?"

"Somewhere off around the corner so you can't see her."

"Let's get closer to the door, and I'll tell you who's who."

"Our faces will catch the light."

"Nobody could see us with the light shining on the other side of that curtain."

"Look," whispered Jack irritably, rising on one elbow, "if you get caught, this will be a schoolgirl prank. If I get caught it's a misdemeanor, or something. You annoy me, brat, and I wish you'd go away."

Kate looked at him with her round face shining dimly in the curtained glow from the door. It turned a barely perceptible shade pinker and two large shimmering tears unexpectedly rolled out of her eyes and formed little canals around the inside rims of her glasses. Her mouth opened in a silent Oh. She rose to her hands and knees and the tears fell to the floor in two quiet little splats.

"Why, cookie!" said Jack in amazement. He made a move toward her, and the coffee table rose irately on two legs. For a moment they juggled it between them like a football in a complicated pass.

"Get down!" whispered Kate suddenly, and they flattened themselves just as an unseen hand opened the door between the porch and the living room. Without their noticing it, the reading was over, and the stream of conversation was babbling on again. ". . . Terribly hot in here . . ." they heard Freda Cramm's voice trailing away from them. For a moment they lay still and flat, afraid of catching the light if they rose. Snatches of conversation reached them: ". . . what perfect little jewels of verse . . ." a female voice. ". . . reminiscent of the earlier Yeats . . ." male. "Don't you find them a little *difficult*?" . . . "Of course I realize that nowadays you young people scorn the pre-Raphaelites . . ."

Jack performed a difficult disengaging movement without raising himself from the floor, and worked his way clear of the coffee table. He gave Kate's ankle a gentle yank. "Let's get behind the sofa here," he whispered urgently.

"Why?" she whispered back. "Then we can't see anything." But he was already disappearing behind the piece of furniture in question, so she rose to her hands and knees and followed, grumbling breathily.

"Now," he said, when she had collected herself in the dark shadow, and planting his lips on hers, maintained this position with her full consent until interrupted by the startling sound of a step on the brick floor of the porch.

They sprang apart as guiltily as a Victorian couple on the parlor sofa, quickly collected themselves, and peered cautiously around opposite ends of the couch. Whoever had come out the door had closed it after him again, once more the light was dimmer. A man's figure was silhouetted against the lighted door. For a moment he seemed to be looking about the floor for something, his face still dark against the light so that they could make out nothing but a pair of protruding ears. At last his glance stopped, and he moved toward where a large brass maple-syrup kettle which was intended for a wastebasket stood by a chair. Out of his pocket he drew a piece of paper, and tearing it into tiny bits, he let them shiver down through the air into the kettle. He looked down at them indecisively for a moment, then, with an indistinguishable exclamation, stooped down and carefully collected them again out of the receptacle, and holding his pocket open with one hand, dropped the bits into it with the other. Suddenly the door was snatched wide open, and Kate and Jack popped back behind the sofa.

"Why, Mr. Marks," said Freda Cramm's voice coyly, "are you hiding from the idiocy of our adulation? You know how well you read, don't you?"

"Oh," came Leonard Marks' voice in a hoarse croak, "—ah—Mrs. Cramm—ah—not at all—just—ah—getting a breath of cool air."

"Well, come in, come in!" pleaded Freda warmly; drew him back into the living room and closed the door.

"Get *that*!" breathed Kate dazedly, but was masterfully recalled to dalliance, and spent the time until the breaking up of the party in what can only be described as necking on the icy brick floor of Freda Cramm's solarium.

THE GUESTS withdrew from the warm turquoise room in a serpentine body, the last stragglers chatting among the chrysanthemums as the first departures extracted their coats from the hall closet by the door. Standing beside Freda, Leonard made feeble motions toward retrieving his wraps, but was detained by her firm hand on his arm. She kept him standing beside her as she said goodbyes, he noted, with amazement, quite as if he were the host, or the guest of honor. Perhaps he was the guest of honor. A substitute, but nevertheless—was that going too far? His head was humming pleasantly with the drinks he had consumed; he was incapable of such weighty decisions.

In twos and threes the English Department passed through the door, each saying some congratulatory word to Leonard on the way out. At last they were all gone—the last was standing on the doorstep mouthing politeness when Leonard made a final effort toward his own departure. But this time Freda firmly and distinctly closed the front door and turned to him with a warm smile. "Ah," she sighed. "Now we can have a drink in peace."

He was seized with a sense of unreality; he thought his head might suddenly grow wings and take off from his neck. "Oh," he said, "oh, ah, yes, that would be nice."

But no matter how much he made an ass of himself, no matter how he stammered and bungled, still she kept smiling and being pleasant to him. It was like a dream—a good dream. He stuffed his hands in his pockets, twitched his moustache, and followed her back into the empty room—beautiful, yet slightly en *déshabille* with empty glasses and full ash trays, like a lovely woman after love. This was a thought worthy of Kevin Boyle, who would have spoken it aloud and collected the kudos due on it, but Leonard could only redden and walk to the fireplace, where he kicked the andiron and stood frowning into the fire.

Freda stood at the table where the decanters, the siphons, the silver thermos bowl of ice were, and mixed their drinks. He studied her broad fleshy back, solid under mauve chiffon, her big haunches, her cushioned elbows, the netted chignon of red hair low on her neck. In her pierced ears little old-fashioned

diamond pendants dangled and swung briskly as she moved.
She turned and came toward him, carrying glasses filled with
whisky and soda. Her face was weary, mischievous, sardonic,
and utterly frank all at once, and for the first time, by God for
the very first time, she seemed to be looking at him as if he
were a human being, not some kind of a—some kind of a
worm, or example of a lower biological order. His hands began
to tremble and he stuffed them deeper in his pockets, then was
obliged to remove one to accept the drink. Facing him, Freda
lifted her glass to eye level. "Skoal," she said, looking him full
in his eyes as if they both knew the same secret. "Skoal," he
imitated, and drank too. Then she set her drink on the coffee
table in front of the sofa, and with a swift gesture, gathered up
her skirts and lay down. "Ah," she breathed, kicked her shoes
to the floor, and raising her quivering arms, began removing
the tortoise-shell pins from her knot of hair. The ice in
Leonard's glass began to tinkle uncontrollably. What was
she—was it possible that—oh, how could he think such things?
He took a big swallow of his drink.

"Leonard darling," she said, "you read beautifully." And at
this he was obliged to set his glass on the mantel, for this was
the first time that anyone at Hollymount—even Kevin Boyle,
who had addressed him as Marks, or Boy, or Lad—had called
him by his first name.

"Thank you," he said weakly.

"But," she went on, "I am so tired of faculty gatherings that
I retch at the thought."

His mind burgeoned with questions. Then why did she live
here? Why did she teach at Hollymount? Surely she could afford not to—that was plain. Why had she given this party tonight? "They seem a bit stuffy, don't they?" he essayed timidly.

She wriggled round on the sofa, passed her hand across her
eyes, and sighed. "Well, we've said Amen over Kevin, and that
relieves me, because it seems uncivilized to me to do without a
funeral—it leaves you with such an unfinished feeling about
the dead. When some kind of last rites have been said you can
put them from your mind and go on to the living."

"I should have thought," he ventured, "that you would find
funerals barbarian."

She threw back her head and laughed so that he could see

the roof of her mouth and several gold fillings in her teeth. "Now, darling, I can see you think of me as one of the conventionally unconventional. You must get that notion out of your head if we're to be friends at all—" his heart leaped—"because I'm the firmest of believers in form and ritual. I'll tell you a secret. I gave out to all of them that the occasion of the reading was to interest Philip Frisbee in Kevin's poems, but the fact is that I knew from the beginning he couldn't come. Oh, I'll give him the poems to read, right enough. But the truth is that I couldn't bear not to have some sort of farewell made to Kevin—I felt that his poor ghost was wandering among us crying and moaning for its last goodbye. You think that's foolishly sentimental?" She paused, and cocked her head.

"No," he said. "Oh no. The whole thing was such a shock. I mean the violence. It's hard to get out of your head. You know, I never saw a dead man before. Not even one I didn't know."

She nodded, her long eyes lustrous with understanding. "Violence that strikes in our midst shakes us in a strange way," she said mysteriously. "Personally, I think there are not enough murders. They feed us in some way. See how avidly we devour all accounts of crime, or detective stories! And after all, the responsibility of giving death is a small one which we regard so seriously in comparison to the responsibility of giving life, which we take so lightly."

"Oh, goodness!" said Leonard incautiously, and blushed. He backed up a little along the mantel, and took another quick swallow of his drink.

"There are two separate pleasures," she went on, not noticing his shock. She removed the last pin from her knot of hair, leaving it to uncoil like a fiery snake down her shoulder. "The pleasure of vicarious violence, and the pleasure at the detection and punishment of the crime of another. In the first we can enjoy the emotional outlet without undertaking the penalty, and in the second we can shiver deliciously with the knowledge that *we* cannot be found out, since our share in the business was secret, and of the mind. Don't you feel, Leonard darling, that you're just a *little* bit guilty of every crime you've ever heard of?"

Liquor was overtaking Leonard, buzzing in his head, throwing down barriers that the mind had set up against the blood. The polish of spurious worldliness was rubbing thin, as the

traditions of his pious middlewestern forefathers shouldered
their way to the surface of his conscious mind. The whore that
sitteth upon the waters! his grandfather's voice thundered in
his ear, and he admitted freely that he was alarmed. "You seem
to have a low opinion of humanity," he remarked with courageous primness.

Freda threw her head back again and laughed her big laugh
while she ran her fingers through her twist of hair, spreading it
around her shoulders like a thick copper serape. "Oh, Leonard
Marks, Leonard Marks!" was all the answer she had to give
him. She took her glass from where she had set it on the carpet, and sipped. Then she went on, "I very much doubt that
there'll be any pleasure of detection in this case, unless some
fictional detective plants himself fortuitously in our midst."

"Who do you think could have done it?" said Leonard,
reeling a little against the mantel.

She shook her head. "I do wish it were some eminent colleague—oh, I do wish it! But that's asking too much of fate, and
it doesn't sound very reasonable. Kevin hadn't been here long
enough to make any good enemies. And some more damning
bit of evidence would already have turned up, I imagine—unless
the police are holding out on us, of course—a probability which
I regard as quite beyond their mental capacity."

"What about the little girl—the student who was interviewed by the *Messenger*?"

"Oh, of course it's a possibility—quite a possibility," considered Freda. "But I rather think that if it's ever solved it will
turn out that some sneak thief came in and was surprised by
Kevin or something of the sort."

"I don't know," said Leonard. "I don't know. It seems awfully unlikely any sneak thief would choose Miss Stone's to
break into. It's not very—very *prosperous* looking. If only I'd
come out when I heard the thud. But boarding houses are full
of thuds, you know—or perhaps you don't." He heard his
voice coming back to him through a slight buzzing in his
blood. He tried to recollect how many drinks he had had, but
wavered between three and four. It seemed to him that Freda
Cramm was looking at him rather sharply, and he grinned back
at her. "He had a rather extensive love life, you know," he said,
and positively leered.

"How do you know?" she demanded.

"He was quite a raconteur," said Leonard happily, shaking his head and enjoying his own sophisticated vocabulary. "Quite a raconteur."

It seemed to him that at this Freda sat up a little straighter on the sofa, but he could not be sure if this were actually the case, or if it was only a part of the general tendency to defy the law of gravity that all objects seemed suddenly to have acquired. At any rate, she did raise her hand to rearrange her heavy veil of hair. "Where do you think *I* might have fitted into his love life, Leonard?" he heard her say with a peculiarly steely coyness. Did she feel that . . . Could she be concerned about . . . He pulled himself to attention and straightened his tuxedo jacket, tilting slightly to the left and staring at her astigmatically in what he intended for a reassuring gaze. "Oh, Mrs. Cramm!" he said seriously (for after all, she had never asked him to call her Freda), "Kevin was a *gentleman*! He never mentioned your name!"

"Now, confess, Leonard," she pursued in a pseudo-jocular tone (but he could hear the anxiety behind it), "surely you must have noticed I was rather a frequent visitor to Kevin's apartment."

In his bosom the springs of chivalry welled warmly. She was, he told himself, a good, a delicate woman. Poor thing, for all her brave talk and pretended brazenness, she was as concerned for her reputation as his own mother. He looked at her long and lovingly. "I knew you were one of Kevin's *very good friends*, Mrs. Cramm," he said in deep, tender, pastor-like tones.

"For all my yelling at him like a banshee and giving Miss Stone's house a bad name?" she pushed on—jovially, she would have had him think, but now, with the new supersensitive vision that had been granted him he could see through this pretense, straight to her worried, womanly heart.

"I'm sure you are accusing yourself unjustly, Mrs. Cramm," he intoned expressively. "I *know* you for the lady that you are."

He would have liked to restate this more definitely, but vague as it was, it caused her to relax, to lie back, though still chewing her lip nervously. Don't worry, *dear* Mrs. Cramm! his chivalrous heart cried out to her. "So, so," she said, her voice coming from a great distance. "You regarded it as a platonic relation. And the great joke of it is, Leonard, that it's true— never touched the hem of my gown, as the saying goes."

"Of course not, of course not, Mrs. Cramm," agreed Leonard earnestly. "Always had the greatest respect for you." He took a swallow of his drink, toasting her in silence.

"He never," she said, "mentioned quarreling with me?"

"Oh, Mrs. Cramm," assured Leonard, "we never discussed you at all!"

Suddenly he saw her sit forward with a rapid movement of which he knew he would be incapable at this moment. "Are you lying?" she said sharply.

"Lying?" he repeated in reproachful bewilderment, "Why should I lie?"

They were silent for a moment while Leonard thought he would like to sit down. Yet he couldn't see where he was to sit and still converse comfortably with Mrs. Cramm except on the sofa beside her feet. Suddenly it was absolutely imperative that he sit down before he fall down. With wavering step he made his way to plump down beside her gold-stockinged extremities. They lay like two gracefully fashioned caramels on the rosy velour cushion. Attached to them were two not ill-favored ankles, and beyond, disappearing into clouds of mauve chiffon, like the members of some Tiepolo goddess, there must unquestionably follow legs. At the termination of this thought stood Leonard's Baptist grandfather, raising a prohibitive hand. Freda lay with her delicately violet-ringed eyes closed like some sleeping Venus, or Brunhilde. Leonard began to tremble. Why not— after all, why not—but before his mind had by any means completed the sentence, a monstrous thing occurred. By a will quite outside his own, his hand was on her ankle and sliding timorously up her calf. He looked down at it in horror. "Oh, Mrs. Cramm!" he cried, and looked at her face for sympathetic amazement at the shocking thing that was taking place. But her features were quite impassive, her eyes slightly open, slumberous yet piercing. As he stared at her, she opened her mouth and thrust her flat creamy arms straight up into the air. "A-ah!" she yawned frankly. "Suddenly I'm completely done in. Leonard, I'm going to send you packing." And she swung her desecrated

limbs to the floor, fished for her shoes, and squeezed her feet
into them. Together they rose, he swaying. "Yes," he said in
relief. "Oh, yes, Mrs. Cramm!"

Out into the hall they swam, his mind reeling with liquor
and the impudicity of what he had nearly done. Freda opened
the coat closet and removed the one masculine garment that
remained there from its hanger. "This must be yours," she said
without expression, and handed it to him. He struggled into it
silently, while she held his new gray felt hat. His head spun and
floated with his exertions. He stared at Freda, standing there
in her graceful robes, on the floor, perhaps, or perhaps on the
air a foot or so above. How beautiful she appeared, how calm
and madonna-like, golden, full bosomed, impassive. Suddenly
the devil took hold of him—how else could one explain such
an atrocity?—he threw his arms around her and implanted his
wet lips on hers. "Oh, Mrs. Cramm!" he breathed reverently,
between embraces, "Oh, Mrs. Cramm!"

She suffered him to hold her, crushing his own hat where
she held it between them. Then she disengaged herself forcibly
and handed him his mashed hat. "You're drunk," she said,
"you—you pipsqueak!" And almost pushed him out into the
chilly night.

H E ROSE abruptly, went to the bathroom and threw up. He tottered back to the bedroom, sat down on the edge of the bed for a moment, his head in his hands. He looked at the clock. Nine-forty-five. He struggled into his bathrobe, rose gingerly, and made his way to the kitchenette with the aid of several pieces of furniture. By great concentration he managed to measure water and coffee into the percolator and set it on the gas plate. With this hope in view he was able to withdraw a jar of tomato juice from the refrigerator and pour out a glass which he drank in small sips. The coffee began to bubble into the little glass dome. He waited as long as he could, then poured out a cupful. He staggered into the living room, slopping the coffee into the saucer. It was a terrible day—the sky was black, the rain pouring. Also, he couldn't see things very well—ah, no wonder, he had forgotten to put on his glasses. He debated the possibility of going into the bedroom to get them, then leaned his head against the back of the chair and closed his eyes. But then the floor began to rock; he was obliged to open them again and drink a large swallow of coffee, which burned his tongue and throat. In response to this attack, his stomach gave a heave, but then subsided. He was able to turn his attention to less tangible effects of debauchery—guilt, shame, and mocking laughter.

He had made a fool of himself, an awful fool. He who hesitates is lost, his mind regurgitated. Faint heart never won fair maiden. Opportunity knocks but once. Fools rush in where angels fear to . . . How happy he had been last evening before going out . . . How miserably, idiotically happy. It seemed life was conspiring to teach him that happiness for him was only a prelude to . . . Pride goeth before a fall. Was it pride? No, it seemed to him he had always been reasonably humble. What he had been proud of were real, tangible accomplishments—a Phi Beta Kappa key, a Ph. D. . . . His father had always said his mother spoiled him. Praise to the face sure disgrace. All the adages of his childhood were coming back to him in gusts, like reminders of an undigested meal. He should never have drunk so much—oh, he knew a great deal better than to drink so much, with the kind of stomach *he* had!

Pipsqueak! He had never heard the expression before, but

he knew at once what it meant. A creature beneath contempt. A sort of larva. The kind of person you ask to serve on the committees that do the most dirty work, the sort of person whom you always interrupt. That was what she really meant. It had all come out.

Because he tried to kiss her? That was odd. Because she had been so—so kind up to then. Was she really a puritan, for all her ribald talk? Plainly she did not want *him* to kiss her, that was plain, but why be so—so brutal about it? She had behaved as if . . . behaved as if . . . His thought stream was muddied and boiling with misery and poisonous secretions . . . And *everyone* had been so kind. Praising him for his reading— saying goodnight to him as if he were guest of honor. Could it all be a gigantic hoax designed to dash him to earth after first elevating him to a great height? It hardly seemed they would have bothered—*she* would have bothered. Oh dear, it was all so confusing! He took a large swallow of coffee.

He must think it out in orderly fashion. It seemed to him that something was afoot, whatever he meant by that, and he wasn't sure. It all began with Kevin Boyle's murder. Now what could such a thing have to do with him, Leonard Marks? Well, he lived across the hall. He had, as a matter of fact, heard the murderer leave after the crime. If he had been a little more curious, in fact, he might have caught the murderer. As it happened, he heard nothing but the most unidentifiable of noises, beyond Kevin's loud No. He did not even know if the footsteps sounding in the hall were those of a man or of a woman. Of a woman? What did that remind him of? . . .

The pleasure of violence, she had said. *There are not enough murders. But the criminal will not be caught this time* . . . He took his spinning head between his hands. Had she really said those things, or had he invented them for her in his cups? But he heard her voice, remembered his own shock. By God, he even remembered thinking of his grandfather preaching about the whore that sitteth upon the waters! He stood up abruptly, pounded one fist on the other palm, and then sat down again, clutching at his forehead. And he had thought she was concerned for her virtue! Ha! His heart had warmed to her, he had thought of her in the same breath with his own mother. Oh, sacrilege! But was it really possible that *she* . . . ?

"*Somebody* has to commit murders," he assured himself aloud, and got up, more cautiously this time, taking his empty cup to the kitchenette for more coffee. He felt a little better, he noticed, but his feet were cold. He looked down at them. No wonder. He had forgotten his slippers. Carrying the coffee back to the living room, he touched a match to the already laid fire, the newspaper caught, and the kindling began to crackle. Why not, why not? He felt very excited. He extended his long bluish toes toward the blaze. Think of her character. She was a woman of self-advertised violence. This in itself, of course, warned caution. Barking dogs never bite. And yet . . . and yet he wouldn't like to have her after *him* with a poker. Not, of course, that she had showed signs of being after him with anything . . . His spirits sank again; he swallowed more coffee and lit a tentative cigarette. Suddenly he sat forward.

What was all that business about quarreling? Yelling like a banshee, she said—wait! It was coming back! He saw her mauve chiffon skirts spilling down from the seat of the sofa like the mist from a waterfall. He saw the enormous creamy orbs of her bosom bursting up from the decolletage of her dress. He saw her leaning forward a little, the snake of hair down one shoulder . . . *He never*, she said, *mentioned quarreling with me?* "Oh boy!" said Leonard aloud, inadvertently, and rose to pace the drafty floor, regardless of his bare feet. Was he rushing to a conclusion? It all seemed so pat. How had he begun this train of thought? Think back . . . By wondering . . . by wondering why Freda had made all the fuss over him. Wondering why she had . . . and then she hadn't. It all could *fit* so neatly, if you accepted the premise. The premise that Freda had murdered Kevin Boyle . . . He stopped dead in the middle of the floor, his feet purple, his mouth agape. And at that moment a knock sounded on his door, as fatefully as if this were the second act of *Macbeth*.

He paused a moment, listening, then girded up his bathrobe and opened the door. There, on his doorsill, stood a sharp-looking young man with horn-rimmed glasses, and his hat on the back of his head. "Mr. Marks?" he said, somehow injecting breeziness into those two words, "I'm from the *Messenger*. Wondered if you'd care to tell me a little something about Mr. Boyle's poetry."

"Oh," said Leonard, aware of his bare feet, his unshaven face, his heavy breath, and his uncertain vision, "uh—all right. Come in."

The young man entered, looking around Leonard's apartment with exaggerated appraisal. "Won't you take off your coat?" said Leonard. "Won't you sit down?" And wondered why he was being so bloody polite, because he had hated this young man on sight.

"Thank you, thank you," said the reporter, and removing his coat, sat down, looking much too much at home in Leonard's own chair.

"Some coffee?" said Leonard, caught inexorably in the compulsion of his manners.

But the young man said he had already breakfasted. "I understand there was a reading of Mr. Boyle's poetry last night."

Leonard sat down in the chair that he thought of as being for visitors and tucked his naked feet under it. "Yes," he affirmed. "Ah, yes, at Mrs. Cramm's house. A sort of memorial gathering, I believe."

"You believe?" said the young man rudely. "I thought you were the one who read the stuff."

"Oh," said Leonard, "ah—yes, of course."

"Well," demanded the questioner, "what do you think of it?"

"Think of it?" echoed Leonard.

"Yeah—what do you think of the poetry?" The young man looked at him inquisitively. "You look a little under the weather," he remarked. "Hung?"

"I beg your pardon?" said Leonard.

"I said," said the young man, raising his voice as if Leonard were deaf, "have you a hangover?"

"Oh," said Leonard. "Oh, ah, that. Ah, yes, I dare say I have." Ever since this young man had come on the scene, things had seemed very strange in a distant way—like a Kafka novel. Somebody walks into your room, and you have a dim feeling that he doesn't belong there, yet it seems altogether too out of order to say, What are you doing here? or Get the hell out . . . and besides, you are not too sure he would go. It might turn out that you were the one who was . . . A wave of nausea came sweeping down on Leonard like a rip tide. He had only time to say "Excuse me," in a strangled voice, and dash for the bathroom.

When he came back he felt very weak, yet somehow stronger. He had washed his face, combed his hair, put on his glasses and his slippers. He had tied the belt to his bathrobe. He had spit on his moustache and swept it to the left and to the right with his fingertips. He felt abler to cope. But he suffered a setback almost immediately when he found the young man making himself quite at home in the kitchenette. He appeared from behind the door carrying in a glass a concoction which resembled some waste product from a surgical operation. "Just swallow this," he said, and Leonard's gorge leaped like a hart in protest. "I know it looks terrible," said the Samaritan (showing his first resemblance to a human being), "but it will settle your stomach."

"But I—" Leonard began feebly.

"Don't quibble, drink it right down."

Leonard found himself clutching the glass and swallowing the slick fluid, which had a certain unity about it, leading Leonard to suppose that it was based on a raw egg. It descended to his stomach as dubiously as a paratrooper entering enemy territory, and then, to his surprise, settled there rather comfortably. "Thank you," he remarked tardily. "Ah—very kind of you."

"I know just how you feel," said the young man, and producing a notebook and pencil, sat down in Leonard's chair again. "Look, I'm sorry to bother you at such a time, but I've got to cook up some kind of tale about this poetry reading before I lose my job. This is a hell of a murder, you know." He was a companionable bastard, thought Leonard bitterly, retiring to the guest chair again. "First I get myself in a jam involving the honor of this virgin up at the Infirmary. My paper thinks the story's wonderful, but unfortunately I have by that time got myself amorously involved with a strange and luscious tomato who can't see things the practical way quite as plainly as she might. Now the paper is after me for more about Molly Morrison, but my newly acquired and highly valued love life says thumbs down, so now I've gotta get a new angle. Any ideas?"

The young man was beginning to appear more bearable to Leonard. His monologue seemed without ulterior motive, and genuinely troubled. As his health improved, Leonard's heart filled with sympathy, and some idea began to work in the back of his mind—when his head really cleared it would be plain just what its nature was. "Perhaps," said Leonard timidly, "you could do a piece about the poetry."

"That," said the young man, "was the general idea. Although how happy my boss is going to be to get a piece of literary criticism instead of a new suspect, I'll leave you to imagine."

"Perhaps," ventured Leonard, with unprecedented boldness, "you may—ah—be able to—ah—supply your—ah—boss with both."

The young man sat forward in his chair. "So?" he said, cocking his cropped head.

Leonard drew himself up in his chair, frowned, and touched his moustache. "Can I trust you not to quote me if I simply relate to you certain notions which have entered my mind as to the possible murderer of Kevin Boyle?"

"I guess you can sue me for libel if I do, since we haven't any witnesses," said the reporter wearily.

"Personally," said Leonard impressively, "I found the entire notion of the poetry reading last night a very suspicious business."

"How so?" said the young man, holding his pencil suspended over his pad.

"For one thing," said Leonard, "the entire English Department was given to understand that part of the purpose of the gathering was to have Philip Frisbee, one of the editors of Cornish House, hear Mr. Boyle's poems read. Yet Mr. Frisbee did not appear."

"Oh, that could be explained very easily, I'm sure," said the reporter, looking disappointed.

"It was explained," pronounced Leonard impressively. "To me. By Mrs. Cramm. After the party. She knew from the beginning that Frisbee was not coming."

"Well," said the young man pensively.

"But that is not all," said Leonard. "She admitted this to me in conjunction with a number of other remarks which seemed to me very much out of the ordinary. About murder. She said to me flatly and in so many words that there were not enough murders, and that in this case the murderer would never be caught." He paused impressively and folded his hands on one knee.

"She may be right on both counts," said the young man, biting his thumbnail.

Leonard sniffed irritably. He was beginning to dislike the young man again. "While mulling over Mrs. Cramm's *very odd* remarks this morning, I was trying to reconstruct my own impressions of the departing steps of the murderer. I heard him—or her—leaving Boyle's apartment, you know."

"Yeah, I know. I interviewed you once before, but it was with a bunch of other reporters. Donelly's my name."

"Oh," said Leonard correctly, "how do you do, Mr. Donelly?"

"Not very well, thank you," said the young man abstractedly. "How's *your* health?"

"Better," replied Leonard. "That—that *thing* helped me."

"What were you going to say about the murderer leaving Boyle's place?"

"*Well*," continued Leonard with renewed eagerness, "I got to thinking about the footsteps. I got to thinking about how there was no way I could remember whether the footsteps were those of a woman or a man. Now if they had been the footsteps of a—well, a *slender* woman, in high heels, it would have been quite simple to distinguish them from those of a man, wouldn't it?"

"Sure, I guess so," said Donelly.

"*However*," said Leonard, leaning forward, "had the steps been those of a *large* woman, wearing brogues, they would have been *very difficult* to distinguish, wouldn't they?" He leaned back triumphantly.

"So?" said Donelly, unimpressed.

It seemed to Leonard that he had gone quite far enough—the reporter's lack of enthusiasm dashed him a bit, but he pulled himself together and went on. "Boyle used to talk to me a good deal," he said. "He used to talk to me about—ah—women. I was quite conversant with the type he preferred. He frequently and graphically described it. Among other less relevant characteristics were those of good legs set off by high heels, and willowiness."

"That's what *I* used to say to myself," said the reporter in a puzzled voice.

"Breathes there a man with soul so dead, Mr. Donelly?" quipped Leonard boldly.

For a moment the reporter's face looked almost irate; Leonard wondered what on earth he had said wrong this time. "Look," said Donelly at last, "are you trying to say you think Mrs. Cramm did Boyle in?"

"I think," said Leonard coldly, "that I have gone quite far enough. You may make what use you like of my deductions."

The reporter rose exhaustedly and put on his coat and hat. "It doesn't cook," he said. "I always knew there was no story in the poetry angle. There isn't any story, and that's the long and the short of it, because there aren't any clues—unless you take this Morrison girl, and I can't take the Morrison girl or I'll lose *my* girl, and I don't think I want to lose my girl," he muttered on in an amazed undertone, "because I *think* I might want to marry her."

Deep pity rose in Leonard's breast for Donelly's troubled spirit. If he had been writing himself in a book, he would have had himself clap Donelly on the shoulder and say, Don't worry, old man, it will all come out in the wash; but in real life this seemed both unrealistic and impertinent. He followed Donelly to the door, commiserating silently. Just as he had his hand on the knob, the reporter turned suddenly on Leonard. "By the way, Marks," he said, "what was that paper you tore up and put in your pocket on the sun porch at Freda Cramm's last night?"

The room reeled, the reporter seemed to leer at him like the wolf from Grandma's bed, the Kafka-esque quality of the encounter increased a thousandfold.

"Paper?" gasped Leonard feebly, "Paper?" and making a hopeless upward gesture, turned and fled to the bathroom, where he threw up the Prairie Oyster in the toilet.

"Dr. FORSTMANN, Mr. Bainbridge," said Miss Seltzer, sticking her head around the door, and disappeared to admit the tall dripping figure of the psychiatrist. Bainbridge came round from behind his desk.

"Hullo, Julian," he said. "I'm as glad to see you as any of your anxious patients."

"A good deal gladder than most, I assure you," said Forstmann, shaking out his trench coat, knocking the drops off the brim of his hat, and standing his wet umbrella in a corner.

"Julian, this business of the Morrison girl becomes more and more pressing. Sit down." Bainbridge went behind his desk again and sat down, passing and repassing his hand over his bald spot. "How am I going to keep that idiot Flaherty from arresting her?"

Forstmann sat down and lit a cigarette. "I suppose that if it were absolutely necessary he could put a police guard outside her door at the Infirmary."

Bainbridge shook his head. "I'd hate that, and so would the trustees. Lord, what a scandal! I wish I could just ship the girl home."

Forstmann grinned. "Flaherty would love that."

"Oh, I know, I know, but I'm at my wit's end. Now you must tell me what *you* think about her."

"Think about her? That's a poser. I think it probable that she could and should undergo a successful analysis. But as to whether she's a murderess or not, I have no more idea than you. Her Rorschach shows her to have a high intelligence, but low productivity. She is very much introverted, and has great difficulty in making contacts with people, even to the point of showing paranoid tendencies."

Bainbridge groaned. "Pity my gray hairs and translate, Julian."

"Delusions of persecution," said Forstmann sharply. "Lucien, do you know what a hepcat is?"

"Why—ah—yes, I believe I do," said Bainbridge, amazed. "It's approximately—ah—a jitterbug, isn't that correct? Good heavens, what has that to do with the Morrison child—"

"It has only to do with your affected ignorance of psychiatric

283

terms which have long since become common parlance, Lucien. From your overprotestations I sometimes suspect that one morning I'll come to the office and find you on my couch."

"Not if I see you first," said Bainbridge colloquially. "And you seem a little touchy yourself."

"If you want to be convinced of my humanity," said Forstmann, "I had a flat tire on the way over, and I'm catching cold."

"Patient shows a tendency to wander away from the subject," murmured Bainbridge.

"All right, all right," said Forstmann. "The picture of Molly Morrison that I've gotten from three visits with her is this: Her father is Miles Morrison, as you know, and a very distinguished painter who is not successful financially. Her mother makes no bones about having married him on the assumption that he would one day be rich and famous; when he failed to become so, she became very much embittered and took out the frustration of her social ambitions on both the father and the child. Wait a minute." He unzipped the brief case that was on his knees and withdrew a manila folder. He scanned a sheet and then began to read from it.

There were constant recriminations, and Morrison evidently felt a good deal of guilt about his own inability to make money, which Molly shared with him. Molly also seems to have gotten the idea that if she had never been born, things would have been easier between her mother and father. She came to Hollymount actually dreading to leave home, but feeling that if she did leave, relations between her mother and father might become smoother. She is strongly attached to her father, and I should imagine that her feeling for Kevin Boyle was a pretty direct transference of her feelings for her father to a nearer object. Her relations with all women are fearful and inhibited, as a reflection of her dealings with her mother—she seems to have had literally no strong relationships outside her home in all her life. When she speaks of her housemother, of the nurses in the Infirmary, or of the students in her dormitory, her sense of persecution is intense—she imagines she is always being ridiculed, scorned, despised. It's interesting, for instance, that her feelings about Flaherty during the interview in which she made the confession are nowhere near so violent as those she has about Miss Sanders taking her to the Infirmary, which she felt was just another move in the conspiracy of women—mothers—to get rid of her.

He broke off, shuffled the pages, began again, "About the confession—she will tell me nothing about it—simply refuses to discuss it. I haven't thought it wise to press the point, because I am most interested, at the moment, in building her confidence in me."

"But Julian, you'll have to," said Bainbridge worriedly. "You'll simply have to find out something about it. Because it's the confession that's Flaherty's entire weapon in the case. And, of course, to a literal mind, it has a striking weight. Even to my literal mind."

Forstmann replaced the papers in the folder, frowned and shook his head. "The confession may be gospel truth or pure confabulation, for all I know. The girl is not psychotic; I can say that fairly flatly. But does that make her incapable of murder? I don't know. Look at suicidal types. There is some truth to the old saying that depressives who talk a great deal about suicide seldom actually kill themselves. Yet the fact remains that once in a while one does destroy himself—perhaps simply by accident. The same is just as probable of murder. I'd say from what I've seen of Molly that it is very unlikely that she killed Boyle. The act seems quite untypical of her personality as I've had occasion to see it. But I've only *had* occasion to see it three times."

Bainbridge picked up a pencil and beat the eraser against his front teeth. "God," he said, and sighed heavily. "God. What kind of people do commit murders, Julian?"

"Murderers," said Forstmann shortly.

"Isn't there a criminal type or something?"

"Balderdash," said Forstmann.

"How about Lombroso, or whatever his name is?"

"Nineteenth-century nonsense."

"Oh dear," said Bainbridge, "I really know a good deal about Milton, you know. Also about seventeenth-century poets. Why did I never turn my mind to some more practical field which would come to my aid now?"

Forstmann shook his head abstractedly, staring out at the level lines of rain.

Suddenly the president extended his pencil at arm's length. "A double personality!" he cried.

"What?"

"Maybe she's a double personality—you know—Dr. Jekyll and Mr. Hyde? Or is that," he finished weakly, "just nonsense —I mean, do people have them?"

"Oh yes—not frequently, but they do."

"Well, how about the Morrison child? Is she the type to have one?"

"Type?" said Forstmann, who was thinking of something else. "Oh, I don't know. You don't see them nowadays. Not in my kind of practice, anyway. Hysterics or schizophrenics."

"Well, could this girl be—what about all those diaries? Aren't they always supposed to do automatic writing and so on?"

"The diaries!" said Forstmann, suddenly galvanized. "That damned tire put them out of my mind. Did you get them?"

Bainbridge shook his head sadly. "Miss Sanders said she turned her room inside out and didn't find anything but school notes and papers. Not even letters from her family."

"Hmm," muttered Forstmann.

Bainbridge rose, came around his desk, and began to pace the floor, his hands in his pockets. Suddenly he stopped in the middle of the carpet and extended his short arms. "Look, Julian," he said, "I wish you'd do something for your fat fee besides sit around and look cryptic."

"I'm wide open to suggestion," said the psychiatrist sadly.

"Well, *do* try to get some kind of answer from her about the confession," said Bainbridge.

"I'll try today," said Forstmann, "but if she says she *did* commit the murder, she'll only be repeating what she's already said to the police. I really can't see how that's going to help you—however, I'll try. Meantime, I think you should conduct a recheck on anyone who might possibly give her an alibi— have the housemother talk to all the girls in the house to see if anyone could definitely state that she had seen her at the time of the murder. Because she might very well admit to me that the confession was false, but what influence would that have on the police?"

Bainbridge sank into one of the armchairs and groaned again. "None at all. I can't think straight. The *Messenger*'s printed another story—*What's Become of the Morrison Girl?* or some such. After my childlike faith in that young man. Although I must say they didn't mention the confession. But you can imagine the frenzy this will stir Flaherty to."

"Well, at least I'll see what I can do," said Forstmann, rising with a loud sneeze. "I'm on my way to the Infirmary now. You see what you can do in the way of getting an alibi. So far as I can see, that's her only real hope, other than having someone else confess to the murder."

"If all else fails, I may as well do that myself," said the president gloomily, helping Forstmann into his sodden coat.

THE BED had been turned so that the foot was toward the window, and Molly, lying propped on pillows, stared out aimlessly over the rolling dun-colored fields that stretched beyond the river to the misty mountains. Forstmann closed the door behind him, took off his hat and coat, and stood his umbrella in a corner. "Hullo," he said.

"Hullo," she answered listlessly, not turning her head.

The wicker chair stood ready for him, a little behind the head of the bed. But today he drew it to where he could see her face, and sat down. For a moment neither of them spoke. Then, a little to his surprise, she broke the silence. "The fields are like a cow," she said in a monotone. "Like an old brown cow, lying down waiting for you to lay your head against its flank and be comforted. With a big warm udder full of milk hidden between her legs and a warm stupid sort of look in her eyes." She paused. "You could just put your head against her and go to sleep." He thought that what she said was almost beautiful, but her voice had the sound of exaggerated grief and self-pity to which he was so used that it voided any emotional content which might have reached him, leaving only the sickness for his mind to deal with. He followed her gaze out the window to the drenched fields. "That would make a painting, too," he said, half jocularly.

"Oh, yes," she said, and turned toward him with a spark of animation in her eyes. "I was thinking that. Like those paintings that are two things at once—a landscape and a face—you know what I mean."

He nodded.

All at once her face turned pink, and she looked down at her hands. "I'm glad you're sitting there," she said. "Where I can see you."

"I'm sitting here because I have something special to say to you," he said, a little wearily.

She looked up, her face pale and drawn again. "What?" she said anxiously.

He smiled at her. "You won't like it."

"All right," she said tensely, "all right. Say it. What is it?"

"About the confession you signed for Flaherty," he brought out, not at all sure that he had been right to go at it quite this

288

way. And as if to confirm his self-doubt, she hid her face in her hands and turned from him.

He looked out at the fields again, and put his hand over his eyes. "Listen," he said, "listen to me for a moment, Molly. I'll try to explain. I shouldn't have to ask you this. You ought to be allowed to take your time, and to talk about this when you get ready to. Psychoanalysis doesn't go on the theory that suffering purifies—it makes it plain that when people have to suffer beyond their strength it warps and scars them, so that it takes them a long time to heal—if they're lucky enough ever to do so." This was not what he had planned—he could not remember what he had planned, but he went on. "It's against anything that I want to push you into a position of making you go back to something which hurts you so deeply as the thought of this confession plainly does. But unfortunately, your cure is not the only issue involved. You have gotten mixed up in a complicated situation over which I have almost no control. You're tangled in the law. And I can't help you unless you help me."

She kept her hands over her face and rolled her head from side to side. "I don't care, I don't care!" she wept. "I don't care what happens to me. It doesn't matter, it doesn't matter!"

He would have liked to put aside his therapeutic imperturbability and tell her not to be a little idiot, just for once in a way. The course he must steer was so delicate, running between the necessities of the police and of his patient—on the one hand a need for immediate action, on the other, the need for infinite patience. He groped and fingered among his thoughts for the right word, the exact degree of gentle firmness. "It matters," he said. "It does matter, but I'm going to have a hard time trying to explain to you how, unless you will listen to me very patiently and trustfully. Yet I am perfectly aware that you have no reason for trusting me—you've only seen me three times in your life. Ordinarily, Molly, you would have the time to try me out and find out whether or not you thought you could count on me before you exposed anything you found painful to expose. But because of the pressure of the police, I have to try to push you, although it's against my better judgment. Will you listen to me, Molly?"

She had turned her head while he was speaking, and drawn

her hands down her face until her eyes stared at him over her fingertips. "I'll listen," she said tragically, through her hands. "But it doesn't matter."

Now he marshalled his forces and blew his nose. He recrossed his long legs, looked at her for a moment. She stared back, her eyes flickering, frightened, but steadfast on his own. "You're saying," he began finally, "that your life doesn't matter—that it doesn't matter whether you live or die. But you're not sure. You have before you in the world too many examples of people who have preferred life to death to be able to say quite flatly that there's little to choose between them, or that death is preferable."

"But—" she began, taking her hands away from her mouth.

He raised his hand to silence her. "Will you just listen for a moment while I lecture?" he said, smiling a little, but firm. "It would be much easier if I could tell you that your life mattered to me, or to your mother, or your father, or some other person. And of course it does, in many ways. But the person to whom your life is really important is yourself. Much more important than your death could possibly be."

She made a little moue of scorn and began to speak, but he went on without letting her. "Death has certain incontrovertible advantages which I shouldn't for a moment undertake to deny. Death is a sure thing, and life is a risk. Death might even represent for you a small but definite improvement on the *status quo*." An amazed look came over her face, and he was childishly pleased. "You're miserable now; if you were dead, you'd at least be at peace." She nodded and nodded, agreeing vehemently. "I've got everything your father ever learned, everything your mother ever learned, and most of the things you ever read to fight when I try to sell you life, Molly. I wish I had a nickel for every time somebody in the last generation and the generation before that said: You can't demand happiness of life. I think you can. Once you've found out that happiness is learning to work with the materials at hand and to grow and develop in proportion with your own abilities. Once you've found out you have a right to your own importance."

Her hands lay on her lap, her white face gazed at him, and a flat look of utter contempt was on it. As he watched her, he saw her raise her eyebrows and shake her head slowly and hopelessly. Outside the rain poured on the windowpane, on the brick terrace, on the dingy fields. He felt tired and mistaken. What he had done was like giving a patient a six-week's dose of medicine in one day. . . . Six weeks . . . six months . . . sixteen . . . "All right," he said wearily. "I know. It sounds idiotic to you. It even sounds idiotic to me. I've tried to give you a *Reader's Digest* version of *War and Peace*, or something like it." He sneezed ignominiously, blew his nose, and rising, took his overcoat.

"You have a cold," her voice came to him suddenly, small, flat, and female.

"I have indeed," he said stuffily.

"You shouldn't run around without rubbers," she said softly. "You're worse than my father."

He stopped in the midst of thrusting his arm through a sleeve, then made himself go on calmly. When he had buttoned his coat and taken his hat and umbrella, he turned. "All the same," he said, "I wish you could have told me about the confession, Molly."

She looked down at her hands, rolling and unrolling the edge of the sheet. "All right," she said, almost inaudibly. "I didn't kill him. Of course, I didn't. But I might as well have. And it doesn't make any difference."

He took a step toward the bed, striving to keep his voice even. "Where were you at the time the murder was being committed, Molly? Do you remember at all?"

"I went back to the house and stayed there all evening," she whispered, bending her head even lower over her moving fingers.

"All right, Molly," he said gently. "That's all. Good girl." Quietly he let himself out the door, without either of them saying goodbye.

Good old transference, he thought irreverently as he strode out of the Infirmary to his car.

As he pushed the big library door and stiffened himself to brave the rain, Hungerford met Leonard Marks, who, with sighs and puffings of relief, was folding his umbrella under the shelter of the vestibule. The younger man looked peaked and drawn with an unattractive oyster-like pallor. Hungerford remembered having been beastly rude to him once when Marks had approached him in his repulsively eager fashion. And he remembered, too, that Marks had been kind to him the night after Kevin's murder. So he made a point of stopping and speaking to him, instead of passing on.

"Hullo," he said, and twisted out a wry friendly smile. "Glorious New England autumn, isn't it?"

"Oh, Christ," said Marks miserably, "it's awful."

"How did the reading go at Freda's?"

"I read," said Marks.

"Yes, I know. How did it go?"

"Oh," said Marks bitterly, "everybody wished it had been you."

"Rats!" said Hungerford, embarrassed and annoyed. "As a matter of fact Miss Austen was just telling me how well you read. How did Frisbee take the poems?"

"He wasn't there," said Marks, a peculiar expression passing across his face.

Hungerford raised his eyebrows. Because he felt sorry for Marks and wanted to make a demonstration of friendliness, he said frankly, "Why the devil do you suppose she gave the thing?"

Marks drew his face into a mask of exaggerated suggestiveness. "That is something I should like to know very much myself," he enunciated.

The poor blundering idiot! Hungerford thought with annoyance. He made it so impossible to be decent to him. What in the world was he trying to imply? Hungerford's own mood of benevolence was not ample enough to impel him to coax out hidden meanings. Instead he sought to change the subject. "Wonder who's to be your new neighbor in Kevin's place," he threw out. "I don't imagine there'll be any difficulty in finding a tenant for it in this enlightened community, in spite of its tragic associations." He felt his face contract for the tic. I'm tired, he thought. I must get home and rest. The constant chill and dampness of the day were enervating. Still and all, he had felt well today—better than for a long time—better than he had since Kevin's death.

He saw Marks' depressing countenance fall into lines of self-abnegation and doglike devotion which would have been moving had they not been so abject. "I wish," said Leonard with humble hopelessness, "that *you'd* move in there, sir. It's an awfully good apartment—sunny and all, and the fireplace."

Hungerford smiled, and made ready to go. "I'm pretty well off where I am," he said. "It's a gloomy old place, but it suits me, somehow. Give me a ring and drop in to see me one of these days." And he was off down the granite steps, erecting his umbrella against the downpour. God, he thought, he'll probably come.

Sometimes, he found, rainy days pleased him. They carried the well-worn childhood recollections of staying indoors by the fire, of reading three and four novels in a day, of having his mother surprise him with a tray of cocoa and cookies as he sat curled in the old wing chair. She had liked the rainy days too, shutting the two of them off from the world. . . . Ah, he knew their relationship had been perverse and warping, but how beautiful, my God, how loving! True, he had grown up like some small white stunted plant beneath a stone, but he had loved the secrecy and privacy of his warm underground world—sometimes he thought the brilliance of that filial passion he had known was worth the torments it had caused him. Things he could not have told a psychiatrist, who would have made them obscene, he treasured as the loveliest moments of his life. Sitting on the stool of his mother's dressing table while she lovingly brushed his long blond curls over her ivory fingers. He could not have been more than four or five—his earliest memory. She had dressed him in kilts—even then a little out of date—and velvet suits. "I wanted a little girl," she had confided to him. "That was before I knew how nice a little boy could be." Their warm, plush-carpeted privacy . . . his mother, her auburn hair tumbling down over her peignoir, coming in to light his gas log as he lay in the big mahogany bed . . . A neurotic, sex-terrified widow, almost insane in her withdrawal from the world. Those things were true, he recognized them. He recognized the irreparable damages her strangeness had wrought on his spirit. Yet how was he ever to explain to anyone, ever, the vivid pure pleasure of their companionship, the mutual harbor of their love? She was the great passion which more than his work, even, had justified his existence; for her he had remained virgin during the fifty years of his life, regretting nothing . . . nothing he had missed.

Wrapped in his thoughts of warmth and love he had walked unnoticing through the dripping streets and found himself at his own doorstep almost before he knew it. The old house held its grim face up to the rain in a kind of bleak resignation; it seemed to him like a person awaiting his return, like some long-faced spinster housekeeper, unsmiling always, yet devoted and welcoming in her own, queer, unyielding way. Silently, he returned the silent greeting.

In the hallway an old-fashioned lamp shaded by a crimson and gold painted glass globe throbbed dimly in the gloom. To the left and right were the closed doors of two apartments occupied by very old ladies. He climbed the stairs to his own rooms. Opposite his own was the apartment of an emaciated and ancient professor emeritus of Greek who ate health foods, and would, if you allowed him, discourse for hours on the benefits of eurythmics and Dalcroze. On the third floor, in what had formerly been the servants' rooms lived Miss Penny, the landlady, who was quite as elderly as the rest. Among them, Hungerford was a youthful sprig, a mere boy of fifty. He smiled as he turned his key in the lock. Downstairs he could hear Miss Belcher's radio tuned to "Orphan Annie," while across the hall Samson Ellerbee engaged in audible slumber. He felt a kind of peace and protection in the queer old place. He snapped on the gooseneck student lamp on his desk. The blotter was neat and vacant; all at once his heart began to pound and he could not catch his breath. He became aware that all his protestations of peace, his memories of protection, had been a barrier erected against fear—the fear that he would find the notebook awaiting his return.

He sat down in his armchair, slumped over like an old man, panting. Fear. Why should he be so frightened? What was there to fear? Was not death the ultimate thing that people feared? And was he afraid of death? No. Then what? Guilt, he thought, involuntarily. What kind of guilt? Of what was he guilty? His breath began to come in heaving, audible gasps. He hid his face in his hands. Of nothing—nothing but his mother's death.

And yet he was not. Surely he was not. That was pure madness to blame himself for what must have come with or without him one day . . . Ah, but it had come without him! He had left her; she had died helpless and alone, surrounded by strangers, calling for him. If he had been there to comfort her, to stay her with his love, perhaps she would have lived again, and died in peace some later day, dropping off to sleep and never waking, as one might hope. There he had been, enjoying heartlessly the things she would so have loved to share with him, basking unabashed in Sicilian sunshine, gone abroad to write on a fellowship, while she lay pierced and gasping with pneumonia in the bitter New England damp. His breath came rasping from his chest. God, had he not paid sufficiently? Since that day, when the cable reached him, he had not written another word. For three years now he had been nothing but a living corpse, waiting to be buried.

He could not stand these thoughts; as if to purge one pain by inflicting another, he rose, went abruptly to the desk, drew out the notebook, and began to turn the pages of mad scrawled writing. Slowly he dropped into the swivel chair at his desk and began to read the entry dated November 5.

George Hungerford [it said], went to Kevin Boyle's tonight. He sat down by his fire and put his feet on his fender. He talked to Kevin Boyle about his work. Oh, says he, in his whining meaching voice, all Christlike, all crucified. You must get away from here. For the sake of your work, he said. Hoh! He said for the sake of his work! If I told all I knew how his fine speeches would fly out the window. The martyr, suffering about so they will comfort him. Oh, no, Mr. Hungerford, don't go there! You're too weak, too feeble—let us take care of you, we understand. So he goes to Kevin Boyle, all love and fawning. I come too. I knock at the door, I beat on the window. Will I tell Kevin Boyle to go away? No, I will not! I will tell him to stay here, to lie on my breast, to know what warmth is—

not sit by the fire with dry old men. Oh, Kevin Boyle! I
cry, but George Hungerford will not let my voice be
heard. He is all Go Away, and For the Sake of Your Work.
Old hypocrite! I will finish you. . . .

The writing was so large that this entry covered five pages.
When Hungerford turned the last of them, his hands were
shaking. He laid the brown-covered notebook on the desk.
Why should it disturb him so—beyond the mere fact of its
presence, which was, to be sure, disturbing in a realistic enough
way. It was hostile, unfriendly, hating. And who should hate
him so? Who was his enemy? And how had his enemy such
secret access to his house? And if to his house, perhaps to his
thoughts . . . Already this had occurred to him. This enemy
seemed almost to read his thought . . .

He rose and paced the floor. The room was gloomy with
only the small puddle of light from the desk lamp to illuminate
it. In the dark corners the furniture loomed threateningly, with
semi-human faces. He wished, for once in a way, to think this
through, scientifically. He tried to remember how each discovery of a new entry in the journal had come about.

The discoveries had these characteristics in common. They
occurred on his return from supper, which he usually ate
downtown, in the cafeteria of the Harlow Hotel. This, of
course, was the logical time for an outsider to gain access to his
room. It had occurred to him that it would also be possible for
the girl—or woman—to enter the room while he took his
regular afternoon nap, but this he had dismissed as too improbable a notion. Besides which, since he had thought of it,
he had taken to propping a chair underneath the knob of the
door which, had it fallen, would have wakened him even from
the drugged sleep he slept. She could even, he thought, as he
walked up and down the floor with a rapid and erratic tread,
write the entries while he slept, for all he would know of it. For
always when he woke his head would be thick, his consciousness muddy; it was his custom to put his clothing and wraps in
meticulous order before lying down so that when he woke
there would be no need for concentration; he could simply
stumble into his things blindly, wash his face, and stagger out
into the night, where the fresh air would revive him. But that

was improbable—highly improbable. No, the most likely thing was that she came while he was at dinner. No one would notice her. The old ladies downstairs were half-blind and deaf, besides which one of them always had a radio roaring. As for Mr. Ellerbee, he was always either sleeping, or practicing Yoga. And Miss Penny, supposing that she heard footsteps or an opening door below, would have no reason to suppose that it was not one of her regular tenants. The question was not so much the how as the why. What a curious and subtle mind had devised this form of torture? Who knew him well enough to know how utterly undone this odd means of persecution would render him? Who cared enough?

For a moment he halted at the rain-streaked window and stared into the thickening twilight. One hunched figure under an umbrella passed on the opposite side of the street; a red truck rumbled by. Yet the strangeness of the thing grew, for though he thought of the torture in terms of a subtle mind, nothing said in the entries indicated subtlety of mind except with regard to means of causing pain to himself. There was one detail of the business which haunted him with such fearsome implications as he dared not think about straight-on. The name of the writer—for she sometimes referred to herself in the third person—or the name she had assumed, was Eloise. Just why this should terrify him so he did not know, yet it made him tremble in his deepest being—Eloise was the name of his sister, who had died when she was six months old, before he was born.

How long was it to go on? How long must he bear it? Something must be done before—before . . . He whirled about and faced the dark room, his hands against the window sill, like a criminal at bay, facing his tormentors. The furniture seemed to take on the appearance of people he knew. The spindle-backed straight chair was Samson Ellerbee, all bones and no flesh; a well-picked skeleton existing in polite madness. The studio couch was Bainbridge, stolid, overstuffed, unperturbed, unheeding. The bookcase was the dog-faced librarian, herself half mad, who lashed out at him in invective when he brought in books that were overdue. The telephone was Leonard Marks, extending his lips in a great black overeager kiss. But in the corner—ah, in the corner! There stood a

square-shouldered, apelike figure, clenching its fists and lowering its head, grinning a broad brass-edged grin, seeming to
move, to swing its weight from hip to hip—the golden maple
highboy, like Freda Cramm, waiting to pounce on him!

He fled across the room and opened the door to the hall.
There too, it was dark, but through the banisters he could see
the hall lamp shining its fiery eye malignantly. Downstairs the
radio had been turned off, and all was very still. It seemed to
him the latch of the outside door clicked gently and a step
sounded in the hall below. In panic he slammed the door and
propped Samson Ellerbee—the straight chair—under the knob.
He switched on the ceiling light, and the room suddenly glared.
He was panting and trembling. He went to the telephone and
thumbed clumsily through the college directory, then dialled a
number. "Hullo," he said breathlessly, at last. "Hullo, Marks?
This is Hungerford. Look, I wondered if you would do me a
favor. Speak to Miss Stone for me about Boyle's apartment. Tell
her to hold it until I see her. On thinking over your suggestion,
it seemed it might not be a bad idea to make the change."

THERE WERE ten tables of six girls each in the dining room. The talk flowed on in a water babble of female voices—you could become fascinated by the collective effect if you ceased to listen to the individual sense. It was bright and warm there, snug with the knowledge that the rain was coming down outside. The dining room was full—no one wanted to eat out when the weather was so horrible, in spite of the meal, which consisted of creamed chipped beef, baked potatoes, beets, and canned fruit cup. There was a short conference among the girls at the head table, then they banged on their glasses with their spoons to quiet the dining room, while Miss Sanders, at the head of the table, rose.

"There will be a short house meeting after dinner in the living room, which it is imperative that you all attend. Roll will be called. It will only last a very few minutes, and it is terribly important."

She sat down again, blinking her pink-rimmed eyes nervously, while the stream of talk took up its course with added volume. The house president, seated at Miss Sanders' table, looked at her in some surprise, since she was usually asked to call any meeting of the girls in the house. "What's the meeting, Miss Sanders?" she asked curiously.

"Why," said Miss Sanders, blinking her eyes almost frenetically, "I'd rather just wait and have you hear it with the rest, if you don't mind, Marjorie."

Slightly wounded in her dignity, Marjorie addressed herself to her fruit cup.

With a short nervous titter, Miss Sanders asked one of the other girls how the tryouts for the Dramatic Association play were coming along, and the conversation resumed its irritatingly innocuous course.

When one of the maids gave her the signal that all the tables had finished their dessert, Miss Sanders rose and conducted the stream of girls out of the dining room. Chattering and jostling they idled after her, the procession held up by the bottleneck created while each girl waited to thrust her rolled-up napkin back in its cubby hole. During the dinner hour the last mail of the day arrived; a second halt occurred in midstream during the trip to the living room when each one stopped to look despairingly or delve triumphantly at her mailbox. At last they were established in the living room, on the couches, on the chairs, on the floor, with Miss Sanders behind the coffee urn and several self-appointed Hebes moving about with demitasse cups, sugar, and cream. A slight stir of curiosity and impatience was beginning when Miss Sanders pulled out a sheet of paper from under the tray, and perching a pair of reading spectacles on her beaklike nose, began to read out the names.

"Ackerman . . . Allen . . . Bastion . . . Bellini . . . Burton. . . ."

Several were missing, in the Infirmary, or out to dinner. These names Miss Sanders carefully marked on her list. When she was done, she folded up her spectacles, looked around at all of them apprehensively, and cleared her throat.

"Girls," she began in her high nasal voice, "I want to ask a question to which you must all give your most serious attention, as it is—ah—in the most *literal* sense a matter of life and death." She paused and looked around at their faces, now frozen utterly dumb with surprise. "I want you each and everyone to try to remember if she saw Molly Morrison on the day that Mr. Boyle was—ah—killed." The silence following her speech was absolute. Faces turned up to her, round and amazed, many of them open mouthed. "If any girl *does* recollect seeing Molly about the house on that day, will she please report to me in my apartment. I'm going to my room now." She rose and left the living room in the midst of a dead silence. After her departure, the talk started up again slowly, first a buzzing murmur around the room, then loud and confused. "God," one little redheaded girl kept saying, "I live right *next* to her and I didn't see her . . . No, I'm sure I didn't see her!" "Do you suppose she *did* it? Do you suppose . . ." Kate Innes, sitting on the sofa beside Honey Sacheveral beat one fist on the other palm. "Oh, Lord," she kept saying over and over. "I *couldn't* have. I was at a meeting of the *Holly*."

"Gee," said Marjorie, the house president, hopelessly, "how can they expect anyone to remember at this point? It's nearly two weeks ago. Anyway, nobody ever noticed her, and that's the truth."

They sat chattering anxiously for some time, then one or two got up and drifted out the door, then more. Each time someone left the room there was a general craning of necks to see if the departing one turned into Miss Sanders' doorway, but none of them did. The rest stayed on, conversing desultorily, draining off little by little. When the room was nearly empty, Honey, who had been staring broodingly into space, turned to Kate with sudden animation. "Did you see the new article about Molly Morrison in the *Messenger*?"

"Yeah," said Kate tonelessly, "I saw it."

"Know what I bet?" said Honey eagerly. "I bet that little ole boy we met in the Harlow wrote those stories. *I* thought *he* was *cute*."

"He's a stinker," said Kate. "An old fourteen-carat stinker from way back. You, Sacheveral, are more or less innocent because you don't know what you're doing. He knows." She rested her elbows on her dungareed knees and put her head in her hands. "They'd never have gotten that stuff about Morrison if it hadn't been for me. *I* did it, I did it all, and then I so miserably misjudged that rat's character . . . oh, I could shoot myself!"

"Don't feel bad, honey," said Honey.

"Why the hell not?" said Kate ungratefully. She pulled viciously at a strand of her drooping hair, then sighed and pushed her glasses up her nose. "If only somebody had seen her. She must have been around here. Somebody must have seen her. It wasn't the time of day when a person's ordinarily out wandering around."

"When was that?" said Honey vaguely. "Was that a Monday?"

"Of course it was a Monday, you cretin. A week ago last Monday."

"Now let me see," said Honey. "On Mondays—yeah, I ride. That's it. When it's rainin', Miss Hoogle comes and picks us up on the corner by The Coffee Shoppe."

"You mean," said Kate, momentarily distracted, "you actually know a character named Hoogle?"

"Oh, honey, she's *real* sweet—she comes from Atlanta."

"Not Miss Scarlett O'Hoogle?"

"Uh-uh," said Honey seriously. "I think her first name is Mary Margaret. She teaches riding, you know."

Kate groaned, but Honey went on undeterred. "Now let me see," she mused, cocking her beautiful head so that the golden feathers of her hair curled over one shoulder of her pale blue sweater. "Did it rain that Monday?"

Kate shook her head abstractedly.

"That means we were in the outdoor ring. Miss Hoogle was teaching us about leads."

"Do you have to call her that—that name?" snapped Kate, rousing momentarily from her reverie.

"Honey, I can't help that's what her name is. And you know what? I think she's queer."

"How do you mean, queer?"

"Oh, *you* know. Regular sort of queer. I mean, she has such a deep voice, and she goes around in pants all the time."

"So do I," said Kate morosely.

"Oh, but honey, you're like my mama says—full busted."

Kate threw her hands in the air and collapsed against the back of the sofa, closing her eyes. In a moment she might have been seen to open one of them a trifle to view her own contours as they were spread before her. Meanwhile, Honey went on placidly.

"O.K., so that Monday we were in the ring. That was until five o'clock, or ten of, or something. Then I walked home from the stables—that takes about twenty minutes, I reckon. Then I took my clothes off and put on my robe—only it seems to me the tubs were all full and I had to wait. Seems to me I went all the way down the hall and Dibby and Jane or somebody had the tubs. No, it couldn't have been Dibby, because it seems to me she has choir practice Mondays . . ."

"Gee," said Kate, "you're awfully boring, but I wish I could be wondering like that what I was doing last Monday. The least I could do would be to produce an alibi for the girl. If only I hadn't been in that damn *Holly* meeting!"

Honey went on as if Kate had not spoken. "And then it seems to me I went back down the hall to my room to wait for the tubs to be empty, and I plucked my eyebrows for a while, and then I came out again and . . ."

Kate got up abruptly and stretched. Honey stopped and looked up at her. "What's the matter with you, have you got a photographic memory or something? People aren't supposed to remember that well what they did two weeks ago."

"Oh," said Honey complacently, "it's very easy. That was the day I fell in love."

"In love?" said Kate, sitting down again and looking more curious than she would have liked.

"With little ole Petey Jones," said Honey dreamily. "Honey, he drove all the way over here from Amherst, and he had two flats on the way. And I was thinking about him, all day. About whether I would fall in love with him or not. And I did."

"So that's the way it happened," said Kate shortly.

"Yes, it did," replied Honey. "Darlin', isn't it *mysterious*?"

The room was empty now. Kate fished in the crevice between the sofa cushions for her cigarettes and pulled herself forward, preparatory to rising.

"Then," said Honey, rolling on like the Mississippi, "when I finished plucking my eyebrows I started back down the hall again, and—"

"Oh, shut up," said Kate rudely, and rose. "You don't take my mind off my troubles worth a nickel."

"But Ka-ate!" cried Honey aggrievedly. "*That* was when I saw that little Morrison drip! Isn't that what I'm supposed to remember?"

"You *what*?" shrieked Kate, and plumped down again. "What time? Where did you see her? What was she doing?"

Honey nodded her flaxen head complacently and smoothed her skirt. "I surely did," she said. "I remember it just as plain, because she nearly took my head off. She was coming out of her room with a great, big, old pile of notebooks, and I said to her, What are you up to, fixin' to make a bonfire? and didn't she just lay into me—what was I doing snooping around her room, and why was everybody always spying, and—oh, I don't know what all. She just blessed me out for sure, and I never did a thing—just was coming down the hall to take a bath and met her with all those papers and stuff she was carrying."

"Well!" gasped Kate. "Well! Could you say—is there any way you could tell what time it was?"

"We-ell," said Honey doubtfully, "I didn't look at the clock or anything. What time *ought* it to be?"

"Between half-past five and six to do her any good."

"Well, honey, it's *got* to be between half-past five and six, because I couldn't have gotten home earlier than ten after five, only more likely it was twenty after, and then I got undressed, only Jane and Dibby were in the tubs—but it couldn't have been Dibby—"

"Oh, the hell with Dibby," said Kate joyfully. "Honey Sacheveral, could you swear all that on a stack of Bibles?"

For answer, Honey turned her blue eyes upward and raised her slender right hand in the air. "I, Honoria Sacheveral, do solemnly swear to tell the truth, the whole truth, and nothing but the truth, so help me God," she intoned dramatically, "that on the night of—Monday night, whenever that was—I saw Molly Morrison in the hall of the second floor of Birnham House at the time the murder was being committed."

"Amen," finished Kate religiously, and taking Honey's arm, dragged her to Miss Sanders' apartment.

WHEN KATE had finished directing Honey's evidence as it was given to the excited Miss Sanders, she slowly climbed the stairs to her floor and locked herself in her room. There she sat down at her desk and stared at the open copy of the *Messenger* that was lying there. WHAT HAS BECOME OF THE MORRISON CLUE the headline read—not a big headline, or on the front page, but still, there it was in plain view. It didn't have a West Lyman dateline. It was mostly a rehash of old stuff. There was no mention of the confession. But who else could have written it? It must have been what needled the police so that it was necessary to find an immediate alibi for Molly. Thank God for Sacheveral. She had really expiated her sins—which was more than some people could say. Deliberately she took off her glasses, laid them on a corner of her desk, put her head down on her arms, and began to cry. How could he be such a heel?

In the middle of a loud snivel, the electric buzzer in her room rang alarmingly. She jumped and put her glasses on, snatched a Kleenex, and blew her nose. The buzzer meant she had a caller, who was, she judged, the man from the printer's here with galley proofs of the December *Holly*. Yes, it must be that, and *whoever* it was, she disdained making up her face for him. She unlocked her door and went thudding down the stairs to the front hall.

Jack stood there, looking somehow dejected, with his hat on the back of his head, reading *PM* as he leaned against the mail desk. Kate stopped halfway down the last flight of stairs. She said very distinctly, "I don't want to talk to you."

Jack looked up at her and folded up the paper. "Yes, you do," he said, without smiling. "Go put your face on and we'll go somewhere."

"I'm sorry," said Kate, "there isn't anything I have to say."

"You don't need to say anything. I'll do the talking."

"You've verbalized quite enough," she said, with excessive dignity, and turned to go upstairs again.

Jack made a sprint and caught her by the wrist. "Look," he said, "I'm in no mood for explanations here and now. Will you go up and make yourself presentable, or shall I take you up and wash your face for you?"

305

She stood quite still, looking into his eyes. "I don't feel like joking," she said, "not about anything, and expecially not about Molly Morrison. I just don't want to see you any more. Will you let me go, please?"

He released her wrist. "I've never seen the dignified side before," he said, sounding a little more natural. She was on the landing when he called after her, "Would it make you feel better if I said I'd lost my job?"

She turned and looked back at him, her face still stern. "When?" she asked.

He laughed shortly. "You ought to be a lawyer," he said, "think of everything. I lost it after I turned in a piece of literary criticism on Kevin Boyle's poetry. The thing you're sore about was written by a colleague who was more willing to ride along with the boss."

"Oh, Jack!" she said, transfixed on the landing.

"Now will you go fix your face for me?" he grinned.

"Yeah," she said, flushing, "yeah!" and turned to fly up the stairs when he caught her on the landing and kissed her re-soundingly.

"Take those damn pants off," he said, smacking the logical place, "and drop them in the nearest incinerator!"

"Young man! Young man!" came a sudden, scandalized voice from the hall below, "Men are *not allowed* on the upper floors of the dormitories!"

"Miss Sanders!" gasped Kate, scarlet.

"Kate Innes!" gasped Miss Sanders, the same color.

"Now, Miss Sanders," said Jack soothingly, ambling down the stairs as Kate fled up them, "I assure you that my intentions were most honorable."

"Well!" sputtered Miss Sanders, "You must remember that appearances count as well as intentions, young man! Although," she remarked over her shoulder as she trailed off toward the dining room, "I must say I've always thought that a little more of that sort of thing was just what an intellectual sort of girl like Kate needed."

In something more than a jiffy, Kate reappeared, looking respectable in a sweater, skirt, and cosmetics. She took her polo coat from the coat rack and they went out the door in silence. When they were in the car, Jack said, "I'll have to be going back to New York."

"You could work for the West Lyman *Star*," said Kate without conviction.

"Not and start saving for Junior," he replied, looking at her so meaningfully that they almost caromed into a traffic light. After this they drove soberly and silently to the Harlow bar.

It had stopped raining, but the raw New England wind ripped around the street corners, whipping at skirts and cutting the breath. As Kate and Jack were precipitated through the glass door of the Harlow by a gust, they ran into a man coming out, head bent to meet the blast.

"'lo," said Jack.

Amazingly, the figure swept off its hat and made a low bow. "My dear sir," it intoned, "the clumsiness is entirely on my side. Think nothing of it, nothing of it!" and went off muttering into the night.

"Why," gasped Kate, "that was Mr. Marks and he was pie-eyed!"

"Drunk as a skunk," said Jack cheerfully, removing his gloves. "Good evening, Stanislas." The bartender nodded morosely.

"But he's the quiet type!" said Kate, unable to get over her surprise. "I mean, you should see him. The most utterly inhibited white mouse you ever saw!"

"I know," said Jack. "We've met. I suspect that somebody suggested a touch of the hair of the dog, and he's been chewing dog hair ever since."

"Since when?" demanded Kate.

"Since Freda Cramm's party."

"Was he potted that night? He sounded perfectly sober when we were listening."

"I regret to inform you, my respected fellow sleuth, that we walked out of that gathering just before things got hot. I deduce from later findings that our Leonard stayed on after the rest of the guests had departed."

"Oh, Jack, that's incredible! You don't mean—"

"My dear young woman, I don't mean any such thing, having a strong sense of reality to balance my highly colored imagination, but when I went to interview him the following morning he was most horribly hung and gave evidence of having had a private chat with Freda such as he had no opportunity to have during the rat race that was going on while we were there."

"Well, well, well!" said Kate.

They sat down in a booth in the taproom, and Jack gave the order for two whiskies with soda. "Beers," said Kate firmly. "This is not on the expense account."

"That's my little woman," said Jack, grinning idiotically.

"Don't be so possessive." Kate pushed her glasses up her nose and leaned on her hand. "Marks," she said pensively. "Leonard Marks."

"Shall I let you in on my secret theory?" asked Jack rhetorically. "I'm suspicious of that guy."

"*Him?*" said Kate.

"Yes," said Jack. "Him. Or *he*, as we used to say back at City College. Here's the story. I went to see him last Saturday morning, after a cold night spent on a sun porch where I was so adequately heated that I failed to catch even the slightest sniffle."

"Shut up," said Kate. "Go on."

"I said I wanted to get some dope on the poetry, which, as a matter of fact, was the God's truth—I wanted anything I could put down on paper that didn't include Molly Morrison."

Kate blushed. "You're very sweet," she said primly, "but just by the way, what ever happened to our Freda Cramm story? I mean, that seems a little more substantial than the poetry reading."

"Nothing at all, dear," said Jack grimly. "It went right into the waste basket. Mrs. Cramm has a nice hunk of *Messenger* stock. Embarrassing, isn't it?"

"Not to me!" said Kate hotly. "Why that's—"

"The way of the world," finished Jack. "Be quiet and listen to my story. I went to Marks' place, as I was saying, and found him green as an uncooked lobster. Hung? says I. Yes, says he, and promptly rushes off to shoot his cookies. So I went into his kitchen and fixed him a little remedy. He swallowed it, it stayed down, and I rose in his estimation. Then he began making mysterious noises around the subject of la Cramm."

"What sort of noises?"

"It was a little hard to make out. That she had made a lot of suspicious remarks to him about murder in general, and this murder in particular, and some sort of wild deduction that since the footsteps of the murderer couldn't be distinguished as either those of a man or a woman, therefore they must be those of a heavy woman. Beer!" Jack broke off irrelevantly.

"Beer!" said Kate, "What's that got to do with it?"

"You can't have beer! It has too many calories!"

"Why you—!" exploded Kate, looking about pointedly for something to shy at him.

But he signaled the waitress and ordered coffee for her with utter disregard of all her splutterings, and then proceeded calmly. "He was trying to pass the buck a little too hard. It sounded very phony. As a parting shot, I asked him what the paper was that he tore up on the porch. His reply was a rush to the bathroom."

"Maybe he really knows something about Cramm. Maybe he really has something on her."

"If he had something on her he would have either spilled it or have been more mysterious," said Jack, shaking his head. "He was trying very hard to make something out of nothing for some ulterior motive. I suspect him."

"Oh!" Kate disagreed. "Really, why do people always have to have the least likely person as a murder suspect? It's sort of a new development in logic, if you like."

"It makes the customers feel they're getting their money's worth, I guess. But I want to know what that paper was he tore up so carefully on the porch there."

"Probably an old cleaner's bill he found stuck on his coat. He's just the type that would be embarrassed about a thing like that. My money's on Freda Cramm. Look at her—she's a big battle-ax who could wield a poker—and please keep your associations to yourself—she's a woman of violent emotions, she hung around Boyle, she has no alibi—alibi! I forgot to tell you that Molly Morrison has an alibi!"

"No!" cried Jack. "What is it?"

"Well, it's the irony of fate, or something. Honey Sacheveral saw her in the corridor at Birnham between five-thirty and six the day of the murder. She couldn't conceivably have walked over to Boyle's place in time to have conked him."

"I should telephone old Knucklehead! I would, too, if I thought he'd reverse the charges for me," said Jack dazedly.

Kate clasped her brow. "Hoogle! Knucklehead! What a day! Who's Knucklehead, and is that really his name?"

"Naturally not, stupid! It's Smith, and he's my ex-boss."

"Well, gee," said Kate concernedly, "oughtn't you really? I mean, isn't it sort of a scoop? You'd probably get your job back."

"Yeah," said Jack, "and get stuck in it for the rest of my life. I believe in fate or something."

"Don't tell me you're now free to write the great American novel," said Kate suspiciously.

"Not at all," snapped Jack. "I'm just tired of being a sob sister, and also of administering digitalis to the entire staff every time the New Deal is mentioned."

"All right, dear," soothed Kate meekly.

Jack leaned across the table, grinning like a monkey. "Baby, you're wonderful."

"Fine," said Kate composedly. "Now I've been sweet for today and I'll have that beer if you don't mind." She collared the mug and deftly substituted the coffee cup in Jack's hand. He sighed resignedly and signaled the waitress.

"Everybody was concealing mysterious papers," mused Kate after a moment's silence. "Molly with her notebooks and Leonard with his cleaner's bill, or whatever it was."

"That was no cleaner's bill," said Jack. "Otherwise why did he scrape up the pieces after he'd already dropped them in the wastebasket?"

"Some unfashionable cleaner, perhaps," suggested Kate.

"You've got foam on your lip, and if you get on the scales tomorrow morning, you'll find out what you're doing to yourself. The trouble with you as a detective, baby, is that you get a preconceived notion of a character which you stick with through thick and thin, at the risk of tossing aside objective clues. You see Leonard Marks as a Caspar Milquetoast, and you refuse to even try to imagine him as a killer. You'll never make the homicide squad that way. You have to let your imagination play."

"Well," said Kate stubbornly, "I just can't see Marks as a killer. It's too unconventional. The notion of the unfavorable publicity would make him faint before he ever picked up the poker."

"Ah, but can't you bring yourself to imagine that in his breast there rages an uncaged beast? Even the rabbit will turn and snarl when cornered!"

"If there's a beast in his breast, a rabbit is just about the size of it. And rabbits don't snarl, Frank Buck, in my recollection they can't even squeak."

"I'd still like to know what that paper was."

"Why don't you search his tuxedo pockets?"

"Maybe I will."

"What I'd like to know—out of idle curiosity rather than detective spirit—is what those notebooks were that Molly had. I'll bet those were psychiatric documents."

"Classroom notes, probably."

"Honey said she carried them downstairs toward the back door. It sounded as if she were taking them to the trash baskets by the kitchen door. And she could ill afford to burn class notes when she was flunking four out of five subjects."

"Maybe she was taking them to the library or somewhere."

"Honey said she had no coat on."

"Well, she's got her alibi now, so it can't matter much."

"Oh, I know, I was just taking a psychologist's interest, in my amateur way."

Kate drained her glass and Jack looked at the clock. "It's ten of ten," he said. "We'll have to start back if I'm going to have a chance to kiss you before lights-out."

"O.K.," said Kate, roseate.

They shouldered their way back to the car through the blustery night and drove through the quiet empty streets to the quadrangle. There the new trees shivered in the blast, in spite of the protection of the neo-Georgian buildings. Now and then a hunched figure pedaled by on a bicycle, or a group of girls rushed by chattering and giggling. Inside Jack's car the heater gushed forth hot air. At ten-fourteen they drew apart, and Kate pushed the handle of the door. But Jack caught her face in one hand and forcibly turned her jaw toward him. She tried unsuccessfully to wiggle away. "Look at me," he said, and she deliberately shut her eyes. "Seems I'm in love with you."

There was a silence, in which a window rattled up in its frame and the electric bells in the dormitories could faintly be heard sounding curfew. Her jaw was beginning to hurt between his fingers. "Seems it's mutual," she said at last, and sliding out the door, ran into the house just as Miss Sanders was locking up.

THERE WAS a row of small, diamond-paned casement windows across the front of the room; the sun poured through them prodigally, illuminating towers of books piled on the floor, and suitcases set in a corner, empty, and ready to be stored in the cellar—or the attic, perhaps, depending on Miss Stone's custom. There was a kind of infantile joyousness in this morning to Hungerford. He found himself particularly sensitive to weather on all occasions; one way or another his mood was always intensified by the day. What he hated most were days of sun and shade, indeterminate, when, in the midst of glorious brightness, clouds passed across the sun and the spirit was dashed to earth even as it rose. Today the heavens were as clear as a blue glass bell; crystals of frost made ferns about the mullions of the windows. He whistled what was intended for a theme from a Mozart sonata as he worked at arranging his books in the book shelves where formerly Kevin Boyle's had stood. He wondered idly what had been done with Boyle's things, since he had no family. For sentiment's sake, there were one or two of Kevin's volumes he should have liked to own—a first edition of Yeats he had noticed. An issue of *transition* with a fragment of Joyce as it had first appeared. He would have liked to have one of these to finger, to say, Kevin Boyle chose these, owned these, thumbed these . . . In retrospect he was surprised at the violence of his feeling when he had first heard of Kevin's death. Now he felt sweetly mournful, for he had enjoyed the boy's company, but no more. Who was he to begrudge a man death, after all? The Mozart theme rose and rose in his head like a fine silver trickle of water in the bright steam-heated air, but his whistle cracked, only air came from between his pursed lips, as in his ear he followed the complications of sound and rhythm. He congratulated himself on owning the New York edition of James as he packed its faded rose and gold volumes evenly into the bottom shelf of one of the bookcases. His mother had given it to him on his fortieth birthday. She had always given the most beautiful sensitive presents in the world. That was an art, if you like. To make a study of those you love so delicately that you anticipate their desires before they are themselves aware of them. He had dedicated his book on James to his mother because it was in the truest sense her book—

somehow, without her gift, he thought he would never have written those pages, have come to love so passionately the high, pure, perverse *noblesse* of Milly Theale, the inflamed voyeurism that inundated *The Sacred Fount*. He had been passionately happy in the writing—passionately! He had found himself singing over and over fragments of an old hymn—

> *Amazing grace—how sweet the sound*
> *To save a wretch like me.*
> *I once was lost, but now am found—*
> *Was blind, but now I see.*

He knew of no better words to explain the passion of creation. It was like divine grace—whatever your virtues you could never be worthy of the joy of it. Each time it flowed was as miraculous as if it had never been before, would never be again . . . His face drew together and twitched sidewise in the tic. He straightened from his work and looked up into the blinding sun.

> *He who has eaten ambition*
> *Accepted it into his person*
> *Cannot un-eat or reject it. . . .*

There was an intent clumsiness about Kevin's words that expressed what had run as an undercurrent to his thinking. The proof of it all was the completeness of the dark when the light of his creativeness had been withdrawn—as if God had turned his head, and the light fell elsewhere . . . as if a shadow had crossed the sun, and the sun remained dim.

He stood up, the backs of his legs stiff from squatting, to light a cigarette. He looked at his mother's ormolu clock, now standing on Kevin Boyle's mantel where the colored postcard of van Gogh's young man in a straw hat had once stood. He remembered somebody saying once that where you found that picture you would find a homosexual, and he could see why that remark had been made—there was a kind of glow of narcissism on the sensitive face—but it certainly bore no reference to Kevin Boyle. He had had the kind of deep self-love that one might mistake for the prelude to—the other, but on the whole—no, it was not so. In spite of the overprotestations of potency. In spite of the role of professional erotic so ardently played. Sometimes he thought that perhaps Kevin Boyle was as pure as himself, though it was hardly probable that this could be. He thought that Kevin must have been pure and timid like some wild animal, making the camouflage of ordinariness, but underneath it primitive, and frightened, and wild . . .

His mind finally took in what the face of the clock was saying to him, and with a muttered, "God!" he went to the bathroom to wash the dust from his hands before going to class. He had fifteen minutes to spare, but he wanted to think over his lecture quietly for a space before plunging out to it. He sat down in the wing chair and riffled through the pile of folded papers that lay on the table beside it, held together by a rubber band. His reader had marked them and he should have looked them over. He skipped past the B's and C's, paused at an A-minus. He pulled it out of the pack, glanced at it. It was a paper on Hawthorne. It said very little that had not already been said better, but this seemed to be the aim of education as it was practiced on the eastern seaboard—and on the western and in the Dust Bowl, for all he knew—to enable the mediocre mind to paraphrase the wise and pseudo-wise. Well, this was no time for bitterness, when he was about to have to go look into their shining young faces . . . Damn it, he was in a good humor this morning! That he had moved—it seemed to prove that he was still capable of action, of decision . . . that he might become able to move again.

A knock sounded at his door. "Come in!" he called cheerfully.

The door, made of panes of frosted glass, opened, revealing Leonard Marks' putty face. "May I come in?" he asked hesitantly.

"Yes, come in, come in!" welcomed Hungerford. "I won't apologize for the mess. I didn't even try to begin putting things away yesterday."

"Of course," said Leonard nervously. "Naturally. I stopped by to see if I could lend a hand."

"That's awfully good of you, but I'm just about to leave for class," said Hungerford. "Are you going toward the campus soon?"

"Yes," said Marks. "I have an eleven o'clock too. But your clock is fast, I think. We have quite a little time. The College Hall clock just struck ten-thirty."

"In that case sit down," said Hungerford. "Have a cigarette."

Marks cleared himself a space on the book-crowded sofa and twitched a cigarette out of the pack Hungerford extended to him. His nervousness began to make Hungerford nervous. "Moving is hell," he said, trying to make some sort of start to set the younger man at his ease. "I'm taking it very slowly, like a convalescent. Yesterday, the actual removal of my belongings occurred. I saw them well strewn over the living room floor, paid the movers, and promptly went to sleep."

"You must have been pretty irritated by your caller," said Marks, smiling a little for the first time.

"Did you knock?" said Hungerford. "I'm terribly sorry, I didn't hear you. I sleep so foully at night that I always take a sedative in order to get a before-dinner nap. That seems to be my best sleeping time."

"Oh, no," said Marks. "I didn't knock. I thought you were probably fed up by then—I was going to, but then I heard your voices and went away."

"As a matter of fact, I was completely done in," said Hungerford, his mind wandering to the pile of papers. Oh well, they were marked—he would hand them back without reading them. He would like to be kind to this Marks, for some reason. He always made one think of the white rabbit in *Alice*—a furtive look of guilt behind his spectacles proclaimed his awareness that somewhere, always, some ever-avenging duchess was furious. "Yesterday I felt depressed as a boulder— fatigue, I guess. Today I am full of hope for the world—I go around congratulating myself on my courageous remove from one house to another over a prodigious space of four blocks."

"It's too bad you had to be bothered yesterday," said Marks shyly.

"If it were done when 'tis done, then 'twere well it were done quickly," said Hungerford banally. Suddenly a sense of confusion entered his mind. He wondered if he had quite un- derstood what Marks had said. "I mean, you were talking about my moving, weren't you?"

"Why, no," said Marks, with an embarrassed laugh. "I meant your caller. You must have been ready to kill her."

"But I had no caller," said Hungerford, his face suddenly drained of expression.

Marks blushed very red, his eyes watered, and he rose. "I'm sorry," he mumbled. "I didn't mean—" he made for the door.

"No! Don't go!" cried Hungerford sharply. "I had no caller. What made you think I did?"

"Oh please!" said Marks, "I didn't mean to be inquisitive."

Hungerford rose, too, and went toward him. "Don't be a fool, man," he said sharply. "Will you please sit down and tell me what gave you the impression that I had a caller?"

"Why, Mr. Hungerford," said Marks, clasping his hands nervously, "I heard her voice."

Suddenly his knees buckled, his face twitched violently, and Hungerford sat down again in the wing chair, his hands dangling between his knees.

"Oh, Mr. Hungerford!" cried Leonard Marks contritely. "It was probably just Miss Stone! What's the matter?"

"Sit down, Marks," said Hungerford dully. "Sit down, sit down! Listen, this is very important. Miss Stone was not here yesterday. This morning she came and apologized profusely for her negligence. It seems she had to go to a church meeting and couldn't oversee my moving, for which I was profoundly grateful. What makes you think this was a woman's voice you heard, and what time did you hear it?"

Leonard paused a moment, seeming to put his thoughts carefully in order so as to answer the questions exactly. "I came back from my last class," he said, "it's a five o'clock class. That means it was over at ten of six, and it takes me just about ten minutes to walk to here from Raleigh. I didn't speak to anyone on the way, so it must have been just about six when I got home. I came in the front door, and I thought I would look in on you and see if I could do anything for you. I—I thought—" he fumbled, "you might be willing to have supper with me. But I heard a woman talking inside, so I went to my rooms instead, thinking you'd have enough confusion with your moving, without two callers."

"Six," said Hungerford dully. "Six. Ordinarily I take my nap at six. Yesterday I was done in and lay down as soon as the movers had gone—at twenty minutes of, or so. I must have been completely out by six o'clock. It's a pretty heavy dose of sedative I take."

"You mean," gasped Leonard, fumbling his way back to the couch at last, "that somebody was in your apartment while you were asleep? Oh, Mr. Hungerford! Hadn't you—I mean, suppose—oughtn't you to tell the police?"

Hungerford did not answer, hearing only the meaningless outline of the words. He rubbed his hand across and across his forehead. At last he rose, warily, and went to a carton that stood in a corner beside the books. The string which had tied it hung loose about it. "I left it tied," Hungerford muttered. "I know I left it tied. And who would have known which—" But just as he had expected, the papers that filled it were disordered, as if someone had gone through them looking for something, and on top of them lay what he had carefully packed at the bottom, the limp, brown, cardboard notebook. He did not open it, but held it in his hand. Then he closed his eyes and began to shudder violently. He held the notebook at arm's length. "Look in it!" he ordered Leonard. "Look at it and see if there's an entry dated with yesterday's date!" He felt the notebook removed from his fingers, and buried his face in his hands.

"Mr. Hungerford," came Marks' questioning voice, "it's a journal—do you want me to—"

"Yes, yes," he said impatiently, "do as I say!"

"Yes, sir," Leonard's answer came to his ears, "there is."

"Oh, God!" said Hungerford.

"Oh, Mr. Hungerford, sir," Leonard Marks' pleading voice came to him in his darkness. "Please, sir, let me do anything I can! I'd do anything for you, anything—I can't tell you how much I've always admired you and your work! If there's *anything*—"

Yes, thought Hungerford, still standing among the towers of books with his hands over his eyes, there is something. You can listen. I have to tell someone. I can't go on alone with it—not if it's to follow me . . . "Listen," he said, "ever since the school year began, that journal has been turning up in my rooms. It's a form of persecution—read it if you like. It's horrible—maybe it won't seem as horrible to you as to me, but somehow it has grown into such a nightmare in my life—I don't know how to describe it. It disgusts me utterly. At first I thought it must be some student who held a grudge against me—though I couldn't think who, or why. Then—then—I didn't know. I don't know. It seems to be someone who hates me so utterly as to be indecent. A person who knows my most secret weaknesses. Each time I find it open again I wonder if she will not have discovered the most secret crime in my heart—the crime which would still be secret to me. It's a woman. She calls herself Eloise. She's insane. That's all I know." He took his hands down from his eyes, and leaning heavily on the corner of the table, on the back of a chair, he made his way back to his seat.

"But Mr. Hungerford!" cried Leonard Marks, the notebook clutched between his palms, his voice thrilling with horror, "why don't you show it to the police?"

"Look at it," said Hungerford wearily. "Glance through it. You'll see why I might not care to."

Hesitantly, Leonard let the notebook fall open, and began to read. His face blanched and his lips parted. "Oh," he said. "Oh." Then he slapped the book shut and rose from the sofa, came and leaned urgently over Hungerford's chair. "Look, sir. This can't go on. But now there'll be two of us to catch her. You must tell me everything—when she comes, how you think she breaks in, everything! Then we can set watches, the two of us, and catch her at it!"

Hungerford's muscles relaxed and he felt a sense of gratitude, even affection for the unattractive young man. "What can we do when we've caught her?" he asked.

"We can have the police on her for housebreaking. We—oh, we wouldn't have to show the notebook, sir! You could have me for a witness that it had existed, and just burn it!"

Hungerford lay back in the chair, exhausted, and looked up into Marks' eager face. He smiled faintly at the younger man's excitement.

"Oh, Mr. Hungerford," said Leonard, leaning down close to Hungerford, "I would do anything for you!"

SINCE THE reading, he did not know how he had lived with himself. It was not the things that he thought, somehow, but the things that he did not think, the things which lurked on the periphery of his consciousness, half-exposing themselves to his awareness, then fleeing back to the shadows of the unknown. And a good thing. For if they had come whole into the light, he should not have been able to bear them—this much he knew. They would have led him to such wholesale self-condemnation as no man can stand. He grouped them under the mass heading of having behaved like a fool, and strove to forget.

He could not forget. It was not how he had behaved. He had not behaved so very badly. Not so badly as many men behaved without harming themselves in the least. It was what he had *thought*. It was what he had dared—albeit tacitly—to *demand*. And she had known. She had looked right through his skull into his brain—he had no illusions about that. She had looked into his most secret hopes and ambitions, his most indecent considerations, with her wicked, x-ray eyes, and had allowed him to go on in his idiocy until she had no more use for him. Then, in a grand gesture of contempt, she had let him know what she had observed, stripped him bare, revealed his silliest delusions of grandeur, and left him derelict on the shore of his own self knowledge. Pipsqueak! she had cried.

And why? For what reason? For if he had behaved like a fool, her own behavior was open to some question. She had led him on. There was no reasonable, rational doubt but that at the first, at least, whatever it was that now shamed him so— his hopes of elevation, his dreams of affection—she had approved and fostered. Had she not asked him to read Kevin Boyle's poems? There were at least five other men in the department who could have read them as well as he. Had she not encouraged him to stay alone with her in her house when the others had left? What meaning had he been expected to read from that, but the obvious one, which she had subsequently so brutally denied? And when had it all changed—how had she become so different?

Are you lying? she had rapped out, rising on her elbows . . .

Lying about what? About whether Kevin Boyle had spoken

of her. Oh, was it not all becoming plainer and plainer? And now this latest. This horrible persecution of George Hungerford.

Leonard Marks' office was in the round tower of one of the older campus buildings; high, hideous, and pseudo-Gothic, it stood at the intersection of one of the campus drives with the little street of shops that ran downhill toward Miss Stone's. From his office window, Leonard could almost see his own roof, could watch the passers-by on the sidewalk of Witherspoon Street—girls jostling and pushing each other at the between-class interval, piling their bicycles like a heap of scrap metal in front of The Coffee Shoppe, or, during class hours, idling past the shop windows where feminine frivolities were displayed. It was four o'clock in the afternoon; dimly, at the edges of the day, twilight was creeping up the sky. Leonard was not sitting at his desk, but had pulled his straight chair to the window, where he sat surveying Witherspoon Street with a vigilant eye. Parked halfway down the narrow way was Freda Cramm's elaborate automobile. Freda herself he had seen disappear into The Coffee Shoppe a half hour ago. He was waiting for her to come out, although he was not sure what he would then do.

No doubt existed in his mind as to whose voice he had heard last night as he stood hesitantly outside Hungerford's door. It had come from far back in the room, so that the words it spoke were indistinguishable. But the tones could have belonged to no one he had ever known but Freda Cramm—low pitched, harsh, almost like a man's for deepness and decisiveness, yet poisonously feminine in their purring persuasion. Oh—the violence of his feeling made him rise from his chair—she was a bad woman! Yet he meant to be calculating and cool, not carried away by emotion. He sat down again.

Coolly and calculatingly he had considered it: it seemed to him ultimately probable that Freda Cramm had murdered Kevin Boyle. She had, he thought, been carrying on illicit relations with the young man. She had been afraid of indiscretions on his part, and had murdered him to shut his mouth.

Here a snag arose in the flow of his reasoning. Why should she fear indiscretion, loud-mouthed advocate of liberty and modernity that she was? Would one not have expected her to override—even to flaunt that sort of revelation? Leonard frowned, his eyes fixed unseeingly on the shining black car. He thought he had the answer. He thought he had hold of the explanation which, if one accepted it, made the premise of Freda as murderess quite tenable. This was that he had not been wrong in his drunken assumption on the night of the reading that under her free talk, Freda was a puritanical woman. He thought he could offer some evidence in behalf of this hypothesis. Otherwise, why had she repelled his own advances? Leonard straightened his glasses and smoothed his moustache to one side and the other. "I am quite," he said to the empty room in a tight voice, "an unrepulsive young man."

At that moment, in the street below, the door of The Coffee Shoppe opened, and a large flame-headed figure in a russet coat came out. Leonard started, and rose, for it was Freda. He did not know what to do—had not made up his mind. If she got in her car, there was no use following her. Impossible. Well, if she got in her car, he would go straight back to his own apartment and keep watch on Hungerford's door. But she was not crossing the street. She was walking straight down Witherspoon Street, lingering at shop windows. In a frenzy of decision, Leonard snatched up his hat and coat and sped down the stairs. There were three long flights; when he reached the street corner, the figure of Freda Cramm was out of sight. He stood panting at the corner, wondering which way to turn. Here Witherspoon Street formed one of the branches of a Y with Main Street the base, and Jeffery Street the other arm. If she had turned down the hill to Main Street, she was simply walking downtown—there was no use following. However, if she had turned up Jeffery, there was a lane she could take, leading straight through the back yards to Miss Stone's. At once he paced determinedly down Jeffery. If he could not see her, he could take the lane himself, give up the chase, and simply get washed for dinner. He would have covered all the possibilities of her reaching Hungerford's apartment unseen. It was, Hungerford had warned him, unlikely that another entry would appear in the journal for weeks. But Leonard did not mean to count on that. He meant to watch her every moment, to prevent its ever happening again, and somehow to expose the whole of her criminality by means of that vicious little manuscript. And he wished he had not said what he did about burning the journal. He thought that it should be preserved as evidence. He thought a handwriting analyst could undoubtedly prove the script to be Freda's, and that then it could be shown to have some bearing on Boyle's murder. He had not read more than the last passage in it, but Hungerford had told him that there was mention of Kevin Boyle earlier— incriminating mention. In any case, he could not entirely understand Hungerford's sensitivity about its being seen. It was vulgar, crass, even obscene, but the references to Hungerford did not appear so serious or shameful to Leonard as they seemed to have struck their subject. They reflected on the writer, after all, not on her innocent prey.

Jeffery Street curved down a hill. To the right was a row of dingy frame houses built at the turn of the century, styleless, graceless. To the left the hillside flowed away to the river bottoms, which were swampy and rush grown, now brightly sanguine with reflection of the evening sun. The sky was pink in the east, flamingo in the west, and overhead, a pale dusty blue. The day's wind had died, but chill was rising in the air. The sidewalk Leonard hurried down was empty except for himself, clear to the curve of the road. He came to the lane to Miss Stone's, where the houses began to be set far apart. Here for the first time he could see round the bend. At quite a distance he made out Freda Cramm, striding easily up the rise that came at the margin of the open farm land around the town. Leonard caught his breath and walked faster.

The houses were all left behind now; he followed the macadam road into the open country. The fields full of outcroppings of rock, the distant mountains, the occasional low-lying farms were all bathed in red evening light. It was a cold redness, cold and bleak, promising snow, although the sky was clear. It was an ominous unfriendly sort of light, not like the midwestern sunsets Leonard could recollect. Near his home, the farm land had been rolling and rich; here it was rocky and poor, stretching miserably to the foot of the Berkshires. The road wound away from the town, out over the flat fields; the macadam ended; a dirt surface began. The river disappeared in a thicket of willows off to the left. The road ran along flat and then began to climb. Far along it, growing dimmer as the

evening deepened, Leonard made out Freda, still stroking
along with a hiker's stride. He was a little winded himself, but
followed bravely.

The woods which had resembled sparse stiff hair on a re-
cumbent animal's side while the hills were in the distance, now
appeared as a heavy copse of saplings and second growth. The
road curved around the foot of the mountain, and Freda disappeared from Leonard's sight. He paused and panted. He had
lost sight of his objective—not only Freda, but why he was
following her. Now he was only consumed by a strange sense
of urgency that seemed to press on him from all sources, from
the bloody sunset, from the darkening woods on the mountain
slope, from the strange luminescence of the pebbly road as it
caught the slanting light. He began to walk faster and faster
until he almost ran around the bend at the foot of the mountain, but still Freda was nowhere to be seen. He felt a sort of
panic. How could he have lost her? Where had she gone? He
could imagine that he would run on and on this foolish way,
pursuing nothing but obsessed with the notion of his pursuit.
Then suddenly there appeared a break in the woods, and a
branch of the road rose up the mountainside. Gasping with
relief, he turned up it and began to climb.

In the woods, darkness had already begun. Darkness collected like a mist round the boles of the trees, rose in a vapor
from the dead leaves that carpeted the forest floor. Suddenly
there was a rustling, a small dark shape ran across the road.
Leonard started, and stood frozen for a moment before he
could reassure himself that it had only been a chipmunk, disturbed by his passing. As he paused he listened for footsteps,
wondering if he were within earshot of Freda. But he heard
nothing—nothing but a vast resounding silence, punctuated
by the small mysterious cracklings of the woods and their secret life. He pushed on, less and less knowing why.

Then suddenly, the air was lighter, the trees thinned, and
Leonard paused, for he could see that ahead of him the road
stopped at the edge of a clearing. Now that the woods had
come to an end, he felt disinclined to leave their protection;
prodded by he knew not what impulse, he struck away from
the road and through the trees, across the floor of leaves to the
edge of the clearing. There, standing a little behind one of the

few old trees in the wood, he looked out at the open field, at
the house that stood there, and at Freda Cramm, suddenly
close enough so that he could make out her features, sitting on
its doorstep.

The house was an ancient saltbox with a fanlight and the
date 1700 carved over its door. Half of the panes of the windows were gone; the rest, facing blindly westward, blazed
crimson into the sunset. Clapboards were warping away, paint
lay only in leprous patches over the walls, and a great black
wound gaped in the shingles of the roof. Freda sat on the only
remaining step of what had once been a flight of three leading
to the front door. She seemed to be staring out at the pan-
orama of river and valley that lay below her. As he watched a
shape detached itself from the woods at the other side of the
field, came streaking across the grass and leaped into Freda's
lap—an enormous tortoiseshell cat, whose head she touched
absently, and murmured.

It seemed to Leonard he had stood for years watching her
stroke the head of that cat and wondering what he was to
do—it seemed a mystery to him that night had not fallen in
the long, long moment of his watching. The strangeness was
too much for him; he could not bear it; he found himself
shaking and clutching the trunk of the tree. Then, without his
intention, the words formed themselves in his mind: I must
get away from here. He saw a star, shining tentatively in the
twilight. The sun was fading from the checkered glass panes of
the windows of the house. He took a step backward and trod
on a dry stick. Suddenly Freda Cramm rose, dropping the big
cat unceremoniously from her lap.

"I hear you!" she cawed out, standing like some big, golden
broody bird in the midst of that lonely place. "Come out of
the woods, there! I hear you!"

He could turn, he could flee, but behind him the woods
were dark and darker. Stumbling, he came out of the trees and
stood at the edge of the clearing, a distance from her.

"Come over here!" she commanded. "Come where I can
see you!"

Like a hypnotized animal, he crossed the desolate yard,
picking his way among the rusted tin cans, and stood before
her. She glared at him as he approached with eyes which

seemed to him as bright as hawk's or owl's. The cat wound it-self purring in and out around her ankles. "Well," she sneered, in her deep harsh voice, "it's little Mr. Marks—our Leonard!"

He was unable to speak, but only stared at her dazed, like a schoolboy caught in a misdemeanor. She set her fists on her hips and looked at him, tilting her head so that she seemed to look down at him, although actually they were of a height.

"Well," she said finally, "what are you doing here?"

He caught his breath. "What are *you*?" he piped.

She looked at him and cocked her head to one side. "I can't see how that concerns you."

The darkness was deepening. Freda's hair shone brazen, catching what little light was left. A chill came over Leonard —he felt himself facing a bare reality—he felt it was now or never; he must speak. "I followed you," he said, his throat dry. "I came after you. I don't know what you're up to, but I won't let you do it. You've done enough. You're a bad woman." His breath was coming fast.

"So?" she said expressionlessly. "How so?"

"Boyle," he said, scarcely able to speak. "Kevin Boyle. And now Hungerford. You leave Hungerford alone or you'll be sorry—I'll make you sorry!"

He thought he saw the shadow of a malicious smile hover on her face. "So you think it was Boyle and then Hungerford," she said. "Oh, my little Leonard Marks!" She seemed to swell and tower over him in the darkness. "Do you know what happens to little peeping Toms like you? Do you know what happens to bad little boys?" She put her face close to his, her lips drawn back from her teeth. He could distinguish each golden blot in the saddle of pale freckles across her nose. The gentle prettiness of her small features was horrifying to him in combination with the malevolence of her expression. She leaned over him as if she had grown taller as she stood there; it seemed to him her hands were moving upward, gauging the roundness of his throat. His knees began to tremble—he imagined her brandishing the poker, striking upward to the base of Kevin's skull. All at once something pressed against his leg, as if hands were reaching up from the ground to pinion him, hold him fast. He gave a wild shameless yell, spun around and ran, kicking the cat in this flight. After him rang the shrill laughter of Freda Cramm, pur-

suing him through the trees, resounding in the darkness as if to
warn him of the hopelessness of escape.

He ran and ran, blindly, stumbling in the ruts of the uneven
road. He could see nothing, he only trusted the feel of the
ground under him. The road through the wood stretched
endlessly—it seemed the trees would never end. Just as he
thought he must fall down for want of breath, his hip struck
something with a metallic sound, he doubled over with pain,
and a hand took his elbow. "Here, here," a voice said softly.
"What goes on?" It was Donelly, the reporter, beside his car.
In a frenzy of relief, Leonard threw his arms about him, like a
French diplomat honoring a hero.

D R. FORSTMANN had made arrangements to have one of the doctor's offices in the Infirmary in which he could see Molly Morrison. The nurse had gone for her. He sat looking over her charts. Her temperature had been normal for two days; nausea had ceased, crying fits during the day had given way to lethargic depression. Sedative still administered at night. He wondered what was to be done with the girl. It seemed unlikely she could continue her college work. He doubted that the family could pay for a sanitarium, and sending her home appeared to him the least advisable course of all. It seemed very strange that the mother had not answered Miss Sanders' letter with some show of concern, but there had been no word from her. He heard footsteps in the corridor and rose. Molly knocked and came in. Her hair hung lankly in oily strands. Her face was white, her lips pale. There was a stain on her sweater, as if she had spilled food. "Hello, Molly," he said, and smiled.

"Hello," she answered dully, her face unmoving. She went to the couch and lay down, like an animal moving mechanically to its stall. Then she pulled something out of the pocket of her skirt, raised herself on one elbow and held it out to him. It was a letter. "Here," she said. "I got this this morning. Read it."

He took the letter and she sank down on the couch.

Dear Molly: [he read], A week or so ago I had a communication from your housemother from which I made out that you were down with something which she vaguely describes as "mental disturbance." I trust you will have become undisturbed again by the time this letter reaches you. It seems to me that you are hardly in a position to allow yourself the luxury of a nervous breakdown, if that is what you have in mind, since your staying in college depends on your scholarship, and the continuation of your scholarship depends on your academic standing.

He stopped reading for a moment and glanced at Molly. She was twisting her hands together, her eyes were closed. He glanced at the envelope, at the postmark, almost to reassure himself that she had not written the letter herself—it fitted almost too perfectly with her expectations of persecution. He had to remind himself that this was the mold in which those expectations had been cast.

    . . . As you are aware, after twenty years of marriage to your father, I am not so inclined to be sympathetic with this sort of "disturbance" as I might once have been. There are always people in the world who can make their moods the excuse for failure and irresponsibility. There are others who are unable—or unwilling—to indulge quite the same moods, because they refuse to make themselves a burden on those around them. You are no longer a child who can lie on the floor and have temper tantrums. If you try to do so, you will find yourself in the embarrassing position of simply being allowed to kick and scream and make as much of a fool of yourself as you like.

    I have kept your housemother's letter from your father. I do not wish to trouble him with it, as there seems to be some chance of his getting one of the post office murals after all, and I do not know what this kind of upset might provoke him to do.

    As I reread this letter, I am aware that you may find it cold and harsh. I must confess frankly that I feel no sympathy for you, only deep irritation. I have lived in poverty and sordidness because of your father's highfalutin notions of his art, being the one who scraped and met the creditors while he indulged his soul. I would feel that I had failed my duty as a mother if I encouraged you in a path which, for the twenty years I have watched your father follow it, has brought nothing but misery to both of us. The scholarship at Hollymount is your chance at some better kind of life than your parents have known. I will not have you pass up an opportunity of that life.

    I am concerned for your welfare only, Molly.

                      Mother

He folded the letter and returned it to its envelope. "Well?" he said.

"Well," she repeated dully.

"Tell me how the letter made you feel," he said.

"How would it have made you feel?"

"Why," he considered, "if I were you, it might have made me feel in one of a number of ways. I might have been very angry at it. I might have been hurt. I might have thought she was right."

"Oh," she said desolately. "You think she's right!"

"No," he said immediately, "I think she's wrong. Because I don't accept the premises and standards from which she argues. But try to tell me how you felt about it, Molly. Tell me how it was when you got the letter—how you felt when you opened it—from the beginning."

"From the beginning?" she said. "Oh . . . well. Miss Justin said I could get up this morning. She said did I want my breakfast in bed. I said I'd get up and dress first. So I did. Then she brought my breakfast on a tray. I was sitting on the chair with the tray on my lap when she brought the letter. She said, You have a letter from your mother. Then I spilled the egg on my sweater." She put her hands over her eyes and began to cry, sobbing without sound, but violently, so that the convulsions shook her body.

"Why does that make you cry?" he asked softly.

"She hates me!" she cried, her voice suddenly loud. "She always hated me! She never would admit it—she was always saying how she loved me! But nothing I ever did ever pleased her—ever! I used to pretend I'd been invited to somebody's house for meals and then go without because she nagged me so. She always said I was sloppy, and I knew she would be watching me to see me spill something, and then I would. I know you think that's silly, I know it's silly, but I can't help it, I can't help it!" She was gagging and gasping, hysterically. He said nothing, at last her sobbing subsided. "Once she found my diaries," she said finally. "That was the worst, I think. I always wrote in them when I was angry with her. I tried to say all the things she would hate most. I tried to describe her the way she was—so cold and accusing and inhuman. I tried to write her so that she would be ashamed to read it if she ever did. She did, all right. But she wasn't ashamed. She just got that terrible cold look on her face. She held the book out to me, and she said, Is this yours? as if it were some stranger's hat she'd picked up in the street. But she wouldn't give it to me. She showed it to my father. She never said anything about it. She never said a word. She just looked at me—just looked at me—as if I were beneath contempt." She had begun to cry again. "And then she took it out on him. She knew that would hurt me most. I heard them in the night. Oh, I hate her so!" She was caught in another convulsion of weeping and could not speak. When she was quieter, she said tensely: "She'd kill me if she dared. Do you know that? I've seen her looking at me as if she were—were taking the measure of my throat—to choke me!"

"Do you really think that's true, Molly?" he said quietly.

"Oh," she cried, "you don't believe me, I knew you wouldn't, but it's true all the same! She wished I'd never been born, and then she could have left my father and married someone who would have made lots of money! But she couldn't bring herself to leave me, too—she couldn't forget her Presbyterian up-bringing to that extent! She couldn't leave me, so she stayed and tortured me the rest of her life! I tell you, she would have liked to kill me!" She paused, drew a grubby handkerchief from her pocket, blew her nose and wiped her eyes. "She was always saying my father was a failure. She never could see he was a great painter—a really great painter! He is! She was al-ways talking about how we lived, how it was so sordid, how he didn't care enough about his family to support us—I don't care! I don't care! He's a great man. It didn't matter if we did live sordidly if he could paint! I'm not ashamed!"

He looked at his watch. "Your way of life may have seemed sordid to your mother because the kind of rewards it offered weren't within her understanding. I imagine from what you say that she doesn't care a great deal about painting."

"Oh, she doesn't, she doesn't!" cried Molly eagerly. "She pretends she does! She used to teach art appreciation in high school before she met my father. Art appreciation! *How* she can talk about brushwork and impasto and chiaroscuro! But just ask her what a painter is saying, or what his work means! Just ask her! She looks as if you'd asked some question that was be-tween obscenity and stupidity . . ."

"Molly," he said, "I want to talk to you a little about plans. Have you thought at all about what might be best to do?"

"Best to do?" she said in a frightened voice. "What do I

have to do? Will I have to leave? Do I have to go back to Birnham? Do I have to go home?"

"You don't want to do either of those things, do you?"

"No, no, I don't, I don't!"

"Your mother's right about one thing, Molly," he said. "It would be a shame to lose your scholarship. I thought of this. I think that in a while you may feel ready to go back to Birnham—but I don't want you to go back before you do feel absolutely ready. I shouldn't like to think of you staying at the Infirmary and doing nothing at all, seeing no one. Dr. Abby tells me that there's a clerical job open that you could do for an hour or two a day if you liked. The rest of the time you could try to get caught up in your school work a bit, and maybe do some painting. And I want you to get out and take a walk once in a while. Talk a little to the other girls in the Infirmary. I won't put you in a ward, but wander around and chat, if you can."

"They don't want to talk to me," she said sullenly.

He leaned forward in his chair. "They have nothing either for or against talking to you," he said. "They will like to chat with you as much as with any other chance acquaintance they make, because they happened to have caught grippe at the same time. You have a great deal to offer, Molly—an unusual background, and an unusual knowledge."

"Very unusual," she said bitterly.

He ignored her. "And get some air. Would you like to do some outdoor sketching?"

"No," she said. "I don't want to go out. I don't want to walk."

"Why not?"

This time there was no sobbing, but the tears began to leak slowly from her eyes. "I want to be very still. I don't want to move myself. When I move, it's like dragging a great stone. I don't want to look at a lot of things. I don't want to look down streets. I want to look at small areas, like my hands, or a page of paper. You know where I like it best? I like it in corridors, when there's nobody there. A corridor is nowhere. It's just a between place. Nothing can happen to you there."

"What are you afraid of having happen to you, Molly?" he asked.

"I don't know," she said. "I don't know."

SHE HAD made the decision. She had been very brave. She had been brave almost beyond her own power. She had taken her coat and scarf and put them on. She had walked to the front door. She had opened it. "Where are you going, Molly?" Miss Justin had cried from the desk, with hygienic cheer. "For a walk," she had answered. For a walk. She had stepped out on the stoop. She did not look down the street, she only looked down at her brown moccasins, her tan socks, her cold bare legs. She watched her own feet walking down the brick walk. She was very tired. She walked slowly and dragged her feet. She was cold, too. Her teeth chattered and her muscles contracted against the wind. She heard a group of girls pass on the other side of the street. She did not look up from her feet. She heard them begin to laugh. They were laughing at her, at what a fool she was, walking there all hunched over with cold, looking at her feet. A lunatic. In the Infirmary because she was crazy. But she wasn't really. If she had been really crazy there would have been some excuse. She was just indulging herself, saying: I can't stand it, when what was really true was that she wouldn't try hard enough. But something had to be worth trying for. You couldn't try in a vacuum, try for nothing. Now she had something to try for—something to take a walk for. She knew where she was going. It took a great deal of courage, but courage was what she must force herself to have. Oh, how she despised the coward that she was!

It was getting to be evening. The winter sun was nearing the horizon, salmon colored among violet clouds, promising snow. For a moment Molly looked up from the ground; it seemed to her the world was turned to a vast, ominous, but beautiful dream landscape. The white frame houses took on a luminousness in the evening light, standing on their drab dead lawns among the skeletons of trees. She had reached the corner and turned out of the side street. Now there were a few more passers-by, bundled against the cold, intent upon their secret errands. And she knew that, as in a dream, though their faces seemed strange to you, you knew that somehow they were your enemies; secretly they peeped at you from under their eyelids, from over their furs, and mentally noting your appearance, your patent guilt, they hurried on with news of your treason to the great mysterious one who held your fate in the hollow of a palm, who totted black marks against you, and would at last pounce, strike . . . She walked faster, hearing footsteps behind. If she walked quickly, got to where she meant to go, warmed herself with a fire, perhaps, and talked—the kind of talk she longed for so, then everything would not seem so threatening and evil.

She recognized the house, set back on its lawn with a dark antique elegance. For a moment when she first saw the iron Saint Bernard, she was stricken with a new fear, thinking that it was real, and she would have to pass it. But as it continued to stand so still, with one paw raised, she saw it was only a statue, and let her breath puff out, milky on the cold air. Now she was close enough to see the lamp gleaming amethyst and ruby through the colored glass panes of the front door. The house towered above her, high and stern, with its flat roof, its beetling eaves, its cupola. It seemed to hold her at a distance, to ask her business. Her heart pounded, she could not catch her breath. "Courage!" she whispered to herself, and turned up the walk. The bell at the high double door was the sort you have to pull. At last she found the trick of it, and heard it pealing, far back in the hollow reaches of the house. Oh please . . . she prayed. She waited a long, long time before footsteps sounded within, far away and slow, then closer and shuffling. Finally the door opened and an old, old woman peered out. She said nothing, but stared at Molly, as if she, too, were participating in the dream.

"Please," said Molly faintly, after a long silence, "is Mr. Hungerford . . . ?"

Still the old woman did not answer, but stood there staring at her in the twilight. At last it seemed true—this was a nightmare, the horror was about to come. Then the old woman spoke. "Well, Miss, speak up!" she said sharply.

Don't be a fool, said Molly to her pounding heart. She's only deaf! "Is Mr. Hungerford in?" she said loudly.

"Doesn't live here any more," said the old woman flatly, and began to close the door.

"Oh, please!" cried Molly, "can you tell me where he lives?"

The old woman drew the door a little farther open again.

"He moved over to West Street," she said grudgingly. "He moved in where that young man lived who got murdered. I don't recollect the number." And closed the door.

She had to stop and press her mittened hands against her breast, standing there on the high step, panting in the cold. He lived at Kevin Boyle's house . . . He had moved there . . . It was beautiful—like a gift! Now she could go, could ring his bell, could go in the room where he had stood, had lain . . . lain dead. She ran down the steps lightly before her weariness caught up with her again. She crossed the street and took the short cut down the hill toward where she knew so well.

As she walked toward Kevin Boyle's house she had no choice but to think of the thing that had brought her out—out of her hole. It was a strange thing, something new, something she could not understand, something terrible, a new kind of death. In the last days she had forgotten Kevin Boyle.

She had forgotten the way he looked. Or how it felt to walk to The Coffee Shoppe with your heart exploding like electric shocks because you did not know if he would be there. Or how it was in class, watching him talk, seeing the way his hands moved. She could remember *that* it had been, but *how* it had been was gone.

The thing that had come over her had begun with grief, but it had been worse than grief, worse than any live pain. It had been like a stone on her heart, a negation of life, of love. She began to wish fiercely that she could feel grief as she had felt it in those first days after his death, but even the memory of the sharpness of it was gone from her. Grief had been a thing like love—clear, and with a certain purity. What had come over her was allied only to death. Depression, Dr. Forstmann would say, who always had the word for everything. Almost she could hate him too, though he was her only friend. Sometimes she felt that if she had not talked to him she might have preserved the beauty of her grief and kept the life from running from it. Now she had two things to mourn—the death of Kevin Boyle and the death of her grief. And since the first was irreparable, it seemed the second was the harder to bear. She would not, *could* not bear it. So she had tried to think of what would be a restorative for her dead grief. She thought if she had a picture of him . . . but she could not think where she would get

one. Or a letter he had written—just some impersonal thing
. . . but that was just as hard. And then the perfect thing had
come to her. A poem. Just a copy of one of his poems. And she
knew where she could find that, too. Only—how many ages
ago?—two weeks ago she had heard him tell, sitting in the
booth at The Coffee Shoppe, Mr. Hungerford was reading his
book of poems, was kind enough to offer to submit it to his
publisher. Mr. Hungerford. He had a kind sad face. And a
poem. A poem was like a painting. In it you said a thing so
dear and tender and secret you could not venture it straight
out in plain words . . . If anything could revive her dead
grief, it would be Kevin Boyle's poem. She had begun to long
and long for it. Longing had made her brave. Longing had
drawn her out . . .

It seemed strange to her to see the college girls pushing
their bicycles up the hill past her, or walking in long striding
steps. A long time ago she had been one of them—in name at
least—sharing their common routine, their meaningless activities. What meaning could they have? To go in a library, to
look in a book, to write words on a paper . . . Was that life?
Was that any sort of preparation for life? Once in her father's
studio there was a young man with a beard, one of the wild-
talking ones who made her want to hide for not knowing what
to say. "What do *you* do for a livelihood?" he had asked, looking down his crooked nose patronizingly, stroking his too thin
beard. "I—I'm going to college in the fall," she had stammered. Suddenly he began to pace around the studio as if he
had gone mad. "College!" he had cried. "Education! All they
care for is knowledge—all knowledge and no wisdom!" At
that moment she had scorned him, had heard her mother's
voice speaking in her own thoughts, saying, Why do artists
think they have to behave like maniacs? Yet he had been right.
That was all that was here. Knowledge, and no wisdom. Now
that Kevin Boyle was dead . . .

She was at the corner of West Street. There was a hedge full
of red berries, running along by the walk. Then the house.
What was she to say? Yet she must speak. She had come so far
. . . She would blind herself to everything . . . She could
scarcely gasp air into her lungs as she plunged round the corner, ran up the steps onto the porch. His name was still on the

mailbox on the card tacked over the bell. She pushed it desperately, and closed her eyes. She heard the door open and looked quickly. There was Mr. Hungerford, his thick gray hair rumpled, his tie loosened, his face haggard. "Yes?" he said, in a strange, faraway voice. Now she was here. Now she must begin.

"Mr. Hungerford?" she said. But of course she knew him. "I'm Molly Morrison. I'm the girl who . . ." but she trailed off, not knowing how to say, I'm the girl whose name was in the paper, I'm the girl who confessed to murdering Kevin Boyle, only it wasn't true, I'm the girl. . . .

"Oh," he said, "yes, of course. Come right in."

Now she knew it was a dream. This was the strangest thing of all. He acted as if he had been waiting for her, as if he had known she was coming. *Of course what?* she wanted to demand of him. But she followed him into the dim hall. This was not a nightmare part of the dream. This was a warm good part. This was the way she would have wished to be welcomed to Kevin Boyle's rooms, as if she belonged there, as if it were natural that she should come.

French doors with glass panes opened off the hall. One of them stood ajar. Preceding her, Mr. Hungerford stood in the entrance and said, "Won't you come in?" She followed him. He turned to her. His face seemed very tired and very kind and very sad. "Excuse the mess," he said. "I'm not properly moved in yet. I was just lying down for a moment." He passed his hand across his eyes. "Then you rang, and I was glad. I couldn't sleep. I can't seem to sleep here—not any more."

She stood clutching her hands together in front of the dying fire. For the first time in days, feeling assailed her heart, as if a half-healed wound had broken, and warm beautiful blood were pouring out once more. She saw everything with terrible intensity, as if each object were surrounded by a ring of light. It was Kevin Boyle's room she was standing in—where he had stood; perhaps where he had died. And Mr. Hungerford there, his face hanging in such weary and despairing folds . . . How she knew that look! How she had lived with it! It was her father's look, standing at the easel, his brush dropped to the floor, staring out the dirty panes of the slanting skylight . . . "Can't you work?" she asked softly.

"Oh," said Mr. Hungerford, a sudden little smile of surprise lighting one corner of his mouth, "that. No. Not for years. My God, child, how did you know?"

She tossed her head in embarrassment. "I just knew."

"Here," he said, "take your coat off. Pull up to the fire. Get warm. Are you one of my students? To tell you the truth, I don't yet know one face from another."

Then she grew cold again inside. No, it was not a dream. It was only a mistake. He thought she was one of his students. She must tell him at once, even if then he would not like her any more. Her face contracted with anxiety. "No," she said, "I'm not one of your students. I'm—I mean—I—" and against all her most fervent intentions, she began to cry. She put her mittens up to cover her face.

"Oh, my goodness, child!" she heard his worried voice saying. "Don't cry. Just tell me what it's all about. You're very welcome, you know. You don't have to be one of my students to call on me!" he gave a little laugh. "I'm delighted to have a strange young woman in . . . my . . ." His words trailed off strangely. She took her hands down from her tear-smeared face. He was looking off into space as if something were behind her shoulder, as if he were haunted. Again her heart grew hot with pity for him.

"Mr. Hungerford," she said reassuringly, sniffling at the remains of her tears. "Is it embarrassing for you to have me here? I'll go away. I didn't know students weren't supposed—"

"My goodness, no!" he said, with heartiness to counteract her sadness. "Take your coat off like a good girl and tell me what it is you want." He put his hand to the knot of his tie and pulled it closer. "Tell you what," he pushed on, "this is really against rules—to offer a student alcohol, but let's have a glass of sherry—by now we both need it." He did not wait for her answer, but took a decanter from the top of a bookcase, and filled two of the glasses that stood by it. She took off her coat and laid it on the couch, then sat down on a stool by the fire, pushing close to the warmth. She stared at the hearth. On these bricks Kevin Boyle had lain. His blood had flowed here. And the truth was . . . The truth was she had forgotten him. Her heart had gone dead. In all the confusion, the drugs, the confession, the weepings to Dr. Forstmann, she had lost the wood in the trees. Nothing was about her but the confusion of the trees of her thought—her mother, her father, the shame of living among the girls at Birnham, Miss Justin, Miss Sanders, the newspaper reporter, the policeman—she wanted to make a sweep of them! She wished she could take a wet cloth and wipe her mind clean as a blackboard. She wanted to go back—go back to the sense of her love. She had lost her love—first she had lost Kevin Boyle, and then her love for him. The second loss was more desolate than the first. The first was human and bearable, in a terrible way. The second she could not stand. She could not bring back Kevin Boyle, but she must bring back her love for him . . . "Here's your sherry," said Mr. Hungerford's voice.

She looked up at him, almost startled, and took the glass. "Thank you," she said.

He pulled forward the chair opposite her and sat down. "Now," he said, raising the glass in silent toast before sipping of it. She sipped too, staring at him. His face was so drawn, so weary. And there was a strange indecency about seeing him with this streaked gray hair, usually so smooth, disarranged. He moved his lips together in little mumbling motions, like an old man. "What's your name?" he asked kindly. "I'm afraid I didn't listen when you told me before."

"Molly Morrison."

He looked at her, waiting for her to go on, she knew, but she was unable . . . "What class are you—shall I call you Miss Morrison, or Molly?"

"Oh, Molly, of course," she said, her tongue suddenly loosened. How kind he was! He seemed—he seemed so much more human, more understanding—something . . . "I'm a Freshman. I was in—I was—" she wanted to say she had been in a class of Kevin Boyle's, but her voice faltered and broke.

"And you aren't in any of my classes, but you came to see me—is it a guessing game?" There was an edge of asperity in his voice at last. His patience was going to end in a moment. She gathered herself together frightenedly. She did not know what to say, though—how to begin. She couldn't just ask him baldly.

"I've been in the Infirmary," she said abruptly. "They seem to think—I've been acting—they think I'm rather unbalanced."

But she did not want to give him a false impression. "I may be, you know," she said earnestly.

Suddenly he laughed, startling her. For a moment she thought her heart had stopped at the thought that he was laughing at her. Then he looked at her, very, very kindly. "That makes a pair of us, Molly," he said. "We should be friends, alone together in this neurasthenic garden spot."

She did not know what he meant, except that they had something in common, and he looked so very kind, so very sad. "I didn't mean to be," she said, saying at last to him what she had wished to say to all of them. "I wanted everything to go right when I came to Hollymount—I wanted to be different, to make people like me, not be shy. But then it wasn't, and I couldn't seem to make it change—they hated me, and laughed at me, and then when—when Mr. Boyle died—" She had done it again. She had begun to cry. She put her face down in her hands and let the tears trickle through her fingers. She cried a moment in silence. Then suddenly she heard a glass crash on the bricks of the hearth, and looked up, all tear-stained as she was.

She had heard the girls talk about the way his face twitched sometimes—how he would have to stop dead in the middle of a lecture to wait for it to be over—but she had not known it was as bad as this. The whole side of his face was drawn together in the most grotesque way—it was so strange and horrifying it almost shocked you to laughter. She saw his hands were shaking, and the sherry glass lay in fragments on the hearth. She felt terribly terribly sorry—she almost had risen to touch him, to comfort him—when suddenly the dream was back. Inwardly she shook herself, she implored herself not to let it come again, but inexorably—as inexorably as if she were asleep—she felt its atmosphere closing in. The warmth of the fire, the warmth of the sherry, the warmth of Mr. Hungerford's kindness—all evaporated until her very bones were shuddering with cold at the knowledge that she was alone in a threatening world, a room in which each object of furniture conspired against her. Outside unknown pursuers were closing in; wicked enemies were ambushed behind the berry-red hedge, and here inside, even Mr. Hungerford, even with his kind sad face, his tragic tic, his trembling hands, his hopelessness . . . She should never have come out. She should have stayed in the safe white room at the Infirmary, where she lay like a corpse, with Miss Justin and Dr. Forstmann praying at her wake. She got to her feet nervously. "I came," she said, because she must get it out at once, "because I heard him—I heard Mr. Boyle say once you had some poems of his. I came to ask—I came—" She was shaking all over, uncontrollably.

On the other side of the fire, Mr. Hungerford got to his feet. Was it true that he was shaking too, or did she only imagine it was so because she shook herself? In any case, his face had not relaxed from its contorting grip, it stared at her gargoyle-like. Impossible to separate true from false—was he glaring at her, or did her fear read anger into kindness? Then suddenly it seemed to her something strange had happened to him. The tic left his face, but left it different, slacker, in strange new lines. His posture changed; everything was different, because of what she imagined she saw. She thought, quite carefully, I am going mad. She thought she must pick up her coat and scarf and leave here before she lost her mind in front of Mr. Hungerford—as if she had to get to the bathroom before throwing up. She knew it was madness now because suddenly, instead of the sad worn intelligence so like her father's that had first clothed his face, she now saw on his features the fierce peering cruelty of her mother—the slack jowls, the drawn brow . . . She slung her coat over her shoulders, mumbling foolishly, keeping her eyes on him, trying not to let him notice. "I'll just—" she said. "I'd better go now, I don't—I'm not feeling very—you'll excuse . . ."

It was useless. Whatever it was that had been holding her together snapped loudly, like a log on the fire and he— she—Mr. Hungerford—her mother—who?—took a step forward, hands raised, the way she had always feared. "Why," said a strange voice, a voice she had never heard before, coming from she knew not where, "you little—it was you—" She closed her eyes to shut herself in darkness. Hands were at her throat as she had always known they would be. Her own hands were wresting at them—or was it her own hands at her throat? A fingernail drew a thin line of pain over her wrist. Back and forth she was battered, like a boat in a storm, battered by waves, caught in undertow—what? "Oh, Mr. Hungerford!"

she gasped. She wanted to say she begged his pardon, but she had no breath.

Then at last she was loose. Something had fallen to the floor—someone—an inert lump. She could not stop to see what it was. It might even be herself lying on the floor there. She flung open the door and fled. The cold night air tore in her lungs. And all the time she ran she was thinking foolishly, He'll never believe me. Meaning Dr. Forstmann. Meaning she was mad.

THE FIRST snow of the season was floating down through the blue air, catching pinkness from neon signs, yellow from shop windows. It lay in unmelted crystals in Kate's hair, gently removing the curl. She blew an upward blast at her forelock to send it out of her eyes, and passed through the glass door of the Harlow bar. Stanislas was, as usual, morosely mopping, but Jack was nowhere to be seen. She pushed on to the gloom of the taproom, where Jack promptly popped out of a booth as soon as she crossed the threshold. "Hello, gorgeous," he said, winking elaborately, "we've got company."

When she came around the back of the booth, she perceived Mr. Marks, drooping low over the table, hiccuping gently. "Good God!" she said, *sotto voce*, clutching Jack's arm, and then loud politely, "Good evening, Mr. Marks."

"Mum mum mum," said Leonard Marks indistinguishably, then suddenly straightened and threw his arms wide. "Good evening," he enunciated, clearly and loudly. Then he relapsed to his former posture. "Mum."

Jack gave Kate a rather hideous wink, and summoned the waitress. "Mr. Marks seems to have a bit of dope on the murder," he said.

"Oh, now listen," said Kate, "fun's fun, but do you have to go digging up old dead murders *every* night? I'm sick to death of it."

"Climbing and climbing," muttered Leonard, looking cross-eyed. "Following and following. Up, up, up. Black as the pit. Like wrestling with Lucifer!" he slumped a little lower.

"Wrestling with Lucifer!" whispered Kate, not quite sure how near to the surface of consciousness Leonard was. "What in hell is he talking about?"

"Beers," said Jack to the waitress, "and a highball for the gentleman. Lucifer, in this instance, is la Cramm. Just keep listening, pet, and a very interesting saga will be unraveled— has been about three times already, and each time it starts over, it has a little something added. He's still holding something back, I don't make out just what."

"If that's the case," said Kate, "for heaven's sake get him coffee, not whisky, before he's out like a light. Look at him!"

Leonard's face leaned closer and closer to the initial-carved

343

table top, a look of utter despair spread over it. "Venusberg!" he said suddenly and distinctly. "The temptress! The whore that sitteth upon the waters!" His eyelids drooped.

"By golly!" cried Jack, suddenly recognizing the danger, and slid out of the booth to run after the waitress.

Suddenly Leonard hoisted himself a notch and looked straight though blearily at Kate. "'Thy ruddy breasts, thy rosy thighs, thy snowy flesh incarnadine!'" he remarked.

Kate turned perfectly scarlet and edged toward the end of the booth. "I beg your pardon?" she inquired desperately.

"The whore that sitteth on the waters!" pronounced Leonard again, and slumped lower.

Jack reappeared, carrying the cup of coffee himself. "Here you are!" he cried briskly. "Swallow this down fast, and you'll feel like a new man!"

"The guilty flee where no man pursueth!" mumbled Leonard, but toyed with the handle of the cup.

"Quick!" cried Jack. "Drink it up!"

Obediently Leonard drank the whole cup down, steaming as it was. Then he passed his hand across his eyes, reeled slightly. A sweat erupted visibly on his brow.

"Let me get this straight again," said Jack, businesslike. "You were following Mrs. Cramm and she *attacked* you, you said?"

"Oh, Mr.—uh—Mr.—uh—well, I really forget your name, but not in the ordinary newspaper sense of the word, I assure you!" cried Leonard earnestly, leaning across the table and swaying gently. Kate recoiled a bit.

"Well, just how *do* you mean?" pressed Jack.

"Oh," groaned Leonard, "it all began that dreadful night, that dreadful, evil night!"

"Which night?" chorused Jack and Kate.

Suddenly Leonard's eyelids went down to half mast again. "Watch it!" cried Kate, but amazingly, Leonard shot to his feet and pressed his right hand to his left breast.

> Thy ruddy breasts, thy rosy thighs, thy snowy flesh
>   incarnadine—
> Oh nymph, thou art a pearl, I'm swine!

he declaimed vociferously, and collapsed again, staring vacantly into his empty coffee cup, the sweat forming in little rivulets on his temples.

"Oh, Jack!" cried Kate. "That's the second time!"

"Baby," said Jack, "it's the first for me. Would you mind repeating that, Marks?"

Suddenly, dismally, Leonard's countenance was contorted as by a drawstring, and, in addition to the perspiration, two tears brimmed over his eyelids. "Oh," he sniveled, "I'm so ashamed! Please forgive me, Miss—ah—Miss—ah—please forgive me! I'm just drunk, that's all, disgracefully, disgustingly drunk!" And he sobbed bitterly.

"Not at all," said Kate, reassured, "I'm very interested. Can you give me the source of that quotation, or can I find it in Bartlett's? Thy—"

"Oh, don't!" wailed Leonard. "Please forget I ever said it! Please! It's that dreadful night! It's that dreadful woman! Please!"

"Now you've *really* got my curiosity roused," said Jack. "What *is* all this—what terrible night?"

Leonard sank his face in his hands. "The reading," he muttered. "The night of the reading. Kevin Boyle. Kevin Boyle's poetry."

"You mean *that* was Kevin Boyle's poetry?" demanded Kate.

Leonard kept his hands over his face. "No," he whispered, "No."

"Then whose *is* it? What's it all about? What's it got to do with—with Freda Cramm?" asked Jack irritably.

At last Leonard raised his face and peered through steamy glasses at Jack and Kate. "It was the beginning of everything," he pronounced. "That poem. You know who wrote that poem? It was in with Kevin Boyle's. *She* read it. *He* read it. They laughed at it. I found it there that terrible night. The night— the night of the reading. I didn't find it until I was right in the middle of the reading. There it was, between two of *his*. I nearly lost my voice when I saw it. I shifted it to the bottom." He paused and panted a moment, then looked at Jack with bloodhound eyes. "Mr.—uh—Mr.—uh—"

"Donelly," said Jack impatiently. "Call me Jack."

"Mr.—uh—Jack, you remember when you came to my place? You remember what you asked me just at the end— before—before you left?"

Jack shook his head No.

"You asked me what was the paper I tore up on Freda Cramm's sunporch. You asked me—*that* was what I tore up."

"*What* was what you tore up?" demanded Jack.

"That poem. I wrote it. Oh," Leonard sobbed brokenly, "I'm so ashamed. One should never be—never be *carnal*!"

"The cleaner's bill!" breathed Kate.

"Anyhow, that cleans that up," replied Jack. "How did it get there, anyway, Marks, and what's so awful about it? A little carnality makes the whole world kin. Did somebody swipe it from you?"

"Oh, no," said Leonard miserably. He took out his handkerchief and blew his nose. His tears seemed to have sobered him up a little. "I gave it to him—to Boyle—to read. I guess he got it mixed in with his own stuff. I can't tell you how awful it makes me feel. It's so—so *private*."

"Not at all," soothed Kate in womanly tones, "it's individual, but it's *also* universal, Mr. Marks. You mustn't feel you're the only sinner in a pure world—you know better."

"Oh, I know," sighed Leonard. "Boyle could do it. Boyle could—get away with it. But I'm different. It's like—I guess it's the way Mr. Hungerford feels about that journal."

"What journal?" said Jack, beckoning to the waitress with his empty beer mug.

"The one Freda Cramm writes and puts in his room."

"*What?*" cried Jack and Kate simultaneously.

"Yes," said Leonard. "Didn't I tell you? That's why I was following her. To catch her at it. I'm *sure* she murdered Boyle now. And she's trying to drive Hungerford insane. She poisons his life with this—I don't know how to tell you. She breaks into his room and writes a journal. Just an ordinary notebook— full of—evil!"

D R. FORSTMANN subdued Miss Justin's flutterings and left her outside the door of the room. The lamp was lighted by the bed. Under the white covering there was a large quivering lump. "Molly!" he said. "What happened?" In response, the quivering stopped and the lump was responsively still. "Please come out, Molly," he said. "I want to hear about it." The lump was still and solid as a boulder. "Miss Justin told me you came in terribly upset from a walk. That's all I know. I have to know more to help you."

"You can't help me," was what he made out of the muffled voice coming from under the covers. "Leave me alone," or "I'm all alone." Something like that.

"That's what I'm here for, so you won't be alone," he said, pulling up the wicker chair and sitting down. "I came over from Springfield just as soon as I heard you needed me. How about it? How about telling me?"

He wasn't sure whether or not she could hear him. He sat silent for several minutes. He was gathering himself to utter some new bromide when the knot under the covers began to loosen; he saw the outline of Molly's legs extend under the blanket, and at last the frowsy top of her head and her two red-rimmed eyes appeared over the sheet. "I'm so frightened," she said urgently. Her mouth was still covered and he couldn't understand her very well. He was surprised at how quickly she had emerged. It put a new complexion on the matter. In a way it troubled him. He had expected a long stubborn struggle before she gave in. "Dr. Forstmann," she was saying. She even took a hand out of hiding and pushed the covers away from her mouth. "Dr. Forstmann, I'm so glad you came really. You can't help me, though. I'm really crazy."

"I doubt it," he said. Inadvertently, the thought of the dinner he had left steaming on his home table crossed his mind and he put more asperity into his answer than he had meant. Her lip quivered. "You went for a walk," he said quickly, with all the gentleness he could summon. "Something upset you. Let's hear about it now."

"Yes," she whispered, "listen. I have delusions, or hallucinations or something. Hallucinations, it must be. That's when

347

you really imagine direct sensations instead of just sort of distant things like persecution, isn't it?"

He nodded, puzzled.

"I imagined," she whispered, and seemed to choke, "I imagined someone was strangling me. That's—" she caught her breath again, "that's pretty far gone, isn't it?"

He was trying to think quickly, to go over the notes he had made about her without having them there to go over. What was this fear of having "gone crazy"? Was it in response to the letter from her mother? Perhaps to convince the mother of the seriousness of her plight, she had produced more violent symptoms . . . Possibly. Yet for some reason he had a feeling that something was unpredictably odd about her behavior. She was somehow too straightforwardly glad to see him, too straightforwardly fearful of the experience she had had, whatever it was . . . Too little conflict . . . Well. He had let a long silence lapse after her last words. Quickly he said, "You've had an upsetting day today, Molly, what with your mother's letter and your first venture out of the Infirmary. Maybe if you could describe your—hallucination, we could piece together a good reason for its appearance."

"Yes," she whispered. "Yes. Listen. I went to see Mr. Hungerford. I walked to his house. But the woman said he didn't live there any more. She said that he had moved to where Kevin Boyle used to live. Oh!" she cried suddenly, "Maybe he hadn't moved at all! Maybe I only dreamed that too! But it seemed so real!"

"Just tell me what happened first," he said. "Why did you want to see Mr. Hungerford?"

She pushed her head farther out of the covers and lay back on the pillow. Her forehead contracted anxiously. "I want to tell you everything," she said. "It's so complicated. He had Kevin Boyle's poems. I thought if I could see them I—" She stopped and looked at him, but for once she did not begin to cry.

"Go on," he said, "you thought if you could see them—what?"

"I thought—if I could have one—I might feel something again," she said in a whisper. "I thought I'd stop being dead."

It was complicated. The roast veal he had been about to

carve when the telephone rang kept coming back to haunt him as if he were an habitual glutton. His stomach uttered a loud and probably psychosomatic protest. "Just tell it right along, Molly," he said gently. "I know there's too much to say all at once. We'll go back and pick up the pieces later."

"All right," she said faintly. "So I went to—to the house where Mr. Hungerford lives now. I rang the bell. Mr.—Mr. Boyle's name was still on the card. Mr. Hungerford let me in. He was awfully nice. He even said I'd waked him up from his nap, but he didn't care. He wasn't trying to make me feel uncomfortable by telling me that. He seemed really glad to see me. We talked, and then I told him why I was there. He gave me a glass of sherry, but I wasn't drunk at all. I was almost—" the tears came up on her eyes but hovered at the brink of the lids. "I was almost happy. He was so nice. He was so human. He wasn't like a professor at all. He was like somebody you know, and you feel fond of—like a father, or an uncle, or something. And then the feeling came back."

She stopped, but he did not prompt her, only waited.

"I guess I should have told you about the feeling I had. I guess it sort of fits in. I didn't want to go out, in a way. It was only thinking of the poems that made me able to go. All the time I walked in the streets I felt as if I were in a dream—when you're not sure what time of day it is, and you aren't certain whether you've seen the people you pass before, but it seems they look at you as if they knew some secret about you, and you know something dreadful is going to happen—they've found out something you've done, and you're going to be punished for it—you know the feeling?"

He nodded. "Who was going to punish you, Molly? For what?"

"Oh, you don't know who, and you don't know for what! It's like when you were little, and your parents found out you had done something wrong, only you didn't know it was wrong, so you didn't know what it was they were angry about, or why they were going to punish you—only it's something worse than your parents that's going to punish you now!" Her voice was rising.

"So when you were talking to Mr. Hungerford about the poems the feeling came back?" he cut in.

"Yes. I told him that that was what I had come for—I wanted him to let me read them. Then his face went funny—he has some sort of tic, you know. I guess that was what frightened me. It drew all to one side for a long time, and he dropped his sherry glass. And then, when his face went back again—that was when it happened." She stopped.

"What happened?"

She closed her eyes and shook her head on the pillow. "I guess I went crazy. I guess there isn't any other way to explain it. He looked all different. Before I had been thinking—" she blushed—"I had been thinking he reminded me of my father. And then all of a sudden he looked like my mother. That just doesn't make sense, you know."

"I think it makes a good deal of sense," said Forstmann slowly, "when you think about the letter you had from your mother today. I don't know yet why you should have thought of her in connection with Mr. Hungerford, but I'll bet you we can find a reason. Was that all?"

"Oh, no!" she cried, suddenly rising on her elbows. "That's only the beginning! I shut my eyes because I was so frightened when—when I thought he looked that way, and all of a sudden somebody was strangling me!"

"Describe how that felt," he said, sitting forward.

"Why," she said, "it felt just like somebody strangling me!"

"Do you mean you had a choking sensation—couldn't swallow or so?"

"Oh, no, no!" she cried. "Somebody's hands were around my throat, and I could feel all the blood swelling in my head, and I was fighting with this—this person, only the terrible thing was—" she paused—"I wasn't sure I wasn't doing it myself, or that nothing had happened at all, or that I'd just dreamed it. And then finally the hands dropped away, and it seemed—" she puzzled a moment, "it seemed that something or somebody fell on the floor. And before that somebody said something. About So you're the one. But it was a strange voice. I'd never heard it before."

"Whose voice does it make you think of? Does it remind you of anyone?"

"Oh," she said, "oh, let me see! I can't think. It was sort of deep. But not a man's voice. Like some woman with a very deep voice. You know who it kind of sounded like? Mrs. Cramm in the English Department. Do you know her?"

"No, I don't. Have you a class with her?"

"No. I used to see her in The Coffee Shoppe sometimes. She was a friend of—of Mr. Boyle's."

Her eyes were wide and her breath was coming fast, but there was a certain calmness, a kind of sureness about her which he didn't understand. Was she relieved at being able to produce so definite a symptom? Did she feel that now she would be justified in the eyes of her mother? Something must be done now about the parents. If he could get her father to come East, to talk to him. He couldn't see keeping her at the Infirmary at this rate. Nor could he think of sending her to the State Hospital. It was possible some arrangement could be made to send her home and put her in the care of someone there—cheaper than a sanitarium. Certain doctors might be willing to take her on a sort of professional discount for the sake of Miles Morrison's work. He'd have to talk to Bainbridge—that was the next thing.

Unexpectedly she broke into his thoughts. "I'm not worried, you know," she said oddly. "I'm the calmest I've been since I've been here. It's sort of the courage of desperation. Now I know the worst. I could even go to sleep now. I even feel sleepy."

"Listen, Molly, the worst isn't so bad as you've made out, that I know—I don't mean you haven't told the truth," he amended hastily, "but I doubt if its significance is so final as you imagine. You've been turning up a lot of violent emotions in the last few days which you've always kept far under the surface of your mind before. It's not altogether surprising if you get some violent reactions. If you can sleep now, I think that's the best thing you could do. I'll get Miss Justin to give you a sleeping tablet to take in case you can't. Tomorrow we'll talk more about this. Sleep's the thing tonight." He rose. "Goodnight," he said.

She even smiled at him. It was almost the first time. "Goodnight," she said. "I'm sorry I made you miss your dinner."

He grinned. "Goodnight," he said again, and left.

WHEN MOLLY woke the white room was filled with dazzling white sun. White as a magnesium flare. She shut her eyes to recapitulate her dream. It was an old dream, almost an old friend of a dream, a nightmare, but this time (as always) with a new twist. She was walking through a wood. It was dark and tangled and dangerous. In the thickets, behind the trees, lurked danger, but what the danger was she never knew. But the sense of it was terrible; sometimes, in the dream, she dropped on the path and lay quivering in a ball, waiting for the danger to take her, to digest her in its inexorable maw. Sometimes she fainted of fear, yet remained conscious all the time, not escaping the danger by her withdrawal from life. But this time she walked on through the forest, in terror. Then all at once, an enormous beast came bounding from out of the bushes, roaring terribly. Suddenly she had turned calm, had drawn her sword and shot him three times, and had wakened, not with a sense of nightmare, but of curious peace.

Lying in the infirmary bed with her eyes closed, she began to laugh. Shot him with her sword! How ridiculous! The laughter took her by surprise, caught her unawares, carried her away. She was so delighted at the surprise of her laughter that the tears rose in her throat, of a kind of gratitude for being able to laugh. She opened her eyes and sighed. Then she realized the significance of the whiteness of the light. It had snowed. The sun was reflecting from snow.

Snow in the night is like a gift, she thought, and wished she had something on which to write this sentence. It came in the night like a gift, like an ineffable largesse of purity. It came like a reaffirmation of hope after despair. Like the premonition of a miracle. Like love. She began to cry with happiness because of the snow. "I'm not dead! I'm not dead!" she said aloud, the tears running down her cheeks. She raised her hands to her cheeks, to cover her face as if she were blushing with love at the approach of her lover. Then she saw it.

Running across the back of her left hand was a long, deep scratch.

It all came back, like part of the dream. The threatening walk through the twilight. The Saint Bernard. The deaf old woman. The haven of Mr. Hungerford's room. The fire. The sherry. And then, like a clap of thunder, everything changed, everything different, Mr. Hungerford transformed to a wicked witch in an enchanted wood, standing on the hearth amid the bits of broken glass. She had closed her eyes at the sight of him—she could not bear that he had changed. And then the hands had been at her throat; she was rocking and struggling, straining to breathe. And all the time thinking: I am mad, I am doing this to myself, this is the final ultimate proof! Out of some skewed notion of self-destruction I am compelled to behave this way, wrestle with my own spirit! A fingernail had drawn a line of pain across the back of her left hand. And here was the scratch.

But her own fingernails were bitten to the quick!

The sun and snow blazed blue light through the windows, dazzling as revelation. "Oh, oh, it was true!" she whispered. It changed everything! It changed the complexion of the whole world! Like the sun, like the snow, like the beast in the dream, like a gift presented to her unexpectedly! It was true, she had been right, and it made her feel nearly mad with excitement. She was not crazy—except almost crazy with happiness—someone—some real person—had actually tried to strangle her!

She leapt out of bed and shut her window. She stripped off her pajamas and put on her clothes very quickly. When she was all dressed except for her sweater, she stopped and began to laugh, shivering in her slip and skirt. It seemed so insanely silly to be happy that someone had tried to strangle you! Maybe she was still crazy, only in another way. But it didn't matter, it didn't matter . . . This time she had been right. It was as if she were vindicated in all the thousand times she had made a stand, had said: You have mistreated me! and they had scoffed, What nonsense, what childishness, what selfishness! . . . This is the birthday of my life, she thought, shivering with excitement.

When Miss Justin knocked on her door with the breakfast tray, her face was burning with anticipation. She ate in hasty gulps. When she was through, she took her coat and muffler from the closet, her mittens from the drawer, and dressed to go out. At once, at once, she must get to Mr. Hungerford! She stopped, one sleeve of her coat still dangling. What a fool she

had been! What a selfish idiot! Had he, too, not been in danger? What had she been thinking of, running off and leaving
him, all cowardly with her own peril! God knows what could
have happened to him by now, in the room like herself with
those gripping hands, that grating voice! Perhaps he was even
now . . . like Kevin Boyle . . . like Kevin Boyle, from her
cowardice! She thrust her arm into the sleeve and ran out the
door down the corridor. Halfway to the front hall she nearly
collided with Miss Justin who was carrying a tray of thermom-
eters and tongue depressors.

"Why Molly!" she exclaimed, looking frightened in a curious way, "Where are you going?"

"Oh," she answered breathlessly, "I'm going for a walk—
I'm—I'm just going for a walk."

Slowly, oddly, Miss Justin was edging in front of her, blocking the corridor. "But, my dear," she said, "there's four or five
inches of snow underfoot and you have no galoshes! None of
the walks will be cleared at this hour."

"It doesn't matter," said Molly, starting to push past. "I'll
stop off at the house for my galoshes and another pair of
shoes."

"But, my dear," said Miss Justin monotonously, "why don't
you let me phone one of the girls to bring over your galoshes?
I mustn't let you go out this way. We're not trying to drum up
trade, you know!" There was a queer little rabbity look under
her falsely facetious smile. No! Molly told herself. I will not
think it! I'm always thinking people are against me. I have to
stop. I have to be reasonable.

"It's all right. I couldn't possibly catch cold in that little
space, Miss Justin. After all, Dr. Forstmann told me I was to go
for walks—and it's a beautiful sunny day." She smiled politely.
There! That ought to convince her! It was probably the first
time she had smiled at her for any reason.

"Oh, I'm sure Dr. Forstmann didn't mean to have you go
out with no overshoes into the wet snow," said Miss Justin.
"We must remember you've been sick for a while, Molly—
your temperature has only been normal a few days."

She was beginning to tremble. She wanted to keep hold of
herself, not slide away from the happiness, the plateau of reason which she had achieved in that waking moment. But al-

ready her face was flushing, her eyes preparing to fill with tears, her hands shaking. She managed to keep her voice even, though. "I don't think he would mind, Miss Justin, really I don't. It's rather important that I go out this morning, you see. I'll tell Dr. Forstmann all about it when I see him later. He—in fact he already knows about it. I assure you it will be all right."

But the rabbity look came even stronger on Miss Justin's face. A look of suspicion and secrecy, and, strangely, of fear. Oh no, no! she thought. I won't see things like that! They're imaginary! And so subtle—who can *really* say what another person's face expresses? Nevertheless, the look was there. Fear, and wiliness. Danger. "Molly," said Miss Justin, "you look a little feverish to me. Just pop this in your mouth, will you?" And drawing a thermometer from its antiseptic bath, she advanced it toward Molly's mouth.

Suddenly a great rage began to break the boundaries in her; she felt like some small cornered beast who finally dares to bare its tiny teeth. "That's fantastic!" she said angrily, backing away from the outstretched thermometer. "Naturally I look feverish when you keep me standing with my coat on in a steamheated hall. Will you please let me pass?"

"I don't think you'd really better—" Miss Justin began.

The tears conquered her. She was too weak. She slid back from the plateau. She covered her eyes with her mittened hand. "He said I could go out!" she sobbed childishly. "You call Dr. Forstmann! He *said* I could go out! You're—you're exceeding your authority! Call him up! You—you horse-faced old bitch!"

"Well!" she heard Miss Justin's outraged voice. "Well, I must say! I never expected to be working in an insane asylum when I came here! I see now . . . Very well, Miss, if you want to know, Dr. Forstmann left instructions that you were not to leave the building. Do you want to go back to your room by yourself, or shall I call another nurse to help me?"

She turned and ran. There was a bolt on her door—they had not thought to remove it. She pushed it into place. Then she threw herself on the bed, coat and all, and sobbed and sobbed. Betrayed. He had betrayed her. Her last, her last . . . This was the end. He believed it too. She was crazy. Dr. Forstmann had said she could not leave. She wept wildly until she was worn out, and then she lay, staring at the patch of bright snow sunlight on the floor. A cool, contemptuous voice began to speak in the back of her head. Well, it said, what do you expect? How do you think you've been acting? Didn't you tell him yourself that you were mad?

But I'm *not*! she returned querulously. I'm not, and now I can prove it! He should have known, he should have known!

But how could he know? said the voice reasonably. You didn't know yourself.

Her eyes were blinded with sun. She raised her hand and looked at the scratch through a green haze of sun blindness. You didn't know yourself. Of course I didn't. He doesn't know about this. This makes it real. He couldn't know that. When he knows . . .

Suppose he does not believe you? Suppose he thinks you have scratched your hand on something else, doesn't believe . . . But I didn't, I didn't! It hurt too much—it was then, I remember! It was then, then!

Suppose it was just part of the dream—as when the alarm clock rings and you weave the ringing into your dream—invent a telephone or a doorbell to explain its voice.

She moaned. "Oh, I must go, I must go!" she said aloud. Only one person could set her mind at rest—Mr. Hungerford. If she could get to him, either he would support her, or tell her it had been illusion. And if it was *not* illusion, then he was in danger. Perhaps he was already dead. Yet if he had . . . It was all too tangled. She must speak to him. She could not sit in solitude through the morning, waiting for Forstmann to set her right. Perhaps he wouldn't believe her anyway. She rose from the bed, her head spinning and swollen with tears. It would be simple to get out. The room was on the ground floor. She had only to open the window and climb over the sill. Outside there was a brick terrace. Then where? Not the street. She would be seen. Across the field to the cover of the little wood that was behind the row of houses across the street. To the path along the river, then up the hill and across the athletic field to the back of Mr. Hungerford's house.

She pushed up the sash, straddled the sill, and set her foot gingerly on the undefiled purity of the new-fallen snow.

"YOU SEE, it's just as sunny as advertised," Leonard Marks said, and laughed nervously. Please, he seemed to plead silently, please, tell me what it is, let me help you!

Hungerford smiled at Leonard weakly, and tried to form a word, but he could not. He could not speak. He sat by the fire in an old dressing gown, unwashed, unshaven. Every now and then he was taken with fits of shivering. The grippe, Leonard said, and tried to persuade him to go to bed. But it was not the grippe, and he would not go to bed. The curious thing, the thing which he could not tell Leonard, was that he himself did not know what the trouble was. He shivered and shook, he was nauseated with dread, he could not bear to be alone, but what it was, how it had come about, that he could not—or would not—conjecture. Since yesterday. Whatever it was had come up yesterday. And he simply could not remember. A girl had come to see him—a student. He had liked her at once. But he could not remember why she had come. And whenever he tried to recall it, he began to shake and shiver—he made Leonard bring him a tumbler half full of whiskey.

The sun was streaming through the small, diamond-paned windows, blue-white. The fire he had lit seemed pallid in the brilliant morning light. He sat before the blaze, one side of his body heated, the other stiff with chill, and he thought irrelevantly of a passage in *Madame Bovary* where Charles comes to see Emma before they are married, and there is a description of the blue light coming down the chimney onto the dead ashes. But that was on a hot day, as he recollected—there followed a description of the beads of sweat on Emma's half uncovered breasts. Hot. So hot you could sweat. So hot your bones were warm—you would not remember that bones could ever be cold. That intestines could run ice water. That feet could ache with cold inside woolen socks. Poor Leonard was looking at him like an anxious bloodhound. No. Dachshund. Well.

"I wish you'd let me call a doctor," he pleaded, breaking the silence. Hungerford said nothing, only smiled weakly again. "Oh, Mr. Hungerford," he finally burst, "*won't* you tell me what it is? Is it—is it something about the journal again?"

Hungerford shook his head, still unable to speak. He opened

357

his mouth. His dry tongue clung to the roof of it. "I seem," he essayed thickly, "I seem to have had—have had some sort of—sort of spell of amnesia. It has—it has rather undone me." He felt the muscles of his face pulling anxiously, wishing to distort his cheek with the tic. But the fact was that he was too cold. It would have been like—like trying to pour molasses in January for his muscles to move his flesh that way.

"*Amnesia!*" Leonard was saying, his eyes starting behind his glasses. "Is that—I mean, has that ever happened before?"

Hungerford shook his head in the negative.

"Then oughtn't you—I mean, really, Mr. Hungerford, really, sir, you've been working too hard! You aren't well enough! *Do* see a doctor!"

Poor Leonard Marks. Poor dear Leonard Marks! He meant so very well. Leonard, my dear, if I could only make you understand. You see . . . But one must participate. One must have experienced to understand . . . One must have realized one's own participation. A mock professional voice spoke in his head. Mental illness, it said. Leonard Marks, he was sure, had had a thousand comparable experiences. He, Hungerford, was no more than a humble stockholder in the neuroses of the times. It was not that it was anything private, personal though it was. But to make it understood to one who was not aware . . . His brain was cold. Thought flowed sluggishly and stiffly through whatever passages thought must flow through.

Marks had risen. "Now really, sir," he was expostulating, "I'm just—I'm just going to *make* you go to bed! You're having a terrible chill! You're shaking like a leaf! Why don't you get covered up and have a hot water bottle and some of that sedative you—"

A force—how else to describe it?—like a hand at the scruff of his neck, lifted Hungerford to his feet. "No!" he was amazed to hear himself shout. Good heavens, he thought to himself, with a rather comic abstraction, what has got into me? Almost, he began to enjoy this illogical scene.

Leonard Marks shrank back—like a Victorian wife whose husband has asserted his authority. Almost visibly quaking, then, he pulled himself together, clasping his hands over the middle button of his vest. "I know I'm being a pest," he said bravely, "but honestly, Mr. Hungerford, I do so *deeply* mean it for your own good!"

Oh dear, oh dear. Better than a doctor, to be sure. But so . . . Suddenly he thought of the girl who had been here yesterday, and an entire scene reappeared in his memory like an enormous bubble bursting on the surface of water. He saw her standing before him, twisting her brown mittens in her hands in an agony of embarrassment. They seem to think, she was saying, they seem to think I am unbalanced. How something frozen in his heart had melted at the sound of those words! How he had loved that child who knew too . . . knew too . . . He would like to talk to *her* now. Though for what purpose he could hardly say. He felt at the same time better and more perturbed for thinking about her. He felt that she was a key to his disturbance of today, if only he could fit her to the proper lock. He would even have sent for her, have made her tell him what had gone between them, if he could have remembered her name. Why had she come to see him? That he could not recollect at all. Perhaps one of his students. Perhaps if he went through the roll calls of his various classes he would recognize a name.

Leonard Marks was looking anxiously between himself and the clock. He wanted to comfort Leonard, somehow, yet he was irritated that he was called upon to do so. "Go along, go along, Marks!" he cried, his tongue finally loosened. "You have a class, I know, and I assure you I'm *quite* all right. If I need anything, I've only to call for Miss Stone. I tell you, I wish you'd put a note on the blackboard that I won't be meeting English 24 this morning. It's in Room 33 of Framingham."

"Oh, of course!" vibrated Leonard, delighted with his little task, yet still undecided as to whether he should leave. "Are you quite sure . . ."

"Go—get out—run!" he cried, trying to make his voice teasing, yet annoyed within. And Leonard left at last, looking a little frightened, a little worried, a little relieved.

Now he was alone with the quiet brilliant sunshine, the blue-white sunshine—blue. That meant it must have snowed. The windows were too high in the wall for him to see the ground from here; the shade to the one facing out on the porch was

pulled down for privacy. But of course, if he had been in a
mood for observation, he would have seen before that the bare
branches that showed through the high panes had each a load
of white, lying soft and precarious. As a child he had often been
too delicate to go out in the snow, to play the rough games of
sliding, wallowing, bombarding. Yet he remembered the sense
of miracle that always came to him when he waked to find it
had snowed in the night. Often he would lie abed until his
mother came in to light the gas log. "It snowed last night," she
would say, in a soft wondering voice. And he would answer,
"Yes, I know," though he had not been out of bed to look
through the window. There would be that whiteness in the air,
that radiance . . . He put another log on the fire and sat
down beside it. He ran his hand over his rough cheek. In a
moment he would shave. He felt better. Less cold. Because it
had snowed, he felt less cold! What a nonsensical mood he was
in today!

And then the doorbell rang. It gave a long sputtering buzz
and stopped. He thought he would not go. He sat staring into
the fire. It buzzed again. Still he sat. Then it occurred to him
that he could peep through the crack of the shade and see who
was on the porch. He rose and went to the window. A girl was
standing at the door with her back to him. She wore a nonde-
script tweed coat, the usual socks and moccasins. Her hair hung
lank over her coat collar—for the life of him he could not recollect ever having seen her. Just as he was about to let the blind
fall back against the window, he saw her turn a little, beating
the back of one brown mitten into the palm of the other.
Brown mittens—brown mittens—probably a hundred pairs on
the campus! But he heard the voice saying again: They think
I'm unbalanced. Oh, he must see her, must speak to her!
Quickly, forgetting his deshabille, he rushed from the window,
out the French doors to the hall and the outer entry. He threw
the door open, and sighed with relief and gratification. It was
she—same face, same heavy bang, same frightened eyes. "Come
in!" he shouted joyously, "Come in!"

She stepped back, looked a little startled by his exuberance,
and by—he finally realized—his appearance. But she came
forward again, crossed the threshold, silently walked through
the hall to his room. He followed her, feeling so warm, so

grateful. He remembered something new. When she had come yesterday, he had not known her name. "Do you know something that's to my shame?" he said, shutting the door to his rooms behind him. "I've forgotten your name again."

But she paid no attention to his remark. She stood in front of the fire as she had yesterday. "Mr. Hungerford, I *had* to see you," she said, her gray eyes clouded with anxiety. "I've run away. They don't know I'm here. I escaped. They really—now they really think I'm crazy. You have to tell me what happened yesterday!"

The strength went from his legs and he had to sit down. He looked up at her, opening and closing his mouth like a fish, unable to make words. She stared back at him, her face making ready for tears. At last he brought out, "You mean you don't remember?"

Dumbly she shook her head, and he thought the floor was rocking under him. For if *she* did not remember, how was he ever . . . "Oh," she said, "I *think* I do. But it's all a hallucination. At least, I thought it was an hallucination. Dr. Forstmann thought so too. He thought I was crazy. He told the nurse not to let me out. But then I found *this*—" she thrust her hand out toward him—"and I couldn't tell any more if it was true or not."

He looked down at the thin back of her left hand, and saw an angry-looking scratch running across the back. He passed his hand across his eyes. He could make nothing of it. "I don't understand," he muttered.

"Then," she said dully, "there was nothing. I *am* crazy. I'd better go back."

She started to move toward the door, her shoulders sunken. He jumped up and caught hold of the mantel to steady himself. "No!" he cried. "Don't go! You mustn't go! Tell me what it is you thought you remembered!"

She turned in the doorway and looked at him pitifully. "Must I?" she said.

He went toward her unsteadily and laid his hands on her shoulders. "Yes," he said urgently, and almost tenderly, "you must! Really you must!"

Obediently she came back into the room. She stood before the fire like a child making ready to recite a piece. Her eyes filled with tears, but she blinked them back. "When I came here yesterday it took a lot of nerve," she said. "I don't know. I don't know if I can tell you."

"Yes, you must, you must!" he urged.

"I'll try," she whispered. "You see, I don't know if you understand—it took such a lot of nerve just to go outdoors. I don't know if you'd understand that. It sounds so crazy. I guess it is crazy."

He laughed a little, almost jubilantly. "My God, of course I know, child! You get to the doorstep, and all you want to do is go back to your room and hide in the bed. You lay your hand on the knob and think you simply cannot . . ."

"Yes," she said in a surprised voice. "That's just it—that's just it! And you're scared to walk in the streets—you think everybody—you think they're looking at you—you think they hate you. Oh, that's silly, I know. I just can't seem to help it."

Hurry, hurry! he wanted to beg her, but instead he said comfortingly, "I know, too well. Will you tell me what happened?"

"I'm sorry, I didn't mean to be so slow," she apologized. "First I went to where you used to live. You weren't there, but the woman told me you were here. So I came here. We were talking, and you were very kind to me, but then all of a sudden everything got . . . I don't know how to—someone choked me! Or that was what I thought! Please, could you tell me what really happened?"

Now the tears were pouring down her face in earnest. He had taken his seat by the fire again. He let his hands drop between his knees. "I don't know what happened," he said. "I can't tell you. I had some sort of fit of amnesia. I can't remember a damned thing that happened. I couldn't remember a thing except that you had been here. I recognized you when I saw you."

"Oh," she said, and stood in an attitude of utter gloom.

"Look," he said. "We must work on this, and maybe more of it will come back. Somebody *choked* you, you say?" All at once he began to be excited again. How had he passed up her words so calmly? "Tell me everything that happened after you came here! What makes you say you're crazy? What did Forstmann say to you? Oh here!" he cried, "Take off your coat and sit down!"

She peeled off her coat and threw it on the couch, then sat

down in the chair opposite his and thrust her feet toward the fire. She clasped her hands in her lap and began, "I came here and you were very nice to me. You gave me a glass of sherry. I thought you looked like my father, and I liked you very much. But then all of a sudden you looked different to me, and I closed my eyes and someone was choking me—or I imagined it—and then I ran away. I thought it was all a dream and that I was really mad, and I told Dr. Forstmann; only this morning, I found the scratch on my hand. You see—" she was getting excited, and so was he—"the sensation of choking was so plain, that I thought I must have done it myself—taken hold of my neck with my own hands, I mean. But I remember very plainly feeling my hand scratched at that time—I remember that it hurt, but I had to keep on struggling, and I couldn't get my breath. Now I couldn't have scratched myself because—" she blushed—"I bite my fingernails so. So I thought that—I imagined that might be a kind of evidence that something had really—oh, and I forgot. I heard a voice. It wasn't you. It was like a woman's voice, only deep."

Suddenly he put his hands to his temples as if to keep his head from falling apart. My God, my God! "She was here!" he said aloud, without meaning to.

"I beg your pardon?" she said.

"What's your name?" he asked, taking his hands down.

"Molly Morrison." Her lower lip began to quiver.

"Molly," he said, "you're not mad. I think it was quite real. I think I see how it was. But I have to think. I have to figure it out. I—" He rose and began to pace the room. "Go back home," he said. "I think—I think I'm going to find other evidence which will convince Dr. Forstmann. Go back to the Infirmary. I'll telephone him today."

She rose, looking bewildered, on the brink of tears. "But—" she began—"I have to know—"

Suddenly he was in a frenzy to have her out, to have her gone, to know for himself. "You will!" he cried. "You will! You must take my word for it! Now run along like a good child! I'll call Dr. Forstmann within an hour."

She took her coat and put it on slowly, biting her lip. She went to the door, turned and looked at him pitifully, her hand on the knob. "You—you will?" she begged.

On an impulse, he rose and went to kiss her cheek. "I will, Molly, I promise," he said. Then she was gone.

A sweet child, a dear—but he had no time; feverishly he had jerked a whole row of books off the shelf and was scrabbling for—ah, he had it! He turned the brown cardboard cover and riffled wildly through the pages, the big scrawl staring up at him like a malignant face. Why had he not thrown it away? Why had he. . . . There it was. Yesterday's date. It began:

> *And she came here, the little bitch, and how brazenly she faces up to me and says, Give me his poems. Ah, I cried, so it was you! And I took her by the throat, and I shook her like a dog in a fight, yes, in another minute I would have snapped her skinny little neck, but she broke away. Oh, the next time will I not succeed, the next time . . .*

Then unconsciousness overtook him, and he read no more.

When he came to, someone was dabbing at his face with a wet cloth. Slowly he became aware of Leonard Marks, looming into his consciousness like a ship over the edge of the horizon. "Leonard," he said faintly but urgently, "now you can call a doctor. Call Dr. Julian Forstmann in Springfield. Call him at once." And as he closed his eyes it seemed strange to him that his first thought should have been of vindicating the little girl instead of calling the police, protecting himself.

FREDA CRAMM was cleaning her desk. It was one of those small necessities which occasionally seem so pleasant as to appear self indulgent. Across the top of the writing space was a row of eight cubbyholes assigned to paid and unpaid bills, answered and unanswered letters, receipts, and a great deal of miscellany—Christmas cards from years back, a wrist watch which needed a new strap, a bunch of luggage keys, and envelopes full of snapshots and negatives. Freda sat precariously on a plump, plush slipper chair, humming and throwing papers on the floor. Sometimes the pile began to sprawl, so she gathered it up and threw it onto the fire that blazed pallidly on the sunny hearth. Then she would go back to the desk, to slit unopened envelopes, examine the contents of those already opened, filing some in the cubbyholes, and throwing the rest on the floor beside her chair. Suddenly she made a little exclamation, and paused, smoothing a scrap of lined paper under her plump ringed hands.

Freda—[said the small ragged writing], You're a big brute of a woman, damn you, and you can put a scare into a man. There it is, humiliating though it be: there is something about you that makes the words wither in my throat and my manhood on the vine. And I'm attracted to you, curse you. Forgive me, and come to tea tomorrow.

K.

She grinned at the paper, mirthlessly, musingly. She picked it up and dropped it on the wastepaper pile, then leaned and took it back again. *Memento mori*. She put it in the pigeon hole with the envelopes of snapshots. She raised her chin in the air and ran her hand along the flabby flesh under it. "I'm getting old," she said aloud to the room. Outside the windows the evergreens nodded, loaded with snow. The sun blazed through the icicles that hung outside the panes. The room was too warm, with the sun, the central heating, and the fire on the hearth. Freda drifted into a half trance, bemused by heat and light. I am getting old, she thought, echoing her spoken words. She was forty-two. She had been a woman of vanity, in her prime, yet she had known so many of the satisfactions of the flesh that she did not grudge the years the weight and the wrinkles they had put on her. She was well aware that a woman's attraction lay in something beyond a slim waist and firm breasts, and if she chose this very day—well, it was no use pretending it was quite so easy as it once had been. But on the other hand, her appetite for experiment had long since been satisfied; she could now take her sex like a gourmet, sampling only the tastiest tidbits. She laughed out loud, drily. She had never gotten a taste of Kevin, and that was the long and the short of it. Nor was it for want of trying, either. As he put it, there it was, humiliating though it be. Yet, when she considered the incident, she doubted very much if she had been as humiliated as Kevin Boyle. She had long since outgrown the capacity for that sort of humiliation, because she had long since learned to estimate her own strength, or attraction or whatever, and she was perfectly sure that it was great. Considering herself as a historical phenomenon, she thought she could stand as a successful example of a woman of the Freudian era—she had entered maturity in the storied twenties, and had been subject matter for a good many stories herself. She had been married, she had been divorced, but the force of the blow of Michael's rejection had been so cushioned by the size of the sum he had settled on her that she could now meet him and his second wife with their growing family as amicably as though intimacy had never been. And if she had felt the need for reassurance, why there had been lovers in Rome, Paris, London, Capri, Hendaye, and other places. Now she was basking in the warmth of her middle years like a fat cat resting after a long night's prowl; she enjoyed playing at being an intellectual, she enjoyed *épatant le bourgeois* in this sleepy little town, and if a charming piece like Kevin Boyle slipped out of her grasp—well, no use mourning spilt milk. It made a good story, too. If only she could have told it to someone who would appreciate it.

She had first seen Kevin in the faculty tea room, cornered by Miss Austen, a colorless young woman from Rhode Island who was also in the English Department. They were discussing their respective sections of Freshman English, from all she had been able to overhear. Miss Austen was making sheep's eyes in a clumsy—even pathetic, if you could sympathize with that sort of thing—way. Freda had borne down on them like an expert polo player galloping in to take the ball, and in no time at all Kevin Boyle was driving home with her to borrow her copy of *The Tropic of Cancer*. In a week they had had three warm discussions of modern literature over her very excellent Amontillado. And then, just when she half expected him to attack, he withdrew. He began disagreeing cantankerously with her. He found fault with her way of life. She decided their relationship was ready to enter a new phase. She begged him to show her his poems.

In the guise of literary critic, she donned a new coloration. From dominating female, she shifted slightly to mother image. She was all warmth and appreciation. She invented new phrases of praise. She worked hard at the task of constructive criticism. As she looked back at it, she thought she had said some damned valuable things to him. His armor dropped. He was frankly adoring—in an impersonal sort of way. He was getting so he could not write without periodic injections of her approval. Then she began to be bored—bored with the amount of energy she was putting into him in proportion to the small returns she was getting. She had had the fullest intentions of sleeping with him from the start. She decided to stop the cat-and-mouse game and bring the thing to a climax.

It had become their daily habit to meet for sherry at her house in the afternoon, or tea at his, or coffee at The Coffee Shoppe. On this particular afternoon it was to be her place; she dressed carefully in a loose tea gown, and spent the afternoon in an astringent cosmetic mask. At four-thirty, when he was to come, the autumn dusk was descending, the fire was lit, the softer lamps were lighted. He arrived. The maid took his coat and hat. She had not risen when he entered the room. She had not even raised her head, but only her telling eyes. She had taken in every inch of him, slowly, consideringly. She remembered his long sinewy hand rising nervously to the knot of his tie.

"Sit down, Kevin, sit down," she had said. And she let him know with every syllable of it what she was up to.

They had sat and talked desultorily, he nervous, she slow and deliberate. At the end of their first glass of sherry, the maid had appeared in the doorway in her hat and coat, and Freda had risen to give her a check. "I'm sending Margaret off

for the week end," she let him know, as the door closed, and
he had shivered, as if a goose had walked over his grave.

They had talked, as usual, about his poetry, but she had put
very little of herself into the discussion this evening, only murmuring abstracted answers, agreeing, assenting. She meant
business, and she thought he might as well know it sooner as
later. She considered that men matured more slowly than
women, and it annoyed her to have to wait for Kevin to bridge
the ten or fifteen years that separated them; nevertheless, looking at his lean, odd sort of beauty, she thought he was worth
the wait. But the talk wore on and on without any sort of
move being made. His gestures grew more and more jerky,
hers more and more unhurried. If he did not say something
within the next five minutes, she thought, she would make the
first move herself. She watched the hands move slowly across
the face of the clock.

"I find you very disturbing, Kevin," she interrupted then.

She had turned down the lamps, the room was in complete
darkness except for the fire. They sat in armchairs, facing each
other, on opposite sides of the hearth. He was slumped low in
his, his knees rising angularly, the shadows emphasizing the
sockets of his eyes, the flickering light catching on his nervous
fingers as they rolled and unrolled the end of his necktie. At
her words, he sat forward with a jerk, his eyebrows flying up
his forehead. "Disturbing?" he echoed, in a high tense voice.
"Why, how is that?"

She rose from her chair and looked down at him in silence a
moment. "I find you very sexually attractive," she said at last.

His jaw dropped a little, then drew close again. "Oh," he
said, "thank you." And sat there, looking up at her. She turned
and left the room.

She stayed in the dark inner reaches of the house, laughing,
and giving him a chance to gather himself together. Every now
and then she would say, "Thank you," out loud to herself, and
giggle uncontrollably. She supposed she *was* a bit of a shock.
She wanted him to have time to get over the instinctive movement of withdrawal, and become a ravening male. When she
judged he should be in that state, she came back to the living
room.

But he was standing on the hearth, wearing his overcoat, with his hat in his hand. She waited on the threshold a moment, taking in the situation. Then she entered the room and went about from lamp to lamp, lighting them all. When the room was bright and decided with electricity, she turned to him and said matter-of-factly, "Must you go?"

"Yes—yes, I must," he stammered. "There's a—that is—I'm asked to a faculty dinner at—ah—at—ah—Barclay House tonight."

"That's too bad," she said. "I had hoped you'd stay for supper."

"Oh," he said, making an almost epileptic gesture with his hat, "that's terribly kind of you, but—"

"Of course," she cut him short. "Well, Kevin, I'll be seeing you at The Coffee Shoppe tomorrow, no doubt." She led him into the hall and opened the door. "Goodnight."

"Good—goodnight, Freda," he said, and stumbled off down the brick walk.

The next day the note she had under her hand had come, and she had gone to his house to tea. But it was not her game to be responsive at this particular move; she had arrived all indignant over her own affairs—had burst into his bravely loving mood (she had seen him steeled to approach her) with the letter over which they had quarreled. She supposed, now that it was so long past, that he had reproached her out of irritation that she had not given him an opening to make up for his cowardice. And she supposed that she had gotten so angry herself out of a kind of misplaced and almost maidenly disappointment. She had meant to make it all up—make it appear to be a sort of lover's quarrel, by becoming his lover. But the next week he was dead.

It was strange how his murder had dropped out of sight in the life of the community, like a stone dropped into water. Only the outermost circles of the ripples it had created now remained to quiver on the surface. Perhaps the police were at work still, unearthing new clues. Perhaps the president had knowledge of new discoveries which were kept secret. But in the town, in the faculty, even the game of conjecturing about who could have killed Kevin and why had palled. It was a nine-days' wonder, and the nine days were long gone. Curious that in so quiet a society, violence should be accepted as a matter of course. She supposed it was because the group in the college was predominantly intellectual and accustomed to living the life of the mind, so called. After all, the drama of Kevin Boyle was a rather shoddy little business if you chose to compare it with similar inventions of Dostoevski, Euripides, or even Poe. And murder, in order to be kept alive, had to be fed, she imagined—with clues, or new murders, or something of the sort. Here, Kevin Boyle had gotten hit on the head with a poker, and that was the end of it. She felt somewhat foolish at her own anxiety over the letter she had left in his rooms. But it had been natural to be hysterical at first.

With a sigh, she rose, gathered up the new pile of papers that had collected beside her chair, and carried them to the black marble fireplace, trailing scraps behind her. Just as she tossed them into the blaze, the doorbell rang, and she went to answer it, hearing the hum of Margaret's vacuum cleaner upstairs. There on her doorstep stood two youthful callers, a very intense looking young man—somehow familiar, wearing regulation college gear, and a roly-poly girl who was obviously a student—who was, in fact, she realized in a moment, Miss Innes, the editor of *The Holly*. "Hullo," said Freda agreeably. "What can I do for you?"

They had the violently defensive look about them that she had seen on the faces of groups of students who feel that their rights have been violated, and who have been indulging their virtuous indignation until they reach such a pitch as to call on sympathetic authorities for aid. Among certain student groups, she herself was regarded as an upholder of free living, and was not infrequently called upon to right real or supposed wrongs of one kind or other. She could not quite figure what the young man had to do with the case—where had she seen his face?—though on second thoughts, of course she could. Instead of answering her, the two of them stood on the stoop, panting a little in the cold, and obviously trying to bring themselves to say something they had not as yet phrased to their own satisfaction. "Well, come in, if the cat has your tongues," she said finally, "before we all freeze."

"Yes, we'd just like to have a word with you, Mrs. Cramm,"

said the young man, suddenly glib and bustling as they crossed the threshold.

They refused to lay their coats as she indicated, refused to sit down when they came into the living room. They had a strange look about them as they stared at her; they began to irritate her a little. "What in the world is the matter with you?" she snapped at last. "You're staring at me as if I showed definite symptoms of smallpox or something. Is my slip showing?"

"Mrs. Cramm," said the young man after a dramatic pause, "I'm Jack Donelly of the *Messenger*." Of course, of course! That impertinent young idiot! "I have a couple of questions I'd like answered about what you were doing in Kevin Boyle's rooms the night we saw you."

Now she felt really annoyed. The whole scene came back to her—how she had come out the front door of Kevin's house and had been half scared out of her wits by these two staring in the window of his apartment. She *had* been a fool about the letter—who would have cared if they had found it? It would have been slightly embarrassing at worst. "What night?" she said sharply, not knowing yet whether she intended to lie or tell the truth.

The young man took a notebook out of his pocket and flipped the leaves. Why the Innes girl was here was more than Freda could make out. She thought she would report her to Bainbridge, since he had made such a point of having the students keep away from reporters. "The night of November seventeenth," said the young man accusingly.

It was too ridiculous. She refused to lower her dignity by lying. "I was looking for a letter I had left there," she threw at the reporter. "I had left it there one day when I left Mr. Boyle's place in a rage because I'd had a fight with him. It was a letter from a poor relative of my late husband's, dunning me for money. Now you know as much as I do, and you may go, because I consider you fantastically impertinent and you are imposing on my hospitality. Miss Innes, I intend to speak to President Bainbridge about your collaboration with the press in a matter which he plainly does not want discussed in print." As she talked, she grew angrier. What a pair of brats!—bursting in on her this way, and what a fool she was, deluded in thinking she was about to aid and abet a pair of errant lovers. And of course, the young man actually was attached to a paper, albeit one on which she was able to exert a certain amount of influence. Still, she could not be quite sure how much.

The young man was looking at her in a peculiar way—a very peculiar way indeed, as if he fancied himself a judge leaning down to lecture the prisoner at the bar. Which reminded her that she would very much like a glass of sherry before lunch, but she had no intention of offering any to *these*. "And that was not your *last* visit to his apartment," he enunciated, in the manner of a district attorney in a Grade B movie.

"*What* was not my last visit there?" Freda snapped back at him. "The day I had the fight? No, it was not. I was at his rooms again on the night of November 17, as you just pointed out, looking for the letter I had left there. I hardly see how this can be of interest to your paper, Mr. Donelly."

"But," the young man pressed in his overdone ominous tone, "you have been back there more recently—*much* more recently!"

"No," said Freda, with rising asperity, "I have not. I think you'd better go, now." She raised one eyebrow and stared at them in her most quelling manner. Miss Innes shrank slightly, and pulled at the young man's elbow, but he stood his ground.

Suddenly, looking at both of them, at their pale tense faces, Donelly's long and irregular, the girl's perfectly round, both of them with identical horn-rimmed glasses sliding down their very different noses, she wanted to laugh at them, but refused to do so. She saw it all now. They had constituted themselves a pair of detectives on the Kevin Boyle Murder Case, and she was their most likely suspect. She supposed the whole notion had grown that night they had caught her slipping out of Kevin's place. She supposed she had looked pretty suspicious. Suddenly her dignity did not seem worth maintaining. She rose abruptly and went to the secretary where the decanter and glasses stood. She poured three glasses and turned. "You're behaving like utter babies," she said amiably, "but I'm so agreeable as to offer you a glass of sherry. Come on, sit down and tell me what this nonsense is all about."

The Innes child had the grace to blush very red, but the reporter squared his jaw. "What have you got against George Hungerford?" he shot at her. "Does he know too much?"

"George Hungerford?" she repeated blankly, and stood still with a glass of sherry in each hand.

At that moment the girl gave a gasp and pointed to the desk. "Look," she half whispered, "look, Jack, it's just like—"

Freda followed her finger, but saw only the mess of envelopes, returned checks, and miscellany that she had just been sorting. But Donelly seemed to know what she meant at once. He dived at the desk and brought forth a brown cardboard notebook containing her monthly accounts. Suddenly she lost her temper completely and screamed. "Here!" she yelled, "what the hell do you think you're doing, rooting through my private papers? You get out of here before I call the police! Miss Innes, don't think you won't be disciplined for this abominable impertinence!"

The young man had actually opened her account book and was thumbing through it. A look of puzzlement came over his face. "Oh," he said weakly. Then he looked up at her. "Is this your writing?"

"Of course it's my writing!" she said irritably, but unable to maintain her fury because of her growing curiosity. "What in God's name did you think it was?"

But the young man's face renewed its fierceness. "It doesn't prove a thing!" he cried. "Anybody can change his writing. I'll just hang onto this. An expert—"

"Look," said Freda. "I won't call the police. I won't tell Bainbridge on Miss Innes. But will you for God's sake sit down and tell me what this is all about?"

"Where were you between five and six the afternoon of November 21?" rapped the reporter, and glared at her, breathing heavily.

Deliberately, Freda set down the sherry glasses and went to her desk, extracted an engagement pad. "I was," she enunciated slowly, "at a meeting of the Library Committee in Room 31 of College Hall. There are five other members of the committee, all of whom were present and will undoubtedly vouch for my presence. If you will call Miss Austen, Mr. Sancton, Mrs. McGill and—um—Mr. Horner and Miss Michaelson you'll find I have an ironclad alibi for that period. And now, my good Holmes and Watson—"

The two looked at each other for a moment and sidled

toward the sofa, sitting uncomfortably on the edge, as if to punish themselves. She handed them each a glass of sherry and sat down herself while they mumbled thanks.

"Well," said Miss Innes resignedly, "I guess it'll just have to be chalked up to reading too many detective stories. But honestly, Mrs. Cramm, you looked like such a good suspect. Even Mr. Marks—oh dear!" She blushed again, shutting her mouth quickly.

Freda lay back in her chair and roared. "Oh, my Lord!" she said at last, limply, "Did Leonard Marks tell you I tried to murder *him*?"

Miss Innes was silent, but the young man, who, on closer observation, was neither as young as he looked, nor as he acted, put in quickly, "It wasn't only that, Mrs. Cramm. Although what you were up to the day you scared the spit out of him up on the mountain is a mystery to me."

Freda looked down at her sherry coyly. "I frequently walk out to that wonderful old ruin. I'm half thinking of buying it. That evening Mr. Marks had come bounding out of the woods like such a beast from the jungle that I half felt I was protecting my virtue."

"Bounding like a big fierce cottontail," murmured Miss Innes, who was recovering her *savoir faire* as she absorbed sherry.

"It wasn't only Marks—or rather it was some other things he said that set us off," said Donelly seriously. "Someone has been systematically persecuting Mr. Hungerford. Someone who was—ah—rather intimate with Boyle. Hungerford won't go to the police about the thing, because the persecution takes the form of a journal which is planted in his room, full of—well, scurrilous statements about him."

"Why in the world should *I* want to make scurrilous statements about George Hungerford, of all people?" said Freda in puzzlement. "And if I did, why should I take the trouble to put them in a journal in his room? It seems to me that if a person wanted to make scurrilous—who started that word, anyway?—statements about another person, she would make them where they'd be heard."

"Oh, I don't know," said Kate Innes eagerly. "It's the same

principle as poison-pen letters; after all, nobody knows about *them* but the writer and the recipient."

"Yes, but—" began Freda, and then threw up her hands. "Well, it's just alien to my nature, that's all I can say. What in the world made you pick on me?"

The Innes girl blushed and played with her skirt, and Donelly cleared his throat. "Well, it was a lot of little things," he said belligerently.

"The story about the fight you and Mr. Hungerford had before he went to the sanitarium was campus gossip," the girl interrupted. "Nobody knew just what it was about, or whether it was a real grudge, or just that he was going off his rocker. And then this person who wrote the journal was a woman. She called herself Eloise, Mr. Marks said. And she—she seemed— that is, she must have known Mr. Boyle pretty well—wrote about it in the journal. And then Mr. Marks heard her. He said—" she stopped and blushed—"well, he *said* she sounded just like you."

But suddenly Freda rose and began to pace the floor. "He actually *heard* the person?"

"That was why he followed you out into the country that day," said the reporter. "The day before, he had heard your voice—or what he thought was your voice—in Hungerford's apartment. On the same day a new entry appeared in the journal. That was when Hungerford told him all about the persecution—he'd been asleep at the time Marks heard the voice."

"How in the world did Leonard hear a voice in Hungerford's apartment?" said Freda suddenly, stopping by the windows. "Does he hang about the halls of that fantastic mansion waiting for Hungerford to appear?"

"Fantastic mansion?" said Kate. "But didn't you know—Mr. Hungerford moved! He moved to Kevin Boyle's apartment— just to escape the journal, he told Mr. Marks. And then it followed him—even there! Maybe *especially* there! The woman actually gets into his rooms to write the thing!"

At last Freda was galvanized into action. She flew out to the coat closet and put on her coat. Then she whisked back to the living room and beckoned to the amazed couple there.

"Come along," she said. "You were quite right to feel some action should be taken. All this should have been in the hands of the police long ago. I'm going to George Hungerford's and get that journal!"

LEONARD HAD got him to bed, but by dint of a ruse, he persuaded him to leave. He promised to go to sleep. He said he would not be able to sleep if he knew Leonard was in the other room. He pleaded that after all Leonard would be just across the hall where he could easily hear him, and in any case the doctor would be here in a half hour or so. But after Leonard finally left, protesting and casting regretful backward looks, he crept from his bed like a naughty child and locked his outer door. For now he could no more lie still than he could cage a tempest. He was on fire, in flight, as dire as night, and everything about him was a little askew, as if the center of gravity had shifted, as if he were climbing to the crest of one wave and down to the trough of the next as he walked across his once perfectly level floor; the imitation oriental carpet which Miss Stone had laid on his floor had suddenly become a jungle rioting with tropical plants and he was walking over the shifting treetops of the solid jungle while the rhymes winged through his head like a flock of parrots, or a flight of pigeons caught in the draft between city buildings. He roamed and paced the rooms. He had a handkerchief in his hands which he was tearing to bits, dropping the shreds on the floor because he had to feel some kind of resistance, otherwise he would explode and fly into a thousand pieces before the doctor even came. At last he dressed. He felt he must dress. He shaved. "Must lay the corpse out properly," he mumbled. But he cut himself with the razor and bled. Corpses do not bleed. His hands shook. He was the corpse and the undertaker all at once. This is the church and this is the steeple. The sunlight coming through the diamond-paned windows was blinding blue, like the pointed rays of acetylene torches, burning through the bits of glass. And the snow, the delicate fragile snow, lying crystal on crystal like a thousand thousand lovers in a common bed, and the blue blue sky, blue as a steam whistle or a loud blast on a brass trumpet. He was strung and humming stripped like catgut, over bridge and around key. He shook and vibrated in response to the breath of the universe like the highest tautest violin string. He put a cigarette in his mouth and tried to light a match. Three times he could not strike the box, and when the little stick caught flame at last, he singed his eyebrow and

did not touch the cigarette. He gave it up. He paced and paced
the living room with an uneven gait. Not the gait of a drunken
man, for drunken men are loose and falling into stupor—but
with the wild twitching limp of an epileptic about to fall into a
fit. In some far off inner cavern of his brain where self-
observation still resided, he knew he was beside himself. But
outwardly he felt a queer joy in his own wildness, illness, madness. Never before had he felt so able to express the power in
him that had gone muffled all these years except in his writing.
It was as if at last the passion of creation could be taken off
paper and put into life. In a rush of ecstasy he took the persecuting notebook and tore out half its pages, scattering them
about the room. This was to symbolize that there was no more
use for that kind of secondhand action, it could no longer
touch him. Now let the murderess come herself, let Eloise attack him directly, for her mere paper words no longer had any
meaning.

But the doctor was coming too. This he knew, and he knew
he had something to say to the doctor, something which was
absolutely imperative for him to say. Or pray this day one way
. . . He went back through the bedroom, pitching against
the bed, steadying himself against the footrail. He clasped the
edge of the basin and guided his hand to the knob of the
medicine chest. By what feat of control he knew not, he extracted one of the sleeping capsules, separated its transparent
halves, spilled out a little of the powder, and swallowed the
rest. Then he went back to the living room and sat down by
the fire. He rocked back and forth in the wing chair, his head
in his hands, simply because he could not be still. Suddenly he
was roused by a pain in his foot. He looked down and saw his
slipper smoking with heat, his foot almost in the fire. He began
to laugh, but his laughter turned to tears, which ran childishly
down his cheeks. On the hearth beside his foot lay a black
curly head, pillowed boyishly on a folded arm. The intimacy of
that hair, with the firelight defining each separate thread of it!
To touch it, to feel it, to say: Kevin, come back . . .

As the drug took hold, he became calmer. It did not make
him drowsy at all, but only relaxed him a bit—thank God,
otherwise he never could have said what he had to say to the
doctor. Finally he would speak of the notebook, he would

clear the girl of the charge of madness, at last he would lay his burden in the hands of authority. He liked Forstmann. If it had not been too late, he would have gone to Forstmann long ago, to be cured. Once he had visited him professionally, indeed, and had approved that calm, sympathetic, recording face. But too late. He was too entrenched in illness by that time to be blasted out. Only in this hour of danger could he call on him. He must tell him of the danger in which they all stood. It menaced everyone, growing larger and larger, like ink spreading across a blotter. First Kevin, then the little girl—Molly—now himself—who next? Anyone, everyone.

On his mother's ormolu clock the minutes curled away. For a moment his mother came and stood beside him, her hand on his hair, in a way she had. But she did not speak. She only came the way she used to come to his study when he was at work, not speaking, not interrupting, but warning him that an interruption was at hand, that he must prepare for a meal, or company. Then the doorbell buzzed. He twitched to his feet, jerked down his jacket, smoothed a hand over his hair. In the room a smell of burnt leather lingered from his scorched slipper.

He tried not to look too queer in greeting Forstmann, but gazing into the man's wide-set eyes, blue and magical as a Siamese cat's in his dark face, he had the feeling that already the doctor knew everything, there was scarcely need to say a word.

"Sit down," he said, when he had ushered Forstmann in, his voice cracked, his hand making a tense upward gesture.

Slowly, gravely, the psychiatrist took his place to one side of the fire, and Hungerford sat opposite. He imagined that in the black brief case on the floor might repose the mysterious implements to be used in administering last rites. Extreme unction. He cleared his throat, and restrained a titter, or a sob, he was not sure which. Like a foetus miscarried before the sex can be determined. No. No sense in this.

"I wanted to talk to you," he said, very slowly and carefully. He opened his mouth, but the wrong words came out. "What's in your bag?"

"Notes," said Forstmann, very calmly. "Papers."

"Oh," he laughed foolishly. "All at once I couldn't imagine

what it would be a psychiatrist would carry. What sorts of implements, I mean."

"What did you imagine might be there?" asked Forstmann conversationally.

"The things—whatever it is a priest carries for dying people," said Hungerford promptly. "Of course, you know that's not what I meant to talk about at all."

"No?" said Forstmann. "What then?"

"It's about that little patient of yours—that little girl—Molly Morrison—is that her name? Strange, I couldn't remember it earlier. Now it's come back."

"Yes, Molly Morrison," said the doctor, twitching at his trouser leg. "She told me about coming to you. I couldn't make much of it. I'd be very much obliged if you could throw some light on the matter." But the cat's eyes were looking at him in frank scrutiny, saying, of course I know that this is not what you wish to talk about at all. However, they held infinite patience and ability to allow him to go his own gait.

Hungerford paused, picking his way among all the galaxies and myriads of dangerous words that swarmed like bees for him to choose from. "First," he said slowly, "I must tell you that I am unable to give a clear account of what happened the day she—the day she first came here, because I seem to have—I seem to have suffered an attack of amnesia for the period of her visit." He drew a breath, but Forstmann only nodded judiciously. "Nevertheless," he pushed on, "I have reason to believe there actually was an attempt made on the girl's life." He stopped. "Just as she described it."

Forstmann moved in his chair and cleared his throat. Would he never show emotion? "You mean," he said, "there actually was an attempt made to strangle her?"

Something took hold of his own throat, as if he too were being strangled. In silence, he nodded. They both sat quietly until he could go on. Strange shiftings and undersea earthquakes were taking place on the floor of his brain, but he tried to maintain a surface calm. "I found evidence," he said at last.

"What sort of evidence?" asked Forstmann.

How was he to explain? It was so bald. "First I must go back a bit," he began, and stopped.

"Yes?" said Forstmann, after allowing him a pause.

He chose his words very carefully. "All during this year," he said, "someone has been persecuting me. A woman. A woman named Eloise." Again he had to stop. Why was it so hard?

"An acquaintance?" asked Forstmann. "Someone whom you believe has reason to dislike you?" He tactfully behaved as if he believed the whole thing.

"She's my sister," blurted Hungerford, and then began to titter, for it had come off his blundering tongue without his having the least intention of saying it. "How silly! I mean to say, she has the same name as a sister who died before my birth. Which leads me to believe this person must know a *great* deal about me—a great deal more than I can explain. I have no idea of who it is. No idea at all."

"What did you say her name was?"

"Eloise," said Hungerford. As he said the name, he suddenly knew what she must look like. Like an idiot girl who had lived in the town where he grew up. Huge and hulking, built like a fat adolescent boy, with big flat feet and a strange walk, little pig's eyes . . .

"What form does this persecution take?" said Forstmann matter-of-factly, quite as if he thought Hungerford were sane. He wanted to go and shake the doctor's hand for his fine performance. But instead he rose from his chair. The notebook was under a table where he had thrown it, with the leaves he had ripped scattered about. He gathered them up and put them between the covers, handed the book to Forstmann. "A journal," he said. "A journal which has been appearing in my rooms ever since the beginning of the college year. I have come to believe this woman must have had something to do with Kevin Boyle's murder. And now that she has made this attempt on the little girl . . ." Suddenly his face contorted in the tic, and he was unable to speak until the tyrannical muscles released their grasp.

Forstmann was thumbing through the notebook. "If you believed this had to do with the murder," he said thoughtfully, "why didn't you show it to the police?"

The tic was doing a new thing. Instead of contracting only his face, it seemed to have taken hold of one whole side of his head, even of his brain, and was squeezing tighter and tighter. But he felt he must answer. "Read—it—" he forced out. "I—

couldn't." He could see Forstmann's eyes staring at him, large and limpid. He heard his own words only faintly. He thought he could count on Forstmann to understand, to carry on, to . . . Because he was at the absolute end. He might even be dying. This time he was not sure. He was being sucked down a corridor by an irresistible draft, to a broad, flat, grassless, treeless plain. And from the plain he looked up to a mountain which stood ominous and purple against the horizon. That mountain was his brain. And as he watched, he saw a crevice begin to open down its side, a terrible wound from which the bowels of the earth in all their foulness came spilling out, engulfing him in their sliminess, stifling him in their stench, like the patient under the ether cone, but his lungs were breathless, he was slipping sidewise into space, his face contorting sidewise, his whole being changing, altering, crying out, Mother! like a dying man. Faintly, through the roar surrounding him, he heard Dr. Forstmann's matter-of-fact voice saying, "And you have no idea who the writer might possibly be?" And then he went altogether away.

"OF COURSE I have," said the voice irritably. "I wrote it myself."

Forstmann's whole being said to him: Don't show surprise! He grasped the notebook more tightly, and sat forward a bit. "I thought you said you didn't know who wrote it," he said very quietly.

"Not at all," said the voice. "I said no such thing. *He* did."

The sun was pouring through the windows behind the chair where George Hungerford sat so that his face was dim in the shadow of the wing chair. But Forstmann could see that the tic had abated, leaving the face curiously lax. Had he known the man better, he would have said that there was something totally uncharacteristic about the expression on his face, but having seen him so seldom, he could not risk such a notion. Still, the face seemed to him to have a curiously secret smug look which drained it of all the tragedy and intelligence that made it so admirable ordinarily. "Who is *he*?" he asked, as quietly as he knew how.

"Hoh," said the voice scornfully, "he, him, Jesus on the Cross, Prince Mishkin, our Georgie. George Hungerford, who else?"

"And who are you?" asked Forstmann, very cautiously, very quietly, scarcely above a whisper.

"Why I'm little sister Eloise," simpered the voice, nearly falsetto now, utterly horrifying in its grotesquerie, issuing from George Hungerford's mouth.

B AINBRIDGE SAT at his desk, his head in his hands. Outside the windows the snow whirled dizzyingly. "Please God," he remarked devoutly, "don't let the newspapers get hold of this."

"I see no reason why they should," said Forstmann. "I see no reason why the police should, either. Let the whole thing simply dribble off, as it would have in any case. Hungerford is in a place where he can't do anyone any harm anyway—there's no reason why he should be taken out of the State Hospital for the Insane, tried, and put back in again. And since he is in a condition which could legally be attested to as insane, there's actually no further evidence that he murdered Kevin Boyle than there was before."

"Yet you're convinced that he did?" said Bainbridge curiously, lifting his head.

"Or that *she* did," said Forstmann. He shook his head incredulously. "Honestly, Bainbridge, this case has Miss Beauchamp, Doris Fischer, Dr. Jekyll, and Mr. Hyde looking like a bunch of malingerers."

"But George *Hungerford*," wailed Bainbridge, "was always the quietest, calmest, least troublesome—that is, with the exception of the nervous breakdown—Forstmann, if this were a joke, I assure you it would be a very bad joke, even in the rowdy medical circles which you frequent."

"It's not a joke," said Forstmann, looking serious. "I've had Hungerford under observation for two weeks. I have placed him under narcotics about once a day. Each time I do so, the second personality—Eloise, as she calls herself—"

"Eloise!" exclaimed Bainbridge disgustedly.

Forstmann sat forward. "That's one of the most fascinating sidelights on the whole thing. In his waking state—or in the role of George Hungerford—he is unable to remember any of the history that obviously gives rise to the second personality— Eloise. But in the guise of Eloise, he tells a perfectly connected story about how as a small child his mother called him by the name of the sister who died in infancy, dressed him in girl's clothes, and encouraged him to assume female characteristics altogether."

"It just doesn't sound reasonable," said Bainbridge, shaking

his head bullishly. "Hungerford has none of the ordinary homosexual mannerisms. God knows we've had enough around
for me to recognize the signs when I see them."

"He rejected the female elements in his nature so violently
that they actually regrouped themselves into a second personality—that's the only way I can think of to describe it," said
Forstmann.

"Why?" said Bainbridge. "Most men have some womanly
characteristics, just as most women have some manly ones.
What's the harm?"

"The harm is when a man has such a large admixture of the
female in his nature that his whole sexual status becomes en-
dangered. As near as I've been able to make out, Hungerford
was encouraged to develop his female potentialities, so called,
far beyond his male ones with his mother. Yet outside the
home, the atmosphere which he lived in was so rigidly conventional that he knew he stood in terrible danger from not only
his schoolmates, but other adults, and, in a strange way, even
his mother. She couldn't have given him a better background
for psychosis if she'd known what she was about. For the first
four or five years of his life he was actually called Eloise by her.
(As Hungerford, he remembers none of this, by the way.)
Then, when it came time to cut off his curls and take him out
of Lord Fauntleroy suits, even his mother recognized that he
must become a boy. So that then she began to rebuke him for
behaving in the way that she had encouraged."

"You *couldn't* be making this up," groaned Bainbridge.

"Well, in a way I am," said Forstmann. "I'm trying to make
something clear to you that isn't clear to me at all—I'm making
very tenuous connections seem strong, and I'm reading in in-
terpretations which may be quite incorrect. I'm taking bits of
other cases of multiple personality and grafting on to this one,
simply because if I couldn't make some sort of sense of the
business there'd be nothing for it but to say the man was possessed of a devil."

"That's much the better explanation," said Bainbridge emphatically.

"It's certainly easier," admitted Forstmann, "and I'll admit
freely that for a moment I might have been tempted to accept
it myself. I always had a great admiration for Hungerford and

his work. When I went to see him that day the first thing I thought was what a noble sort of head he has—like a Roman medallion. He was obviously extremely confused and on the border of some sort of manic state. But when I heard that eerie falsetto voice coming out of his mouth, saying, I'm Eloise, I must confess that my hair rose on my head."

Bainbridge sighed and shook his head. "Well," he began again, "Why hasn't Eloise appeared before? You mean she's been—I mean, he's had a double personality all this time and it never came out before? How is that?"

"I would take a guess that there may previously have been some sort of minor somnambulistic state in which she appeared, but never with the same distinctness as after his return from the sanitarium when he began to use nembutal to put him to sleep in the afternoons. It's possible that the reason for his insomnia at night at this time was the fact that Hungerford felt that Eloise was more out of his control than ever before, and he feared what she would do when she made her appearance."

"Why should she have gotten worse all of a sudden? What happened to him?"

"I don't think it was all of a sudden. First came the death of his mother, about which he had terrible and quite conscious guilt feelings. His lifetime devotion to her stands as nothing in his mind beside the fact that he was not at her deathbed. This cut off his creative ability—evidently as a form of self-punishment he found himself unable to write after her death. Then his life was terribly empty of affection without her, until Kevin Boyle came to the college. In the role of George Hungerford he became very fond of him. In the role of Eloise, he fell madly in love with him."

"But as Eloise, how did he know about Kevin Boyle? Eloise never saw him, did she?"

"He had what is not uncommon in cases of dissociated personality—partial amnesia. As Hungerford he had no recollection of the existence of Eloise, but as Eloise, he had total recall of his life as George Hungerford. In fact, Eloise seems to regard herself as existing at the same time as George Hungerford, but under a sort of spell, so that she cannot act."

Bainbridge, who had been frantically rearranging his desk,

twisting bits of paper, and sharpening pencils with his pen knife, now could sit still no longer, but rose from his swivel chair and paced around the desk to lean over Forstmann who sat deep in his chair, his knees jutting. "Julian," he said desperately, "may I smell your breath?"

"Certainly," said Forstmann, grinning, and blew at him.

Bainbridge sighed and went back behind his desk. "The world would have seemed so much more *stable*," he said wistfully, "if you had been drinking."

Forstmann stopped smiling and spoke soberly. "Hungerford used a phrase that impressed me very much. The poetry of unreason. He said he had been unable to come to a psychiatrist, even though he knew he was mentally ill, because he never found one who could grasp the poetry of unreason. Well, I could make a different diagnosis of why he didn't come, but what he said would remain true. Because psychiatrists aren't intended to be poets, they're scientists, they're obliged professionally to take the dew off the rose and analyze it as H_2O. That's their function. But when, on my busman's holidays, I've thought of madness, it seems most easily explained to me as poetry in action. A life of symbol rather than reality. On paper one can understand Gulliver, or Kafka, or Dante. But let a man go about *behaving* as if he were a giant or a midget, or caught in a cosmic plot directed at himself, or in heaven or hell, and we feel horror—we want to disavow him, to proclaim him as far removed as possible from ourselves." He stopped suddenly and looked at Bainbridge. "For God's sake, Lucien, stop staring at me with your mouth hanging open as if you took my every word for gospel!"

Bainbridge shut his mouth and made a noise which sounded like "humph." "Well," he said more audibly, "and when did he—she—tell you about killing Boyle?"

"Almost immediately," said Forstmann. "We were talking about the notebook. First Hungerford was speaking as Hungerford. Suddenly that very distorting tic he had came over his face and he reappeared in the personality of Eloise."

"Wait a minute," cried Bainbridge. "I thought Eloise only appeared when he was asleep or under the influence of a drug."

"It later appeared, when we examined him, that he had taken some nembutal before my arrival. Not enough to put him to sleep, but enough to release the personality of Eloise, who must have been awfully close to the surface even before he took the drug, to judge from Leonard Marks' description of the state he was in earlier in the morning."

"What sort of person is Eloise?" asked Bainbridge curiously. "I mean, can you tell?"

"She's a pretty unattractive female," said Forstmann, "if you'll pardon the loose use of the term. She is, I should say, brutal, ruthless, cunning, passionate—a real Mr. Hyde type."

"But that's so opposite to anything Hungerford could ever possibly be!" cried Bainbridge.

"Maybe if he'd found it easier to be some of those things he wouldn't have found it necessary to develop Eloise," said Forstmann. "Do you want me to give a lecture on the protestant ethic in education and its role in the formation of neuroses of our culture, or shall I just make out a reading list?"

"Spare me," said Bainbridge quickly, "I'm too old. But I still want to know about the murder."

"Well," said Forstmann, leaning forward and opening the zipper of his brief case, "read this." He pulled out a few lined sheets of paper, covered with great toppling calligraphy and handed them to Bainbridge. "Begin here."

Bainbridge frowned, looked at the sheets, pulled a pair of reading glasses out of a leather case and set them on his nose. He formed the words with his lips, trying to make out the strange writing, and then he began to read aloud:

Dear Dr. Forstman, old kid old coffin-face old mortality, this is the letter of how I killed Kevin Boyle—my sweet my lovely, but he would not have me no, he turned his face away. Listen, I said to him, I said Listen Kevin, I am your love your lovely, but he could not see me, he could not see me for the Other One that was without, that enemy, that tomb of ice in which I lay betrayed, our Hungerford. Listen, Kevin, I said, I am free, now no one can stop me (for this was the first time of my coming into the light) but he could see none of me, he turned from me, from my woman's heart, he turned and I could see that he hated me, that there was disgust and horror in his face and this I could not stand. You do not know how terrible this is because your heart is ice, you do not know how it is to be a woman, you are nothing but a nothing a nothing a no. So I took the poker up from the hearth and crushed his head in as he was going to the door. How did I do it? Simply like this. I took the poker and I hit him. And there he lay with his dear sweet head mashed in like a tender little eggshell, like an egg with the chick all unborn and oozing out the crevices. . . .

Bainbridge laid the papers down on the desk and whistled long and low.

"The poetry of unreason," said Forstmann softly.

"The poetry of unreason," echoed Bainbridge.

HONEY SACHEVERAL sat in the Harlow Taproom looking like an angel and drinking an Alexander. Petey Jones of Amherst, sitting opposite her, heaved a sigh which caused the button of his dizzyingly plaid jacket to fly open. "Gee, Honey," he said. "If I sat on that side, I could hold your hand. If I sit on this side I can look at you. Gee, Honey, I don't know *what* to do." In desperation, he drank off half his glass of beer.

Honey giggled, threw back her plumes of hair, and finished her Alexander. "Silly," she said, "you could hold my hand *across* the table. Can I have another Alexayunduh?"

Petey Jones sighed again and took the white hand (magenta tipped) which she extended in one of his own rather grubby paws. With the other he surreptitiously counted ready cash under the table.

"Know what?" said Honey complacently, after Petey had summoned the waitress and ordered her drink, "Mr. Hungerford's gone crazy. They took him to the State Hospital."

"Gee," said Petey, "*George* Hungerford?"

"Uh-huh," said Honey.

"Gosh," said Petey reverently, "we used a book of his in a Sophomore English course. Crazy, huh?"

"Uh-huh," said Honey. "But then, intellectual people are more likely to go crazy than other people."

"Yeah," said Petey, dazzled, "I guess they are, at that."

"It's because they *think* too much," Honey elaborated. "I don't think it's a good idea for a person to think too much. Even for a man."

"Kinda wears your brain out, I guess," said Petey, and swallowed some beer.

"That's right," said Honey. "My mama says a girl never should think too much. Just have a good time and leave the thinking to the men. My mama says a woman's place is in the home, and who in the world wants to just sit around home and *think*?"

Petey Jones leaned over the table ardently. When he felt ardent, and also when he drank beer, his left eye became slightly crossed. "I like my women *feminine*!" he said, as if he were supporting a harem.

"My mama always brought me up to be a feminine sort of girl," said Honey complacently. "Can I have another Alexayunduh?"

"Sure," said Petey nervously, feeling in his pocket to where there was a dollar and seven cents in change.

"But," said Honey contemplatively, "you can't honestly say an intellectual girl *never* gets a man. Now you take Kate Innes."

Petey signalled the waitress for another Alexander and took a very small sip of his beer. "Innes?" he said. "Do I know her?"

"I don't guess so," said Honey. "She's the editor of *The Holly*. Now she's a right messy lookin' sort of a girl, and *real* smart, so's you'd never expect her to do anything—well, you know, *foolish*. But I'm blessed if she didn't up and elope with this cute little ole reporter we met right here in this very booth!"

"You mean right *here?*" asked Petey meaningfully. "Maybe it's an omen!"

"Omen?" questioned Honey.

"*You* know," explained Petey, "like there they were in this very booth and *they* eloped, and now here we are, too."

"Why, Petey!" said Honey appreciatively, "That's right romantic of you! Can I have another Alexayunduh?"

"Gee, Honey," said Petey nervously, "do you think you ought to? You've already had three and it's only nine o'clock."

"Oh Petey!" cried Honey reproachfully, "The Sacheverals always carry their liquor like gentlemen and ladies!"

"All right," sighed Petey. "Wait till the waitress comes around this way again."

"And speakin' of crazy people," said Honey, "they let that little Morrison girl come right back to Birnham House. Now I call that right silly. She might murder us all in our beds, for all we know."

"Oh," said Petey knowingly, "that's the one they had the piece about in the *Messenger*—about did she murder Kevin Boyle."

"Well," said Honey doubtfully, "they said she couldn't have because I saw her in Birnham on the day of the murder between five and six or something, but how do they ever figure it out about a thing like that? I mean, maybe she did it some other time, or something." Honey's smoky eyelashes were hanging low over her halcyon eyes. "Oh, Petey!" she mumbled, yawning as frankly as a kitten, "I'm *so* sleepy. That ole Alexayunduh better hurry up!" She rested her flower head on her rosy palm.

"Maybe they—had some sort of other evidence," said Petey distractedly. "Listen, Honey, don't go to sleep—don't you want some coffee or something?"

"Don't want—nothing'—but—a—little ole—Alexayunduh," murmured Honey, drooping lower over the table.

"Listen, Honey!" cried Petey desperately, "let's dance—come on—I'll put some real jive on the box!"

But Honey was out like a light, her Botticelli countenance flushed, her cheek pillowed on her hand.

"Wake up! Wake up!" cried Petey frantically. "Honey, you can't—" and then, as the waitress came down between the tables, he tried to look as if he were interested only in his few drops of beer. When she was out of sight again, he raised his honest whiskerless countenance to the ceiling and whispered to nobody in particular, "Gee, what are you supposed to do when your girl passes out?"

IN A LONELY PLACE

Dorothy B. Hughes

For

CHARLOTTE

———————————

"It's in a lonesome place you do have to be talking with someone, and looking for someone, in the evening of the day."

J. M. Synge

I

IT WAS good standing there on the promontory overlooking the evening sea, the fog lifting itself like gauzy veils to touch his face. There was something in it akin to flying; the sense of being lifted high above crawling earth, of being a part of the wildness of air. Something too of being closed within an unknown and strange world of mist and cloud and wind. He'd liked flying at night; he'd missed it after the war had crashed to a finish and dribbled to an end. It wasn't the same flying a little private crate. He'd tried it; it was like returning to the stone ax after precision tools. He had found nothing yet to take the place of flying wild.

It wasn't often he could capture any part of that feeling of power and exhilaration and freedom that came with loneness in the sky. There was a touch of it here, looking down at the ocean rolling endlessly in from the horizon; here high above the beach road with its crawling traffic, its dotting of lights. The outline of beach houses zigzagged against the sky but did not obscure the pale waste of sand, the dark restless waters beyond.

He didn't know why he hadn't come out here before. It wasn't far. He didn't even know why he'd come tonight. When he got on the bus, he had no destination. Just the restlessness. And the bus brought him here.

He put out his hand to the mossy fog as if he would capture it, but his hand went through the gauze and he smiled. That too was good, his hand was a plane passing through a cloud. The sea air was good to smell, the darkness was soft closed around him. He swooped his hand again through the restless fog.

He did not like it when on the street behind him a sudden bus spattered his peace with its ugly sound and smell and light. He was sharply angry at the intrusion. His head darted around to vent his scowl. As if the lumbering box had life as well as motion and would shrink from his displeasure. But as his head turned, he saw the girl. She was just stepping off the bus. She couldn't see him because he was no more than a figure in the fog and dark; she couldn't know he was drawing her on his mind as on a piece of paper.

She was small, dark haired, with a rounded face. She was more than pretty, she was nice looking, a nice girl. Sketched in browns, the brown hair, brown suit, brown pumps and bag, even a small brown felt hat. He started thinking about her as she was stepping off the bus; she wasn't coming home from shopping, no parcels; she wasn't going to a party, the tailored suit, sensible shoes. She must be coming from work; that meant she descended from the Brentwood bus at this lonely corner every night at—he glanced to the luminous dial of his watch—seven-twenty. Possibly she had worked late tonight but that could be checked easily. More probably she was employed at a studio, close at six, an hour to get home.

While he was thinking of her, the bus had bumbled away and she was crossing the slant intersection, coming directly towards him. Not to him; she didn't know he was there in the high foggy dark. He saw her face again as she passed under the yellow fog light, saw that she didn't like the darkness and fog and loneness. She started down the California Incline; he could hear her heels striking hard on the warped pavement as if the sound brought her some reassurance.

He didn't follow her at once. Actually he didn't intend to follow her. It was entirely without volition that he found himself moving down the slant, winding walk. He didn't walk hard, as she did, nor did he walk fast. Yet she heard him coming behind her. He knew she heard him for her heel struck an extra beat, as if she had half stumbled, and her steps went faster. He didn't walk faster, he continued to saunter but he lengthened his stride, smiling slightly. She was afraid.

He could have caught up to her with ease but he didn't. It was too soon. Better to hold back until he had passed the humped midsection of the walk, then to close in. She'd give a little scream, perhaps only a gasp, when he came up beside her. And he would say softly, "Hello." Only "Hello," but she would be more afraid.

She had just passed over the mid hump, she was on the final stretch of down grade. Walking fast. But as he reached that section, a car turned at the corner below, throwing its blatant light up on her, on him. Again anger plucked at his face; his steps slowed. The car speeded up the Incline, passed him, but the damage was done, the darkness had broken. As if it were a parade, the stream of cars followed the first car, scratching their light over the path and the road and the high earthen Palisades across. The girl was safe; he could feel the relaxation in her footsteps. Anger beat him like a drum.

When he reached the corner, she was already crossing the street, a brown figure under the yellow fog light marking the intersection. He watched her cross, reach the opposite pavement and disappear behind the dark gate of one of the three houses huddled together there. He could have followed but the houses were lighted, someone was waiting for her in the home light. He would have no excuse to follow to her door.

As he stood there, a pale blue bus slid up to the corner; a middle-aged woman got out. He boarded it. He didn't care where it was going; it would carry him away from the fog light. There were only a few passengers, all women, drab women. The driver was an angular, farm-looking man; he spun his change box with a ratcheting noise and looked into the night. The fare was a nickel.

Within the lighted box they slid past the dark cliffs. Across the width of the road were the massive beach houses and clubs, shutting away the sea. Fog stalked silently past the windows. The bus made no stops until it reached the end of that particular section of road where it turned an abrupt corner. He got out when it stopped. Obviously it was leaving the sea now, turning up into the dark canyon. He stepped out and he walked the short block to a little business section. He didn't know why until he reached that corner, looked up the street. There were several eating places, hamburger stands; there was a small drugstore and there was a bar. He wanted a drink.

It was a nice bar, from the ship's prow that jutted upon the sidewalk to the dim ship's interior. It was a man's bar, although there was a dark-haired, squawk-voiced woman in it. She was with two men and they were noisy. He didn't like them. But he liked the old man with the white chin whiskers behind the bar. The man had the quiet competent air of a sea captain.

He ordered straight rye but when the old man set it in front of him, he didn't want it. He drank it neat but he didn't want it. He hadn't needed a drink; he'd relaxed on the bus. He wasn't angry with anyone any more. Not even with the three noisy sons of bitches up front at the bar.

The ship's bells behind the bar rang out the hour, eight bells. Eight o'clock. There was no place he wanted to go, nothing he wanted to do. He didn't care about the little brown girl any more. He ordered another straight rye. He didn't drink it when it came, he left it there in front of him, not even wanting to drink it.

He could go across to the beach, sit in the sand, and smell the fog and sea. It would be quiet and dark there. The sea had appeared again just before the bus turned; there was open beach across. But he didn't move. He was comfortable where he was. He lit a cigarette and idly turned the jigger of rye upon the polished wood of the bar. Turned it without spilling a drop.

It was his ear caught the word spoken by the harsh-voiced woman. He wasn't listening to her but the word spun and he thought the word was "Brub." He remembered then that Brub lived out this way. He hadn't seen Brub for almost two years; he'd spoken to him only once, months ago when he arrived on the coast. He'd promised to let Brub know when he was settled but he hadn't.

Brub lived in Santa Monica Canyon. He left his drink on the bar and went quickly to the phone booth in the corner. The book was tattered but it was a Santa Monica book and there was the name, Brub Nicolai. He found a nickel and clanged it in the slot, asked the number.

A woman answered; he held on while she called Brub. Then Brub's voice, a little curious, "Hello."

He was excited just hearing the voice. There wasn't anyone like Brub, those years in England wouldn't have been real without Brub. He was gay as a boy, calling, "Hello there, Brub," wanting Brub to guess or to sense who it was. But Brub didn't know. He was puzzled; he asked, "Who's calling?"

Excitement titivated him. "Who do you think's calling?" he demanded. And he cried, "It's Dix. Dix Steele."

It was a good moment. It was the way he'd known it would be, Brub taking a gulp, then shouting, "Dix! Where you been hiding out? Thought you'd gone back East."

"No," he said. He was warm and comfortable in Brub's

pleasure. "I've been sort of busy. You know how it is. Always something here. Something there."

"Yeah, I know." Brub asked, "Where are you now? What are you doing?"

"I'm sitting in a bar," he said and heard Brub's answering crow. They'd spent most of their free time sitting in bars; they'd needed it in those days. Brub didn't know Dix no longer depended on liquor; he had a lot of things to tell Brub. Big brother Brub. "It's down by the ocean, has a ship's prow by the door—"

Brub had cut in. "You're practically here! We only live on Mesa Road, couple of blocks from there. Can you come up?"

"I'm practically there." He hung up, checked the street number in the phone book, returned to the bar and swallowed the rye. This time it tasted good.

He was out on the street before he realized that he didn't have his car. He'd been walking up the street this afternoon and he'd climbed on a Wilshire-Santa Monica bus and he was in Santa Monica. He hadn't thought of Brub for months and a scarecrow dame in a bar said what sounded like "Brub." She hadn't said it at all; she'd been calling the scarecrow guy with her "Bud," but he'd thought of Brub. Now he was going to see him.

Because it was meant to be, a taxi was held just then by the red light. At first he didn't recognize it as a cab; it was a dark, battered car with a young guy, hatless, driving it. It was empty. He read the lettering on it, "Santa Monica Cab Co.," even as the lights turned, and he ran out into the lonely street calling, "Hey, Taxi."

Because it was meant to be, the driver stopped, waited for him. "Do you know where Mesa Road is?" His hand was on the door.

"You want to go there?"

"I sure do." He climbed in, still in his happiness. "Five-twenty."

The driver turned and drove back the way he'd come, a few blocks up the hill, a left turn and a steeper hill. The fog lay a deep and dirty white in the canyon, the windshield wiper pushed away the moisture. "This is Nicolai's," the driver said.

He was pleasantly surprised that the driver knew where he

was going. It was a good omen; it meant Brub wouldn't have changed. Brub still knew everyone, everyone knew him. He watched the driver's fog lights circle, turn, and head down the hill. It was unconscious, the waiting and watching; in his thoughts was only the look of the amber swinging across the pillow of fog.

There was a gate to open; and the mailbox was white beside it. Lettered in black was B. Nicolai, 520 Mesa Road. He embraced the name. The house was high above the flowered terrace, but there was a light of welcome, amber as a fog light, in the front window. He climbed the winding flagstone steps to the door. He waited a second before he touched the brass knocker, again without consciousness, only a savoring of the moment before the event. He had no sooner touched it than the door was flung wide and Brub was there.

Brub hadn't changed. The same short-cut, dark, curly hair, the same square face with the grin on the mouth and in the shining black eyes. The same square shoulders and the look of the sea on him; he rolled like a sailor when he walked. Or like a fighter. A good fighter. That was Brub.

He was looking up at Dix and his hand was a warm grip on Dix's hand. "Hello, you old son of a sea cook," he said. "What do you mean by not calling us before now? Let me see you."

He knew exactly what Brub saw, as if Brub were a mirror he was standing before. A young fellow, just an average young fellow. Tanned, medium light hair with a little curl, medium tall and enough weight for height. Eyes, hazel; nose and mouth right for the face, a good-looking face but nothing to remember, nothing to set it apart from the usual. Good gabardine suit, he'd paid plenty to have it made, open-necked tan sports shirt. Maybe the face was sharpened at the moment by excitement and happiness, the excitement and happiness of seeing an old and favored friend. Ordinarily it wasn't one to remember.

"Let me look at you," he echoed. Brub was half a head shorter and he looked down at Brub as Brub looked up at him. They made the survey silently, both satisfied with what they saw, both breaking silence together. "You haven't changed a bit."

"Come on in." Brub took his arm and ushered him out of the dim, pleasant hallway into the lighted living room. He broke step as they crossed the comfortable lamp-lighted room. Things weren't the same. There was a girl there, a girl who had a right to be there.

He saw her as he would always see her, a slender girl in a simple beige dress, curled in a large wing chair by the white fireplace. The chair was a gaudy piece patterned in greens and purples, like tropical flowers, with a scrawl of cerise breaking the pattern. Her hair was the color of palest gold, a silvery gold, and she wore it pulled away from her face into a curl at the back of her neck. She had a fine face, nothing pretty-pretty about it, a strong face with high cheek bones and a straight nose. Her eyes were beautiful, sea blue, slanted like wings; and her mouth was a beautiful curve. Yet she wasn't beautiful; you wouldn't look at her in a room of pretty women, in a bar or night spot. You wouldn't notice her; she'd be too quiet; she was a lady and she wouldn't want to be noticed.

She was at home here; she was mistress of the house and she was beautiful in her content. Before either spoke, he knew she was Brub's wife. The way she was smiling as the two of them entered, the way her smile strengthened as Brub spoke. "This is Dix, Sylvia. Dickson Steele."

She put out her hand and finished the sentence, "—of whom I've heard you speak constantly. Hello, Dix."

Dix stepped forward to match her smile, to take her hand. Except for that first moment, he hadn't shown anything. Even that wouldn't have been noticed. "Hello, Sylvia," he said. She was tall standing, as tall as Brub. He held her hand while he turned to Brub, a prideful, smiling Brub. "Why didn't you tell me you were married?" he demanded. "Why hide this beautiful creature under the blanket of your indifference?"

Sylvia withdrew her hand and Brub laughed. "You sound just like the Dix I've heard about," she retorted. She had a nice voice, shining as her pale hair. "Beer with us or whiskey as a stubborn individualist?"

He said, "Much to Brub's surprise, I'll take beer."

It was so comfortable. The room was a good one, only the chair was gaudy, the couch was like green grass and another couch the yellow of sunlight. There was pale matting on the polished floor; there was a big green chair and heavy white drapes across the Venetian blinds. Good prints, O'Keeffe and

Rivera. The bar was of light wood—convenient and unobtrusive in the corner. There must have been an ice chest, the beer was damp with cold.

Sylvia uncapped his bottle, poured half into a tall frosted glass and put it on an end table beside him. She brought Brub a bottle, poured a glass for herself. Her hands were lovely, slim and quiet and accurate; she moved quietly and with the same accuracy. She was probably a wonderful woman to bed with; no waste motion, quietness.

When he knew what he was thinking, he repeated, "Why didn't you tell me you were married?"

"Tell you!" Brub roared. "You called me up seven months ago, last February, the eighth to be exact, told me you'd just got in and would let me know soon as you were located. That's the last I've heard of you. You checked out of the Ambassador three days later and you didn't leave a forwarding address. How could I tell you anything?"

He smiled, his eyes lowered to his beer. "Keeping tabs on me, Brub?"

"Trying to locate you, you crazy lug," Brub said happily.

"Like the old days," Dix said. "Brub took care of me like a big brother, Sylvia."

"You needed a caretaker."

He switched back. "How long have you been married?"

"Two years this spring," Sylvia told him.

"One week and three days after I got home," Brub said. "It took her that long to get a beauty-shop appointment."

"Which she didn't need," Dix smiled.

Sylvia smiled to him. "It took him that long to raise the money for a license. Talk of drunken sailors! He spent every cent on flowers and presents and forgot all about the price of wedding."

Comfortable room and talk and beer. Two men. And a lovely woman.

Brub said, "Why do you think I fought the war? To get back to Sylvia."

"And why did you fight the war, Mr. Steele?" Sylvia's smile wasn't demure; she made it that way.

"For weekend passes to London," Brub suggested.

He stepped on Brub's words answering her thoughtfully. He

wanted to make an impression on her. "I've wondered about it frequently, Sylvia. Why did I or anyone else fight the war? Because we had to isn't good enough. I didn't have to when I enlisted. I think it was because it was the thing to do. And the Air Corps was the thing to do. All of us in college were nuts about flying. I was a sophomore at Princeton when things were starting. I didn't want to be left out of any excitement."

"Brub was at Berkeley," she remembered. "You're right, it was the thing to do."

They were steered to safe channels, to serious discussion. Brub opened another beer for the men.

Brub said, "It was the thing to do or that was the rationalization. We're a casual generation, Dix, we don't want anyone to know we bleed if we're pricked. But self defense is one of the few prime instincts left. Despite the cover-up, it was self defense. And we knew it."

Dix agreed, lazily. You could agree or disagree in this house. No one got his back up whatever was said. There was no anger here, no cause for anger. Even with a woman. Perhaps because of the woman. She was gentle.

He heard Sylvia's amused voice as from afar, as through a film of gray mist. "Brub's always looking for the hidden motive power. That's because he's a policeman."

He came sharply into focus. The word had been a cold spear deliberately thrust into his brain. He heard his voice speak the cold, hard word. "Policeman?" But they didn't notice anything. They thought him surprised, as he was, more than surprised, startled and shocked. They were accustomed to that reaction. For they weren't jesting; they were speaking the truth. Brub with an apologetic grin; his wife with pride under her laughter.

"He really is," she was saying.

And Brub was saying, "Not a policeman now, darling, a detective."

They'd played the scene often; it was in their ease. He was the one who needed prompting, needed cue for the next speech. He repeated, "Policeman," with disbelief, but the first numbing shock had passed. He was prepared to be correctly amused.

Brub said, "Detective. I don't know why. Everyone wants to know why and I don't know."

"He hasn't found the underlying motive yet," Sylvia said.

Brub shrugged. "I know that one well enough. Anything to keep from working. That's the motto of the Nicolais. Graven on their crest."

"A big healthy man reclining," Sylvia added.

They were like a radio team, exchanging patter with seemingly effortless ease.

"My old man was a land baron, never did a lick of work. But land baroneering is outmoded, so I couldn't do that. The girls all married money." He fixed Sylvia with his eye. "I don't know why I didn't think of that. Raoul, my oldest brother, is an investment broker. That's what it says on his gold-lettered office door. Investment broker."

"Brub," Sylvia warned but she smiled.

"Up and to the office by ten," Brub proclaimed. "Maybe a bit after. Open the mail. To the club for two quick games of squash. Shower, shave, trim, and lunch. Leisurely, of course. A quiet nap after, a bit of bridge—and the day's over. Very wearing."

Brub took a swallow of beer. "Then there's Tom—he plays golf. A lawyer on the side. He only takes cases dealing with the ravages of pterodactyls to the tidelands. The pterodactyls having little time for ravaging the tidelands, he has plenty of time for golf." He drank again. "I'm a detective."

Dix had listened with his face, a half smile, but he kept his eyes on his beer glass. His mouth was sharp with questions, they were like tacks pricking his tongue. Brub had finished and was waiting for him to speak. He said easily, "So you took the easy job. No investments or law for you. Sherlock Nicolai. And were you right?"

"No, damn it," Brub wailed. "I work."

"You know Brub," Sylvia sighed. "Whatever he does, he does with both heads. He's full fathoms deep in detecting."

Dix laughed, setting down his beer glass. It was time to go. Time to put space between himself and the Nicolais. "Brub should have taken up my racket." To their questioning eyebrows, he elucidated, "Like ninety-three and one-half per cent of the ex-armed forces, I'm writing a book."

"Another author," Sylvia mused.

"Unlike ninety-two and one-half per cent I'm not writing a book on the war. Or even my autobiography. Just trying to do a novel." A wonderful racket; neither of them knew what a smart choice he'd made. Not haphazardly, no. Coldly, with sane reasoning. He stretched like a dog, preliminary to rising. "That's why you haven't seen me before. When you're trying to write, there isn't time to run around. I stick pretty close to the old machine." He smiled frankly at Brub. "My uncle is giving me a year to see what I can do. So I work." He was on his feet. He had meant to ask the use of the phone, to call a cab. But Brub wouldn't allow it; he'd insist on taking him to the busline; he'd want to know where Dix was living. Dix didn't mind a walk. He'd find his own way to town.

He said, "And I'd better be getting back on the job."

They demurred but they didn't mind. They were young and they were one, and Brub had to get up in the morning. He slipped the question in sideways. "After all Brub has to have his rest to detect for the glory of Santa Monica, doesn't he?"

"Santa Monica! I'm on the L. A. force," Brub boasted mildly.

He'd wanted to know; he knew. The L. A. force.

"Then you do need sleep. Plenty of work in L. A., no?"

Brub's face lost its humor, became a little tired. "Plenty," he agreed.

Dix smiled, a small smile. Brub wouldn't know why; Brub had been his big brother but he hadn't known everything there was to know. Some things a man kept secret. It was amusing to keep some things secret.

"I'll be seeing you," he said easily. His hand opened the door. But he didn't get away.

"Wait," Brub said. "We don't have your number."

He had to give it. He did without seeming reluctance. Brub would have noticed reluctance. Brub or the clear-eyed woman behind him, watching him quietly. He gave his telephone number and he repeated his goodnight. Then he was alone, feeling his way off the porch and down the path into the darkness and the moist opaque fog.

2

He walked into the night not knowing the way, not caring. He'd moved more than once during his seven months in

California. He could move again. It wasn't easy to find quarters, the right ones for him. He liked the place he had now; he'd been lucky about it. A fellow he'd known years ago, in college. Years, aeons ago. He hadn't cared for Mel Terriss then; he'd cared even less for him on running into him that night last July. Terriss was going to pouches; under his chin and eyes, in his belly. He had alcoholic eyes and they were smearing the blonde with Dix. He didn't get an introduction. But he blatted waiting for it and Dix had found the flat he'd been waiting for. He was sick and tired of the second-rate hotel off Westlake Park. It smelled. Terriss was telling everyone about being off to Rio for a year, a fat job to go with his fat head.

He could move again but he was damned if he would. He liked Beverly Hills; a pleasant neighborhood. A safe neighborhood. It was possible he could change his phone number, Terriss' number. Get an unlisted one. He'd considered that before now. But Terriss' number was as good as being unlisted. There was no Dix Steele in the book.

Automatically he walked out of the small canyon, down to the beach road. He crossed to the oceanside; he could hear the crash of waves beyond the dark sands. He considered walking back along the waterfront but sand walking was difficult and he was all at once tired. He turned in the direction of the Incline. There was no bus, no taxi, and no car stopped for him. He walked on, in the street most of the way because there was no sidewalk, keeping close to the buildings because in the fog he was no more than a moving blur. He was damned if he'd move or even bother to change his number. He didn't have to see Brub and his woman again. He'd proffered his excuse before it was needed. He was writing a book; he had no time for evenings like this, gab and beer.

He walked on, quiet as the fog. It had been pleasant. It was the first pleasant evening he'd had in so long. So terribly long. He tried to remember how long. Those early days in England when he and Brub knew each other so well.

He hardened his jaw and he trudged on towards the yellow ring of fog light on the pavement ahead. He watched the light, watched it come closer as he moved silently towards it. He shut out thought, clamping it between his set teeth. It wasn't until he reached the light that he saw the Incline looming slantly across. And realized that the house into which the brown girl had disappeared lay just beyond. He stopped there, in the shadow of the clubhouse. The club's parking lot, wire fenced, empty of cars, lay between him and the huddle of houses. The pounding of the sea recurred in changeless rhythm and he could smell the salt far beyond the wire fence.

He had to walk up to the three houses; that was where the white lanes of the crosswalk lay on the highway. He smiled a little as he started forward. He was halfway past the fenced lot when the hideous noise of an oil truck, ignoring the stop sign, thundered past. A second one speeded after the first, and a third, blasting the quietness with thumping wheels, clanging chains. Spewing greasy smoke into the fog. He stood there trembling in anger until they passed. He was still trembling when he reached the huddle of houses, and when he saw what he saw his anger mounted. There was no way to know beyond which brown gate the brown girl had vanished. The gates of the first and second houses stood side by side. Abruptly he crossed the street and started up the Incline. He had been so certain she had entered the center house. And now he didn't know. He'd have to watch again.

He was to the midsection, to the hump of the walk, before he was calmed again. He stopped there and looked out over the stone railing. There was a small replica of the Palisades on this other side of the railing. And here, just over the rail, was a broken place in the wild shrubbery, even the pressure of a footpath down the cliff. A place where a man could wait at night. He smiled and was easy again.

He walked on up the Incline, undisturbed when a car heading downwards splashed light on him. He wouldn't move from Terriss' flat. He was satisfied there. There was something amusing about Brub Nicolai being able to lay hands on him whenever he wished. Amusing and more exciting than anything that had happened in a long time. The hunter and the hunted arm in arm. The hunt sweetened by danger. At the top of the Incline he looked back down at the houses and the sand and the sea. But they were all helpless now, lost in the fog.

He went on, not knowing how he would get back to Beverly, not caring. He was surprised crossing to Wilshire to see the lights of a bus approaching. He waited for it. It was the

Wilshire-L. A. bus. After he boarded it, he saw by his watch
that it was still early, a little past eleven o'clock. There were
only two passengers, working men in working clothes. Dix sat
in the front seat, his face turned to the window. Away from the
dull lights of the interior. Others boarded the bus as it rumbled
along Wilshire through Santa Monica, into Westwood. He
didn't turn his head to look at the others but he could see their
reflections in the window pane. There was no one worth looking at.

The fog thinned as the bus left Westwood and hurried
through the dark lane framed by the woodland golf course. At
Beverly you could see street corners again, as through a gray
mesh. You could see the shop windows and the people on the
streets. Only there were no people, the little city was as deserted as a small town. Dix kept his face pressed to the window.

At Camden Drive he saw her. A girl, an unknown girl,
standing alone, waiting alone there, by the bench which meant
a crosstown bus would eventually come along. At night busses
didn't run often. Dix pulled the buzzer cord but he was too
late for Camden. He got off at the next stop, two blocks away.
He didn't mind much. He crossed the boulevard and he was
smiling with his lips as he started back. His stride was long; his
steps were quiet.

3

The phone was a jangle tearing sleep from a man's face. It was
the scream of bus brakes, the clanging chain of an ugly oil
truck on a beach road, the whine of a spiraling bomb. Dix
opened his cramped eyes. He didn't know how long the phone
had been ringing. It stopped when his eyes opened but as soon
as he'd closed them again the fretful noise began anew. This
time he didn't open his eyes. With his outstretched hand he
knocked the phone from its cradle, ending the sound. He buried his head in the pillow, grasped at waning sleep. He didn't
want to talk to anyone this early. He didn't care who was on
the other end of the phone. No one important. No one important had his number.

His eyes reopened. He'd forgotten Brub Nicolai. He'd given
Brub his phone number last night. For a solitary moment the

coldness of fear gripped his entrails. As quickly the moment passed. He was without fear. But sleep had gone. He turned his head to look at the bedside clock. It wasn't so early. Eleven thirty-five. He'd had almost eight hours' sleep.

He needed eight hours more. God knows he needed it. He'd fallen into bed in complete exhaustion. It took more than eight hours to refuel a body exhausted. But his curiosity could not let him return to sleep now. He shoved away the covers, and pulled on his bathrobe. He didn't bother with his slippers. He walked barefoot through the living room to the front door, opened it and brought in the morning *Times* from his doorstep. His hands were eager but he closed the door before opening the paper.

There was nothing unusual on the front page. The ways of civilization, international and national strife, wars and strikes, political propagandizing. Nothing he was expecting on the second page. That meant there'd be nothing. He thrust the paper under his arm. There'd been no reason to leave his bed. But now that he was up, he wanted coffee. He padded to the kitchen. Terriss had good stuff; he plugged in the electric percolator and opened the kitchen door to bring in the cream. The apartment was a corner one, easy for a man to keep to himself and to hold his affairs his own. No snoopy neighbors here. Most of them were connected with the studios; Terriss had told him that, told him with Terriss' fathead pride. They kept themselves private too.

While he was waiting for the coffee he began to read the paper. He drank three cups, finishing his reading. He left the spread paper and the coffee cup on the kitchen table. There was maid service; he made it a point to be out during that period. The maid was a shapeless sack with heavy feet. She came to this apartment between two and three in the afternoon. He didn't know the maid's name; he wouldn't have recognized her on the street.

He returned to the bedroom. There wouldn't be time for good sleep before she came plodding in. If he were asleep, she wouldn't do the bedroom and he didn't like an unmade bed. He sat down on the edge of it, noticed the phone and replaced it in the cradle. He just sat there for minutes, not thinking, not seeing. Then he got up and went into the bathroom. His face

in the mirror was the usual face, drawn from sleep, his hair
rumpled. He'd feel better after a shower and a shave. He was
taking his razor from the case when the phone rang.

He wasn't going to answer it and then the quickening of
curiosity stirred him. He took his time returning to it. Again
he sat down on the rumpled bed. His hesitation before lifting
the phone was so minute, his hand didn't realize it. He said,
"Hello."

"Dix?"

It was a woman's voice, a woman querying, "Dix?"

He took a breath. Only one woman could be calling. Sylvia
Nicolai. He forced life into his voice. "Speaking. Sylvia?" He'd
surprised her.

"How did you know?"

"Recognized your voice," he said amusedly. She would believe him.

"Where have you been? I've been trying all morning to
reach you."

He didn't like having to account. Nor did she care; it was
conversational gambit. Because he didn't like it, he lied. "I've
been right here. Working. Phone didn't ring."

She said, "Phones," then went on in her cool, lovely voice,
"Brub and I wondered if you'd like to join us for dinner at the
club tonight?"

He didn't know what to say. He didn't know whether he
wanted to be with them or not tonight. He was tired, too tired
for decision. It was always easy to lie, so easy. He asked, "Could
I ring you back, Sylvia? I've a tiresome date tonight, business.
If I can get free of it, I'd much rather join you." The charm
was in his voice, he turned it on. But she didn't match it. She
was businesslike, as if she were Brub's secretary, not his wife.
As if she preferred his refusal. "Yes, do call back. If you can't
make it, we'll try it another time."

He echoed her goodbye and set back the phone. She didn't
want him along tonight. It was Brub's idea and she'd said, "If
you want him, Brub," because she was in love with Brub, the
new hadn't been rubbed off their marriage. He wouldn't go.
He wouldn't intrude on their oneness. They had happiness
and happiness was so rare in this day of the present. More rare

than precious things, jewels and myrrh. Once he'd had happiness but for so brief a time; happiness was made of quicksilver, it ran out of your hand like quicksilver. There was the heat of tears suddenly in his eyes and he shook his head angrily. He would not think about it, he would never think of that again. It was long ago, in an ancient past. To hell with happiness. More important was excitement and power and the hot stir of lust. Those made you forget. They made happiness a pink marshmallow.

He stood up again, rubbing his untidy hair. He wouldn't go out with the Nicolais to their lace-panty club. He'd go out alone. The lone wolf. There was a savage delight in being a lone wolf. It wasn't happiness. It was the reverse of the coin, as hate was the reverse of love. Only a thin press of metal between the sides of a coin. He was a lone wolf; he didn't have to account to anyone nor did he intend to. Sylvia Nicolai wanting to know where he was this morning. It was none of her damn business. This morning she didn't care, but get mixed up with the Nicolais and she would care. Women were snoopy. He hated women. Brub would be snoopy too; he was a detective.

Yet the game would be heightened if he teamed up with a detective. Dix went into the bathroom, plugged in the razor and began to shave. Hating the noise, the grinding buzz of noise. He could have used a safety razor but there were mornings when his hands had the shakes. He didn't know when those mornings would occur. Better the buzz than to have people noticing the cuts on your cheeks and chin. His hands were steady as iron this morning.

He finished shaving as quickly as possible, scrubbed his teeth and sloshed mouth wash. He was feeling better. Under the shower he felt considerably better. It might be definitely amusing to be with the Nicolais tonight. It might be that Sylvia was the one who wanted him along, that her play of indifference was a cover-up. He was clinically aware of his appeal to women. He'd seen their eyes sharpen as they looked at him. Sylvia's hadn't, true, but she was smart. She wouldn't let it happen with Brub there. He'd like to see Sylvia again.

He thought of her as he stood scrubbing himself with the towel. The long lines of her, the silvery look and sound of her.

He'd like to know a woman of her caliber. Brub was lucky. He flung the towel on the floor. Brub was born lucky. For an instant he stiffened, as if a cold hand had touched his spine.

His laugh shot from his throat. He was lucky too; he was more than lucky, he was smart. He strode out of the bathroom. It was close to two; he'd have to hump it to get out before the ugly beldame of the brooms showed up.

He put on a blue sports shirt, blue slacks, comfortable loafers. No jacket. From the open windows he knew the day was a sultry one, September was summer in California. He transferred his wallet and keys and other stuff from the crumpled gabardines he'd worn last night. He rolled the gabardines, opened his closet and gathered up the other suits and odd trousers needing a cleaner's attention. He'd beaten the maid; he was ready to leave. The phone started to ring as he reached the front door. He ignored it and left the apartment.

The garages were in back of the court. His was almost a half block away. Just another of the advantages of Terriss' quarters. No insomniacs sitting up in bed checking you in and out. The garages fronted on an alley; a vacant lot across. He unlocked the one housing Terriss' car. A nice car Terriss had left for his use. He'd have preferred something flashier, a convertible or open brougham, but there was advantage in a black coupe. All black coupes looked alike at night. He drove away.

He dropped the bundle of clothes at the cleaner's on Olympic, then drove leisurely up Beverly Drive, parking near the delicatessen. He was hungry. He bought an early edition of the *News* at the corner and he read it while he ate two smoked turkey sandwiches and drank a bottle of beer. The delicatessen was fairly crowded even this late. It was a popular place and a pleasant one. Noise was a blur here, like in a club.

There was nothing in the paper. After checking the headlines, he read the comics, the café columnists and Kirby, Weinstock, and Pearson, loitering with his beer. He looked over the movie ads, sometimes he went to a movie in the afternoons. It was too late today. He had to phone Sylvia Nicolai.

He walked down to the Owl after eating and bought a carton of Philip Morris. It was after three then. The beldame would be out of his apartment, he could return, call Sylvia, and catch a nap before joining the Nicolais at their club. The afternoon heat and the beer had made him sleepy again. Or he could get the letter written to Uncle Fergus. Damned old fool expected a letter once a week. It had been two weeks since Dix had written him. He wouldn't put it past Uncle Fergus to stop sending checks if he didn't get his damn letter from Dix pretty soon. He'd say he'd been sick. Maybe he could jack up the income for medical expenses. Something needing treatment, something acquired overseas. A back or a kidney. Not anything that would jerk the strings, drag him back East.

He got in his car, backed out, and drove a little too fast around the block. Uncle Fergus didn't have to be so dirty cheap; he didn't have another living relative. Two hundred and fifty a month was pennies. Medical treatment was a good idea, he should have thought of it before. He could get three hundred for sure, maybe three fifty. He'd write a whale of a letter. He was the boy could do it. He knew Uncle Fergus like the palm of his hand. He felt all hopped up returning to the apartment.

He flung the Philip Morrises on the divan, got out the portable and opened it on the desk. He rolled in the paper and started, "Dear Uncle Fergus," before he remembered the phone call to Sylvia. He left the desk and went to the bedroom. Before dialing—Terriss had extended service of course, Terriss had everything easy—he lit a cigarette.

Sylvia answered the phone. Her hello was natural. When he said, "Sylvia? It's Dix," her voice became a bit more formal. She was conscious of him all right. She was fighting that consciousness. He'd played the game so often of breaking down that withdrawal but never with this variation, the wife of his best friend. It stimulated him.

He asked, "Do you still want me tonight?"

She was conscious of his phrasing because there was a minute hesitancy before she counter-asked, "You mean you can join us for dinner?"

"If I'm still invited."

"Yes, indeed." She acted pleased. "Can you make it about seven? That will give us time for a drink before we go to the club."

"I'll be there."

He was pleased that he had decided to go. He lay back on the bed to finish his cigarette. He was still leisurely there when the phone sounded. He was surprised, more so when it was Sylvia again. Her voice wasn't standoffish now. "Dix? I forgot to say, don't dress. We're informal at the beach."

"Thanks," he said. "You eased my mind. My dinner coat is out at the seams. It shrank while I was away flying."

"Brub's too. They fed you gentlemen altogether too well," she laughed.

They had some easy conversation before ringing off. He didn't want to return to the damn typewriter. He was comfortable here on his spine; he wasn't sleepy now, just restful. It was just such delaying tactics that had let two weeks go by without writing the old skinflint. He pushed himself up and returned to the machine. Today there was incentive. He needed money for medical treatments.

Inspiration returned to him at the typewriter. He wrote a peach of a letter; it was just right, not too much nor too little. He didn't ask for money. He was certain his back would be all right without the treatments the doctor ordered. Stuff like that. He reread the letter twice before putting it in the envelope. He decided to go and mail it now. It was a little after five. Before sealing the envelope, he drew the letter out and read it again. Yes, it was right. He sealed it quickly, put on an airmail stamp, and left the apartment.

He was walking fast. That was why he didn't see the girl until he almost collided with her at the arched street entrance of the patio. It shocked him that he hadn't noticed her, that he hadn't been aware. He stepped back quickly. "I beg your pardon," he said. It wasn't a formality as he said it; shock made each word apology for a grave error.

The girl didn't move for a moment. She stood in his way and looked him over slowly, from crown to toe. The way a man looked over a woman, not the reverse. Her eyes were slant, her lashes curved long and golden dark. She had redgold hair, flaming hair, flung back from her amber face, falling to her shoulders. Her mouth was too heavy with lipstick, a copper-red mouth, a sultry mouth painted to call attention to its premise. She was dressed severely, a rigid tailored suit, but it accentuated the lift of her breasts, the curl of her hips. She wasn't beautiful, her face was too narrow for beauty, but she was dynamite. He stood like a dolt, gawking at her.

After she'd finished looking him over, she gave him a small insolent smile. As if he were a dolt, not Dix Steele. "Granted," she said and she walked past him into the patio.

He didn't move. He stood and watched her, his mouth still open. She walked like a model, swaying her small buttocks. She had exquisite legs. She knew he was watching her and she didn't care. She expected it. She took her time, skirting the small sky-blue oblong of the pool which lay in the center of the patio. She started up the stairway to the balcony of the second-floor apartments.

He swung out the archway fast. He wouldn't let her reach the balcony, look over the balustrade and see him standing there. He'd find out about her some other way, if she lived here, or whom she visited. He'd left his car down the block a bit, by the curb. Although he'd intended driving to the Beverly postoffice to mail the letter, he didn't. He half ran across the street to the corner mail box, clanged in the letter and ran back to the court. He was too late. She was already out of sight.

He went back into his own apartment, sauntered in as if he weren't damning luck. If he'd bumped into her on his return from the box, he could have bungled at his doorway for the key, discovered which apartment she entered. He walked inside, slamming the door after him. It had been years since he'd seen a girl who could set him jumping. The redhead was it. He went out to the kitchen and although he didn't want a drink, he poured a double jigger of rye and drank it neat. The slug calmed him but he wandered back into the front room, wanting an excuse to slip out into the patio, to look up at the second-floor balcony.

The excuse came as he wished for it. He heard, just short of the doorstep, the thud of the flung newspaper. He moved quick as a cat. But as soon as he picked up the paper, unfolding it, he forgot why he'd hurried outdoors. He saw only the headline: *Strangler Strikes Again.*

II

I T WAS quarter past seven when Dix pulled up in front of
Nicolai's gate. There was no woolly fog tonight, only a thin
mistiness lay in the canyon. It was like gauze across the windshield. He could see the flagstoned steps clearly, even the geranium border framing them. The windows of the house were
golden with light; the porch light was also on to welcome him.

He was again pleased that he had decided to come. He had
dressed for deliberate effect, an eastern friend of the Nicolais,
well off, the right background, even to ex-Air Corps. Gray
flannel suit; an expensive tie, patterned in navy, maroon, and
white; a white shirt; well-polished brown shoes, English shoes.
He settled his tie before climbing to the porch. He didn't
hesitate before ringing the bell and there was no hesitation in
the opening door.

Sylvia was standing in the doorway. She had on her coat, a
soft blue coat, and her bag, a white envelope, was under her
arm. "Hello, Dix," she said. "I'll be right with you."

She didn't ask him in; the screen door was between them
and she didn't push it open. She left him standing there on the
lighted porch while she turned back into the hall and switched
off some overhead lights. There was dim light still glowing in
hall and living room when she came outside.

"We're meeting Brub at the club," she said in her high, clear
voice as she started down the steps. "He called and asked me
to bring you there for drinks. He couldn't make it home."

He followed her. He had to raise his voice to speak to her,
she was that far ahead of him. She was accustomed to the steps;
he must watch them. "Brub pretty busy?"

"Yes," she said but she didn't continue on that. "Do you
want to take your car or mine? It isn't far, only a few blocks."

She wasn't talking particularly fast yet there was a breathless-
ness to it, as if she didn't want any silence between them, as if
she were too conscious of him. She stood there by his car, tall
and cool and lovely, but not quiet as she was last night.

He smiled at her; he put no intimacy into the smile. "We
might as well take mine, it's here. You can direct me."

416

"All right," she agreed.

He helped her in and went around, took his place at the wheel. She'd rolled the window down on her side, and she rested her arm on the frame. She remained there in the far corner as she gave directions. "Just down to the beach road, turn left, the club's on the ocean side."

It didn't take five minutes to get there, no time for the furthering of acquaintance. She talked of club friends, names he didn't know. There was no silence on the short ride. On direction, he drove through the pillared gateway into the parking court. She let herself out of the car, not waiting for him to help her.

The clubhouse wasn't large. There was a young feel to it, like an officers' club, the couples in the entrance hall, in the lounge beyond, were the kind you'd expect the Nicolais to know. A pattern you found all over the country, decent, attractive young people. The norm. They didn't look dull to Dix tonight. He was warmed by their safeness.

Sylvia said, "I'll drop my coat." She smiled at him, an open, friendly smile. "Be right back, Dix."

She wasn't long. She looked lovely, her dress was cream color, an expensively simple dress. He had pride entering the lounge with her.

"Brub doesn't seem to have shown up yet. Unless he's beaten us to the bar." She nodded to several couples as they crossed the room. There were more couples in the nautical bar but Brub wasn't there. "I'll substitute for Brub and buy you a drink while we wait," she said.

"I approve the substitution. But I'll buy the drink," he told her.

She moved away from him to a table. "You can't. Not at the club. This is Brub's party."

She introduced him to all who stopped by their table. The question of the passers-by was inevitably the same, "Where's Brub?" It didn't occur to any of them that she had any interest in Dix.

Her answer was always the same. "He'll be along soon." And her introduction never varied. ". . . Dix Steele. Brub's best friend in England." Only once did she show any disturbance. She said it quietly, "I wonder what's keeping him."

At eight the bar was emptied of all but those whose goal was alcoholism. Her nervousness lay near the surface now. She pushed away from the table. "We might as well go to dinner. I'm sure he'll be here any moment."

He deliberately broke through the commonplaces then. "Don't apologize, Sylvia. I'm not missing Brub." His voice smiled at her. "I'm enjoying you—quite as much as I would Brub."

She laughed. And she said with a small moue, "I'm missing him. I haven't seen him since morning."

He mock sighed. "Still on your honeymoon."

"Definitely."

But he'd broken through, only a wedge perhaps, yet enough for a starter.

He waited until they were at the dinner table before he asked the question casually. "Is he on a big case?"

She looked at him. Her eyes were anxious. Then she looked away. "I don't know," she admitted. "He didn't say. Only he'd been delayed."

She hadn't seen the evening paper. He could have told her but he didn't. Let Brub tell her. What she feared.

He saw Brub at that moment crossing the room. Brub looked worn, he put on a smile in answer to greetings as he passed the various tables, but it was a thin smile, it slipped away as quickly as it came.

Sylvia saw him almost as soon as Dix did. Anxiety sharpened her face. They were tacitly silent until Brub reached the table. He bent and kissed Sylvia. "Sorry I'm so late, darling." He didn't smile at them; he didn't need to pretend with his wife and best friend. He put out his hand to Dix, "Glad you could join us," then he sat down, dog tiredness in every muscle. His suit was dog tired too and his linen showed the wilt of the day. His dark hair was crumpled. "I didn't have time to change." He smiled at Sylvia. "You can pretend I'm your chauffeur."

The waiter, a young colored man, whiter of skin than the beach-brown guests, was unobtrusive at the table.

Brub looked up. "Hello, Malcolm. Do you suppose you could get me a double Scotch from the bar before you start my dinner? I've just come from work and I need it."

"I'm sure I can, Mr. Nicolai," Malcolm smiled. He went away.

Sylvia's hand covered Brub's on the table. "Hard day, darling?" She'd started casual but she couldn't keep it up. Something about the set of Brub's mouth released her fear in a little gust. "It wasn't another—"

Brub's mouth was tight; his voice deliberately matter of fact. "Yes, another one."

"Brub!" She whispered it.

He began to light a cigarette, the flame wavered slightly. Dix watched the two with the proper attentiveness, and the proper curiosity. When neither spoke, he let his curiosity become audible. "What's it all about?"

"Another woman killed . . . The same way."

Sylvia's hands were clenched.

Malcolm brought the drink.

"Thanks," Brub said and saw Dix. "I'm sorry, chum. How about you?"

"The same," he grinned. He didn't want it for himself; an extra for Brub. To relax Brub. He began on his shrimp cocktail. "Are you assigned to the case?"

"Everyone in the department is on it," Brub said. He drank again and he grimaced. "No, it's not my case, Dix. They don't put juniors on big stuff." He turned to Sylvia. "The commissioner called in the whole department. We've been with him since five, since I called you. Even hizzoner the mayor sat in." His mouth tightened. "We've got to stop it."

"Yes," Sylvia said. Her eyes were frightened, the color under her tan was gone. It was as if she had personal fright, as if the horror were close to her.

Dix said, "Someone important who was killed?" Malcolm set down the highball. "Thanks."

"No." Brub was halfway through his drink. "It's never anyone important." Again he realized he was talking to someone, not thinking aloud. "I forgot. You wouldn't know about it. Being a visitor." He could speak about it calmly; it seemed to relax him as much as a highball would. "The first one was about six months ago. March to be exact."

"March sixteenth," Sylvia said. "The night before the St. Patrick's party."

"We didn't know it was only the first then. It was a girl down on Skid Row. She was a nice enough kid for the life she lived, I guess. Danced in a bump-and-grind house down there. We found her in an alley. Strangled." He picked up his glass, emptied it. "No clues. Nothing. We wrote that one off as the neighborhood even though we didn't get any leads. You usually can on Skid Row. The next one was in April." His hand reached for his empty glass.

Dix shoved his across. "Take mine. The shrimp are too good to dilute. Try them, Sylvia."

"Yes, don't wait for me," Brub said.

Sylvia picked up her fork but she didn't do anything with it. Just held it loosely, her eyes on Brub's face.

He took a drink before continuing. "In April. We found her in Westlake Park. There wasn't any reason for it. She was a nice normal girl, young, attractive. She'd been to a movie with a couple of girl friends. She lived in the Wilshire district, blocks from the park. No clues. She'd been killed the same way." He looked at Dix angrily. "There wasn't any reason for her to be killed. There's been no reason for any of them." Again he drank.

"There've been others?"

"Last night was the sixth," Brub said heavily. "One a month. Since March."

"Except last month," Sylvia said quickly. "There was none in August."

Brub continued, "No motive. No connection between any of them. Never the same neighborhood."

"Last night's—" Sylvia's voice was hushed, as if she dreaded the question.

Brub said, "A new neighborhood. Beverly Glen Canyon—up where it's country. She wasn't found until late this morning. She was lying in the brush at the side of the road." Anger clanged in his voice again. "It's like hunting a needle in a haystack. Los Angeles is too big—too sprawling. You can't patrol every street every night, all night. He's safe. A maniac walking the streets, looking just as normal as you or me, more normal probably."

"You'll get him," Sylvia said, pushing conviction into her wish.

"We'll get him." Brub believed it. "But how many women will be murdered first?" He tipped up the glass.

"You'd better eat, dear," Sylvia said. She forced herself to start eating.

"Yeah." Brub began spearing the shrimp, eating hurriedly, not tasting the food. "Take this girl last night. A nice girl like the others—except perhaps the first was a different cut. This one was a stenographer. Worked downtown. Lived in Hollywood. She'd been playing bridge with friends in Beverly. On South Camden. Just four girls. They played once a week, rotating the meeting place. They always quit early. None of them wanted to be out late, alone that way. Last night they stopped around eleven. The three left together, walked up to Wilshire together. The other two lived downtown farther. They took the Wilshire bus. Mildred was taking the Hollywoodland bus. Her name was Mildred Atkinson. She was still waiting when the girls' bus came along. She waved goodbye to them. No one saw her after that."

Sylvia had stopped eating. "It's horrible," she said.

"Yes, it's horrible," Brub agreed. "There's no reason for the pattern. If we could just get at what's behind it."

Dix put on a thoughtful frown. "Have you no leads at all?"

"Not much," Brub said. "There are no clues, there never are; no fingerprints or footprints, God, how we'd like just one fingerprint!" He returned to monotone. "We've double checked all the known sex offenders."

"It's a sex crime?" Dix interrupted.

Brub nodded. "That's a part of it."

Sylvia's shiver was slight.

He continued, "We know one thing, of course. He works from a car."

Malcolm brought the chowder.

"How do you know that?" Dix asked.

"He has to. Take last night, for instance. The place is inaccessible without a car."

Dix scowled. "Can't you check tire prints?"

"We can't check every car in L. A.," Brub said helplessly. "It's the same as footprints. We can't check every pair of shoes in L. A."

"I understand that," Dix nodded. "Excellent chowder." But

they'd have the tire tracks in plaster. If you could get them off concrete.

"We have an excellent chef at the club," Sylvia said. She had no appetite. Her soup was barely tasted when Malcolm brought the abalone steaks.

Dix began on his with relish. "What you know then is that there is a man and he has a car—"

"Yes. In the fourth case, he was seen."

Dix's eyebrows lifted. He held his fork in mid-air. "You mean you have a description?"

Brub sighed. "The fourth girl was seen leaving a movie with a man. As for description, hell!" He gestured. "The guy who noticed them, a tailor waiting for a street car, was half a block away. All he knew was the man was kind of young and sort of tall and normal looking. Only one head and no fangs!"

Dix smiled slightly. "Maybe he saw two other people."

"He saw them all right. But he was so busy looking at the girl's red suit, he didn't notice the man."

"No one else has ever seen him?"

"If they have, they've taken a vow of silence. You'd think he—"

Sylvia broke in, "Brub, let's talk about something else. Please, Brub. We asked Dix to a party, not a postmortem."

"Okay, sweetheart." He patted her hand. "I'm sorry. Sorry, Dix. How about another drink? Malcolm!"

Dix smiled. "I'll have another with you." He hid his annoyance. Just like a woman, interfering, imposing her whims on the party.

"Who's here tonight?" Brub edged his chair to look around. He lifted his hand to the group at the next table. "Hi, there."

Dix lit a cigarette and also surveyed the room. Nice people, healthy and wealthy. Normal as you and me. Normal as Sylvia when she didn't have the megrims. But you didn't know what was beneath beach-tanned faces and simple expensive clothes. You didn't ever know about thoughts. They were easy hidden. You didn't have to give away what you were thinking. No one exchanging pleasantries now with Brub would know that the man's mind was raw with murder. No one watching Sylvia replacing her lip rouge, smiling over the mirror of her bleached wooden compact, would know that fear was ravel-

ing her nerves. Even he, permitted as friend to know that
there was fear in her veins, didn't know whether the fear was
for Brub's safety or her own. Or an atavistic fear of reasonless
death.

The color under her sunbrown had returned as she did the
little normal things of lipstick, cigarette. He could make it re-
cede so easily, a word, or one more question on the subject.
He could make her heart stop beating as easily. With a simple
statement. His lips smiled. And his eyes again turned to the
room. Away from temptation.

It was then that he saw her, the little brown girl. It almost
shocked him for a moment. She didn't belong here; she belonged out in the dark. She wasn't a brown girl tonight, save
for her healthy beach color. She was in starchy white, an evening dress, cut low on her brown back, flaring to her white
sandals. She had a young, laughing face, short brown curly
hair. She was at the table directly across the floor. He should
have seen her earlier. He had, he realized, but only the brown
back and white pique dress. She'd shifted her chair as Brub
had, bringing her face to the room.

He took a long draw on his cigarette before he asked, deliberately casual, "Who's the girl over there?"

Brub turned back to their table. "Which one?"

Sylvia followed Dix's gesture.

"Over there. In white."

Brub peered. "Oh, that one. I've seen her—who is she,
Sylvia?"

Sylvia had placed the girl. "Betsy Banning. You know, Brub.
The Bannings bought the Henry house up the beach." Sylvia
said to Dix, "I've met her but I don't really know her." She
smiled, "Or I'd introduce you."

Dix laughed. "Don't start match-making. I'm happy. She
looked familiar, that was all. Is she in pictures?"

"No," Sylvia answered. "She's at the university, I believe."
She smiled. "She doesn't need the pictures; the Bannings are
Texas oil, floating in it. Otis Banning, her father, is the bald
one. They say he has seven millions in a little black box. No
doubt an exaggeration."

Brub said, "Sylvia ought to be the detective in the family.
She knows everything about everybody."

"Otis and I share the same dentist, darling."

"She's a cute kid." Brub was again looking across at the girl.

"You're married now," Dix reminded him.

"To me," Sylvia added sweetly. "I may not be a cute kid but I'm nice."

They exchanged that happy intimate look. Then Brub turned his eyes again to the Banning girl. "You're right, though. She does look familiar." He was scenting her, the way a detective would, narrowed eyes, his brows pulled slightly together, his nose keen.

"Come on home," Dix laughed.

Brub's head snapped to Dix quickly. His dark eyes were lighted. "That's it! You know who she looks like? Brucie!"

The name was spoken before he could warn Brub not to speak it. He'd known in that split second of Brub's remembering, in the second before the name. It was said and for the moment he could see nothing, only the red blur before his eyes and the dread roaring of sound in his ears. He didn't know his knuckles were white knobs gripping the table, his cigarette mashed between his fingers. The moment passed and he was in control of himself again. He let the cigarette brush to the floor. In another moment he could speak.

Sylvia spoke first. "And who is Brucie, darling?"

"A girl we knew in England. She was a Red Cross worker when we were stationed near Dover. Scotch—that's where the Bruce, Brucie, came from. Cute as a button."

Brub had noticed nothing. But he wasn't sure about Sylvia. Behind her civilized attention, her humor, her casualness, he wasn't certain. Something was there behind the curtain of her eyes, something in the way she looked at Dix, a look behind the look. She might have been watching him at that wrong moment.

Dix said, "She was, all of that." His voice wasn't thick; it was as casual as Sylvia's.

"Wonder what ever happened to her? She was sure a cute kid. You kind of went for her, didn't you, Dix?"

Dix laughed, a normal laugh. "You kind of liked her yourself, didn't you?"

"Brub!" Sylvia's eyes opened, wide surprise. She was pretending. She was too level-headed, too secure to care.

"You bet I liked her. I guess every man in the platoon sort of liked Brucie. But you needn't worry, honey. No one had a chance with old lady-killer Steele present."

Dix was very careful lighting his cigarette. Because Sylvia was watching him. With the look behind the look.

"You ever hear from her, Dix?"

He shook his head. He was surprised at how easy it was to talk. "No, Brub, I never did."

"Out of sight, out of mind. That's the great Steele. Don't ever fall for a guy like that, Sylvia." Brub began on his neglected ice cream.

"No, darling," Sylvia murmured. She wasn't looking at him, yet Dix had a feeling she was seeing him. And probing him with her mind.

"If I'd had a girl like Sylvia," he began, and he realized there was some honesty in the play, "I wouldn't have looked at anyone else. I wouldn't have been like you, ogling all those U.S.O. legs."

"I'm learning things." Sylvia nodded a severe head. "Go on, Dix, tell me more."

He invented lazily but his mind wasn't there. It was remembering Brucie and the ache in him was the ache of a wound torn open. His face covered his mind, as his voice covered the pain crying from his throat. "Remember the redhead contortionist?" and he remembered the redhead in the patio this afternoon. With a woman like that, he might be able to forget. Nothing else brought forgetfulness, only for a brief time. Another section of his mind moved as the brown girl stood up from her table with her young crew-cut escort. The look of Brucie, not the face, the swagger of her shoulders, the echo of laughter. Perhaps married to seven million dollars you could forget. You could have fast cars, fast boats, a good plane to climb up there into the vastness of eternity. Brub and Sylvia were happy. Marriage could be happy.

He realized there was music when the brown girl and her partner began to dance. He should ask Sylvia to dance. But he didn't want to. He wanted to get out of here, to go home. He couldn't leave abruptly, not two nights in a row. However, he didn't think the Nicolais would stay much longer, off guard their faces returned to somberness. He could nudge them. He said abruptly, "You're tired, Brub."

Brub nodded. "Yeah. But I've got to go back to work."

"No, Brub," Sylvia cried.

"I shouldn't have left when I did."

"You're worn out now. You can't, darling. It's an hour's drive downtown—"

He interrupted, "I don't have to go downtown, Sylvia. To the Beverly Hills station is all. That isn't fifteen minutes. Why don't you keep Dix—"

Sylvia shook her head.

Dix said, "I ought to get back to work myself. So don't be polite."

Sylvia said, "I couldn't stay. You understand."

He gave her an appreciative smile. "I understand."

"It's been a punk evening for you, Dix," Brub was apologetic. "We'll make it up to you."

They almost hurried from the dining room into the lounge. As if, once it had been admitted, all three could make up with haste for the spent time. Sylvia said, "I'll get my coat." She hesitated, "You are on the case, Brub?"

He admitted ruefully, "Just a little bit, honey."

She didn't say anything, simply turned and went to the cloakroom. Brub watched her go.

"Why is she afraid?" Dix asked.

Brub started. "Wha—" He realized Dix's question. "I guess it's pretty much my fault. Ever since this thing started, I've been afraid for her. She's lived in the canyon all her life. She never had any fear, wandered all over it, any time of day. But the canyon at night, the way the fogs come in—it's a place for *him.*" His face was again angry, helplessly angry. "I've scared her. She's alone so much. I never know what hours I have to keep. We have good neighbors, a couple of our best friends are right across the road. But you know our street. It's dark and lonely and the way our house is set up there—" He broke off. "I'm the one who's scared; I've infected her. And I can't help it. I can't pretend. Until we've caught him—"

Sylvia was coming into the hall. She looked herself again, tall and lovely and unruffled, her gilt hair smooth, her movements unhurried.

Brub said under his breath, "If we could only find the why of the pattern—" He didn't finish because she was there, and the three were moving out of the club into the sea-fresh darkness. The swish of the breakers was liquid against the night.

"I could take Sylvia—" Dix began.

"No, I'll run her home, get her settled. Unless you'd like to sit with her until I—"

"Dix has to work," Sylvia said. "And I'm tired." She put out her hand. "Another time we'll do better, Dix."

"We certainly will," Brub vowed.

He watched Brub wheel the car out of the drive. In a hurry, hurried to get back to the Beverly Hills police station. He would take Sylvia into the house, make sure there was no shadowy stranger lurking. They would cling together for a moment, fear in both of them. The woman fearing to have her man sniffing the spoor of a murderer, fearing lest he catch up with evil. Fearing less for herself; only the unease she must feel, infected by Brub's fear for her. Brub fearing for her because she was a woman, because she was his woman, and women were being stalked in the night. Fearing, he would yet leave her, and quickly, because he was a hunter and this was a big hunt. For wild game.

Dix circled back to his car, Terriss' car. The plain black coupe. He warmed the engine. It was a good car and he kept it functioning smoothly. He released the brake. Fifteen minutes at the outside and Brub would be gone. He could go there then; she'd let him in. Brub's friend. He could have excuse, Brub could have infected him too with the fear. She'd be glad to see him. He could coax her into driving up to Malibu. For a drink. For fresh air. She wouldn't be afraid—at first.

He slid the car to the gates. Left lay the canyon. Left lay Malibu. Right was the California Incline. Right was Wilshire, the road back to town. She was Brub's wife. Brub was his friend. Brub, the hunter.

He was very tired. He hadn't had much sleep last night. He turned to the right.

2

The morning paper had columns on the case. Having been scooped by the afternoon papers on the original story, this sheet at least was making up its loss by intensive research. It had pictures of the girl, Mildred, of her family, of the apartment house where she'd played bridge, of the lonely spot in Beverly Glen Canyon where her body was found.

Her name was Mildred Atkinson and she had led a very stupid life. Grade school, high school—Hollywood High but she was no beauty queen—business college and a job in an insurance office. She was twenty-six years old and she was a good girl, her parents sobbed. She played bridge with girl friends and she once taught a Sunday-school class. She didn't have any particular gentleman friend, she went out with several. Not often, you could bet. The only exciting thing that had ever happened to her was to be raped and murdered. Even then she'd only been subbing for someone else.

The sleuths had found that she and the man had had a cup of coffee about midnight in a near drive-in. The couple had been served inside, not in a car. She'd been standing there alone, waiting for a bus. Her girl friends had waved goodbye to her. The man had seen her standing there alone, a little nervous. He'd said, "Busses don't run often at night," as if he too were waiting. She hadn't wanted to talk; she'd been brought up not to talk to strange men. "Mildred was a good girl," the parents sobbed. She'd never let a man pick her up, her girl friends chorused, but they wondered how much they hadn't known about Mildred. "Not unless she knew him." The cops were scouring the town now, talking to every man Mildred had known. They'd be thorough; they'd check every man who'd passed through that insurance office. Believing they had a lead at last on a man apparently as normal as you or I, who tracked women at night. The lead editorial called him Jack the Ripper and demanded more and better police protection. The editorial—it was a non-administration paper—sneered politics and got in some snide cracks about the mayor.

She didn't want to talk but he was a decent-looking young fellow waiting for a bus. And the mist grew cold on the lonely corner. When he knew she was ripe for the suggestion, he mentioned coffee at the drive-in up at the corner of Linden Drive. The pert car-hop remembered Mildred when she saw the picture in the paper. She'd been carrying out a tray when they entered. Remembered possibly because by then Mildred was pleased at having coffee with a good-looking young fellow. She'd preened a little.

The car-hop told the other girls, "That's her"; the boss heard the gabble and he called the Beverly Hills police. The car-hop couldn't describe the man, sort of tall, nice looking, in a tan suit. She was sure he couldn't be the strangler; he wasn't that kind of a man at all. She would always be sure that what happened to Mildred happened after she left her drive-in escort.

He read every line of every story in the morning paper. He felt good today after last night's sleep. It was a wonderful summer day. He stretched out in bed lazily and he thought about the redhead. She would be poison but it wouldn't hurt to think about her. He couldn't get mixed up with a woman, with a damn snooping dame. But God, she'd be worth knowing. It had been so long a time since he'd had a woman to hold to. He hadn't wanted one.

He didn't want one now; it was hangover from seeing Sylvia and Brub looking at each other. Maybe the crazy thought that had flickered in his mind about the little brown girl and her seven million dollars. It would be a good day to lie on the beach at Santa Monica. In front of Betsy Banning's house at the foot of the California Incline. He might even find out which house was Banning's.

He stretched off the bed. If he were going to sun on the beach, it might be smart to call Brub. Brub shouldn't be working on Sunday. He should be beaching. Talking about the case. New developments. He smiled. It was neat to have a source of information on a case.

A quick shot of thought jabbed him. The tires. They were good tires, no patches, no distinguishing marks. Only somewhere in the back of his mind, he remembered that all tires had distinguishing marks, like fingerprints. Could they get a cast of tire marks from dry concrete? He doubted it. As he had doubted it last night. But he should make sure.

Certain gambles were legitimate. Like appearing in a lighted place with Mildred. Gambling on the muddled memory of waitresses and countermen who served hundreds of average-looking men and women every day, every night. Risks were spice. Stunt flying. As long as you used them like spice, spar-ingly; like stunts, planning them with precision, carrying them out boldly.

He fingered his lip. He could grow a mustache. No reason why he should. He didn't like lip brushes. He looked like a thousand other men. He'd never been in that drive-in before. He never intended to go in it again. Risks he took; mistakes he didn't make.

It would be better to call up the Nicolais. He could find out where the Bannings lived easily enough. If he was going to marry the girl he'd have to find out where she lived. Too bad she wasn't a pal of Sylvia's. That would make it easy. He lifted the phone, dialed the Santa Monica number. There was no answer, only metallic ringing. Too late; they'd probably already gone to the beach. It was past one o'clock.

He wasn't too disappointed. He dressed leisurely, tan gabar-dine slacks, a white T-shirt. He left the house by the front door. On the balcony were open doors, musical radios, laugh-ter. If she lived in Virginibus Arms—he was certain she did; she hadn't walked like a visitor—he'd run into her again. Plenty of time. Mel Terriss wouldn't be back for a long time.

He walked around the block to the garage, opened the noiseless doors. Before taking out the car he circled it, kicking the tires. They were in good shape, not worn, good solid tires. He didn't need new ones; there was no reason to go to that expense. Brub had said it: the police couldn't check every pair of tires in L. A.

He backed out and swung over to Wilshire, turned west. The road to the beach. About three million other drivers had the same idea on this blue-sky, golden-warm day in late September. He took the San Vicente cut-off, as he turned noting the eucalyptus grove with one small corner of his mind. Not exactly secluded, yet late enough . . . At Fourth Street in Santa Monica he right turned again, descending into the canyon. The sign pointed this as an alternate road to the beach. He was prospecting. This descent would be pretty well de-serted at night. But no underbrush except fenced. He dropped into the canyon and found Mesa Road. He didn't expect to find the Nicolais at home, but it was worth a try.

It was well worth it; the door was open, through the screen

he could see into the hallway. He pushed the bell, pleased with himself, relaxed, comfortable. It was Sylvia who answered and she was surprised to see him. By her startled look, you'd think he was someone unexpectedly returned from Limbo.

"Hello," he said easily. "Anyone home?"

"Dix—" She unhooked the screen, pushing it open. "I didn't recognize you at first. The sun behind you." She had an open white beach robe over brief white shorts and a white cleft brassiere. Her skin was deep tan and her gilt hair was loose about her shoulders. Without the cool poise she seemed much younger. She was flustered. "Excuse the way I look." Her feet were bare and dappled with sand. "We've just come up from the beach and Brub beat me to the shower. I didn't expect you. Some friends were coming over—"

He cut her off, "I'm a friend too."

She colored. "Of course, you are. I mean, old friends." She sighed. "I'm making it worse. Go on in and get comfortable. Help yourself to a drink. I'll tell Brub." She went quickly, too quickly.

Maybe his open admiration embarrassed her. He didn't understand Sylvia. She was too many women. He settled himself on the living-room couch. Friends coming in. He wouldn't stay on. He'd have a dinner date.

Brub wasn't long. His face lighted when he saw Dix, it had been heavy at the doorway. "Where's that drink? Sylvia said you were mixing them."

"What am I, the bartender?" Dix lounged off the couch. "Name it."

"No," Brub waved him down. "I'll do it. I'm handy."

He felt too good to bother with a drink. "I don't care. Whatever you're having."

"Then you'll settle for Scotch and splash," Brub said from behind the bar. "That's the only English I learned in the service. We'll have it with ice though." He filled the glasses. "What you been doing all day?"

"Working," Dix answered. "Tried to reach you earlier. I wanted to play hookey on the beach." He took the glass. "Thanks. I thought you were probably on the job."

Brub frowned a little. "I worked this morning." He pushed away the frown. "Spent the afternoon on the beach."

Dix tasted his highball. "How's the case coming?" He had just the right casual curiosity in his voice. It pleased him.

The frown returned to Brub's forehead. "It's not. Right where it was."

Dix's foot edged the paper on the floor. "But you found someone who saw her with the man."

"Yeah." Brub's voice was flat. "Maybe if he'd walk in again, that car-hop would remember him." He was disgusted. "She's looked through the files of every known offender and she can't even describe the guy any more. She thinks he was this and maybe he was that. She doesn't even know the color of his eyes."

"That's too bad." Dix was gravely sympathetic. "No one else noticed the couple?"

"If they did, they've got stage fright. No one else has volunteered any information. And it was a crowded time at the drive-in. The after-movie crowd. Somebody else must have seen them."

"Yeah," Dix said. "Though you can see people without noticing them." He enlarged on it as if he'd never thought of it before. "How many times in a restaurant do you notice people around you? You don't pay any attention to them when they come or when they go. At least I don't."

"That's it," Brub agreed. He went on, "There's one thing we do know."

Dix lifted his eyes with renewed interest.

"We know he was in Beverly Hills on Friday night." Brub was sardonic. "But whether he was in the neighborhood for an evening's pleasure"—he bit his lip—"or whether he lives there, we don't know. He can't live all over Southern California. He's probably never operated in his own neighborhood; he'd be too cagey for that."

Sylvia came in on the end of his sentence. "Brub, you're not talking the case again. I can't take it." She was as different from the girl who'd opened the screen door as from the frightened woman of last night. She looked glowing, slim as a birch, in pale gray slacks, a brilliant green sweater. Her damp hair was braided on top of her head. "That's all I've heard this afternoon. Everyone on the beach hounding Brub for details. Do I get a drink, darling?"

"You do. Same as us?" Brub went to the bar again.

"Please, darling." Sylvia dumped ash trays with zeal. "Why people are so damn morbid," she returned to the subject with emphasis. She'd set up a hearty defense mechanism to battle her fears.

Dix remonstrated. "I don't know that it's exactly morbidity. Isn't it rather self-importance?" He grinned. "It isn't everyone who can get a first-hand account from the detective in the case."

Brub said, "Yeah, Junior G-Man tells all. He don't know nothing but he gotta say something." He swizzled the soda.

Dix smiled into his drink. "I'm different. I have a personal interest in the case." He let his eyes lift lazily as he spoke. Sylvia had frozen where she stood, her eyes alone moving, her eyes slewing swiftly to his face as if he'd suddenly revealed himself as the strangler. Brub went on swizzling.

"You see, I'm writing a detective novel," Dix added.

Sylvia moved then, setting down the ash tray she held. It made a small clack on the glass-topped end table.

Brub brought her the highball. "Here you are, skipper." He sat down, hanging his feet over the arm of the green chair. "So that's what you're writing. Who you stealing from, Chandler or Hammett or Gardner?"

"Little of each," Dix agreed. "With a touch of Queen and Carr."

"It should be a best-seller if you combine all those," Sylvia said. She sat opposite Brub.

"Can't miss," Dix admitted. "But for God's sake don't tell Uncle Fergus what I'm doing. He thinks I'm writing literature."

"I don't know Uncle Fergus," Sylvia murmured.

"You wouldn't like him. He's vehemently conservative. He hasn't relaxed since Hoover left Washington," he added cheerfully. "He won't mind what I've written when the royalties roll in. He won't read it anyway." She tried to stymie him on his questioning; he'd fixed that. He said, "Now you take that business about tire tracks that Brub mentioned last night. Instead of beating my brains out at the library, all I have to do is ask him. It's a good touch for a story. Makes you sound like an expert." He lifted his glass. "Do they really make plaster casts of tracks, Brub?"

"They try," Brub said gloomily. "But it takes cooperation. For good ones you need skid marks or mud or virgin territory. No chance this time. There weren't more than several hundred tracks superimposed on that particular stretch. Not worth lifting them."

"But you lifted them, didn't you?" Dix wondered. "The thoroughness of the police—"

"Sure," Brub grunted. "Thorough as hell. Maybe next time—" He broke off. Sylvia had gone tense. "There mustn't be a next time," he said heatedly. "Only now—"

Dix said seriously, "Let's skip it, Brub. With you working on it, feeling the way you do, you'll get him." Sylvia's eyes were grateful. "I'll take a refill and I'll tell you about the redhead at my apartment. You still like redheads?"

Sylvia's gratefulness was gay. "He'd better not."

"Who is she?" Brub played up, taking Dix's glass and his own. But it was an effort, he was pulling by his bootstraps.

"Well, I haven't met her yet," Dix laughed. "But I'm working on it." He knew better than to be talking about a woman publicly; he knew he shouldn't even think about her. "As soon as I find which apartment is hers, I'm going to get a job reading the light meter or delivering laundry. She's the sweetest built job I've seen in Hollywood."

"You better have me look her over before you make any commitments," Brub said. "Don't forget that blonde in London. Whew!"

"How was I to know her husband was a brass hat? With brass knuckles." He wanted the second drink less than the first but it tasted good.

"You'd better let me look her over," Sylvia suggested. "I don't trust Brub's taste. He just looks at the envelope. Now I'm a psychologist. I find out what's inside."

"You're both invited. As soon as I read the meter."

"That shouldn't take you long," Brub railed. "Unless you're getting old." He squinted his eyes. "You don't show much wear."

Voices clacked on the porch.

"That'll be Maude and Cary," Sylvia said. She called, "Come on in."

They were about what Dix had expected. A cute, babbling

brunette, big-eyed, hips too wide for her salmon slacks. A nice, empty-looking guy in gabardine slacks and a sports shirt. The Jepsons. Maude liked Dix. She baby-eyed him while she headed for the couch. He'd finish the drink and get out.

She said, "You're the ace, aren't you? I've heard all about you." There was a Texas drawl in her voice. She put a cigarette in her mouth and waited for him to light it. She smelled of perfume and liquor. "Make mine weak, Brub. We had one before leaving." She turned back to Dix. "You were in England with Brub." She babbled at Dix until Brub put the drink in her hand. She started on Brub then; it was inevitable what she would say.

"Have you caught that man yet, Brub? I tell you I'm so scared I don't know what to do. I won't let Cary leave me alone for a minute. I tell him—"

She ought to be scared. It would be a pleasure to throttle her.

"Anything new?" Cary put in.

"No," Brub said.

Sylvia said firmly, "We're not going to talk about it tonight."

Maude ignored her. "Why can't the police catch him?" She was highly indignant. "Nobody's safe with him running around loose." She whispered in sepulchre tones, "The strangler." She shivered closer to Dix. She was having a swell time.

Sylvia took a preparatory breath but Maude raced on, "How are we supposed to know who he is? He could be anybody. I tell Cary maybe he's our grocery man or the bus driver or those dreadful beach athletes. We don't know. Even the police don't know. You'd think they could find out."

Sylvia said desperately, "For God's sake, Maude. Don't you think they're trying?"

"I don't know." Maude tossed her head. "Maybe it's one of their own men. Well, it could be," she insisted to the rejection on the faces of the others. "How do we know? It's simply silly to think that this nice-looking fellow she had coffee with is the one. How did he get her into Beverly Glen Canyon?" she demanded. "Did they walk?"

Cary grunted, "He had a car, of course, Maude."

"Ah." She pounced on it. "But he didn't have a car. They went into the drive-in for coffee." She cocked her triumph at all of them. Her husband looked tired of it all but a thin layer of fear came over Sylvia's doubt.

Brub was scowling. He said, "That's just one of the things we're trying to find out, Maude. He must have had a car."

"I don't get it," Dix admitted.

"Our effete Easterner." Brub seized the diversion. "Dix is from New Jersey," he explained and turned to Dix again. "No one goes into a drive-in for a cup of coffee. Not if he has a car to sit outside in."

"But I've seen people in the drive-ins," Dix argued.

"Kids without a car. Or folks who've walked to the neighborhood movie. Or someone who's after a full meal, something he doesn't want to balance on a tray. But not for a shake or a cup of coffee. That's the point of a drive-in. You don't have to get out of your car."

"If you don't have a car, then you have to sit inside," Maude wagged her head. "He couldn't have had a car. Because," she took a deep breath, "because if he was the strangler and had a car, he never would have taken her inside where people could identify him. That man didn't have a car. But the one who killed her did have a car or she wouldn't have been found up Beverly Glen." Her triumph skittered joyfully. "There has to be another man with a car."

Dix narrowed his eyes, as if with the others he was pondering her conviction.

Sylvia broke the pause. "You think then that there was a second man, an accomplice." She looked quickly at Brub.

Brub shook his head. "He works alone." There was certainty in him.

Dix didn't jump on the statement. He asked simply, "How do you know that?"

"His kind of killer always works alone. He can't risk an accomplice."

Cary said, "He's insane, of course."

Dix turned his glass in his hand. Cary Jepson was a clod. He wouldn't be married to a stupid little talking machine if he had any spirit. The obvious reach of his imagination was, "He's insane, of course." It would never occur to him that any reason other than insanity could make a man a killer. That's what all the dolts around town would be parroting: *he's insane of course he's insane of course.* It took imagination to think of a man, sane as you or I, who killed. He hid against his highball glass the smile forming on his lips.

Brub was explaining, "—but doubtless he's a loony only in that respect. Otherwise he's probably an everyday citizen. Going about his business like any of us. Looking normal, acting normal until that urge comes on him."

"About once a month," Maude said goggle-eyed and then she screamed, "Oh."

Dix moved slightly away to look down at her. There was nothing wrong, she was just acting up. Sylvia didn't like it. Sylvia's face was granite. Dix didn't like it either; he was getting out of here.

Brub said, "Just don't be out alone at night, Maude, and you needn't worry." He added almost to himself, "We'll get him. He'll make a mistake yet." His mouth was grim.

"Suppose he doesn't," Maude wailed. She savored it, "Suppose it goes on and on—"

"Maude!" her husband complained wearily. "She keeps raving like that—"

Sylvia said definitely, "She isn't going to rave here. That's all, Maude. It's a truce—no more talk about crime tonight." She put on a bright smile. "Where will we eat? Ted's for steak? Carl's for shrimp? Jack's for chowder?"

He could leave now. Dix glanced at his watch and stood upright fast. "Why didn't someone tell me? I've a dinner date in Hollywood at seven. I've got to beat it."

Maude pushed out her spoiled underlip. "Break it."

"With a redhead?" Brub grinned.

Dix grinned back. "Not yet. I'll keep you informed. Thanks, Sylvia. Ring me, Brub. We'll have lunch." He nodded goodbye to the Jepsons, not saying it was a pleasure to meet them; it hadn't been.

He took a deep breath outside to expel the odor of Maude from his lungs. He'd like to meet her on a dark corner. It would be a service to humanity.

He drove the beach road to the Incline, casually glancing towards the three houses there. The traffic was still fairly heavy, on Wilshire it became irritating, at Sepulveda's intersection it was a slow-moving mass. Enough to make anyone's nerves short. He left turned at Westwood Boulevard, cutting sharp, just missing a right-turning car. He saw the motorcycle cop as the brakes of the other car screamed. But the cop didn't come after him.

He drove slowly up through the university gates and onto Sunset. Only one stop sign, at Beverly Glen. Sunset seemed deserted after Wilshire, he picked up speed. The light was against him at the intersection. He glanced casually at the Bel-Air gates; the road north jogged here, dividing into Bel-Air Road and, just beyond, Beverly Glen.

His hands tightened on the wheel. Cops again. Not on cycles; in a prowl car. Parked there watching the cars. He slid with the change to Go, not gathering speed until he had rounded the corner of the twisting woodland Sunset stretch. The rear-view mirrow showed no car following. His hands relaxed and he wanted to laugh. Out loud, noisy.

The cops were as unimaginative as that Jepson. Could they actually believe the killer would return to the scene of the crime? He did laugh and loud. He could see them sitting there all day, waiting for a loony to drive up the canyon. Fools.

He cut south at Rodeo, swinging back to Wilshire. He had nothing to do with himself and tonight he didn't want to be alone. The routine dullness of his nights, eat alone, go to a movie, go home—or, skip the movie, go home and read, write a little sometimes. The end, the same. Take some dope to sleep. Unless he could sleep the sleep of exhaustion. That wasn't often.

A man couldn't live alone; he needed friends. He needed a woman, a real woman. Like Brub and Sylvia. Like that stupid Cary had that stupid Maude. Better than being alone.

It wasn't often it hit him hard. It was the balmy night and the early dusk and the look of lamps through opened windows and the sound of music from radios in the lighted rooms. He'd eschewed human relationship for something stronger, something a hell of a lot better.

The car had followed its lead to the apartment; he hadn't intended to come back here yet. He parked at the curb; he'd have to go out to eat. Later.

He didn't have to give up normal living; that had been his one mistake. Brub and Sylvia proved it. He could be with them and be himself and not give away any secrets. His nerves were steady, his eyes level. It was time to gather friends again. Someone besides Brub and Sylvia. He couldn't be so constant at their home. They might start wondering. Sometimes Sylvia's eyes were disturbing, they were so wise. As if she could see under the covering of a man. Ridiculous, of course. You didn't ever have to give yourself away. Not if you were smart.

His spirits had jutted back up to a normal level. It wasn't often he got the dumps. His life was good, a slick apartment, a solid car; income without working for it, not half enough, but he could get by. Freedom, plenty of freedom. Nobody telling him what to do, nobody snooping.

He pulled the keys from the ignition and walked, tinkling them, the few paces to the court entrance. It was amusing to enter boldly, announcing his entrance with the metallic percussion. He didn't let into actual consciousness the thought that the redhead might be on her balcony.

The first time he'd seen the patio, he hadn't believed it. He hadn't been long enough in Southern California to believe it. It wasn't real; it was a stage set, a stagy stage set. In the center was the oblong blue pool. By day the pool was sky blue, it was tiled in that color, the water in it had to look that blue. By night it was moonlight blue. Two blue spotlights, one at either end of the balcony, made certain of that.

Dix had never seen anyone swimming in the pool by day or by night. He'd never seen anyone lounging in the bright, striped gliders or around the gaudy umbrella tables. The idea was good, the semi-tropical flowers spotted in the corners of the square prettied it up still more, the high oleander hedge was protection from street eyes, but nobody used the patio. The people in the Spanish bungalows boxing the court on three sides, and those upstairs off the Spanish-Colonial balcony, weren't clubby. Dix hadn't laid eyes on a couple of them in the weeks he'd been here.

He was thinking about the artificial moonlight in the artificial patio when behind him the blare of a horn jabbed. Jangle of voices scraped across his nerves. Anger shook him; for a moment he was tempted to turn out of the court and raise hell. Instead he tightened his fists and walked to his door, the first bungalow on the left. He was only at the door when he heard the heels clicking across the flagstone patio. Before he turned he was certain whom he would see.

She hadn't noticed him standing there by his door, she was hurrying. In the blue light her hair and her slacks and jacket were all blue, different depths of blue.

What he did was out of impulse, without thought. Thought would have rejected the idea. With long stride he quietly circled the pool. He was at the stairs almost as quickly as she. She was only on the third step when he spoke to her.

"I beg your pardon."

She wasn't startled although she hadn't known he was there. She stood arrested in motion of ascent, her head turning without any haste until she could look back down at him. When she saw it was a man, the glint of dare touched her mouth, her eyes.

"Did you drop something?" he continued. He held one hand cupped before him.

She looked down at herself, at her purse, touched her blown hair. "Did I?" she puzzled.

Quickly, impudently, he thrust both hands in his pockets. He looked up boldly at her. "I don't know. I was hoping so."

Her eyes narrowed over him slowly, in the way they had last night. She liked the look of him. Her eyes lengthened and she began to smile her lips. "Why?" she countered.

"I just lost my dinner date. I thought maybe you'd lost yours too."

She stopped smiling and she froze up just a little, not much. His eyes didn't waver; they held on to hers until she smiled again. "Sorry."

"I'm your neighbor. One A." His head gestured. He didn't want her to think he was a stranger, trying for a pickup.

"Sorry," she repeated and she moved up to the fourth step. "My dinner date will be here any minute and I'm not dressed. I'm rushing."

"I'm sorry too," Dix said. He said it warmly, with all the charm he could summon, and only a touch of arrogance for diversion.

She broke in, "If I ever lose a dinner date, I'll let you know." She ran up the stairs lightly, not looking back at him.

He shrugged. He hadn't expected success, therefore he wasn't disappointed. He'd made the preliminary maneuver, the question now was of time. He was stimulated by merely talking with her; she was a lure, even with that ghostly blue light coating her face. He moved back to his own quarters. Hearing again the tap of her heels, he swung suddenly and looked up to the balcony. She was just entering her apartment, the darkened one, the third. He continued, content, to his bungalow. He'd made headway. He knew now where to find her.

3

He didn't have to hurry. As a matter of fact, he needn't leave the apartment. There were tins of food, crackers, some cheese and fruit, cold meat in the ice box. He could get comfortable, cheese and beer were good enough for any man on the evening of a scorcher day. But he didn't want to get comfortable; he wanted something lively. Something amusing and stimulating and male.

He switched on the radio, found music, and fetched himself a cold beer from the kitchen. He was sprawled on the couch, half listening to the program, half thinking about the things he'd like to do tonight. If he had the money and the woman.

The slow beer was half gone when his front doorbell sounded. It startled him momentarily; his front bell was never rung. Slowly he got to his feet. He didn't delay moving to answer it. But he didn't hurry. He walked with caution.

The breath he took before setting his hand to the knob wasn't deliberate. Not until he flung open the door and heard the breath expelled did he realize he'd been holding it.

On the doorstep was the redhead. She said, "I've just lost a dinner date."

He tried not to sound too foolishly pleased. "Come in. Maybe you'll find him here."

"I hope not," she said dryly. She moved past him into the living room. She was eyeing it. It didn't look so good, the Sunday papers crushed on the couch, spilling over to the floor. The limp sofa cushions. The ash trays dirty, the beer bottle standing on the rug. Yet even in disarray it was class. The gray-green walls might have been indigenous to Virginibus Arms but the furniture was handpicked by Terriss. All modern bleached wood and glass and chrome, upholstery in yellow and crimson and gray. Terriss had boasted of his decorating taste. It wasn't personal taste, it was money; with Terriss' money you were steered to taste. You couldn't go wrong.

Dix said, "Tillie doesn't come on Sundays."

"You should see my place." She slid down in the wing chair as if she belonged there. She was still wearing the slacks; the outfit wasn't shades of moonlight blue but pale yellow, the pullover deeper yellow; the jacket, loose over her shoulders, was white. And her hair wasn't red, it was burnt sienna with shimmer of gold dusting it. She'd done over her hair and her face but she hadn't taken time to change.

Dix held out the cigarette box to her. "What do you mean you hope not?"

She put the cigarette in her mouth, lifted her face, waited for the light. From the thin gold lighter, Mel's lighter. "Because I told him I had a lousy headache and was going to bed." She blew the plume of smoke directly up at Dix. "And that I was disconnecting the phone."

He laughed. She was bold as her rust-red mouth and her slanted eyes, sharp as her painted tapering nails. She was what he'd needed. She was what he wanted. "Drink?"

"No. I want dinner. I had enough cocktails before I came home." She moved her body in the chair. "Maybe that's why I'm here." Her eyes studied the room.

"Mind if I finish my beer?"

"Not at all."

He returned to the couch and picked up the bottle. He didn't bother to pick up the newspapers. The way the first section had fallen revealed half of Mildred's whey face. He rested his foot on the paper.

The redhead turned her eyes suddenly back to him. "This is Mel Terriss' apartment." It wasn't a question.

"Yes. He's in South America. He turned it over to me while he's away."

"Who are you?" she demanded.

He smiled slightly. "I'm Dix Steele." In turn demanded, "Who are you?"

She wasn't accustomed to being given her own treatment. She didn't know whether she liked it. She tossed back her au-

IN A LONELY PLACE

tumn hair and waited, her eyes watching him. And then accepted his equality. "Laurel Gray."

He inclined his head. "How d'y'do." Exaggerated politeness. He switched to impudence. "Married?"

She bridled. Retort was on her tongue but she withheld it, her eyes going over him again in that slow slant fashion. There was no wedding ring on her finger, there was a lump of twisted gold, channeled with rubies and diamonds. A glittering bauble, the kind that cost fat money, the kind you looked at in jeweler's windows on Beverly Drive. You looked through the thick plate glass of the windows and wondered about those jeweled hunks. Wondered how a man could get his hands on the kind of dough it took to touch.

Somebody had put it on her finger. But there wasn't a wedding ring beside it.

She answered coolly, "It's none of your business, son, but since you asked, not now." She lifted her chin and he knew what she was about to say. He didn't want it said, he fended it away quickly.

"You were a friend of Mel Terriss?" The ring might have come from Terriss.

"Not much." She stubbed her cigarette into the ash tray. "Dropped in on a couple of his parties." She eyed him. "You a friend of Mel's?"

She was like all women, curious about your private life. He laughed at her; she'd find out only as much as he wished. "An old friend," he laughed. "Pre-war. Princeton." Princeton meant money and social position to her, calculation came that quickly under her skin. She was greedy and callous and a bitch, but she was fire and a man needed fire. "I'm from New York," he threw in carelessly. It sounded better than New Jersey.

"So you looked up old friend Mel when you came to the coast," her voice mocked.

"What do you think?" He saw the way her leg curved and lengthened into thigh. "Terriss isn't the kind of guy you look up. He's the kind you run into." She had taken another cigarette into her mouth. He crossed to light it. Her perfume was of flesh as he bent over her, and her eyes were wide and bold. It was too soon. He snapped shut the lighter, but he stood over her for a moment longer, smelling her. "You won't change your mind about a drink?"

"It's food I want." She didn't want food, she wanted what he wanted.

"You'll get it," he told her. But not yet. He was comfortable. He didn't want to start out again. He wanted to sit here opposite her, feeling for knowledge of her in his mind. He knew her; he had known her on that first evening when he'd bumped into her. But it was satisfying to corroborate the knowledge. He said, "First, I'm going to have a drink."

She gave in. "Make it two."

He smiled to himself as he went to the kitchen. He'd thought she would change her mind. A couple of drinks and they'd get acquainted faster. When he returned to the living room with the drinks, she was still curved in the chair. As if she hadn't stirred but were waiting for him to infuse movement into her.

She had moved. The paper his foot had trodden was by her chair. She took the glass from him and she said, "I see where the strangler's been at it again." She wasn't very interested; it was conversation, nothing more. "Someday maybe those dopes will learn not to pick up strange men."

"You picked me up."

She'd taken a long swallow of the highball. As he spoke, she lifted her eyebrows. "You picked me up, Princeton." She purred, "Besides, you're no stranger." She knew it too, the instinct of one for the other. "Mel's liquor is good as ever."

He said, "Yes, he left a good cellar for me." He went on, "I ran into him in a bar."

"And you had an old-home week."

"He was potted and trying to make my girl." His eyes spoke meaning beyond the words he slurred. "A blonde."

"That you'd picked up somewhere," she retorted.

He lied, "Friend of mine from home. She was just here for a week. Not Mel's type." He drank. He couldn't even remember the girl or her name. "Did you ever try to get rid of Mel when he was soused?"

"When wasn't he?"

"Well," he shrugged. "I promised to lunch with him next day. I lunched with him. I was trying to find an apartment. He was going to Rio on this new job. So—"

"Wait a minute," she called out. "Not Mel. Not a job in Rio."

"That's what he told me," Dix said. That's what Mel had said. He could have gone on a job. Some alcoholics tried to make a new start.

She was laughing to herself. "So you moved in."

"Yes, I moved in." He wasn't irritated. She didn't mean he was a charity case; she wouldn't be here drinking with him if she didn't think he had the stuff to spend. She probably thought he was another stinking rich loafer like Mel Terriss. He was casual. "I needed a quiet place for my work."

She was still laughing within her. "What do you do? Invent bombs?"

"I'm a writer." He didn't let her put the question. It was time again for her to answer questions. "I suppose you're in pictures?"

"Not often. I don't like getting up mornings." She knew all the tricks, to speak in commonplace phrases, to say more than words could say. He wondered who was keeping her. He could see the guy, fat-paunched, fat-jowled, balding. Too old, too ugly to get without paying for it. Paying plenty. A guy with nothing on his side but money. A bad idea slapped him. Could Terriss have been the guy? He didn't fit the picture of Old Moneybags. But if you revised the picture. A younger fellow, dopey with drink, his looks ravaged by the booze, a dullard always, even before alcohol narcotized what he had for a brain. And that stinking ego. He could just hear Terriss boasting about his girl, wearing her in public the way she wore that hunk of a ring; making himself believe he didn't have to buy it, he was just treating the gal right.

It couldn't have been Terriss. Terriss would have bragged about her. At least he'd have mentioned her. It wasn't Terriss. But doubts were worms crawling in his mind. She could twist a man about those taloned fingers, a man like Terriss. She could have excuses to keep her name out of it. Her career. A jealous ex. A divorce not quite complete.

She hadn't been talking. She'd been having her drink, eyeing him. Nor had his thoughts run across his face. It was trained to remain expressionless.

He finished his drink. "I don't like mornings either," he said. "That's why I'm a writer."

"Trying to break into pictures?"

He laughed at her. "I write books, lady. When I try to break into screen work, it will be because I need the money." He'd said the right thing, some of the speculation about him went out of her that quickly. There was an imperceptible relaxing of her muscular tension. He watched her over the edge of his glass as he tilted it, finished his drink. "Another?"

"Not now—"

He broke in, "I know, you're hungry. Wait'll I get a jacket and we'll be on our way." He didn't take a minute, catching up the heavy tweed jacket, a fuzzy, wiry tweed, rich brown, rich stuff. He slipped into the coat—he had about twenty dollars, enough for a Sunday-night dinner. Not a dress-up dinner, not in slacks.

She had retouched her lips, combed out her hair, resettled the white coat over the yellow sweater. She looked as fresh as if she'd just tubbed. She turned from the mirror as he reentered, the mirror near the desk. Her bag was on the desk. Good thing he'd mailed Uncle Fergus' letter. She was the kind who wouldn't care how she got her information on a man.

"Ready?"

She nodded and she walked towards the door. He came up behind her. In time to open the door. She looked up at him. "Do you have Mel's address in Rio?" The question was sudden. Why the hell couldn't she forget Mel Terriss?

"I'll give it to you when we get back," he told her. He opened the door. They went together into the night.

He touched her then for the first time, his hand against her elbow, escorting her into the blue courtyard.

He asked, "How would you like to drive up to Malibu?"

III

S HE WASN'T afraid. She rested herself carelessly against the
seat of the car, her left knee half-turned towards his thigh.
In the rounding of a corner she would touch him. She knew it;
she curled herself deliberately in this fashion. It was one of her
tricks. Yet, even knowing it was trick, he was stimulated, waiting for that pressure.

This was the beginning of something good, so good that he
was enjoying its immediacy without thought, without plan.
She was beside him, that was enough. He had needed her for
so long a time. He had always needed her.

It was a dream. A dream he had not dared dream, a woman
like this. A tawny-haired woman; a high-breasted, smooth-
hipped, scented woman; a wise woman. He didn't want to go
to Malibu, he wanted to swing the car around, return to the
apartment. He could wait. It was better to wait. She knew
that.

The traffic lanes were quieter at this early evening hour. He
followed Wilshire to the eucalyptus grove of San Vicente. The
spice of eucalyptus scented the darkness. San Vicente was a
dark street, he hadn't noticed before. And the smell of the sea
came in to meet them long before they reached the hill that
dropped into the canyon, long before they reached the sound
of the sea.

She was quiet on the drive. He was grateful for her quietness. He wondered if she were feeling for knowledge of him in
her quietness or if she were only tired. She didn't speak until
he turned into the canyon.

She remarked then, "You know the back roads."

"You recognize them," he smiled.

The touch of her knee on his thigh was more deliberate. She
tossed back her hair. "I've driven them often enough," she said
in that slow, husky way which gave words meaning. She
laughed. "I've friends in Malibu."

"The particular friend?"

"Which one?" she countered.

"Isn't there a particular one?" Curiosity nagged him. He

447

wanted to know about her. But he couldn't ask questions, not open questions. She was like him; she'd lie.

"There usually is," she said. They had reached the ocean road, turn right to Malibu. "Where will we eat?"

"Any place you say. You know Malibu."

"I don't want to go to Malibu."

He turned his head, puzzled at her abruptness. Afraid for the moment that this was to be the end of it, that she would put him off as she had the other man. Afraid that he'd said the wrong thing or done the wrong thing although he didn't know where he'd gone wrong. But she was still relaxed. She said, "I'm too hungry to drive that far. Let's stop at Carl's."

Anything that she said. The neon sign of Carl's slatted over the road ahead. He remembered the Nicolais and their friends had mentioned a Carl's or Joe's or Sam's. He wouldn't want to run into them. He wanted Laurel alone, unshared. Not touched by the anger and terror which entangled the Nicolais. He didn't ever want her touched by ugly things.

Yet he had no reason to reject Carl's. No reason to instil controversy in what had been between them, quiet, uncluttered. If Carl's had been the Nicolais' dinner choice, they would be gone by now. It had been more than two hours since he left them; they were planning to eat at that time. A car was pulling out from the front of the restaurant. Instinct avoided the lights. He drew up in the road at the side of the building, parked there.

She said, "I'll slide through." He stood there watching her come to him, taking her hand, touching her waist as he helped her from the car. The sea was a surge and a hush in the darkness across the road. She stood close to him for a moment, too close, before he removed his hand. She said, "You don't mind stopping here? The shrimp's good."

She led him around to the steps and they went up into the dining room. There were few in it, his quick look saw that he knew no one. Nor did she. Her look was quick as his own.

It was a spacious room, warm with light, circled with windows overlooking the dark sea. They sat facing each other and it was good. To be with a woman. To be opposite her, to have his fill of her face, the shape of it, the texture of it, the bone structure beneath the amber flesh. The set of her eyes and the shape of her mouth . . . her fire-tipped mouth.

"You think you'll know me the next time you see me?"

He returned to her actuality. He laughed but his words weren't made of laughter. "I knew you before I ever saw you."

Her eyes widened.

"And you knew me."

She let her lashes fall. They curved long as a child's, russet against her cheeks. She said, "You're pretty sure of yourself, aren't you, Dix?"

"Never before."

Her eyes opened full again and laughter echoed through her. "Oh, brother!" she breathed.

He didn't answer her, only with the look in his eyes. He hadn't been sure-footed with her before. He was now. He knew how to play it. She was brittle only on the surface. Underneath she too was seeking. Exhilaration heightened him. He knew then the rightness of this; she was for him.

The waitress came to the table before he could further it. He said, "You order, Laurel. I'll double it. Drink first?" He was irritated by the interruption. The waitress was a little chit, too much hair and flat face.

"No drinks." Laurel ordered for both, competently, without fuss. "Bring the coffee now, will you?"

The waitress went away but she was back too quickly. She poured the coffee. This time she'd be away longer.

Laurel said, "If you don't want your coffee now, I'll drink both, Princeton."

"You're out of luck." She knew what a man wanted, coffee, now, not later. He lighted her cigarette, realizing her as he leaned across the table. She was real, not a begging dream in his loneness. She was a woman.

She settled herself in comfort. "How long have you been living at Mel's place?" She was deliberately veering from intimacy. It didn't matter; postponement added zest.

He tried to remember. "About two months—six weeks, I guess."

"Funny I haven't run into you."

"Yes." Yet it wasn't. He'd used the back door, short cut to

the garage. He hadn't been in the blue patio half a dozen times. "I thought you were a visitor when I bumped into you last night. Have you been away?"

"No."

"Guess our hours didn't coincide. They will now."

"They might," she admitted.

"They will," he said with certainty.

Again she veered. "When did Mel leave?"

He figured it in his mind. "August. Around about the first. Before I moved in."

The waitress divided them again. She wasn't too long about it, and she was agreeable despite her flat face. The shrimp looked good and she poured more coffee without request.

He waited only until she was out of hearing. "Why the interest in Mel? I thought you'd only been in his place a couple of times." It wasn't jealousy but she'd think there was a twinge of it in him. She was thinking it now, maybe that was why she kept harping on Mel. Just another trick, not actual curiosity. "You weren't carrying the torch there?"

"Good Lord, Princeton!" That ended that. She needn't try that trick again.

He smiled slightly. "I was beginning to think he might have been the jeweler." His forefinger touched the mass of gold and ruby.

Her lip curled. "Mel was more careful of his money than that. Liquor was the only thing he could bear to spend it on." Her eyes touched the ring. "My ex."

He lifted his eyebrows. "It's a nice piece."

She said suddenly, "Don't ever marry money. It isn't worth it." She began to eat as if her hunger had reawakened.

"I've always thought it might be a good racket." He added, "For a woman."

"There's nothing wrong with the money. It's what goes with it." Her face was stony. "Bastards."

"Ex's?"

"Rich men. And women. They believe the earth was created for them. They don't have to think or feel—all they have to do is buy it. God, how I hate them!" She shook her head. "Shut up, Laurel."

He smiled patiently. "I don't believe that's true of all of them." As if he were a rich guy himself, one of the dirty bastards himself.

She said, "I can smell them a mile off. They're all alike."

"They aren't all like Mel—or your ex."

She went on eating. As if she hadn't heard him. And he had to know. If Mel had been in on the rent. He seized it. "After all they pay the rent. And the jeweler."

"They don't pay mine," she said savagely. Then she smiled. "I said shut up, Laurel. But I'm surprised Mel went off without saying goodbye. He was always in my hair."

"I'm surprised he didn't take you with him," Dix said.

She grimaced. "I told you I'd learned my lesson. Don't marry money."

No one was paying her rent. She was on her own; the ex, the rich one, must have settled up. She'd see to that; she and a battery of expensive lawyers. He said lightly, "It's the man who pays and pays. It couldn't have been too bad. You can sleep mornings and not have to worry about the roof over your head."

She said, "Yes," and the hardness came about her mouth. "As long as I don't marry again."

He understood her bitterness, but, understanding, he was disturbed. There could be someone she wanted, the way he was going to want her. She wouldn't have the hatred of the ex if there weren't a reason; she had his money to live on and free of him. Dix couldn't go on asking questions; he'd asked too many now. He was prying and she'd know it when the anger went out of her. He smiled at her again. "I'm glad that's the way it is," he said.

"Why?" She flashed at him.

"Because I wouldn't have found you in time—if it hadn't been that way."

Because she was desired, she softened. Giving him the look and the dare. She said, "Why, Princeton!"

"Or am I in time?"

She smiled, the inscrutable smile of a woman who knew the ways of a woman. She didn't answer him. There could be someone else. But at the moment, here with her, he was sure of his own prowess. Because he knew this was intended; that he and she should meet and in meeting become enmeshed. It was to be; it was.

They were the last guests to leave the restaurant. Again in the dark, sea-scented night, he was filled with power and excitement and rhythm. But tonight it was good. Because he was with her.

He didn't want to turn back to the city. He wanted to go on with her into this darkness, with the sound of water echoing the beat of his heart. He wanted to keep her with him always in this oneness of the two. He wanted to lift her with him into the vastness of the night sky. He said, "Shall we drive on up to Malibu?"

But he didn't want to drive, he didn't want to be occupied with the mechanics of a car. He was relieved when she refused.

"Let's keep away from Malibu."

He turned back, but driving without plan, he found the place where he could silence the car. An open stretch overlooking the dark beach and the sea. He said, "Do you mind? I just want to smell the salt."

Her eyebrows quirked. She'd thought he was parking the way a kid parked with his girl. She liked it that he hadn't meant it for that. She said suddenly, "Let's go down where we can really smell it."

The wind caught at them as they left the car and descended to the beach. The wind and the deep sand pushed at them but they struggled on, down to the water's edge. Waves were frost on the dark churning waters. Stars pricked through the curved sky. The rhythm pulsed, the crash and the slurring swish repeated endlessly, the smell of the sea was sharp. Spindrift salted their lips.

He had taken her hand as they walked to the water, he held it now, and she didn't withdraw it from his. She said, "I haven't done this for a long, long time." Her voice wasn't brittle; she wasn't playing a game with him. She was alone here, with him but alone. The wind swirled her hair across her face until he could see only the slant of her forehead and her cheek. Happiness rose like a spire within him. He hadn't expected ever to know happiness again. His voice stirred, "Laurel—"

She turned her head, slowly, as if surprised that he was there. The wind blew her hair like mist across her face. She lifted her face and for the first time, there in the light of the sea and the stars, he knew the color of her eyes. The color of dusk and mist rising from the sea, with the amber of stars flecking them.

"Laurel," he said, and she came to him the way he had known from the beginning it must be. "Laurel," he cried, as if the word were the act. And there became a silence around them, a silence more vast than the thunderous ecstasy of the hungry sea.

2

To sleep, perchance to dream and dreaming wake . . . To sleep and to wake. To sleep in peace, without the red evil of dreaming. To wake without need to struggle through fog to reach the sunlight. To find sleep good and waking more good. It was the ringing phone that woke him. He reached for it and he felt her stir beside him.

He spoke into it quietly, not wishing to wake her. Yet he willed her to wake, to open her eyes as he had opened his, into the full sunshine. "Hello."

"Dix? Did I interrupt your work?"

It was Brub Nicolai. For the instant there was a waning of the sun, as if a cold hand had pushed against it. Dix softened his voice to answer. "Not at all."

Brub didn't sound depressed today; it could have been the old Brub speaking. "Who was that redhead I seen you with last night? Was that the redhead?"

He couldn't answer quickly. It was impossible for Brub to have seen him last night with Laurel. Unless Brub were having him followed. That was more impossible. That would be incredible. He asked, "What are you talking about?"

"The redhead, Dickson. Not the blonde you were meeting in Hollywood. The redhead. Was that—"

Dix said, "Hm, a peeping Tom. Where were you hiding, Tom?"

Brub laughed. As if he hadn't a care in the world. "You didn't see us. We were pulling out of Carl's when you went in. It was Sylvia spotted you. I spotted the redhead."

The car he had avoided by parking at the side of the building. There were always eyes. A little tailor on his way home from a movie. A waitress in a drive-in. A butcher-boy on a bicycle. A room clerk with a wet pointed nose. A detective's wife who was alert, too alert. Whose eyes saw too much.

There were always eyes but they didn't see. He had proved it. His hand relaxed on the phone. "You would. And what did the little woman say to that?"

"I couldn't repeat such language." There was an imperceptible change in Brub's voice. Back to business. "How about lunch with me? You bring the redhead."

He could hear the stir of her breath. She was awake but she was silent. "She's tied up." He wouldn't put her and Brub together. She belonged in a different compartment from the Nicolais.

"Then you're not, I take it. How about lunch?"

He could refuse. But he didn't want to. Even to be with her. Because the game with Brub was important; it had to be played. There was renewed zest of the game in having Brub make the approach today.

"Sure," he agreed. "What time and where?" He noted the clock. It was past eleven.

"Noon? I'm at the Beverly Hills station."

His pulses leaped. The game was growing better. To walk into the police station, to be the guest of Homicide for lunch. But he didn't want to hurry. He wanted to watch her rise from sleep, to see her woman-ways, the clothing of her, the combing of her hair. He asked, "Can you make it one or do you punch a time clock?"

"One's okay. Meet me here?"

"I'll be there, Brub." He replaced the phone and turned to look on her. She was beautiful, she was younger than he'd thought her on first meeting; she was beautiful in the morning after sleep. Her hair was cobweb on the pillow, her dusky amber-flecked eyes were wide. She didn't smile up at him, she looked at him with that long wondering look.

She said, "Who's first on the shower?"

He put his fingers to her cheek. He wanted to tell her how beautiful she was. He wanted to tell her all that she was to him, all that she must be. He said, "The one who doesn't fix the coffee."

She stirred, lazy as a cat. "I don't cook."

"Then you do the scrubbing, Lady. And don't take all day."

"You have a lunch date," she mocked.

"Business."

"It sounded like it."

He didn't dare touch her, not if he were to make it to Brub. He slid away his fingers, slowly, with reluctance. Yet there was a pleasure in the reluctance, in the renunciation. This moment would come again and he would not let it pass. Postponing it would make it the sweeter.

"Go on," she urged. "Make the coffee."

She didn't believe that he meant to leave. He surprised her when he rose obediently, wrapped his bathrobe about him. He wanted to surprise her; he wanted her interest. She knew men so well although she was too young to know so well. Only by whetting her interest would she remain with him long enough to become entangled with him. Because she was spoiled and wise and suspicious.

He put on the coffee in the kitchen and then he went to the front door. The paper had hit the doorstep today, he didn't have to step outside for it. It was habit that unfolded it and looked at the front page. He didn't really care what was on it. The story wasn't there; it was on the second page, the police quizzing friends of the dead Mildred, the police admitting this early that there were no leads. He read the story scantly. He could hear the downpour of the shower. There was no mail in the slot. Too soon to hear from Uncle Fergus. The old buzzard had better come through. He'd need money to take Laurel where she should be taken. To expensive places where she could be displayed as she should be.

He flung down the paper, went back to the bedroom, impatient to see her again. She was still in the bathroom but the shower was turned off. He called, "How do you take your coffee?" Touching the soft yellow of her sweater there on the chair. Wanting to look on her, to smell her freshness.

She opened the door. She was wrapped in a borrowed white terry bathrobe, it was a cocoon enfolding her. Her face was shining and her damp hair was massed on top of her head. She came to the quick take of his breath, came to him and he held her. "Oh, God," he said. Deliberately he set her away. "I've got a business luncheon in one hour. How do you want your coffee?"

Her eyes slanted. "Sweet and black."

He hurried as she sat down at the dressing table, hurried to return to her. She was still there when he brought the coffee, she was combing out her hair, her fiery gold hair. He put the coffee down for her and he carried his own across the room.

"You'd better shower, Dix. You don't want to be late for that business appointment."

"It is business. Someday I'll tell you all about it." He drank his coffee, watching the way she swirled her hair below her shoulders. Watching the way she painted her lips, brushed her lashes. As if she belonged here. Jealousy flecked him. She knew her way around, had she been here before? He couldn't bear it if Mel Terriss had touched her. Yet he knew she had been touched by other men; there was no innocence in her.

Abruptly he left her, long enough to shower. He couldn't stay with her, not with the anger rising in him. It washed away in the shower. Mel Terriss wasn't here. She couldn't have had anything to do with Terriss. She wouldn't ever have been that hard up. He opened the door when he'd finished showering, fearing that she might have slipped away from him. But she was there, almost in the doorway. "I brought you more coffee," she said.

"Thanks, baby. Mind the noise of a razor?"

"I can take it." She was dressed now. She sat on the edge of the tub with her coffee, watching him shave. As if she couldn't bear to leave him. As if it was the same with her as with him. The burring didn't annoy with her there. He could talk through it, gaily. "I knew you'd be busy. That's why I said okay."

"And if I weren't?"

"Aren't you?"

"I have a voice lesson at two," she admitted.

"What time will you be home?"

"Why?" she mocked.

He didn't bother to answer, only with his eyes. He finished shaving, cleaned the razor. "Busy tonight?"

"Why?" she repeated.

"I might be free," he said.

"Call me."

"I'll camp on your doorstep."

She frowned slightly, ever so slightly. He might have imagined it. Only she said, "I'll come here." And she curved her lips. "If I'm free."

She didn't want him to come to her place. It could be the ex, yet how could it be? It could be she was tied up with someone else. She could have lied. There might be a Mr. Big in the background. The man she'd lied to last night.

He said definitely, "If you aren't here, I'll be on your doorstep."

She followed him into the bedroom again, lounged on the edge of the bed while he dressed. Gray slacks, a blue shirt—he wouldn't need a coat, warmth filled the room. From the back of the chair he took the tweed jacket he'd worn last night. He'd forgotten to hang it.

She said, "That looks like Mel's jacket. He was a good dresser."

He turned with it in his hands. She hadn't meant anything, it was just a remark. He admitted, "It's Mel's." Casually but boldly. "In Rio it's summer. Mel was going to buy up all the best Palm Beach. He left his old stuff here, told me to help myself." He explained it, continuing into the closet, the closet filled with Mel's expensive clothes. "My own things shrank when I was in the service. And thanks to the shortages, I arrived here practically destitute."

She said, "I'm surprised anything of Mel's would fit you."

He closed the closet door. "His backlog before he developed that paunch. He was skinny enough at Nassau."

He transferred his billfold and car keys.

She said, "He even left you his car. You must have done him a favor once. I never thought he'd give away an old toothpick."

He smiled. "He's making up for all of it on the sublease. But I did do him several favors."

"At Nassau," she mimicked.

"Yeah. I used to speak to him." He took her arm, steered her to the door. "Is your phone still disconnected?"

"Why?"

"Because I'll start calling you the minute I'm back here."

"I'll call you when I get back."

They were at the front door and she turned to him, into his arms. Her mouth was like her hair, flame. This time she broke from him. "You have a business date," she reminded.

"Yeah." He took his handkerchief, wiped his lips. "Somebody might be in that empty patio."

She laughed. "The nice part about departing at noon, Dix, is that no one knows what time you arrived."

They left together and he heard her footsteps passing the pool to her staircase. He knew he was behaving like a love-smitten sophomore but he waited by the entrance until she was on her balcony, until she lifted her hand to him in goodbye.

He'd left his car standing in the street. There hadn't been time last night to put it away. He was pleased it was there, that he didn't have to go through the back alley to get it out. He felt too good to do more than step into it and swing away on its power. He was even on time for the appointment with Brub.

He drove up Beverly Drive, turning over to the city hall. It looked more like a university hall than headquarters for the police, a white-winged building with a center tower. It was set in green grass, bordered with shrubs and flowers. There was nothing about it that said police save that the huge bronze lamps on either side of the door burned green. He climbed the stone steps and entered the door.

The corridor inside was clean and businesslike. A sign directed to the police quarters. He went up to the desk, it might have been the desk in any office. If it hadn't been for the dark blue uniform of the man just leaving, it would be hard to believe this was the Beverly Hills police station. The pleasant young man behind the desk wore a brown plaid sports coat and tan slacks.

Dix said, "Brub Nicolai?" He didn't know a title. "Detective Nicolai. He's expecting me."

He followed the young man's directions up the hall, entered another businesslike room. Brub was sitting in a chair. There were a couple of other men present, a little older than Brub, in plain business suits. They didn't look any different than ordinary men. They were L. A. Homicide.

Brub's face brightened when he saw Dix. "You made it."

"I'm seven minutes early."

"And I'm hungry." Brub turned to the other men, the tall, lean one and the smaller, heavier-set one. "See you later." He didn't introduce Dix. But they were Homicide. It was in the way their eyes looked at a man, even a friend of one of their own. Memorizing him. Brub said, "Come on, Dix. Before I start eating the leg of a chair."

Dix said, "Sawdust will give you a bay window if you aren't careful."

They walked down the corridor, out into the sunshine. "My car's here."

Brub said, "Might as well walk. We can't park much nearer. Where do you usually eat?"

"If you're hungry and don't want to stand in line, we'll go to my favorite delicatessen. Or the Ice House."

They walked together the few blocks. The sun was warm and the air smelled good. It was like a small town, the unhurried workers of the village greeting each other in the noon, standing on the corners talking in the good-smelling sunshine. He chose the Ice House, it was the nearer, just around the corner on Beverly. Man-food in it. He was surprised that he too had an appetite. Good sleep meant good appetite.

He grinned across the table at Brub. "For a moment this morning you startled me. I thought you were clairvoyant."

"About your redhead?" Brub whistled. "That's a piece of goods. How did you arrange to meet her?"

He could talk of her to Brub. And like a love-smitten swain he wanted to talk of her. "It's time the Virginibus Arms had a good-neighbor policy."

"Virginibus Arms? Not bad," Brub said.

He realized then that Brub hadn't known his address until now. He'd given his phone number, not his address.

"Yeah, I was lucky. Sublease. From Mel Terriss." Brub didn't know Mel. "Fellow I went to school with at Princeton. Ran into him out here just when he was leaving on a job."

"Damn lucky," Brub said. "And the redhead went with it?"

He grinned again, like a silly ass. "Wish I'd known it sooner."

"Is she in pictures?"

"She's done a little." He knew so little about her. "She's studying."

"What's her name?"

Brub wasn't prying; this was the old Brub. Brub and Dix. The two Musketeers. A part of each other's lives.

"Laurel," he said, and saying the name his heart quickened. "Laurel Gray."

"Bring her out some night. Sylvia would like to meet her."

"Sylvia, my eye. You don't think I'd expose Laurel to your wolfish charms, do you?"

"I'm married, son. I'm safe."

"Maybe. What about that little gal yesterday? Wasn't she cooing at you?"

Brub said, "Maude would coo at a pair of stilts. Cary's sort of a sixth cousin of Sylvia. That's why we get together. Maude thought you were wonderful, hero."

"Did she ever stop talking?"

"No, she never stops. Although after she saw you with Redhead, she subdued a bit."

It was good to know that it didn't matter how many saw him with Laurel. That he could appear with her everywhere, show her everywhere; there was no danger in it. Only he wouldn't take her to Nicolai's. Not to face Sylvia's cool appraisal. Sylvia would look at her through Sylvia's own standards, through long-handled eye glasses.

"She was certainly hipped on your case," Dix said. It was time to steer the conversation. "How's it coming?"

"Dead end."

"You mean you're closing the books?"

"We don't ever close the books, Dix." Brub's face was serious. "After the newspapers and the Maudes and all the rest of them forget it, our books are open. That's the way it is."

"That's the way it has to be," Dix agreed as seriously.

"There've been tough cases before now. Maybe ten, twelve years the department has had to work on them. In the end we find the answer."

"Not always," Dix said.

"Not always," Brub admitted. "But more often than you'd think. Sometimes the cases are still unsolved on paper but we have the answer. Sometimes it's waiting for the next move."

"The criminal doesn't escape." Dix smiled wryly.

Brub said, "I won't say that. Although I honestly don't think he ever does escape. He has to live with himself. He's caught there in that lonely place. And when he sees he can't get away—" Brub shrugged. "Maybe suicide, or the nut house—I don't know. But I don't think there's any escape."

"What about Jack the Ripper?"

"What about him? A body fished out of the river, an accident case. A new inmate of an asylum. Nobody knows. One thing you can know, he didn't suddenly stop his career. He was stopped."

Dix argued, "Maybe he did stop it. Maybe he'd had enough."

"He couldn't stop," Brub denied. "He was a murderer."

Dix lifted his eyebrows. "You mean a murderer is a murderer? As a detective is a detective? A waiter a waiter?"

"No. Those are selected professions. A detective or a waiter can change to another field. I mean a murderer is a murderer as . . . an actor is an actor. He can stop acting professionally but he's still an actor. He acts. Or an artist. If he never picks up another brush, he will still see and think and react as an artist."

"I believe," Dix said slowly, "you could get some arguments on that."

"Plenty," Brub agreed cheerfully. "But that's the way I see it." He attacked his pie.

Dix put sugar in his coffee. Black and sweet. And hot. He smiled, thinking of her. "What about this new Ripper? You think he's a nut?"

"Sure," Brub agreed.

The quick agreement rankled. Brub should be brighter than that. "He's been pretty smart for a nut, hasn't he? No clues."

"That doesn't mean anything," Brub said. "The insane are much more clever about their business, and more careful too, than the sane. It's normal for them to be sly and secretive. That's part of the mania. It makes them difficult to catch up with. But they give themselves away."

"They do? How?"

"When is more important. But plenty of ways. Repetition of the pattern." Brub finished off the pie and lit a cigarette. "The pattern is clear enough with the strangler. It's the motive that's hard to fix on."

"Does an insane man need a motive? Does he have one?" He lit a cigarette.

"Within the mania, yes."

Dix said offside, "This is fascinating to me, Brub. You say you have the pattern. Doesn't that in a way incorporate the motive?"

"In a way, yes. But you take this case. The pattern has emerged. Not too clearly but in a fuzzy way, yes. It's a girl alone. At night. She doesn't know the man. At least we're reasonably sure of that. This last girl, as far as we can find out, couldn't possibly have known the man. And there's no slight connection between the girls. All right then: it's a pickup. A girl waiting for a bus, or walking home. He comes along in a car and she accepts a ride."

"I thought you were figuring he didn't have a car. What were you talking about?"—he appeared to try to remember—"Going into a drive-in to eat—"

Brub broke in. "He had to have a car. Not in every case but definitely in the last ones." His eyes looked seriously into Dix's. "My own theory is that he doesn't make the approach from the car. Because girls are wary about getting into a car with strangers. The danger of that has been too well publicized. I think he makes the approach on foot and after he has the lamb lulled, he mentions he's on his way to get his car. Take this last one. She's waiting for a bus. He's waiting on the same corner. Busses don't run often that time of night. They get talking. He invites her to have a cup of coffee. It was a foggy night, pretty chilly. By the time they've had coffee, he mentions his car isn't far away and he'll give her a lift."

Dix set down his coffee cup carefully. "That's how you're figuring it," he nodded his head. "It sounds reasonable." He looked at Brub again. "Do your colleagues agree?"

"They think I may be on the right track."

"And the motive?"

"That's anybody's guess." Brub scowled. "Maybe he doesn't like women. Maybe some girl did him dirt and he's getting even with all of them."

Dix said, "That sounds absurd." He laughed, "It wouldn't hold water in my book."

"You're forgetting. It's mania; not sanity. Now you or I, if we wanted to strike back at a girl, we'd get us another one.

Show the other gal what she'd lost. But a mind off the trolley doesn't figure that way."

"Any other motives?" Dix laughed.

"Religious mania, perhaps. There've always been plenty of that kind of nut out here. But it all comes back to one focal point, the man is a killer, he has to kill. As an actor has to act."

"And he can't stop?" Dix murmured.

"He can't stop," Brub said flatly. He glanced at his watch. "I've got to go up Beverly Glen. Want to come along?"

Dix's eyebrows questioned.

"To the scene of the crime," Brub explained. "Would you like to have a look at it? It'll tell you more than I can in words of what we're working against."

His pulse leaped at the idea of it. To the scene of the crime. For book material. He said, "Yeah, I think I will." He glanced at his own watch. Two-twenty. "I can take another hour from work. Particularly since I can charge it up to research."

Brub picked up the checks. At Dix's demurring, he said, "This is on me. In the line of business."

The cold touch at the base of his spine was imaginary. He laughed. "You mean detectives have a swindle sheet? Authors aren't so lucky."

"I'll put it down: conferring with an expert." He queried, "All mystery authors claim to be crime experts, don't they?"

"I'll dedicate the book to the dick who bought me a lunch."

He and Brub emerged into the sunshine of Beverly Drive. The lunch hour was done; the workers had returned to their offices. Women shoppers were beginning to stroll the street. They clustered at the shop windows. They held little children by the hand. They chattered as they went about their aimless female business. There wasn't a brilliant red head in sight.

The news vendor on the corner talked the races with a passing customer. His folded papers, the early edition of the *News*, lay stacked on the sidewalk beside a cigar box holding coins. Dix's eyes fell to the papers but he didn't buy one. There wouldn't be any fresh news anyway. He was with the source of news.

They returned to the city hall. "Shall we take your car or mine?" Brub asked.

The cold hand touched him quickly again. How could he

know? Brub couldn't be suspicious of him. There wasn't a shred of reason for thinking it. Brub included Dix with himself, "normal as you and I." Yet how could he be sure? Brub had once known him so well. That was long ago. No one could read him now. Not even Laurel.

Did Brub want him to take his car back up the Beverly Glen Canyon? Was this luncheon arranged; were the two ordinary men, who were L. A. Homicide, waiting for Brub to report back to them? He had hesitated long enough in answering, too long. It couldn't matter which car. There couldn't be eyes waiting to identify a black coupe, a coupe like a thousand others. It couldn't be tire marks they were after; they were unable to get marks off a clean, paved road. Brub had said so. Had intimated so. Too many cars had passed that way.

He pretended to come to. "Did you say something? Sorry."

Brub grinned. "Thinking about the redhead? I said, whose car shall we take? Yours or mine?"

"It doesn't matter," he answered promptly. But he knew as he answered that he preferred to take his own. He'd been a panty-waist to have considered anything but that. That was what quickened his mind, that was what put zest into the game. To take the dare. "Might as well use mine."

Brub said, "Okay," but he stopped at the doors to the building. "I'll go in and see if Lochner wants to ride up with us. You don't mind another passenger?"

"Not at all." He followed Brub. To watch faces, to see if there were interchange of expression.

Only one of the Homicide men was left. He was talking to a couple of motorcycle cops in uniform. Talking about the local baseball club. Brub said, "Want to go up Beverly Glen, Loch?" He made the introductions then. "Jack Lochner—my friend, Dix Steele."

Lochner was the tall, thin man. His clothes were a little too big for him, as if he'd lost weight worrying. His face was lined. He looked like just an ordinary man, not too successful. He didn't give Brub any special glance. He didn't examine Dix now as he had earlier; he shook hands and said, "Nice to know you, Mr. Steele." His voice was tired.

Brub said, "Dix is a mystery writer, Loch. He wants to go along. You don't mind?"

"Not at all." Lochner tried to smile but he wasn't a man used to smiling. Just used to worry. "Nothing to see. I don't know why we're going back. Except Brub wants to. And the Beverly Hills bunch seems to think he's on the right track."

Dix raised one eyebrow. "So you do have some ideas?"

Brub's laugh was embarrassed. "Don't you start riding me too. All I've got is a feeling."

"Psychic," Lochner droned.

"No," Brub denied fast. "But I can't help feeling we're on the right track here in Beverly." He explained to Dix, "The Beverly bunch sort of feels the same way. That's why we're hanging around here. Beverly has its own force, you know, separate from L. A., but they're doing everything they can to help us."

"And they know how to help," Loch said. "A smart bunch."

They left the building together. Dix said, "We're taking my car." He steered them to it. He wasn't going in a police car. Only a man off his trolley would consider riding around in a police car with Homicide. Homicide with psychic hunches.

"Do you know the way?" Lochner asked.

"I know where Beverly Glen is. You can direct me from there." With the dare taken, his mind was sharp, cold and clear and sharp as a winter wind back East. They could direct. Not a muscle would twitch to indicate he knew the place. He began laughing to himself. Actually he didn't know the place. He didn't even have to worry about making the unwary move.

"Go over to Sunset," Brub directed. "Turn right on Beverly Glen."

"That much I know." He swung the car easily towards Sunset, enjoying the power of the motor, the smoothness of the drive. A good car. He held it back. You shouldn't speed up with cops in your car. "There were a couple of cops guarding the portals when I went by Sunday. On my way home after I left your place, Brub." Were those the same cops Lochner had had in the office? Were they there to look him over? He was getting slap-happy. The cops couldn't have picked him out of all the drivers passing that intersection Sunday afternoon. Just him, one man. His fingers tightened on the wheel. Did the police know more than they had told? Had there been someone else in the canyon on Friday night? He went on talking.

"What were they doing? Waiting for the killer to return to the scene of the crime?"

"They were checking traffic," Lochner said in his disinterested voice. "I never knew a killer yet who went back. Make it easy for us if they did. We wouldn't have to beat our brains out all over town."

"All we'd have to do was post a couple of the boys and wait," Brub enlarged. "They could play checkers until he came along—easy."

"How would you know him from the sightseers?" Dix joined the game.

"That is an angle." Brub looked at Lochner.

The older man said, "He'd be the one who was too normal."

"No fangs? No drooling?" Dix laughed.

"Of course, he wouldn't know the cops were watching," Brub said.

They'd reached Beverly Glen and Dix turned right. "You can direct me now."

"Just keep on going," Brub said. "We'll tell you when."

It was a pretty little road to start, rather like a New England lane with the leaves turning and beginning to fall from the trees. He had no tension, perhaps a slight fear that he might recognize the place, that muscular reaction might be transferred from him to Brub seated close beside him. He relaxed. He said, "This reminds me of home. Autumn in New York, or Connecticut, or Massachusetts."

"I'm from the East myself," Lochner said. "I've been away twenty years."

It wasn't pretty for long. A few estates and it became a road of shacks, little places such as men built in the mountains before the rich discovered their privacy and ousted them. And then the shacks were left behind and the road became a curving pass through the canyon to some valley beyond.

It would be lonely up here at night; there were deep culverts, heavy brush, on the side of the road. It was lonely up here now and they passed no cars. It was as if they had entered into a forbidden valley, a valley guarded by the police. Keeping the sightseers away. Only the hunters and the hunted allowed to enter. The walls of the canyon laid shadows over the road. There was a chill in the air, the sun was far away.

He drove on, waiting for them to give the word to stop. They weren't talking, either of them; they were on the case now, a case that had them angry and bitter and worried. He kept quiet, it wasn't the time for a conversation piece. He realized his fingers were tightened on the wheel and again he relaxed them. He didn't know if the detectives would shout a sudden stop command or if they'd give warning or just how it would be done. He kept the speed down to twenty and he watched the road ahead, not the culverts with leaves like brown droppings in them. He didn't recognize any of the road. That was the good part of it.

It was Lochner who said, "Here we are. Just pull up along here, Mr. Steele, if you will."

This stretch of the road was no different than the others. There was nothing marking it as the place where a girl had been found.

The detectives got out, and he got out on the other side of the car. He walked beside them across the road. "He came this far, and then he turned around," Brub said. "Or he may have been on his way back to town."

"This is where you found her?" Dix wasn't nervous. He was an author in search of material, a man along just for the ride.

Brub had stepped up into the rustling brown leaves. He said, "It's a little heavier here. He could have known that. He could have figured she wouldn't be found for a long time, with the leaves falling on her, covering her."

Brub was scuffing through the rustle, as if he expected to find something under the sound. A clue. An inspiration. "Every day there'd be more leaves. Not many people look off at the side of the road when they're driving. Not unless there's something scenic there. Nothing scenic about this thicket."

Lochner stood with his hands in his pockets, with the worry lines in his tired face. Stood beside Dix.

Dix could ask questions, he was supposed to ask questions. He said, "How was it she was found so quickly then?"

"Luck," Brub said. He stood in the ditch, leaves to his ankles. "The milkman had a flat right at this point."

Lochner said, "He picked this place on purpose."

"The milkman?" Dix looked incredulous.

"The killer. Take a look at it. The way the road curves

here—he can see any lights coming from behind, two loops below. And he can look up to the top of the hill, see the lights of a car approaching him when it makes the first of those two curves. He can sit with her in the car, looking like a spooner, until the other car goes by." His eyes squinted up the road and back down again. "Not much chance of traffic here in the middle of the night. He was pretty safe." His voice had no inflection. "He does it. He opens the door of the car and rolls her out and he's away. No chance of being caught at it. Strangling's the easiest way. And the safest."

Brub had stooped and brushed aside the leaves.

Dix moved closer to the edge of the thicket, looked up at him. "Find something?" he asked with the proper cheerful curiosity.

Lochner monotoned, "The experts have been over every inch with a microscope. He won't find anything. Only he wanted to come back up so I said I'd come along." He put a cigarette in his mouth, cupped his hands about the match. "The only place we'll find anything is in his car."

A wind had come up, a small sharp wind. Lochner wouldn't have cupped the match if it hadn't. It wasn't imaginary. Dix said, with the proper regret, "And you've not been able to get a description of the car yet?"

"Not yet," Lochner said. In that tired way, but there was a tang underneath the inflection. Not yet, but they would. Because they never closed the books. Because a murderer had to murder. Dix wanted to laugh. They knew so little, with all their science and intuition; they were babes in toyland.

"When you do, you mean you might find a hairpin or a lipstick or something?"

Brub did laugh. There in the brush it sounded hollow. "Good Lord, Dix. You're old hat. Girls don't wear hairpins. You ought to know that."

"Dust," Lochner said.

"Dust?" He was puzzled now.

Brub climbed down from the thicket, one big step down. He began brushing the crumpled brown leaves from his trouser legs.

"That's dust," Lochner said. He turned back to the car. "We've got dust from the drive-in. We've got the dust from her clothes and her shoes. There'll be some of that same dust in his car."

Dix held the mask over his face. He shook his head, his expression one of awe and admiration. "And even if it's ten or twelve years, the dust will be the same?"

"Some of it will," Lochner said.

They all got back in the car. Dix started the engine. He asked, "Is there a better place to turn than here?" They were supposed to know. The police cars had been all over this territory. They'd drawn circles around it and carried laboratory technicians into it. They'd done everything but dig it up and carry it to headquarters.

"Go on a bit," Brub said. "There's a side road a little further on."

Dix ran the car up the hill. He saw the side road and he turned in. The side road wasn't paved. If there were any suspicion, this could be a trap, to check on his tires. Behind the brush, there could be the two cops, playing checkers, watching. Cops with plaster, ready to make casts. But they were wrong. He hadn't turned here before. There was a better place farther on. He maneuvered the car, headed back towards town.

He could be talkative now. He was supposed to be impressed and curious. He said, "Did you find anything, Brub?"

Brub shook his head. "No. I didn't expect to. It's just—I get closer to him when I do what he did. What he might have done. I've got a picture of him but it's—it's clouded over. It's like seeing a man in the fog. The kind of a fog that hangs in our canyon."

Dix said cheerfully, "The kind you had when I was out at your place Friday night."

"Yeah," Brub said.

Lochner said, "He's from the East."

Dix's nerves were in strict control. Not one nerve end twitched. Rather was he stimulated by the sharp and cold blade of danger. He said, "That's a bit of information you've kept to yourselves, isn't it? Did the waitress recognize an Eastern accent?"

"It isn't information," Brub answered. "He talked just like anybody else. No accent. No particular quality of voice. That's Loch's reconstruction."

Lochner repeated, "He's from the East. I know that." He was deliberate. "He's a mugger."

"What's a mugger?" Dix asked quickly.

"Certain gangs used to operate in New York," Brub explained. He illustrated on himself with his right arm. "One man would get the victim so, the others would rob him. Until they found out it could be a one-man job. You don't need more than two fingers to strangle a man. Or woman."

"He's a mugger," Lochner repeated. "He doesn't use his fingers. There's no finger marks. He uses his arm. He's from the East."

Dix said, "As a fellow Easterner, Mr. Lochner, you might admit that a Westerner could have learned the trick."

Lochner repeated, "I've seen the way they did it in New York. He knows how. The same way."

They came out of the shadowed canyon, out into the sunshine, into the city again. But the sun had faded. There were clouds graying the blueness of sky. And the winding road of Sunset to Beverly was heavy with shadows of the late afternoon. It was almost four o'clock when they reached the city hall.

Dix pulled up and Lochner got out. He intoned, "Thanks for the lift, Mr. Steele."

Dix said, "Thank you for letting me go along." He shook his head. "It's pretty gruesome though. I don't think I'd go for police work."

Lochner walked away to the hall. Brub leaned against the car door. He was frowning. "It isn't pleasant," he said. "It's damned unpleasant. But it's there, you can't just close your eyes and pretend it isn't. There are killers and they've got to be caught, they've got to be stopped. I don't like killing. I saw too much of it, same as you did. I hated it then, the callous way we'd sit around and map out our plans to kill people. People who didn't want to die any more than we wanted to die. And we'd come back afterwards and talk it over, check over how many we'd got that night. As if we'd been killing ants, not men." His eyes were intense. "I hate killers. I want the world to be a good place, a safe place. For me and my wife and my friends, and my kids when I have them. I guess that's why I'm a policeman. To help make one little corner of the world a safer place."

Dix said, "That's like you, Brub." He meant it. It didn't matter how unpleasant a job was, Brub would take it on if in the end it meant the righting of something wrong.

Brub pushed back his hat. He laughed, a short laugh. "Junior G-man rides his white horse. I suppose in a couple of years I'll be as stale as Loch. But right now it's personal. I want to get that killer." His laugh repeated. It was apology for his emotion. He said, "Hang around till I check in and I'll buy you a drink."

"Sorry." Dix put his hands on the wheel. "I'm late now. We'll do it again. And thanks for a valuable afternoon, Brub."

"Okay, fellow. See you soon." Brub's hand lifted and he rolled off, like a sailor on the sea. Like a policeman tracking an unknown foe.

IV

He rang Laurel as soon as he reached the apartment. Before he fixed a drink, before even lighting a cigarette. There was no answer to the call. He rang her every fifteen minutes after that, and at six, when the dusk was moving across the open windows, and when there was still no answer to his call, he stepped out into the courtyard where he could look up at her apartment. But there were no lights in it.

His toe stubbed the evening paper as he returned to his apartment. He'd forgotten it. His impatience to reach her had made him forget the news. He lighted the lamps in the living room when he reentered. He'd had two drinks and he didn't want another. He wanted her. He took the paper with him back into the bedroom where he could lounge on the bed, where the phone was close to hand. He turned on the bed light and he looked through the paper until he found the story. It was on an inside page tonight. There was nothing new. The police were still working on the case. That was true. They had valuable leads. That was a lot of eyewash. He read the sports page and the comics and he rang her again. And again to no avail.

He was beginning to be upset. If she hadn't intended to come home this evening, she could have told him. She'd said she was going for a singing lesson. No singing lesson lasted until this time of night. She knew he was expecting her. She could have called him if she'd been delayed. He tried to look at it reasonably. Honestly tried. She had a lot of friends, of course she did. A girl with her body and hair and strange, lovely face would have more friends than she could handle. He was a newcomer, a nobody in her life. After all, she hadn't met him until yesterday. She couldn't be expected to drop everyone else and devote herself to him alone. She didn't know yet how it was going to be between them. She didn't know it was to be just these two. Two that were one. Until she understood as he did, he couldn't be disturbed that she had other obligations. But she could have told him. She needn't have left him here hanging on the phone, afraid to go out lest it ring. Lying around here without food, smoking too much, reading every line of the damn dull newspaper, waiting for the phone to ring. Wearing out his finger dialing.

The door buzzer sounded with an insolent suddenness while he was still lying there, trying to put down his anger, trying to see it reasonably. He jumped off the bed, and he almost ran to answer. He was angry, yes; he'd tell her plenty, but the heat of it was already dissipated in the eagerness to see her. In the joy of rushing to behold her. He opened the door, and his hand tightened over the knob as he held it wide. Sylvia Nicolai was on the threshold.

"Am I interrupting anything, Dix?" She stood there, tall and slim, at ease, her hands thrust into the deep pockets of her cashmere Burberry, her gilt hair pulled smoothly away from her slender face.

He couldn't believe it because it wasn't she he expected. It was as if the fire of Laurel had faded, had become polite and cool and ladywise. He recovered himself quickly. He was hearty. "Come in, Sylvia."

"You're quite sure I'm not interrupting you?" She hesitated on the doorstep, looking beyond him into the room as if she expected Laurel there. He knew then, whatever the explanation would be, why Sylvia had come. To get a good look at Laurel.

"Not a bit. I'm not doing a darn thing. Sitting around thinking about dinner and too lazy to start out. I suppose you've eaten?"

She came in, still slightly hesitant. She looked at the room the way a woman looked at a room, sizing it, and approving this one. She loosed her coat with her hands in the pockets, remained standing there on her high-heeled pumps, politely, but easily. Like a family friend. Like Brub's wife, who wouldn't want to be an intrusion into a man's privacy. "Oh, yes," she said. "We ate early. We were just starting to Beverly to see a movie when Brub got a call." A slight cloud fleeted over her eyes.

"Not another one?" he asked somberly.

"Oh no." She shook her head hard. As if she couldn't bear to consider that. "Lochner wanted to see him, that was all." She put a smile on her wide, pleasant mouth. "So Brub suggested I run in here and let you amuse me until he could get back. He said it wouldn't take long."

Fleetingly he wondered if it had been Brub's suggestion, or if it had been Sylvia's. She had withdrawn from him previously, she didn't now. She was forwarding herself, her smile at him wasn't reluctant as it had been. It was free. He would have been interested day before yesterday. Now he only feigned it. "I'm delighted, Sylvia. Let me have your coat." She allowed him to help her. She had on a brown sweater and a slim check-ered skirt in browns. She was made long and lovely, like a birch tree. Laurel was made lush and warm, like a woman.

She sat down on the couch. "You have a nice place."

"Yes, it is. I was lucky to get it. You'll at least have a drink, won't you?"

"I'll have a coke. If you have one?"

"I'll join you." He passed her a cigarette, lit it, and left her to get the cokes. He wondered what Lochner wanted with Brub, important enough to interrupt his evening. He'd find out, for Brub would come here from Lochner. He'd want to talk about it. It was a break. If only they'd be out of here be-fore Laurel returned.

He brought in the cokes. "Did Brub tell you he and Lochner let me go along today with them?"

"Yes. Thanks." She took the coke. "How did you like Loch?"

"He seemed bored with it all. Is that his cover-up for being the best bloodhound on the force?"

She said, "He has a wonderful record." Her mouth widened. "As a bloodhound, as you say. He's head of Homicide."

His eyes opened. "He's the head man?" He smiled. "I would never have guessed it."

"That's what Brub says. He seems so different. I've never met him."

"He's worth meeting." Dix relaxed comfortably in the arm chair. Head of Homicide. That worried old boy. "A character." He felt easy. "I still can't get used to Brub being a policeman."

"It's funny," Sylvia said seriously. "He always wanted to be one. I suppose lots of little boys did when you and Brub were little boys. Nowadays they want to be jet-propelled pilots, from what I can gather. But Brub never gave up wanting it. And when he asked me if I'd mind, I said I'd be delighted."

"So you're responsible for it," he said with mock solemnity.

"No," she laughed. "But he asked me and I said I'd be delighted and I meant it. Anything he wanted, I'd be delighted. It isn't much of a life. Like a doctor, twenty-four hours a day. And you never know when the phone will ring."

"Like tonight."

"Yes." There hadn't been that underlying fear in her until now. It was just a twinge; she'd recovered from the terror that had closed over her Saturday night and yesterday. She could put it away tonight. She could lose it in a bright change of subject. "We saw you last night."

"So Brub told me."

She was to the reason for her visit now. She was eager. "Who was she? The one you were telling us about?"

"Same one. She lives in this house."

"How did you meet her?" She was asking for romance.

He said, "I picked her up."

She made a little face at him.

"As I told Brub, it's the Virginibus Arms' good-neighbor policy," he said. "And high time there was one. It's bad as New York here. There you see your neighbors but don't speak; here you don't even see them."

"You saw her."

"And I picked her up," he said impudently.

"What's her name?"

"Laurel Gray."

"Is she in the movies? She's gorgeous enough to be, from what I saw of her."

"She's done some movies." Again he was struck by how little he knew of her. "She doesn't care much about it. Too early in the mornings for her." He said it with deliberate meaning; she understood.

She said after a moment, "Will you bring her out some evening? We'd like to meet her."

"We'll fix up a date." It was so easy to say, and so easy to avoid doing it. He was feeling better all the time. It had been right that Laurel was delayed. It was in order that she wouldn't have to be inspected by Sylvia. Sylvia wouldn't like Laurel; they weren't cut out of the same goods. Even as he was sure of the rightness, the telephone rang. He excused himself and went to answer, certain it wouldn't be she. It was time for Brub to check back in.

He was so certain it wouldn't be she that he left the bed-room door open. And it was Laurel.

She said, "What are you doing, Dix?"

"Where have you been?" Irritation gnatted him again; she'd stayed out until—after nine o'clock now by the clock. And she turned up asking lightly what he was doing!

"At dinner."

"I thought you were having dinner with me."

"Really? I must have forgotten."

Anger threatened him.

"Why don't you come up?" she asked.

He couldn't. Not now. He said, "I can't."

"Why not?"

"I have company." His anger lurched at Sylvia then for being here, at Brub for sending her here.

There was a sharpness came into her voice. "Who's the girl?"

"What girl?"

"The one on your couch, sweetheart."

She'd seen Sylvia. She must have come to the door and she'd seen Sylvia and gone away. That explained the insolence in her voice. She was annoyed about it. And again the anger went out of him in the upwelling of emotion; she didn't like his having another woman here.

He couldn't talk openly; the bedroom was too close to the living room. The door open. And Sylvia sitting there silently, listening. Trying not to listen because she was a lady but being unable to miss what he was saying.

"An old friend," he said.

"Business, I presume?" She was sharp.

"As a matter of fact, it is," he agreed.

"In that case, I'll come down."

"No!" He didn't want her to come here. Not until Sylvia and Brub had gone. She must understand. But he couldn't speak out. He spoke as quietly as possible into the mouthpiece. "I'll come up as soon as I'm free."

"What's the matter with my coming down?" she demanded. "Don't you think I'm good enough for your friends?"

He wondered if she'd been drinking. Belligerence wasn't like her, she was slow and sultry and she didn't give a damn for him or anyone. That was in her last night. And tonight, brushing him off for something better or more amusing. Now she was deliberately possessive. There was a reason and he didn't know the reason. He wanted to shake the hell out of her. She must have known he couldn't talk openly.

"Well?" she demanded.

He said, "I'm busy. I'll see you as soon as I can."

She hung up; the crack smote his eardrum. He was infuriated; he'd wanted to hang up on her but he hadn't. She'd done it. He went back into the living room scowling, forgetting that he shouldn't scowl, that he wasn't alone.

Sylvia was apologetic. "I am intruding."

"No." He said it flatly. Without explanation. "No." He meant it, he had no objection now to her presence. All anger was transferred to Laurel. The ear she had smote stung sharply. When he saw Sylvia studying his anger, he smiled at her. The smile was hard to come, it pained when it cracked the hard mold of his face. He said, "As a matter of fact, I'm delighted you dropped in, Sylvia. It gives me a feeling of belonging. I think it calls for a celebration—or perhaps a plaque: On this night at this spot Dickson Steele was no more the stranger from the East. After long months, he was at home." He was talking idly, to get that look, that seeking look out of Sylvia's eyes. He wasn't doing half bad.

Most of it was gone when she said, "You've been lonely."

"I expected it." She wasn't trying so hard now. Pity had expelled calculation. He didn't want the pity and he spoke lightly. "It takes time in a new place. I knew that before I came."

"You could have called on us sooner." It was all gone now, the look and the search.

"Now, would you?" he demanded. "You know how it is. There's always the knowledge that you're making a forced entry into the other fellow's life. Sometimes friendship survives it. More often it only spoils a good memory."

"It's worth trying," she said. "How else can—"

The doorbell rang. Brub, and it hadn't taken long. The business with Loch couldn't have been too important. He went to the door talking, breaking in on Sylvia's words. Wanting Brub to see how ordinary this had been. "Sometimes the dissent isn't mutual, Sylvia. The fellow who closes the door feels a hell of a lot worse than the eager beaver. I wouldn't want to be—"

Laurel stood there. Because she had been angry, because she had hung up on him in anger, he was so amazed that his words didn't dissipate; they became an utter void. He didn't realize he was scowling at her until she mirrored it ludicrously. "And what did the big bad wolf say then to Little Red Riding Hood, darling?" Deliberately she stepped past him and went into the room while he stood there scowling and empty-mouthed.

They were together, Sylvia and Laurel. Each had come for that reason, to look upon the other. He didn't know exactly why it mattered to either of them. He wasn't a sweepstake. Sylvia didn't care at all; Laurel cared little enough. They were eyeing each other in the faint patronizing manner of all women to women, no matter the stake, when he turned into the living room.

He'd had a slight apprehension over the phone that Laurel might have been drinking. She hadn't been. Her scent was perfumed, not alcoholic; she had never looked more glowing. She was in white, all white but for her radiant hair and painted mouth and eyes. Before her Sylvia was colorless and yet before Sylvia, Laurel was too richly colored. Between them was the gulf of a circumstance of birth and a pattern of living.

He said, "Sylvia, this is Laurel." And to Laurel, "This is Sylvia. My friend, Brub Nicolai's, wife."

They acknowledged the introduction in monotone, in the same manner of social courtesy, but it did not diminish the gulf. There was nothing could diminish the gulf.

He said, "Let me take your coat, Laurel. Drink?"

"No, thanks. I've just had dinner." Her eyes were strange amber flowers. She opened them full on him. "I've been trying to call you for hours. Where have you been?"

She was a dirty little liar. She was trying to tell Sylvia it hadn't been she on the phone getting the brush-off. He looked at Sylvia and his mouth quirked. She wasn't fooling Sylvia. You didn't fool Sylvia. She burrowed under words, under the way of a face and a smile for the actuality. He was suddenly cold. For he knew, was certain of the fact, that Sylvia had been burrowing beneath his surface since the night he had come out of the fog into her existence. Irritation heated him. She had no business trying to find an under self in him; she should have taken him as he was taken, an average young fellow, pleasant company; beyond that, her husband's old friend. It couldn't have been Brub who set her on him. There could have been no suspicion when he came to Brub's house that night. Nor was there; yet Sylvia had searched his face and the way he spoke—and she hadn't liked him.

He knew it with cold clarity, he'd sensed it from the first moment of meeting, she didn't like him. He didn't like her either with her damn prying mind. Her bitching, high-toned mind. Brub was all right; she wasn't going to spoil Brub with Dix. She wasn't going to be allowed.

He said to Laurel, "I've been right here since five o'clock." He lit her cigarette. "Maybe you had the wrong number."

"Maybe I did." She took her eyes from him and laid them again on Sylvia. She didn't think any more of Sylvia than Sylvia of her. She was more open about it, that was the way of her, the way that couldn't be helped. Yet she had a fear of Sylvia that had no echo in Brub's wife. She was harder than Sylvia could ever be but she wasn't fine steel; she could be broken. She said to Sylvia and the smear of insolence was under the surface, "Where's your husband?" She let it rest until Sylvia was ready to answer and then she didn't wait for the answer. "I've wanted to meet him. I've heard so much about him."

A dirty little liar. He'd not told her much or little of Brub. Brub's name hadn't been spoken between them.

Sylvia said, "He'll be along. He had some business and I decided Dix would be more amusing than business." She gave him a woman smile. Not for him, for Laurel because she scorned Laurel.

"And Dix wasn't," Dix said, waiting for her disavowal.

She was provocative as Laurel would have been. "I don't know," she said.

"Is your husband on the Mildred Atkinson thing?" Laurel asked abruptly.

He hadn't thought she knew who Brub Nicolai was but she had known. And she'd brought up from the shadows that which Sylvia and Dix had been pretending didn't exist there.

She didn't care; all she was attempting was destruction of their mood. Succeeding better than she could know.

"Yes, he's working on it." Sylvia didn't like the mention of the case. That quickly the tightness was in her fingers, the set of her lips. She didn't dissemble well.

"Gorgon told me he was," Laurel nodded. She didn't explain Gorgon nor did Sylvia. But Sylvia knew the name; she admitted knowledge by accepting Gorgon as casually as he was offered. Laurel went on, "He was talking about it tonight. He says Brub Nicolai's the smartest young dick in the department."

He felt Sylvia's cringe at Laurel's use of the word dick for detective. He didn't see it; he saw nothing. His mind was knotted too tightly, so tightly the room was a blur. He steadied himself against the table.

It was good that Sylvia was there; that he was not alone with Laurel. She had been out with someone named Gorgon while Dix waited here for her. The desperate need to be alone with Laurel, to force truth from her, began hammering against his temples until he wanted to cry out from the pain of it. He had to stand there, holding himself by the pressure of his palms on the table, while the two made conversation about Brub, Brub who should be here and take his wife away.

He had to stand braced there listening to Laurel quote Gorgon to Sylvia, all of Gorgon's damn omniscience about Brub Nicolai's growing prowess as a detective.

He couldn't have endured much longer. The door buzzer reprieved him. He left the two women without excusing himself. They didn't know he was there. It was Brub at last; the Brub of these days, a frown between his eyebrows, a distant look on his face until he saw Dix and smiled.

"Hello. Sylvia still here?"

"Yeah. We've been gabbing. Come on in." He let Brub precede him into the living room. He didn't want to hear any more about Gorgon. He didn't have to. By the time he rounded into the room, Sylvia was making introductions.

"Brub, this is Laurel Gray. My husband, Mr. Nicolai."

Laurel's eyes took stock of Brub in the same way they had taken stock of Dix on first meeting. Thoroughly, boldly, despite Sylvia's presence. It might be Laurel knew no better, it might be unconscious. The only way she knew to look at a man. Sylvia watched, but she wasn't disturbed. Not about Laurel. Only when Brub had acknowledged the introduction and turned to his wife did the waver of fear come to her.

Her voice was controlled but the fear cooled it. "Everything . . . all right, darling?"

He nodded, his smile reassured her. But it wasn't real, it came and it went. As brief as a flicker of light in the darkness.

Dix said heartily, "How about a drink, Brub?"

"Thanks." The response was automatic, without thought for with thought Brub shook his head. "But not tonight." As if that had been what he meant to say in the first place. "I'm too tired. Ready, Sylvia?"

"Yes." She spoke brightly as if unaware of Brub's depression.

Dix didn't attempt to delay them. He knew Brub had information on the case to impart; he knew Brub would talk if he remained for a drink. The case wasn't important to Dix at the moment; he wanted one thing only, to be alone with Laurel.

He only said, "Sorry," putting real feeling into it, as real as if it were honest. "You better take it easy a few days, you do look tired. Can't you fence him in, Sylvia?"

"I wish I could." But she too was acting, her thoughts were on Brub only.

She and Laurel said the false and polite things required. Brub nodded; he was in a hurry to be gone. His arm held Sylvia's closely.

"I'll give you a ring," Dix promised. He held the door ajar until they had crossed the patio, until they walked under the arch to the street. He closed it then, definitely. One stride carried him to the entrance to the living room.

Laurel coiled in the chair, her eyes smoldering, her mouth insolent, ready to strike.

He struck first. "Who is Gorgon?"

She didn't answer him. "What's the idea of that woman here?" she demanded.

He repeated, "Who is Gorgon?"

"Giving me the runaround, telling me not to come down here. Business!" Her voice spat.

He only repeated, "Who is Gorgon?" He began to move towards her then. There was no sound of him crossing the room.

There was no sound but her voice berating, "You can't play me that way. There isn't any man I'll take that from. God knows, I won't take it from you."

He was standing over her. "Who is Gorgon?" The knots in his head were tightening. He couldn't stand the tightness. His hands reached down, clamped on her shoulders and he pulled her out of the chair. "Who—"

She spoke with cold nastiness. "If you don't take your hands off me, you won't be any good to any woman any more." Through her shoulders, he felt the shift of her weight and he released her, stepped away quickly. She had meant the words. The knots loosened as quickly, the shock of her intent was as ice flung in his face. With the diminishing of pain, he was weakened, his forehead was wet. He drew his sleeve across it, across the dampness of his eyes.

He heard her say, "I'm getting to hell out of here."

He couldn't have stopped her, weakened as he was. His voice was husky. "Don't go."

He didn't even look at her. He didn't know why she didn't leave; curiosity, perhaps. It couldn't have been pity, she wasn't a woman to have pity on a man.

He was surprised at the sound of her voice; it wasn't hating now, it shrugged. "I think we both need a drink."

He heard her go to the kitchen and he flung himself face down on the couch, his fingers gripped tight into his palms. He had wanted to kill her.

When he heard the sound of her returning, he turned. She was standing over him and she held out the glass. "Thanks, Laurel."

She went back to the chair, sat down, and drank.

He took a swallow from his glass, another. She'd mixed it strong.

"Feel better?" she asked.

"Yes. I needed this."

"Shall we start all over?"

His eyes went quickly to her. She meant it. He was ashamed of his anger; it hadn't been he; some stranger had performed that way. But the stranger was himself.

"Let's do."

"You want to know who Gorgon is. He's my lawyer."

He was more ashamed. He didn't say anything.

"I ran into him when I was leaving the studio. He wanted to talk over some business. It was nearly six." Her eyes hardened. "I figured it wouldn't hurt him to buy me a meal." She looked away. "I couldn't call you, Dix. I didn't want him—snooping."

It was all explained. Warmth filled him, good and tender warmth. She'd wanted to be with him, to run back to him. Wanted it as much as he. He hadn't been wrong; they were meant to co-exist. He was ready to rush to her when she hardened again. "What about her?"

He laughed. "It's as dull as yours. Brub dropped her off while he went on business. I didn't want her here."

Her words barbed. "Then why did you try to keep me away? Didn't you think I was good enough to meet her?"

"Good God, Laurel!" He was exasperated, the more so because she wasn't up to Sylvia's par. Yet she soared above Sylvia.

"Didn't you?" she demanded.

He wasn't going to get angry again. He wouldn't let her make him angry. "Listen," he said, "I didn't want you let in on something that would bore the tar out of you. That's point one. Two, I was sore at you for not showing up."

"You expected me?"

"You know damn well I expected you. We were going to have dinner together—"

"Three?"

She was pleased, there was an upcurve of her rich mouth, the mockery was again in her golden eyes.

"Three, I wanted you alone, for myself, all alone, not cluttered up with a lot of dumb people." His voice wasn't steady, nor was he as he pushed up to his feet. Yet he could move and he went to her, pulling her again out of the chair. His hands were strong this time, not cruel.

She said, "Wait a minute, Dix." Her palms pushed against his shoulders, her body twisted but he didn't let her go. His mouth closed over hers and he held her until she quieted. He held her for a long time.

When he released her, there was laughter in him where there had been pain. Exultant laughter. He said, "That's the way it is, Laurel. That's the way it has to be. You—and me."

She was as beautiful as if set aflame. Her eyes slanted up at

him, even her eyes were aflame. She pushed back her hair. "I
guess you're right," she said. She rubbed at her arm. "But
don't try the rough stuff again. I won't take it."

"I'm sorry." He was, and for a moment he tightened. He
was more than sorry, he was afraid. He might have hurt her.
He might have lost her. With her he must remember, he must
never take a chance of losing her. If it had happened—he
shook his head and a tremble went over him.

She said anxiously, "What's the matter?"

He didn't answer, he took her into his arms and held her.
Held her without explanation until he was quieted again.

2

It was morning and the sun lay bright blue against the open
window. And the sun lay mildly gold where her hair had flamed
on the white pillow, where again her head would rest. The
room was swirling with sun and he rested there content in
brightness. It was good to wake to sun, to warmth, and remembrance of warmth and bright beauty. It was good to know
she would return after her little errands and business appointments and lessons were done, would return eagerly to his eagerness. For him there were the hours of day to pass, but they
would trickle through his hands as quietly, as simply as sand.
The sun and the day would pass; there would come night. And
the night would flame with a radiance surpassing the sun.

The day passed and there was the night and another day and
another night and another. Until he did not know the count of
the hours or of the days. Or of the nights. They were one unto
the other, a circle whirling evenly, effortlessly, endlessly. He
knew beauty and the intensity of a dream and he was meshed
in a womb he called happiness. He did not think: This must
come to an end in time. A circle had no beginning or end; it
existed. He did not allow thought to enter the hours that he
waited for her, laved in memory of her presence. He seldom
left the apartment in those days. In the outside world there
was time; in time, there was impatience. Better to remain
within the dream. Even the broom-and-mop harridan could
little disturb the dream.

He did not say: This will not endure forever. He did not face the awakening. There was the morning when the fleet of clouds passed over the sun but he did not accept the augury. He did not admit to mind the chill that came through the windows of an afternoon even as he closed the windows. He did not admit the scrim of gray shutting away the stars on that night.

He knew but he did not admit. It might have been a week, it might have been a day or two, or perhaps there was no time. But the restlessness was coming into her. She could not be content too long to be bound within the confines of this dream. It might have been the way her shoulders moved to a dance orchestra over the radio. It might have been the small frown as they sat again for dinner in the living room. It could have been her evasion to his questions about her hours of that particular day. Or the way in which she stood at the doorway, looking out into the night.

He had known from the beginning she was meant to be displayed. She could not be hidden away long in the cave of his dream. Yet he could not admit. She had to be the one to speak.

She telephoned him. Late, five o'clock or later. She said, "Dix, I can't meet you for dinner tonight . . . It's business."

He knew a little more about her now, not much, a little. She didn't talk of herself, no more than did he. There had been slight need of words within the cave. But he knew she was studying and waiting for the big chance. Her sights were high; others had been discovered by the magical screen. She intended to be. Talent wasn't of the same import as knowing the right guardians of the portal. The philosopher's stone was contacts.

He couldn't let her know his disappointment. They hadn't played it that way. They hadn't been soft lovers; they'd been aware of worldly needs. He wouldn't have dared let her know his adolescent urgency. He said, "Sorry," as if it didn't matter. "See you later?"

He could sense her hesitation.

"If I'm not too late. There's a party after." There was definite hesitation now, if slight. "I'm to sing."

He knew better but he demanded, "No matter how late, come. Wake me up."

She didn't say yes or no; she said nothing in a rush of words.

After she had rung off, it began. Slowly at first. Like fog wisping into his mind. Only a small doubt. He could, at first, brush it away. But it moved in thicker; tightening around the coils of his brain, blotting out reason.

She was with another man. Someone with money to spend on her, big money. Uncle Fergus! Dix almost ran to the desk. He hadn't looked at mail during these days, once or twice maybe he'd riffled for a Princeton postmark, not finding it, finding nothing but bills for Mel Terriss. Then he had forgotten mail, forgotten the dunning bills, forgotten everything in her. He pawed through the neat stack of envelopes and he found it, the letter from Uncle Fergus. There was a check inside, he glanced at the figures, two hundred and fifty dollars. He pushed open the brief typewritten letter. It said:

Dear Dickson,
    If you have a bad back and are not just inventing same to get out of work, I suggest you apply to the Veterans' Hospital for treatment. As for my sending you additional funds, the idea is as stupid as yours usually . . .

He crumpled the letter into a tight angry ball and hurled it across the room. He didn't even finish reading it, he knew too well the pious platitudes about work and pay, he'd heard them all his life. When other fellows had cars and clothes and free spending, he had platitudes. It wasn't that the old skinflint didn't have it. There was plenty of money for stocks and bonds, real estate. Everything salted away for an old man's idea about being a solid citizen. You'd think Uncle Fergus would have recognized the need for the things that made living worth living. He'd been a poor clod, son of a dirt farmer. He'd never had anything either, starting to work in a Princeton hardware store when he was fourteen (how well Dickson knew every step of Uncle Fergus' meager life; he could recite it like a nursery rhyme), studying nights to get himself into the university. Dickson could see him, one of those poor boobs, peasants, owning one dark, ill-fitting suit and a pair of heavy-soled shoes, clumping to class, study, and work, and nobody knew he was in Princeton but the other peasants. Not even coming out of it cum laude, the needed touch for a big success story. Nothing, just grubbing through, worrying along to graduation; getting nothing but a diploma and a fixed belief that to be a Princeton man was like being a senator or maybe Jehovah.

Dix hadn't wanted to be a Princeton man. Not that kind. If it could have been right, if he could have been one of the fellows he saw around town, driving a fast car, careless about expensive clothes and money and girls, club fellows, he'd have grabbed it. He might as well have wanted to be senator or the Jehovah, he was Fergus Steele's nephew, and he worked in the hardware store after hours all through high school. Either he worked or he had nothing to spend. That was Uncle Fergus' hand-embroidered, gold-framed motto: No work, no money.

A fellow had to have money, you couldn't get a girl without money in your pockets. A girl didn't notice your looks or your sharp personality, not unless you could take her to the movies or the Saturday night dance. And feed her after the show.

Dix hadn't learned then how to get money without working for it. Except maybe filching a dime or a quarter from the cash register now and again. Lying about it. Once he took five dollars; he needed it, too. You couldn't take a girl to the Junior Prom without sending her flowers. Uncle Fergus fired a delivery boy for that one.

Dix knew damn well he'd go through hell at the university. He did. He suffered, God how he suffered, that first year. He'd have quit, he'd have flunked out quick but the alternative was far worse; being packed off like a piece of cattle to a farm Uncle Fergus owned in western Pennsylvania. Either he had to be a gentleman, according to Uncle Fergus' standards, or he could revert to the peasantry. Dix was smart enough to know he couldn't get a job, stand on his own feet. He didn't want to work that hard. He took the first year, working in the hardware store after school, afraid to look anyone in the eye, afraid he'd see the sneers openly, or the pity.

It was along in the spring that he started getting wise. Latching on to boys with money, rich stinkers who hadn't any better place in the university scheme than Dix himself. They really were stinkers; Mel Terriss was a good example of the breed. But they had money. They were good for a tip if you knew a place to get a bottle of booze after hours, or took their cars to be serviced, or picked up their cleaning. They were good for a cash loan in return for a hard-luck story. You could wear their clothes, smoke their cigarettes, drink their liquor. As long as you toadied, you had a pretty good life. It notched them up higher if they could sneer at a boob of a townsman who had less than they. He took the sneers with the tips and the second year wasn't so bad.

The second year he found Mel Terriss who hadn't even made the stinkers' set. He got Mel into the circle and he saw that Mel repaid him. It was easy sailing for Dix after that, with Mel's clothes and Mel's car and the babes thinking Dix was the rich guy and Mel the stooge. Dix had the looks and the air; he had everything Mel needed. Mel was kept soothed by Dix bringing him the women that Dix couldn't be bothered with. And by booze. Mel was headed straight for alcoholism even then, a kid in college. The booze made him believe he was what he alone thought he was, not a stinker. Only it made him a worse stinker, of course. End of the term, Dix was Mel's only friend. That suited Dix. It looked like two good years ahead if he could keep Mel in college; so far he'd showed Mel how to manage it with Mel's money, paying grubs to tutor Mel through. He and Mel hated each other's guts but each without the other was lost. They stuck together.

That was the summer when the young men knew war was fact. The only question was when it would be acknowledged. And that summer Dix enlisted in the Air Corps. All the top men of the campus were enlisting.

The war years were the first happy years he'd ever known. You didn't have to kowtow to the stinking rich, you were all equal in pay; and before long you were the rich guy. Because you didn't give a damn and you were the best God-damned pilot in the company with promotions coming fast. You wore swell tailored uniforms, high polish on your shoes. You didn't need a car, you had something better, sleek powerful planes. You were the Mister, you were what you'd always wanted to be, class. You could have any woman you wanted in Africa or India or England or Australia or the United States, or any place in the world. The world was yours.

That life was so real that there wasn't any other life. Even when the war was over there was no realization of another life.

Not until he stood again in the small, dark living room of his uncle's home. It came as shock, the return to Uncle Fergus; he hadn't really known it wasn't going to be always the way it had been in the war years. He had mistaken interlude for life span.

Uncle Fergus had done well for himself too during the war years. He'd invented some kind of nail or screw or tool and manufactured it. But getting richer hadn't made a change in the old man. He lived the way he always had lived, in the same uncomfortable house, with the same slovenly old housekeeper, the same badly cooked meals, and bad lighting. The only difference was more stocks and bonds and real estate. It was in a bathos of patriotism that Uncle Fergus consented to Dix's year in California to write a book. Oh, Dix had had to do some fast talk. The old skinflint thought he was living with friends who could help him, who would keep him in line. He explained the frequent change of address as difficulties in getting office space. Once the offer was made, Uncle Fergus regretted his generosity; that was obvious. But it was too late, Dix didn't let him withdraw.

In excess of anger Dix took the measly check now and tore it into little pieces, tore it and retore it and scattered it all over Mel's rug. The usual check, the pittance on which to exist another month. Go to a Veterans' Hospital. Beg, you're a veteran, aren't you?

He sat there at the desk, holding his hot head with his steeled fingers. Seeing through his fingers the stack of bills addressed to Mel Terriss. It was rotten luck running into Mel that night. Why couldn't he have met Mel during the war years, when he could have sneered down at him the way he'd wanted to all his life? But Mel had been hiding out in some factory; even the Army hadn't wanted Mel. When they met, the war was long over and Mel was a rich stinker again.

Dix had tried not to speak to Mel in the bar that night, he'd avoided the recognition, forgetting you couldn't avoid an ass like Mel. Mel had to weave over and poke his fat, stupid face across the table. Dix could see what was churning in Mel's mind as he looked at the blonde. Ready to start over the same old way, let Dix do the dirty work, procure the girls in exchange for tips. Well, it hadn't worked that way; he'd stopped boot-licking six years ago. And maybe it wasn't so bad running into Mel. Dix had the apartment and the car and the clothes; the charge accounts wouldn't hold out forever but they were still good enough. That was the sort of money Mel had. And Mel was in Rio, good old Mel!

Without Mel, there would have been no Laurel. His brain cooling, the hunger for Laurel began gnawing again. Maybe she had had a chance to sing at some big event; she wouldn't turn it down, he knew that, even if she hungered for him as he for her. She was like him that way, she was after big time. The only difference was she wasn't looking for money; she wanted a spotlight.

Hatred of Uncle Fergus surged anew. Unless Dix could help Laurel get that spotlight, he'd be sloughed. As soon as the new wore off him. As soon as she found out he was broke. He couldn't lose her, she was the only thing he had, the only right thing he'd had since he took off his uniform. In shame he got down on his hands and knees and began gathering up the tiny pieces of the check. He had to have this much money; it wouldn't last long but it would prolong things for another week, maybe by that time he could raise more. There must be ways to get gravy out here; there were sure to be, only he hadn't been looking for them. He hadn't needed to, the two-fifty did well enough before he met Laurel. Delicately he picked up each small piece, being careful not to crumple them. And then came the fear that Laurel would return suddenly, find him in this ridiculous position. He began to work faster, nervously. When he had retrieved all the scraps, his hands were wet and shaking. He had to wipe the palms on his shirt before he dared piece the check together. He was careful despite his shaking fingers, putting each small piece in its proper place. Until they were put together and one piece missing. It had to be a piece of value, the "Fergu" of the signature. Frantically he searched for it, crawling on the floor like a baby, trembling with the fear that she or someone would come before it was found.

He spied it finally, under the desk chair. He had the check again! He didn't know if a bank would accept it, whether it would be necessary to write again to Uncle Fergus with some excuse about its destruction. The maid mixing it with advertising folders, tearing it up. Uncle Fergus wouldn't believe his story. He'd stop payment on the first check and then he'd wait to make sure it hadn't been cashed before he sent a second. It would be a month at least before Uncle Fergus would return a check to Dix, a month with not more than a ten spot left in his pocket.

Worrying about what could happen, a sickness came over him, so real that he felt weak as a cat. He could scarcely make it to the couch. He flopped there, his eyes closed, his fingers tight in his palms. He couldn't lose Laurel. He wouldn't lose her. No matter what he did. He could go to work. There must be plenty of jobs. Laurel knew a lot of rich people; maybe he could give her a story about needing to get into something. Not for money. For research. Or Brub. Brub might get him on the police force.

He could smile at that; and he then felt better. Only what would Laurel be doing while Dix was on call twenty-four hours a day? She wouldn't be sitting at home; she wasn't a Sylvia.

He couldn't go to work; there were other ways of getting money. If Laurel would only introduce him to some of her friends; the easiest way to get money was through those who had money. He knew how to do it that way. Why was Laurel keeping him hidden? Anger was rising; he mustn't get angry now. He couldn't take another spasm. He went to the bar and he poured a heavy slug of the stuff; he didn't want it but it settled his stomach.

If he knew where Laurel was, he'd go to her now. If she cared anything about him she'd have wanted him there tonight to hear her sing. He didn't believe she was singing. She had another man; whenever she got a chance to be with that man, she didn't care whom she knocked down.

He couldn't remain here all evening thinking these thoughts, suffering these agonies. He'd go nuts. He had to get out, go where he could breathe. Go hide himself in the night.

He caught his breath. He didn't dare. It was too soon. The police were still on the alert. And there was Laurel. He didn't dare do anything that might spoil what he had with Laurel. But he couldn't stay here. He had to get away from thinking his thoughts.

He went to the bedroom, seized the telephone. He didn't know how many times Brub had called during these days, these weeks. Dix had abruptly turned down all advances. But he'd left the door open. When the surge of work was over, he'd call Brub. He didn't notice the time until after he'd dialed; he was relieved to see that it wasn't late at all, not quite nine o'clock.

It was Sylvia who answered. She sounded not only surprised to hear from him but almost as if she'd never before heard his voice. He asked for Brub. "Is he home? Thought I might run out for a little if he isn't busy."

By that time she seemed to know him again. She was cordial. "Do come out. We've been wondering when you'd get your nose out of that book."

"Sure you don't mind?"

"We welcome you," she said quickly. "And I do mean it. Brub was so bored just sitting around with me, he's gone next door to borrow a rake or a deck of cards or something."

"He isn't at home?"

"He will be before you get here," she said with certainty. "Come along."

He felt better right away, he felt himself again. Sure of himself, happy, easy. He'd stayed in too closely with Laurel; that wasn't good for a man. Maybe she'd felt it too. Maybe that was why she'd taken this job tonight. But she couldn't have felt too shut in, she'd been out every day on lessons or beauty appointments or some excuse.

He didn't bother to change his clothes. He grabbed the nearest jacket, putting it on as he returned to the living room. He had to delay there. The torn check was on the desk. He wouldn't want Laurel to see it. He scooped the pieces into an envelope, sealed it to make certain he wouldn't lose any precious bit, and stuck it in his jacket pocket. He looked down at the stack of bills addressed to Mel, wondering if Laurel had noticed them, and if she had, why she hadn't said anything. Someone had stacked them in that neat pile, not he. It could have been the slattern, but it could have been Laurel. It probably had been Laurel; he could see her hands now arranging the paper and the magazines on the table. Idly, deliberately. She could have done the same to the mail while he was dressing or putting on the coffee. Idly, but she would have noticed.

Noticed and wondered. He swept the mail into the drawer, banging it shut. He wasn't going to think in circles; he was going to Brub's and forget.

3

He left the apartment by the back door. It gave him a good feeling as soon as he stepped into the night; he was doing something familiar. The night too was good; there were no stars, only hazy darkness. He went softly through the alley to the garage. The sound of the door opening couldn't carry back to the apartments. The hinges were well oiled.

The car looked good. He hadn't had it out for days, and it felt good to be at the wheel. He didn't have to back out quietly, he let it purr; he was going to visit his friend, his friend the policeman.

By the time he reached the Nicolais' there was no anger, no tension left in him. He whistled his way up the walk. Brub opened the door and things were good again, the way they'd been that first night. Brub in sneakers and a pair of pants as wrinkled as his own. Holding out his hand saying, "You're a sight for sore eyes. What's the idea of the brush-off, Genius?"

It was all good until they came into the living room together, as they had on that first night. And as on the first night, Sylvia was there. Filling the room, for all her quietness. Fading out the bright colors for all the monotone of her silver-gray slack suit, her pale gold hair, her pale, serious face. There was no welcome in her eyes for him, she was looking at him as at a stranger. In an instant she smiled, but the smile was a pale thing and in her eyes there was no smile. He felt himself an intruder and he was angry; if she hadn't wanted him to come here tonight she could have said so, she could have said Brub was out and let it go at that. But she'd urged him to come; she'd even called Brub home for his coming.

When she spoke, it was better. "Finished that book?" she asked as if they'd been together daily. "I'm dying to read it." Yet in the midst of her words, she chilled again. And recovered, giving him a wider smile. "How about a beer?"

"Let me," Dix said, but she was already up from the chair,

crying, "I'm the official beer-getter around here. You sit down." She wasn't smooth and polished in her motions tonight; there was a nervousness as she went to the bar. Maybe she and Brub had had a scrap; maybe that was why he'd gone to the neighbors, and why she'd urged Dix to come, to get them past the awkward stage. At any rate there was no difference in Brub, good old Brub, reclining himself on the couch and saying, "I was afraid you'd skipped back East, Dix."

"Just work," he answered. He sounded like anyone who worked, regretful of the time it took, almost apologetic.

"Finished?"

"God, no!" He laughed easily. "But the heat was off so I decided a break was in order." Sylvia set the glass and bottle at hand on the end table. Dix took the opposite side of the couch, pushing Brub's sneakers aside. He smiled up at Sylvia. "That's why I barged in on you. Hope I'm not in the way."

"Not at all! I told you we were bored, didn't I?" She looked down at Brub. "Beer, darling?"

"Might as well."

But there wasn't the smilingness between them as on that first night, not the ease and two-is-one perfection. Something was wrong. Dix didn't care about their troubles. He'd needed a quiet evening like this, with beer and Brub gabbing about his boat. Brub was a kid about boats. Dix didn't want to talk; he wanted only to be lulled by this kind of aimless conversation.

There was no mention of the case; there was no case until Dix mentioned it. Until he said, "How's the case coming?"

Under his eyes he watched Sylvia, waited her reaction. He was disappointed. There wasn't a reaction tonight. She was too quiet, too colorless to be more quiet or of less color. There was no change in her at all.

"Nothing new," Brub answered. "It's stymied. Same as the others. No clues, no fresh evidence, no hints."

Brub wasn't lying to him. Brub was disgusted but he wasn't discouraged as he had been before. The life had gone out of the case. It wasn't closed because the police didn't close the books, but it was as good as closed. Brub even switched the subject. "Remember Ad Tyne, Dix?"

He didn't.

Brub insisted, "Sure you do. Adam Tyne. The flight commander from Bath. Nice quiet fellow. We saw a lot of him that spring of forty-three. The blonde one."

He searched for memory but he didn't find Adam Tyne. There'd been a lot of good fellows, Adam Tyne could have been any of them. Not that it was important. Brub was continuing, "Had a letter from him the first of the week. I wrote him when I got back but hadn't heard a thing. He's married, settled down. Wish I had the letter here, darn it, but I left it at the office." Brub's voice changed, became grave. The transition was so sudden that there was no time to attune to the change before the words were spoken. "He had a sad piece of news. Brucie is dead."

Brucie is dead. The words quivered in the vacuum of quietness. *Brucie is dead.* They resounded thunderously in the silence. *Brucie is dead.*

When he could, he began to echo them as he should, with proper shock, with the right incredulity. "Brucie is—" He couldn't finish above a whisper. His voice broke, "—dead." The tears were rolling down his cheeks; he covered his face, tried to withhold the sobs that were clawing him. *Brucie is dead.* The words had never been spoken before. He had not known what would happen when they were spoken.

He heard from a far-off place Sylvia's little, hurt cry, "Dix!" He heard Brub's embarrassed apology, "Dix, I didn't know—"

He couldn't answer them. He couldn't stop crying. It was a long time before he could stop; it seemed eternity within the confines of the shocked silence. He lifted his head when he could and said huskily, "I'm sorry." It released Sylvia and Brub. They didn't know the agony raking his heart.

"I didn't know," Brub said again. He blew his nose loudly. "I didn't know you—and Brucie—"

He said simply, "She meant everything in the world to me." *Brucie*, his soul wept; *Brucie*. He took out his handkerchief and blew his nose. Sylvia's eyes were large as moons, pale moons, sad. "We didn't know," she whispered.

"No," he shook his head. "I guess no one knew. It was all over." He put the handkerchief away. He could talk all right now; they didn't know anything he was thinking. "How did she die? Buzz bombs?"

Brub said, "She was murdered."

He could show shock because he was shocked. He had never expected to hear it said. It was so long ago. He echoed, "Murdered."

Brub nodded. His face looked as if it hurt.

Dix had to ask. Painfully as it should be asked by a man who'd loved her. "How did it—what happened—who did it?"

Brub said, "The police have never found out." He blew his nose again. "Better not talk about it, Dix."

His jaw was firm. "I want to know." His eyes promised that he could take it.

"She was down for a weekend at a small beach place. Her husband was coming to join her. At least that's what she told the landlady." Brub told it with starts and stops; he didn't want to tell it. Dix was forcing him to tell it. "Her husband didn't come. Or if he did, no one saw him. She went out Saturday evening alone; she didn't come back. She wasn't found for several weeks. In a rocky cove—she'd been strangled."

Dix couldn't speak. He could only look at Brub out of unseeing eyes.

"It was some time before she was identified. She hadn't signed the register under her own name." Brub said almost apologetically, "I wouldn't have dreamed she was that kind of a girl. She was always gay—but she was so—so nice—you know, like a girl from home."

"She wasn't that kind," Dix choked. "She wasn't."

Sylvia wanted to say something but she didn't. She just sat there like a ghost with her sad, luminous eyes on Dix. He knew he had to get out, before he broke down again. He didn't know how to leave.

"They never found any trace of the husband. It must have happened just after our outfit left England. That's why we didn't know, why we never heard about it." And he said what was true. "There'd been so much killing, one more wasn't news."

Brucie had died but no one cared, only he. All of them had lost so many, dear as brothers, as their own selves, they had learned not to talk about death. They had refused to think about death being death. Even in the heart's inmost core where each dwelled alone, they did not admit death.

Dix said unsteadily, "I'd better go." He tried to smile at them. "Sorry."

They tried to stop him. They wanted him to stay and forget in their sympathy and their understanding, in their love for him at this moment. He couldn't stay. He had to get out, to be alone in his lonely place. To remember and to forget. He brushed aside their urging the way you brushed away smoke; knowing it would recur but you could again brush it away. He went into the night while they stood close to each other in the doorway. Together. Never alone.

He drove away not knowing where he was going or why. Only to get away. He did not know how far he drove or how long. There was no thinking in his mind; there was only sound, the swish of the dark wet water over the cold sand, colder than Brucie; the water was the voice of a girl, a voice hushed by fear, repeating over and over, *no . . . no . . . no . . .* Fear wasn't a jagged split of light cleaving you; fear wasn't a cold fist in your entrails; fear wasn't something you could face and demolish with your arrogance. Fear was the fog, creeping about you, winding its tendrils about you, seeping into your pores and flesh and bone. Fear was a girl whispering a word over and again, a small word you refused to hear although the whisper was a scream in your ears, a dreadful scream you could never forget. You heard it over and again and the fog was a ripe red veil you could not tear away from your eyes. Brucie was dead. Brucie whom he had loved, who was his only love.

She had loved him! If there hadn't been a marriage, one of those secret war marriages. Only she couldn't see it was unimportant; she loved Dix but she loved that unknown husband too. She didn't know the unknown one would die so soon. Somewhere over Germany. So many died. She was all mixed up; she wasn't bad. She was good! He didn't know until she died how good she was. She hadn't done anything wrong; it wasn't wrong to love. When you were filled with love, overflowing with love, you had to give love. If it weren't for that boy who was to die over Germany. If Dix had only known. The swish of the waves whispering *if . . . if . . . if . . .* And Brucie dead. Little Brucie.

How long, how far he drove, he didn't know. With his fingers clenching the wheel and the waves crashing in his ears. He didn't once stop the car. He drove until emotional exhaustion left him empty as a gourd. Until no tears, no rage, no pity had meaning for him. At some point he turned the car to home. He had no memory of the act until he reached his garage, rolled the car into it. He was so tired he walked like one drugged, dragging his leaden body through the dark alley to the dark apartment. He went in through the kitchen, pushing one heavy foot after the other. It wasn't until he entered the bedroom and saw her that he remembered the existence of Laurel. Until he remembered with agonized relief that he was no longer alone.

She must have heard him coming for she'd turned on the bedside lamp and she was standing by the bed holding the yellow chiffon of her negligee tightly about her. Even in his exhaustion he realized the fear on her face. It was gone before the realization.

"I didn't know it was you," she said, then her voice sharpened. "Where have you been all night?"

He was too weary to answer questions, to ask them. He stumbled to her, she couldn't back away more than a step, the table halted her. He put his arms around her and he held her, holding her warmth and the life that flowed beneath her flesh. He held her and he said, "Help me. I'm tired—so tired."

4

It was afternoon before he awoke. There was no sun on the windows, outside was grayness, the sky was watered gray silk.

He wasn't rested, he was heavy, tired, although his sleep had been dreamless. He took a cigarette from his pack on the bed table, lighted it. He wondered where Laurel was. Without her last night, or this morning, he wouldn't have dared sleep, fearing the dream. She had known; she hadn't asked questions after that first one. She had given comfort, helping him undress, laying back the covers, laying herself and her warmth beside him, within his arms.

He ought to get up, not lie here in the comfort of bed. Shower, shave, dress before she returned. She'd come back as soon as she'd finished her business. She wouldn't call, she'd come, she knew he needed her. She had cared for him last night. Laying back the covers . . .

She hadn't been to bed! She'd just come in; she too had been out all night.

He didn't lose his temper. He lay there calmly, considering it. Weighing it the way a judge would, quite calm and objective, almost coldly. She hadn't been in long enough to lay back the covers. That was all there was to it. It was no reason for anger. She would explain where she had been and the why of it; she might lie about it but she would explain. He would know if she were lying. He would have no difficulty in nailing the lie.

She'd been afraid of him when he came in last night. Because she had a guilty conscience? Not necessarily. He was still being calm about it. She had feared because she hadn't known it was he, his dragging steps were those of a stranger. It was fear of the unknown; not fear of him.

Her conscience hadn't been guilty. Because she'd demanded explanation of him, where had he been. She had a legitimate reason for her lateness, she'd come directly to him to explain. And he hadn't been there. Yet she'd forgiven him. She'd asked no further questions; she had taken him to comfort.

It was well after four when he stopped thinking, arose and dressed. He hurried then, the shower and shave. He dressed in the suit he liked best; he didn't wear it often. It was distinctive, a British wool, gray with a faint overplaid of lighter gray, a touch of dim red. It fit him as well as had his dress uniforms; he'd had it made up for himself at Mel's tailors, when Mel first went to Rio leaving his credit at its peak.

When he was dressed, he went into the living room. It was neat, everything in place; the sloven must have been here while he slept. The kitchen too was spotless. He decided to mix martinis, she liked them. This was a celebration night. They'd do it big; go out to dinner at some place swell, maybe Ciro's. He didn't have dinner clothes; he'd never bothered to have Mel's altered. He must see to that; he and Laurel were going to put on a campaign although she didn't know it yet. He could help her as much as she could help him. A good-looking fellow who knew how to get what he wanted was what she needed. He'd get the spotlight for her and be satisfied to pick up the gold pieces that slid off the outer rim.

He mixed the cocktails, sampled one and found its coldness

good. Only one. He hadn't eaten and he didn't want to spoil the evening by starting too soon. He brought in the evening paper from the doorstep, smiling to think how once the news had been more important to him than anything else. He smoked a cigarette, being careful to drop the ashes neatly into the tray, being careful to keep the chair in its place, the creases in his best suit. One cigarette and a careless reading of the paper; almost seven o'clock and she hadn't come, hadn't called.

She couldn't be going to stay away again. She wouldn't stay away without letting him know. For fifteen more minutes he riffled through the paper, reading with his eyes alone, wondering, anger beginning to take shape within his mind. Yet the words in his mind reiterated, she wouldn't, she couldn't.

Against his will, on stiff legs he stalked to the door, flung it open and stepped out into the dim blue courtyard. He was afraid to look up to the balcony, the muscles of his eyes moved stiffly as his bones. He let out his breath in a slow, strangely relieved sigh. Her apartment was dark.

He returned to his, and he heard the phone ringing as he stepped into the hallway. He ran to answer, bumping against the doorway, wondering if it had been ringing long, fearing this too might be laid on him, missing her call.

He shouted his "Hello," and heard the answering "Hello," with irritation. A man's voice, Brub's voice. Brub saying a jumble of words, sorry to call so late, just got in, going to the club for dinner, could Dix make it?

He had no wish to make it. To sit in their goody-goody club through a wasted evening, with Sylvia staring at him and Brub trying to act as if he hadn't been made different by being chained to a woman. Even as Dix was making excuse, he heard the front door, and he revised his excuses quickly. He was a quick thinker, changing, "I'm afraid not, Brub," to "I'll tell you what, if I can I'll meet you there. You go on ahead. I have to find out what Laurel has up her sleeve." As if he too were chained. Quick thinking. If he could take Laurel to the club, as Brub's guests, he'd give her a big night and he wouldn't have to borrow the money from her to pay for it. Dix ended the conversation fast; his nerves jumping with the reasonless fear that she would leave before he could see her.

As he was hurrying to her, he wondered why she hadn't

come to the bedroom. Wondering, his steps slowed and he stopped in the doorway, a reasonless and terrifying fear chilling him. There might come a day when he would face strangers, quiet, businesslike strangers.

He called out, questioning, "Laurel?"

"Who were you expecting?"

It was Laurel and he went in happily despite the quarrel underlying her voice. She was stretched out on the couch, her arms behind her head. She'd evidently just returned from whatever her afternoon business was; she was wearing a pin-checked sorrel suit; she'd unfastened the jacket; the narrow skirt was wrinkled above her long tapering legs. Her slant amber eyes were hostile on him. Her lip curled. "Going someplace?"

He didn't want to quarrel; he looked on her and was immediately filled with realization of his love for her. He loved her more than he had ever loved before. More than Brucie. For the first time he could think of Brucie while he thought of another woman. And he knew he loved this other woman.

"Sure," he smiled. But he didn't go to her. "How about a cocktail?" Get her in a good humor first; he didn't want to be pushed away. "I mixed martinis."

"Who with?"

For a moment he didn't get it. When he did, his smile was wide. She was jealous! She thought he had another woman. He wanted to laugh.

"With you, Baby. Who else?" He did laugh then. "I'll get the mixings."

He felt so good, he whistled as he went to the icebox for the shaker. He caught up two glasses. She hadn't moved and her eyes were no less hostile. "You haven't dressed up for me before," she said.

"We're going places tonight, Baby," he told her. He poured carefully, the dry, dewy liquid. It even smelled good.

"Where? To a drive-in?"

His hand was steady. Only one drop spilled. She couldn't mean anything. She was trying to start a fight because she was jealous. Because he'd never taken her out and she thought he took other women out. He turned slowly, holding her glass.

"No drive-ins." Carefully he handed the glass to her. His

eyes beheld her beauty but he didn't touch her. "You aren't the drive-in type," he smiled down on her body.

She tasted the drink. "What type am I?" she asked sullenly. "The kind you wouldn't be caught dead with in a public place?"

He wouldn't quarrel. He'd keep his good nature. He went back to the chair with his drink. He smiled over the glass, "Definitely the bedroom type, Beautiful. Haven't you enjoyed the honeymoon?"

"So it's over."

He had her where he'd wanted her all along. With him holding the reins. He'd been afraid before that she'd leave him; he'd been jumping through her hoops. It was good to be top man. "You weren't tired of it?"

She didn't answer; she demanded, "Where were you last night?"

He could have played it along but he didn't. He didn't want to prolong her anger. "At Nicolai's," he said. Last night seemed years away. Brucie was dead but it didn't matter any longer. Laurel was his love. "Drink up, Baby, we've got to hurry. They're expecting us."

Deliberately she set her glass on the floor. "Who's expecting us?"

"Nicolais. We're to meet them at their beach club for dinner."

Her dark eyes were cold jewels. "So she's the one. That stiff-necked clothes horse."

"Oh, Laurel!" he sighed. "What on earth are you getting at?"

She put down the words one after the other, like thuds on a drum. "You aren't the kind of man to stay out all night alone."

"Listen, Laurel." He was patient, even long-suffering. "Brub Nicolai was my best friend in the A.A.F. He's my best friend out here. His wife is his wife and I'm no more interested in her than I am in the dame who sells me cigarettes at the drugstore or the old cow that manages these apartments and right now I couldn't tell you what they look like. I went out to see the Nicolais last night only because you weren't here. They've asked us to have dinner with them tonight at their club. Now will you drink up that cocktail and get dressed so we can get to the club before it's too late?"

She picked up her glass and drained it slowly, set it back on the rug. "I'm not going," she said.

"But Laurel—" She ought to be beaten like a rug. "Why not?"

"Because I don't like stinking rich bastards and their stinking rich clubs."

"Laurel!" He was still patient; he clutched his patience. "They're not stinking rich bastards. They live in a little house and their club is just a little informal club."

She snorted, "I know the Nicolais."

"Certainly, Laurel, the Nicolai family—"

"Rich society bastards."

"Will you listen to me?" He raised his voice. "Just because the family had money, doesn't mean Brub has it. He doesn't. He just has his salary, his salary as a cop, that's all. God knows that can't be much. He and Sylvia don't have as much money as you have." He added quickly, "Or as I have."

"So now you've got money?" Her mouth was a sneer. "Did your check come in?"

"My check did come in," he said, holding his anger. "As a matter of fact, I got dressed thinking you'd be in early and we could celebrate tonight. Ciro's or any place you wanted. Then Brub called and I thought you might prefer that. We can go to Ciro's any time."

She yawned, insolently stretching her mouth wide. "I'm not going any place tonight," she said. "I'm going to eat something and go to bed. I'm tired."

He held in the words only for a moment. When he spoke they came out cold, quiet. "I guess you are. After your night out."

She hadn't known that he knew it. She turned her head. "What do you mean?"

"You didn't beat me home last night by very long, did you? Not even time to warm the bed."

Sullenness settled over her face like a hood. "It's none of your business," she said evenly.

He didn't speak. At that moment he couldn't trust himself to speak. He couldn't trust himself to look at her, at her insolent length, her stubborn mouth. It was his business. She was his woman; she belonged to him. He waited for her to say more but only silence roiled about them. He knew better than to turn his eyes in her direction; when he did, he was walking towards her and he could feel the pain of his steeled fingers. There was no sound of his measured steps on the carpet. He was there standing over her before he knew. And his voice was one from far away, from out of the fog. "Laurel," it said. "Don't say that, Laurel."

Her smooth, cold eyes didn't waver. Yet something like a flicker of light or scrap of cloud went into them and out of them. So quickly you could not say it was there, because that quickly it was not there. Something that might have become fear. And he turned away his head. He had almost become angry; she was trying to make him angry but he wouldn't let it happen. He was stronger than she. He stooped over and picked up her cocktail glass. His voice was closer in now. "How about another?"

"Might as well," she grudged.

He walked carefully to the table, poured the cocktail for her, carried it back to her.

"Thanks," she said. Not graciously. As sullen as before, the same sullen insolence in her eyes.

He smiled down at her. The bad moment was over and he could smile. "How about it, Baby? Think that one will put you back on your feet? It might be fun to drive out to the beach club—"

"It would stink." Deliberately she yawned. "If you can't be happy without your precious Nicolais, go on. I'm not going."

He drew a deep breath and forced a smile. She was acting like a two-year old, you had to treat her like one. Ignore the tantrum. "Not without you. I'm taking you to dinner. If you feel that way, I'll phone Brub we can't make it." He started to the bedroom. "Shall I call Ciro's and reserve a table for"—he glanced at his watch—"ten o'clock?"

"Save your money," she yawned. "You can take me to a drive-in tonight." She was still yawning.

He stopped short. Slowly he turned to look at her. "I won't take you to a drive-in." He stated it flatly.

She flared, "Why not? What's the matter with a drive-in?"

"Nothing," he admitted readily. "But you're tired. You need a good dinner tonight. Not drive-in stuff."

"What's the matter with drive-in stuff? I eat at Simon's all the time, up on Wilshire."

It couldn't be deliberate. It was still part of the tantrum. He spoke slowly, carefully. "We're not going to eat there tonight."

She turned on the couch, lifted herself to one elbow. "What's the matter?" she demanded. "Are you afraid someone might see you there?"

She didn't mean a thing. She meant his big-shot friends, his rich friends like Mel. Someone might see him and think he was broke.

As if he had put the name in her mouth, she said, "You don't have to be afraid. Even Mel used to eat there when he was rocky."

He breathed easily. "I'm not rocky. I got a check today." She could get someone to cash it for him, or she could loan him enough for tonight. He built it. "Look, I get all dressed up to go places and do things. Come on, let's celebrate. We don't have to go to Ciro's. We'll go any place you say—the Kings, Tropics—"

She broke in again, "You look. I'm tired. I'm pooped. I don't want to get dressed up and go places. All I want is to go up to the drive-in—"

"We're not going up to the drive-in!" He didn't mean to shout. It came out in spite of himself. He closed his throat and he kept his lips together in a tight line. His hands had begun to shake; quickly he thrust them into his coat pockets.

She was just looking at him out of her lozenge eyes, slyly looking at him, pleased that she'd made him lose his temper. "Okay," she said finally. "We'll go to the beach club."

He didn't believe what she'd said. His mouth fell open as if he were a character in a cartoon strip.

She said, "I changed my mind. We'll join the Nicolais." She got off the couch. She stretched like an animal, one of the big cats, a young golden puma. She came over to him there in the doorway. "Call and see if we're too late while I go change." She stood there beside him but she didn't touch him. And he didn't touch her. There wasn't time. Not if they were to make it to the beach club. And he didn't want to go; unpredictably he had changed. Because she had? Because he wondered why she had. After she'd been so insistent about the drive-in.

He watched her walk away to the front door. She said, "Go on, call. I won't be long." And she went out.

He wanted to cry her back, to rush after her and bring her back here. They didn't have to go out. It was better for them to be alone, together. He had a feeling of desolation as she closed the door, as if she were gone forever. Although he knew she'd only run up to her own apartment to change, although he knew she would return, it was as if never again would she return to him.

He even took a step after her but he reversed at once and went to the bedroom phone. He should have gone upstairs with her; he could have called from her phone. At least he should have tried to go with her. He'd never been in her apartment. He couldn't see what difference it would make; she came to his, but she insisted that the woman manager was a snoop. The old bag would throw them out if she thought anything went on between them. And the old bag's own apartment was at the right of the stairs; she knew everyone who went up and down those stairs, Laurel said. Mel's apartment was safer, isolated from prying eyes.

This wasn't the night to take issue with Laurel over any of her notions. He'd coddled her into a fairly decent humor, try to keep her there.

He looked up the beach club, dialed, waited while someone went to find Brub. He hoped it was too late, that the Nicolais had long ago gone home to bed. But it was only nine o'clock and Brub's voice denied his hope.

"What happened to you?" Brub asked.

"Laurel was delayed. Are we too late?" He hoped they were too late but he couldn't deliberately try to call it off. Because he'd won the scrap with Laurel; he couldn't pull out of it now.

Brub said, "No. It's buffet tonight. We're serving until ten. Can you make it by then?"

"We'll be there right off."

"I'll try to hide out a couple of plates. Hurry up."

He hung up; they were committed now. He lit a cigarette and went back to the living room. There was still half a martini in the shaker. He drank it; it wasn't very good.

There was no reason to stand around here waiting. The old bag couldn't get her morals up if a man went to his girl's doorway to fetch her. Yet he didn't go. He started twice but he didn't go. He didn't want another fight precipitated.

He was pushing out his second cigarette when she returned. He hadn't seen this dress before; it was some knit stuff, dull amber like her flesh, and it clung like flesh. It was cut low, sleeveless, and the short coat about her shoulders was corn-flower blue. He whispered, "You're wonderful."

He went to her but she sidestepped. "Later, Dix. There's no time to make up all over again. Let's go."

They were outside in the court before he remembered that his car was in the garage. "Do you want to wait here until I get it? Or shall we take yours?"

"I put mine up."

She went with him; he didn't want it, through the alley, the block to the far garage. But she was stubborn and again there was the fear she would vanish if she weren't at his fingertips. She didn't say a word until they reached the garage, until he was opening the noiseless door. Then she said, "No one at the snoopery would ever hear what time you got home."

He laughed it off. "It's rather a jaunt."

She didn't go into the dark garage with him; she waited until he'd backed out before she got in the car. He headed to Wilshire. He said, "I'm surprised Mel would walk that far."

"He never put the car up. When's he coming back?"

"Who? Mel?"

"Yes."

"I don't know." He headed west on Wilshire. There was a faint haze in the night, the approaching headlights had a misty look. A few coming in from the beach showed golden fog lights.

"Don't you hear from him?"

"Good God, no." He laughed at the idea. "Can you imagine Mel writing me?"

"He might like to know how his apartment's getting along. And his car."

She was being deliberately nasty again. He said, "The rent I'm paying him, he should worry."

"You never gave me his address."

"I don't have it," he said. Why did she have to get on Mel? Why had he mentioned Mel tonight?

"You told me you'd give it to me."

"When I got it. He said he'd send it but he never has."

"Is that why you're holding his mail?"

She had snooped. His jaw was tight. He snapped, "That's why." She had snooped so she knew what kind of mail was coming for Mel. He said, "Maybe he doesn't want his bills, maybe that's why he doesn't send his address." He said, "I still don't know why you want his address."

"You don't know why," she slurred. Then her voice edged. "I'll tell you why. Because he went off owing me seven hundred dollars, that's why."

Dix was honestly amazed. "Mel owed you seven hundred dollars!"

"Yes. And I'd like to collect."

"Was Mel broke?" He couldn't believe it.

"He was always broke at the end of the quarter. Before his check came. This is the first time he didn't pay up as soon as it came."

They were in Santa Monica, and the haze was a little heavier. Not too much. The fronds of the palms in the parkway on the Palisades were dark against the mist-gray sky. The fog smelled of sea.

"Mel was a heel but he paid his debts."

Again she could be meaning something, but her face, as the car rolled through the orange fog light on Ocean Avenue, meant nothing.

"It's probably the Rio mails," Dix dismissed it. He pushed the car right on the avenue, and down the California Incline to the beach road. The car rolled down the dark, lonely Incline. No one walking there tonight. He said briskly, "I hope Brub saved us a lot of food. I'm hungry." He reached over and put his hand on her thigh. "I'm glad you decided to come, Baby."

She hadn't thawed. She said, "I just came for the ride. But maybe I can entertain your best friend while you muse with his fancy wife."

He withdrew his hand. He said from his heart, "I don't want anyone but you, Baby."

She was silent. Even her face said nothing.

V

THE CLUB doors opened as if they had been seen approaching. They hadn't been, it was dark in the mist-hung forecourt and they had been silent as they left the car. The opening of the door, too, was quiet and some trick of silence held sound within the clubhouse for the moment before the girl appeared.

It was trick again that she appeared alone and within the veilings of mist assumed another's form and face.

He choked, "Brucie," yet beneath his breath the word was aloud.

He knew at once, even before speaking the word, that this was no apparition of Brucie. The word was no more than reflex. This was the little brown girl, the Banning girl, and she was not alone. Two young fellows followed her. They didn't notice Laurel and Dix standing in the mist and the night; the trio cut across to a car on the opposite side of the court, laughing together.

He knew that Laurel had heard the name even before she spoke. "Who's Brucie?"

"A girl—I used to know." He walked away quickly from the words and the memory. Into the lighted club, the clear, unmisted light of the living. He didn't know or care that Laurel followed him. Yet he was grateful to find her there. He was all right again in the light, he smiled at her. "Come on, let's find Brub fast. I'm starving."

Brub lifted a greeting hand from a table by the far windows of the dining room. Dix took Laurel's arm. "There they are." Laurel hadn't softened any; there was a sulkiness in the arm he touched. She'd get over the mood; put some food into her and she'd cheer up. She hadn't come along just to stage a scene; that hadn't been the purpose of her reversal of mood. Yet he looked at her with a touch of apprehension as they reached the table. He was reassured; Laurel was civilized. She had on the same company-polite smile that Sylvia was wearing.

She didn't revert until after dinner and leisurely coffee. Until he asked her to dance. Even then he was the only one could know. "You've forgotten your manners, Dix," she said, so sweetly, so ladylike. "A guest dances first with his hostess."

It was mild enough and he played up. "If Sylvia will do me the honor."

"He's a wonderful dancer," Laurel cooed.

She didn't know; she'd never danced with him. But as long as she didn't act up any more than this, he was satisfied.

Sylvia's long and lovely lines fit well against him just as he'd known they would the first time he saw her. He was stirred by the touch of her, almost exulted by it. If she were not Brub's wife, if he were to be alone with her—the fact that she consciously withheld herself from intimacy was knowledge that she too was aware of body. They danced well and easily, whatever awareness lay beneath the mind and perceptions.

He knew the absurdity of his reaction; he had a woman, a far richer woman than this. He had no need of Sylvia, and yet there was need, the sensual need of pitting his mind against the mind of another. Until this moment he had not realized his itch for the chase, deprivation had made him jumpy these last days. Even in this incident which could not be furthered, he had begun to soar. He was breathing as a man could breathe when he was lifted into the vastness of sky, when he knew himself to be a unit of power, complete in himself, powerful in himself.

Sylvia said, "Laurel is very lovely, Dix."

Her commonplace words brought him thudding to earth. Brought him to annoying consciousness of the noisy room, the disturbing shuffle of dancers' feet, the coils and scraps of conversation, the metallic music of the phonograph. He said, "Yes," although for the moment he hardly knew to what he was assenting. His inner ear echoed her statement and he said with more enthusiasm, "Yes, isn't she? Something special." He turned Sylvia in order that he too might look upon Laurel, he had not ever seen her in dance motion. She should be something special.

She was not dancing. She was sitting with Brub at the table, their heads together, their words intent. He didn't understand, he knew that Brub had risen to dance with Laurel as Sylvia and Dix left the table. But they hadn't danced; they had remained together to talk; they were talking as if they had waited a long time for this moment. "You've known Laurel before!" he said quickly. He didn't mean it to sound suspicious but he spoke too quickly.

Sylvia's answer was unperturbed. "We've met her. When she was married to Henry St. Andrews. I didn't realize it when you introduced me at your apartment. Not until she mentioned Gorgon. We met her at Gorgon's."

"Who is Gorgon?"

"He's a lawyer." She wasn't as easy now, she was making up words. "A friend of Henry St. Andrews. And Raoul Nicolai, Brub's oldest brother. We don't know them well, we don't travel in that crowd. Can't afford it."

He remembered it now. Gorgon had had opinions on the case. Laurel had quoted Gorgon's opinions. And he remembered he'd seen the name, it must be the same name. Thomas Gorgonzola. Criminal lawyer. A name to conjure with in L. A. courts, a name that meant a feature to the newspapers. He smiled; not Sylvia, not anyone would know the meaning of that smile. Laurel's friend, the great criminal lawyer.

"What is St. Andrews like?" he asked curiously.

"I didn't like him," Sylvia answered. She wasn't hesitant longer; she was on even keel. "One of those spoiled young men, too much money, mamma's darling, an ego inflated by too much attention and absolutely no discipline all of his life."

"Heavy drinker?" St. Andrews sounded like Mel. Laurel hated the first; it was a cinch she hadn't had any doings with Mel.

"That goes without saying. Liquor is such a nice substitute for facing adult life. I understand Laurel took quite a beating."

"Yes," he agreed. "She doesn't say much, but I gathered that."

"She wasn't good enough for the sacrosanct St. Andrews. And anyone with a functioning mind is an insult to their irrationality. You know, before I met Brub I was afraid he'd be that kind. The Nicolais and the St. Andrews—all that clan."

"Aren't you?" He was a little surprised.

She laughed. "What you said! My grandfather was delivering babies, and not getting paid for it, while the clans were grabbing everything that might turn into silver dollars. No, I'm

just a poor girl, Dix. And fortunately Brub's a throw-back to
when the Nicolais worked for a living."

The music ended. He would have liked to continue the talk,
to ask more about Gorgon. But she started to the table and he
followed. The dark head of Brub and the glowing head of
Laurel separated as they approached. He put Sylvia in her
chair. "Thank you," he said with mock formality. "It was indeed a pleasure." He sat down beside her. "Now that my
manners have been made, let me tell you it really was a pleasure." There was a drink in front of him and he sampled it.
"What's the matter, Brub? Laurel step on your new shoes?"

Laurel said, "I was tired. I didn't want to dance." She hadn't
lost her hostility although her words seemed simple statement
of fact. Her eyes were watching him with the same intensity as
earlier. He ignored it. He said pleasantly, "I'm sorry. I wanted
to dance with you. Couldn't you take one little spin?"

"I'm too tired," she said. She wasn't sorry. She had no intention of dancing with him, of giving in to him.

It didn't matter. He could handle her later. He could handle
anyone. He was Dix Steele, there was power in him.

"Who is Brucie?"

He was shocked that she would ask, that she would deliberately instigate a quarrel before Brub and Sylvia. He'd even
forgotten the episode in the doorway; she too should have
forgotten it until later tonight when they were alone, when he
could explain it in private. His eyes went quickly to her but she
wasn't asking the question of him, and he realized she'd tricked
it in a small, curious voice, asked it to all.

Brub could have answered her, Sylvia could have, but both
were silent. Brub was looking into his drink, turning it in his
worried hand. Sylvia was shocked as Dix, her eyes were wide on
him. It was up to him to answer. He said it quietly, "She was a
girl I knew a long time ago. That Brub and I knew. In England."
He was furious but he was quiet. He'd told her that much
outside, she shouldn't have nuzzled the name, kept it alive in
her consciousness. He completed her knowledge. "She's dead."

He opened his eyes on her as he spoke and he saw the shock
come into hers. He wanted to shock her. He wouldn't have
said it otherwise, not bluntly, not out like that. He didn't know
if there were fear in her as well as shock; you couldn't tell; it

was hard to tell what lay behind gem-smooth, gem-hard, amber eyes.

"Dead," she repeated, as if she didn't believe him. "But she was—"

He smiled, "That girl wasn't Brucie." He explained to Sylvia, to Brub who had looked up at him again. "As we were coming in tonight, we saw that girl, the one who was here that other evening. You knew her name, Sylvia, and she reminded you of Brucie, remember, Brub?"

Sylvia said, "The Banning girl."

"Yes." His voice wasn't quite steady remembering that moment in the mystery of the night and fog. "She looked so much like Brucie tonight, it—" He smiled ruefully. "It was rather startling."

He was pleased now that Laurel had brought up the name when she did. Brub and Sylvia were corroboration of the fact that there was no Brucie in his life; Laurel might have doubted him if he'd explained it away in private. He was pleased too that the name had remained with her, that it had given her jealousy. He was still important to her. She had thought he was shaken because he'd run into a girl out of his past.

Again he asked her to dance and this time she didn't refuse. He held her closely, he said to her hair, "You didn't think there was anyone else for me, did you, Baby?"

"I don't know what I thought," she said. "How does anyone ever know what they really think?" She was defensive but she was weary, it was in the strands of her voice.

He said, "Let's go home."

"All right," she agreed.

He didn't wait for the music to end; he danced her to the table and saw Sylvia and Brub move apart, in the same fashion that Laurel and Brub had earlier. He didn't wonder at the repetition; only briefly did it occur to him that Brub must be in one of his confidential moods. And that Brub too must be tired tonight, otherwise he'd be cutting capers on the dance floor.

2

It didn't occur to Dix to wonder why Brub was tired. Not until he and Laurel had ridden in the silence of her weariness almost to the apartment. He'd been thinking of Laurel, watching her as she rested there in the corner of the seat, her eyes closed, her lips parted as if she slept. He'd been thinking of her beauty and her fire, and tonight, her lack of fire. Thinking without thoughts, conscious of her and of the fact that this many mist-dulled streets must be covered before he could put the car at the curb, until he and Laurel could be alone.

He didn't consciously bring Brub to memory. It was one of those minnows of thought, darting through the unruffled pond of his thinking. But why should Brub be beaten? The case was closed, insofar as work activity was concerned. In the files of unfinished business there was an entry; girl murdered, murderer unknown. There were plenty of like entries, another wouldn't mean that a young fellow playing cop should have all the high spirits knocked out of him. Plenty of reasons why Brub could have been tired, he could have thrown one the night before, he could have sat up reading all night; he and Sylvia could have continued their dissension, if there had been one, far into the dawn. Or they could have pitied Dix far into the dawn. Because of Brucie.

And that had been only last night, the revelation of Brucie's death. Dix should have been the one holding his head in his hands. But he knew how to get away from trouble, from grief and from fear. He knew better than to indwell with it. He was smart.

He said aloud, "I don't know why everyone should be so tuckered tonight, I'm not."

She wasn't asleep. She didn't open her eyes but she said, "Why should you be? You slept all day."

It wasn't much further home. And he waited to answer, waited until they could be alone. It wasn't worth while to whittle off little edges of disagreement; you must get at the roots. As soon as he found out what was in back of her hostility, he would uproot it. They'd have it out tonight, before she slept.

He said, "We're here."

He held the door and she slid under the wheel to get out of the car. She might have slept on the way home, her eyes were half-closed yet. She walked ahead of him under the arch into the blue-lighted patio, dulled in tonight's mist. She must have been half asleep for she didn't turn to Mel's apartment, she was starting back to the steps when he caught her arm, asking softly, "Where you going, Baby?" He turned her, holding her arm, "You're walking in your sleep."

She stood there quietly while he opened the door, but she waited to enter, waited until he touched her again and explained, "We're home, honey. Wake up."

He had left the lamp burning in the living room. He shut out the blue mist and turned to the welcome of the light. It was good to be home. With her. "Go get undressed and I'll fix you a drink."

"I don't want a drink," she said. A little shiver twisted her shoulders.

"Something hot," he said. "Milk? Coffee?"

"Coffee," she said. "I'd like coffee. Hot, black coffee."

"Coming up!" He filled the electric percolator in the kitchen, he'd make it in the bedroom. With her. He fixed the tray and hurried back to her.

She hadn't started to undress. She was sitting on the edge of the bed, just sitting there looking into the monotone of the rug.

He plugged in the percolator. "Be ready in a minute. Why don't you get undressed while it's perking? I'll serve you in bed, solid comfort."

She didn't make any move, not even to take off her coat. She just looked up at him. Not saying anything, not even with her eyes. Not even hostility now in her eyes.

He came over to her and he sat down beside her on the bed. "Look," he said gently. "Get it off your chest. What's bothering you?"

She shook her head and her hair fell across her cheek. As if mist were bright as sun, it obscured her face.

"It isn't fair not to tell me, Laurel," he continued. "You don't give me a chance. How can I explain if you don't let me know what's the trouble?"

Her sigh was audible. She started to say, "What's the good—" but he stopped her, turning her to face him.

"You're the most important thing in the world to me, Laurel. No matter what it is, I want to get it right with you." He didn't mean to say much, he meant to keep it light, but he couldn't when he had touched her, when he was looking into her face. "I couldn't bear to lose you, Laurel. I couldn't take it."

She studied his face while she released her shoulders gently from his hands. She could see in him truth of what he had said. Her voice was very tired. "All right, Dix," she said. "Let's talk about it. Let's start at the beginning. Where were you last night?"

That was easy. "But I told you. At Nicolai's."

"Where were you after you left Nicolai's?"

She'd been checking up on him. He got up from the bed and began to walk the room. She was Laurel, but she was a woman and she was snooping on him. His laugh was short. "So you didn't believe me. You checked with Brub. That's what you two were talking about."

"That was part of it," she admitted.

"What did Brub tell you?"

"You needn't get annoyed. I didn't ask him outright. I simply found out you'd been there early and left early."

"You didn't believe me," he accused.

"I didn't believe you'd come from Nicolai's at four in the morning in the shape you were in," she said flatly.

The coffee was beginning to bubble. It was a small sound, a bubble forming, breaking, a small, annoying sound. He shut it out of his ears. He wouldn't let it start roaring. He didn't have to listen to sounds any longer; he had Laurel. He had her voice and her presence to shut away sound. He could explain to her and he didn't mind explaining. He didn't mind anything that would keep Laurel near to him.

"How much did Brub tell you?" he asked. "Did he tell you the news he gave me last night?" If Brub had, she wouldn't be asking these questions. She'd be avoiding the subject as did Brub and Sylvia. He was pleased that Brub had kept silent; it was better that he tell Laurel himself; it was another tie to her. "No, I didn't come right home from Nicolai's. I couldn't. You see Brub had just told me that Brucie was dead."

Her eyes widened. With a kind of terror of disbelief.

"I couldn't see anyone. I was too shocked. I drove. Just drove. I don't know where, up the beach, I guess. I remember hearing the water." The shush of the water, the hush of a girl's voice. His own voice was uneven. "That's why I came home—the way I did."

She said, "No." In disbelief. In pity. And then she said, "Brucie must have meant a lot to you."

"She did."

"More than anyone."

He came to her swiftly, knelt before her, taking her hands. "That was true until I met you, Laurel. But there's never been anyone like you. Not ever." His hands tightened over hers. "Marry me, Laurel. Will you? We're meant for each other, you know it. You knew it the first time we looked at each other just the way I knew it. Will you, Laurel?"

She had released her hands. And the weariness on her face wasn't because she was tired, it was because she was sad. She shook her head. "It's no good, Dix. If I married you, I wouldn't have a dime."

"But I—" He didn't get a chance to build a dream.

She looked at him out of seeing eyes. "You don't have a dime either, Dix. Don't bother to lie. I know you. Yes, I knew you the first time I looked at you just like you knew me. Because we're just alike. We're out to get it, and we don't care how we get it."

He had left her, he was walking around again, listening to what she had to say, hating what she knew, hating that there wasn't truth with which to demolish it. Because he couldn't lie to her now. She knew too much.

"I thought I could get it marrying St. Andrews. All the money in the world and a position where I could look down my nose at the small-town big shots that looked down their noses at me when I was a kid. I didn't know how hard it was. I couldn't take it. The St. Andrews weren't a bit different from the Buckmeisters back in Nebraska, they just had more money and bigger noses. So I got out. But I'm still going after what I want. And I'll get it. I'll get it on their money, and don't think that doesn't burn them. And when I get there I'll be up so high I won't even know they're down there under my nose." There was an excitement in her as well as hate. She was getting there. That was all the business she'd been attending to while he slept; she knew she was getting there. When she did, she'd carry him along. But he couldn't risk waiting; when she did, there might be someone else. He walked around trying to figure what he could do. If he had Uncle Fergus' money, he could have her right now. They'd go to the top together. If there were some way to get the money that was his, that was going to be his. He heard her voice again.

"—I don't know how you got rid of Mel so you could take over here. I don't even care. But I know you're living on borrowed time. I know Mel will come back from wherever he is—"

"He's in Rio."

"Rio or taking the cure again, I don't know."

"He's in Rio," he insisted.

"Maybe he finally went. He'd been talking Rio ever since I met him three years ago, and before that. The big job he was going to take over in Rio. Next week. Next month. Maybe you got him to take it, I don't know. Anyway you fell into the apartment and the clothes he didn't want and his car. How you wangled it, I don't know; he wouldn't give his best friend the cork out of a bottle. But he's going to come back and take them all again and then what are you going to do? Move in on somebody else? You can't carry a wife with you living that way. Get a job? You don't want a job. And you couldn't get one that would pay enough to keep me in war paint. I'm expensive, Dix."

He was choked up. "My uncle—"

"What uncle?"

"My uncle, back in Princeton. You're wrong about that, I've got an uncle and he's got the chips."

"You haven't got them," she said cruelly. "Don't try to tell me he's cutting you in. I know guys in the chips. They don't keep a girl cooped up in an apartment, they're out spending."

In the silence, the roar of the coffee percolator blurred his ears. He saw her as she walked over to the table, he was grateful when she shut out the sound. She drew two cups, handed one to him.

"Let's face it, Dix. It's been swell but—"

Panic made his voice too loud. "You're not calling quits?"

She spoke quickly, stammering a little. "No, no. I didn't

mean that. But it can't be for keeps, Dix. You know that as well as I. I'm not saying that if you had half the money that stinker of an ex had, I wouldn't marry you. Want to marry you." She finished her coffee and drew another cup.

Automatically, he said, "Don't drink too much of that. You won't be able to sleep."

"I don't expect to sleep very well." There was sadness in her voice again.

She moved to the dressing-table bench as he went to the end table. He put sugar and cream in his coffee. He stirred it, the spoon whorled the liquid, churned it as a storm churned the sea. He put away the spoon and he drank some of the coffee. He said, "You're not telling me everything, Laurel. You're keeping something back. You're through with me."

"No, no, I'm not," she protested quickly. He ought to tell her to stop saying that—*no, no, no.*

She went on haltingly, "There's only one thing. If I land what I'm after, it'll mean leaving town."

He waited until he could speak quietly. "What kind of a job is it?"

"It's a show. Musical. They're casting it here on the coast. I've got a good chance." Life returned to her eyes. "It means Broadway—after that, the pictures. Starring, not a peasant in the background."

"Broadway." He could go back East, he could get things fixed up with Uncle Fergus! Everything was going to be all right. He was sick of California anyhow. "Broadway," he repeated and he smiled. "Baby, that's wonderful. Wonderful."

A childish surprise came into her face at his reaction. He finished his coffee, set down the cup. He walked with excitement. "That's terrific, Laurel. Why didn't you tell me? I've got to go back home in a couple of months anyway. You're right about my uncle. The old skinflint has hardly given me enough to eat on, that's why I've been pinching the pennies. And if it weren't for Mel letting me use this place, I'd have been in a furnished room somewhere, I'd never have had a chance to lay eyes on you. Good old Mel."

He was burned up with the radiant promise of the future. Even if he couldn't fix things with Uncle Fergus, by that time she'd have so much money she wouldn't need the St. Andrews' income, she wouldn't need Dix's income. She'd move him in and he'd get a chance to pick off the outer leaves of dough. The rightness of it all laid a sanctity on it. And he could embellish a bit now, because of the rightness it would ring true. "We'll be hitting the east coast about the same time. You're wrong about my not wanting a job, I'm used to working. I was raised on work." He laughed. "You don't know my Uncle Fergus! The only reason I've been laying off a year was to get a chance at writing a book. Now I'll go back and take on the job he wants to give me, and it'll pay for more than your war paint. He's got a factory that turns out stocks and bonds. He wants me to handle the advertising. That means New York, Baby," he grinned, "and I think by the time your run is over with we'll be doing some California advertising. I'll be around, Laurel!" She laid down her cup just in time. He caught her tightly in his arms. "Laurel," he was laughing, he was half-crying, "Laurel, I knew we were meant to be. Forever. For always."

She didn't say anything. She couldn't say anything. She was trembling within the cup of his arms.

                                   3

His sleep was restless. Even with her beside him, dreams drove him fretfully to the surface of the night. Too often. She too was restless. For he heard her stirring each time he half-awakened, heard her breath of wakefulness, not sleep. The dreams were shapes in the mist, he could not remember them when he awoke at last from the final stretch of deep if uneasy sleep.

He hadn't slept long enough. She was gone, as she was always gone when he awoke these days. There was no sun in which to remember her. The morning was a dirty gray rag. He felt cramped within the misshapen room. The dregged coffee cups were there, one on the dressing table, one by the tray.

He had to get out of here. He showered, hating the sound of the rushing water; shaved, hating the buzz of the razor. He dressed quickly, not caring what he put on. He had no plan, only to get out of this room, to get away from the unremembered shape of his dreams.

He didn't take the car. In order to breathe, in order to put motion into the staleness of his body. He didn't know why he should feel this way; everything had been right, everything was going to be right. Laurel had made it right. There'd be a few weeks of separation while she was on the road but that was unimportant. A separation would whet the emotions of both. Absence was a heady spice.

He felt better by the time he'd walked as far as Wilshire, and he continued up Beverly Drive to his favorite delicatessen. He turned in there, he was suddenly hungry. He was a little ahead of the noon crowd, he ordered salami and swiss on rye and a lot of coffee. It was when he was paying for it, breaking his last ten, that he realized he must do something about the torn check. The envelope was in his pocket, he had automatically transferred it with the rest of his stuff when he dressed.

He was pretty sure he'd need help to cash it. He'd only been in the bank twice in Beverly; no one knew him well enough to accept a mutilated check. The deal called for Brub's help, a Nicolai and a cop ought to throw a little weight.

He finished eating, left the delicatessen, and went into the nearest drugstore. He called Santa Monica first but there was no answer. It was a guess but he called the Beverly Hills station. It wasn't Brub's bailiwick but at least they could steer him to the right number.

The cop who answered said Detective Nicolai wasn't there. Dix hadn't expected Brub to be there. He said, "I know. I just want to find out what number to call to get in touch with him." He thought the cop was stupid but the cop was thinking the same thing of him; it finally cleared up, Brub was in Beverly but he'd gone out to lunch. The cop didn't know where.

Dix was irritated when he left the booth. It shouldn't have taken that long to find out that Brub was in the neighborhood. He didn't want to go sit in the police station to wait; he wasn't in the mood for that kind of amusement today. He hadn't anything to do. He could probably run into Brub if he made the rounds of the near-by eating spots. It would be better to run into him instead of seeking him out. Make it casual.

He was lucky. He found Brub in the second place, the one he called the Ice House. Always a carved cake of ice in the window. Dix said surprised, "Well, look who's here!" Before he saw the other man, the lean-visaged Lochner. Before he wondered why the two were together again in Beverly Hills.

Brub was surprised to see Dix. "Where'd you come from?"

"A guy gets hungry." He spoke to Lochner, "How d'you do, Captain Lochner."

Brub moved over in the booth and Dix sat by him. It was invitation to join them. He had to eat again but he didn't care, he ordered a chicken sandwich and a bottle of beer. It was a good omen, running into Brub as he'd wanted, not having to seek him out. It made him feel more cheerful. "More trouble in Beverly?" he asked.

"No," Brub shook his head, took a big bite of spaghetti, blurring his words. "Same old case."

"You're still working on that?" He was surprised.

"We don't give up," Lochner said in his flat voice.

He really was surprised. "It's still important enough that the head of Homicide is giving special attention to it?"

Lochner said, "We aren't going to let it happen again."

"Then you honestly believe it stems from this neighborhood."

Lochner shrugged. "It's the last clue we have."

"Seems rather hopeless," Dix said kindly.

Brub's words were audible again. "We pick up a little every time we check."

Dix didn't show any disturbance. He was as calm as an innocent bystander. "But where do you check? How?"

"We've been talking to the help again. At the drive-in where he stopped with her that night."

He was more calm. When there was anything to face he could play up to it. "Any luck?"

There wasn't. He could tell by Brub's expression. Lochner said, "There may be. Nicolai's got a good idea there." The chief left it for Brub to tell.

Brub said, "I don't know that it will amount to anything. But in these neighborhood spots, a lot of the same faces recur pretty regularly. Down at Doc Law's, for instance, in the canyon, you get to know people just seeing them over and again. I got to thinking about it. There must have been some of the regulars around that night when he took Mildred in for coffee." He let out a gust of breath. "God, the nerve of him! Walking in there, facing all those lights and gambling no one would remember what he looked like."

"Like you and me," Dix dared, "an ordinary man."

Brub nodded slowly. "Yeah. An ordinary man. With the nerve of a jet pilot." He took another bite of spaghetti fast and talked through it. "My idea, whatever good it is, is to have the help ask questions of the regulars when they come in. Were they at the drive-in the night of the murder, and did they notice the couple?"

"Not bad," Dix said, as if he were thinking about it. "And I suppose you're hoping this fellow is a repeater too."

"Yeah. That would be a break." Brub was exasperated quickly. "What a break, but no chance. Except for his nerve."

"You mean he might have the nerve to walk in again."

"Yeah."

"And you think the help would spot him in that case."

"I'm sure they would. At least I think they would. They're keyed up to remember. The little girl, Gene, her name is, is sure she'd know him if he came in again. She says she'd know him if she ever saw him. Only she can't describe him."

"The trouble with people in these cases," Lochner droned, "is that they're not articulate."

"What about the tailor?" Dix asked.

"What tailor?" Brub frowned.

"The one you told me about. The one that saw this fellow and that earlier girl come out of the movie in Hollywood." He'd nearly said the Paramount. He took a swallow of his beer. "Are you working on him too?"

Brub shook his head. "He wasn't close enough to them to be any good at identification. The guy could go in and be measured for a suit and he wouldn't know."

"He might," Dix smiled. "Mightn't he? A tailor might be expected to recognize the shoulders or the body length, don't you think?"

Lochner hmmed and Brub thought that the tailor might. Dix had given them an idea. And welcome to it. Brub was thinking out loud again, "Walking right into that battery of lights. What a nerve!"

Dix said, "Maybe he didn't intend to do anything to her. Maybe it wasn't so much nerve but no intention."

"We've considered that," Brub said thoughtfully. "But it doesn't fit the pattern. He picked them up to kill them. It wasn't ever without intention."

"According to your reconstruction."

Brub's smile was a little abashed. "I don't think I'm far off base. He's first of all a killer, that we know. He kills because he's a killer." He tallied on. "He's a gambler. He's reckless, I mean he'll take chances, like that drive-in, or taking the other girl to the movies. But he's not so reckless that he doesn't realize his chances; it's the recklessness we had at the sticks during the war, we took chances but we were sure, God willing, that we'd pull out of them."

"He's an ex-serviceman," Lochner supplied.

Dix raised his eyebrows. When Lochner didn't explain, he said, "That's something new."

"Ten to one," Lochner said. "He's the right age, good healthy specimen, average. The average were in the service."

"He's a nice-looking fellow, nice clothes," Brub said. "We know that from our inarticulate observers. He's well off, he has a car. He has a pleasant approach, we know that too or these girls wouldn't have let him pick them up. Except maybe that first one."

"What was a fellow like you reconstruct doing on Skid Row?"

"That's one of the things we don't know," Brub admitted.

"Maybe he was slumming," Lochner said.

"Maybe he knew he was off on a kill," Brub was feeling it out, "maybe he didn't want to do it. Maybe he thought it wouldn't matter so much if he picked a girl that didn't matter."

"And after the first time, he didn't care?" Dix asked soberly.

"It wasn't the first time," Lochner said with authority.

Dix's eyes slewed to him, letting his surprise show through.

"It was too professional," Lochner explained. He picked up his check. "I'm going back to the station and go over those Bruce reports again. Coming?"

Bruce reports. Bruce wasn't an uncommon name. There must be a hundred thousand Bruces in the United States. Hundreds in L. A. Dix didn't show any reaction to the name. He went right on eating the sandwich. They could have been examining him, putting out this information to get reaction from him. There was no reason for them to have any suspicion of him. There was nothing at all that made him open to suspicion. Absolutely nothing.

"I'll be along shortly," Brub said. "Soon as I finish eating."

He'd ordered apple pie and coffee, the girl was bringing them now.

Dix waited until Lochner was at the door. "Smart guy," he said.

"The best." Brub was testing the pie.

Dix got away from the subject, onto a natural one. "You and Laurel hit it up pretty chummy last night, didn't you?"

Brub didn't grin it off. He said seriously, "I like her."

"I didn't realize you and Sylvia had known her before."

"Just met. Never had a chance to talk to her until last night."

"You did pretty well last night. Looked like a serious confab." He was fishing. But he could fish openly; Laurel was his girl. He didn't catch anything.

Brub said, "I have my serious moments."

Dix said, "Won't do you any good. Looks like Laurel and I aren't going to be around much longer."

Brub wiped his mouth. His eyes were opened in surprise.

"Didn't she tell you about the show she's going into? And it's about time for me to head back to New York."

"You're going back East?" Brub was surprised. He added with mock rue, "Just when I thought we had you sold on California." He took another bite. "What's the trouble? Mel Terriss coming home?"

Laurel had talked to Brub about Mel Terriss. Brub wouldn't have had the name so glibly if she hadn't. Harping on Mel. Wondering aloud to Brub if Mel was in Rio? He bit his anger between his teeth. "I haven't heard from Mel. No telling about him. I've got to go back and get refinanced." He remembered the check. "By the way, Brub, wonder if you could help me out?" He was quick. "This isn't a touch, pal. I tore up my check, got the envelope mixed in with a bunch of ads. I'm too stony to wait for Uncle Fergus to send another, and the old boy wouldn't wire money if I were selling pencils. Would you want to vouch for me at the bank here?"

"Sure. I don't know the rules but it's worth a try." Brub picked up both tabs. Dix took them out of his hand. "I'm not that stony. My turn."

The gray day settled over them as they emerged. It was depressing; no matter how good you'd been feeling, to step into this dirty wash was depressing.

The bank was only across the street. He'd borrowed trouble about the check. There was none. Brub's identity was good. The bank manager was pleasant, saying, "I don't know why anyone should be penalized for making a mistake. As long as you have all the parts." You could tell by his manner he considered Dix an honest young fellow, a friend of the Nicolais was certain to be all of that.

He felt better with the two fifty in his billfold. The day even looked brighter. He said, "Thanks, Brub. Thanks a million." He was ready to go. He'd buy a present for Laurel, he'd never given her anything. He couldn't splurge, not on these peanuts, but he could buy her something, if only one orchid. He'd drape her in orchids someday.

It was Brub who was making the delay. Brub who blurted it out, "Those reports."

He knew what was coming. He felt the gray close in on him again but he showed only polite courtesy.

"Would you want to look them over? They're the reports on Brucie." Brub was rattling. He was embarrassed. Expecting Dix to break down? Or ashamed that he was suspecting a friend, a friend he had no reason to suspect? A shocked, grave look was the right one from Dix.

"I was talking to Lochner about her. I couldn't help talking about her, I was knocked off my pins when I heard the news. He cabled for a report on the case from the London police." Brub was speaking more slowly now. Because Dix hadn't burst into sobs? Because he was warning Dix? "He thought it might help us out. That maybe Brucie was one of a series, like our series. It's far-fetched, but the killer might have been an American, England was full of G.I.'s at that time. Maybe even a California man."

He asked only one question. "Was she one of a series?"

Brub's face was torn. "They don't know. There was a series but it didn't start right after Brucie. A couple of months—and then it began. The same pattern. A strangler."

"He was never caught?"

"No, he was never caught." Brub hesitated. "After six months it stopped. As suddenly as it had begun. Maybe he was shipped back home."

"And did it start then, over on this side?" It was a good question.

Brub slurred it. "N-no."

No series, no pattern. Isolated cases. They hadn't caught up with the isolated cases. On the east coast. Or had they? Was Brub keeping quiet because it might sound too pointed? Why should Brub suspect him?

He knew he'd better get away. He was beginning to grow angry. Brub had no business suspecting him. Yet he didn't believe that was any part of it. Only a part of his own depression. He said, "I don't think I could take the reports, Brub. You understand?"

"Yes, Dix." Brub's face showed sympathy. "See you soon."

He watched Brub's stocky figure roll away in the crowd. He shook his head, regretfully. Poor guy. Going around in circles trying to find an invisible man. Brub must be desperate if he were suspecting his best friend. Dix felt better. He rambled down Beverly Drive, shopping the windows as if he were one of the chattering females obstructing the walks. At Leonard's he took a chance, turned in. The moment he'd decided to chance it, he felt right. The whole trouble with these past weeks was playing it safe; that was what love did to you, love and being stony; and the result, the megrims.

He walked in and he put it over smooth. Too bad he couldn't get a suit out of it but he did well enough. Several jackets, navy flannel, white tweed, gabardine in tan, pinks was what it was called a couple of years ago; shirts, ties, a nice haul all wrapped up to be shipped to Rio. Dix Steele signing for it, he'd established that fact when he first moved into Mel's. Dix Steele taking care of Mel's affairs while Mel was in Rio. Maybe the credit was strained a bit but he brushed that off, first of the month, check coming any day now. And Mel wanting some of Leonard's good stuff, Rio togs didn't suit him. A dust of flattery and man-to-man and gab, and he'd mail the box himself as he was on his way to the post office. His car just around the corner.

He wished for the car as he lugged the heavy box down the street. He'd get the address label ripped off as soon as he got home, before Laurel snooped around and saw it. She might try writing Mel at Avenida de Perez, nice-sounding street. Letters could go astray. However, she might be anxious enough to cable. Not so good. Besides he'd said he hadn't known Mel's address.

He shifted the box. He should have had it delivered. But he wanted the navy flannel jacket for tonight, wanted to show her that the check was bigger than she thought it was. He shifted it again as he passed the Beverly Theatre. And he stopped. It was only four o'clock. Laurel didn't ever return until six, nearer seven. There was a special showing of some big picture, hence there was continuous run. He hadn't seen a picture in weeks. He went in.

It was after six when he came out. The street lamps were lighted in the early, hazy dark. He was a damn fool for walking, not bringing the car. There was no crosstown bus line that serviced his neighborhood. He had to walk it, carrying the awkward box. No taxis in sight.

It wasn't far but his arms ached when he reached the dark apartment. Automatically he looked to the balcony, her apartment too was dark. He went in and lighted his. He wondered if she'd tried to call, to tell him she'd be late. Not tonight. After the wrangle of last night, she'd get home tonight. She'd go places with him. He took another shower, leaving the door open to listen for the phone.

He dressed elegantly, the gray flannels, the navy coat. He looked like a million dollars. And felt like it. Although it was past seven and she still hadn't phoned. He was certain that she was coming, otherwise he'd have heard from her before now.

He went out and mixed himself a tall, comfortable highball. He stretched comfortably in the chair, took up the evening paper. Tonight he wasn't going to get annoyed waiting for her, he felt good.

She didn't come at all.

4

Discomfort wakened him. He'd fallen asleep in the chair, his legs were cramped, his neck was rigid. He turned off the lamp and the windows became gray. He didn't care what time it was, he didn't think about time. There was no reason to go again into the court, to gaze up at her apartment. He wouldn't know if she were there or not. She hadn't been there at four. Her lights wouldn't be on now if she had slunk back like the alley cat she was.

She could wait. He was too foggy now to knock her awake and demand explanation. Even if foggy, he was smart. No one in the Virginibus Arms was going to remember him at Laurel Gray's door.

He flung himself fully dressed on the bed. If he could sleep without taking anything, he would. He didn't want to be put out, he must be alerted for the ringing of the telephone.

His sleep was sodden although much too brief. The gray of daylight was still pasty on the panes. He felt dirty and sick. The new flannel jacket was a sweaty mass. He peeled it off and hurled it to the floor. The best gray slacks were crumpled like an ocarina. He pulled off the heavy brogues that leaded his feet. They were good shoes; he'd bought them in England. When he had money and position. When the best was none too good for Colonel Steele. He rubbed his fist hard across his upper lip. No tears. He hadn't the strength for tears.

He pulled off the slacks, left them where they fell. A shower would revive him, at least enough to put him on his feet for a few hours, until she came home.

He stayed under the gentle shower for a long time. The water was soothing, even the sound of it was soothing. He'd always, all of his life, loved the sound of breaking water. Nothing that had happened had changed that. The crawling of water over sand, the hush of a word *no . . . no . . . no . . .* not even that had changed his love of the power of the sea.

He put off shaving. His hands were trembling when he picked up the razor, he knew what the rasp of it would do to his nerves. Undo the good of the water. Yet he must shave. A man didn't look like just any ordinary man unless he were clean-shaven.

It was almost six o'clock before he was dressed. In the protective coloring of tan gabardines, a white sports shirt. Too late to take the discarded clothes to the cleaners. He wadded them into a bundle and pushed them in the closet. It hurt him to see the navy-blue flannel jacket, the good-looking, high-style jacket, dumped there. He rubbed his lip again. He'd wear it yet, he'd wear it to the best places in town, the places where that kind of a jacket ought to be worn. He was through living in a hole; he was going places and doing things. Big places and big things.

He lit a cigarette and took a deep drag. His head felt light as mist. No wonder, he hadn't eaten since noon the day before, a couple of sandwiches then. He wasn't hungry. His mouth tasted stale as the smoke of the cigarette. He didn't want to go out into Mel's kitchen, eat the old stuff that had been in the refrigerator for days. If only she would come.

There was no reason to believe that she wouldn't come. Something she couldn't foresee had happened last night. Maybe a job out of town. He hadn't returned to the apartment until almost seven. She must have called him all afternoon, then had to leave without getting word to him. There was no way that she could leave a message. No possible way.

She'd return any minute now. She'd explain as she had the other time—and what had her explanation been? He'd explained to her but had she ever explained to him? She'd said it was none of his business. She'd talked about the big show she might land. But she hadn't said where she was all night.

She'd meant to. And he'd meant to question her after he explained himself. But the conversation had channeled; they'd never returned to the subject. It didn't mean that she hadn't a simple and reasonable explanation, as she had the night when she'd been caught by her lawyer.

She'd come in pretty soon now. She'd be full of news about the show. There wouldn't be any wrangle tonight; they'd talk it all over, make plans for New York. God, it would be good to be back in New York again! Where no one knew you; where there weren't Nicolais parking on your doorstep. Brub was a great guy—the old Brub. But marriage changed a man. Being a cop changed a man.

The phone hadn't rung all day. It wasn't going to ring now, not while he stood here in the bedroom looking at it. There wasn't any girl worth getting upset over. They were all alike, cheats, liars, whores. Even the pious ones were only waiting for a chance to cheat and lie and whore. He'd proved it, he'd proved it over and again. There wasn't a decent one among them. There'd only been one decent one and she was dead. Brucie was dead.

Laurel couldn't disappoint him. He'd known what she was
the first time he'd looked at her. Known he couldn't trust her,
known she was a bitchy dame, cruel as her eyes and her taloned
nails. Cruel as her cat body and her sullen tongue. Known he
couldn't hurt her and she couldn't hurt him. Because neither
of them gave a damn about anyone or anything except their
own skins.

He was neither surprised nor disappointed that she hadn't
turned up. He'd expected it. He wasn't going to fight with her
when she came back; he was going to take her out and show
her the town. Whatever she was, she was his. She was what he
wanted.

He wouldn't sit around any longer, yenning at the phone.
He turned on his heel, half-expecting its ring to summon him
back, and he went into the kitchen. The bread was dry, the
cheese hard, but he put together a sandwich. His throat closed
to the tasteless stuff; he was hungry, he needed a well-cooked
dinner, something good to eat, served in style. He threw away
most of the sandwich; he couldn't stomach it.

It was after seven, way after, and she hadn't come, hadn't
called. He wouldn't wait around any longer. He was hungry.
He strode through the living room and out the front door
into the blue courtyard. There were no lights in her desolate
apartment; she wasn't there, she hadn't been there.

Slowly he went back into his apartment. At the door he
sprinted; he thought he heard the phone, but the ringing was
only in his mind, the apartment was quiet as dust. She wasn't
coming. She hadn't come last night and she wasn't coming
tonight. Only a fool, only a mawkish loon would hang around
waiting for her to come.

This time he did quit the apartment, definitely, defiantly.
Without leaving a note behind. The car was in the garage, he
hadn't had it out for two days, time it was moving again. The
garage doors opened in smooth silence. He backed out the
car, left the motor running while he closed the doors after
him. Just in case he didn't get back until late. Just in case his
garage neighbors, not one of whom he'd laid eyes on, were the
kind who'd wonder what a fellow was doing out so late.

He drove over to Wilshire, not knowing where he'd eat. The
Savoy, on up Rodeo, Romanoff's, the Tropics. He was after

good food but he didn't want to waste a lot of money on it. Not until Laurel went with him to those spots. There was always the Derby or Sheetz—not for tonight. Neither could fill the hollow within him.

He passed Judson's, and the brilliant lights of the drive-in, Simon's drive-in, glittered ahead. He thought only for a moment, a brilliant gash of thought that splintered his indecision. Quickly he slewed the car into the parking space.

It was a dare, a magnificent dare. He and he alone of those outside the case knew the police were watching Simon's, knew the help was alerted for the face of an average young fellow. It was the kind of dare he needed, to return here openly, to take the chance. Knowing they were watching for a man of a certain height, of a certain look under the garish lights of the circular counter. They weren't looking for a fellow in a big black coupe, shadowed in the twilight of a car. The same fellow and they couldn't know.

Simon's was always busy; even at this early hour cars were circled close in to the car hops' pavement. There were a couple of holes and he pulled in boldly, cut his lights and waited for the hop. A middle-aged couple, a bleached blonde and a balding man, were in the car on his right. Two young fellows in the car on his left. He was certain neither was of the police. It would have amused him to smell cop. He was never more certain of himself than when he attacked. Cringing in corners alone was fearful. He was through with that stuff.

The girl who came with a menu and bright "Good evening" was young and pretty, as young as sixteen. Pert nose, blue eyes, long, light brown hair under her ugly brown cap.

He smiled at her. "Hello," he said as if he'd been here often, as if he were one of the regulars. "I'm sure hungry tonight," he told her before she went to service another car. He wanted to be noticed, wanted her to remember him as something usual.

Dust. Lochner and his dust. Dix would have plenty of Simon's Drive-In dust in his car. He lived in the neighborhood; he could eat here often. Even the rich Mel Terriss ate here. Even Laurel Gray.

He wondered what name was on the identification card the girl had left on the outside of the windshield. He wasn't foolish enough to investigate. But he hoped it was Gene, the girl who'd recognized Mildred from her picture in the paper. He wasn't the same fellow.

She returned with her pad and he ordered steak, french fries, tomato-and-avocado salad, coffee. Cars pushed in and out on the lot. The late diners left and the first show crowd moved in. Constant motion, comings and goings, the counter men too busy to look up, the girl hops too busy running from car to counter to car to know whom they served. He was as safe as in a church.

The food was okay. He flicked the lights, ordered a chocolate shake for dessert. He wasn't in any hurry. He'd give any and all of them a chance to look him over. He wished the police were here to look him over. But he didn't go into the lighted building. He liked a chance but he was too smart for a risk.

No one paid any attention to him. When he drove out of the lot, no car followed. As soon as he was away from the lights, depression settled on him again. His hands itched to turn the wheel back towards the apartment. She might be there by now, waiting for him. He set the car forward. Let her wait. He'd waited enough for her.

He didn't consciously plan to drive out Wilshire to the sea. But the car was set on its course and the road led to the dark, wet horizon. The fog blew in at Fourteenth Street and he should have turned back then. He didn't. He went on, through the opaque cloud, until he had passed into the yellow spray that, falling into a pool, marked the Ocean Avenue intersection.

He knew then what he was going to do. He swung left and pulled in at the curb by the Palisades park. Out of the fog light glow, all things became an indistinguishable blur in the night. He left the car. The fog was cool and sweet as he drifted through it. Into the park, the benches, the trees assuming shape as he neared them. He walked to the stone balustrade. He could hear the boom of the breakers far below, he could smell the sea smell in the fog. There was no visibility, save for the yellow pools of fog light on the road below, and the suggested skyline of the beach houses. There was a soft fog-hung silence, broken only by the thump of the water and the far-off cry of the fog horn.

He drifted through the park on quiet feet, looking for the

shape of a living thing, of a woman. But he was alone, the living were huddled behind closed doors, warming their fears of the night in the reassurance of lighted lamps. He came to the corner that jutted out over the cliffs, to the corner which was the beginning of the California Incline. He stood there quietly for a long time, waiting, remembering the night he had stood in the same place almost a month ago. The night he had pretended his hand was a plane swooping through the fog; the night he had seen the little brown girl. He waited, without allowing himself to know why. He kept his hands dug into his pockets, and he leaned over the edge of the balustrade, his back to the avenue. But no bus came to shatter the silence and the fog. There were not even cars abroad, not at this particular time and place.

He tired pretending after a time and he began to walk, down the Incline, past the mid-hump, pausing there to examine the beaten brush where, in the sunshine of the day, kids took the short cut down the hill to the beach. It wasn't a good cave, too small and shallow; it offered too little protection from the lights of cars traveling up or down on the Incline. Less protection from the beach road below. There were better places, places of seclusion, of quietness. He thought of the spiny trees in the eucalyptus grove, of the winding road that dipped down into the canyon.

And he walked on, down the Incline to the pool of fog light at the intersection. He didn't hesitate, crossing the deserted road to where the three houses huddled together in the night. He passed them slowly, as if reluctant to accept the closed gates, barring the intruders of the night. He went on to the open lot through which, in sunlight, the beach crowds passed over the broad sands to the sea beyond. He knew where he was going. He sludged through the sand until he stood in front of the third of the huddling houses. It was a tall peaked house, standing dark in the thick fog. He knew this was not the one, the brown girl had entered one of the two gates that stood side by side, the first or the second house.

He scraped through the damp sand to the center house, two stories, both pouring broad bands of light into the fog. There was warmth and gaiety within, through the downstairs window he could see young people gathered around a piano, their singing mocking the forces abroad on this cruel night. She was there, protected by happiness and song and the good. He was separated from her only by a sand yard and a dark fence, by a lighted window and by her protectors.

He stood there until he was trembling with pity and rage. Then he fled, but his flight was slow as flight in a dream, impeded by the deep sand and the blurring hands of the fog. He fled from the goodness of that home, and his hatred for Laurel throttled his brain. If she had come back to him, he would not be shut out, an outcast in a strange, cold world. He would have been safe in the bright warmth of her. He plowed on up the beach, to where there was no light, where the empty beach clubs loomed in the dark. Groping on, his feet chained in the sand, he stumbled and fell to one knee. He didn't get up again, instead he slumped down there on the slope of a dune, and he buried his head in his arms.

He was there for a long time. Lost in a world of swirling fog and crashing wave, a world empty of all but these things and his grief and the keening of the fog horn far at sea. Lost in a lonely place. And the red knots tightened in his brain.

He was there for a long time but there was no time in this sad, empty shell of the night. He was there for so long that he was startled when he heard something running; almost frightened when the small dark shape hurtled upon him. He realized quickly that it was a dog, a friendly terrier. He said, "Hello, fellow," and the dog nosed his hand. He wanted to cry. He said again, "Hello, fellow."

And then he heard footsteps coming over the sand, and he no longer wanted comfort of tears. Excitement charged him; where there was a dog there was a master . . . or a mistress. His hand slowly stroked the dog's curly head. "Nice fellow," he said.

The dog was nuzzling him when the girl came out of the fog. Dix looked up at her and he said, "Hello." She wasn't afraid. She said carelessly, "Hello."

He smiled. She didn't know that behind that smile lay his hatred of Laurel, hatred of Brub and Sylvia, of Mel Terriss, of old Fergus Steele, of everyone in the living world, of everyone but Brucie. And Brucie was dead.

VI

SHE HADN'T returned. All night again she had been away. The apartment was empty and cold. He put out the lights before the gray fog of night became the gray fog of morning. He sat there in the dark bedroom waiting for the morning.

He did not dare sleep. Not until he had covered the mistake. The first mistake he had made. The mistake of sand. For sand was an evil and penetrating thing, no matter how much of it you brushed away, particles adhered as if cemented, particles leered where there had been none a moment before. If dust divulged a story, sand screamed its secrets.

It hadn't mattered before. When he could walk away from it, when he need answer to no one. Now uncertainty riddled him. Not knowing how much was in his mind alone, how much was real. It had been a mistake to look up Brub Nicolai, to embrace friendship. If he had remained lone, he wouldn't have had to worry about sand. It was good he was leaving for New York soon. He'd had enough of this neighborhood. He was getting nervous. It was nothing but nerves. Yet he'd take no chance on sand fouling him up.

He didn't smoke much while he waited. He was too physically exhausted even for that. He could have slept easily, slept long and deep, yet it was not hard to remain awake. His mind was alert. He knew exactly what he had to do and how he would do it. It was only necessary for morning to break. And for no one to come here until after what must be done, was done. He did not even want to see Laurel until he was again safe.

Safe. He was safe! He had no fear, no anxiety. He had never permitted fear to engage him. His annoyance at the occurrence of the word safe in his mind reawakened him and he saw it was morning. He stretched his arms and his body in the first pale gray of light. He felt as if he'd been cramped in a foxhole all night.

He scrubbed his face and hands again, scrubbed his teeth. His suit looked as if he'd lain all night on the sand. That was all right too. He took off the trousers now, put on bathing trunks, and pulled his trousers back over them. The trunks weren't new, he'd bought them when he first came to California. He'd expected to spend quite a bit of the past summer on the beach. But he hadn't had a car and he couldn't take being packed into an ill-smelling bus or clanging streetcar. His swimming had been done at the community pools in the various neighborhoods where he'd lived. He hadn't had a chance to enjoy the city until Mel's car became available for use.

It angered him that he'd wasted so much time, hanging around public swimming pools and cheap eating houses and neighborhood movies. If he'd known how to get started sooner, he'd be established by now, living high, clubbing with the right people, the people who had money and leisure. There was always room for a good fellow in those circles. For a moment he half-wished for Mel.

The day was lightening and it looked as if the break for which he'd dared not hope was coming his way. It looked as if the fog was clearing.

He fixed coffee at eight, drank two cups black. He was edgy now. No one ever came to the apartment in the morning, yet the very fact that he was up and about at this hour could draw a passer-by. There was yet one more thing he must do before leaving. He was reluctant, not afraid, merely reluctant to bring in the morning paper. Yet for his plan, it must be done.

He didn't get a break on that. The delinquent who delivered the paper hadn't left it on the doorstep. From the living-room window he could see it, not even on the porch but on the walk beyond. He waited at the window until a man he had never seen before hurried out of the patio. An oaf on his way to work, just a little late.

It was the wrong hour for Dix to be up, the hour when the members of Virginibus Arms set out to their jobs. Twice again he started to the door and each time he was forced to wait until a closing door and retreating footsteps were silenced. He finally opened his door a small wedge and watched from behind it. He could go put on his bathrobe, it would bolster his story of working all night, but he didn't want to waste the time. He was in a nervous frenzy to get away, to do what must be done before it was too late. And there was within him still the fear of Laurel returning. He could not face a scene with her this morning. He hadn't time.

He chose his moment to duck out for the paper. He didn't hurry the act. He made it a matter of everyday business, something a man did without deliberation. He was lucky; he saw no one. But he didn't know how many were watching behind their living-room windows, wondering what the young fellow in Mel Terriss' apartment was doing up so early. Well, he had the answer to that one too. He'd worked all night. Finished his book! That angle hadn't occurred to him before; it was a good one. He'd worked all night, finished his book. He'd been exhausted but too keyed up to sleep. He'd decided to go out to the beach, it wasn't too good a day but it looked as if it might clear and there was nothing more relaxing than lying in the sand, listening to the roll of the water. So he'd packed up the manuscript, mailed it on his way, and gone to the beach.

For Christ's sake, for whom was he plotting this minute alibi? He wasn't going to be questioned. He was nuts to think he had to account for his time, as if he were a reform-school kid on parole or a henpecked husband. He didn't have to do a damn thing but climb into bed, take a couple of pills and get the dreamless sleep he needed. Who cared what he'd done all night and today? Who in hell cared why he'd done it?

The answer was no one and he certainly wasn't boob enough to proffer an alibi to Brub. He wasn't reaching for trouble; there was only one reason for going to the beach, to put a day, today, on the sand which was in the car and imbedded in his shoes and tucked in unseen crevices of his suit. It wasn't he had nerves; it was because he was smart, because he didn't miss bets.

He had been standing in the middle of the living room, holding the folded paper in his hands. One thing more to do and he did. He opened the paper and looked at the front page.

Relief bathed him, relief flowed gently, excitingly, over him and through him. There was nothing on the front page of the paper, nothing. There was no way he could know what happened. He was off to the beach.

He flung down the paper on the couch, part of it spilled to the floor. Good. As if he'd been reading it. He started for the kitchen but he hesitated. In case he should run into anyone at the garage, he needed a prop. He pulled out a large manila envelope, gave it bulk with some magazines, sealed it and carried it under his arm. He needed nothing more. The apartment would tell no story to anyone who came in while he was away. Who the hell was going to come in? Not even Laurel hung around any more.

He didn't need the prop. He saw no one on his way back to the garage. No one showed up while he was taking out the car. He was on his way. Not as early as he'd expected to start out but this was better. He wouldn't have to sit so long on the God-damned cold beach.

He had to stop at a post office somewhere along the line. Better to avoid the Beverly one, too much danger of running into Brub. The police station was too near the post office in Beverly. There were Westwood and Santa Monica offices. He decided on the latter; he knew where it was located. There was the danger of hearing rumors, but what if he did? It would make no difference now.

He drove Olympic to Sepulveda, then north to Wilshire, thus avoiding easily the Beverly business district. The road to Santa Monica was a new one by day, even on this dull day with a watery sun trying to break through the overcast. He didn't have to hurry, there was no hurry now, no hurry at all.

He maneuvered the car into the inner lane. There wasn't much traffic at this hour but he was careful. He couldn't afford an accident or a near accident, he couldn't chance attention from a cop. It annoyed him that such an idea should enter his consciousness, and in annoyance he swerved too quickly. It was luck that nothing went wrong on the swerve. Pure luck. But it meant that luck was with him again. He could stop jittering.

He pulled in at the post office. There were people wandering in and out, like extras in a movie. No one who knew him, no one who would notice him. He addressed the envelope in the car. He hesitated over the address, wanting to make sure that this mail fodder would never turn up again. He rejected sending it to himself either at Mel's, to General Delivery, or back to Princeton. If by any outside chance his mail should be checked, it wouldn't be good. Not in his own handwriting; not in disguised handwriting, too many experts; not from a Santa Monica address. He rejected addressing it to Uncle Fergus or to Mel Terriss for the same reasons. He hit on the solution without particular thought and wrote out the name, a fellow who'd died over Italy a long time ago. The name dribbled into his mind, a simple name, Tommy Johns. The address, General Delivery, Chicago, Illinois. No return address; it would end in the dead letter department, where it wryly belonged.

He took it in to be weighed. The post office was fairly busy, he was third in line at one of the windows. No one knew him, no one noticed him. He paid for the stamps and took the envelope back to a desk as if to write on the return address. The desk he chose had no one at it; he affixed the stamp and mailed the envelope.

Nothing could have been more anonymous than the transaction yet the palms of his hands were wet when he returned to the car. He'd never had nerves like this; he couldn't understand it. Yet looking at it rationally, it could be understood. He'd been under a terrific strain; that, followed by no sleep, would make anyone jumpy. Before he'd always been able to sleep long and heavily; he'd never had to go through stunts like this. He damned the circumstances which necessitated this stunt.

He was careful to avoid the California Incline approach to the beach; he was taking no chances on getting mixed up with a police inquiry. He drove on down Ocean Front and followed the winding canyon way to the beach. He wasn't the only one who had come for a day on the sands. There were a fair dozen cars parked in the enclosure by State Beach. He parked his own car and went down the concrete steps to the sand.

The beach wasn't crowded. There were a couple of fellows and girls, sweaters over their bathing suits, backed against the concrete wall. They were playing cards, a portable radio giving out music. There was a heavy set man and his scrawny wife farther down the sands. A scattering of young men, singly and together, beach athletes. Dix chose a place against the wall on the other side of the lifeguard station. He took off his coat, folded it, laid it on the sand. He took off his trousers, folded them on top of the coat. He kept his shirt on, the off-shore wind was chill under the streaked sky. He took off his socks and shoes, set them aside, and stretched out, his head on his folded suit. The ocean was a hushed sound, the sun was beginning to break through, even faint strips of blue were appearing in the sky. He closed his eyes and he slept.

On waking he was amazed. He had evidently dropped into

the pit of sleep as soon as he lay down for he had no memory past that moment. Luck was with him that he hadn't slept too long, it was only a little past three. Discomfort had evidently aroused him for the afternoon had turned chill, the sky was completely grayed again. Dix shook out his clothes and put them on, their wrinkles, their sand were legitimate now. The same was true of his shoes and socks. He could take all these clothes to the cleaners not caring who might snoop. He could go home, have a warm shower, clean things, sleep in a comfortable bed.

First he must make certain that he was remembered. He had planned that last night. He drove the car into the gas station across, said to the dark-haired owner, "Fill her up, will you?" and as if in afterthought, said, "If you don't mind I'll phone while you're filling her." The gas-station operator might not remember him, but he could be reminded by the call. He called his own number; when there was no answer, his coins were returned.

The car was ready; Dix drove away. He would have liked to stop at the hamburger stand for food and coffee, particularly coffee. He was chilled from his sleep on the cold sand. But he didn't want to chance running into Sylvia or even Brub; this was their corner. He drove on, winding up through the canyon to San Vicente. There were no eating places on this boulevard, nor were there any drive-ins until he reached Beverly. He had no intention of dropping into Simon's at this odd hour, no intention of forcing his luck. Thinking about food had made him ravenous, yet he could not face going into a restaurant until he'd changed clothes. He wouldn't pass unnoted at any place in Beverly in his doubly wrinkled suit. By now everyone would be babbling about the latest murder, anything out of line might be suspicious. Anything sandy would be suspicious to the yokels.

He drove on back to the apartment. He didn't want to put the car away; he'd be going out again as soon as he was clean. It was double work putting up the car, yet it meant getting into the apartment without walking openly through the patio. He preferred entering without being observed.

Reviling the need of precautions, he went through the routine. Brake the car in front of the garage, get out of the car, open the garage doors, get in the car, unloose the brake, run the car into the garage, get out of the car, close the garage doors. Doggedly he walked through the alley to the rear door of his apartment. He slowed his walk as he approached. He wasn't unobserved. A yahoo was trimming the hedge just beyond his doors. A little measly Mexican fellow in faded overalls, a battered hat bending his ears, a mustache drooping over his mouth. The shears were bigger than the man. Clip, clip, clip clip, the shears chopped with Dix's approaching footsteps. The fellow looked up as Dix reached the back door. " 'Allo," he said brightly.

Dix didn't say hello, he nodded only, and he went into his apartment. He wouldn't have been surprised to find something wrong, he'd been thrown that much off beat by the unexpected gardener. But the apartment was unchanged. The slattern had been in and cleaned, that was all. The coffee pot and cup were clean, the newspaper in the living room was folded on the table. The ash trays in the bedroom had been emptied, the bed he hadn't slept in was smoothed. Everything was okay.

He restrained himself from looking out to see if the evening paper had come; he knew it was too early. The paper didn't arrive until past five o'clock. He peeled off his clothes, added them to the bundle on the closet floor and he took a long and hot shower. He shaved without hearing the electricity. He was beginning to feel great. While he dressed, dressed well in a dark tweed, a white sweater under his jacket, he wondered if she would return tonight. Surely she would. She'd been away two nights now. He hoped she would come tonight; he wasn't angry with her. She had a good reason for her absence. He would accept her reason without recriminations. He'd accept anything if she'd just show up, join him for a big feed, come home with him after it.

He decided he might as well wait an hour to see if she'd come. Postponing food had taken the edge off his appetite. He poured a shot of rye, drank it straight. Not that he had need of it, he felt swell. It was a fillip to top his good spirits.

He switched on the radio, earlier in the day he hadn't thought of that news source. He rolled the stations but there was nothing but music and kids' adventure yarns; he was be-

tween news reports. He turned off the nervous sounds, he
preferred the quietness of the apartment.

It was possible the paper had come early. He needed to
know what had happened, not have it sprung on him. He
opened the door, stepped out and looked on the porch and
walk. No paper. But the Virginibus Arms had suddenly gone
in for gardening in a big way. There was another peasant out
here in front, doing something to the flower beds. This one
was younger, a tall, skinny character, but his face was just as
droopy as the little fellow in back. He didn't say hello; he
looked at Dix and returned his attention to his spadework.

Dix went back into the living room. If she hadn't shown up
by six, he'd go on to dinner. He wouldn't wait around tonight.
She definitely must have gone out of town on a job. Probably
afraid he'd raise a fuss if she mentioned it in advance. He was
pretty sure she'd show up tonight and he wasn't surprised at all
when the doorbell rang. It didn't occur to him to wonder why
she'd ring instead of walking in until he was opening the door.
And in that split second he was amused by it; she was returning
humbly, not on her high horse.

Thus he opened the door and faced Brub Nicolai across the
threshold.

2

Brub said, "Hello, Dix." He wasn't smiling; he was standing
there, a stocky, foreboding figure.

The cold breath of danger whistled into the inmost crannies
of Dix's spirit. He answered mechanically, "Hello."

There was then a moment when neither man spoke, when
they remained unmoving, looking each into the other's face. A
moment when each knew the other for what he was, the
hunter and the hunted.

It was broken when they spoke together, Brub asking,
"Aren't you going to ask me in?" and Dix crying, "For Pete's
sake, what are you standing out there for? Come on in."

They could feign ignorance of each other's identity after
that. They could pretend they were two old pals getting together for a drink. Brub rolled in on his stocky legs, dropped

down on the couch and sailed his hat towards a chair. "I could use a drink."

"Good idea. What'll it be?"

"Scotch. Soda if it's handy."

"There ought to be some around." He stood the scotch and rye bottles on the small bar, found a soda and opened it. "I'll get some ice."

Brub's voice followed him to the kitchen. "You aren't the two-fisted grogger you used to be, are you? Imagine having two kinds of liquor at your place."

Dix pulled out the ice tray, pressed up the cubes. "You're not such a souse yourself since you grew up, are you, chum?"

But it was hollow interchange. It died before he had the drinks mixed. He tried again, lifting his own highball. "To our youth," he toasted. "Those careless rapture days seem kind of far away, don't they?"

"Like they were of another world," Brub said gravely.

Again silence moved in on them. In the void, he heard the faint plop of the evening paper flung at his door. He couldn't go for it now. Not until he knew why Brub had come. He could even hear far away, or thought he could, the clip-clip of the gardener's shears.

He couldn't take the emptiness which should be filled with man talk. He asked, "What's the trouble, Brub? You look beat."

"You should ask. I am beat."

"I'm asking." He didn't know a thing. He hadn't seen the paper, hadn't heard a radio. He threw a curve, "Is it Sylvia?"

Brub's eyebrows slanted quickly. "What about Sylvia?"

Dix said apologetically, "I thought the last time I was at your place that maybe you were having a little trouble. There was sort of a strained feeling—"

Brub had started to laugh as Dix spoke. It was a real laugh, a laugh at something funny. When Dix broke off, Brub said, "You couldn't be further off the beam. Sylvia is—she's Sylvia." He didn't have to say any more. The whole was in Brub's face and on his tongue and in his heart.

Dix murmured, "That's good." He took another drink from his glass. "What is it then? What's the trouble?"

"You mean you don't know what's happened?"

Dix said with mock exasperation, "I mean I don't know from nothing. I've been out at the beach all day—"

He had only to say "beach" and Brub tightened. He had said it deliberately. He went right on, "I just got in about an hour ago, cleaned up, had a quick one and settled down to wait for Laurel." He glanced at his watch. "I hope she won't be too long tonight. I'm starved."

"You were at the beach all day." Brub said it with wonder, almost with awe.

It was what Dix wanted. He relaxed in his chair, comfortable in his well-being, enjoying his drink. "Yes, I'd worked all night, finished my book," he threw in with modest pride. "I was worn to a pulp but I was too high to sleep so I decided to go out to the beach. Looked as if it might clear—what's happened to the California sunshine? I'm sick of this gray stuff—but it didn't." He took another drink, he wasn't talking too fast or too emphatically. He was rambling like a man enjoying the cocktail hour. No alibi, just discussion of the day. "It did relax me though, enough that I took a nap out there. Wonderful what the briny will do for a man, even on a day like today. I feel like a million dollars tonight." It was exciting to sit there behind the pleasant mask and watch the suspicion simmer out of the hunter.

Brub exclaimed, "Finished the book! That's great. Going to let Sylvia and me have a look at it?" He was trying to re-orient his thinking while he made expected talk.

Dix shook a rueful head. "I've already shipped it East. This morning. I'll send you an autographed copy when and if it's published. I promised you one for your help, didn't I?"

"Help?" Brub tried to remember.

"Sure. About tire tracks, and that day you let me go up the canyon with you. I appreciated that."

Brub remembered. Remembered more. Depression settled heavily on him again.

"Now, what's your trouble?" Dix demanded. "Here, let me fix you another." He took Brub's glass. His own wasn't half empty. He was watching it. With no food and his already high spirits, he didn't need alcohol. He talked while he poured a fairly stiff one. "Tell me what's weighting your strong shoulders." He carried the drink to Brub. "Try this."

"Thanks." Brub looked up at him. "You haven't seen the papers?"

He went back over to the easy chair. "I had a quick look at the *Times* this morning—" He broke off, getting it out of Brub's eyes. "Brub—you don't mean—"

Brub nodded heavily. There wasn't an atom of suspicion left in him. If there ever had been. "Yes. Another one."

Dix let out his breath. He exclaimed softly, in shocked disbelief, "God!"

Brub kept on nodding his head.

"When—where— Was it . . . ?" Dix stammered.

"It was," Brub said grimly. "The same thing."

"The strangler," Dix murmured. He waited for Brub to go on with the story. It wasn't a time for questions, only for shocked silence. Brub would talk; he was too tightly crammed with it to keep from talking. He had to have the release of words.

"It was last night," Brub began. He was having a hard time getting started. He wasn't a cop at all, he was a man all choked up, swallowing the tears in his throat. "Last night or sometime early this morning." His voice broke. "It was Betsy Banning. . . ."

Dix let the horror mount in his face. "Bets . . . the little . . . the girl who looked . . . like Brucie . . ." He didn't have to control his voice.

Anger, the hard iron of anger, clanged in Brub. "I'd kill him with my bare hands if I could lay them on him."

Had Brub come to kill? On ungrounded, fathomless suspicion?

Dix waited for him to go on. Brub was steady now, steadied by the iron anger that was holding him rigid. "Wiletta Bohnen and Paul Chaney found her."

Wiletta Bohnen and Paul Chaney were top picture stars, Bohnen was Mrs. Chaney. The publicity on this one would be a feast to the peasants who got their thrills through the newspapers.

"They walk their poodles on the beach every morning at eight o'clock. Walk from their house, it's the old Fairbanks place, up to the pier and back." Brub took a swallow from his glass. "They didn't see her on the way up. They had their dogs on leash and they cut across slantwise several houses to the water. But the dogs were running free on the way back . . . the dogs found her. Almost in front of the Fairbanks house, just a little above the high-tide mark."

It was hard for Brub to talk. He had to stop and swallow his throat more than once.

Dix made his own voice husky. "That's—that's all you know?"

"We know she went out a little after eleven," Brub said angrily. "She had friends there earlier, college friends of hers . . . the boy she was going to marry. She always took her dog out for a run at night, no matter what time it was. Usually it was earlier. She wasn't afraid—she was like Sylvia, the ocean was always something safe, something good. Her father—" Brub swallowed again. "Her father sometimes worried—especially these last few months—but she wasn't afraid." There were angry tears in Brub's eyes. "And she had her dog."

"The dog—"

Brub said jerkily, without intonation, "We found him. Buried in the sand. Dead . . . strangled."

"Poor fellow," Dix said from his heart.

"One thing," Brub spurted with hard anger, "nothing had happened to her." Then he laughed, a short, grating laugh. "Nothing but death." He said with irony, using that weapon to combat tears, "It's some comfort to her father and the boy—nothing happened to her."

"Was it the same man?" Dix asked dubiously.

"Who else?" Brub demanded belligerently. "It's been just about a month. Every month. Every damn stinking month—" He wiped the back of his hand across his eyes without shame. Then he picked up his glass and drank a third of its contents.

Dix looked at him with sorrow. "God!" he repeated. It was terrific, the most terrific show of all. With Brub here weeping and flailing impotent anger at an unknown, a killer who killed and went quietly away into the night. And Brub would never know.

Dix asked, "No clues?" as if he were certain this defeat too followed the pattern.

"On the sand?" Brub snorted. "No, no clues. No buttons, no fingerprints, no cigarette stubs, no match folders, not even a calling card."

Dix rubbed his cheek. It was apology for a foolish question. "Mind if I use your phone?" Brub asked abruptly.

"Go right ahead. In the bedroom. Can I fix you another—"

"No, I've got to get on downtown to headquarters." Brub left the couch and went into the bedroom. He didn't close the door. He wasn't going in to snoop; a lot of good it would do him to snoop.

Dix was quiet, deliberately listening to the call.

"Sylvia?"

Dix relaxed but he listened.

"I'm calling from Dix Steele's . . . No, Sylvia! No, I can't come home yet, I have to go down to headquarters . . . I dropped in on Dix for a drink and a few minutes' rest from . . . Nothing . . . No . . . Absolutely nothing . . . You'll stay there until I come for you? . . . Be sure to wait for me . . . Goodbye, darling. Goodbye."

Dix didn't pretend he hadn't heard the call. Brub knew that every word was audible in a small apartment. Brub didn't care; he'd left the door open. Dix asked, "Sylvia frightened?"

"I am," Brub said. He walked over and picked up his hat. "She's not staying alone at night until we catch the murderer."

"I don't blame you," Dix agreed. "Can't I give you a quick one before you leave?"

"No, I'd better not." He seemed reluctant to go, to face the blank wall again. There would be ants scurrying around the wall, with plaster casts and fingerprint powder and chemical test tubes, but it wouldn't change the blankness of the wall.

"Come again, Brub." Dix said it with true urgency. "Come any time. Anything I can do to help you out—"

"Thanks." He put out his hand, clasped Dix's. "Thanks. You've helped me over a rough spot, fellow. And I'm not kidding."

Dix smiled. The inner smile didn't show, the outer one was a little embarrassed. The way a man is embarrassed at any show of emotion from a friend. "The bottles aren't empty. Come back."

"Oke." At the door, Brub hesitated. "Leaving town soon?"

Dix was surprised at the question. As much as if it had been a police warning. He remembered then and he laughed easily. "Now that the book's done? Oh, I'll be around a couple of more weeks at least. Maybe longer. Depends on Laurel's plans."

From the doorstep he watched Brub start away. Watched Brub stoop on the walk and a splinter of doubt again chilled him. But Brub turned back to him at once. "Here's your paper," he said.

He didn't want the paper. He didn't want to look at it. The moment it was opened in his hands, there again in the solitude of his living room, he was sickened. He'd never felt this way before. He hadn't felt this way when Brub was talking about it. Actually he hadn't thought then, he'd been too busy playing the required part.

He didn't want to read about the girl and her dog, he didn't want to look at the smile on her clean-looking, vital face. Even with the same morbid curiosity of the peasants tickling him, he didn't want to read about it. He put the paper down with trembling hands.

He hadn't needed a drink for a long time, not the way he needed it now. He'd had enough. Another might be too much, might be the edge to start him on a binge. He didn't dare go on a binge. He didn't dare anything other than complete alertness in all of his senses.

What he needed was dinner, a big, hearty, tasty dinner. Steak and french fries and asparagus and a huge fresh green salad, then a smoke and coffee and something special for dessert, strawberry tart or a fancy pastry and more coffee.

Hunger ached in him. If only Laurel were here. He knew damn well she wasn't coming; he'd known it all along but he'd been kidding himself. Teasing himself with hope. Wherever she was, whatever guy she'd gone off with, she didn't think enough of Dix even to let him know. She'd never cared for him; she'd made him a convenience while Lover Boy was tied up with some kind of ropes. Once Mr. Big was loose, she didn't even say goodbye. The old couplet taunted him . . . *she didn't even, say she was leavin'* . . . and he was furious at its popping into his head. The situation wasn't funny. It hurt. It would hurt if he weren't angry.

Well, he wasn't hanging around any longer waiting for Laurel. He was going to eat. He went fast, strode out the back door, down the alley to the garage. It was annoying to have to go through the whole stupid routine again. He shouldn't have put the car up. Tonight he wouldn't. If the police wanted to pry into the dust he'd make it easy for them. The car would be at the curb.

There was a young fellow peering into the works of a Chevvie in the alley. He didn't turn around to look at Dix. Or to say hello. Dix jutted his car out and drove away fast. He didn't bother to close the garage doors. He hesitated at the Derby but he wanted something better tonight. Something as good as the Savoy. He could afford it. He had two hundred and fifty bucks, damn near, and he was hungry.

This was the kind of a place in which to dine. These were the kind of people a man wanted to be a part of. People who knew the gentleman who seated you, who spoke to him by name. This was the way he was going to live someday. Nothing but the best. No worry about money. Or about nosey cops.

He ordered a rich meal, and he ate it leisurely, appreciating every well-cheffed bite. He lingered as long as he possibly could, he didn't want to leave this haven. Eventually there was nothing to do but go out again into the thin cold night. The fog had dissipated but there were no stars in the covered sky. And now? Not back to the unutterable loneliness of the apartment. There was always a movie. He drove down Wilshire slowly; he'd seen the Beverly, he parked around the corner from Warner's. He didn't care what the picture was; it was a place to pass time.

There was a double bill. A mild comedy; a tear-jerking problem story. Neither was absorbing, he could scarcely stay awake during the tear-jerker. But the time was passed; it was midnight when he came out of the theatre. There was nowhere else to go now, the streets of Beverly were quiet as the streets of a nine-o'clock town. Nowhere but back to the apartment.

He dreaded sleep, sleep and dreams. If only she would come back, if only she'd take him and comfort him as she had on that other night. He didn't tell himself a tall tale now, that she might be waiting for him, in all her beauty and warmth. He went into the soda fountain next to the theatre. It was closing but he didn't care. He gathered a handful of magazines from the stand, the only kind of magazines there, movie stuff, crime stuff.

Anything to keep his mind serviced until he was forced into sleep.

He didn't put the car up. It didn't matter who saw him coming in. And he wasn't going out again. If he changed his mind and did want to go out again, it was nobody's business.

He came to a sudden stop just inside the patio. It wasn't lone and desolate, a figment of a blue dream. Someone was there. A dull red circlet was burning in the shadows, back by the rear apartments. For a moment he thought it might be Laurel, but in the silence he heard the flat-paced steps of a man, an unknown man.

Dix covered his pause, stooping down as if he'd dropped something on the ground. Something small that had fallen without sound. Feeling for it until he found it, perhaps his latchkey or a packet of matches. Without another glance to the red circlet, he went to his own place, entered and shut the door, shut away the menace that might lie in the night. He was breathing heavily.

It was ridiculous to have let the presence of a man affect him simply because there had not before been a man waiting in the shadows. How did he know but that this man had a last cigarette nightly in the patio before turning in? How could he know? He, Dix, always came the back way when he was late. The man might be a musician just home from work, pumping the stale air out of his lungs before bed. Maybe it wasn't a guy who walked nightly, maybe he was locked out tonight and waiting for his wife to get home. Or it could be a guest, somebody's uncle or cousin, who beat the family home. Dix could think up a thousand and one explanations. Any of them good. Any of them stamped with logic. Any except the first one that had hit him, that for some unfathomable reason the man had been put there to find out what time Dix Steele came in. As if anyone would care.

He was all right now. He dropped the magazines on the couch and made for the bar. He'd have a nightcap, a small one before turning in. He was slightly chilled; there was a definite hint of autumn, if only the mildness of California autumn, in the air tonight.

The guy might be, he smiled, a private dick. Somebody's ex might have put him there to see how the lady was behaving.

Maybe Dix wasn't the only one wondering where Laurel was keeping herself. There was something funny about the divorce relationship between Laurel and her ex; she was so damn careful to keep men out of her apartment.

He tossed off the drink, gathered up the magazines, and put out the lights in the living room. He needn't worry about the man outside, it wasn't someone interested in— He heard the footsteps then, the flat, muffled footsteps. They were coming this way. Panic squeezed him. Unhurried, inexorable, the footsteps were bringing the man up the portal to Dix's door. Without sound, Dix quickly crossed to the window, flattening himself against the long drape. He could see out; the man could not see Dix even if he stopped and peered into the room.

Dix stood, not breathing, not having breath. Listening, seeing the shadow, the approach of the red dot, the shape of the man himself, a dumpy, shapeless shape topped by a shapeless hat. The man did not pause. He walked past Dix's door and out into the patio, crossed to the opposite portal and started again to the rear.

Dix leaned weakly against the curtain. Within his head his thoughts sounded shrill, falsetto. No one cared what he did. No one cared. No one cared. . . .

He left the window, walked the silent blue-dark room to his bedroom. He didn't put on the lights, he lay on the bed with the darkness broken only by the red dot of his own cigarette. No one cared; Laurel didn't care. She'd gone off without saying goodbye. She'd known, known that night that it was their farewell. He'd almost known it himself—he'd even questioned her. And she'd denied. She'd lied in his face, lied in his arms. . . .

He hated her. She was a cheat and a liar and a whore, and he hated her while the tears rolled from his eyes down his cheeks to salt his mouth. No one cared, no one had ever cared. Only Brucie. Brucie who had gone away leaving him alone, alone forever, for all of his life.

He ground out the cigarette. It wasn't ended with Laurel. He didn't end things that way. She'd find that out. She'd come back; she had to come back. She wouldn't walk off and leave everything in her apartment, her clothes would be important to her if nothing else was. If no person was. When she came back, he'd be waiting. He'd end it his way, the only way that meant a thing was finished.

3

Startled out of sleep, he snatched up the phone, with the wild lurch of hope that it was she. The humming of dial tone answered his shout, "Hello." And the long sound of the buzzer brought him fully awake, it was the door, not the phone, which had wakened him.

The door at nine in the morning, with dreams heavy in his mouth and smarting in his eyes. Sometime in the night he had undressed, sometime he had fallen into frightful sleep.

He pushed out of bed. Taking his time. Knowing that nothing of meaning to him could be leaning on the door buzzer at this morning hour. Knowing he did not want to answer the summons. Yet knowing that he must. It might be a wire from her. It might be Brub.

He grumbled, "Keep your shirt on," while he roped the belt of the silken Paisley robe about him, slid his feet into the morocco leather scuffs. He plodded into the living room, any man disturbed at his rightful slumbers, making no pretense at a smile as he flung open the front door.

There were two men waiting outside; he had never seen either of them before. One was a portly man in a brown suit, a man with a heavy inexpressive face and spaniel-brown eyes. The other was a young fellow in gray, a neat-looking young fellow with bright gray eyes. The portly man wore a shapeless gray hat with a faded hatband; the young fellow wore a well-shaped brown fedora. It wasn't that each hat belonged to the opposite suit; it was that they wore hats at all. Men didn't wear hats in Beverly Hills. These men were strangers, strangers with purpose.

The younger said, "We're looking for Mel Terriss."

Dix didn't say anything. He didn't believe what he heard for the moment, it was shock but it was a dull shock. Whatever he had been expecting, it wasn't this. After a moment he managed to say, "He isn't here."

"This is his place, isn't it?"

"Yes," Dix said. "But he isn't here."

The young fellow looked a little disappointed or maybe he was perplexed. He seemed to be trying to figure it out. He said finally, "Mind if we come in? I'm Harley Springer." He gestured to his partner. "And Joe Yates."

Dix didn't want them in. He didn't want to talk about Mel Terriss at any time, certainly not now before his eyes were open, before his brain was quick. But there was nothing he could do outside of shutting the door on Harley Springer's foot. The young fellow had it in the door.

Dix said, "Yes, come on in. I'm Dix Steele."

"Looks like we got you out of bed," the big Yates commented. He had a snicker in the corner of his mouth.

"You did," Dix agreed. He wasn't going to get angry at this pair. Not until he found out why they'd come to him. And he wondered if Laurel had set them on it, Laurel with her stubborn determination to get Mel's address. He didn't believe Mel owed her any seven hundred. She'd put that in hoping Dix would think it was important enough to give out with the address. Thinking money would tempt him.

He led the way into the living room. A neat living room, he hadn't hung around it last night. "Sit down," he said. There were no cigarettes in his pocket, none on the tables. He had to have a cigarette. A drink would help too but he couldn't take a drink at this hour. It wouldn't be a good tale for them to carry back to whoever had sent them. A cigarette was essential.

He said, "Excuse me while I get my cigarettes, will you?" He went quickly into the bedroom, gathered up a pack and his lighter, returned before the men could have had time to walk over to the desk. They were still on the couch, the younger man with his leg crossed one way, the big fellow with his crossed the other. They hadn't moved, only to light cigarettes of their own. He took the chair across from them. He was as much at ease as a man could be, dragged out of bed, entertaining a couple of strangers while he was wrapped in a bathrobe. Entertaining without knowing why. But he smiled at them. "What can I do for you?"

The young one, Harley Springer, took off his hat. As if he should have remembered to do it before. As if he were a cop, someone from the D.A.'s office, not used to taking off his hat when he invaded a man's privacy. He repeated then his first remark, "We're looking for Mel Terriss."

"And he isn't here," Dix smiled.

"Where is he?" Yates flipped.

The young Springer gave Yates a look, a look that meant: Shut up, let me handle this. A look that meant: You're an oaf and this guy's a gent, let a gent handle it.

Dix was actually beginning to feel at ease. He didn't have to worry about being on his toes with Springer and Yates. They weren't that well coordinated; it wasn't like being with Lochner and Brub. He answered Yates as if Yates weren't oafish. "He's in Rio," he told him. "He went down there on some big job. I subleased from him before he left."

The two exchanged a look. Dix waited. Let them explain it. Make them do the talking. He'd changed his mind about these two being cops, more like from a collection agency, trying to get on Mel's trail over those unpaid accounts.

"You're sure he went to Rio?" Springer frowned.

Dix laughed. "Well, I didn't fly him down and get him settled. But he told me he was going there. I took his word for it. I don't know why he should have told me that if it weren't true." He laughed again. It was his turn now. Time for their explanation. He stopped laughing. "Are you friends of his?" he demanded.

"Nah," Yates said.

Springer gave his partner another shut-up look. He said, "We're from Anson, Bergman and Gorgonzola. Lawyers. Our firm handles Mel Terriss' trust."

It was time to walk softly. He didn't know about trusts.

Springer continued, "We haven't heard from Mel Terriss since July." Evidently it was unusual. The way that Springer said it. "He hasn't even been around for his check."

"He didn't communicate with you from Rio?" Dix showed surprise.

"No. We had no idea he'd gone to Rio until recently. Mr. Anson or Mr. Bergman heard something about it."

Or Mr. Gorgonzola. From an alley cat who'd blabbed, who for some reason wanted to get in touch with Mel Terriss. Bad enough to ask her lawyer about him. Her lawyer and Mel's lawyer. There wouldn't be two Gorgonzolas prominent in legal circles.

"It's strange he didn't communicate with Mr. Anson before leaving. Or since. Particularly since it was Mr. Anson who had so often urged he go there."

Yates said, "Anson thought he might straighten up if he got out of town."

Harley Springer gave a light sigh.

Yates went on doggedly, "Mel's been gassing about getting a job in Rio long as I can remember. Every time he was extra loopy. He never had no intention of going to work."

Springer cut in quickly, "Do you know when he left?"

"He told me I could move in the first of August. He'd be gone before then."

"You don't know by any chance if he went by boat or plane?"

"I don't," Dix smiled slightly. They were going to check passenger lists. "He did say something about going by freighter, a sea voyage to get in trim." He shrugged, widened his smile. "I can't say I believed him. He was too fond of comfort for such rigors." Let them try to check all the freighters that steamed out from the California ports. They'd get nowhere.

He'd had enough of this. He wanted his coffee. He wanted peace. He prodded them, "I'm sorry I can't help you any more than this, gentlemen." He rose. "I didn't know Terriss particularly well. He'd hardly confide his plans to me. I'm a tenant, that's all."

Yates was going to stick his big foot into it again. There was a malicious look in his soulful brown eyes. "The trust pays Mel's rent in advance. To keep him off the street. How'd you arrange to pay him?"

Even Springer's embarrassment didn't quiet the rage in Dix. He smiled wryly as if it were none of Yates' business to so question a gentleman, but being asked, he would reply. "I gave him a check for a year's rent, Mr. Yates. He said he intended to be away at least that long." This time he was polite but firm. "If that is all—"

He waited for them to rise. Springer made apology. "I'm sorry to have had to bother you, Mr. Steele. You understand it's a job—when Mr. Anson—"

"Or Mr. Bergman or Mr. Gorgonzola," Dix smiled wholeheartedly. "I understand." He didn't include Yates in his understanding. He moved the two men to the door, opened it. Yates went on outside. Springer stopped on the doorstep. "Thanks for your help."

"Little enough," Dix said.

Springer had another question. He'd been holding it, now he sprang it. "What about his mail?"

It came too fast for preparation. But Dix could think fast. He could always think fast in a pinch. "I suppose some has been coming," he said as if it had never occurred to him. "I'll ask my secretary—" He laughed, "She keeps everything so efficiently I wouldn't know where to look. I'll tell you, leave your address and I'll have her forward it." He accepted the card from Springer, said goodbye. Yates was already out in the patio, watching the gardener plow up geraniums.

Dix shut the door with a thud. He crushed the card in his fist. Damn snoops. Why should they or anyone care what had happened to Mel Terriss? Stupid, sodden, alcoholic Mel. The world was better off without Mel Terrisses in it. Why should Laurel care? Unless she were trying to get Dix into trouble.

Let them prove, let them try to prove he didn't have a secretary. He'd go through the bills and the ads. Send the harmless ones, the ones without purchases after July. He shouldn't have used the charge accounts, but it was an easy way to do it. So easy.

It was Mel, fat-headed Mel, who was going to run him out of California. Before he was ready to go. Before Laurel came back. He'd be damned if he would. He'd settle with Laurel before he left. They couldn't hang a man for using a friend's charge accounts. Particularly if the friend had told him to make use of them. No one could prove Mel hadn't told him that.

He wanted a drink more than ever; he was so angry he was rigid. Again he didn't dare. At least not until lunch time. It was legitimate then, not before, unless you were a confirmed alcoholic like your friend, Mel.

He should have asked them about another disappearing client. He should have said: By the by, what's happened to your client, Laurel Gray? She's missing too, didn't you know? Maybe she's gone to join Mel.

His face darkened with rage. He flung the crumpled card

into the basket. He wasn't going to sit around and be questioned by any lugs who happened by. He'd dress and get out of here. Quick.

But the phone stopped him. The silent phone by his bed. He sat down and he dialed Laurel's number. The sound of ringing went on and on until he hung up. She hadn't sneaked back in. There was an idea nagging at the back of his mind; it had been there last night; it was there again now. It had to be faced. Laurel could have moved out of the Virginibus Arms.

He didn't dare go to the manager's apartment and ask. The old bag might start thinking up her questions about Mel. He'd had enough of Mel today. He could go up to Laurel's apartment; that he would dare. But it was pointless; she wasn't at home. She'd answer the phone if she were; she'd be afraid not to, afraid it might be a business call. He picked up the phone book, then laid it down. He wouldn't phone the manager from here. Not and chance having the call traced. Go out to a booth, disguise his voice. Not that the manager would know it, but someone might be around who did.

He was thinking as if it were Laurel the lawyer's narks were asking about. As if it were Laurel's life the cops were prying into. He could ask anything he wanted about Laurel. It was perfectly safe. Yet he didn't pick up the phone.

He was just starting to the shower when the doorbell buzzed again. His fists clenched. It couldn't be those two back again. It couldn't be anything important. Yet he must answer. Slowly he returned to the living room.

There was only one man on the doorstep this time. And he didn't look like he'd come from the cops or the lawyers. He was hatless, coatless, an ordinary guy in pants and shirt. "I'm from the telephone company," he stated.

Dix had the door half closed as he spoke, "You have the wrong apartment. There's nothing wrong with my phone."

"Yeah?" The man talked fast before the door was further closed. "There's something wrong with the lines running into these apartments. We got orders to check."

"Come in," Dix said wearily. "The phone's in the bedroom." He led the way, pointed it out. "There."

The fellow had a black satchel, like a plumber's satchel. He was going to rasp and ring bells and yell to Joe somewhere on the line. Dix said, "Listen, I'm late. If you don't mind, I'll start getting dressed."

"Sure, go ahead," the man said comfortably. He was already taking the phone apart.

Dix went into the bathroom, closed the door and locked it. With the shower running he didn't have to listen to the racket. When he'd finished bathing and shaving, he opened the door. The man was just repacking wire in his little black bag.

"Find any bugs?" Dix asked.

"Not here. Thanks. Shall I let myself out?"

"Go ahead."

Dix lit a cigarette. Maybe there'd been something wrong with his phone. Maybe Laurel had been trying every night to get in touch. It was fixed now, if that were it. That was no longer excuse.

He heard the front door close and at the same time he heard the clip-clip of the gardener outside the window. If he didn't get out of here, his head would split. He hadn't noticed the weather, he'd had too much on his mind. It was still gray, but there were splits of blue in it. Clearing. He put on the same tweeds he'd worn last night. He didn't know where he was going but he'd be dressed for no matter what. He knew the first stop, the cleaners. With the sandy gabardines, and the sweaty clothes in which he'd slept two nights ago, two hundred nights ago. He rolled the bundle of clothes under his arm, left by the back door. The goofy, mustached gardener offered his daily bright saying, " 'Allo."

Dix acknowledged it with a nod, striding on down the alley to the garage. The garage doors were closed. He swung them open. The car wasn't there. It was shock. And then he remembered; he hadn't put it up last night. He hadn't even closed the garage. He began to tremble. With sick anger, sick, frustrated anger. He couldn't pass the gardener again. He'd smash the man's stupid face to a pulp if he heard, " 'Allo."

He walked out of the alley, all the way around the long block to the walk in front of the apartment. The car was where he'd left it. He got in, threw the clothes on the floor, and drove rapidly away. He drove too fast to the cleaners on Olympic. He wasn't picked up. The cops were all out at the beach or hanging around the drive-in. He ought to go up there and eat, see how many he could spot. That would be a laugh. Or out to the beach with the curious.

He dumped the clothes. He'd forgotten he had others here, now he had to drive around with them hung over the seat. He asked for a special on this load, three-day service. In case he left town soon, he wasn't going without that new navy jacket.

He drove on up the boulevard, not knowing where he was going. Not caring. When he saw a corner drugstore he remembered the phone call and drew up at the curb. There wasn't anyone much in the store, a couple of women at the lipsticks, a few young fellows at the soda counter. Dix closed himself in a booth, looked up the Virginibus Arms number. While he was waiting for the call, he took his handkerchief from his pocket. He didn't hang it over the phone, someone might look in and wonder. But he held it to his mouth, his back turned to the folding door. It would muffle his voice just enough.

The manager's voice was strident to match the strident hennaed head he remembered.

"I understand you have an apartment to rent," he began.

She was as annoyed as if he'd asked for a loan. She not only had all the apartments rented but on long lease. She wondered where he ever got such an idea.

He said, "A friend of my wife's understood that Miss Gray's apartment was for rent."

Her voice was suspicious. "Who said that?"

"A friend of my wife," he repeated. "She said that Miss Gray was moving."

"Well, it's the first I've heard of it. She's paid up—who is this?" she suddenly demanded.

He said, "Lawrence. A. B. Lawrence," reading initials penciled on the wall. He had no idea where the Lawrence sprang from. "Thank you." He hung up before she could ask more. He had what he was after, information. And no one to know he'd called.

He came out of the booth, ordered coffee and a toasted cheese sandwich at the counter. It wouldn't be very good from the looks of the place but it was better than nothing. While he was waiting, he took a morning paper from the rack. He hadn't had a chance to bring his in from the doorstep.

The murder was still front-page copy. The police were doing

the usual, following every clue. Captain Jack Lochner of the
L. A. force was working with the Santa Monica force. Captain
Lochner was quoted as believing this was another of the stran-
gler murders.

Dix didn't read all the drivel. The L. A. police were rounding up a maria full of known suspicious characters. The Santa
Monica police were rounding up beach bums. There was a lot
of questioning going on and no answers. No one had noticed
any cars parked along the beach road that night. No one had
noticed anything. They never did.

Dix finished his poor breakfast and left. There was more
blue in the sky now. The sun was bringing warmth into the
day. It was nothing to him. It was an empty day, a day to be
passed, before another night would come. Another empty
night, and yet another empty day to follow. He ought to leave
town at once, not wait for his clothes to be returned by the
cleaner, not wait for a woman who would not come again.

He swung the car over to Santa Monica Boulevard, drove
into Santa Monica. He intended stopping at the Santa Fe office,
to find out about railroad tickets east. He'd have to hold out
enough money for return fare. But there was no place to park
and in irritation he drove away, cutting across to Wilshire. He
had no intention of turning west, yet he did. And he followed
the avenue to the Incline, down the Incline to the beach road.
It didn't look any different. There were no police lines. There
were perhaps more cars than usual parked along the street. Yet
perhaps not. With the day warming, the beach regulars would
be out in force. Dix didn't slow the car. He drove on down the
road, turned off into the canyon and back to town.

He didn't realize that he was being followed until he was
held by the light at the San Vicente eucalyptus grove. Until he
remembered that the shabby sedan that drew up beside him
had been behind him when he turned to the beach. Digging
back, he knew it had been behind him when he left the drugstore; uncertainly, he remembered seeing it before then. His
hands were cold against the wheel. It couldn't be.

And he was right, it couldn't be. The two men in the sedan
were ordinary, and the car didn't wait for Dix to turn, it headed
out ahead of him on the green. It was nerves, induced by the
early morning visit of Springer and Yates, by the irritation of

the gardeners and the lineman and forgetting where he'd left the car. You couldn't drive many blocks without running into a shabby black sedan with two men in it, Wilshire was full of like cars right now.

He wasn't being followed. Yet he drove back to the apartment. If there'd been anything he wanted to do, he wouldn't have cared how many cars were following him. But he was tired. Too tired to fight traffic for no reason. He would go home and sleep.

The front gardener had at last finished with Dix's side of the patio. He was leaning against a pillar, laying off with a cigarette. If anyone was hanging around, trying to find out what Dix had done with himself this morning, it was obvious. A trip to the cleaners, here was the evidence. A stop at a drugstore and if anyone wanted to know what call he'd made there, he'd have an answer. He'd called to see if Laurel was in. On to Santa Monica to the ticket office but no place to park. The drive down the beach? Simple curiosity. It was legitimate. He wouldn't be the only man in town with curiosity.

He picked up his paper off the walk, let himself into the apartment. He'd forgotten the cleaning woman. She was flicking the dust off the living-room tables as he entered. She was no more pleased to see him than he to see her. She didn't speak, she substituted a surly bob of her head.

He gave her a like bob as he carried his clothes into the bedroom to hang them. Hoping she would have started with the bedroom but she hadn't. It was still in ugly disarray. He left it abruptly, wanting to snarl at her, to ask her why she hadn't done the bed and bath first. Knowing why, because too often he was asleep at this hour.

Even as he stood there, hating her, the hideous siren of the vacuum cleaner whined suddenly in the next room. He rushed to the doorway. "Get out!" he shouted. She didn't turn off the infernal machine, she only glanced up at him dully. "Get out," he screamed. "Take that thing and get out!"

Her eyes bugged at him then, her slack mouth opened. But she didn't speak. She pulled out the cord fast, gathered her dust cloths, and scurried out the kitchen way. He heard the door bang behind her.

He steadied himself for a moment against the wall. He

shouldn't have lost his temper. He was left with a slovenly bed, an unkempt bathroom. He held himself rigid until he had stopped shaking. Slowly he walked into the kitchen and bolted the back door. He knew the front was locked but he returned to it, made sure. He had to have sleep, undisturbed sleep. Slowly he plodded back to the bedroom, drew the curtains against the sun. He was desperate for sleep.

He tried to pull the bedcovers into some shape but his hands were witless. He did manage to slip out of his jacket and kick off his shoes before flinging himself face down, begging for oblivion.

He lay there, trying to quiet his thoughts, pleading to any gods who might heed to give him rest. And he heard it begin, clip-clip, clip-clip. Outside his windows, clip-clip, clip-clip. His breath hissed from between his set teeth. It had begun and it wouldn't stop. It would go on, louder and louder, sharper and sharper. He began to tremble. He wouldn't dare order the man away, he couldn't risk having another employee run to the manager with tales. He tried to stop up his ears with his tight fists, he sandwiched his head between the pillows, he tried to will his ears to close. But the inexorable rhythm continued, clip-clip, clip-clip.

He began to weep. He couldn't help it, he tried to laugh but tears oozed from his smarting lids. His whole body was shaken. He twisted the covers in his clenched fists. He couldn't stand it. He'd go crazy if he lay here longer.

Shaking, he moved into the living room, dropped weakly on the couch. He thought he could still hear the shears but he couldn't. It was only echo in his brain; it would go away. If he closed his eyes, lay quietly, it would go away. His hand fell on the newspaper; he'd dropped it automatically on the couch when he came in with the cleaning. He didn't want to look at it. He knew what it said. He knew all about it. But he found himself opening the sheet, staring at the black headlines. He'd read the story once, but he found himself reading it again, reading every word, every tired word. Strength returned to him and he crushed the paper, hurled it across the room. He turned over on the cramped couch, turned his back to the room, clamped his eyes as tightly as his teeth. He must find sleep.

Even as he turned, the door buzzer began its sickening rasp. He ignored the first three drones. Lying there rigidly, willing whoever it was to go away. The buzz continued, in longer pressings now, like a drill boring into his tortured head. Whoever it was had no intention of going away. Whoever it was knew that he was within. There was to be no sleep. It didn't matter now. Even the need of it was no longer alive. He got up and padded in his sock feet to the door. He opened it without hesitation. He didn't care who was outside.

Two men. Two men in plain suits and hats and shoes, plain faces to match. Two quiet men. Before either spoke, he knew them for what they were.

4

He stood aside to let the men come in. He refused to know why they were here.

One of them said, "Mr. Steele?"

"Yes?"

One of them said, "Captain Lochner sent us to see if you'd mind coming up to the station, Mr. Steele."

He had no defenses. He said, "Certainly not." No matter how pleasantly it was offered, it was a command. "Will you wait while I get my jacket?" He felt naked without his shoes; he was ashamed to mention them.

"Take your time," one of the men said. He was the one who moved over to the desk as Dix left the room. The other one moved to the windows.

He put on the tweed jacket, pushed his feet into the brown loafers, brushed his trousers with his hands. They weren't badly wrinkled, not as they would have been had he slept. His hair was tousled. He took time—they'd said, take your time—to brush it. Cigarettes, in his pocket. His lighter—it wasn't his, it was Mel's, narrow, gold, real gold. No initials, no identification. He slipped it into his pocket.

The two plain men turned to meet him. They let him lead the way out of the apartment, walked beside him casually, not one on each side, not clamping his arms. The car at the curb was a plain sedan, not a police car. One of the men said, "Maybe you'd rather follow us in your own car."

Dix caught his breath. He didn't understand; they couldn't
be offering him a getaway. He couldn't get away. Not in the
fastest car made. He could delay them but he couldn't escape
them.

He said, "It doesn't matter."

"You might as well take yours. You know the way?"

"Sure." He didn't get it. And he didn't like it. It wasn't until
he was following them up Beverly Drive that he did get it. This
wasn't an arrest. How could it be, they had no charge to place
against him. They hadn't a thing on him. But this did put his
car into their hands where they could get their God-damned
dust. He had to laugh at that. Little good the dust would get
them. And if they took casts of the tires while he was in the
office, little good that would do them.

The laugh had picked him up. Enough so that he felt himself
as he parked across from the station. The two plain men had
pulled up just beyond him. Not in the police drive. He joined
them to cross the street. He didn't ask what Lochner wanted.
He could have now, but it might point up his silence before.
Therefore he was silent, going along with them into the flowered grounds, up the stone steps, beyond the door flanked by
the great bronze lamps holding green light.

He showed his ease by knowing the way to the office. He
was certain it would be the private office; it was. He was surprised to find that Lochner wasn't alone, to find Brub there
with him. Somehow he hadn't expected Brub to be in on this.
His hands twitched slightly. Why hadn't Brub come for him
instead of sending the two zombies? Nevertheless, he gave
Brub a wide smile as he spoke, "Good afternoon, Captain
Lochner. You wanted to see me?"

"Yeah. Sit down."

Dix sat down and he calmed down; this wasn't Brub's show.
Lochner was the boss. Brub looked like a clerk, sitting there at
the table surrounded with papers. Dix didn't see the plain men
leave the room; he only realized they had gone when they
were gone.

Lochner gave him a chance to settle down. The Homicide
chief was as drab as before, as tired of it all. He waited for Dix
to light a cigarette before he spoke. "Thought maybe you
could help us, Mr. Steele."

Dix lifted his eyebrows. He didn't have to pretend to be puzzled. "I'd be glad to. But how?"

"It's that Bruce case."

His hands didn't twitch. He lifted his cigarette calmly to his lips.

"Nicolai told you something about it."

"Yes." He might have spoken too quickly. He added, "You mean the English case?"

"Yeah. You knew the girl?"

"Yes." He directed a small glance at Brub. "We both knew her. A wonderful girl." Lochner was waiting for him to say something more. Dix didn't fumble. There were several things he could have said. He chose a surprised one. "Are you taking over that case, Captain Lochner?"

"Uh-uh," Lochner said. "But I got to thinking—"

Dix nodded. "Brub told me your idea. It could have been the same man."

"I got a list." Lochner rooted out a paper from under Brub's hands. "These men were friendly with the Bruce girl. All Americans. All in England when it happened. Now I wonder if you'd look it over." He held onto the paper, swinging it in his hand. "Just read it over, see what you can remember about these men. Anything they might have said or done. Anything you can remember, no matter what it is." He pushed the paper at Dix suddenly. "Here."

Dix got up from his chair, walked to the table. He didn't look at the list as he carried it again to his chair. There was a trick in this. Some kind of a trick. He hadn't been called in to look over a list. He took his time studying the names, keeping his expression grave, thoughtful. Time to think. To get ready for questions. When he was ready, he smiled up at Lochner, moved the smile to Brub. "My name's on it," he said.

"Yeah," Lochner nodded.

Brub said, "But you'd been transferred before then, Dix. I told Jack."

"My transfer wasn't completed until after I returned from Scotland," Dix explained, as if surprised that Brub didn't know. "I had a month's leave, accumulated." Brub hadn't known. Brub had been shipped out before the changes.

"You came home after that?" Lochner asked.

"No," Dix answered. Walk softly. "I was sent to Paris and into Germany. On the clean-up. I was overseas another year." Say nothing of the months in London. He'd been proud of the cushy job. Adjutant to the general. Say nothing. Lochner was too snoopy. Dix's war record was none of his business.

"Then you saw something of those men?"

He couldn't deny knowing the names. Brub knew them too. They were, most of them, part of the old gang. Some he'd liked; some he'd have liked to kick in the teeth. For instance, Will Brevet. If Brub weren't sitting here, he could send Lochner looking into Brevet. But with Brub present, he couldn't. Brub knew the louse had tried to grab off Brucie.

Dix shook his head. "I'm sorry but I didn't. I was transferred immediately after my leave. I didn't run into any of these men after I left." Sure he'd run into Brevet in London, he'd even pubbed with him one lonely night. He could lie about that. Lochner wasn't going to track down all these guys.

Whatever the purpose of this summons, it wasn't to look into the whereabouts of a bunch of harmless guys or of Will Brevet. It was funny, in this small world, that Dix hadn't run into any of them after he left London. Not even after he got back to the States. But that was how it turned out, even in the small world.

He walked over and handed the list back to Lochner. He faced the chief squarely. "I don't know a thing against any man on this list. They were all swell guys. There isn't a one of them that could have had anything to do with—with what you think." He'd delivered the defense stirringly; he meant what he said. Brub's eyes applauded. "Is there anything else?" Dix asked quietly.

"That's all." Lochner's big forefinger rubbed over the names. "I guess that's all, Mr. Steele." For a moment, his eyes weren't sleepy. "You can't blame a guy for trying," he said.

He took his list then and walked out of the room, through a communicating door. Dix looked at Brub.

Brub tilted back his chair. "I've tried to tell him. He wouldn't take my word for it." He brought the chair forward again. The legs hit hard on the floor. "You can't blame him for trying. Even if the administration weren't riding him, he'd feel the same. It's a personal failure. That these things could be happening while he's the chief."

Dix sat on the edge of the table. "Yes, I can see how he'd feel." He took out another cigarette, lit it, pushed the pack to Brub and held the lighter. Held the lighter right under Brub's nose. "It's hard lines. For you, too."

"We'll get him," Brub said. There was fight in him, no defeat now.

"Keep me posted. I'll want to know how you brought it off. The tec who solved the perfect crimes."

"They aren't perfect," Brub said softly. Then he turned his head fast to look at Dix. "You're going back East soon? Thought you said you'd be around some weeks more—or months."

"I may have to take off sooner than I expect," Dix grimaced. "The beckoning hands of business."

"Don't just disappear," Brub warned. "I want to give you an aloha ball. That'll bring you back."

"I'll make my farewells." He slid off the table. "I won't take up any more of your valuable time now, Brub. Give me a ring and we'll have lunch or dinner in a day or so. How about it?"

"Sure." Brub walked with him to the door. When they reached it, he asked, "How was Scotland?"

He'd forgotten that tangent, it took him a minute to balance the question. He answered, "It was wonderful."

"I didn't know you traveled there."

"Yes." He was thinking about it, not the way it was, the way he'd wanted it to be. "She loved it so. She talked so much about it. It was everything she said." And she was dead, but no one had known. Brub was thinking, and Brucie was then dead but Dix hadn't known.

Dix lifted his shoulders, lifted the memory away. "So long, Brub." He didn't look back; he let Brub remember him as a strong man, a man who could, after a first shock, keep his sorrow in check.

He'd carried the whole thing off well. If Lochner had been playing a hunch, he'd lost his wad. He knew now there was nothing to get out of Dix Steele. There was nothing damning in being in Scotland when Brucie died. There was nothing damning in having been in London afterwards. Except that he'd told Brub he knew nothing of what had happened. He might have been expected to know from London. Actually there'd not been a thing in the papers to tie unrelated crimes with the death of Brucie. He'd never seen Brucie's name in print. But he didn't want to go into such explanations, they sounded like alibis. He had no alibis; he needed none.

The car was where he'd left it. If the police had gone after dust, they hadn't taken much. The floor mat was no cleaner than it had been. He felt swell only he was hungry. It was too early for dinner, not more than a bit after four. A big delicatessen sandwich and a bottle of beer wouldn't spoil his dinner. Not after the starvation wages he'd been on today.

He was lucky, finding a parking place directly in front of the delicatessen. He was always lucky. He ought to kick himself for the megrims he'd had these last couple of days. Something must be wrong with his liver. Or perhaps he was coming down with a cold. From that nap on the beach. Actually he knew what was wrong. It was having Laurel walk out on him. If she'd been around he wouldn't have had a case of nerves.

He ordered salami and swiss on rye with his beer. Someone had discarded an afternoon paper in the next booth. He reached out for it, folded it back to its regular paging, first page first. The story was still on first. The police had given up questioning the fiancé and the college friends and the father; they were satisfied none of them knew any more about the Banning case than did the police themselves. The police were talking fingerprints now. That was a lot of eyewash. Sand didn't take fingerprints.

Lochner was probably having the force develop fingerprints off that piece of paper right now. Because Lochner would be thorough. Or maybe he'd had them lifted off the steering wheel, you could get dandies off a steering wheel. Only trouble was he had nothing to match them up with. A beachful of sand.

Dix enjoyed the sandwich. The beer tasted fine. So good that he considered another but he didn't want to hang around here. The phone might be ringing at the apartment. Laurel might be waiting there. He bought a couple of bottles to take out and he hurried away. His luck had turned, and that meant Laurel was coming home.

He was left-turning off the drive when he caught sight of the car. The same shabby black sedan with the same two average men in it. He was certain it was the same. He slowed his speed, eased his car around the block. He drove the entire block and the car didn't show up behind him. Rage flushed him. It was reasonless to imagine such things now. He'd come through the interview with banners flying, he'd had a good snack, all the indications were that luck had caught up with him. He couldn't revert, even for an imagined moment, to the weaknesses of these last days. He wouldn't let it happen.

As he was crossing the intersection, he saw the car again. It hadn't followed him around the block. It had come the other way to meet him. It followed him to the apartment. It was almost as if the men didn't care if he knew they were following. As if they wanted him to know.

When he parked in front of the apartment the other car plodded past. He didn't get a good enough look at the men to recognize them again. They didn't have faces to be remembered: they were background men, familiar only in their own setting, in the front seat of an old sedan.

Slowly he entered the patio, thinking, trying to understand. He'd passed Lochner's examination; he was sure of it. Why should he still be followed? He hit on explanation, the men didn't know it as yet, Lochner hadn't had time to call them off. He took a deep breath of relief. Luck hadn't defaulted, she was still along with him.

Automatically he raised his eyes to the balcony. He stopped short, his eyes widening in disbelief. The door to Laurel's apartment was ajar. He didn't think about who might be watching, he didn't care. Laurel had returned.

He covered the patio quickly, ran up the stairs, reached the door in seven-league strides. He was about to tap but he let his hand fall. He'd walk in on her, surprise her. He still carried the sack of beer. They would celebrate.

Softly he entered the small foyer, moved through the arch into her living room. It was better than Mel's living room; she'd had an even better decorator. It was as exciting as Laurel herself, silver-gray and gold and touches of bronze; in this room Laurel would glow, it had been fitted to display her as a Reingold window displayed a precious jewel. The room was empty. But the apartment wasn't empty; he could hear the water running in the bath. She'd come home! She was getting bathed and then she'd dress and they'd have a swell evening.

He was so excited that he couldn't have called out to her if he'd wanted. But he wanted to surprise her. He set the beer down on the couch, carefully, so that the bottles wouldn't clink. And he started softly towards the bedroom door.

He passed the piano, a magnificent baby grand of a strange, bronze-looking wood. The piano had caught his eye before. It was meant to. He must have noticed the photograph, but he hadn't seen it. He'd taken it for granted, a picture of Laurel or of someone in her family. It wasn't. He saw it now. A too handsome, patent-leather-haired gigolo, smiling his too pretty smile, holding the inevitable cigarette wisping smoke. It was a theatrical photo and it was inscribed in bold and banal theatrical style. "To the only one, the wonderful one, Laurel. With all the love of Jess."

Dix was turned into stone. He knew he had been turned into stone, he was fully conscious of it. The heaviness, the coldness, the roughness of stone. He was perfectly normal otherwise. He could think more clearly than ever. This photograph wasn't something old, someone discarded. It still held the place of honor. Nor was it something new. Not that new. The look of the ink wasn't that new.

He was surprised that stone could have movement. Movement that was noiseless. He entered the bedroom, her bedroom, as lush, as feral as she. From the dressing table, that face smirked at him. From the bed table that face leered. From the chest of drawers, whichever way her eyes would lift on waking, she could see only that face. As if the man were a god, her household god. And she'd cheated on him! She'd cheated even on her god.

The sound of running water had ceased in the bathroom. There were only little sounds, the gathering up of towels, the closing of a medicine cabinet. He stood there waiting.

VII

WHEN THE door opened he was as silent as stone, only his eyes had movement. The door opened and the cleaning woman came out. She took one look at him. Her face twisted, her voice was shrill. "What you doing here? Don't you look at me like that! Don't you yell at me!" She lifted the bath brush, threatened him.

He spoke with quiet dignity, "I thought Miss Gray had returned." He turned and stalked out, leaving her standing there brandishing the brush. He stalked out of the apartment. But he picked up the beer as he passed the couch. He wouldn't leave it for the vicious old harridan.

He didn't relax until he was within his own apartment. The hag would go running to the manager. Sniveling about a man yelling at her, about a man following her to Miss Gray's apartment. A certain man. The one in Mr. Terriss' apartment. He wouldn't deny he'd spoken to her sharply. Not yelled at her, a gentleman didn't yell at a charwoman. He'd spoken to her courteously, asked her not to use the vacuum cleaner this day. That was perfectly reasonable. He wasn't the only man who couldn't stand that infernal din. As for his following her to Miss Gray's apartment, that was absurd. He'd gone upstairs to see if Miss Gray had returned from her trip. He would deny, of course, that he'd entered the bedroom. He had been in the living room when the char appeared and started berating him. His word was certainly better than that of a desiccated old hag.

He put the beer on ice. He didn't want it now. He was cold, too cold. He poured a shot of rye. To warm him, for no other reason. He didn't taste it when it went down his throat.

There had been another man all along, a man she loved, the way Dix loved her. Perhaps the way in which her husband had loved her. There had always been this other man. She couldn't marry him, Henry St. Andrews had fixed that. It explained her bitterness against St. Andrews. She couldn't marry Jess because he didn't have enough money to give her what she wanted. She didn't love even Jess enough to give up the luxury she'd learned with the rich man.

Why had she played Dix? Why had she given him what she
had, where had Jess been then? Dix rocked his head between
his tight palms. Why? She alone could tell him; if there'd been
a lovers' quarrel, if Jess had been on tour, if she and Jess had
decided to split up and do better for themselves. But it hadn't
worked. She'd gone back to her love, her little tin god.

And after she got into it with Dix, she'd been afraid to tell
him. Because she knew him too well. Because she knew that he
wasn't a man to give up what was his. She had been his; brief as
it was, in that time, she had belonged to him. She'd even cared
for him. He knew it, he wasn't fooling himself on that angle.
That was the hardest part of it to face. She had cared for him.
The way in which Brucie had. But he'd been second best. He'd
been good enough only if the number one was out of the way.

He sat there while the early twilight dimmed the room. Sat
there and hurt and bled until he was again cold and tough and
unyielding as stone. Until even the hot blade of anger gave
him no warmth.

He sat there trying to understand. So many things. Why he
had been born to live under the rules of Uncle Fergus. Why
he couldn't have had what Terriss had, what St. Andrews and
the Nicolais had without raising a finger. Why Sylvia had
distrusted him. From the first moment he'd walked into their
house, he'd known she raised a barricade against him. Why?
Why had she been suspicious of him, without any faint reason
to arouse her suspicion?

Brub had said it once: Sylvia looks underneath people. Yet
how could she see what was beneath the façade? Brub had not
been suspicious; even now Brub didn't trust his suspicion. Yet
Brub listened to Sylvia and passed it on to Lochner in line of
duty. How could they suspect him? He could open the pages
of his life to them; they would find nothing there. Why, why
should they suspect?

There were no slips, no mistakes. There had never been.
There would never be. He had no fear, no reason to fear. They
could not hold him. He would go back East. He'd get the
trunk off tomorrow by express. He'd go by plane. He'd tell
Brub goodbye. Goodbye Brub, goodbye Sylvia. Thanks for
the buggy ride.

He could find a room, not too far away, a room to hole up

in for just a few days. Once he was gone, Laurel would come back to her apartment. He'd be in the shadows watching. He'd take care of Laurel before he actually left town. He would take care of Laurel.

The room was dark now, he sat there in the heavy darkness. His fingers ached, clenched in his hands. His head was banded with iron. He'd been hounded all of his life by idiot fate. He'd had to smash it in the face ever to get anything good. He wasn't licked. He could still smash, walk over the broken pieces, come up bigger than ever. Bigger and smarter and tougher than anyone. He was going to get what he wanted. He was going to have money and he knew where he was going to get it. Once he had his hands on the money, there'd be no more second best for him. He'd be the top man wherever he wanted to go. No one would put him in second place again.

While he sat there he heard the steps in the patio. He swung around quickly and looked out. It wasn't Laurel. It was some man coming in from the office, brief case in hand. The man entered one of the apartments across the court.

Tonight Dix would watch. Tonight she might come. Because he'd been cleared by the police; he'd even cleared himself with the lawyers she'd set on him. Because no one need be afraid of him tonight.

He watched. A man and woman went out, dressed to the teeth. A couple of fellows went out talking about their dates. Another man and a petulant woman who railed at him for being late. It was Saturday night. Everybody going out, putting on the dog, Saturday night out.

He watched the mist begin to fall over the blue light of the patio. To fall and to hang there, listlessly, silently. He waited there in his dark room, behind the dark window. Waited and watched.

His anger didn't diminish. Not even when the hopelessness of his vigil filled him as mist had filled the patio. Even then the spire of his anger was hot and sharp. Yet so heavily did the hopelessness hang on him that the sound of a woman's footsteps wasn't communicated to his anger until she was within the patio. High pointed heels. Slacks, a careless coat over the shoulders, the color washed out by the blue mist. A scarf to mask her flaming hair. He moved swiftly, moved before recognition was telegraphed to his anger. He was out the door, softly through the shadows.

He came up behind her just as she reached the steps. "So you decided to come back," he said quietly.

He had startled her, she swung around in quick terror. It wasn't Laurel. He looked into the face of Sylvia Nicolai. "What are you doing here?" he asked. And he saw that he was not mistaken, this was the very coat that Laurel had worn so often. It had the feel of her coat.

Sylvia shrank away from his touch. She didn't answer him. Fear alone spoke from her wide blue eyes.

"Where's Laurel?" He demanded again, still softly but more sharply, "Where's Laurel? What have you done with her?"

Sylvia was caught there, backed against the step. She wanted to move away from him but she couldn't; she was trapped. She found her voice. "Laurel's all right," she said gently.

"Where is she?" He caught her shoulders. His hands tightened over them. He held her eyes. "*Where is she?*"

"She—" Her voice failed. And then swiftly she moved. She twisted, catching him off guard, breaking through. Leaving the coat in his hands.

He turned. She hadn't run away. She hadn't sense enough to run away. She was standing there, only a slight distance from him, there by the blue pool. Her breath was coming in little gusts. She spoke clearly, "She isn't coming back, Dix. She's safe. She's going to stay safe."

He unclenched his hands and the coat fell. It lay there on the ground, slumped there. He said, "You've poisoned her against me. You've always hated me. From the beginning you hated me." He took one step towards her.

She backed from him. "No, Dix. I've never hated you. I don't hate you, even now."

"From that first night, from the beginning—" He was about to step towards her but she was ready for him. He didn't move. He wouldn't warn her when he moved again.

"From the beginning I knew there was something wrong with you. From the first night you walked into our living room and looked at me, I knew there was something wrong. Something terribly wrong."

He denied it. "You didn't know. You couldn't know."

Neither had to fill in; both knew they spoke of the same terror. He jeered, "You were jealous. Because you wanted all of Brub. You didn't even want a friend to have a part of him."

She didn't get angry. She shook her head, a little sadly.

"But that wasn't enough. You had to take Laurel from me too. Because you hated me so."

She spoke now. Without emotion. "Laurel came to Brub. Because she was afraid. Afraid of the way you looked at her. That night she asked you to take her to the drive-in."

He gripped his hands. "And you lied to her."

Sylvia ignored him. "It wasn't the first time she'd been afraid. But it was beginning to grow. Every time she spoke of Mel—"

"Damn Mel!" he cut in.

"What happened to Mel?" Her voice lifted. "Where is he? Without his car—and his clothes—without the cigarette lighter Laurel gave him, the cigarette lighter he wouldn't let out of his hands?"

He watched her, watched her in her little moment of triumph.

"What happened to Brucie?" she went on, softly now. "What happened to the girl who drank coffee in the drive-in with you? What happened to the girl in Westlake Park, to the girl who let you take her to the Paramount, to the girl on Spring Street—"

He broke in again. It didn't sound like his voice when he whispered, "I'm going to kill you." He leaped as he spoke. He didn't telegraph the movement and he was on her, his hands on her throat before she knew. It was his hands that failed him. Because they were shaking, because before he could strengthen them enough, she was screaming and screaming. By the time he'd throttled the scream, the men were running to close in on him. One from the patio entrance, one from the shadows beyond the steps, one from the shadows behind him. He didn't release his grip, not until he saw who it was running full towards him. Brub. And Brub's face was the face of a killer.

It was Sylvia who saved Dix. Because she whirled and went into Brub's arms, clung to him, keeping him from killing. She wasn't hysterical. What she cried was bell clear. "It worked," she cried in her husky voice. "It worked!"

————

They took him into his own apartment. Into Mel's apartment. Brub and Sylvia, although they didn't want Sylvia to come. They wanted to protect her from the ugliness they expected. Brub and Sylvia and Captain Lochner who had come from the shadows. The shapeless man with the cigarette who had come from other shadows. And the two cops who had driven him to the Beverly station earlier today. They'd come from somewhere.

They turned on the lights and they sat him down on his own couch. They stood around him like vultures, looking down on him, looking down their noses at him. All but Sylvia. They stood between him and the chair where Sylvia was huddled.

Lochner said, "I'm arresting you on suspicion of the murder of Mel Terriss."

He laughed. He said, "Mel's in Rio."

Lochner went on, "And suspicion of the murder of Mildred Atkinson."

He laughed again.

"And suspicion of the murder of Elizabeth Banning."

They didn't have anything on him. Not a thing.

"And the attempted murder of Sylvia Nicolai."

He hadn't hurt Sylvia. He'd lost his temper over her vicious taunts but he hadn't done anything to her. A good lawyer would take care of that one.

"Have you anything to say?"

He looked straight at Lochner. "Yes. I think you're crazy."

The shapeless man said, "The girls were safe in August. You killed Mel Terriss in August, didn't you?"

"Mel Terriss is in Rio," Dix sneered.

It was Brub who began talking to him as if he were a human being. "It's no use, Dix. We have Mildred Atkinson's fingerprints in your car. There's only one way they could get there."

Brub was lying, trying to trap him. They hadn't had time to take all the fingerprints out of that car while they talked with him today. They had time to take them while the car stood in the garage or at the curb, while a gardener guarded each door of the apartment by day, while men in the shadows watched the doors at night.

"We have the dust—"

He'd covered the dust. His lawyer would make a monkey of the dust expert.

"—lint from the Atkinson girl's coat—"

His eyes lifted too quickly to Brub's impassive face.

"—hairs from the Banning's Kerry Blue on the suit you took to the cleaners this morning—"

You couldn't think of everything. When you were rushed. When your luck had run out.

For one moment the old Brub broke through the deadly, grim-visaged cop. The old Brub cried out in agony, "For God's sake, why did you do it, Dix?"

He sat there very quietly, trying not to hear, not to speak, not to feel. But the tears rose in his throat, matted his eyes, he could not withhold them longer.

He wept, "I killed Brucie."

THE BLANK WALL

Elisabeth Sanxay Holding

To L. W.

Chapter One

LUCIA HOLLEY wrote every night to her husband, who was somewhere in the Pacific. They were very dull letters, as she knew; they gave Commander Holley a picture of a life placid and sunny as a little mountain lake.

"Dear Tom," she wrote. "It is pouring rain tonight."

She crossed it out, and sat for a moment looking at the window where the rain slid down the glass in a silvery torrent. There's no use telling him that, she thought. It might sound rather dreary. "The crocuses are just up," she wrote, and stopped again. The crocuses are up again for the third spring without you to see them. And your daughter, your idolized little Bee, has grown up without you. Tom, I need you. Tom, I'm frightened.

It was one of her small deceptions to pretend that she had lost her taste for smoking. Cigarettes were very hard to get. It was difficult to keep her father supplied. She would sit by while he smoked, and refuse to join him. No, thanks, Father, I really don't seem to care for them any more.

Yet, hidden in her own room, she always kept a few cigarettes, for special moments. She got one out now and lit it, leaning back in her chair, a tall woman, slight, almost thin, very young looking for her thirty-eight years, with a dark, serious face, and beautiful dark eyes. A pretty woman, if you thought about it, but she herself had almost forgotten that, had lost any coquetry she had ever had.

The house was very quiet this rainy night. Her son David had gone to bed early; old Mr. Harper, her father, was reading in the sitting room. Sibyl, the maid, had stopped creaking about in the room overhead.

Bee was shut in her own room, rebellious, furious; perhaps she was crying. I'm not handling this properly, Lucia Holley thought. If only I were one of those wise, humorous, tolerant mothers in plays and books. But I haven't been wise about this and I'm not tolerant about the man. I hate him.

If Tom were here, she thought, he'd get rid of that beast. If David were older . . . Or if Father were younger . . . But there's nobody. I've got to handle it alone. And I'm doing it badly.

She remembered, with a heart like lead, the visit to New York, to the dingy little midtown hotel where Ted Darby lived. She remembered how she had felt, and how she had looked standing at the desk, asking the pale and supercilious clerk to tell Mr. Darby there was a lady here to see him. Countrified, in her old tweed coat, gray cotton gloves, and round felt hat, she was already at a disadvantage. She did not even look like the wise, humorous, woman-of-the-world mother she so wished to be.

"Mr. Darby'll be right down," said the clerk.

She had sat down on a bench covered with green plush, and waited and waited, in the gloomy little lobby. Presently, as the doorman in uniform sat down beside her, she realized that the bench was for him and his colleagues. He was quite an elderly man, and she thought it might hurt his feelings if she got up and went away too quickly, so that she was still sitting there beside him when Ted Darby came out of the other elevator.

He had come straight toward her, holding out his hand.

"You must be Bee's mother," he had said.

She had taken his hand and that was a mistake. Only, she had never yet refused an outstretched hand; she had acted before thinking.

"Suppose we go into the cocktail lounge?" he had suggested. "It's quiet in there, this time of day."

It was a very small room, dimly lit, smelling of beer and varnish. They had sat at a table in a corner, and after one quick and apprehensive look at him, she had been silent. He was so much worse than she had expected, blond, thin, with an amused smile. Puny, she had thought, and dressed with a sort of theatrical nonchalance, in a powder-blue coat, darker blue flannels, and suède moccasins.

She had refused a drink, and he had ordered a rye for himself, and this had given him another advantage over her. He had been easy and relaxed and she had been in misery.

"I don't want my daughter to see you again, Mr. Darby," she had said, at last.

"My dear lady, isn't that for Bee to decide?" he had asked.

"No," Lucia had said. "She's only a child. Only seventeen."

"She'll be eighteen next month, I believe."

"That doesn't matter, Mr. Darby. If you don't stop seeing Beatrice, I'll have to put this in my lawyer's hands."

"But put what, dear lady?"

"I understand that you're married," she had said.

"But, my dear lady," he said laughing, "what will your lawyer do about that? After all, it's not a crime."

"It's altogether wrong for you to see Beatrice."

"Well, really . . ." he protested. "The poor kid tells me her life is miserably dull. She likes to get around, meet interesting people, and I'm very happy to take her around. She knows I'm getting a divorce, but she doesn't think that's any reason for refusing to see me."

Her visit had been not only utterly useless, but harmful. Ted had told Bee about it and she had been bitterly angry.

"Ted's so good-natured that he only laughed," she had told her mother. "But it doesn't make me laugh. It's the most humiliating, horrible thing that ever happened to me."

"Bee," Lucia had said, "unless you promise not to see him again, you'll have to stop going to art school."

"I *won't* stop going, and I *won't* promise."

"Bee," Lucia said, "Bee, darling, why won't you trust me? I'm only thinking of what's best for you."

"Why don't *you* trust *me*?" Bee had cried. "Ted's the most interesting person I've ever met. He knows all sorts of people, artists, and actors, all sorts of people. I'm *not* having a nasty love affair with him."

"I know you're not," Lucia had said. "But, Bee, you must believe me. Bee—he's not the right sort of man for you to know."

"Well, I *don't* believe you," Bee had said. "You think you know, but you're just terribly old-fashioned. You couldn't possibly understand anyone like Ted."

Then Lucia Holley had used her last weapon, with heavy reluctance.

"Bee, if you don't promise me not to see him, I shan't give you any carfare, any allowance at all."

"You *couldn't* do that!" Bee had cried.

"There's nothing I wouldn't do, to stop this thing," Lucia replied.

She meant that. A week ago, her cousin Vera Ridgewood had telephoned her.

"Lucia, angel, I wonder if you know that your precious child is playing around with a *quite* sinister-looking character. I've seen them *twice* in Marino's bar together and today I saw them going into a place on Madison Avenue."

It doesn't mean anything, Lucia had thought, and she had spoken to Bee about it with very little anxiety.

"Bee, dear, is there someone in the art school you go to bars with?"

"That's Ted Darby," Bee had answered. "He doesn't go to art school. He's in the theatrical business."

"I'd rather you didn't go in bars with anyone, Bee."

"I never take anything but ginger ale."

"But I don't like you going to bars, dear. You could go to a drugstore with this boy."

"He isn't a boy," Bee had said. "He's thirty-five."

Lucia had been anxious now.

"Ask him out here, Bee," she had said.

"I wouldn't ask him under false pretenses," Bee had said. "He wouldn't come like that, either. We talked about it, and I told him that if you knew he was married, you'd never let him set foot in the house."

I didn't say the right things to her, Lucia thought, watching the rain against the window. I've made so many mistakes with Bee, even when she was a little girl. I've objected to her friends. I've been upset when she changed her mind about things. I've done so much better with David. If Tom was here, he'd know just what to say to Bee. Here, now, Duckling . . . ! She did use to look like a little yellow duckling, all ruffled . . .

She got up, and went over to the window, restless and heavyhearted. The rain was streaming down the glass, glittering, with an oily look, the trees swayed a little. At the end of the path stood the queer long shape of the boathouse and beyond that lay the invisible water.

It's too lonely here, she thought. It was a mistake to come here. There aren't enough young people. David doesn't much care, but if Bee had met some nice boys, perhaps this wouldn't have happened. Perhaps.

There was someone in the boathouse. She saw a little flame

spring out and slant sidewise and die. She saw another one that was steady for an instant. Someone was striking matches in there. A tramp? she thought. A drunken man, who'll set fire to the place? I'd better tell . . .

No, I'm not going to tell Father, or David, and let them take risks. I'm not going myself, either. If he does set fire to the place, the rain will put it out long before it could reach here. As long as nobody can get in here . . .

She wanted to make sure the doors were all locked, the safety catches on the windows. She went out of her room, moving swiftly, her feet in slippers, and along the hall to the stairs. And in the hall below, she saw Bee, cautiously sliding the chain off the door. She ran down to her.

"Bee," she said, very low. "Where are you going?"

"Out," Bee answered.

She was wearing a transparent, light blue raincoat, her pale blonde hair, parted on the side, hung loose to her shoulders, her blue eyes were narrowed, her mouth had a scornful twist. She looked beautiful and terrible, to Lucia.

"It's raining, Bee. I don't want you to go out."

"I'm sorry, but I'm going," said Bee.

It was plain enough now.

"No," Lucia said. "You can't."

Bee began to turn the doorknob, but Lucia caught her wrist.

"Bee, you want to meet that man."

"All right, I am going to meet Ted," Bee said. "You won't let me go in to New York any more, but I called him up and told him to come here. At least I'm going to explain to him."

"What's this! What's this!" cried old Mr. Harper from the doorway of the sitting room.

Nobody answered him. He stood there, lean and soldierly, with his neat white mustache and his clear blue eyes, an open book in one hand.

"What's this?" he asked again.

"Mother refuses to let me go out of this house," said Bee.

"Your mother's right, Beatrice. Too late, and it's pouring rain."

"Grandpa," Bee said. "I've got a special reason for going out and Mother knows it."

Lucia could see now what the child's tactics were to be. She was counting upon her grandfather's immense indulgence for her, hoping to use it against her mother.

"You take your mother's advice, Beatrice," he said. "Best thing."

"It's *not*! She doesn't understand anything about this. She hasn't any faith in me. She thinks I'm a sort of juvenile delinquent."

"Come, now!" said Mr. Harper.

"She does! Ted's come all the way out here to see me."

"A man?" asked Mr. Harper. "Where is he?"

"In the boathouse. I want to see him for a few moments."

"Your mother's perfectly right, Beatrice. If you want to see this fellow, have him come to the house."

"He couldn't. Not after the way Mother's treated him."

"Beatrice, if your mother doesn't approve of this fellow, she has some good reason, you can be sure of that."

"No!" cried Bee. "I asked him to come, and I'm going to see him, just for a few moments."

"Afraid not, m'dear."

Oh, Bee, darling! Don't look like that! Lucia cried in her heart. As if we were enemies . . . Under the light in the ceiling the child's pale hair glistened, the blue raincoat glittered, she looked so beautiful, so delicate, and so desperate.

"Do you mean," Bee said slowly, "that you and Mother would stop me by force from doing what I think is right?"

"It's not going to come to that, m'dear," he said. "You're going to be a sensible girl and not worry your mother. You know she's thinking only of——"

"Oh, *stop* it!" Bee cried, stamping her foot. "I *won't* . . . I won't . . ."

She began to cry, she tossed her head as if the tears stung her; she turned around and went running up the stairs. Her door slammed.

I hope she won't wake up David, Lucia thought. I shouldn't like him to know anything at all about this.

"Now . . ." her father said. He laid his hand on her shoulder, and a great sense of comfort came to her. "Have you a nice book to read, Lucia?"

"I'm writing to Tom, Father."

"Run along and finish your letter, m'dear," he said. "I'll be down here to see that everything's all right."

She understood what his words implied. He would stay in the sitting room, in a spot where he could watch the stairs, all night if he thought it was necessary. She trusted him as she trusted her own heart. She trusted even his thoughts. He would not misjudge that poor, reckless, furious child.

She kissed him on the cheek. "Good night, Father," she said, and went up the stairs to her own room.

DEAR TOM:
   David is sending you some snaps he took of this house, so that you'll have a better idea. It's really very nice. The victory garden isn't doing so very well, though. The soil is too sandy. But the tomatoes are coming along . . .

Her writing was neat and small. It took so very many words to fill a V-mail page. I'm so *slow*, she thought. I'm stupid. I've done so badly with Bee.

The wind had died down and the rain fell straight now, pattering on the roof. A door closed. That's the front door! she thought. Ted's got in!

She hurried out into the hall and from the head of the stairs she saw her father taking off his overcoat. She ran down.

"I went to the boathouse, m'dear," he said. "I had a few words with this fellow. Very unsavory character, I'd call him. Inclined to be troublesome. When I told him to leave the premises, he refused. But I dealt with him. To tell you the truth, I pushed him off into the water."

He was pleased with himself.

"Water's no more than four feet deep there," he said. "Wouldn't drown a child. Won't do the fellow any harm. Do him good. Cool him off."

He patted her shoulder.

"Yes . . ." he said. "I sent him off with a flea in his ear."

Chapter Two

To wake up extra early in the morning was always a delight to Lucia Holley. It gave her an exquisite sense of freedom and privacy. She could do whatever she pleased, while all the others were sleeping.

This morning she waked at five o'clock. For a moment she lay thinking with a heavy heart about Bee; but life and energy were strong in her, and she could not lie still. She got up and put on a black wool bathing suit and a white rubber helmet. She took her rope sandals in her hand and went down the stairs barefoot. David made such a fuss about her swimming alone.

"Anyone that's water-wise," he said, severely, "wouldn't do that."

"I *am* water-wise," Lucia said. "I've been swimming since I was a baby."

"Nobody ought to go swimming all alone," he said. "And anyway, the water's too cold the beginning of May. I wish you wouldn't *do* it."

She felt sorry to do anything that might worry David. But he never wakes up before half-past seven or eight, she thought, and by that time I'll be all dried and dressed. He'll never know, and this is such a wonderful time of day.

She unchained the front door and went out, and sitting on the steps, she put on her sandals. It was a gray morning, but fresh and somehow promising, not like the beginning of a rainy day. I'll row out a little way, she thought. And she thought that when she would be swimming in the gray water, under the soft sky, she would think of some new and better way to talk to Bee.

Something else to offer her, she thought. If I don't let the poor child go in to her art school, what *is* she going to do? I'll have to branch out. I'll have to meet some of the people here, on Bee's account. But I'm so poor at that. It's so hard without Tom.

She had married at eighteen, and she had never gone any-where without Tom, never had thought of such a thing. And before her marriage, she lived with her mother and father, a tranquil, happy home life with very little going out. She was by nature friendly and uncritical, but she had very little to say for herself. She had no talent for social life and no desire for it.

And that's wrong, she thought. With a daughter Bee's age, it's my *duty* to do things. Maybe I could get Father to go around with me and call on people . . . Maybe Father and I could join the Yacht Club here.

The boathouse was a queer-looking structure, a long wooden tunnel over a cement basin where the boats were moored, and attached to it, on the landward end, a little two-storied cottage with a porch. Ideal for a chauffeur or a couple, the real-estate agent had said, only Lucia had no chauffeur or couple, only Sibyl, who did not care to live out here.

The wooden wall of the tunnel led to an opening with a ramp. She went down this, into the dimness where the row-boat, the canoe, and the motorboat were moored to iron sta-ples. They had all swung out to the end of their ropes, following the ebb tide, and she began to pull in the rowboat. It came as if reluctant, and as she stepped into it, she saw the body.

It was a man, face down in the motorboat, in a strange and dreadful position, his legs sprawled across the thwart, his head and shoulders raised by something. She could not see his face, but something about him, the shape of his head perhaps, made her almost sure it was Ted Darby. And she was almost sure he was dead.

Almost sure was not good enough. She stepped into the motorboat, and it was Ted Darby, and he was dead. He had fallen on a spare anchor, half upended on the seat, and it had pierced his throat.

Father did that, she thought.

She stood in the gently rocking boat, feet apart for balance, tall and long-legged in her white robe. Of course it means the police, she thought. Then Father will have to know that he did this. They'll find out why Ted came here, and Bee will be dragged into it. And I shan't be able to keep it from Tom. Not possibly. It'll be in the tabloids.

It will be so horrible, she thought. For poor little Bee. For Tom. For David. But worst of all for Father. He'll have to go to court. He'll be blamed. He'll be so shocked, so humiliated.

If I were able to get rid of Ted, she thought, I would do it. If I could think of any way to save us all . . .

I could do it, she thought, if I could get him off the anchor.

Standing there, swaying a little as the boat rocked, she knew that she could get him off. She had the resourcefulness of the mother, the domestic woman, accustomed to emergencies. Again and again she had had to deal with accidents, sudden illnesses, breakdowns. For years she had been the person who was responsible in an emergency. She had enough physical strength for this job. What she lacked was the spirit for it. I *couldn't* touch him, she thought.

That's nonsense, she told herself. I thought I couldn't possibly kill old Tiger with gas. But I did. When that laundress had a fit and we were all alone, in the house, I did something about it. When David fell down the cellar stairs and just lay there with blood all over his eyes . . . No, I can do this.

It was very difficult, for the body had begun to stiffen. It was very dreadful. When she got Ted down in the bottom of the boat, her breathing was like sobbing. She got a tarpaulin out of a locker, and spread it over him; then she cast off and started the engine.

The noise was stupendous, terrifying in this enclosed space, in the early-morning quiet. She had trouble, too. The engine started and stopped and started again. Bang, *bang*, putt-puttputt. *Bang*. They'll hear it at the house and somebody will come, she thought. Even when she was under way, the noise was atrociously loud.

She steered through the narrow inlet through the reeds and out into the open water of the Sound, in a world gray, soft, and quiet. There was no other craft in sight. She had already made up her mind to take Ted to Simm's Island. She had decided upon the best spot. On the side of the small island that faced the mainland there was a row of bleached little summer bungalows, all empty, as far as she knew. But I shan't go near them, she thought.

She and David and Bee had come here for a picnic lunch a week ago. They had been looking then for a nice place. She was looking now for a half-remembered place, so far from nice that no one would be likely to go there. It would be dreadful if a child were to find him, she thought.

Here was the place, a narrow strip of sand, and behind it a stretch of marsh where the tall reeds stirred in the breeze. She stopped the engine, and dropped the anchor. She drew a long breath and set to work.

Ted was very slight, but even at that, it was hard enough to lift him out of the boat. Then she took him under the shoulders and dragged him to the marsh, well in among the tall reeds. He looked grotesque and horrible with his arms and legs sprawled out; she tried to straighten him and could not, and she began to cry. There he lay, staring at the sky.

I can't leave him like this, she thought. There was a big blue bandanna in the pocket of her terry robe. She took it out and dried her eyes with it, and spread it over his face. But the breeze lifted it at once. There were no stones here to anchor it down. She knelt beside him frowning, still crying. Then with her strong sharp teeth she tore two corners of the bandanna into strips, and tied it, catercornered over his face, to two reeds.

It's better than nothing, she thought, and went back to the boat. The engine started easily this time. When she was out in the open water she stopped it again and cleaned the bottom of the boat with an oily rag. There was very little blood. I hope it was quick, she thought. I hope he wasn't there a long time— alone . . .

She tied the robe tight around her waist and turned in the lapels across her chest, for the breeze seemed chilly now. She started the engine, headed for home. It's done, she told herself. I'm going to put it out of my mind. But suddenly she thought of the bandanna. Well, nobody could identify it, she thought. It's just one I bought in the ten-cent store ages ago. There must be thousands and thousands exactly like it. Fingerprints? I don't think they get fingerprints from cloth of any kind. Anyhow I could say I'd left the bandanna on the island the day we had the picnic.

Anyhow, I can't help it now. It's done. And I'm not going to brood about it. I'm not going to think about it at all.

As she approached the boathouse, she felt a faint shock of dismay to see David standing there, thin and slouching, in blue trunks and a khaki windbreaker. But she recovered herself at once. It's just as well to have to start right in, she thought.

"Hello, David," she said, cheerfully.

"Hello," he said unsmiling.

As the boat glided into the tunnel, he moved along to the ramp, and was waiting to help her out.

"I couldn't believe my ears," he said, "when I heard the engine start. I thought someone was stealing the boat and I got down here as quick as I could, and I saw you scooting away."

"I like the early morning," she said.

"That's all right," said David. "But why didn't you take the rowboat, like you always do?"

"Well, I thought I'd like the motorboat for a change."

"Well, I ask you not to do it again," said David. "It's dangerous. You don't know one darn thing about that engine. If it stalled or even the least little thing went wrong, you'd be absolutely helpless."

"I didn't go far," said Lucia.

"Well, I ask you not to do it," said David. "It's darned eccentric, anyhow."

"There's nothing so terrible about being eccentric once in a while," said Lucia.

"Personally," said David, "I shouldn't like any of the fellows I know out here to see you scooting around in a motorboat at half-past five in the morning."

David's like Father, Lucia thought. But he looks like Tom with those furry ginger eyelashes and those nice green eyes. He's only fifteen. Only a child. But in three more years . . . if the war goes on for three more years . . .

Again and again and again that thought would come to her, piercing her heart. She put her arms around his thin shoulders.

"I'm quite sure none of your friends saw me, dear," she said. "But I won't do it again, if it worries you."

"Well, that's good," he said.

"Let's go along to the house and get some breakfast."

"Sibyl won't be down yet."

"I can manage," said Lucia.

She took her arm away from his shoulders and they walked in side by side.

"What's the matter with Bee?" he asked.

"What do you mean, David?"

"You certainly must have noticed it," he said. "Of course most of it's an act. She's always putting on an act. But something's been bothering her lately, all right."

"Doesn't she ever talk to you about things, David? You used to talk everything over together."

"I don't encourage that," said David.

"It does people good to talk over their troubles to——"

"Well, it doesn't do me good to listen to them," he said with unexpected vehemence. "I don't like anything that's sappy and emotional and all, and I don't want to get mixed up in things like that. Not now, or any other time."

He held open the screen door and she went past him into Sibyl's beautiful kitchen. The sun was breaking through the clouds; a shaft lay upon the green and white linoleum floor. It was a lovely thing to be getting breakfast for David.

Chapter Three

"WE COULD wait till tomorrow," said Sibyl. "Only this is the day for the chicken man."

"Then I'll get you a taxi," said Lucia.

"Better if you go, ma'am," said Sibyl, standing by the kitchen table, tall, portly, her dark face impassive.

"You're a much better marketer than I am," said Lucia.

"My business to be so," said Sibyl, quietly. "But the chicken man don't like colored people. Don't hesitate to say so."

"Has he ever said anything to you, Sibyl?"

"Yes, ma'am," said Sibyl.

"We won't deal with him any more," said Lucia.

"He's the only one got any chickens," said Sibyl.

"Then we'll do without chickens for the rest of the summer."

Sibyl smiled a smile, gentle, infinitely affectionate.

"No, ma'am," she said. "If you go, maybe you can get us two nice roasting chickens and I'll cook them Saturday and we'll have a chicken salad Sunday. I'll give you the list, ma'am."

They had been together, day in and day out, for eight years, in complete harmony. Sibyl knew that Lucia was not the wise, thrifty housewife the family believed her to be. Sibyl remembered the things Lucia forgot, found the things that Lucia lost, covered up Lucia's absent-mindedness, advised her, warned her. She had lent Lucia money, to conceal a shockingly careless overdraft, and had herself gone to the police about the chauffeur Lucia could not bring herself to accuse.

She knew Lucia better than any one else did. But Lucia knew curiously little about Sibyl. She did not know Sibyl's age, or where she had been born, what family she had, or what friends. She had no idea where Sibyl went on her afternoons off, or what she did. Simply, she loved and trusted Sibyl without reservation.

"Well, maybe I can speak to the chicken man," she said.

"No, ma'am," said Sibyl. "Can't change this world."

From where she stood, Lucia could see her father at his breakfast in the dining room, the soft collar of his blue shirt revealing his lean old neck. He was wearing the black and white checked jacket he had bought in London years ago, and cherished so fondly, getting it relined and patched up again and again. Rather have a really decent jacket like this even if it was a bit shabby than a cheap flimsy new one, he often said.

He could very well have got himself a new one, not cheap and flimsy, but his daughter never pointed this out to him. He thinks it's more English to be shabby, she thought, and why shouldn't he if he wants?

I'm so glad I was able to get Ted away, she thought. Now no matter what happens, I don't see how Father could even find out what he did last night, or be connected with it in any way. Nobody will ever know.

She went in and kissed the top of his neat white head.

"Father," she said, "I think it would be better not to let Bee know that you saw that man last night."

"I didn't see him," said Mr. Harper.

"But, Father . . . !"

"Too dark," said he, pleased with the joke. "Don't worry, my dear. I shan't tell Beatrice. And I don't think we'll be troubled again by the young gentleman."

Bee was coming down the stairs. She came straight into the kitchen.

"Good morning, Mother," she said. "Good morning, Sibyl. Is my orange juice in the icebox?"

"Yes, Miss Bee."

Bee brought out the bowl that held the full pint of orange and lemon juice combined which was an essential part of her new Vitabelle diet and carried it into the dining room.

"Good morning, Grandpa," she said.

This, obviously, was to be her attitude, polite, cool, aloof; no smiles for her oppressors.

"Going in to your school today?" Harper asked, surprised by her appearance in blue overalls and white shirt.

"I'm not allowed to go any more," Bee answered, very clearly.

"Oh . . . I see!" he said. "Number of pretty scenes around here that you could paint, I should think."

She gave the smile Lucia, watching from the kitchen, hated to see. The child was so lovely, with her soft fair hair, her delicate skin, her fine little features, but she rouged her mouth into a sort of square, and when she smiled this way, with her lips scarcely parted, and her eyes narrowed, she looked almost ugly.

She couldn't really have cared so very much for a man like Ted, Lucia thought. Of course she'll be terribly upset when she hears that he's dead, but she'll get over it. She's so *very* young. Poor Bee . . . I must do something about branching out, finding more friends for her. And there's no reason now why she shouldn't go back to the art school, only that I can't tell her. Can I just say I changed my mind? Or had I better wait until Ted gets into the papers?

She telephoned for a taxi and changed into a costume suitable for the village, a blue and white checked gingham dress, a blue belt, blue sandals, a wide black straw hat. Sibyl had the list ready for her and when the cab came, off she went, with the big green denim market bag.

I'll tell Bee this afternoon that I've changed my mind, she thought. Then she can go in to her school tomorrow. It may be quite a while before Ted gets into the papers, and there's no reason why she should stay home, poor child. Is she going to mind very much, when she finds out? It's so hard to understand how she could possibly have cared, even the least little bit, for a man like that. So cheap and sneering . . .

It was a morning of frustration. The chicken man would sell her only one chicken, and a smallish one at that. There was no margarine, no sugar. She could not get the brand of soap flakes Sibyl particularly wanted. The only potatoes she found were old and soft and sprouting. The only cigarettes were an unheard-of variety.

She could not get the tooth paste her father wanted. She could not get the magazines David had asked for. Bee's shoes, promised for last week by the shoemaker, still stood untouched, on a shelf. She went from one shop to another, the bag growing heavier and heavier. She was hot, flushed and tired, but still with her air of earnest politeness. She stood patiently in line at counters, she engaged in conversation with other housewives, she was zealous with her ration stamps.

When she had got what she could, she had a big paper bag in addition to the market bag. They'd hate me too much in the bus with all this, she thought, and crossed the main street of the village, pulled down by the bag, to the railway station, where three taxis stood.

"Got to wait for the train, lady," the first driver said.

He could put three or even four passengers in together; he was not interested in this single fare.

"If I drive you out to Plattsville," said the second, "I got to come all the way back empty. It don't pay me."

"Well, suppose I pay a little extra . . . ?" Lucia said, hot and tired.

"Well . . ." said the driver, "we're not supposed to do that. I'd have to charge you two dollars and a half."

That was outrageous. For a moment she contemplated trying the third, but he would realize that he was the last resort and he might take advantage of it. He might be worse.

"All right," she said, and got into the cab.

Just at that moment the train came in and her driver waited. A little crowd of people descended; the two other cabs pulled up to drive away, and a man came, leisurely and deliberately, toward Lucia's taxi. He was a stout man, in a gray suit with the jacket open. He walked with a sort of roll, bearing his portly stomach proudly.

"Know where some people named Holley live, son?" he asked the driver.

"Nope," said the driver. "You might ask the ticket office."

"You run along and do the asking, son," said the stout man.

Lucia sat back in a corner, looking at him in unreasoning dismay. His eyes . . . she said to herself. They were very pale eyes, light-lashed, with a curious blankness, as if he were blind. He's a detective, she thought, and he's come about Ted.

"I got a fare," said the driver, "the other cabs'll be coming back."

"You go find out where the Holleys live, son," said the stout man, in the same even, indifferent voice, and it increased Lucia's dismay to see that the far from obliging young driver was prepared to do as he was told. Everyone would do what that man said.

"I'm going out there," she said.

The stout man gave her a glance, a thorough one from head to foot.

"You told me the Maxwell place," cried the driver, shocked and aggrieved.

"I know," Lucia said. "But we've rented it."

The stout man opened the door of the cab and got in. He sat down beside Lucia with his knees apart, taking up a good deal of room.

"Get going, son," he said.

He's one of those horrible detectives that you see in the movies, Lucia thought. He's . . . the word sprang up in her mind. He's merciless, she thought. He'd be merciless to Father.

"Your name Holley?" he asked.

"Yes."

"You got a sister or daughter name of Beatrice?"

"Yes," she answered again.

"She's the one I want to see," he said.

"Well . . . what about?"

"I'll take it up with her," he said.

"I'd rather you didn't," said Lucia. "I'm her mother. I can tell you anything she could tell you."

"She's the one I came out to see," he said. "Beatrice Holley."

"You might as well tell me what you want to see her about. She'll tell me herself, later on."

"Think so?"

"Yes, I know it. I wish you wouldn't talk to her. If you'd please talk to me instead . . . ?"

"It's Beatrice Holley I want," he said.

Something like panic assailed Lucia. He'll tell Bee that Ted's been found, she thought. It must be that. What else could bring him here? He'll ask her questions and questions, and she'll tell him things that'll get in the papers. I can't let her see this man, alone.

"My daughter's a minor," she said. "I'm sorry but I can't let you see her."

He turned his head and gave her another glance, his light lashes flickering up and down. Then he turned away again.

"That won't work," he said.

It was intolerable that Bee should have to endure this.

"I'm going to send for my lawyer," said Lucia.

He did not trouble to answer that; he sat with his double

chin resting on his chest, looking straight before him, thinking his own thoughts. Lucia was of absolutely no interest to him.

They were in sight of the house now. David was strolling across the lawn of coarse grass; when he saw the cab he stopped and waited.

"What's the fare?" said the stout man.

"Dollar," said the driver, and the stout man gave him a dollar, no tip. He opened the door of the cab and got out without a glance at Lucia. He was speaking to David before she got her dollar out of her purse.

"Two-fifty was the rate," said the driver.

She gave him another fifty cents and got out, with her two big bags. The stout man was standing in front of the house.

"If you talk to my daughter, I'm going to be there, too," she said.

He didn't answer her. She stood there with the bags, utterly at a loss, but determined to protect Bee as best she could. The screen door opened and Bee came out. She looked with a frown of surprise at the two standing on the lawn, and ran down the steps.

"You wanted to see me?" she asked.

"You Beatrice Holley?"

"Bee—" Lucia began. "Don't."

"It's just something about the school, Mother," said Bee.

"It isn't!" said Lucia.

"It isn't," said the man. "I told the boy that. Makes it easier. No. I came to ask about my good friend Ted Darby."

"Well . . . Who are you?" Bee asked.

"The name's Nagle."

"Well . . . What do you want to ask?"

"Bee . . . !" said Lucia. "Don't!"

He's not a detective, she thought. He's—I don't know—a crook, a gangster, something horrible.

"Ted came out to see you last night," said Nagle.

"What if he did?" said Bee.

"He never came home again," said Nagle.

The statement was shocking to Lucia and frightening. But Bee was not alarmed.

"You mean he didn't go back to his hotel?" she said. "Then he probably went to visit someone. He has plenty of friends."

"Did he tell you he was going to visit somebody?"

"My daughter didn't see him last night," said Lucia.

"You saw him?"

"No. Nobody saw him."

"You're saying he didn't come here?"

"I don't know whether he came or not. I'm just saying that none of us saw him."

He turned to Bee.

"You called him up," he said. "You asked him to come out here last night. Well?"

"Well?" Bee replied. "I can't see what right you have to come here and ask me questions."

She was not in the least afraid of Nagle. She met his pale eyes steadily.

"Why didn't you see him?" asked Nagle.

"That's my own business," she said. "Come in, Mother, let's——"

"Wait!" said Nagle. "It's not that easy. I want everything you've got about my good friend Ted Darby. Names of any friends he's told you——"

"I'm not going to tell you anything at all," said Bee. "You can wait till he gets back and ask him."

"If you know where he is," said Nagle, "you'd better tell me."

"I'll take the bags in, ma'am," said Sibyl's voice behind Lucia.

She took the bags and walked away, erect and stately.

"I shan't tell you anything at all," said Bee.

"That's just too bad," said Nagle. "That's too bad for Ted."

"What do you mean?" Bee demanded. "Are you threatening him?"

"I ask questions," said Nagle. "I don't answer."

"That goes for me too," said Bee.

She's—tough, Lucia thought astonished. That slender girl in slacks, her light hair down to her shoulders, that child, who had lived all her life at home, protected and cherished, was talking now like a tough girl in a movie, looking like one, too, with her eyes narrowed and her fine mouth scornful.

"Okay! Okay!" said Nagle, and turned away.

Lucia stood looking after him, with dread and dismay in her heart. He'll come back, she thought. This is only the beginning. . . .

Chapter Four

"DEAR TOM," Lucia wrote, "it was so very nice to get an air-mail from you this afternoon, especially a letter telling about the details of your life and your friends and your men. Things like that seem to bring you so much closer, Tom."

Only they didn't, really. I haven't much imagination, she thought, regretfully. I can't imagine Tom being a naval officer. I think of him as he was before he left, over two years ago, and probably he's not like that any more. No, he'll have changed, and I'll be just the same.

She went on with her dull, earnest, loving letter. Thank goodness Tom doesn't expect me to be wonderful, she thought. He knows what I'm like. When Tom had first met her she had been seventeen and still in school, a very earnest student but never excelling in anything, never a leader in anything. She liked everyone and was interested in no one. You're the hardest girl in the world to make love to, Tom had told her once. You're just so blamed friendly.

When she was eighteen they were married. When she was nineteen Bee had been born, and that was that. She had always been faintly disappointed in herself, disappointed in school because she had not been remarkable, disappointed when she married because she had not become the perfect housekeeper, most of all disappointed in herself as a mother. Whenever she visited her children's school she felt singularly inept among the other mothers. Simply not *real*, she thought.

I don't cope with things. That Nagle . . . Bee wasn't at all afraid of him. But I was. I am now. Suppose he tells the police that Ted was coming here . . . ? Well, I'll say he didn't come. But if they start asking Father questions . . . I'm pretty sure he's never heard Ted's name. But he'd say, yes, there was a man, and I sent him away with a flea in his ear.

If Father knew he'd killed Ted, he'd tell the police at once. He's like that. I know just how he'd talk. My dear, I am always prepared to accept the consequences of my acts. The full consequences. And then, of course, Bee would be dragged into it.

And Tom would have to know. Why can't I look after my own daughter?

Lying in bed in the dark, a desperate, almost panic compulsion *to do something* rose in her. But she mastered it at once. Don't be frantic, she told herself. Just one day at a time. Just take things as they come.

She got up and lit a cigarette; when it was finished, she stubbed it out carefully and closed her eyes. I'm going to wake up at five o'clock, she told herself.

So she did, but to a morning of wild wind and rain. I'd love a little swim in this weather, she thought, but I'd worry David too much. No . . . I'll take a little walk out of sight of the house.

The idea was strong in her mind that she must stand guard over the house, that she must protect the inmates. She dressed in an old blue flannel skirt, a black sweater and tennis shoes. She tied a white scarf over her hair and went stealthily down the stairs and out of the house.

And out in the rain and the rough wind, she forgot her fears and distress. She went down the drive to the highway and walked up and down, as if patrolling, her skirt flattened against her long legs, her dark face wet and glowing.

"You look like a gypsy," her father said, benevolently, when she came back to the house.

The morning routine went on. The newspaper came and there was nothing about Ted. Old Mr. Harper went out for his constitutional. David went off in the motorboat to visit some friends he had made; Bee was shut in her own room. And Lucia did the things appointed to be done on Thursday. She stripped all the beds, she made out the laundry list. She tidied and dusted the sitting room and the bathroom she shared with Bee. In a blue cotton pinafore, she had an air of serious efficiency; nobody would know that all this was arranged entirely by Sibyl.

Before lunch, she knocked on Bee's door.

"Come in!" said Bee.

She was sitting at a table by the window, drawing, in a candy-striped play suit, her silky hair pushed back from her forehead.

"Bee," said Lucia. "I've been thinking things over . . . I can't bear for you to stay away from your art school, Bee. Go back tomorrow, dear, and I'll simply trust to your . . ."

"If you think you'll stop me from seeing Ted by saying you 'trust' me," said Bee, "you're mistaken."

"Bee, you don't need to be so hostile. Not to me."

"Mother," said Bee, and was silent for a time. "I know you're terribly fond of me. I know you think you're doing what's best for me. But I don't agree with you about *any*thing."

"Bee, you do!"

"No. I'm not a fool about Ted. I realize he isn't our kind of person. Daddy wouldn't like him any more than you do. But I want to know all kinds of people. I want to live out in the world. I'd just as soon be *dead*, as have a life like you."

"Bee!" said Lucia, startled, even shocked. "I've got all the things that are most worth having in the world."

"I think your life is *awful*," said Bee. "I'd rather——"

"Lunch!" called David from the hall, and Bee rose promptly.

"I'm sorry, Mother," Bee went on with a sort of stern regret. "But I'm not like you. I'm not going to have a life like yours. If you can call it a life. Getting married at eighteen, right from school. Never really seeing anything or doing anything. No adventure, no color. I suppose you like feeling safe. Well, *I* don't want to be safe."

"Come on, Mother!" called David.

He was always a little irritated by the private conversations that Lucia had with his sister. He himself never sought private conversations. He was willing to talk to anyone about anything. When the clergyman had come to call, he had shown a disposition to discuss religion with him which Lucia had had trouble in suppressing.

At the lunch table, he discussed the Pacific campaign with his grandfather while Bee sat silent, with a look of faintly amused boredom. I think he's very intelligent, Lucia said to herself. I like the way men talk.

As they were about to leave the table, Sibyl appeared in the doorway.

"The refrigerator is gone again, ma'am," she said, evenly.

"I don't know what you people *do* to that icebox," said Mr. Harper, frowning.

It was an unbreakable convention that whenever the refrigerator went out of order, nobody but Mr. Harper could turn off the gas properly. He now did this, and it was all he could do. He was not at all handy about the house. Neither was David, who was further disqualified by being candidly indifferent.

"Why worry?" he said. "People didn't use to have mechanical iceboxes, and they got on all right."

"Then they had cakes of ice," said Lucia.

"No," said David, reasonably. "Grandpa's told me, plenty of times, that when he was a boy in England, they *never* had any ice. If they specially needed it, if anyone was sick or anything, they had to send to the fishmonger's."

"Well, that's a different climate," said Lucia.

"The temperature's only sixty-six now," said David. "You couldn't call that so very hot."

He strolled away. Mr. Harper had already gone.

"I'll telephone the company," said Lucia.

"Yes, ma'am," said Sibyl, with the same doubt and heaviness. This recurring trouble with the icebox was a catastrophe they both dreaded. Lucia went to the telephone and she got that girl.

"Holley?" said the girl. "All right. I'll put it down."

"When do you think the man will come?"

"I haven't any idea," said the girl. "He takes all the calls in order. You'll just have to wait for your turn."

"Naturally," said Lucia, coldly. "I simply wanted to know if you could give me any idea . . ."

"He'll come when it's your turn," said the girl. "This company doesn't play any favorites."

"Damn you," said Lucia, but not aloud, and returned to the kitchen. "They won't say when he's coming," she told Sibyl. "I suppose we'd better have the fish tonight . . . ?"

"Better had," said Sibyl. "They won't like fish two nights running, but if the man doesn't come this afternoon . . ."

They both knew he would not come this afternoon.

"Well, as long as he comes before the week end . . ." said Lucia, and was silent for a moment, thinking about it. "I think I'll take a little nap," she said, apologetically. "But call me if anything turns up."

"Yes, ma'am," said Sibyl, with indulgence. She approved of Lucia's taking naps.

But Lucia was longer than usual in falling asleep today. If

the Nagle man comes back, she thought, I don't want Bee to see him alone. I don't want Father to see him at all. Ever. Maybe I ought to stay awake, in case something happens . . .

In the end, drowsiness overwhelmed her. She lay stretched out, long and lean in a shrunken gray flannel dressing gown, her hands clasped over her head.

"Mrs. Holley, ma'am . . . !" Sibyl's voice said, insistently.

"Yes?" said Lucia, sitting up.

Sibyl stood beside her, grave and impassive.

"There's a man here wants to see you," she said.

"What man, Sibyl?"

"Wouldn't give his name," said Sibyl. "Just said he wanted to see you about something personal."

Their eyes met in a long look.

"Sibyl . . . What's he like?"

They were still looking straight at each other, and into Sibyl's amber-flecked dark eyes came a troubled shadow. She was a reticent woman. It was hard for her to find words for her thoughts.

"He don't look like a man you'd know," she said.

It's Nagle, Lucia thought. I knew he'd come back.

"He's on the veranda," Sibyl went on. "I can send him away."

"I'd better see him," said Lucia and got up, standing tall and straight on her narrow bare feet.

"You don't have to, ma'am," said Sibyl. "Told him I didn't know if you were in."

"No. I'd better see him," Lucia repeated. "Tell him I'll be down in a moment, please."

"Let him in?" Sibyl asked, and again their eyes met.

"Yes. Yes, please," said Lucia.

She had to let him into her house, for she dared not keep him out. She stood motionless until she heard the front door close, and then she began to dress quickly and carelessly, in the checked gingham dress that was limp now. He's in, she said to herself. He's in the house.

She went down the stairs and into the sitting room. But the man who stood there was not Nagle.

"Mrs. Holley?" he asked.

He was a big man, broad shouldered and narrow flanked,

very well dressed, in a dark suit, a sober and expensive necktie. He was a handsome man, or could be, or had been. But there was something curiously blurred about him, like a fine drawing partly erased. His strong-boned face looked tired. His dark blue eyes looked somehow dim.

"My name is Donnelly," he said and his voice was muffled.

"Yes?" said Lucia evenly.

Maybe it's nothing, she told herself. Maybe it's just about the insurance. Or selling War Bonds. Or, something just ordinary.

But she could not believe it. He came from some other world, the world of Ted Darby and Nagle, strange and unknown to her as the banks of Lethe.

"I'd like a few words with you," he said, and jerked his dark head toward the open door behind her.

"Well . . . what about?" she asked, with an attempt at defiance.

He moved light on his feet, he reached past her and closed the door.

"You'll be wanting these letters," he said.

"What letters?"

They were standing close to each other, facing each other; she looked up at him, still attempting that defiance, and he looked at her absently.

"The letters your daughter wrote to Ted Darby," he said. "The price is five thousand dollars. Cash."

Chapter Five

SHE WAS aware that she was not really thinking at all. Not yet.

"Well . . . Sit down, please," she said.

He waited until she was seated, and then he drew up a chair, facing her, and sat down, carefully hitching up his trousers. He was remarkably neat, his dark hair neat on his narrow skull, his big hands well kept, his shoes gleaming. He was so strangely, so dreadfully indifferent, simply waiting. A blackmailer, she thought. This is blackmail.

"My daughter . . ." she said. "There's nothing in her letters . . ."

"Would you like to see one?" he asked.

He took a handsome pigskin wallet out of an inside pocket, drew out a sheaf of folded papers, and looked through them. He selected one and handed it to her.

TED:

I just wasn't alive until I met you. But you came like a fresh wind blowing through a stuffy room. I don't know, Ted, if I can make up my mind to do what you asked yesterday. But just the fact that you *did* ask, and that you thought I had the courage to take such a chance makes me feel proud.

Ted, I'm thinking about it. I'm not sentimental; you know that. But just the same it is hard to break entirely with the past, and go against everyone and everything you were taught.

See you Friday, Ted, and maybe by that time I'll have made up my mind.

BEATRICE

The clear beautiful printing Bee used made the words so stark . . .

"That doesn't mean anything," said Lucia. "She's only a child. That doesn't mean—anything."

"It looks like something," he said, and held out his hand for the letter.

"No!" she said, putting it behind her. "I shan't give it to you. I—the police will make you give me those letters."

He didn't bother to answer that. He sat leaning forward a little, holding the handsome wallet open on his knee. Simply waiting.

"I'm going to put this in my lawyer's hands," Lucia said. And she had a vision of Albert Hendry, Tom's lawyer, ineffably distinguished, listening to the story of Bee's disastrous folly.

"Why do you not pay the money and forget all about it?" asked Donnelly. "There's nothing else you can do at all."

"No!" said Lucia. "I wouldn't pay blackmail. Never!"

"There's someone else will," he said.

"Who?"

"Your father, maybe."

"No!" she cried. "No! You can't . . . No!"

She checked herself. She tried to breathe evenly. She tried to think.

"How did *you* get hold of these letters?" she asked.

"Darby wanted to borrow a bit," said Donnelly, "and he left me the letters till he'd pay me back."

"Do you mean that *he*——?"

"Oh, he had it in mind to make the girl pay for them," said Donnelly.

His tone was not at all threatening. There was no hint of violence in him. But his matter-of-fact acceptance of this incredible treachery, this criminal demand, seemed to her infinitely more alarming than violence and infinitely more difficult to meet. The word "blackmail" disturbed him not at all.

"Darby's run out on me now," he said, as if explaining a business affair. "He went off without a word. And I cannot afford to lose what I lent him."

He doesn't know what happened to Ted, she thought. When he finds out, will that change things? Make this better? Or worse? If I could only, *only* think this out.

The rain rattled against the window, the room seemed close, filled with a gray light. Here she sat with this man, this criminal, so well dressed, so unclamorous . . .

"I'll have to have time to think this over," she said coldly.

"I'm going to Montreal," he said, again with that reasonable air of explaining matters to her. "I'll need the money before I go."

"I haven't got five thousand dollars," she said.

"You'll think of a way to lay hands on it," he said.

"No . . . No. When you get that, you'll ask for more."

"I would not," he said, simply.

"No! There's nothing in those letters. Nothing at all wrong."

"They would look wrong," he said.

"Don't you realize," she began, when the door opened and old Mr. Harper entered.

"Oh," he said, "sorry, m'dear. I didn't know . . . Getting near teatime, I thought . . ."

Donnelly had risen; he stood there, like any polite stranger, waiting to be introduced.

"Father . . ." she said, "this is Mr. Donnelly."

"How d'you do, sir?" said Mr. Harper.

But he was not satisfied with this. He wanted, naturally, to know who Mr. Donnelly was and why he was here.

"From Tom's office," she said, in her desperation.

"Ha! From Tom's office," said Mr. Harper, and held out his hand. "Glad to see you, sir. Sit down! Sit down!"

No! No! No! Lucia cried to herself.

"Mr. Donnelly's just leaving, Father," she said.

"You can wait for a cup of tea, eh, Donnelly? Or a highball?"

"Thank you, sir," said Donnelly, and sat down again.

"How is everything in the office?" asked Mr. Harper.

"I couldn't tell you," Donnelly answered, "for I left there three years ago. Government work."

"I see!" said Mr. Harper. "Lucia, m'dear, d'you think you could ask Sibyl to bring along the tea? Or if you'd prefer a whisky and soda, Donnelly?"

"Tea, if you please," said Donnelly.

There were no bells in the house to summon Sibyl. Lucia rose and went out to the kitchen. As she pushed open the swing door, she saw Sibyl standing at a table under the window, cutting raw carrots into little flowers, her dark face in profile was proud and melancholy. She turned at the sound of Lucia's step.

"Sibyl . . ." Lucia said, and could get no further. She was crushed and overwhelmed by this catastrophe.

"What's wrong, ma'am?" asked Sibyl with compassion in her eyes.

"He's staying . . ." Lucia answered.

"That man?"

"Yes. Father's asked him to tea."

Sibyl, too, was silent for a moment.

"We must just do the best we can," said Sibyl. "Don't fret, ma'am."

"But he's———"

"Yes, ma'am," said Sibyl. "I know."

She turned and put the carrots into a bowl of cold water.

"You go back now, ma'am. I'll bring in the tea. Don't fret, ma'am. Sometimes there's good luck in this life. No harm to hope for it."

That was language Lucia could understand. Her father and her husband never spoke like that. In the blackest days of the war, old Mr. Harper had never had the slightest doubt of England's victory; he considered doubt to be a form of treason. And Tom, when he went away, had had the same resolute optimism.

"I'll come through all right," he had said, looking at her pale, averted face. "It's half the battle, Lucia," he had said, "to feel hopeful. Sure that you're lucky."

She did not believe that. She believed that a shell or a bullet could strike a brave and hopeful man as readily as a miserable one. She did not believe that the guilty were always punished; or the innocent always spared. She believed, like Sibyl, that life was incalculable, and that the only shield against injustice was courage.

She had courage.

"All right, Sibyl," she said and turned away.

Old Mr. Harper was having a good time. He was talking about the First World War to Donnelly who, it seemed, had been in it. In France and Belgium he had seen some of the English regiments whose names were glorious and almost sacred to the old man. Donnelly was far from eloquent, but his few words entirely satisfied Mr. Harper.

"Have you ever been in England, Donnelly?"

"I was in and out of Liverpool for nearly a year, sir."

"Oh, Liverpool . . ." said Mr. Harper, politely dismissing that city. "Never been there myself. But London . . . Ever been in London, Donnelly?"

"I have, sir. It is a fine city."

"I imagine it very changed now, Donnelly."

"It has a right to be," said Donnelly, gravely.

Lucia sat on the sofa with the tea table drawn up before her. She poured tea; when her father remembered to include her in the conversation, she responded quickly, with a bright smile. If I could only go out and take a walk, she thought, I'd be able to think. I've got to think. I've got to find a way out of this. I've got to stop being so stupid and dazed.

And then, to complete the nightmare, Bee came downstairs.

"Oh . . . !" she said from the doorway, as if surprised to see a stranger here.

But Lucia noticed that she was much more carefully got up than was natural for an ordinary afternoon at home. She was wearing a lemon-colored organdy blouse and a black skirt; she had blue mascara on her lashes and fresh make-up on her mouth.

Go away! Lucia cried in her heart. Don't you come in here . . .

Mr. Harper waited, but his daughter was drinking tea, her eyes lowered.

"This is Mr. Donnelly, Beatrice," he said. "From your father's office. My granddaughter, Donnelly."

Donnelly rose.

"Oh . . . How do you do?" said Bee, and he gave a slight bow.

She sat down on the sofa beside her mother, and lit a cigarette.

"No tea, thank you, Mother. Is there any grape juice?"

"It's too many points," said Lucia.

"Then could I have some iced tea, Mother?"

"I'm sorry, but there's no ice. The refrigerator's out of order."

"What a life!" said Bee laughing.

She wanted to get the attention of this stranger. It would have irritated David, but to Lucia it was heartbreaking. She saw Donnelly glance at her lovely child, an unreadable glance, and then turn to listen to old Mr. Harper, and a fierce, desperate rebellion rose in her.

I let him get in, she thought. There he is, with Bee's letters in his pocket. Trying to blackmail me. I'll get those letters somehow. I'll do something.

Donnelly rose.

"I'll have to be going," he said, "but I'll be in the neighborhood for a while."

"Oh, stopping out here?"

"It is business," said Donnelly. "Mrs. Holley, could I stop by in my car tomorrow around eleven, maybe, and drive you to see the old house we were speaking about?"

His effrontery was beyond belief. Here, under her own roof, in the presence of her father and her daughter, he dared propose this rendezvous. But she had let him get in, and her home was no longer safe.

All right! she thought. All right! She raised her dark eyes and looked straight at him, a hot color in her cheeks, a defiance in her heart.

"Thanks. That would be very nice," she said.

I'll settle with you, all right, she thought. I'll think of something. Just wait and see.

Chapter Six

ALL RIGHT! All right! she thought. Let him take the letters to Father, and see what happens. Just let him try to blackmail Father.

It will be hard for Bee. But Father'll know that there's really nothing to those letters. No matter how they sound. She went to sleep with that in her mind, defiant and resolute.

But when she waked in the early morning, all that was gone. I simply can't trust Father, she thought. He's so upright. He'd probably want to go to the police. We must see this through, my dear. And then the police would connect Bee with Ted, and when they found Ted . . .

No. I'll put Donnelly off. I'll pretend I'm getting the money for him. That'll give me a little more time.

And what was she going to do with this time? Think of something. Do something.

It was a soft, mild morning of pale sunshine. With a regretful thought for David, she put on her bathing suit and went quietly out of the house, and down to the boathouse. She took the rowboat this time; she went out through the tunnel at the narrow inlet through the reeds into the open water. Oh, this is the best thing! she thought and laying the oars in the bottom of the boat, she made a shallow dive into the water.

"Hey!" she cried aloud, because it was so cold. But, in a moment, as she swam, the water no longer felt cold, only exquisitely refreshing. There were gulls flying overhead, and she turned on her back and floated, to watch them, one swooped so low that she could see its fierce face.

She lay floating in the sparkling water, looking with half-closed eyes at the gulls and the little clouds in the soft blue sky. She turned over and swam around the boat twice, happy in the smooth rhythm of her muscles. Just for practice she swam under the boat, in cold shadow for a moment, and came up with the sun again.

A motorboat had started somewhere. David, coming after me? she thought and climbed hastily into the rowboat. But the motorboat was now behind her. It was coming from the island.

As she took up the oars she saw it. There was a policeman in uniform behind the wheel and in the stern sat another police-man, and a young man in a gray suit, a big young man with big, outstanding ears and a big bony nose. Motionless, she sat watching them, and the young man turned his head, looking at her; as they passed, she met his eyes, dark, gentle and a little sad.

Then they were gone. The rowboat rocked violently in the swell. They'd found Ted, she thought. *Now* what's going to happen?

She began to row homeward. All right. All right. I'll take things as they come. One at a time. I'm not going to worry. I'm not going to borrow trouble. I'll manage, all right. She took off her rubber cap and let her dark hair blow loose in the wind. She rowed slowly, and let the sun dry her woolen suit.

And if the police come asking questions about Ted, I'll say he never came near us. Father doesn't know who it was he spoke to. I'd better tell him something this morning.

She got back to her room, unheard by David. She dressed and sat down by the open window. Now, if anybody comes, I'm ready, she thought. I don't care what I say. I don't care how many lies I tell.

She heard Sibyl go creaking down the stairs and a few mo-ments later she followed.

"Certainly hope that laundry man comes today," said Sibyl. "I don't know how Mr. Harper's going to hold out, with only one clean shirt to last him a whole week."

It was like gears meshing. This was the day beginning. This was life.

"I'd better go into New York and try again to get him some more shirts," she said. "And David, too. But they're so scarce and so expensive."

"We could manage," said Sibyl, "if the laundry man'll do what he said he'd do. But it's nearly two weeks since he came. Doesn't bring back what he's got. Doesn't pick up what we got ready for him."

"If he doesn't come today, I suppose I'd better telephone . . . ?" said Lucia.

"Better had, ma'am," said Sibyl.

She drank a cup of coffee in the kitchen, waiting, very restless, for old Mr. Harper to come down. She was waiting for him in the hall.

"Father," she said, "you know that man who came to the boathouse night before last . . . ? I thought I'd better tell you something about him."

"No need to, m'dear. Not unless he comes again, and I don't think that's likely. No, I don't think he'll be back in a hurry. I sent him——"

"Yes, I know you did, Father. His name is Stanley Schmidt."

"Schmidt, eh! German name."

"He is a German. He's a very queer, shady sort of man, Father, and I shouldn't like it ever to get known that Bee had had anything to do with him."

"What d'you mean, Lucia? How is he—shady?"

"I think he's a Nazi agent," said Lucia, readily.

"What! What! Then he ought to be reported."

"I did. I sent an anonymous letter to the F.B.I.," said Lucia. "Only you can see that we can't possibly let Bee get involved in this."

"No. No, of course not. Have you told her your opinion of the fellow, Lucia?"

"I thought it was better not to," said Lucia in a special tone, quiet, very significant.

It was a tone she had used on Tom, too. It implied that she and she alone could understand the mystery of a young girl's heart. It had always made Tom uneasy and it had the same effect now upon old Mr. Harper.

"Well . . . I dare say you know best," he said.

David came down now, followed a few minutes later by his sister. They all sat at the table together; a steady breeze blew in at the open windows; the sun made the glass and silver twinkle. Lucia glanced at her father's silvery hair, Bee's soft fair mane, David's sandy hair, rough on his stubborn skull. Let them alone! she cried in her heart. Let them *alone*!

"Here comes the postman!" said David, pushing back his chair. "Let's see if there's anything from Dad."

He went out, letting the swing door bang behind him, and came back with the mail.

"Four," he announced. "Two for you, Mother, and one for

Bee, and one for me. V-mails. Newspaper for Grandpa and a letter for Sibyl, and some bills and stuff."

He and Bee opened their letters at once, but Lucia kept hers to read when she was alone. Old Mr. Harper opened his New York paper.

"Fair and warmer," he read. "High time, too. Most unseasonable weather we've been having. Let's see now . . . Things look very promising in Europe. Here's Monty . . . A good man . . . What's this? Ha! Body of Slain Art Dealer found on Simm's Island."

"Go on!" said David, looking up.

"'The Horton County police report the discovery yesterday in an isolated swamp on Simm's Island of the body of Ted Darby, 34, whose name——'"

"Give it to me!" cried Bee.

"What?" said Mr. Harper.

"Give it to me!" she cried again.

"I want to read it," he began, but she snatched it out of his hand, and ran out of the room and up the stairs.

"What's the matter with her?" asked Mr. Harper.

"Probably someone she's heard of," said David. "She knows a lot of those arty people."

"She needn't have snatched the paper out of my hands," said Mr. Harper.

"She'll have a fine time now," said David. "She'll call up all the girls she knows. My *dear*! Have you *heard* about What's-his-name?"

"Nevertheless," said Mr. Harper, "she could have waited a few moments."

"Oh, you know how girls are with a nice juicy bit of gossip," said David, man to man.

Does he know anything? Lucia thought. Or is he just being loyal to Bee?

She did not permit herself to show any impatience or haste, but as soon as breakfast was finished, she went upstairs and knocked on Bee's door.

"It's me, Bee. Let me in, dear."

The key turned in the lock and Bee opened the door.

"Well, you win," she said, with that square, scornful smile.

Lucia went in, closing the door after her.

"I don't want to 'win,'" she said. "It's just——"

"You have won, though," said Bee. "I'm finished."

"Bee, you're *not*! Anyone can make a mistake."

"Not quite such a big mistake. I suppose what they've got in the paper is true . . . !"

"I haven't seen it yet."

"He was arrested, just before the war. He had some sort of little art gallery, where he sold obscene pictures. The police locked up the gallery but somehow he got into it before the trial, and daubed all over the pictures. Amusing, isn't it? What's more, he's already been divorced once, and his first wife accused him of swindling her out of all her money. I suppose you knew all this."

"No, I didn't, Bee. I didn't know anything about him."

"Then how did you know he was so—awful?"

"But when I saw him, Bee, I knew."

"How?"

"Well, I did . . ." said Lucia.

"But *how*? I saw a lot of Ted, and I'd never have thought he was—like that. I mean, he was so gay, and he seemed to be so careless. Not like anyone who'd plot things . . . Mother, I'd like to know how *you*—caught on to him when *I* didn't?"

"But, Bee, I'm so much older——"

"But you've never been anywhere. You've never seen anything of life."

"That's rather silly, Bee. I'm married and I have two children."

"That's nothing," said Bee. "You told me how you met Daddy when you were still in school. I don't suppose you ever even *thought* of another man. You got engaged at seventeen."

"You're only seventeen yourself," said Lucia.

"It's a different era. Girls are different. They're not brought up in that sheltered way." She paused. "I want to get away," she said.

"What d'you mean, Bee?"

"I couldn't *stand* staying here!" Bee cried. "I don't want to see anybody I know. I'm never going back to that art school."

"Bee, you didn't tell anyone about Ted, did you?"

"Oh, not by name. But everyone knew I had a beau . . . I used to mention places we'd been—things like that. God! If anyone ever finds out that I fell for someone like Ted, I'll—I don't know. I'd rather be *dead*."

"Don't say that, Bee."

"That happens to be exactly how I feel. God!"

"Bee, don't swear, dear."

"Oh, what does it matter? When I think that I let him kiss me—*lots* of times . . . I tell you I'd rather be *dead*, than have people know that."

Her blue eyes looked dark, in her face that was white as paper. She was stung to desperation by this pain, this shame.

"I want to get *away*!" she said.

"Bee," said Lucia. "Bee, darling, the only way to stand things is to face them, take the consequences . . ."

"You're talking like *Grandpa*!"

I feel like him, thought Lucia.

"I suppose you've told Grandpa about Ted?"

"I haven't told anyone. I never intend to. You ought to know that, Bee."

"Well, I don't! I don't know *what* your ideas might be. You might think it was your 'duty' to tell Grandpa and Daddy. To teach me a lesson, or something."

"If you can think that . . ." said Lucia.

"I know you always do what you think is *best* for me," said Bee. "But you don't understand me."

Lucia said nothing.

"Will you help me to get away?" Bee demanded.

"Yes," said Lucia. "Let me see the paper, will you, Bee?"

"You'll help me to get away—at once?"

"Yes. We'll talk it over later. I'd like to see the paper, Bee."

She took it into her own room, and sat down on the edge of the unmade bed. The details of Ted Darby's past did not interest her. She was looking for something else.

The body was discovered yesterday afternoon by Henry Peters, 42, electrician, of Rockview, Conn. While walking along the shore, Mr. Peters was led, by the insistent barking of his dog, to enter the marsh . . .

Lieutenant Levy, of the Horton County police, stated the death had been caused by a wound in the throat with some pointed instrument, from twenty-four to thirty-six

hours previous to the discovery. The police are following
several clues.

What clues? Lucia thought. If they trace it back to me, back
to Father, then nothing could save Bee. And those letters . . . ?
Those letters! If I could somehow raise five thousand dollars
. . . But there'd be nothing to stop him from asking for more,
later on. He could hold back some of the letters. I wouldn't
know.

She left the paper on the bed and went over to the window.
Maybe that was Lieutenant Levy I saw this morning in the
launch, she thought. He looked rather nice. Suppose I go to
him and tell him the whole thing? After all, none of us has
done anything criminal. It was probably illegal to take Ted
away like that, but I wasn't covering up a crime, just an accident. It would be dreadfully hard on Father, but he can take it.

Only not Bee. She had a vision of Bee, standing up in a
court, looking so tough and scornful. But, at heart, so desperate and wretched. Miss Holley, you had asked this man to meet
you in the boathouse? You had visited this man in his hotel?

No! Lucia said to herself. I don't want Bee to face things,
and take the consequence of things. I'm going to get her
away somewhere. Angela, in Montreal? Unless you have to
have papers to go to Canada in wartime . . . Well, then,
there's Gracie's camp in Maine. I could telephone Gracie,
right now.

Only she couldn't. Her father might hear her telephoning, or
David might. No privacy was possible for her. It never had been,
she thought, wondering. All my life, people have known everything I did, everywhere I went. I don't mean that anyone's ever
been snooping or suspicious, it's just that somehow I've always
lived in such a sort of public way, right out in the open.

I'll go into the village and telephone from the drugstore,
she thought. I'll——

Sibyl was coming up the stairs, creaking, sighing a little.
Reluctant to speak to anyone, Lucia hurried to the bathroom,
to hide in there, but the door was locked.

"Just a moment!" said Bee, in a loud, choked voice.

Lucia hurried out into the hall.

"I think I'll do a little weeding," she said to Sibyl.

"Yes, ma'am," said Sibyl.

Gardening had no appeal for Lucia. She did it because it was a duty to have a victory garden. She put on a big burnt-straw hat and her heavy gloves. She took up the basket with shears and trowel, and went out of the back door to the patch the local gardener had dug and planted for her.

She was not at all sure which sprouting things were weeds. It's queer, she thought. Father and Bee and David all take it for granted I know what I'm doing. Only Sibyl knows better. There was another implement in the basket, a stubby little rakelike tool with curved prongs. She did not know the name of it, or its purpose, but it was her favorite. You couldn't do much harm with this, she thought, kneeling in the hot sun and scratching gently at the earth.

Mr. Donnelly can stop at the drugstore, she thought. I'll pop in and telephone to Gracie and arrange for Bee to go there at once. I'll tell Father and David that Gracie suddenly needed another counselor. Sibyl can do up a couple of wash dresses for Bee, and she can take my little gray coat for the train. We can send the other things after her. I've got enough cash.

"Mother . . ." said David.

She looked up at him and saw him frowning.

"There's a man who calls himself Donnelly," he said. "Says he's come to take you out for a drive."

"Well, yes," said Lucia, rising.

"You mean you're going out for a drive *alone* with him?"

"Why not?" said Lucia. "He was here to tea yesterday."

"So I heard," said David. "Well, suit yourself. But I think it's a mistake."

There was no time to argue with David now. Lucia ran upstairs to wash and change her dress. A hat, she thought; it looks better, and she put on the new hat Bee had persuaded her to buy in New York, a sort of sailor with an edging of white eyelet embroidery on the brim. She put on white gloves, too, glancing in the mirror. It seemed to her that she looked altogether correct and dignified.

"What time for lunch, ma'am?" Sibyl asked as she reached the lower hall.

"Oh . . . one o'clock as usual, Sibyl," Lucia answered. "I shan't be gone long."

I'm just going to take a little drive with a blackmailer, she thought. It's—hard to believe.

Donnelly was standing in the driveway, with one foot on the running board of a superb roadster. He was wearing a dark gray flannel jacket and slacks of a lighter gray. He looked handsome, aloof, and distinguished.

"Good morning!" Lucia said.

"Good morning," he answered, not smiling, and helped her into the car.

He drove off, down to the highway, with nonchalant skill.

"Would you mind stopping at the drugstore?" she asked. "We can't use our car until we get the next coupons; and things pile up so."

"Certainly. If you'll call the turns . . . ?"

"Next turn right," she said, "and then straight ahead."

Isn't he even nervous? she thought. Doing a thing like this—a crime that could send him to prison for years? Isn't he the least bit ashamed? When they reached the village, she caught a glimpse of them in the plate-glass window of the furniture store, and it was astonishing. The big, well-dressed, well-groomed man, and beside him a lady with gloves and a stylish hat. Nobody would *believe* it, she thought.

"There's the drugstore, on the corner," she said. "I'll only be a minute."

She was mistaken. It took a long time to get the camp in Maine, and it took still longer to get Gracie Matthews, the proprietor.

"I *think* Miss Matthews is out on the lake," said the polished, anxious voice that answered the telephone. "I'll send after her."

It was hot in the booth and there was a very unpleasant smell. Lucia's hands grew damp, sweat came out on her forehead and her upper lip. Oh hurry up! Hurry up! she cried in her heart. I don't want to irritate him by making him wait so long.

Gracie, when at last she came, was very trying.

"Certainly, Lucia. I'd love to have the child. But not today. We couldn't meet the train. The station wagon's laid up. Say Monday."

"I'd like—she'd like to come today, Gracie."

"But what's the hurry, Lucia?"

"It just came into her head . . ."

"Well, tell her it'll be just as nice on Monday."

"Can't you arrange for tomorrow, Gracie?"

"Well, I could!" said Gracie. "But why? I'll have to arrange with the Camp Weelikeus people to pick her up at the station, and I don't like to do that if I can help it. We'll have our own station wagon on Monday, and I don't see *why* she can't wait till Monday. It's Friday already."

"You know how it is when you're young."

"I do not!" said Gracie, with her usual vigor. "When I was young, I didn't *expect* people to cater to my whims."

"Bee hasn't been too well. I don't think this climate——"

"If there's anything wrong with the child, don't send her here, Lucia. I've got thirty-eight girls and no trained nurse. I'm short two counselors."

"Bee would love to be a counselor, Gracie."

"She wouldn't do at all!" said Gracie. "She doesn't know anything about handling people. Too self-centered."

"She's not," said Lucia, mechanically. "Well, if you won't let her come tomorrow——"

"All right!" said Gracie. "Let her come. But it's only for *your* sake, Lucia. Personally, *I* wouldn't give in to an adolescent whim."

They spoke a little, about trains, about equipment.

"Two blankets," said Gracie. "A pillow. And—are you writing this down, Lucia?"

"Yes," said Lucia, lying without a qualm.

It was a long list.

"And if she has any hobbies, stamp album, scrapbook, knitting, water colors; anything like that, tell her to bring them along."

"I will, Gracie. I do appreciate this."

"I think you're very foolish," said Gracie, "to give in to your family the way you do. You can take my word for it, Lucia, that they'd think twice as much of you if you'd stand up to them."

"Maybe you're right," said Lucia. "But thanks ever so much, Gracie. I'll write."

She hung up the telephone and opened the door of the booth. I've been ages . . . she thought. And I didn't want to irritate him. He did not seem irritated. He got out politely and helped her into the car. He set off again through the village and along a tree-shaded road unfamiliar to her.

"Have you the money ready?" he asked.

"I couldn't," she said. "I couldn't get into town to the bank without everyone asking questions. I just want a little more time."

He drove on in silence for a way.

"Things are changed," he said, "with Darby dead."

"Yes," she said. "Yes, I suppose so."

"That makes it worse for the girl," he said.

"Not much," said Lucia, evenly. "It couldn't be."

"It will be worse," he said, "with all that will come out at the trial."

"What trial?"

"They will try the man who killed Darby," said Donnelly. "It was a good job he did, but they will try him."

"If they catch him."

"There's no great mystery in it, at all," said Donnelly. "There's a dozen people know the man."

Oh, no! Lucia thought. They can't. They *mustn't* arrest the wrong man.

"They could be mistaken," she said.

"You mean there are others would be glad to see him out of the way?" he asked, and for the first time she saw him smile, a bleak and fleeting smile.

"Or it could have been an accident," she said.

He turned the car up a side road and slowed down.

"There's a roadhouse along here," he said. "It is a good one. Respectable. Would you have lunch with me there?"

"Oh, thank you," she said, startled. "But I've got to be home to lunch. I really ought to be getting home now."

"Any way you like it," he said, and backed the car down to the road. "Will you have the money tomorrow?" he asked.

"Monday," she said. "I can't do anything until Monday."

"I wouldn't be bothering you so," he said. "Only there's someone else in it."

"Someone else . . . ?"

"My partner," he said. "If it was me alone, I would drop the thing altogether. I would let you alone."

It's the oldest trick in the world, Lucia told herself, pretending to have a partner to blame things on.

"If I don't get the money," Donnelly went on, "he'll be out again after it."

"Again?" she asked. "You mean it's Nagle—Mr. Nagle?"

"You're quick," he said, glancing at her sidelong, and the blueness of his eyes surprised her.

"He's a horrible man," she said.

"Do you think so, now?" he asked. "He's been a good friend to me. It was him gave me my start when I first came over here."

"Did you come from the other side?"

"From Ireland," he said. "I had a great idea of this country, from all I'd heard. I ran away from home when I was fifteen, and I shipped as a cabin boy, the way I'd get here. But it took me near three years. I got here, right enough, on the first voyage, but the mate would not let me go ashore. He'd seen it in my eyes, maybe, that I was intending to jump ship. So there I was, standing on the deck, looking at the Statue of Liberty."

He fell silent, with the shadow of a smile on his face.

"Well, how did you get here?" Lucia asked.

"It would be tejus for you to hear," he said, modestly.

"I'd like to hear," she said.

That was true. She wanted to know what manner of man this was, so that she might deal with him better.

"Back we went, to Liverpool," he said. "I was down on the docks one day, looking for a ship would take me back here, when a stranger comes up, very civil. We talk for a while and then he says, 'Come and have a drink.' I was sixteen then, but I looked older. I never had had a drink and to tell you the truth, I was afraid of it, from all I'd heard. But I went along with him, to see what would come of it. The next I knew I was in a ship bound for Singapore. To China we went, to Japan. When we got back to Liverpool, my head was full of the wonders I'd seen, and I wanted more. I got another ship sailing east, Egypt, India . . ."

He was silent again for a time.

"It is a queer thing," he said. "When I'd the money to go traveling in style, I went back to those places. But they were not the same. Well . . . Maybe it was youth that was missing."

"But how did you get to New York?"

"There's no story to that," he said. "I saved my pay and bought a ticket."

And how did you get to be a blackmailer? she thought. He must have been an adventurous and romantic boy, and how had he come to this?

"What did you do when you got here?" she asked.

"It's a thing you wouldn't believe," he said. "I knew I'd a cousin in Brooklyn. That's all I knew; no address, nothing at all but his name. I thought I could look him up, and off I went to Brooklyn, thinking it would be a small town. You wouldn't believe it . . . I walked up and down the streets, asking here and there: Did you ever hear of a Mr. Mulligan from County Clare? After a while I asked a policeman. There's a club near by, he says, for the men of County Clare. Go there, he says, and maybe you'll learn something. Well, my cousin was well known there. Someone took me out to the saloon he had, and my troubles were over, the first day I set foot in the country."

"Did you go to work for your cousin?" Lucia asked.

"No . . ." he said. "That wasn't quite the way of it. Y'see, he made book on the side——"

"What's that?"

"He took bets on the horse races," Donnelly explained. "He took me out to Belmont Park with him and I met a lot of his friends, and they'd put me on to one thing or another. Then I got in with the ward boss. I got in with everyone."

"But didn't you have a job? A regular job?"

"I did not," he said, with a certain pride. "I've never had a job in my life, since the three voyages I made."

"But didn't you ever want a regular job with a salary?"

"I did not," he said. "That's not in my nature."

And what is your nature? she thought. She could not understand him at all. She could not even imagine what his life had been, or what sort of world he lived in. He doesn't seem like a really *bad* man, she thought. Could I possibly talk him out of this?

But her own house was in sight now. There was no more time.

"I'll ask my partner will he wait till Monday," said Donnelly, "but I don't know . . . Are you sure you'll have it Monday?"

"Yes," said Lucia.

By Monday Bee would be gone. And I'll think of something . . . she told herself. Some way out of this.

When they turned into the drive, there was a high van drawn up before the house. Eagle Laundry. The driver was standing beside it, and Sibyl stood on the steps above him.

"Says he's only coming once a month," she said.

"A *month*!" cried Lucia. "But we can't possibly manage——"

"Best we can do," said the driver, a lean, dark young man in a visored cap. "Haven't got the gas, haven't got the tires, haven't got the men to make a pickup any oftener."

"I'll do it *myself*," said Sibyl, with a sort of passion, "before I wait a *month*."

"Okay!" said the driver and got back into his van.

He backed and turned and drove off. Donnelly got out and helped Lucia to descend.

"I'll get in touch with you," he said, standing hat in hand.

She was surprised to see him turn to Sibyl with a smile and a gesture like a salute.

Chapter Seven

"WHAT'S THE *idea*?" Bee demanded. "It's not *like* you, Mother, to go running around with that man."

"I'm not running around," said Lucia. "He wanted to show me an old house. Historic. We'd better make a list, Bee, of what you'll need. Aunt Gracie said blankets and a pillow."

"I can't carry all that," said Bee. "And there aren't any porters any more. Anyhow, Gracie's sure to have some spares, she's so damned efficient."

"Bee, don't swear. You know how Daddy hates it. And Aunt Gracie."

"She's not an aunt, thank God."

"She loves you and David to call her 'Aunt.'"

"We haven't, for years. Personally, I'm not crazy about her at all. I wouldn't go near her gruesome camp, if I didn't have to get away from here."

Lucia was sitting on the bed in Bee's room, and Bee stood before her, barefoot, in an ivory satin slip, so lovely, and so remote. How much did she care for Ted Darby? Lucia thought. How much does all this mean to her? I don't know. She's very nervous. She didn't eat anything for lunch. But is she sad about it?

I *ought* to know. I ought to be able to talk to my own child.

"David took me over to the Yacht Club this morning," Bee began.

"But how could he? We don't belong to it."

"He knows people there. He's rather good at making friends. There was rather a nice crowd there, not all kids, either. I'd have had a nice time there, only I kept thinking all the time. Suppose any of them ever heard about Ted and me. It makes me *hate* him."

"Bee! He's dead."

"I hate him!" said Bee. "I'll never forgive him for the harm he's done me."

"Bee, what harm, darling?"

"He's made it so I can never trust a man again."

"He hasn't, Bee. Just think of your father and Grandpa and David."

627

"You don't realize," said Bee, "how rare they are. You don't realize how lucky you've been. Your life may have been stodgy, but at least you've never been deceived and humiliated. What's that Donnelly man like?"

"Oh, he's very pleasant," said Lucia. "Now let's get out your list, Bee."

"He's good-looking," said Bee. "But *I* think he's a wolf."

"Well, it doesn't matter," said Lucia. "You'll take your flannel dressing gown, of course."

"The thing is, *you* wouldn't *know* if he was a wolf."

"Certainly I should. I'm not an idiot."

"Mother, did you *ever* have anyone proposition you?"

"I shouldn't tell you if I had," said Lucia.

"That's where you make a mistake," said Bee. "Pretending to be superhuman."

"I don't pretend to be superhuman."

"But you do. You wouldn't let anyone see you shed a single tear when Daddy left."

"Why should I let people see me if I'm not happy?"

"It would be a lot better if you did. If you weren't so darned inhibited, I could *talk* to you."

Oh, Bee! Can't you talk to me? Lucia cried in her heart. I want that so. I do understand things.

David was springing up the stairs.

"Mother," he said, from the hall. "Someone wants to see you." His voice was ominous.

"Oh, who, David?"

"He says Mr. Donnelly sent him. I'll stick around," said David. "Keep an eye on the spoons. He's on the porch."

"Try on that brown skirt of mine, Bee," said Lucia. "I'll be right back."

"Mother, what goes on?" Bee demanded. "Who *is* this Donnelly man anyhow?"

"I told you," said Lucia. "I'll be back in a moment."

From a window in the sitting room, Lucia could see the man on the porch, and her heart sank. He was the worst yet, far the worst, the most obviously shady and suspect. He was young, a boy, in a dark red sweater clinging tight to his skinny torso; he had a rough mop of black hair, and small black eyes set too close to a broad nose.

I suppose there's a gang, she thought. A whole gang of blackmailers. They'll keep on and on . . . Well, the first thing is to get Bee away. Then I'll see. Then I'll think.

Cold with dismay, she opened the door and went out.

"You want to see me?" she asked.

"Yeah," said the boy. "Regal Snowdrop."

"What?" said Lucia.

"Regal Snowdrop," he replied, impatiently. "Mr. Donnelly tole me to come. To pick up your laundry."

"Oh . . . laundry?" she repeated.

"Yeah. Laundry."

She was silent, trying to understand. This must be a sort of code, she thought. He must have come to get money, or a check, or something. And suppose he won't go away without it?

"Mr. Donnelly said tomorrow," she said cautiously.

"Well, he tole us today. Said we got to make dis a special job. Pick it up today, bring it back Tuesday."

"You *mean* laundry?"

"Well, jeez, lady, didn't I *say*? Laundry. What gets washed and ironed. Laundry."

"Mr. Donnelly sent you?"

"He said youse was having problems."

"But how can you take it?"

"I got a car here," he said, jerking his head, and she saw, parked down the drive, a very shabby little blue coupé. "Listen!" he said. "I haven't got all night, lady."

"No," she said. "I'll get it for you."

She went into the house, a little dazed, into the kitchen to Sibyl.

"There's a boy here for the laundry," she said. "They're going to send it back Tuesday."

"It's a new laundry, ma'am?" asked Sibyl.

It seemed to Lucia that Sibyl was looking at her in an odd way.

"Yes," she answered, in a matter-of-fact way. "It's the Regal Snowdrop. If you'll give it to the boy, please, Sibyl."

David was waiting in the hall.

"What gives?" he asked briefly.

"Why, nothing," said Lucia. "It's simply a boy for the laundry."

"Why hasn't he got a van?"

"I don't know. I don't care, either."

"What's the Donnelly man got to do with our laundry?"

"He knew of this laundry, and he wanted to be obliging."

"He can oblige me by keeping away from here," said David.

"Don't be silly," said Lucia, mechanically, and went up the stairs to Bee.

"Who was it?" Bee asked.

"Oh, it was a boy for the laundry."

"How did Mr. Donnelly get into it?"

"He knew about the laundry, and sent the boy."

"Well, why?"

"Why *not*? I'm tired of all these questions!" cried Lucia.

"Mother!" said Bee, shocked. "I never saw you like this before."

"Like what?" Lucia asked coldly. "Turn around, Bee, and let me see how that skirt is in the back."

This won't do, she told herself. It's not like me to get so irritable. Only I'm—I don't know. I feel tired, I guess. But I've got to keep hold of myself or they'll all notice.

They were all dangerous to her, her father, her daughter and her son. And Sibyl? I don't know, she thought. But I've got to be let alone, to handle this thing. I've got to think it out carefully. I'll get Bee away. And I wish I could get Father away.

It seemed to her that if only she could hide them somewhere, in safety, she could cope with the growing menace of her problems. If they were away, I could think, she told herself, and knew in her heart that she had not been thinking, that she had no plans at all. Nothing but this quite useless, stupid impulse to put things off, to gain one more day from Donnelly and Nagle. I couldn't possibly get hold of five thousand dollars, she thought.

But if I have to?

No, it wouldn't do any good. Blackmailers never stop. They wouldn't give me back all the letters. I couldn't know. She was in her own room, sewing a sash on Bee's house coat, a sweet little house coat, of dusty pink rayon, faintly fragrant of perfume. It made her want to cry; she did begin to cry a little.

But that had to be stopped. Someone would come and see her. Someone always came. There was always a knock at the door. Everyone had a right to come to her; that was what she was for, that was her function, her reason for being. There was never an hour that belonged to her.

The knock came and it was Sibyl.

"Mr. Harper's got a man from the police downstairs, ma'am," she said. "He's asked him to stay to tea."

"From the police?" Lucia cried.

"Yes, ma'am," said Sibyl. "But I don't think there's anything to worry about. He came right to the back door and he spoke to me first. Says he's going to all the people in this neighborhood, got to see if anybody knew Mr. Darby."

Was that compassion in Sibyl's voice, and in her amber-flecked eyes? Did she know anything? Or everything? Don't ask her. Don't try to find out.

"Is—where's Miss Bee?" she asked.

"She went out walking with a young man, ma'am."

"*What* young man?"

"Only the neighbors, ma'am. Seems to be a *nice* young man," said Sibyl.

It was compassion in her voice, and understanding.

"A *nice* young man," she repeated.

"I'll go down," said Lucia.

"Yes, ma'am. Mr. Harper's pleased to have company for tea. He doesn't worry about the police, ma'am. Got nothing on his conscience."

So you know? Lucia thought. But she could not be sure, and she did not want to be. She washed, and brushed her hair, and put on a fresh dress, and hastened down to the sitting room.

"Oh, Lucia . . ." said her father. "This is Lieutenant Levy, from the Horton County police. Lieutenant, my daughter, Mrs. Holley."

The lieutenant had risen, a tall young man with big feet and big, rather outstanding ears. He was not in uniform; in a neat gray suit he was not formidable, his smile was friendly, his dark eyes were thoughtful and mild. But she was very greatly afraid of him.

"The lieutenant is making some routine inquiries," said Mr. Harper. "He's investigating a homicide."

That *you* committed, Lucia thought.

Chapter Eight

THE POSTMAN came, while they were at tea, and there was a V-mail from Tom. Lucia kept it, unopened, in her hand. There was comfort in it, and in the thought of Tom, who was so definite about things, so uncomplicated. Here, I'll look after this, Lucia, he would say. And if he saw that she had dreadfully mismanaged things, he would not be angry, or reproachful, or impatient. I think you made a bit of a mistake right here, Lucia . . .

She was very thankful that Levy asked her no questions at all. He didn't even want to talk about Ted. But Mr. Harper did.

"I read about the case in the newspapers," he said. "Didn't mention it, because I didn't want to alarm you or Bee. Too near home, what? But it looks very like one of these gangster murders to me."

"Let's not talk about it," said Lucia suddenly, and more loudly than she meant.

"Certainly, m'dear. Certainly," said her father, instantly contrite.

It was as Sibyl had said, he was pleased to have company for tea. He's lonely, Lucia thought. He misses his office and his club. And he misses Tom so very much. They used to talk. He's lonely and he's getting old . . .

He was getting old in such a clean, fine way, his silver hair cropped close, his nails so neatly clipped, his necktie pressed that morning, a brown and a yellow check . . . I could cry, she thought, and was shocked at herself.

Levy asked her if she had read a certain book very popular just then.

"Well, no," she answered. "Have you?"

He had, and he talked a little about it. He's not—right, she thought. He's not like a policeman. Suppose he really isn't one? Suppose he's someone that Nagle sent?

Her home was invaded, it was no longer a safe refuge for her people. If I could only put Father on his guard somehow, she thought, so that he wouldn't say anything . . . But maybe he had already 'said something,' had, in his innocence, completely betrayed himself?

She looked and looked at Levy, trying to read his face. In vain. He looked mild, a little sad, nothing more. If he was a policeman, why did he stay and stay and stay, like this? To trap someone.

He stayed and stayed, and Bee came home. She brought a boy with her, and he seemed to Lucia a sinister boy, dark and unsmiling; his shoulders were too broad, he looked powerful and aggressive.

"Mother," Bee said, "this is Owen Lloyd."

Owen took her outstretched hand in a grip that made her wince. He then shook hands in turn with Mr. Harper and Lieutenant Levy.

"You're looking into that case over on the island, sir?" he asked Levy. "This Darby?"

Lucia was stricken with terror to see how white Bee grew. If Levy looked at her *now* . . . she thought.

"Oh, we have our routine," Levy answered. "We're visiting everyone in the neighborhood, to see if we can pick up any information."

"My mother'll give you plenty, sir," said Owen. "She's been wanting to go to the police with her story. She says that early Wednesday morning she looked out of her window, and she saw a man and a woman, standing up in a motorboat between here and the island. Struggling, she says they were. She turned away to get her glasses and when she found them, and looked again, the man had disappeared, and the woman was heading for the island."

"Why didn't your mother come to us, Mr. Lloyd?"

"My father and I put her off it," said Lloyd. "We thought maybe she was mistaken, and she'd get herself all upset for nothing. She's pretty high-strung, you know."

"I see!" said Levy.

He finished his second cup of tea and rose.

"Thanks very much, Mrs. Holley," he said. "It's been very enjoyable."

"Stop in again, sir," said old Mr. Harper. "I'd be very interested to hear anything about this case you feel at liberty to tell."

"I will, Mr. Harper!" said Levy, earnestly.

Now it was the boy Owen who stayed and stayed, and Lucia stayed, too, until her father left to take his before-dinner stroll. Then she went up to her own room, longing for the solace of Tom's letter.

But it was one of his queer letters, filled with an almost wild hilarity. She had had two or three others like this and they had disturbed her profoundly. Tom never drinks too much, she thought. It's not that. Is it battle that makes him so excited?

She tried to think of her good-humored, nonchalant Tom in battle. She recalled the battles she had seen in newsreels. Flames, smoke, hideous noises, whining, droning, screaming, shattering crashes. I can't . . . she thought. It's no use. He's too far away . . .

She sat on a chest by the window, in a curious apathy, until David came knocking at the door.

"Sibyl says you got a letter from Dad," he said. "What does he say?"

"Why, nothing very special, dear," she said. "Of course he's not able to tell anything much."

"Owen was in the Pacific zone," David said.

He glanced at Lucia, frowning a little.

"Well, if it isn't over pretty soon," he said, "it'll be my turn."

He had never spoken of that before, he said it now as if it were a question, as if he were asking her, what is this? What shall I think about life and war and death?

He looked so young, so slight. No! she said in her heart. *No!*

And who was she saying that to? She had no power to protect her own people, her own children. The walls of her home were falling down; there was no refuge.

"Have you got a clean shirt for dinner, dear?" she asked. "Give that one to me when you take it off. The collar . . ." She touched the collar at the back of his thin young neck. "It's a little frayed . . ."

"Oh, all right," he said with a sigh and went away disappointed.

Chapter Nine

LUCIA SAT up in bed to read over the letter she had written the night before.

DEAR TOM:
   Bee is going to Gracie's camp for a week or two. I think it will do her good. It really is pretty dull here.

Dull . . . she repeated to herself, but she let it stand.

   You ask how the car is standing up. We scarcely ever use it on account of tires and gas, so it will be in nice shape when you get back. I told Sibyl you sent her your best regards and she said to tell you she prays for you every night. She *means* it, too, Tom. I don't know what I'd do without Sibyl.

She leaned back against the pillows, thinking of Sibyl and what she might know. It was a sparkling morning, but she had no thought of going out. She had to stay here, right here, inside the house, so that nothing could happen. I will stop things, too, she told herself. I don't know now just what I'll do, but as they come up . . .
   Nagle and Donnelly and Levy . . . Five thousand dollars . . . My jewelry! she thought suddenly. She had her diamond engagement ring, an emerald ring her father had given her on her twenty-first birthday, a string of pearls her mother had left her, her grandmother's diamond bracelet, all in the safe-deposit box in the New York bank. I could borrow on them, she thought. Or if it comes to the worst, I could even sell them.
   To pay blackmail? Yes, she thought. It may be terribly stupid, but that's what I'm going to do. It'll keep those men quiet for a while, anyhow. It'll gain time.
   And time must be her ally. She clung to that belief. She lived by it, now. Every day made the end of the war nearer, every day that no telegram came about Tom was a day gained. She lived as if holding her breath. Just get through this day.

She got a book and read it in bed, with stubborn determination. It was a mystery story she had got out of the lending library for her father, and she was not fond of mystery stories. Nobody in them ever seems to feel *sorry* about murders, she had said. They're presented as a problem, m'dear, her father said. What's more, they generally show the murdered person as someone you can't waste any pity on. *I'm* sorry for them, she said, I hate it when they're found with daggers sticking in them and their eyes all staring from poison and things like that.

Yet how little pity did she feel for Ted Darby! I really did that, she thought amazed. I concealed a body. Anyhow I took it away. And when I came back—after that—nobody could see anything wrong with me—anything queer. Maybe I haven't got so much feeling, after all. Maybe I'm rather too tough.

I'd better be, too, she thought, as she rose and began to dress.

Breakfast that morning had an unusual quality. She was surprised to find all her family so cheerful and talkative. Surprised but not pleased; it worried her. They were too innocent. They seemed this morning like victims, pitiably unaware of what darkly menaced them.

She saw the menace more vividly now than ever before. Her father standing in the dock. My dear, I don't like to be hurried, she'd heard him say all her life. But, once accused, he could be hurried. Question after question would be shot at him. She pictured him growing a little confused, indignant. She could imagine his overwhelming shame when he heard of Bee's folly. He and David. Tom would be different, she thought. He'd just be so sorry for Bee.

"Owen's mother wants to call on you," said David.

"Owen? Owen?" said Mr. Harper. "Oh, yes! Nice lad."

"He's twenty-three," said David. "And he was in the Army two years."

"His mother's a frightful nitwit," said Bee. "But she's rather nice. They're quite a nice family."

"Rolling in money," said David, complacently. "Absolutely rolling. I found them."

"Oh, you're a marvel!" said Bee, with scornful good humor.

"I know the art of making friends," said David. "Mother, the Lloyds asked me to lunch today. That all right with you?"

"Perfectly, dear," said Lucia. "Have you got a clean shirt?"

She went into the kitchen to consult with Sibyl.

"If that icebox man doesn't come today," said Sibyl, "I don't know how we're going to keep a thing over Sunday."

They stood in gloomy silence for a moment.

"I'd better get to market early," said Sibyl. "Better leave everything and get the nine o'clock bus."

"I'll do the marketing, Sibyl."

"No, ma'am," said Sibyl. "Better for me to do it Saturday. I'll go early and get back in time to iron those little things for Miss Bee." She thought for a time. "Best give me twenty dollars, ma'am."

"I'll send for a taxi," Lucia said. "And you'd better keep it, Sibyl. I'll pay it by the hour."

Bee wanted to go to the village, too; she and Sibyl set off in the cab. David had gone already; old Mr. Harper was taking his walk. Lucia put on an apron and was starting to wash the breakfast dishes when the telephone rang. She dried her hands and went to answer.

"Mrs. Holley, please," said a man's muffled voice.

"This is me," said Lucia.

"Donnelly speaking. I'd like to see you this morning for a few moments, Mrs. Holley. What time could I come?"

"Oh . . . !" she cried. "I'm afraid . . . You'd really better not come *here*."

"Well, I must see you somewhere, then."

"I don't know . . . I don't see . . ."

"Down at the railroad station, maybe. I am there now."

"I couldn't. I couldn't get away."

"I am sorry to bother you," he said.

"Can't you tell me what it is on the telephone?"

"It is not a good thing to be talking too much on the telephone," he said.

"I don't see *how* I can meet you *anywhere*."

"It is important," he said. "Else I shouldn't be bothering you. Is there someplace maybe near by where you can see me for a moment?"

"Wait," she said. "Let me think . . . There's the boathouse here. If you go by the shore road and then along a little path, you can get into it without anyone seeing you."

"What time will I be there?"

"Oh . . . It's very hard for me to say . . . I mean, I'll have to wait for a chance to slip out."

"I'll go there now," he said, "and I'll wait."

"Wait upstairs, please," she said. "I'll try to come right away, but I *might* be delayed."

"Don't worry," he said. "I'll wait."

She hung up the telephone and stood beside it, irresolute, flustered. There are such a lot of things . . . she thought. People are *idiots* to talk about getting married and being your own mistress, so much more free than women with jobs.

If Bee comes back and finds the dishes in the sink . . . Even unsuspicious Father would think that was queer . . . What reason can I give anyone for running out of the house?

"Oh, I don't know!" she cried aloud in angry desperation. "It's nobody's business."

She decided to finish washing the dishes, and leave them draining. Then I'll tell them, if they ask me, that I felt like being alone. I'll say I wanted to *think*. Why shouldn't I? Other people do.

She ran upstairs to powder her face and her anger increased, to see herself flushed and disheveled. Anger at them, her father, her children, and Sibyl. It's none of their business if I feel like leaving the house for a few moments. And the beds not made . . . I've got to make Father's bed. He's so neat. He'd hate to come back and find it not done.

Bee ought to make her own bed. Oh, Bee, my darling . . . ! Nagle and Mr. Donnelly, and maybe other people, horrible people, reading your poor silly letters. Trying to make money out of them . . .

This afternoon Bee would be going away, perhaps for weeks. Perhaps this trouble couldn't be kept away from her. I've got to make her bed, Lucia thought. Or she'd think I didn't love her.

She could not stop. She made David's bed too. She picked up, she tidied up the bathroom. David had left a ring in the tub. She took up the scouring powder and the rag. No! she told herself. I've got to see Mr. Donnelly and hear whatever it is. This is silly.

But she had to clean the tub. She ran down the stairs, and she nearly cried, because she wanted so terribly to empty the ash trays and straighten up the sitting room. She ran across the lawn and into the cottage part of the boathouse, hot, angry, miserable.

She went through the sitting room on the ground floor and up the stairs, and Donnelly stood on the landing waiting for her.

"I'm sorry I kept you waiting," she said briefly. "But I was very busy this morning."

"You hurried too much," he said. "You're out of breath and all. I did not mind waiting."

"Well . . . Let's go in here," she said, and led the way into one of the two bedrooms, a big room, dimly lit through the grimy windows, with two sagging couches against the wall, everything covered thick with dust.

Lucia sat down in a rocking chair with a torn and discolored antimacassar on the back, and Donnelly stood before her.

"Why is it the ladies don't carry fans any more?" he asked.

"Well, I don't think I ever did," Lucia answered.

"No. You're too young. I remember a long time ago, I was in New Orleans and there was a girl there, French, she was, and dark like yourself, and she'd a little fan, purple, maybe. I don't know the names of those pretty, light colors."

He was trying to give her time to grow calmer, and she responded courteously.

"There's mauve," she said, "and lavender and violet."

"They are pretty names."

There was a silence. She rocked and the floor boards squeaked. Donnelly stood before her, arms at his sides, his head averted, immaculate and elegant in his dark suit and handsome olive-green tie.

"I am sorry this ever began at all," he said. "If I was in it alone, I'd hand you the letters and you'd hear no more about it."

"Well . . ." she said with a sigh.

"I told Nagle you said give you till Monday. He did not like that. It was all I could do to keep him from coming here himself."

"That wouldn't do him any good. It would only make things worse."

"That's what he wants. He wants to keep after you till you'll be desperate and get the money one way or another."

"But not *you*, of course!" she cried.

"Not me," he said.

A great anger was rising in her against Donnelly. He's a crook, she thought, and probably a very smart one. He's trying to trap me in some way. He's trying to deceive me. He's— I don't know what he's trying to do but it's something horrible.

"So Mr. Nagle's to blame for *all* of this?" she said, with a faint smile.

"Well, no . . ." Donnelly said. "No. I couldn't say that. When he first brought it up, I didn't make any objections."

"But now you've changed. You've got very high-minded about it."

"Now I wish to God I could stop it all," he said. "Only I cannot. Nagle is a man hard to handle. There'll be money coming to us from this deal we made. But things are bad now for the two of us, and he is nervous. He likes to have a bit of ready cash by him, in case anything'll be going wrong."

"But not *you*. *You* don't want this money, this blackmail!"

"I do not," he said. "Only I cannot hold Nagle off longer than Monday. Are you sure you can get the money that day?"

"Yes," she said carelessly, recklessly.

Bee would get away this afternoon, and there would be all Sunday to think things over, to make a plan.

"Will I come out here to get it?" he asked. "Or would you rather meet me in New York?"

"I'll meet you in New York," she said.

"When would it suit you?"

"I'll meet you outside Stern's on Forty-second Street," she said, "at noon."

She rose.

"There's one little thing more . . ." he said. "You'll only need bring forty-five hundred with you."

"Oh! How *nice* of Mr. Nagle!" she cried. "How kind and nice of him to let me off five hundred dollars!"

"I gave him five hundred," said Donnelly. "I told him it was you sent it. I did that, that way he wouldn't be out here bothering you."

She looked straight into his face that was as it always was, handsome, strong boned, but blurred and veiled by something.

"I don't believe you," she said. "I don't believe any of this."

He said nothing and she went past him, out of the room and down the stairs. Liar! she cried to herself. Liar! I hate him!

She had never felt anything like this turmoil of the spirit, this anger. He's the one who brought the letters here. He's the one I'm to pay the blackmail to. And he says he did that. For me. Liar. Blackmailer. Contemptible crook. I hate him so . . .

She went back to the house, thinking of nothing but her anger. I will go to the police, she thought. I'll manage some way to keep Father out of it. The police will see to it that nobody ever knows anything about Bee's letters. They'll just arrest those men. That man!

She opened the front door and Bee came out of the sitting room. And at the sight of her child, all the other things rose in Lucia like a rushing tide. Getting Bee's clothes ready, packing, the lunch, the familiar feeling of things undone, things demanding attention.

"Oh, you're back, dear?" she said. "Did you get the things you wanted?"

"No," Bee answered. "But it doesn't matter. I'm not going to the camp, Mother. I sent Aunt Gracie a telegram."

"Bee! But why?"

Bee stood facing her, slight and lovely and curiously stern, all in white.

"I'm too much worried and upset about you," she said. "I'm shocked."

"What are you talking about?" cried Lucia.

"That man," Bee said. "The way you're acting with that man."

Chapter Ten

LUCIA HAD felt irritated by her children now and then, and sometimes—not often—impatient. But this was anger.

"Don't talk like that," she said, curtly.

"How do you think I feel—we feel—David and I?"

"David would never be so silly and offensive."

"He feels just the way I do. When we found out that you'd sneaked out of the house to meet that man——"

"Don't say 'sneaked'!"

"You did! The moment we were gone——"

"I have things to talk over with Mr. Donnelly, and I'll see him when and where I think best."

"*What* things to talk over?"

"I certainly don't have to account to you," said Lucia. "And I'm not going to listen to any more of this. You'll have to go to the camp, as we arranged——"

"I'm not going. Not unless you promise me you won't see that man again. Ever."

"How can you dare to talk like that?" cried Lucia. "As if you had absolutely no confidence in your own mother."

"I met David in the village," said Bee, in a cold, even voice, "and that Halford kid gave us a lift home. You weren't in the house, and David thought maybe you'd taken out one of the boats. So we went to see. We thought we heard voices in the boathouse, and we opened the door——"

"You stood there listening!"

"We didn't. We came right out. We were absolutely shocked."

"Then you're both very silly—and offensive. I don't want to hear another word about this."

"David and I consider that we have an obligation to Daddy——"

"Shut up!" said Lucia, and went past Bee, into the house and up the stairs to her room.

I shouldn't have said that, she told herself. It was vulgar and horrible. Only, I don't care. My own children turning against me like that. I can't believe David would have ideas like that. I'm going to speak to him now, this instant.

But she did not move.

I can't speak to David about such a thing, she thought. About meeting a man. It's impossible. But David couldn't possibly think I was "shocking." Suppose I did step out to the boathouse to see Mr. Donnelly for a few moments, because I had things to talk over with him . . .

Then she remembered what it was that she had to talk over with Mr. Donnelly. Oh, no! she cried to herself. Let the children be shocked. Let them be exasperating, and offensive, anything at all. Anything was better than that they should know the truth. David would never get over it, she thought, if he knew that his sister had written letters like that to Ted Darby. And Bee would never, never get over it, if she knew that that Darby man didn't really care for her at all. That he was just planning to make money out of her.

I said I'd get the money by Monday, she thought. Mr. Donnelly said that if I didn't, he couldn't keep Nagle from coming out here. I can't let that happen.

Then I'll have to get the money. Four thousand, five hundred dollars. I've got eight hundred, about, in my account now, and there'll be the allotment check and Mr. Fuller's check next month. But I have to pay the rent and the food and the storage on our furniture, and all the other things. My jewelry? I don't know how much it's worth. Thousands, maybe. But maybe not.

Those people who make loans . . . That's the thing! She remembered seeing advertisements in newspapers; she remembered hearing something on the radio. Privacy, they said. Your personal signature alone.

I know how stupid and wrong it is to pay money to blackmailers. But that's what I'm going to do. I want *time*. Time to get Bee away. Time for—other things. I don't know just what. Only, if I keep that Nagle man away, even for a while, there's a chance of something happening. He might have to run away. Mr. Donnelly said so.

A sort of fever possessed her. Her anger against Bee was forgotten; she was desperately impatient for Monday to come, so that she could get the money, and pay Nagle, and have peace. For a time.

There was a knock at the door.

"Who is it?" she called, with an unusual sharpness.

"Me," answered David's voice.

"Well, do you want anything special, David?" she asked. "I've got a headache."

"It's important," he said, and she opened the door.

"Now, if you're going to begin to nag, David——" she said.

"I'm not," he said. "I think you're making a big mistake, taking up with that fellow, but I told Bee I was darn sure there was no real harm in it. Just folly."

His extreme calmness was as exasperating and as humiliating as Bee's shocked indignation.

"I'm not going to be talked to like this by a boy of fifteen," she said. "I know what I'm doing——"

"All right! All right!" he said, soothingly. "I came to tell you that Mrs. Lloyd's downstairs."

"Who is Mrs. Lloyd?"

"She's Owen's mother. She's got another son, around my age, and a daughter. They're nice people. They've got two cars and a chauffeur. They've got a swell cabin cruiser."

"What does she want?"

"Why, I suppose she just wants to see you," said David.

"I can't see her now. This time of the morning—and I'm not dressed."

"You look all right," said David. "Anyhow, she won't care."

"No, I can't!" said Lucia. "I'll—tell her I'll come to call on her."

"Mother, she's *right here*!" said David. "I can't tell her you won't come downstairs."

David was shocked now, and, in a way, he was not to be blamed. I'm being—very queer, Lucia thought.

She stopped being queer, at once.

"I'll be very glad to see your Mrs. Lloyd, dear," she said. "I'll be down in a minute."

Mrs. Lloyd was a thin woman, with rouge daubed carelessly on her hollow cheeks, and light hair in a thick, careless bun at the nape of her neck. She wore a white blouse too big for her, with cuffs that half covered her hands, and a bunchy gray skirt, and emerald-green wedgies. But she had a sweet voice, a sweet, triangular smile. Like a cat, Lucia thought. A mother cat, letting the kittens walk all over her.

"It's a *fearsome* time to come bothering you," she said. "But Owen and Phyllis and Nick got at me. I've been wanting to call—but really I never get around to anything." She paused. "I really don't know what I do all day," she said, with a sort of wonder.

"The days just go," said Lucia.

"Yes, *don't* they?" said Mrs. Lloyd. "Do you think you could possibly lunch with me at the Yacht Club some day soon? It's rather sweet there. You sit on the lawn—if it isn't *raining*, of course—and they bring little trays with fishes on them. *Painted* on them, I mean. A really very wonderful girl paints them. She supports her mother and her great-aunt in a tiny little cottage, and she paints simply anything. You send things to her, or she comes to the house. I didn't seem to have anything to send her, so I put her in our sun porch, and she painted simply adorable little fishes all over, on tables, you know, and on the walls. She does flowers, too, if you ask for them. And she did a simply huge horse's head for Mrs. Wynn, almost *too* huge, I thought, right over the mantelpiece. Do you paint, Mrs. Holley?"

"Why, no, I don't," Lucia answered, soothed and pleased by this most amiable guest.

"I don't, either, but I'd love to. Or play the piano, or something like that. When the children were little, they went to the Dame Nature School, and they played in a little orchestra. All the children did. It would be rather lovely if everyone kept *on* playing in orchestras, all their lives, don't you think? But do you think you could possibly come to lunch at the Yacht Club?"

"I'd love to," said Lucia.

"Tomorrow, perhaps? We could have their Sunday brunch. And David says your father is here with you. We should so love to have him—and there's a bar in the clubhouse. He'd like that, don't you think?"

"I'm sure he would," said Lucia.

"Then may we call by, tomorrow? The station wagon will hold us all. Twelve, do you think? I've tried to train myself to sleep late on Sunday mornings, but I can't do it. I seem to be so *hungry*. And then, it's rather charming, somehow, to go prowling around in the house, with everyone else asleep. Do you think I might ask that policeman to lunch with us? If you like him, that is."

"Well, what policeman?" asked Lucia.

"That Lieutenant Levy. I think he's so kind. And it would be nice to have another man. I'm so glad that really sinister case is settled, aren't you? That man on Simm's Island, I mean."

"Settled . . . ?" said Lucia.

"They've caught the murderer, and I'm *very* glad, because my Phyllis is only nineteen, and I do hate the thought of a murderer in the neighborhood."

"Do you know what man they've arrested?"

"I really know quite a lot about it," said Mrs. Lloyd. "We had Lieutenant Levy in for cocktails yesterday and he told us. It's a horrible man, named Murray. Underworld, you know. He was an enemy of that poor Darby man, and they came out here together on the same train. Imagine, in that teeming rain! I was rather surprised, because *I* thought he'd been killed by a woman."

"Oh! Did you?"

"Yes. Nick went over to the island, with another boy. Boys that age seem strangely gruesome, don't you think? Nick found this list there, in the reeds."

"A list?"

"A market list. Quite pathetic, somehow. I mean, grated cheese, two points, and things like that. You simply felt sure it was a *nice* woman, not black market, of course, with those points all written down. I thought it was probably someone goaded to frenzy."

"That's very interesting," said Lucia. "I'd love to see the list, if you'd let me."

"But I gave it to Lieutenant Levy. It did seem to be a clue, don't you think?"

"Oh, I do!" said Lucia.

It must have been one of my lists, she thought. An old one. I must have pulled it out of my pocket with the bandanna. And Lieutenant Levy's got it. He'll know ways to trace it back to me; he'll know I was there.

But they arrested a man—after they'd got the list. So they can't think the list is very important.

"This Murray they've arrested . . ." she asked. "Is he a criminal?"

"Oh, heavens, yes!" said Mrs. Lloyd. "He'd just come out of

another prison. He's a dope-peddler, and what untold harm they do, don't they?"

"Yes, they *do*!" said Lucia, earnestly.

"I was rather surprised," Mrs. Lloyd went on, "because I'd felt quite sure those two women had had something to do with it."

"What two women?"

"Oh, didn't I tell you? Well, you know, the morning the poor man was killed, I got up frightfully early, about half-past five, and I went out on my little balcony. And I saw a little motorboat, a little launch, like yours, you know, and two women were standing up in it, having a struggle."

But you didn't! Lucia thought. If there'd been another motorboat out, I'd have seen it. Certainly I'd have heard it. And there wasn't any. I could swear to that.

Mrs. Lloyd rose.

"I so look forward to our brunch tomorrow," she said. "You and your father and your two children. And shall I ask the policeman?"

"Oh, I think he's very nice," said Lucia.

David was not home to lunch, and Lucia sat at the table with her father and Bee, in a dream. It seemed to her that the world could offer nothing more desirable than Mrs. Lloyd's Sunday brunch. She had a remarkably clear vision of it in her mind; all of them sitting on a shady lawn, holding trays upon which fishes were painted, red and gold; Bee in her blue dress, she thought, and the sky pure blue, the calm sea a deeper blue. Father will enjoy it, she thought. And Bee . . . It's exactly the sort of thing Bee needs. There'll be Owen, and the daughter who's nineteen, and maybe other people will come. Maybe this is the beginning of a really happy summer for her.

"What did you think of Mrs. Lloyd?" Bee asked, with cold formality.

"I like her very much," said Lucia. "*Very* much. I don't know when I've met anyone I liked more."

"I don't think she's all that wonderful," said Bee, a little surprised, and still cold. "Of course, she's goodhearted and all that, but I think she's pretty silly. And irresponsible."

"'Irresponsible'?" old Mr. Harper repeated. "That's a strong word, m'dear."

"Well, I mean muddled," said Bee. "For instance, one time

when I met her in the village, she asked me if I'd seen *Life with Father*. I said no, and she said she'd seen it just the week before, and she told me things out of it. But what she told me about wasn't *Life with Father* at all. It was a boring little play I'd seen with Sammy before we came out here."

"Well," said Mr. Harper, "considering the sort of plays they produce nowadays, I can't say that I blame the good lady."

"Honestly, Grandpa!" said Bee.

She always took him up on things like that; she began now to defend the theater of her own day, and old Mr. Harper was quite as ready to praise, and to describe, plays he had seen in London, in his boyhood. Lucia waited impatiently for the first pause.

"Mrs. Lloyd's asked us all to brunch with them tomorrow at the Yacht Club," she said. "She specially wants you, Father."

"Me?" he said, with a short laugh. He was pleased.

"I think it would be very nice," said Lucia.

"Well, they do know how to have a good time, the whole family," said Bee. "They're all popular, too. There's always a lot going on in their house, people coming and going and the telephone ringing."

"Ha . . . shouldn't care for that, myself," said Mr. Harper.

"I love it," said Bee. "This house is like a graveyard."

That's meant for me, thought Lucia. All right; I know I'm not popular.

"They're calling for us at twelve," she said.

Now it was done. She was letting Murray stay in prison.

Only over the week end, she told herself. I want Bee to get a little established with the Lloyds. I want them to see what she's really like. Then, later on, if they hear anything—about Ted Darby, or anything else, they'll see . . . Just this brunch, and then I'll tell Lieutenant Levy.

That Murray has been in prison before. A few days won't seem so terrible, to him. He's a criminal, anyhow. Being a dope-peddler is as bad as being a murderer. It's murdering people's souls.

I mustn't talk that way to myself. Like a cheap movie. I don't know anything about Murray, except what Mrs. Lloyd said, and maybe she is a little—irresponsible. All I really know is, that he's in jail for something he didn't do. I could get him out. And I'm letting him stay there.

That's a sin, she said to herself.

A car was coming up the drive; someone was mounting the steps. It's the police, she thought. They've traced that market list.

"I'll go, Sibyl!" she called, and pushed back her chair.

A small delivery van stood outside the house and the driver, a burly man in a singlet, stood leaning against the porch rail.

"Holley?" he asked.

"Yes."

"Package," he said, and went back to the truck, returning with a big bundle clumsily wrapped in brown paper.

"Well, but from where?" Lucia asked.

"Wouldn't know," he said. "I was tole to deliver it to Mrs. Holley."

He held it out to her and she took it, and was surprised by its heaviness. The driver turned away, got into his truck, and drove off.

"What is it, Mother?" asked Bee, standing beside her.

"It's probably something Sibyl ordered," said Lucia. "I'll take it into the kitchen. Go on with your lunch."

But Bee followed her into the kitchen; she began to pick at the string on the package when Lucia set it down on the table.

"Why are you so inquisitive?" cried Lucia. "*Do* go back to your lunch, Bee!"

Sibyl stood by the window, silent.

"Good lord!" cried Bee. "It's a ham! A simply huge ham!"

"Came from my nephew," said Sibyl. "Told me he'd send one, soon as he could."

"Without any red points?" Bee demanded.

"I've got plenty of red points, Miss Bee," said Sibyl, mildly.

Bee followed her mother into the hall.

"I hope Sibyl isn't mixed up in any black market business," she said. "I *despise* that."

"You ought to know Sibyl better than that," said Lucia.

"Well, just the same, I call it very queer," said Bee. "A simply huge ham arriving, and nobody asking for red points, or money, or anything."

Lucia sat down at the table again. I don't know where that ham came from, she thought. And I'm not going to think about it. Ever.

Chapter Eleven

DEAR TOM: We've met some very nice people here, named Lloyd. It was David who found them, of course; he's like you about making friends. Mrs. Lloyd's asked us all to brunch with them tomorrow at the Yacht Club, and it ought to be fun. Mrs. Lloyd says they serve lunch on little trays with fishes painted on them by a girl . . .

This is nonsense, she thought. How can I write drivel like this to Tom? Tom—in a war? But I don't know what to write to him. If he knew what I'd done . . . What I'm doing *now*. Letting an innocent man stay in prison.

It's a sin. What I did about Ted Darby was illegal. I dare say it was foolhardy. But this is a sin. It's bearing false witness against your neighbor, not to speak when you know the truth. Suppose Mrs. Lloyd is mistaken, and Murray isn't a criminal and a dope-peddler? Suppose he's a perfectly innocent man?

She had to get the letter finished, some sort of letter. But she was troubled by visions, very foreign to her. She imagined Tom standing on the deck of a ship that was rushing through the water; she could see his blunt-featured face raised to a sky sparkling with southern stars. She knew, in some way, that he was not thinking of her, but beyond that she could not go; she could not imagine the thoughts of a man with battle and death before him and behind him. She felt desolately remote from him, as never before.

That's because of what I've done, she thought. It's made a separation.

She took up her pen and finished the letter, fluently, quickly, and pointlessly. It was late, and she took a bath and got into bed, and turned out the light. And then she had visions of Murray. He was shaking the bars of his cell and shouting. Before God, I am innocent! I am an innocent man! His head was shaved and he was wearing a shapeless gray uniform. I am an innocent man! he cried. But nobody believed him.

Suppose he kills himself? she thought, and sat up in bed,

aghast. The prisoner hanged himself in his cell last night. The prisoner cut his wrists. The prisoner went violently insane.

I'll have to tell Lieutenant Levy now, she thought. But I'll have to tell Father first. And then we'll get Lieutenant Levy on the telephone, and they'll let Murray out tonight.

She went along the hall to her father's room; she stood outside it, barefoot, in her pajamas, her black hair loose on her shoulders. Then she heard him cough a little, an elderly cough. A lonely cough. Did he lie awake in the nights, and think of his wife, who had lain beside him for twenty years? Did he think of the days when his life had been vigorous and stirring, and not lonely?

I won't do it! she said to herself. Not at this hour of the night. I won't do it.

And when she got back into bed again, she made up her mind that she would not do it until after that brunch. All right! she told herself. I'll take a chance. A chance that Murray won't get desperate. I'm gambling with a human life. That sounds like something out of a movie, but it's the truth.

On Sunday afternoon I'll tell Lieutenant Levy. No, I won't. On Monday morning I'll go to see that finance company, and if they won't lend me enough, I'll pawn my jewelry. I've got to get those letters back before the police get into this. It's going to be bad enough as it is, with all that shock and misery for Father. But I won't have Bee disgraced. I'm sorry about Murray. I'm so sorry . . .

Her visions of Murray so troubled her that she could not sleep; she got up and took two aspirins. You can see how people start taking drugs, she thought. Not from grief. I could bear it when Tom went away, when Mother died. It's this feeling of guilt, this horrible, shameful worry.

She waked later than usual; she dressed and went downstairs, and Sibyl was in the kitchen.

"Got the ham boiling," said Sibyl. "Then round about ten o'clock, I'll put it in the oven. Got some cloves left over, in a little jar. Got a little brown sugar. If you could spare a little sherry, ma'am?"

"Yes, of course," said Lucia.

She stood leaning against the doorway, heavy-eyed, oppressed. I suppose I ought to know . . . she thought. It's cowardly not to ask.

"Sibyl," she said. "Did your nephew really send that ham?"

"No, ma'am," Sibyl answered, without emphasis.

It seemed to Lucia necessary to go on with this.

"Well, have you any idea where it did come from, Sibyl?" she asked.

"No sense to look a gift horse in the mouth, ma'am," said Sibyl.

"Well, no . . ." said Lucia, and went into the dining room.

They took three newspapers on Sunday; one was especially for Mr. Harper; one had been requested by David, for certain comics he followed; the third was a sort of communal one. Lucia went through this one in haste, and found what she sought.

> The Horton County police have arrested Joseph "Miami" Murray in connection with the slaying of Theodore Darby on Simm's Island. . . . Five years ago Darby figured in the news as a dealer in pornographic art. . . . "Miami" Murray has twice been convicted on drug-peddling charges. . . .

It's like one of David's comic strips, she thought. They're so *very* criminal. Why should people like Father and Bee have to suffer, just to clear a man like that Murray?

She had learned that answer by the time she was ten years old. Because it was right to tell the truth, and wrong to hide it. Because it was wrong to let anyone be blamed, unjustly, for anything. It was as simple as that. *Thou shalt not bear false witness against thy neighbour.*

That drug-peddler isn't my "neighbor"! she cried to herself. And I'm not bearing any kind of witness against him.

She could not eat anything. She drank the two cups of coffee from the little pot Sibyl had brought in, and then she went into the kitchen.

"Sibyl," she said, "I think I'd like another cup of coffee."

"Never knew you to take three, ma'am."

I never did, Lucia thought. I never wanted to. Only, today I want to be—nice. I want to be gay and pleasant. I want the Lloyds to think we're a nice family.

A nice family? she thought. When Father killed Ted Darby, and Bee wrote him those letters, and I took Ted to the island, and now I'm paying blackmail. Why, if anybody knew about us, we'd be—outcasts.

Nobody's going to know, she thought. I'm not going to think about that Murray any more today. I've made my decision, and I'll stick to it. And not think.

She was curiously undecided about what to wear for the brunch. It was a problem which, as a rule, concerned her very little, only now she felt sure of nothing. She did not even feel like Mrs. Holley.

I want to look nice, she thought. But not too formal. And thinking about this, she was inspired to remember a picture in a magazine, and that was how she wished to look. She put on a black blouse with a high neckline and a white skirt; she looked in the mirror and was pleased with the debonair and somehow soldierly effect.

Mr. Harper was waiting for her in the sitting room.

"I suppose," he said, "that as long as these people have invited me, I'd better go. But I'm a bit past the age for enjoying alfresco meals." He laughed a little. "I prefer my tea—without ants," he said.

Lucia laughed, too. Oh, you darling! she thought, with a pang. You're dying to go. And you look so nice and handsome and pleased.

"Are the children ready, do you think?" she asked.

"Oh, yes. Yes. On the veranda, reading the news," he said. "Quite a little family excursion, eh? All four of us."

He's proud of us, Lucia thought, and it touched her almost unbearably. Everything about this day had pain in it, and, with the pain, a feeling of reckless triumph. She had got this day for them; she had bought it for them, at a price she could not begin to compute. There could never be another day like it; it had, for her, the heartbreaking clarity of a lovely scene never to be revisited.

The Lloyds were bathed in this clear light. Mrs. Lloyd, her hair blowing wildly about her thin, rouged cheeks, sat among her children, with her sweet mother-cat smile, and they were gentle to her. There were Owen, and a vivid, pretty daughter, and a nimble boy of fourteen, all of them good-looking, polite,

and at ease. More at ease, politer, gentler than David and Bee.
Well, I dare say she's brought them up better, Lucia thought.
But I do think David and Bee are more remarkable, somehow.

The brunch had style. A table was set ready for them on the
terraced lawn overlooking the bright water; the chauffeur
brought cocktails in a thermos jug.

"The bar doesn't open till one," Mrs. Lloyd explained. "And
anyway, the ones you make at home are generally a little nicer,
don't you think?"

"In this case, I agree with you," said Mr. Harper. "Smooth
as velvet."

"I'm so *glad*!" said Mrs. Lloyd. "Lieutenant Levy doesn't
seem to be here, does he? But he said he never could be sure."

"'A policeman's lot is not a happy one,'" Mr. Harper quoted,
and he and Mrs. Lloyd both laughed at that.

Lucia could have listened to them and watched them all for
hours. It's the loveliest day . . . she told herself. David was
talking, with amiable condescension, to the younger Lloyd
boy; Bee and the daughter Phyllis were talking together. It
interrupted her dreamlike pleasure when Owen sat down beside her and began to talk, with an obvious effort.

He talked about himself. He was, he said, going back to
Harvard, to take his senior year, and then there would be a job
waiting for him in New York.

"It's a pretty good job," he said. "It's only three thousand to
start, but the possibilities are practically unlimited."

"Oh, that's nice!" said Lucia.

He went on and on, in a curiously boring way for someone so
young. He told her about his fraternity, about his Army record,
he told her about sailing trophies he had won. I must say he's
rather egotistic, Lucia thought. And then, suddenly, it occurred
to her that he was telling her these things for a reason. He was
trying to explain his qualifications as a suitor of Bee's. Oh, no!
Lucia thought, in a panic. Bee's only seventeen, and he's much
too young, too. No! He mustn't——

"There's the Lieutenant!" said Phyllis Lloyd.

The brunch had been cleared away by this time, and they all
strolled down to the beach, a mild and amiable herd. They
scattered there, the young people went away; Mrs. Lloyd gave
all her attention to Mr. Harper, and Levy sat on the sand be-

side Lucia. She did not want him there. His presence made her remember everything that she wanted to forget. She wanted this day to be an interlude, all sunny and clear, and Levy made her remember Murray, in prison.

He talked to her in his quiet and gentle way; he talked about sea gulls and snipe and sandpipers.

"What a lot you know about birds!" said Lucia, politely.

"Well, since I've come here, I've got interested," he said. "I'm making a study of the shore birds, taking photographs of them, and so on."

That's an attractive thing to do, Lucia thought. Too nice for a policeman.

"Do you *like* police work?" she asked.

"Not always," he answered. "I started out to be a lawyer, you know. I was admitted to the bar. But police work appeals to me more."

"I should think it would be horrible," said Lucia. "Hunting people down, trying to get them punished."

"The function of the police is protection, Mrs. Holley," he said. "It's not punitive. I have nothing to do with punishing anyone. I enforce the law, that's all."

"I don't think so much of 'the law,'" said Lucia. "I think it's often very stupid and unjust."

"It's all we have, Mrs. Holley," he said. "It's the only thing that can preserve anything at all of our civilization. Whether it's religious law, or civil law, as long as it's something we've all agreed upon, and something we all understand—in advance——"

"*I* don't understand the law," said Lucia.

"You made it, Mrs. Holley," he said. "If we have any laws of which you don't approve, you have the right to work for their repeal."

"Yes, I know," she said, secretly rebellious.

"Women, above all, should value government by law," he said. "It's the one protection you and your family have against aggressive and predatory people."

"Oh, yes, I'm sure you're quite right," said Lucia.

She did not like him when he talked about his precious law, and she stopped listening to him. She leaned back, with both palms flat on the sand, and she allowed herself to relax. Far down the beach she could see her children, with the young Lloyds and some others they had met; she could hear her father's voice, talking contentedly with Mrs. Lloyd. Nice friends for them to have, she thought. I'm very glad this happened, right now. It was an immeasurable comfort to her that it should be like this, a golden, tranquil day, friendly, and a little de luxe. No matter what happens to me, she thought, I'm pretty sure the Lloyds would stand by Bee and David and Father.

She believed that something was going to happen to her. She had no formed idea of what it would be; only it was as if, in a few hours, she was going to walk out of this sunny world into darkness. She was not frightened, simply resigned, and tired.

It's rather soothing to hear Lieutenant Levy droning on like this, she said to herself. I think he likes me. I'm sure he'd never suspect me of breaking any of his precious laws. He's—when you come to think of it, he talks like a grown-up David. Maybe David will be a lawyer. Or a policeman.

Then she realized that Levy had been silent for some time, and, like most shy people, she was afraid of silence. She glanced at him, and he was pouring sand through the open fingers of one hand, a fine, narrow hand; his head was bent, his face in profile was grave, even melancholy.

"I'd like to see a flamingo sometime," she said, anxiously. "They must be beautiful."

"They are," he said, looking up. "I've seen them, in Florida."

"Oh, you've been in Florida?"

"I went down there, after a man," he said. "However, I like our own birds better. Sandpipers . . . D'you often go over to Simm's Island, Mrs. Holley?"

"Why, no," she answered. "Only—once."

She hoped that this hesitation was not noticeable.

"We went there for a picnic," she went on, "but we didn't like it very much."

"Lots of sandpipers there," he said. "Did you find a fairly good place for your picnic, Mrs. Holley?"

"It was just a strip of beach."

"Most of the island is marshy," said Levy.

"Yes, it is," said Lucia.

"Still," he said, "there are a lot of inlets. It wouldn't be hard to get a boat well into the marshes."

She was afraid to look at him. A trap? she thought.

"But who'd want to?" she asked.

"To study the birds," he explained.

"Oh, yes!" said Lucia. "Yes, of course."

I don't think he means anything, she thought. I think he's too nice to want to trap me. Especially at a sort of little party like this. He's come here to relax and enjoy himself. Not as a policeman.

But he was a policeman.

He offered her a cigarette, and lit it for her and one for himself.

"My housekeeper's getting tough with me," he said, sadly. "She wants *me* to go to market for her."

"That's not right," said Lucia.

"She thinks I get preferential treatment," he said. "She tells me that whenever I take the list to the store, I get things she couldn't get."

"Well, it could be like that," said Lucia. "Someone in the police . . ."

"She says—let's hope it's not true, but she says they don't take enough points from me. Very unethical, that would be."

"I suppose it would be."

"For instance," he said, "how many points should I give for half a pound of Royal Grenadier cheese?"

"Twelve red points," said Lucia.

"Is it a good brand?"

"Oh, yes! We like it best of all."

He turned his head quickly.

"I see!" he said.

But he did not raise his eyes, to look at her. It was as if what he had heard was enough.

He did mean something. She had said something to make him prick up his ears.

Chapter Twelve

"I'VE GOT to go in to New York this morning," Lucia said, at the breakfast table.

There was a silence; her family sat as if stunned.

"But, Mother! You never said a word . . . !" Bee protested.

"Well, why should I, dear?" said Lucia. "I've just got to run in, to look after some business."

"Business?" said her father. "I expect to be going in to town myself, later in the week. Maybe I could attend to things for you, m'dear."

"No, thank you, Father. It's just some little details."

There was another silence, and she resented it. Other people go to New York, she thought, and nobody's so amazed. I bet Mrs. Lloyd goes to New York whenever she feels like it. She made for herself a picture of Mrs. Lloyd at *her* breakfast table. Children, she said, I'm going in to New York this morning. Oh, are you, Mother? said her children.

"What train will you get back, Mother?" asked David.

"I don't know exactly, David. Early in the afternoon."

"If you'll make up your mind now," David said, "I'll meet you with the car."

"There's no sense wasting gas, when we're so short, David. I'll take a taxi."

"Very well," he said, stiffly.

"Mother," said Bee, "I think I'll go in with you."

"Well, not today, dear."

"I want to look at coats, little short coats. You can go ahead and attend to this 'business,' whatever it is, and I'll meet you for lunch."

"I'm having lunch," Lucia said, "with Mrs. Polk."

"For Pete's sake!" cried David. "What d'you want to see that old harpy for?"

Lucia regretted having chosen Mrs. Polk, a simpering white-haired lady of great culture, who had managed the lending library they had patronized in New York.

"You said she'd gone to Washington," said Bee.

Oh, let me alone! Lucia cried in her heart. Ask me no questions and I'll tell you no lies.

"Well, you wouldn't mind my being along, if it's only Mrs. Polk," said Bee.

"She said she wanted to talk to me about something rather special," said Lucia. "We'll go together someday very soon, Bee."

"But what could Mrs. Polk possibly want to talk to *you* about?" asked Bee. "You hardly know her."

"I wish you wouldn't keep *on* at me so!" cried Lucia. "I have absolutely no freedom at all! I can't do the simplest thing without all this nagging——"

She stopped short, well aware that she had shocked all of them, her father and her children. My disposition is getting horrible, she thought. Well, I'm sorry, but I can't help it.

"Will you telephone for a taxi, please, David?" she asked, with cold dignity.

All the way to the station, her anger occupied her mind. Good heavens! Can't I even go in to town, without all this silly fuss? I'm not a child, or an idiot. I'm not a slave, either. I can go to New York whenever I think best, and I don't intend to be cross-examined by my own children. They ought to have confidence in me, and so should Father. Complete confidence.

But when she got on the train, she realized, with a faint shock, that what she ought to be doing, and must do, was to plan the day before her. First I'll go to the bank, she thought, and get my jewelry out of the safe-deposit. Then I'll go to that finance company. If I can't get enough from them, I'll have to pawn my things, to make up the difference. Anyhow, then I'll meet Mr. Donnelly and give him the money. Then I'll call up Lieutenant Levy. No. I'll have to warn Father first. Oh, how can I? How can I tell him he killed Ted Darby? They'll question him, and maybe they won't believe what he says.

They'll ask, why did you go to the boathouse to see deceased? I'll have to tell him not to mention Bee. I'll say I saw a light there, and I thought it was a prowler. That's a funny word, but everybody uses it. The lawn mower was taken by a prowler. There are prowlers in the neighborhood. I wonder if the police use it, write it down? John Doe, charged with prowling. I wonder if there are any women prowlers.

Stick to the point, you fool. Remember what this means. I could get Father to promise not to mention Bee, but I'd never, never be able to get him to tell a lie. He'd just be silent. Mr. Harper, why did you go to the boathouse? All by yourself, in the pouring rain? I refuse to answer that question, sir. Then we'll lock you up until you do answer.

Suppose they lock me up, too? For taking away the body. The children would be left alone. I know Sibyl would look after them, but think of the disgrace . . .

Oh, it can't be true! Things like this don't happen to people like us. I can't tell Lieutenant Levy. But I cannot let that Murray man stay in jail, not even one more night. Taking Ted away was breaking some sort of law, I suppose. But letting that Murray man stay in jail, when I know he's innocent, is really evil. It's a sin.

This was like a fever. Her thoughts came too fast; they merged one into another, in panic confusion. This won't do, she told herself. One thing at a time. First I've got to get the money, so that I can buy back poor little Bee's letters. That's the first thing. First things first. I can't afford to be so flustered.

When the train entered the tunnel, she looked at herself in the window, and she was dismayed. She had taken great pains with her dressing; a black suit, the little black hat with a veil, a white blouse, white gloves. Sophisticated, she had thought, and rather businesslike. But the image she saw in the black window looked idiotic; a white face, the collar of the blouse like a clown's ruffle, the little hat perching too high. Fool! she called herself. If I wasn't a fool, I wouldn't be in this position.

She took a taxi to the bank, and it was her misfortune that she kept on feeling like a fool, a clown. She felt that the man she spoke to was amazed at her and her request. Another man went with her, down to the strange, sinister vaults; a guard with a revolver in a holster opened the door for her and waited outside while she went in alone, to get out the jewelry. It was in a manila envelope, and on it was written, in Tom's handwriting, "Lucia's jewelry."

Oh, Tom! Oh, Tom! Everything so carefully arranged for me—so that there wouldn't be any trouble—if you didn't come back . . . A loud sob came, and a sudden rush of tears; she fought them furiously; she dried her eyes and came out.

The distinguished elderly man who had escorted her gave her a form to sign. "*Thank* you!" she said, and hurried away.

She took another taxi to the offices of the Individual Loan Service Association, and now she had no illusion left of seeming sophisticated and businesslike.

"You want to pay off on a loan?" a drowsy, dark-eyed boy asked her.

"I want to get a loan," she said. "Make a loan. I mean, get one."

"Aw right!" he said, and went away, leaving her in a stately high-ceilinged hall set with Renaissance furniture. A young woman came out, and led her to a table, a young woman with round, rouged cheeks and modishly waved white hair.

"What amount did you wish to borrow?" she asked.

"Oh . . . Five thousand dollars," Lucia answered.

"That's quite a lot of money," said the white-haired young woman. "Where are you employed, Mrs. . . . ?"

"Holley," said Lucia. "I'm not employed anywhere. Not just now."

"What is the purpose of this loan, Mrs. Holley?"

"Well, I need the money," said Lucia.

"Doctors' bills? Paying off a mortgage?"

"Well, your ad says, no red tape."

"We have to protect ourselves, Mrs. Holley. Especially in the case of such a large amount. Have you a weekly or monthly income, Mrs. Holley?"

"Yes."

"What is the source of this income, Mrs. Holley?"

"It's from my husband."

"Will you give me the name and occupation of your husband, please?"

"I'd rather not," said Lucia. "You said you'd lend money on a note. All right. I'll sign a note."

"How much is your income, Mrs. Holley?"

"Well, it's around five hundred a month."

"How much do you think you could repay every month?"

"Well . . . Fifty dollars?"

"Do you realize how long it would take you to repay five thousand dollars at that rate, Mrs. Holley?"

"Yes!" said Lucia, loudly.

"I'm afraid we couldn't consider it, Mrs. Holley. Unless you have collateral. D'you own any property? A car?"

"I've got a car."

"In your own name?"

Tom did that. The car's in your name, Lucia, so that if you ever want to sell it, or trade it in, you won't have any trouble. So that if he didn't come back . . .

"What's the make of your car, Mrs. Holley? How old is it?"

She had to go on with this, but she had no hope left.

"Well, why don't you do this?" said the white-haired young woman. "Drive the car in someday, and we'll get someone to look it over. Ask for me. Miss Poser."

"Your ad said, no delay."

"But we have to protect ourselves, Mrs. Holley," said Miss Poser.

Against *me*? Lucia thought. As if I was a crook?

"Well, how much do you think they'd let me have on the car?" she asked.

Miss Poser said it depended upon the condition of the car, and upon other things.

"But what's the most I could get?" Lucia asked.

If everything was satisfactory, it might, Miss Poser said, come to five hundred dollars.

"Five *hundred*!" said Lucia.

Miss Poser rose.

"You drive the car around sometime," she said, pleasantly enough.

It was a dismissal. For the first time in her life, Lucia was a person to be got rid of, a queer, troublesome, suspect person. Coming around here, trying to get five thousand dollars. Did you ever!

"Would you like to see some jewelry?" Lucia asked.

"Why, no. No, thanks," said Miss Poser.

She was obviously startled and uneasy.

"We don't make loans on personal effects," she said.

"I see!" said Lucia. "Well, thanks!"

She went over to Madison Avenue and walked uptown, looking in vain for a pawnshop. It's getting late, she thought. Mr. Donnelly won't wait. He'll go away. She signaled a taxi and got into it.

"D'you know where there's a pawnshop?" she asked the driver. "A—reliable one?"

"Sure," said the driver.

She was glad that he showed no surprise, not even any interest. It probably doesn't seem queer to him, she thought. He probably knows about society women and duchesses and people like that pawning their jewels. Only Father'd be terribly upset. He has all those little jokes about hock shops, and cockneys hocking their Sunday clothes every Monday and getting them out on Saturday, and things like that. He'd hate me to be doing this.

I don't like it much, myself. But I don't care, if only they won't be rude to me. I didn't know I was so sensitive. It's rather disgusting, to be so sensitive. I thought I was pretty tough. But I'm not. Not when I get out in the world. Then I'm a nincompoop. If one of those reporters stopped me in the street and asked me what I thought about Russia, or something like that, he'd put me down as Mrs. Lucia Holley, Housewife.

Why is it "housewife"? What would I call myself if we lived in a hotel? Nobody ever puts down just "wife," or even just "mother." If you haven't got a job, and you don't keep house, then you aren't anything, apparently. I wish I was something else. I mean, besides keeping house, I wish I was a designer, for instance. The children would think a lot more of me, if I was a designer. Maybe Tom would, too.

No! Tom likes me the way I am. Only, if I could be even a little different when he comes back? I don't mean bustling off to an office every morning. He wouldn't like that. But if I could go to an office or a store now and then, meet outside people. Have interesting little things to tell at dinner. Not be—just me, year after year . . .

"Here you are!" said the driver, stopping before a place on Sixth Avenue.

"Will you wait, please?" Lucia asked.

"Okay," said the driver.

She was frightened. It was such a queer little place, with a metal grille over the window in which was displayed a crazy jumble of things, a mandolin, clocks, candlesticks, a fur neckpiece, an old-fashioned pearl stickpin in a box lined with purple plush. Do they put everything in the window? she thought. I'd hate my things to be there. Mother's pearls, and the ring Tom gave me. I hate this! I hate all this! It's worse than taking Ted over to the island.

It was dim inside the shop, and so queer. A dark, moon-faced young man in shirt sleeves came behind the counter; she thought he looked scornful, and she put on a manner of cold aloofness.

"I'd like to borrow some money on some jewelry," she said.

He said nothing. She opened her purse and took out the long envelope; she handed him the little boxes and he emptied them onto the counter.

"How much do you want?" he asked.

"Well, as much as possible," said Lucia.

The rings, the bracelet, the clasps, the necklace lying on the counter looked, she thought, like junk, worthless and dull. He gathered them up and took them to a little table by a window; he weighed them, looked at them through a glass in his eye, and she stood at the counter, waiting, in cold despair. It's my last chance, she thought. Whatever he gives me is all I'll have for Nagle, and it can't possibly be enough. Maybe he'll say ten dollars. Maybe he'll cheat me. I don't know. I don't care.

He brought the things back to the counter.

"They're very nice," he said. "The settings are nice."

She was startled by his words, and his tone, mild and kind.

"Pretty old, these two," he said. "I guess you think a lot of them."

Tears came into her eyes. All she could do was to ignore them, and keep on looking at him.

"Maybe you'd rather have a smaller loan," he said, "so it'll be easier to get them back?"

She shook her head.

"No, thank you," she said, unsteadily. "As much as possible, please."

"I can let you have six hundred and twenty-five on these," he said.

"Okay!" she said, suddenly and clearly.

"Or maybe we could bring it up to six-fifty," he said, looking down at the things.

"Thank you," said Lucia. "Can I get the money today?"

"Right now," he said.

"Will you—are you going to put them into the window?" she asked, still ignoring the tears on her cheeks.

"Oh, no!" he said. "That's only the things for sale." He glanced up. "Y'see, if you don't redeem the things, or you fail to pay the interest for a certain length of time, why, we're allowed to sell them."

"I see!" she said. "It seems—sort of pathetic, doesn't it? People's funny things."

"Sometimes," he said, "it's very pathetic. But mostly, well, you're doing a service. If anyone needs money in a hurry, well, here's where they can get it. There's been cases I know of where a man would have committed suicide if he couldn't get forty-fifty dollars quick. Then somebody'll come in here that would get put out in the street if he can't pay his rent. Well, the landlord won't take his fine watch. The landlord, naturally, he don't know the value of things. Then, say the next week, this man gets a good job. Soon as he gets his pay, he's back here, redeems his watch, and all is well."

Lucia was very much touched. I like him! she thought. He's trying to make me see that it isn't horrible and comic to be a pawnbroker. He wants it to seem sort of romantic.

She wished to help him in this; she wanted to show an interest in his business.

"Do you ever get wedding rings?" she asked.

"Well, not so many," he said. "People have a lot of sentiment about them and a wedding ring hasn't got much actual value, as a rule. Although you'd be surprised how many women throw away their wedding rings."

"But why?"

"Well, they're getting a divorce, or they're mad at their husbands, or one thing or another, and they throw away their rings."

"I saw a baby's silver mug in the window."

"The father's a drunk," he said. "That's a bad case. Well, I'll get your money for you now."

He brought it to her, all in bills.

"Good luck!" he said.

The taxi driver sat in the cab, smoking a cigarette.

"Do you know where I could get any cigarettes?" Lucia asked.

"Lady," he said, "if I knew that, I'd be rich. I can let you have one."

"Thank you!" she said. "Now I'd like to go to Stern's, please, on Forty-second Street."

He gave her a cigarette; he struck a match and held it for her, and she leaned back, relaxed, savoring the cigarette with something like bliss. It's all over, she thought. I haven't got the money, and I can't get it, ever.

I wonder if this is a little the way people feel sometimes when they're going to die, she thought. When the doctor says there's no hope, and there's nothing you can do but just let go. It would be a rather good way to die, not fighting and struggling, just letting go.

She had a picture of herself at home, lying comfortably in bed, with everything over. Nothing to be done, about anything.

But the children! she thought. And Father . . . They'd have to send a cable to Tom . . . Oh, no! You never can stop fighting and struggling.

The cab turned into Forty-second Street, and looking at her watch, she saw that she was over half an hour late. Maybe Mr. Donnelly's gone, she thought. You couldn't blame him.

But he was there, standing outside the entrance, tall, outstandingly neat, in a dark blue, double-breasted suit and a gray felt hat; not smoking, not fidgeting, not glancing around; just waiting. He certainly doesn't look like a crook, she thought. He's quite distinguished looking. Quite handsome.

As she was getting out of the cab he came forward, hat in hand.

"We could keep the cab," he said. "There's a place in the Fifties I think you would like."

She settled back in the cab and as he got in beside her, he gave the driver an address.

"I haven't got the money," she said, at once. "I never can get it."

He was silent, and she turned to look at him; she found him looking at her, with his curiously clouded blue eyes.

"Be easy," he said. "Take it easy."

Chapter Thirteen

THERE WAS no reason to feel reassured by this, but she did feel so.

"This place where we are going," he said. "There's a small room in it we can have to ourselves. Unless you'd rather eat out with the other people?"

"Maybe we could talk better by ourselves," she said.

"That's what I'd thought of," he said.

It was strange, she thought, that she had no hesitation about lunching alone with him in whatever place he had chosen. She remembered things she had read in old-fashioned novels about private dining rooms, always the scene of some amorous adventure, a seduction, drugged wine, a conniving waiter. But Mr. Donnelly isn't like that, she thought.

The cab stopped before a little restaurant of rather smart appearance, with a dark blue canopy over the entrance on which was lettered Café Colorado; a doorman in uniform came forward to open the door of the taxi. Donnelly took a bill out of his wallet and passed it to the driver.

"All right," he said.

"*What?*" said the driver. "Well, thanks. Thanks a lot."

They went down a few steps, to a carpeted restaurant with lighted lamps on small tables, and at one end a bar with a mirror lined by blue fluorescent lights. The place was well filled with people; nothing at all queer about it, she thought. An elderly waiter came hurrying up to Donnelly.

"*Bon jour, madame, monsieur!*"

"Tell the boss I am here, will you?" said Donnelly.

"*Mais oui, monsieur!*" said the waiter, and hurried away.

Very promptly a man came across the room to them, stout and swarthy, with a black mustache and sorrowful eyes.

"Ah . . . !" he said. "Ze room, Marty?"

"*Parfaitement*," said Donnelly.

"Zis way, madame!"

They followed him through the restaurant, and he opened a door beside the bar, leading to a dark little passage. At the end of this he opened another door.

667

"*Voilà!*" he said, with an air of pride.

"*C'est assez bien*," said Donnelly, and went on talking in French, of which Lucia had only a schoolgirl knowledge. She gathered, though, that he was talking about the lunch, and that the other man was called Gogo.

The room itself made her want to laugh, it was so exactly like something from one of those old-fashioned books; a small room without windows, a round table right in the center, set for two, with a bowl of red roses in the middle; there was even a couch, covered with blue and gold brocade.

"*Alors . . .*" said Gogo, and bowed and smiled and went out, closing the door after him.

"I did not introduce him," said Donnelly. "I did not think you'd be wanting to know him."

"Well, why not? Is he—?" She paused for a word. "Is he— questionable?"

"He is a good friend of mine," Donnelly said. "Only, he's not the class you're used to."

"Class"? she thought. What "class" would you call Donnelly? According to his own words, he came of peasant stock; he had had no education; he was a blackmailer and God knew what else. But he had a courtesy that was natural and effortless; his speech had a correctness, a rhythm like that of a carefully trained foreigner. I don't know what he is, she thought.

He drew back a chair for her.

"I ordered a Martini for you," he said. "Will that be what you like?"

"Oh, yes, thanks!"

"Will you have a cigarette?" he said. "While you're waiting?"

He lit one for her, and one for himself; he moved an ash tray nearer to her, and sat down across the table from her.

"You speak French very fluently, don't you?" she said.

"It is fluent enough," he said, "but I don't know at all if it is very good. I picked it up in Quebec."

"Did you live in Quebec?"

"I was in a monastery near there for more than a year."

"In a monastery?"

"It was in my mind, those days, that I'd study to be a priest."

"Oh! Did you change your mind?"

"I had no vocation," he said, and after a pause, "the world was too much with me."

It seemed to Lucia then that this big, stalwart man, of unimaginable experiences, was a creature infinitely more sensitive and more fragile than herself. She had thought that often about David, about her father, about Tom; she had felt herself to be tougher, more flexible, better able to endure what must come.

"Didn't you ever marry?" she asked.

"I wanted to marry," he said, "but I never found a girl would suit me."

A slight resentment rose in her, against this male arrogance.

"You never found anyone good enough?" she asked.

"I did not," he answered, with simplicity.

The waiter came in then, with one cocktail on a tray.

"Aren't you having one?" she asked.

"I never take a drink till five o'clock."

"Why not?" she asked, a little sharply.

"There was a time when I drank too much," he said. "For three years I went roaring around, till I had the d.t.'s. It is a terrible thing. You'd never forget it. To Bellevue, they took me, and I saw the others that were in it. Old men, some of them, with their lives all drunk away and wasted." He paused. "Now I am moderate," he said.

"You've had quite a lot of experience . . ." she said, lightly.

"I have that," he said.

She sipped the cocktail, feeling an odd new strength in herself, a sense of power she had not known before. I can manage *him*, all right, she thought.

"You look very charming," he said. "It is a nice little hat you're wearing, and the white gloves, and all."

Then it all came back to her.

"I don't feel charming," she said, bitterly. "I've—failed. I can't get that money."

"You were trying?"

"I went to a loan company I saw advertised," she said. "They said they lent money on your note, without any red tape. Well, they wouldn't." She was silent for a moment, remembering Miss Poser. She opened her purse and took out the manila envelope, into which she had put the money. "Here's six hundred and fifty dollars," she said. "That's all I can get. *All.*"

"Did you draw that out of your bank?"

"No. I haven't anything in the bank except what I have to use. No. I pawned some jewelry I had."

"Give me the ticket," he said.

"But—why?"

"Give me the ticket," he said, with a ring in his voice.

"But why? I don't want to."

"Give it me!" he said, rising.

"No! I won't!"

He stood over her, his hand outstretched, and she was startled, and almost frightened, by the power of the man, the concentrated force in him. His face was not blurred now; the angle of his jaw was sharp; his eyes were clear and cold.

"Give it me! Get it out of your purse."

She took the ticket out of her purse, reluctant and angry.

"Well, why?" she demanded.

"I will get your things back for you," he said. "Every damn one of them."

"They're not important. I don't care about them."

He began walking up and down the room.

"I will get them back for you," he said.

"I don't care about them!" she cried. "I only want to stop that Nagle."

"I will do that, too," he said.

"Oh! But can you?"

"I didn't know how it was——" he began, when the waiter came in, with shrimp cocktails set in ice.

"Bring the lady another Martini," said Donnelly, and she made no protest.

He sat down at the table.

"I didn't know it would be so bad for you," he said. "Carlie—Nagle, that is, told me he'd looked into it. He said you'd plenty of money; your father, too."

"I haven't any money," she said. "Only what I have to use."

"It's a wonder they wouldn't give you some."

"They do! My father and my husband have always given me anything I wanted."

"It is not enough," he said.

"You mean I ought to have a little special fund—to pay blackmail out of?"

She could see that that hit him, hard, and she was glad.

"I don't care about those bits of jewelry," she said. "I only care about saving my daughter from a miserable scandal."

"I'm not worrying about your daughter. She would get over a scandal."

The waiter came back with the second Martini and set it before her.

"I'll have a talk with Nagle," he said. "I will try to make him wait till the money comes in from the deal we've got on. I'd pay him for you now, only the two of us are hard up, putting all we could lay hands on into this new thing. The trouble is, Nagle is always nervous if he hasn't a good sum in the bank. Drink your cocktail."

"I don't want it."

"Then eat your lunch."

"I can't."

"Look!" he said. "If I cannot keep Nagle quiet, then let him go ahead. He will take the letters to your father——"

"No! He can't! He mustn't!"

"Your father is a fine old gentleman, by what I saw. He will not be too hard on the girl."

"No! No!" she said. "My father *mustn't* know."

"You take it too hard. Let Nagle go ahead. It will soon be over——"

"No!" she cried, again. "You don't understand. Father can't know anything at all about Ted Darby."

She pushed back her chair, but she did not rise; she sat there rigid, thinking fast. If I tell Lieutenant Levy, Father'll have to know. Have to know about Bee and Ted; have to know that he killed Ted. And I can't let that Murray stay in jail. I've got to tell Lieutenant Levy, unless . . .

Unless somehow Murray could be got out of prison—without my telling the police.

"What is it?" Donnelly asked. "What is it worrying you?"

She glanced quickly at him, and the look in his face was clear to her. She did not care to put it into words for herself; simply she knew that she could trust him with anything at all. She knew that she could make use of all the strength and the force in him.

"Father would go straight to the police, if Mr. Nagle saw him," she said. "And if the police find out about my daughter and Ted Darby——"

"They would not care about that," he said. "When it is people like yourselves, they'd try to keep the girl's name out of it. Her letters have nothing to do with Darby's killing."

"But suppose they have?"

"They have not."

Her heart was beating in a quick, erratic way that made her breath come too fast.

"Suppose it wasn't Murray who killed Ted?" she said.

"I know damn well it was not Murray," he said. "Murray was framed."

"But he's in jail for it. He'll be tried for it."

"He will go to the chair for it," said Donnelly. "I would not lose a night's sleep over that. He and Darby, the two of them, were dirty, double-crossing——" He checked himself. "They are rats," he said.

"Murray can't be punished—executed—for something he didn't do."

"Don't worry about him. He is not worth it."

"Could you get Murray off, if you wanted?"

"I would not want to."

"But *could* you, if you tried? Please answer!"

"I might," he said. "Why do you want to know?"

The waiter came in, and hesitated, seeing the untouched shrimps.

"Wait a while," said Donnelly. "Is there a bell in it? There? Then take it easy till I'll ring for you."

The man went out, closing the door behind him.

"You could get Murray freed?" she asked.

"Maybe. Only I would not lift a finger to do it."

She had the most vivid image in her mind of yesterday's brunch, the blue water, the green trees, the sunny tranquillity; Mrs. Lloyd's smile, the way Owen had watched Bee. Bee, and David, and her father, and Tom so very far away, all of them so innocent, all of them threatened by these dark, horrible shadows from another world, Ted Darby, Nagle, Murray, criminals, all of them, cruel, dangerous as wild beasts.

"What is it worrying you?" Donnelly asked.

"Well . . . Suppose I told you *I* killed Ted Darby?" she said.

Chapter Fourteen

H E GAVE her a quick sidelong look.
"No," he said. "You could not kill anyone."

"It was an accident. He was—I got angry at him, about the letters. I pushed him, and he fell. It was in the boathouse, and he fell into the launch, on the anchor. It killed him."

He gave her another of those sidelong looks, wary and alert.

"Swallow your drink," he said. "It will do you good."

She shook her head.

"I didn't know he was dead, until the morning," she said. "Then I found him there. Then I took him over to the island. It was . . . It was—" She paused a moment. "I had—to get him off the anchor. It was . . . And then I had—to get him out of the boat."

Her voice was unsteady, her mouth trembled. Remembering it was worse than the doing of it.

"You'll have to believe me," she said.

She looked up at him; their eyes met for a long moment.

"I do believe you," he said. "There's no saint in heaven would do more than you'd do for your family."

"I was—never going to tell anyone," she said. "But now—I can't let Murray pay for it."

"You can that," he said. "Murray's no good at all."

"That doesn't matter. I can't let him suffer for something that's my fault."

"You can."

"No," she said. "I won't. It's a sin."

"A sin?" he repeated, as if startled. "It's hard, now, to know what's a sin and what isn't."

"It's never hard," she said. "You always know in your own heart what's right."

"Ah . . ." he said. "It's not that easy. You have to look at all sides of it. Now, there's your family. They're good people. They do good in the world. What's the sense in sacrificing them for a rat like Murray? You have to think out what's going to do the most good."

"No," she said. "You have to do what's right, no matter what comes of it."

"There are many don't agree with that," he said. "There are many believe you have to study out what's going to do the most good in the end."

"That's——" she began, and stopped herself. That's Jesuitical, she had been going to say, but maybe that was his belief. "I can't see things that way," she said. "I can't let Murray stay in jail. No matter what happens to us. I'd rather be in jail myself."

"You'll not go to jail," he said. "Look, now. Will you not try to eat a little? I've ordered a steak, but if there's something else——"

"That man's in prison this moment—while I sit here."

"Look, now. It doesn't mean to him what it would mean to you. He's been in it before."

"Oh, can't you understand how I feel?" she cried. "I can't sit here—eating . . . I don't know what to do. I don't know where to turn."

"Turn to me," he said.

She looked at him. He pushed back his chair and rose, and began to walk up and down the room again. He was a big man, and heavy, but his heel-and-toe walk was very light; his gleaming shoes seemed more flexible than anyone else's.

"It's my punishment," he said. "I've been a fool with my money, and worse. And now, when I need it, I haven't it. I'd give the eyes out of my head if I could pay off Nagle now. Or if I'd the money to pay Isaacs or Jimmy Downey to get Murray off." At the end of the room he turned and came back toward her. "Only don't be eating your heart out," he said. "I will do it."

"How?"

"I will work on Nagle," he said. "He knows we'll be getting this money before long, and I will pay him out of the share that's coming to me."

"Why should you?" she demanded, angrily. "Why should *you* pay blackmail to that horrible man, if he's your partner, or whatever you call him?"

"Well, you see," he said, "it was Nagle got the letters from Darby. Nagle thought up the whole thing. He has a right——"

"You can't talk like that! As if it was an ordinary business thing. It's—don't you realize it's a *crime*?"

He was coming toward her, so big, light-footed, his eyes blank. He was menacing. Then he wheeled round and went away from her.

"Yes . . ." he said. "Yes, you're right. God help me, I hardly know any more what's right from what's wrong."

"Everyone knows."

"Yes," he said. "But I cannot go back on Nagle now."

"Even when you realize that he's a criminal?"

"I am a criminal myself," he said.

"You're not," said Lucia. "Not really."

"I've broken the law," he said. "I've done wrong enough. Only, God be praised, I never killed anyone." He was down at the end of the room now, with his back to her. "Only in the war," he said, "the first war, I mean. And the killing in the war is not accounted a sin." He was silent for a time. "But I wasn't easy about it," he said. "I was young then, and when I'd see some of the Boches—that's what we called them, in those days—when I'd see them lying dead in a field or maybe a forest, I'd think, was it me did that? And now, when you see the young lads going off again . . . You'd think the devil rules the world."

He came back to her.

"There's yourself," he said. "So good—and look at the trouble that's come to you. But I'll get you free of it. I'll work on Nagle, and I will see Isaacs or Downey, about getting Murray out."

"But how can they? Unless they find someone else?"

"Isaacs can get anyone off," said Donnelly.

"But what will you tell him? Will you have to say that you know someone else did it?"

"I will tell him nothing at all. He'll go to see Murray, and they will fix it up together." He paused a moment. "Will you trust me?" he asked.

"Yes . . ." she said.

"There is nothing I would not do for you," he said. "Nothing in the world."

She lowered her eyes, not to see the look in his face.

"Could we have the steak?" she asked. "I've got to be getting home."

He rang the bell at once.

"Did you ever get a ham?" he asked.

"Oh, yes!" she said, and added, "Thank you."

"There's a roast of beef on the way," he said. "And three pounds of bacon."

"Mr. Donnelly——"

"Yes?"

"I'd rather you didn't send anything more. It's—hard to explain them. And——"

"Yes?"

"Well, they're black market, aren't they?"

"I suppose you'd call them that," he said. "But there's no need for it to be on your conscience at all. They are a present to you."

"Thank you very much, but please don't send the beef. Please don't send anything."

"I'm afraid they're on the way, if they're not there already."

The waiter brought in the steak, French fried potatoes, peas, a salad; he moved saltcellars, emptied the ash tray, and went away.

"That Sibyl is a fine woman," said Donnelly.

"But you don't know her!"

"I had a bit of a talk with her yesterday, when you were not home," he said. "She is a fine woman."

"Yes. She is."

"I asked her to let me know if ever I was needed," he said. "I gave her my telephone number."

How could you be "needed"? Lucia thought. But she did not say it.

"Eat, will you not?" he asked, anxiously. "You're pale. Eat a bit of the red meat. And take it easy. I will get Murray out of jail for you, and I will keep Nagle off your neck. He'll give you the letters back. Trust me, will you not?"

"I do trust you," she said.

He gave a sigh, as if a weight were lifted. But he did not eat, nor could she. This room without windows was quiet, too quiet; she felt unbearably restless. She did something unusual to her; she opened her purse and took out a little mirror and looked at herself.

She did not look flustered and frightened now. It was true that she was pale, her hair a little disordered, but there was something in her face she had not seen in it before, a sorrowful and quiet beauty. That's how I look to him, she thought.

Chapter Fifteen

THEY DID not want the dessert; he waved it away. No check was brought to him; he left some bills on the table, and they went out of the room, through the restaurant, and into the street. He stopped a taxi and took her to the train.

"You'll be hearing from me," he said. "And you'll take it easy, will you not? I'll look after everything."

She stood silent, her lashes lowered. She knew that he was looking at her; she knew that she was dark, slender and lovely; she knew he was waiting for her to look up, and presently she raised her eyes.

"Thank you," she said.

"Could I come to the house?" he asked. "Just once more? Stop by, maybe, and bring a bottle of Scotch for your father?"

"I'm sorry," she said, "I'm very sorry, but—not possibly."

"Can I see you once more?" he said. "When I've settled all this, would you have lunch with me, the way it was today?"

She did not answer.

"Just the once, when it's all settled?" he asked. "I know how it is with you. You have your family and your—social position to think of. But if you'd give me just one more sight of you . . . ?"

There were people moving and hurrying all around them; a prodigious voice was announcing trains. But they were some-how isolated. He did not urge her any more; he simply waited, in a dreadful humility. The gate of her platform was opening, but still she stood there, with her lashes lowered.

Suddenly she held out her white-gloved hand, and looked at him.

"Yes," she said. "I'll be very pleased to have lunch with you someday."

She did not smile; they never smiled at each other. He held her hand for a moment, very lightly.

"Be easy," he said.

She went along the dim platform, in a silent, smooth-moving crowd; she got into a car. It was a smoker, and she decided to stay in it and have a cigarette. She sat down beside a man and opened her purse; she took out her pack, but it was empty; she felt in the corners; she turned it upside down.

"Have one of mine!" said the man beside her.

"Oh, but really . . . ! When they're so hard to get . . ."

"Not hard for *me*," he said. "Take one! Take one!"

He lit it for her; a burly man with a red face and bright little blue eyes.

"This shortage'll be over in a week or so," he said. "But in the meantime it doesn't bother *me* any. I've got connections in just about every line of business *you* ever heard of. Why, only the other day, this fellow I know was squawking about an alarm clock. Couldn't find one anywhere. I'll get you one this afternoon, I told him. Hey, no black market stuff for me, he says. I don't use the black market, brother, I tell him. I use *this*."

He tapped his temple with his third finger and raised his thin brows; he smiled, with his lips closed. And he was trying to impress her. His little bright eyes flickered over her, not boldly, but with admiration.

"Here!" he said. "Let's change seats. You young ladies always like to sit by the window."

When he stood up, he put his hand into his pocket, and brought out two packs of cigarettes, Mr. Harper's favorite brand.

"Just slip these in your purse," he said.

"Oh, I couldn't!"

"Plenty more where they came from," he said. "You take them. You'll be doing me a favor."

He settled down cozily beside her.

"No, sir," he said, "I never married. I see you're wearing the badge of servitude." He laughed. "That's the way it goes," he said. "Every time I meet an attractive young lady, she's got a husband. Didn't bother to wait for me."

Now he got around to asking questions, and she had no objection to telling him that she had a husband overseas, that she had two children. Just like somebody in a magazine story, she thought.

"It's hard," he said, gravely, "it's very hard. Attractive young lady."

He's a wolf, she thought. But not a bad one. Sort of pathetic. She could see what he was getting around to now.

"I could meet you somewhere . . ." he said. "We could have a little dinner, go somewhere to dance. Do you good."

"I can't leave the children," she said. "I never go out in the evenings."

"Mistake," he said. "Great mistake. You could get one of these high-school kids to sit with the children."

He obviously pictured two small children, and let him, Lucia thought. She was surprised at herself for the bland enjoyment she found in his company. But she would not tell him her name.

"No," she said, looking into his eyes. "Really I can't."

"I'll give you my card," he said, "and if ever you change your mind——"

Mr. Richard Hoopendyke. Representing the Shilley Mfg. Co.

"Change your mind!" he said, rising when she did.

"Well, maybe . . ." said Lucia.

When she got out at the familiar station, it was strange to see the sunny afternoon quiet. It seemed to her that she had been gone so long, so very long; she felt timid about going home, as if she had in some way changed. She got into a taxi with two other people, a man and a woman, and they rode in grim silence. They don't like me, Lucia told herself. They think I'm queer. An Undesirable Acquaintance. Well, maybe I am.

She felt queer. She was the first one to get out, and she told the driver to stop at the corner; she walked down the road, feeling strangely solitary. Such a long day, she thought, and so much has happened.

But, after all, what really had happened? She had tried to get a loan, and failed; she had pawned her jewelry. And then I had lunch . . . she thought. There's nothing so wonderful in all that. Only, I never can tell anyone about it. Certainly not Father and the children, and not even Tom. Tom would know there wasn't anything wrong, but he wouldn't like it. Lunch in a private room. With a crook. Tom wouldn't like that man in the smoker, and neither would Father or the children. They don't think I'm like that.

The house seemed unwelcoming in the late afternoon sun. It's nice when someone comes out to meet you, she thought. When the children were little, they always rushed out. That was nice. But then I always had some little present for them.

And she was empty-handed now; she felt it. She was bringing back nothing. The front door was unlocked, as usual; she
opened it and went in, and Mr. Harper spoke, from the sitting
room.

"Lucia?"

"It's me, Father."

He was sitting in an armchair, with a book in his hand, an
empty teacup on the table beside him.

"Oh . . . Sibyl gave you your tea?" she said.

"Never forgets," he said.

She came up behind him, and kissed his silver head.

"Ha . . ." he said, pleased. "Have a good day, m'dear?"

"Yes, thank you, Father."

"Shopping, I suppose," he said. "Your mother used to come
home, say she was exhausted, shopping all day. I'd ask her what
she'd bought, and half the time she'd say she hadn't bought
anything at all."

He laughed, his eyes fixed upon nothing; as if in his mind he
could see that absurd and beloved figure. Lucia handed him
one of the packs of cigarettes Mr. Hoopendyke had given her.

"That's very nice," he said. "Very welcome, m'dear. By the
way, that Lloyd boy was here. Wanted my permission to put
my name up at the Yacht Club. I told him my sailing days were
a thing of the past. I shouldn't make much use of the club. But
I didn't like to rebuff the boy. Nice lad. And the dues are no
great matter. I told him to go ahead, if he liked."

He wants to belong to the club, Lucia thought. He's lonely.
I don't keep him from being lonely. I haven't any time. I don't
know what I do with myself, but I never have any time.

"You'll be on a committee inside a week," she said. "You
always are."

"Nonsense!" he said. "At my age——"

"Nonsense yourself!" she said. "People always have such
confidence in you, Daddy."

"'Daddy' . . ." he repeated. She had not used that name
for a long time, and it seemed to echo for both of them. Tears
came into her eyes and she winked them away.

"I've got to see Sibyl," she said.

Sibyl was standing at the cabinet, in a dazzle of sun, breaking eggs, letting the whites slip into one fluted blue bowl, and

the golden yolks into a green one. It was a delicate operation, and beautiful. She dealt with the egg in hand, and then looked up, with her tender, slow smile.

"Oh, you're back, ma'am?"

"Yes, I'm back. We're having the cold ham tonight, aren't we, Sibyl?"

"Thought I'd better cook the beef tonight, ma'am."

"The beef . . . ?"

"It came just in time," said Sibyl. "And I'll make the Yorkshire pudding Mr. Harper likes."

No questions about that beef. No questions, ever, about anything. But what does she *think?* Lucia asked herself. Above everything in the world, she wanted to know what Sibyl thought.

"It was a present," she said.

"Yes, ma'am," said Sibyl.

"You must have been surprised, when the beef came," Lucia said.

"No, ma'am."

"Well, why not?"

"Mr. Donnelly told me he was sending it, ma'am. Asked me, what would Mrs. Holley like. Said he'd get anything you wanted, any time."

The words, in Sibyl's soft voice, had an impact that made Lucia catch her breath. Nobody should say that. Nobody should know that.

"I've told him not to send anything more," she said. "I've told him not to come here again."

"Yes, ma'am," said Sibyl.

Now drop it! Lucia told herself. Let well enough alone.

But she could not.

"He's not the sort of person to have here," she said.

"He's unfortunate," said Sibyl.

"What do you mean, Sibyl?"

"Got in bad company," said Sibyl.

"He's a free agent. He could choose his company, like anyone else."

"We don't always know what we're doing, ma'am," said Sibyl. "Till it's too late."

"It's never too late to—change," said Lucia.

"That's what my husband says, all the time. But I don't think people change much."

"I didn't know you'd been married, Sibyl."

"Yes, ma'am. He's in jail, in Georgia."

"Oh, Sibyl!"

"Been there eighteen years," Sibyl said, "and got seven more to go. Unless he gets a parole. And he won't."

"And you're—waiting for him?" Lucia asked.

"Obliged to," Sibyl answered, somberly. "Bill never did me any wrong. Not that he knew of. When they took him away, I told him I'd wait for him, and I have."

"Eighteen years!" Lucia said. "That must have been terribly hard for you, Sibyl."

"Yes, ma'am," said Sibyl. "And I don't know if it was sensible, either."

"You mean you've changed your mind about him, Sibyl?"

"It just didn't do him much good," Sibyl said. "He's got a hopeful nature. Thinks he can come out of jail, when he's fifty-four years old, and start a fine new life for us. Gets more and more philosophical."

"Well . . ." Lucia said, anxiously. "That's probably a good thing, Sibyl."

"Maybe so, ma'am," said Sibyl, with courteous deference. "The philosophy Bill's got, it's that everything that happens is for the best. He doesn't study about injustice. He's not bitter, shut up there all the best years of his life for what wasn't wrong at all."

"What was it, Sibyl?"

"Bill was a sailor," said Sibyl. "I reckon that's why I married him; I was just so crazy to travel. Don't know how it got in my head, but even when I was a little girl, I used to think about it. Maybe it was out of books. The white people my mother worked for used to lend me books. I used to think, if I could ever get up to the frozen North, big, white fields of snow, those lights in the sky . . . And Paris. Bill told me it's all true about Paris. Colored people can go anywhere, see all the sights. Bill said we'd get to take trips."

"Didn't you ever?"

"No, ma'am. First thing we got married, I started to have a baby. And he gave up going to sea. He got a job in the mill;

said he wanted to be near me, case there was any trouble. I lost
the baby, and there he was. We had some money saved, and he
said we'd take a trip. Went to a steamship office to buy us a
ticket. Man said they didn't want any niggers on their ships.
Bill said it was the law that he could buy a ticket if he had the
money. The man hit him, and Bill hit him back. Assault with
intent to kill, they called it. But the man didn't die, and Bill
didn't ever think to kill him. He just hit back. He had a knife
on him, but he always did, ever since the days when he was at
sea."

"Maybe when he gets out, you can take a trip."

"No, ma'am," said Sibyl. "Bill'll be fifty-four, and I don't
know if he can get him a decent job. He's got kind of queer,
shut up in that jail. I reckon I'll have to support him. Well, I
can do it, if I keep my health."

"Well . . ." Lucia said. "You must have been a wonderful
help and comfort to your husband, all this while."

"I don't know . . ." said Sibyl. "He's got that philosophical
nature . . . If I'd said I wouldn't be waiting for him, he'd
have found some other kind of comfort. And I'd have found
some way to see the world."

Lucia was silent, deeply impressed by this glimpse into
Sibyl's nature. All these years, while she had gone about her
work so quietly and competently, there had been in her this
passionate longing to see the world. I never had that, Lucia
thought. I never specially thought about traveling. I never
wanted anything like that. *What did I want?*

She had wanted a husband and children, and she had got
them. Ever since she could remember, everything she had
wanted had been given to her. If she had wanted a doll, a bicycle, a new dress, her parents had given it to her. The husband
she wanted had appeared while she was still in school; the son
and the daughter she wanted had come to her without too
much pain and effort.

Was she, then, a creature uniquely favored? Or was she a
creature, not favored, but scorned and dismissed by life, denied
what other people had? There was David, filled with his uneasy
hopes, Bee and her stormy follies, Tom going through the experience he could never share with her. Even Sibyl. Even
Donnelly . . .

I'm like a doll, she thought. I'm not real. As she sat at dinner with her family, this sense of unreality became almost frightening. They told about things that had happened to them today, and it was all real, and crystal-clear, to be understood by anyone. But her day was like a dream; if she should try to describe it, who would believe or understand about the vaults, the loan office, the pawnshop, the private dining room, even Mr. Hoopendyke in the smoker?

She sat down to write to Tom, with the same sense of numbed unreality. Who was this, trying to write a letter?

DEAR TOM:
   I don't know where you are. I don't know who I am. Tom, I'm in such trouble . . .

Take it easy, Donnelly had said. I'll get Murray out, he had said. I'll keep Nagle quiet. But she could not take it easy. She was caught in a current that was carrying her farther and farther from the shore.

Her restless dreams that night were all of the sea. She dreamed that she was swimming, in a race with Mrs. Lloyd, and everyone she loved best was standing on the shore, watching. Mrs. Lloyd, in a little hat of purple violets, went through the water with incredible speed and ease, and Lucia went laboring after her, disappointing her own people so by her clumsy floundering.

She waked from that, and got up in haste, to look at the letter she had written to Tom, to make sure that she had not really written anything about "trouble," or even anything he might read between the lines. I don't think so . . . she said to herself. It seems to me just like my other letters. Just babbling.

She went back to bed, and she dreamed that she was in a rowboat, with an enormous rock on the thwarts. She pulled on the oars with all her strength, but she could not move the boat with that great weight in it. And she had to move; she had to hurry. At first it was because something was coming after her, out of the dark boathouse, something dangerous and dreadful. But, as she strained at the oars, she became aware that the danger was the rock itself. If she did not hurry, did not get to the place of safety, the rock was going to change into something else.

It was beginning already. Two things like ears were shaping on its top; it shifted a little, and she thought it sighed. Then it rolled toward her, and she waked, in a sweat of terror. There was a great wind blowing, and rain was driving in at the open window; there was a noise, as if the night itself were roaring.

She sprang up and closed her window and barefoot, in her pajamas, went out into the hall, to Bee's room. It was dark in there, and filled with the rushing wind, and her daughter lay there, unconscious, helpless. She closed that window, and went to David's room. He too was asleep, and the rain was driving straight on his back. She pulled off the damp sheet and covered him with a blanket, and he did not stir.

Tears were running down her face, it so pierced her heart to think of her children lying unprotected in the rain. She went along the hall to her father's room, and there was a light showing under the door; she knocked and he said "Come in! Come in!" in his steady old voice.

He was standing by the window in his flannel dressing gown, smoking a cigarette.

"'Oh, pilot, 'tis a fearful night,' what, what?" he said.

"Yes, it *is*!" said Lucia.

"What's this? What's this? Are you crying, m'dear?"

"It's just the rain. I was closing the children's windows."

"Sit down and have a cigarette," he said. "I've got that pack you brought me, m'dear. Here! Sit down here. Very comfortable chair."

Chapter Sixteen

"I WISH you'd ask Mrs. Lloyd to tea," Bee said at breakfast, with a hint of reproach.

"Well, I will," said Lucia. "I'll call her up after breakfast."

"There's the postman!" cried David, jumping up.

He went to the door, and came back leisurely, looking through the sheaf of letters he carried.

"Oh, hurry up!" said Bee. "Is there anything for me?"

"Take it easy!" said David.

"Mother, tell him to hurry up!" said Bee.

"*Take* it easy! *Take* it easy!" said David. "Four for you, Mother; two V-mails from Dad. One for you, Grandpa. Letter for me from Dad. And here's the vitally important mail for Miss Beatrice Holley. Letter from your alumnae association, letter from Boothbay—that must be Edna. Oh, gosh! Here's a letter from Jerry, Bee. Open it and let's see if he's still in China."

"When I'm good and ready," said Bee.

They all sat at the table, opening their letters. The V-mails from Tom looked queer, Lucia thought; his sharp, clear writing was unfamiliar in this diminished form. These were not the actual letters he had written; this was not the paper his hand had touched; these dwarf letters had been handled and read by heaven knew how many people.

> Have written to David sending some snaps. I'd be very glad to get pictures of the house. Glad to think of you all there, out of the city. Don't worry about your letters being "dull," old girl. They're just what I want. They give me the feeling of our life going on, the same old way. I lived in heaven, but I didn't know it. End of paper. Love to you, kids, Granddad. Most to you.

In the second letter he wrote:

> Like to hear all the little details. Other men tell me their wives complain of shortages, meat, butter, and so

on. How are you getting on? You never say anything much, old girl.

Tom . . . she kept saying to herself. Tom . . . And she thought that if he were to walk into the room this moment, she would have nothing else to say to him. Only his name; only Tom.

"Will you call up Mrs. Lloyd now, Mother?" Bee asked. "If you don't, you'll forget all about it."

"I don't forget everything," said Lucia.

"Oh, Mother!" Bee protested, laughing.

"I don't find your mother forgetful," said Mr. Harper. "On the contrary. Remembers everything, it seems to me. You must realize, young lady, that a woman with a family and a house to look after has a great deal on her mind. Like an executive in an office."

"Yes, I know, Grandpa. I was only teasing her."

"Well . . ." said Mr. Harper, somewhat mollified. "You'll understand, one of these days, Beatrice, when you have a home of your own."

"Excuse me?" said David. "I promised to meet a kid."

"Wait a minute!" Bee said, and ran after him; Lucia could see them talking in the hall.

Their friendship pleased her beyond measure, but it was always a little surprising. She remembered a day, long ago, when they had been little more than babies, perhaps three and five. She had been writing a letter in the sitting room, and they had been in their nursery, with the door open. And, while she sought something to put into the letter, she had heard them talking. Those two baby creatures, that she had brought into the world, were living a life of their own, independent of her. They could talk to each other.

She had listened to them with rapture; it was a thing so thrilling that even now she remembered their talk. They had been making a baby plan. "You get your horse, David," Bee had said, "and I'll get Lilacker." That was her favorite, sacred doll, kept in a drawer; before this, she had always played alone with Lilacker; only now was the little brother admitted. Why, even if I died, they'd go on! Lucia had thought, delighted.

Why do you talk so damn much about "if you died"? Tom

had asked her once. I can't say I enjoy it. Well . . . she had
said. I don't exactly know. Maybe having children makes you
feel like that. It doesn't make me feel like that, Tom had said.
I've got insurance for you all; I've made the best arrangements
I can. But I don't keep thinking about dying, all the time.

It's probably morbid, Lucia thought. It's probably some sort
of enormous conceit. But it doesn't go away. When they were
little, I used to feel that nobody else could understand how Bee
felt about Lilacker. I used to think that nobody else would understand why David wouldn't say his prayers right. He just
couldn't say "I pray the Lord my soul to take." He always said
"keep." He didn't want anyone to "take" his soul. It frightened
him. I'm still like that. I still think I'm the only one . . .

She telephoned to Mrs. Lloyd.

"I'd love to come!" said Mrs. Lloyd. "This afternoon? But
I'm afraid Phyllis can't come; she has a dancing lesson. Would
half-past four be too early? Because if I'm not home at *least*
an hour before dinner, everything gets so queer. *Why* is it that
just when dinner is served everyone locks itself up in a bathroom? They read; I know that. Or if they don't do that, they
start making simply endless telephone calls. It must be
psychological—but why *should* everyone be so psychological
about not wanting dinner the moment it's put on the table?"

Mrs. Lloyd soothed Lucia; she liked her.

"Mrs. Lloyd is coming to tea," she told Sibyl. "Could you
make some of those tiny biscuits, Sibyl?"

"Make popovers, ma'am," said Sibyl. "They don't take any
shortening. Or we could have nice little ham sandwiches."

"Well, no," said Lucia.

She could not offer any of that ham to Mrs. Lloyd; it would
be improper, even treacherous.

"Now, about the marketing?" she said. "I'll go this morning."

"Not much to get today," said Sibyl, with an air of satisfaction. "Got plenty of meat in the house. And now we can use
more red points for butter."

She read off the list she had written.

"And if you'd stop in the gas company office, ma'am," she
said, "maybe you could make them send a man about the icebox."

"I'll try," said Lucia.

She was surprised when Bee volunteered to go with her.

"I've got some things to get in the drugstore," Bee said. "Let's take the car."

"No," said Lucia. "I'd rather save the gas for sometime when we really need it."

They were both ready and waiting when the taxi came; Lucia in an old red and white checked gingham dress, stiffly starched, Bee in gray slacks and a white shirt, and that look she sometimes had of severely perfect grooming, her blonde hair pinned up under a blue bandanna, her arched, delicate brows a little darkened. She looked older this way; only when she turned away her head Lucia noted the sweet contour of her cheek, her childish neck.

"You're going to be disappointed, Mother," she said, "but I don't want to study art any more."

"I shan't be disappointed, dear."

"I'll tell you what I want to do, Mother. I want to go to Miss Kearney's, for her two-year secretarial course."

"Everyone says it's a very good school."

"It's the best," said Bee. "If you graduate from Kearney you're practically certain to get a job, no matter how bad conditions are."

"Well, I think that's a good idea, darling."

"Daddy won't think so," said Bee. "He'll kick like a steer."

"I'm sure he won't," said Lucia.

"Mother, honestly . . . ! You know how Father talks about career women. He's always saying that they miss out on all the best things in life."

"Well, you probably wouldn't want to be a career woman, dear."

"Yes, I do," said Bee. "I intend to keep on working after I get married."

"But if you have children——"

"I'd get a good nurse for them, and they'd be a damn sight better off than if I was home with them all the time."

"Don't swear, dear," said Lucia. "I don't see why they'd be better off. I don't see why a mother couldn't be as good as a nurse."

"Because the sort of mother who simply stays home and has no outside life can't help being narrow-minded," said Bee.

"Well, most nurses aren't so wonderfully broad-minded, that I can see," said Lucia.

"What's more, I think every woman ought to be able to support her children," said Bee. "Nobody knows what kind of world it's going to be, after this war. If you're going to take a chance and bring children into the world, you ought to be able to look after them, no matter what happens."

"Oh, yes . . ." said Lucia.

Anything rather than be like me, she thought. I'm simply a horrible example.

They rode in silence for a time.

"This new shampoo I'm going to get says it's specially good for dry hair," said Bee. "My hair's getting frightfully dry."

"You wash it too often," said Lucia.

This was a very familiar topic.

"I read an article about some women somewhere who wash their hair every single day," said Bee. "And they're famous for their beautiful hair."

"I never wash mine more than once a week," said Lucia, "and sometimes I let it go longer than that. And you'll have to admit that it's in pretty good condition."

"That's different," said Bee.

As if I were too old to *have* any hair, Lucia thought.

"I don't see why it's different," she said, coldly. "As a matter of fact, I've got rather remarkable hair. Hairdressers always speak of it. It's very thick, and it's very healthy."

Bee glanced at her.

"I know it is, Mother," she said, gently. "David and I always say so."

She kept on looking and looking at her mother.

"Don't stare so, Bee!" cried Lucia.

"Sorry, Mother," said Bee, and turned away her gaze.

They got out of the taxi at the market.

"I'll whip over to the drugstore, and come back for you," Bee said. "Will you be long, Mother?"

"Oh, hours, probably," said Lucia.

It was not, in theory, a self-service market, but it was under-staffed, and the customers had been trained to go about and find their own things, to weigh the fruit and vegetables. Then you tried to get a place at the counter, to spread out the unwieldy hoard, and if you were not alert, people pushed in ahead of you and cut you off from your supplies; they planked down their things, and sometimes knocked yours off the counter. I hate this! Lucia thought. I wish I was immensely rich and arrogant, so that people *had* to be polite to me, no matter how they felt.

"No paper towels," said the clerk. "Try on Tuesday. No sugar today. Only cheese we got is pimento, and you're lucky to get that."

The telephone rang and he went away to answer it; Lucia was still waiting his return when Bee came for her.

The girl in the gas company's office was distrait and superior.

"Oh, hasn't the man been yet?" she said. "I'll check on it, to see if he came."

"He *didn't* come," said Lucia.

"Maybe you were out," said the girl.

"We're never all out."

"Well, maybe he's been busy with emergency calls," said the girl.

"Ours is an emergency," said Lucia.

"No," said the girl, flatly. "We don't call yours an emergency. I'll check on it."

"Will you let me know when to expect the man?"

"We don't do that," said the girl. "He takes the calls in turn."

The taxi driver was an unfamiliar one, and odious.

"They ought to leave us make a charge for them big grocery bags," he said. "If trucks get paid for bundles, why not us? But no. People fill up the cab with them heavy bundles that are hard on the springs and all, and when they get out, it's a ten-cent tip."

"Give him ten cents!" Bee whispered.

"No! I might have to take him again," Lucia whispered back.

He stopped the cab before the house and Lucia leaned forward to pay the fare and give him a quarter tip. He said nothing.

"I can't get the door open!" said Bee.

"Pull the handle *down!*" said he. "Pull it hard."

"I suppose it would kill you to open the door," said Bee.

"No," he said, "and it wouldn't kill you, neither."

"Hush!" whispered Lucia.

Bee got the door open and they descended, and carried the big bags into the kitchen.

"Master David said could we have lunch a little early?" said Sibyl. "He wants to go out."

"Why, yes," said Lucia. "Half-past twelve, Bee?"

"All right," said Bee, moving away.

Lucia was about to follow her, but Sibyl came to her side.

"Mr. Nagle's here, ma'am," she said, very low.

Lucia looked at her.

"Ma'am . . . !" said Sibyl. "Sit down! There! Drink some cold water, ma'am."

"Where is he, Sibyl?"

"Put him upstairs in the boathouse, ma'am. Nobody else saw him. Told him he might have to wait quite a while, till you got a chance to see him."

Lucia sipped the water, fighting against a dreadful weakness that weighed upon her. I can't, she told herself. I can't talk to him. I can't see him. I can't—I really can't do anything. If I don't go, he'll go away.

He would not go away. She was certain of that. If she did not go to him, he would come here, to the house. I'll have to see him, she thought. I'll have to.

A furious anger sprang up in her. What's Mr. Donnelly doing? she cried to herself. What does he *mean* by saying not to worry, that *he'll* look after things?

What the *hell's* the matter with him? she thought.

Chapter Seventeen

This anger helped her.

"I'll go and see him now," she said, rising.

The swing door opened and David came into the kitchen.

"Say, look, Mother!" he said. "Just glance over this, will you?"

"What is it, dear?"

"Take a look!" he said, holding out a sheaf of papers.

"But what is it, David?" she asked. "Won't after lunch do?"

"All right," he said. "Don't bother. I've got to post it right after lunch."

He was hurt.

"Oh, then I want to see it now!" said Lucia. "Give it to me, David!"

He hesitated, but only for a moment; he held out the papers again, neatly typed pages stapled together.

Ubu stood at the mouth of the cave and turned his shaggy head from side to side. Over his shoulders was thrown a rough garment of wolf-skin and in his hand he held a stone club weighing around fifteen pounds. The cave was on a mountainside and below him stretched the jungle, where roamed the saber-toothed tiger and other wild beasts who were the enemies of him and his.

"Is it a story, David?" she asked, glancing up.

"Sort of a good start, isn't it?" he asked. "I mean, you get interested in Ubu, don't you?"

"Oh, yes, you *do*!"

"I'll tell you what it's for," he said. "You know that Vigorex Gum program on the radio? Well, they're having a contest. Anyone under sixteen can send in a story, up to a thousand words, about any of the great inventions that changed the life of mankind. The first prize is a thousand-dollar War Bond. I bet you practically everybody will do stories about the printing press, telephone, things like that. Well, I've done the wheel. You'll see how I've worked it out."

"David, how interesting!" Lucia said. "Let's go into the sitting room while I finish it."

Nagle can just wait, she thought. Even if I was mean enough not to read David's story, I couldn't get out to the boathouse now. David would want to come with me—and what could I say?

Mr. Harper was in the sitting room, reading.

"When you've finished it, Mother," David said, "maybe Grandpa'd like to glance at it."

"Certainly! Certainly! What is it? A letter?"

"Well, it's a sort of story, in a way," David answered, laughing a little. "Don't worry, Grandpa. I'm not trying to be an author, or anything like that. I just thought I'd have a try for this prize."

Lucia sat down to read the story.

"Gosh, you're a slow reader!" said David.

"I know," said Lucia.

She was trying to make her distracted mind understand the words she read.

Ikko came out of the cave, bearing in her arms the infant just born, wrapped lovingly in the skin of a giant hare.

"Ikko! Look! Stone!" cried Ubu.

As Ubu stood watching the almost perfectly round Wonderstone rolling down the mountainside, into his brain was born the great principle of the Wheel. He saw how round stones like this could be used to transport the bodies of slain beasts . . .

"Lunch is served, ma'am," said Sibyl.

"Just a moment," said Lucia, and finished the last page. "It's *awfully* good, David."

"The thing is, is it interesting?" he asked.

"It's awfully interesting!"

"The deadline's the day after tomorrow," said David. "I didn't mean to be so late with it, but I couldn't get it right. I've got to mail it right after lunch, but I'd like Grandpa to take a look."

"I'll read it at the table, if your mother doesn't object," said Mr. Harper.

Bee came into the dining room, with a towel pinned over her hair like a Red Cross nurse.

"I tried that shampoo——" she began.

"Hush, dear!" said Lucia. "David's written a story——"

"I've read it," said Bee. "I must say I think it's pretty darn good."

"Remarkably good," said Mr. Harper. "Yes . . . The thing is, my boy, have you got all your facts straight? I mean to say, these prehistoric animals—they all existed in the same era?"

"Yes, sir," said David. "I looked them up in the library. I did quite a lot of research for this thing."

I think I have a fever, Lucia said to herself. I feel so hot. I feel so—queer. I've got to see Nagle. Suppose he gets tired of waiting? Suppose he comes here?

As soon as he had finished lunch, David left the house, and Bee went out on the veranda, to dry her hair in the sun. I'll have to go by the back way, Lucia thought, and went into the kitchen. Through the window there she saw her father pacing leisurely up and down the lawn, hands clasped behind his back. I can't go that way, either, she thought. He'd ask me where I was going.

I must make up an excuse. I've got to get to the boathouse.

"Took some lunch out to Mr. Nagle, ma'am," said Sibyl. "Took him some of Mr. Harper's whisky."

"Oh, Sibyl, what a good idea! Was he—how was he?"

"He's quiet now, ma'am," said Sibyl.

As if he were a dangerous animal, quiet only for this moment.

"If you'll go up and lie down, ma'am," said Sibyl, "I'll tell you, soon as Mr. Harper stops his walking."

Lucia went up to her room, but she could not lie down, or even sit down. She stood by the window where she could see the boathouse.

Donnelly . . . she thought. He told me not to worry. What the hell's the matter with him? Damn him. He let this happen. He's no good. He's nothing but a crook, a liar. I hate him. Damn him.

She glanced at her watch, and panic swept over. Half-past one! It isn't good for Father to walk so long, at his age . . .

But that was his habit. On a stormy day, he would walk up and down a room for an hour or more. Oh, don't let him do that today! Or make Bee come in. I've got to get out.

She kept her eyes upon her watch now. That's a mistake, she told herself. I ought to read—or mend something. This way makes the time seem twice as long. Twenty to two . . . He *can't* walk this long.

It was a quarter to two when Sibyl knocked at the door.

"Mr. Harper's come in, ma'am," she said.

Lucia went past her and ran down the stairs, through the kitchen and out by the back door. Her father or Bee might be looking out of a window; they must not see her running. I don't want to run, anyhow, she thought. Nagle can just wait, damn him.

She walked across the grass to the boathouse and up on to the little porch; she opened the door and entered into the moldy dimness. There was no one in the room; there was not a sound to be heard. She closed the door and stood holding the knob.

"Mr. Nagle?" she called.

There was no answer. Is he—hiding? she thought. No. He's upstairs. Just sitting up there? If I go upstairs, suppose he's standing behind the door?

Suppose he tries to kill me? she thought.

That seemed to her quite possible. Nagle was mysterious to her as a creature from another planet; she did not think of him as a man, a human being; only as something wholly evil and dangerous. He's come for money, of course, she thought, and if he doesn't get any, maybe he'll try to kill me.

But suppose he wasn't there at all? Suppose he had got tired of waiting and had gone away?

Too good to be true, she told herself.

"Mr. Nagle?" she called again.

"Come up!" he called back.

The only thing to do was, to go quickly, without thinking. He was sitting in a wicker chair, in the upstairs sitting room, in shirt sleeves and lavender suspenders, his soft hat on the back of his head. The lunch tray was on the floor, and on the table beside him was a bottle of whisky and a glass.

"You took your time, all right," he said.

"I couldn't help it," said Lucia.

"All right," he said. "I've done all the waiting I'm going to do. It's ten thousand now—and I mean now."

"I can't get it."

"You can get it, off your father. I checked on him."

"No. I couldn't."

"You get it—or else."

"Or else what?"

"I take one of your girl's letters to this guy I know on a newspaper."

"Go ahead," said Lucia. "No newspaper would ever publish a letter like that."

"Wait a minute, duchess," he said. "Wait a minute. Who's talking about printing any letters? All I want is, to get this guy after you. Just let me tip him off there's a good-looking blonde mixed up in the Darby case, and he'll do the rest."

"What good do you think that's going to do you?" Lucia asked.

"Plenty, duchess. Plenty."

He wants to do me harm, she thought. He wants that, much more than he wants the money. He hates me.

And that, somehow, took away all her fear of him. He wouldn't dream of killing me, she thought, scornfully, looking at him as he sat there with his hat on the back of his head, drinking her father's whisky. I'd like to hit him, she thought. I'd like to hurt him.

"Well?" he asked. "What about it, duchess?"

"Nothing," she said. "I can't give you ten thousand dollars. Or even one thousand."

"All right," he said. "Then you and that blonde girl of yours get the first train out of here, and stay out of here."

"What a crazy idea!" said Lucia.

"Get the hell out of this town and stay out of it. Or you'll wish you was never born."

He's just bluffing, Lucia thought, surprised, and still more scornful. Just trying to frighten me. He can't really do anything.

"You needn't wait," she said. "You won't get anything."

"I'll go when I'm ready," he said. "Just now, I'm not ready."

"Suppose I call the police?"

"Go ahead! Go right ahead and call the police, duchess. I'm a friend of Ted Darby's. I know he was mixed up with that blonde girl of yours, and I'm here to see can I find out anything. So I give the cops one of her letters. And they'll make her talk."

Well, that could very well happen, if I called the police, Lucia thought. It's funny, when you think of it, but I really don't want the police getting into this, any more than he does.

"Well, duchess?" he cried.

"Stop calling me that!" she said, sharply.

"So you don't like it? That's just too bad, duchess. That's one mistake I never made, to get myself mixed up with one of you goddam society bitches."

"'Society'?" Lucia cried. "If you think I'm a 'society woman,' you're a fool."

"Oh, no," he said. "I'm no fool. I know your kind, all right. I seen friends of mine fall for them. You're just no goddam good, any of you. Any man that gets mixed up with one of you is finished. Look at Darby and——"

"Stop it!" Lucia said. "Get out of here!"

"When I'm ready, duchess. When I'm ready."

"You——" she began, and stopped, with a chill of terror at the sound of a step on the stairs.

Father? she thought. No, no! Oh, don't let it be Father!

It was Donnelly, tall and elegant, in a slate-gray suit, with a blue cornflower in his buttonhole.

"What's this?" he asked. "I could hear the two of you from outside."

"He's going to give the letters to a newspaperman——" said Lucia.

"Shut up!" said Nagle.

"Let her alone," said Donnelly. "What are you doing here at all, Carlie? It is a dirty, underhanded thing for you to do, when we had it all fixed up."

He spoke with severity, but not angrily.

"You got your money," he said. "Why wouldn't that be enough for you, Carlie? You'd no right to come here."

"Now you look here, Marty," said Nagle, rising. "If we got to have a showdown, we got to have a showdown. I come here, because some way I got to get this woman off your neck. You don't see it, but I do. She's going to ruin you."

"Let her alone," said Donnelly, still without anger. "It is a thing beyond your understanding, entirely."

"The hell it is!" said Nagle. "Look what she done to you already. A man like you, a man with a name—and yesterday you were passing the hat, getting a couple of hundred here, couple of hundred there. D'you think I want the money you got that way? Listen. We went in this together; we were cutting fifty-fifty. And when she won't come across, what do you do? Pass the hat—to pay *me*. Like I was holding you up. I am not. I don't want your money."

"Well, you took it," said Donnelly, "and you told me you'd let her alone. You are a liar, Carlie."

"So I'm a liar. Okay. I'm not going to let her alone."

"You will have to," Donnelly said.

Lucia moved aside, so that she could lean against the wall. The two men stood facing each other; Nagle was shorter, he was overweight, he looked older, but there was a powerful energy about him, in the pugnacious set of his head, in the way he stood, with his rear thrust out. And Donnelly was blurred, vague; he showed no energy, only that severe patience.

But he'll settle things, she thought. One way or another. She leaned against the wall, completely passive. There was nothing for her to do, or to say; for the moment there was nothing she need think about. The two men were talking, but she did not listen to them. She was waiting; she was resting.

Until a note in Donnelly's voice startled her. She glanced at him, and his blurred look was gone; he was wary, his head a little bent, like a listening animal.

"What did yez say?" he asked.

"You heard me," said Nagle.

They're afraid of each other, Lucia thought, seeing in Nagle the same alertness, the same bodily stillness. As if the least little movement might make the other pounce.

"You told me Eddy and Moe were talking about it," said Donnelly. "Then it was you told them."

"It was not. Do you think you can go around in New York like you was invisible? You take her to Gogo's place. Champagne——"

"There was no champagne!"

"Okay, so there was no champagne. Okay. It was Pop that seen you there."

"Pop, was it?" said Donnelly. "And it was Pop told Eddy and Moe?"

"That's right," said Nagle. "It was natural that he'd tell them. She is the same woman they saw over in Darby's hotel, and Eddy and Moe were good friends of Darby's."

"Sure it was natural," said Donnelly. "Only that Pop is in Buffalo."

Nagle made a slight move, a shift of the feet.

"Maybe he wrote them a letter."

"He would not write anybody a letter. And he did not see me at Gogo's place. He went to Buffalo last Thursday. You are a liar, Carlie."

"Now, look here, Marty——"

"If Eddy and Moe were talking, it was you told them, Carlie."

Something was happening, something was changing in the two men who did not move.

"I did not tell them," said Nagle.

"You are a liar," Donnelly said again. "If they were talking, it was you set them on to it. I'll never forgive it you."

"All right. They were not talking. I only told you that to make you see what you were doing. You can't keep this thing hid; you can't do it. They'll find out, and it's going to get them worried. You play around with this society bitch, and she gets you talking. Okay. One day you talk too much, and she turns you up. And the rest of us, too. For God's sake, Marty, drop her! You never let a woman throw you before. For God's sake, show some sense!"

"It's in your mind to set the others on her," said Donnelly.

"Then let her get the hell out of here. We——"

Donnelly struck, without any warning; his arm shot out straight from the shoulder, his fist caught Nagle on the point of the jaw, and sent him stumbling backward, with little running steps. He crashed into a chair and fell on the floor, with a thud that shook the house. As quick as a cat, Donnelly was on his knees beside him.

"Is he hurt?" Lucia asked, in a flat voice.

"No," said Donnelly. "Go back to your house."

He was bending over Nagle, and she moved, to see what he was doing.

"Marty . . . !" she cried. She tried to scream, but her throat contracted. "Marty . . ." she said, in a whisper.

"Be quiet!" he said, his teeth clenched. "Go home!"

She caught his arm, but it was like steel, like stone. His fingers were tight around Nagle's throat, and Nagle's pale eyes were bulging, his tongue showed between his gasping lips, his face was darkening.

"Marty . . ." she said, pulling at his arm with both hands. "Stop . . . I beg you . . . I beg you . . ."

She herself was choking. With her eyes fixed upon Nagle's awful face, she put her hands to her neck. She was choking and she was blind now, looking into blackness.

Donnelly lifted her onto the sagging couch. He raised her head and held a glass to her lips.

"Drink a little," he said. "It will help you."

The whisky had a rank, sour smell. She took a few sips; then she pushed the glass away, so violently that it fell out of his hand onto the floor.

"His glass . . ." she said.

She lay back, for a little time; then she sat up. Donnelly stood beside her, smoking a cigarette.

"As soon as you're able," he said, "go back to your house. Try now; can you get up?"

"Nagle . . . ?" she said, with a great effort.

"I will look after him."

"You killed him," she said. "You killed him. You choked him."

"I had to do it," he said.

"You killed him. You choked him——"

"Let you get back to your house now," he said.

"You killed him. You choked him——"

"Don't be saying that, darlin'," he said.

"How *could* you? How *could* you?" she demanded, beginning to cry.

"I had to do it. It was in his mind to set the two of them on you."

"Better . . ." she said. "Much better . . ." She was sobbing. "Anything—would be better—than that. Than *that*."

"Look!" he said, sitting down on the couch beside her. "It is hard for you, but you'll have to have courage. You'll have to stop crying. Suppose, now, somebody was to call you, and you'd have to go downstairs?"

"O God!" she cried, in despair.

No matter what happened to her, no matter how she felt, her first thought must always be, how to face her world. Her little world, her children, her father.

"I'd like some more whisky, please," she said. "Could I drink out of the bottle?"

"You could," he said. "Only go easy."

She took a few swallows.

"Have you a cigarette?" she asked.

He gave her one and lit it for her.

"Thank you," she said.

"You're welcome," he said.

They spoke with formality, as they had in the past. She smoked for a time, sitting up straight, growing quieter, growing stronger.

"What will you do—with him?"

"Leave it to me," he said. "Go back now to your house, and if they ask you any questions, tell them this. Tell them you'd invited me to take a cup of tea before I'd be off to Montreal. Then, while you were out this morning, Nagle comes, asking for me, and you sent him off to the boathouse to wait. Well, after a while you get to wondering is he still there, and you walk out, and you hear the two of us, having an argument. You wait awhile, and then you're off, leaving us at it."

"All right!" she said, frowning. "But what are you going to do with him?"

"Say it for me once, will you not?" he asked. "I mean, the way you'll tell it, if they ask you any questions."

"No. I'll remember."

"Say it once, will you not?"

"Oh . . . I'll say I asked you to tea, and Nagle came, asking for you, and I told him to wait in the boathouse, and I heard you having an argument. Now I want to know what you're going to do with him."

"I will take him in your boat and row off with him."

"That's ridiculous!" she said. "There are always lots of people out on the water, this time of day."

"I will manage," he said.

"Not that way. There's no place you could take him."

"I will leave him here, then, where he won't be seen, and I
will come back for him later."

"Here? No. Can't you think of anything better than that?"

"I cannot," he said.

"Then I will. The——" She looked up at him, frightened to
see him blurred and vague again. "Don't you realize the danger you're in?"

"I will manage."

"Your plans are—simply idiotic. If you're found with him,
you won't have a chance. I'm sure any doctor would know
how he'd been killed. You want me to tell people I left you
having an 'argument' with him. I suppose you mean to swear
you killed him in self-defense. Well, nobody would believe
that. Not when you choked him."

"I will manage," he said.

He stood there, so big, so slow, so vague.

"You're a perfect fool!" she cried. "You've got to get him
away. I'll bring my car to the door, and you——"

"I cannot drive," he said.

"Yes, you can. You drove me——"

"I cannot drive now," he said. "My arm has gone dead on
me."

"What do you mean?"

"My arm," he explained. "I cannot use it at all."

She noticed then that his right arm hung limp at his side.

"You've got to use it," she said. "That's all just psychological."

"How's that?" he asked, anxiously.

"It's just imagination. You can use it."

"It is a judgment on me," he said.

"What!" she cried. "You *can't* be so ignorant and stupid.
I'm going to bring the car here, and you've got to get him into
it, and take him away. You've got to leave him somewhere, and
then go home. Nobody ever needs know what happened to
him. *Don't* be so spineless! Aren't you man enough to fight for
your own life?"

"I cannot move my arm at all," he said. "It was done to me, so I could not get away. Go back to your house now——"

"You fool! You idiot! You coward!" she cried. "Snap out of it!"

He did not answer.

"Then I'll get you out of it," she said.

Chapter Eighteen

"Now look here!" she said. "I'll bring the car to the door and we——"

"No," he said. "I will not let you get into this."

"If you won't help me," she said, "I'll do it all alone. I'll get him down the stairs and into the car alone."

"Go back to your house," said Donnelly. "Leave me to manage my own way."

"I won't. You've got a chance, and you'll have to take it. I'll get the car, and you look around for something to—wrap him in."

"For the love of God, will you let me alone?" he cried.

"No. I won't. I'll do it all by myself if you're not man enough to help me."

"I will help you," he said, with an effort. He sighed, very deeply, and raised his head. "Have you a trunk, maybe?" he asked.

"Not here. But wait! There's that chest."

He looked where she pointed, at a long window seat, the top padded and covered with faded, moldering chintz. He went over to it and raised the lid.

"It will do," he said. "Only there are things in it, tools, and the like."

"Get them out," she said. "Oh, *try* to use your right hand . . . ! Here!"

She leaned over the chest, and brought out a trowel, two empty flashlight cases, a tangled mass of wire and rope and threw them on the floor; she was so fast, and he was so slow.

"Now we'll get him in," she said.

"You cannot!" said Donnelly, with a sort of horror.

"Oh, yes, I can!" she said.

"You don't know——"

"I picked up Rex—he was David's dog—I picked up Rex after he'd been run over. I carried him to the house," she said, proudly and arrogantly. "I can do anything I have to do."

"Not this," he said.

She turned then to look at Nagle. He was only a mound on the floor, covered with a dark green chenille tablecloth.

"Come on!" she said. "We've got to hurry."

Donnelly turned the chest over on its side.

"Hold open the lid," he said.

Using only his left arm, he pulled Nagle to the chest; he got him into it, lying on his back, with his knees raised high, because the chest was too short. He pushed the box upright, and Nagle shifted, with a faint thud.

"Now, while I'm getting the car," Lucia said, "do something with the tray and the whisky bottle. And the tools. Make the place look all right."

"I will," he said.

She ran down the stairs and opened the door. And out in the brilliant sunshine, terror seized her. Someone will see me, she thought. What can I say? What can I say?

She must not run. She must not look behind her. *Think!* Think of something to say to them. You must think.

She opened the garage door and got into the car. Think! You can't get away with this. Someone is going to ask you where you're going. Someone will come to the boathouse. To see you and Martin dragging that chest down the stairs. What are you going to say?

She drove the car to the boathouse, and left the engine running when she got out. I *knew* I ought to save the gas, she thought. I knew something would turn up . . .

She opened the door, and saw Donnelly halfway down the stairs. He had wrapped the chest in the chenille cover and tied one end of it like the mouth of a sack; he held this in his left hand, letting the chest slide bumping down the steps ahead of him.

"That was a good thing to think of!" she said, pleased. "Now we'll get it into the car."

They could not. It was far too heavy for her, and he was of little use without his right hand.

"Can't you try?" she cried.

"God knows I would like to," he said.

They stood on the grass before the boathouse, with the chest at their feet, and they could not lift it into the car.

"Wait here!" she said. "I'm going to get Sibyl."

Sibyl was sitting in her neat, clean kitchen, reading a magazine. The sun was shining in, the wartime alarm clock ticked loudly.

"Sibyl," Lucia said, "help me, please. I've got to get a box into the car, and it's too heavy."

"Yes, ma'am," said Sibyl.

They walked to the boathouse, side by side.

"Mr. Donnelly's hurt his arm," Lucia said. "But I think we can manage, Sibyl."

It was very difficult, but they did manage. The chest was in the back of the car.

"Thank you, Sibyl," said Lucia. "You'd better get in front with me, Mr. Donnelly."

"*Mother!*"

It had happened. Bee was here, standing beside the car, her newly washed hair like silver in the sun.

"Mr. Donnelly wants to borrow an old engine I found in the boathouse," said Lucia. "He thinks he can fix it."

It was no trouble to say that. It was not necessary to think. The words simply came, when you needed them.

"But, Mother, where are you *going*?"

"To the station," said Lucia.

"But, Mother, Mrs. Lloyd'll be here——"

"Oh, I'll be back," said Lucia, carelessly.

"But, Mother, we can get a cab for—Mr. Donnelly——"

"No, dear," said Lucia. She started the car; they went down the drive and onto the highway.

"Holy Mother of God!" said Donnelly. "There was never another like you in the world."

"Can you think of any place to take the chest?"

"I don't know these parts at all."

"I don't, either," she said. "I haven't done any driving around. I suppose I'd better just go ahead . . . ?"

"You had. I'll keep my eyes open, for a lane or a byroad."

It's done, she thought. I got him out of it. She drove along, steadily, tranquilly, with an untroubled mind. The sweet air blew in her face; cars and trucks were rolling along the highway, each in its right lane, all so orderly. It's like riding in a procession.

It's done. I've got him out of it, the idiot. Sibyl will never say anything. Even if she knew . . . And maybe she does. I don't know. It doesn't matter. Anyhow, here he is.

Here he was, sitting beside her, riding along in the procession. The big parade . . . she said to herself. I got him out of it.

"You'd better really go to Montreal, right away," she said.

"I will," he said.

She glanced at him, and she did not trust him.

"You don't mean that," she said. "You haven't any intention of going to Montreal."

"I was just thinking . . ." he said, with humility.

A great pity for him rose in her. He was so helpless, so remote from her. He mustn't brood, she thought. I've got to get him talking.

There was only one thing in the world that *they* could talk about.

"Why did you come out here today?" she asked.

"Sibyl called me up. She told me Nagle was there."

"Why do you trust Sibyl so," she asked, "when you hardly know her?"

"It's a sort of idea I have," he said, with the same humility. "There's a kind of wisdom in her." He paused. "She is a realist," he said.

Strange word for him to use, she thought. Now he was silent again, and she did not like that.

"If you'd talk . . ." she said. "If we talked—about this . . ."

"I cannot talk at all," he said. "I'm sorry, but I cannot."

"We can't go on like this. We can't—just ignore it."

"I hope you'll forget it," he said. "Try, will you not?"

"Forget it?" she said, scornfully. "Not till the last day I live."

"I had to do it," he said. "You see, Carlie was a strange man. He was a grand friend to the ones he liked, but there were not many of those. And if anyone did him a wrong, he'd never forget it. He was still talking about a teacher he'd had when he was a boy, over in Brooklyn. She's over eighty years of age now, but he was still trying to find a way to get back at her. He'd never have let up on you."

"But I never did him any harm!"

"He thought you did. He thought you wanted to break up the friendship there was between him and me."

There was a long moment's silence.

"There were other elements in it, too," he went on. "The first time he went out to see you, he came back very bitter. He was hurt."

"Hurt? That man?"

"He told me you looked down on him, you and your girl. He told me you were haughty to him. Like the dirt under your feet, he told me."

"I was afraid of him."

"Then you did not show it. Anyhow, he'd a great hatred for society women."

"*You* know better than to call me a 'society woman.'"

"It was the only word he had for it," said Donnelly, grave and gentle. "What they call 'the gentry,' in the old country. What he meant was, a woman with a standing in the world, a woman with a family, a good name. It was his conviction they'd always sell a man out, to keep what they had."

"He was a vindictive, ignorant man."

"Maybe," said Donnelly. "He always held it against his parents that they did not give him a good education, did not send him to college. They had him working for his father, that was a butcher, when he was fourteen, and it made him bitter. He was a smart man. It is a pity he did not get a good education."

"Did you—like him?"

"I did," he said.

"But——"

"I had to do it," he said. "Once he had an idea in his head, he'd never let go of it. And he gave himself away. He let me see what he had in his mind. If he'd set Eddy and Moe onto you, it would be the worst thing could ever happen to you."

"Why? What could they have done?"

"You would not understand, the way you've never met anyone like those two, and never will."

"Are they—gunmen?" she asked, timidly, afraid of hurting his feelings, but desperately curious.

"They are not," he said.

"But—what are they?"

"You would not understand."

"You could explain," she said.

"I will not," he said.

After a moment, he spoke again.

"There's a lane to the left," he said. "What do you think of it?"

She slowed down the car, and looked along the road that ran downhill from the highway, a pretty lane, with trees meeting overhead. There were no buildings to be seen, no traffic.

"We might try it," she said.

"We don't want to waste any time," he said.

"Why? Why do you say that?"

"You ought to be getting home," he said.

That's a strange thing to say, she thought, startled. A strange thing for him to be thinking, when there's this other thing . . .

Nagle is here, she thought, with a shock. In the car. In that chest.

She was driving along this quiet lane, with a dead man in the car, a murdered man. If the least thing went wrong, it would mean—God knew what. We can't do this! she thought. This is madness. We can't possibly get away with this.

She glanced at him. His head was turned away; he was looking into the woodland that bordered the lane. Think what could happen to him . . .

"Mr. Donnelly . . ." she said, a little loudly, "we've got to talk about this. We've got to have a plan, a story. It'll have to be self-defense."

"Oh, I'll think of a story," he said.

"We've got to have the same story, don't you see?"

"There's no need for you to be thinking about a story," he said. "No one's going to bother you about this."

"That's silly. Something could go wrong, any minute. You've got to think this out, carefully."

"I will."

"But now! Lieutenant Levy's been to see me already about —Ted Darby. He might very well come again, and ask questions. He—I think he's very clever."

"Lieutenant Levy? The police, is it?"

"The Horton County police. Suppose he goes into the boathouse? He might find something there—something we hadn't thought about?"

"Look!" Donnelly said. "There's a bit of a lake, around the bend of the road. You can see it from here."

The road was level now, along the floor of a little valley. She accelerated.

"Slow down!" he said, mildly. "There is a curve ahead."

And a car came around the curve, a roadster, with two soldiers in it.

"They saw us!" she said. "They could identify us!"

"Don't be nervous," said Donnelly. "You're trembling."

"Let's hurry!"

The engine backfired, and she gave a sort of scream.

"Don't! Don't!" he said, in distress.

It backfired again, and stopped, and started. Donnelly leaned forward.

"Your gauge is broken," he said.

"I know."

The car stopped. She pressed the starter, and nothing happened.

"I'll get out and crank it," she said.

"It will do you no good," he said. "You're out of gas."

"God damn it!" she cried.

"Don't! Don't!" he said. "It's not like you."

"What can we do? What in God's name can we do?"

"We are fine," he said. "We couldn't have found a better spot. Let you be easy now. Here! Have a cigarette!"

"There's a car coming!"

"Let it come. They'll see nothing at all but the two of us, having a little smoke."

"The chest!"

"People are taking around queer things in their cars, these days."

"Oh, *don't* you see? All these people can say they saw us here. After they've found—that."

"They will not find it. Smoke your cigarette now, and I'll tell you what we'll do."

I'm shaking, she thought. I wasn't, before. But this is the worst. Just to sit here, until someone gets us.

"We can't get away with this," she said.

"Wait, now!" he said. "Listen to what I'm saying, will you not? We can get away with this, if you'll do your part right. You'll have to pull yourself together."

"What can I do? What is there——?"

"Come!" he said. "We'll walk a little way, up the road."

"Leave—that?"

He got out of the car; he held out his hand, his left hand, to her; she took it, and got out beside him. Still holding her hand, he began to walk away.

"Listen now to what you've got to do," he said. "You've got to do it right. If you don't, we're sunk, the two of us. You've got to go home, as fast as you can."

"And leave you—like this?" she said. "I won't."

"Listen, will you not? Your girl said there was someone coming to visit you. Mrs.—" He paused a moment. "Mrs. Lloyd."

"How can you remember that?"

"I'm a good one for remembering. If you don't go home, your family'll be worrying. If you're away out of it too long, they'll have the police looking for you."

"Oh . . . !" she cried, angrily.

"You wouldn't want that," he said. "You'll have to get home as quick as ever you can. Here's how you'll do it. We passed a filling station on the highway, just a bit before we turned off here. It is not a long walk. Go there, and tell them to send for a taxi to take you to the railroad station. Don't say anything about your car being stuck. You could give a kind of idea that the man you were driving with began to make trouble."

"I can't."

"Ah, you can!" he said. "Look how you answered your girl, quick as a flash. Now, when you get home— Are you paying heed to me?"

"Yes."

"Forget the story about us having an argument and all that. It will not do now. Here's the story you'll tell. Are you listening, dear?"

"Yes."

"Sibyl told you Nagle had come and she had sent him into the boathouse to wait. Well, you'd seen Nagle before and you did not like him much. You thought he had something to do with the black market. So you didn't hurry out to see him. You let him wait, hoping maybe he'd go away. Have you got that clear?"

"Yes."

"Then there's myself. Was there ever an old engine in the boathouse?"

"Yes."

"As soon as you've a chance, get rid of it. Throw it down into the water. Well, you'd told me I could take the engine, to see could I fix it. So, after your lunch, when you thought Nagle would be gone, you went out to the boathouse, to have a look at the engine. And, sure enough, Nagle is gone. You did not see him at all. Then I come along, and you say you'll give me a lift to the station. Well, we're driving along, and you ask me where am I taking the engine, and I tell you to a sort of a boat yard where a friend of mine is going to work on it. You'll remember all this?"

"Yes," she said, resisting every word of the story in her mind.

"Well, I have hurt my arm, and in the kindness of your heart, you say you will drive me to the boat yard. The gauge in the car is broke, and you don't know the gas is low until the car stops on you. When that happens, you know you've got to get home, or they'll be worrying. You leave the car with me, to go on to the boat yard, and you take the train."

"And what about you?"

"I'll wait a bit, till you're out of it. Then I'll go along to the filling station and telephone a friend of mine in New York. He'll drive out, and he'll bring gas for me. He'll help me with the chest, and we'll drive back to New York. Then I will get a late train to Montreal."

"No," she said.

"Now, what do you mean, at all?" he asked.

"I can't . . . How is your arm?"

"It is better."

"Can you move it now?"

"A little, I can."

"Let me see you," she said.

She was startled to hear him laugh.

"And what's so funny?" she demanded.

"The way you talk to me."

"I'm sorry," she said, coldly.

"I like it," he said. "Only, don't you be worrying about me. I've been looking after myself a good long while."

"I know," she said. "But . . ."

She remembered him in the boathouse, so helpless, so vague. It is a judgment on me, he had said.

"I'd like to see you move your arm," she said.

"Well, maybe I cannot, just now," he said. "It comes and goes. But whatever it is, it is passing off."

"Suppose the friend you're going to call up isn't home?"

"I've plenty of others."

"It'll be a long time, hours, before anyone can drive out here from New York."

"Well, I've a nice shady spot to wait in. I've cigarettes on me, and a bottle of whisky in my pocket."

"You mustn't *drink*!" she cried. "That'll make you do wrong, stupid things. You mustn't touch it!"

"I wouldn't take too much," he said. "But a drop of good whisky . . . I was thinking you'd take a little yourself, you're that pale."

A car was coming from the direction of the highway.

"O God! He'll go right past my car!" she cried.

"Let him," said Donnelly.

"But if he sees the car there, with no one in it, he might stop. He might get out, and look in the chest——"

"Now, why would he be doing that, dear? He won't stop at all. You want to remember this. There's no one else in the world knows what's in that box, and if you do your part right, there's no reason why anybody would ever know."

She wanted to stop until the car had passed, but he took her hand and led her on, toward the highway. When the car had gone, he dropped her hand, and reached into a breast pocket.

"Here's something you might be glad of," he said, and held out three little capsules, bright yellow.

"What are they?"

"They're little sleeping pills," he said. "One will do you. Swallow one of them, and you'll have a good night's sleep."

"Do *you* take things like that?"

"I do," he said.

"It's a terribly bad habit."

"I don't like to be lying awake," he said.

She dropped the capsules into the pocket of her dress, and he brought out a wallet from another breast pocket. He flipped it open, and leaning it against his chest, he drew out some bills.

"You're not using your right arm!" she said.

"You've no money on you," he said. "You'd better take this."

She put the bills into her pocket without looking at them. They were getting nearer to the highway now.

"Send me a wire from Montreal," she said.

"I will," he said. "And take it easy. There's nobody else in the world knows about Nagle. He won't be missed for a day or two, the way he moves around so much. And it'll be longer than that before ever he's found. When he is found—and maybe that'll never happen—he won't be in the box. Nobody'll know where he came to his end."

Now she could see a big green truck going along the highway.

"The filling station's only a bit of a way, to the left," he said. "You'll go home now—and you'll remember the story, will you not?"

"I can't," she said, stopping short. "I just can't. I'm—tired, or something. I can't go on."

From a side pocket he brought out a bottle of whisky.

"You've got to go home," he said. "You know that, don't you, darlin'?"

"Yes . . ." she said.

"I didn't drink from the bottle," he said, anxiously. "Nobody's touched it at all since you had a swallow."

She took a sip, and it seemed weak, almost tasteless. She went on, one sip after another.

"I wouldn't take any more," he said. "It'd make you drowsy, maybe. It is good Scotch, the real McCoy. You know what to buy, don't you?"

"It's my father's," she said.

And, in speaking his name, amazement overwhelmed her. I *can't* be drinking Father's whisky—here! she thought. This can't be true. Not possibly. Not possibly.

"Now you'll go home, will you not?" he asked.

"Yes . . ."

"You've saved my life this day," he said. "I'd lost my wits entirely. I'd never have got him out of the place, if you hadn't saved me."

You killed him for me, she thought. So that I'd be safe.

"To your left," he said. "It's not far."

"Yes . . ." she said. "Good-by. You'll—be careful, won't you?"

"I will that," he said. "Good-by now, and God bless you."

Chapter Nineteen

S HE COULD see the house now, through the taxi window. She was coming back just as she had left, hatless, in the red and white checked gingham dress; she had no purse with her, no powder, no mirror, no comb. She did not know how strange, how dreadful she might be looking.

It seemed to her completely beyond her strength to mount the few steps to the veranda. The cab drove off, and she did not move.

The door opened, and Bee came running down to her.

"Mother!" she cried, in an unsteady voice. "I've been almost crazy with worry. Mother, what were you *thinking* of? Mrs. Lloyd waited nearly an hour——"

"We ran out of gas," said Lucia.

"But why did you go at all? *Why* did you go off with that man?"

"I don't intend to answer any more questions," said Lucia.

"All right! Just think—how I feel! I gave Mrs. Lloyd tea—and I tried to talk to her." Bee was crying now. "I kept telling her—you'd be back any minute. I said—something must have happened to the car—and that's what I kept thinking. An *accident* . . ."

"I'm sorry you were worried," said Lucia, and moved forward. "But I'm tired now, Bee. I want to wash——"

"Mother, there's liquor on your breath! Mother, you've been *drinking*!"

She stood facing her mother, her eyes dilated, tears on her cheeks.

"Don't you dare to talk like that," said Lucia, evenly. "If I choose to take a cocktail now and then, I intend to do so. And don't you dare to call it 'drinking.'"

I drank out of a bottle, in a country lane, she thought. I must be let alone.

"Let me pass, please," she said. "I want to rest a little, before dinner."

"Lieutenant Levy's here!" said Bee.

719

Let me alone! Let me alone! Lucia cried to herself. She waited a moment.

"I'm too tired now," she said. "Ask him to come back to-morrow."

"You've *got* to see him, Mother," said Bee. "He's a police-man. You can't put him off."

"Certainly I can," said Lucia. "It's nothing important."

"Mother," said Bee, "you've made things queer enough, as it is. When Lieutenant Levy asked me when you were coming home, I couldn't tell him. *I didn't know where you were!*"

"Well, why should you always know where I am?"

"*Mother!*"

That word was like a wave, like a tide beating against her. Mother! Where have you been? What were you doing? Open your door, when I knock. Answer, when I ask. Be there, al-ways, every moment, when I want you. It's—inhuman . . . she thought.

"I'll see Lieutenant Levy," she said, briefly. "Tell him I'll be down in a moment."

Her father came into the hall as she entered the house.

"Well, m'dear!" he said. "We were quite anxious——"

"Hello, Father!" she said, in a loud, cheerful voice, and went past him, up the stairs to her own room. She turned the key in the lock, and stood before the mirror.

She had thought of herself as bedraggled, grimy, pale, strange. But it was not so. Her hair was a little rough; there were faint smudges on her cheekbones, but, on the whole, she looked neat enough; a rather countrified housewife in a ging-ham dress.

She washed, and brushed her hair; she changed into a brown rayon dress with a ruffled peplum, ruffles on the sleeves. Fancy little number, David had called it, with disapproval. She did not like it herself, but what did it matter? She put on lipstick, more than usual, and, for some unrecognized reason, a neck-lace of green beads.

It's more about Ted Darby, she thought. I've just got to go through with it. Only, the whole Ted Darby episode seemed so far in the past, so unimportant. If it weren't for Father, she thought, I'd tell Lieutenant Levy the truth about it right now. There's nothing really horrible about it; nothing criminal.

Levy rose as she came into the room; he stood before her, tall, a little clumsy, with his big feet, his big nose, his big ears, yet with the mild, half-melancholy dignity that never left him.

"I'm sorry to bother you again, Mrs. Holley," he said. "But that's my job. I'm generally unwelcome."

"Oh, no!" Lucia said, warmly. "Not here! Smoke, if you like, Lieutenant."

"No, thank you," he said, and after she was seated, he sat down. "My housekeeper gives me a good idea of how hard things are for you ladies, these days," he said. "It must take the greater part of your day, just to get supplies."

"Well, you see, I have Sibyl," said Lucia. "She's wonderful."

"Does she do all the marketing?"

"Oh, I go sometimes," said Lucia. "But she's much better than I am."

"My housekeeper says you have to stick to one store, where they know you, if you want to get anything."

"Yes, you do," Lucia agreed.

I wish he'd get on with whatever he wants to ask, she thought. This is pretty boring.

But she appreciated his effort to establish a pleasant, easy atmosphere. It's the most sensible thing he could do, she thought, if he wants to get me talking, and off my guard. He had, she thought, a very good personality for disarming people, a slow, quiet voice, a gentle smile, a very courteous way of listening to every word you spoke. But she was on guard, and she would stay so; she would notice the first, the lightest change in his tone, in the drift of his talk.

He was talking on about his housekeeper; a Czech, she was, and a fine woman. She had been left a widow at twenty-five, in a strange country, with three children; she had brought them up, seen that they all got a good education. The two sons were in the Navy now; the daughter was married.

"But she keeps on working as hard as ever," he said. "The only thing that really upsets her is the shortage of soap. She was very apologetic about it, but she asked me to try, whenever I could, to get her a box of soap flakes. I haven't been able to find any of the three brands she wants, in spite of my exalted position." He smiled a little. "In one store they offered to sell me something called Silverglo. D'you think it would do?"

"Well . . ." said Lucia, "I don't think there's any real soap in it, but it seems to get things clean, and it's certainly easier to get."

"Silverglo . . ." he repeated, and reached in his pocket.

He's going to take notes about it, Lucia thought, amused.

"Is this yours, Mrs. Holley?" he asked, holding out a dirty little scrap of paper.

She did not want to take that paper into her hand. She looked at him, but she could read nothing in his face.

"Will you look at this, please, Mrs. Holley?" he asked.

She did not want to look at it. She was afraid. But that would be the worst mistake I could make, she thought. To say—I didn't want to look at it.

She took the paper, still with her eyes fixed on his face. Then, with heavy reluctance, she opened it. It was an old market list of hers. Mrs. Lloyd had told her about a market list found by Ted Darby's body. *This one?* she thought.

Or was this just a trap, something subtle and complicated, designed to make her talk? But he can't make me talk, she thought, and I won't lie, either. That's what he wants, for me to lie, and get all mixed up.

"Why, yes!" she said, as if surprised. "It's an old market list of mine. Where in the world did you find it, Lieutenant?"

"It was found under Darby's body," he said.

That's supposed to shock me, she thought.

"Good heavens! On the island?" she asked. "We went over there for a picnic, and I must have dropped it."

"I don't think so, Mrs. Holley. Your picnic was nearly two weeks ago, and this paper hasn't been out in any rain."

"It looks as if it had," she said. "It's frightfully dirty."

"Mrs. Holley, can you tell me on what day you wrote this list?"

"Not possibly," she said. "There are things that are on almost all my lists. Oranges, whole-wheat bread——"

"You'll notice that the list says 'Try Silverglo?' Does that suggest anything to you, Mrs. Holley?"

"No, it doesn't," she said. "I often put that down about things."

"I have information that the first advertisement for Silverglo appeared in the newspapers on the sixteenth. Does that refresh your memory, Mrs. Holley?"

"Why, no. I'm sorry, but it doesn't."

She saw what it meant. The list could not have been written before the sixteenth, and Ted Darby's body had been found on the eighteenth.

"Can you suggest any way in which this paper could have got on the island, Mrs. Holley?"

"Why, no, Lieutenant. When I've finished with a list, I don't bother with it. I throw it away, just anywhere. It could blow away."

Over a mile, across the water, straight to Ted Darby's body?

"Or someone—anyone could pick it up," she said.

"Yes," he agreed, politely, and waited. But she said nothing.

"Mrs. Holley," he said, "I understand that you took out your motorboat, early on the morning of the seventeenth."

"I don't remember dates, Lieutenant, but it's possible. I often get up very early. I like to."

"Did you, on this occasion, see anyone on the island?"

"I didn't look at the island," she said, airily. "I just went scooting past."

"Mrs. Lloyd has made a statement," he said. "She states that early on the morning of the seventeenth, sometime between five and six, she saw a motorboat in the bay, with two women in it. She has the impression that the two women were engaged in some sort of struggle. Did you see this boat with two women in it, Mrs. Holley?"

Lucia was silent for a moment, seized by astonishment. Maybe I'd better say I did see two women in a boat, she thought. It might help me.

But she could not do that. Her astonishment was turning into a curious anger. You can't let people get away with things like that, she thought. Mrs. Lloyd just says anything that comes into her head, and she can't *do* that.

"If there'd been another boat out," she said, "I couldn't have helped seeing it, or at least hearing it. Well, there wasn't any. Mrs. Lloyd may be nearsighted. I stood up once, to button my coat. Perhaps that's what she saw."

"She seems very definite about what she saw, Mrs. Holley."

"But she's mistaken," said Lucia. "I *know* there wasn't any such boat, with two women in it. Not between five and six in the morning. I *know* it."

Looking at Levy's face, she felt a curious fear. He was grave and patient, but he was not convinced. But can't he see what Mrs. Lloyd is like? she thought. She's sweet, but she's feather-brained. I dare say she thinks she saw two women struggling in a boat—but she didn't. I *know* she didn't.

It came into her mind that things like this must happen sometimes during a trial. Suppose you were being tried for your life, she thought, and someone got up and made a statement like that? Suppose someone said—and really believed it—that they'd seen you in some place where you hadn't been? And maybe you couldn't prove you hadn't been there. Maybe all you could do was, to deny it.

She remembered David coming home from school one day, when he was a little boy.

"Miss Jesser said I scribbled in Petey's geography book," he had told her, pale, his eyes narrowed. "I didn't. But she won't believe me. I hate her! She's an old skunk!"

Lucia had gone to see Miss Jesser, but she had not been able to convince her.

"I don't want to make an issue of it, Mrs. Holley," she had said. "After all, it's not serious. At David's age, a child scarcely knows the difference between truth and falsehood."

Lucia had never been able to get any satisfaction for David. He had been falsely accused, and he had never been able to clear himself. Maybe he had forgotten about that—and maybe he had not. Maybe that happened to every child, at some time, leaving in every adult's mind the fear that she felt now, the fear of an utterly baseless accusation, coming like a bolt from the blue, and impossible to disprove.

"There wasn't any such boat," she said.

"Mrs. Holley," he said, "you understand that, no matter how reluctant I may be, it's my duty to enforce the law——"

"All laws?" she said. "Whether they're good or bad?"

"The laws in this country are made by the consent of the people. They can't be 'bad.' What the people decide for themselves is right, is, by that decision, right."

They were coming to something; she knew that. Everything

they said was leading to a destined end. He was driving her—somewhere, and she had to resist.

"You don't care how unjust a law might be to an individual?" she asked, scornfully.

"The law isn't necessarily synonymous with justice, Mrs. Holley. After all, we don't know very much about justice. And we'd need wiser men than we're likely to get, to apply justice to everyone. What we have is a code, a written code, accessible to everyone."

"D'you think that's so wonderful?" she demanded.

"Yes," he said. "You wouldn't admit that even God had the right to punish or reward, if He never let anyone know what the laws were."

His words frightened her, and silenced her.

"Mrs. Holley," he said, "I suggest that your daughter was with you in the boat, on the morning of the seventeenth."

"My *daughter* . . . ?"

"Darby was not killed in the place where his body was found, Mrs. Holley. We're certain of that. We also know that Darby was in your boathouse at some time. We've found his fingerprints on several objects."

"Anyone could get in there. Anyone. But you said—you said Murray . . ."

"We've let Murray go, Mrs. Holley. One of the smartest criminal lawyers in New York came out last night to take his case—and it wasn't a very good case, anyhow. He's out now."

"But my daughter . . . Why are you trying to drag her into this?"

"Your daughter is attempting to shield you, Mrs. Holley. That's obvious. I've questioned her, and she was extremely evasive."

"And what's she supposed to be shielding me from?" Lucia asked.

"Mrs. Holley, it's my duty to inform you that you are not obliged to answer my questions. It is furthermore my duty to inform you that anything you say may——"

"Don't *talk* like that!" she cried.

He rose, and stood before her, and he was so immensely, toweringly tall that she could not see his face.

"Mrs. Holley. I have evidence that Darby was in your boathouse. I have good reason to believe that he was killed there and his body later removed to the island. I have reason to believe that this afternoon Donnelly assisted you to remove from the boathouse some object or objects which you feared might tend to incriminate you."

"No," Lucia said. "No, I didn't."

"I haven't applied for a warrant, Mrs. Holley——"

"A warrant?" she cried. "For—me?"

"I'd certainly be justified, Mrs. Holley, in holding you, and your daughter for questioning. You're both withholding information."

"My daughter . . . ?"

"Your daughter is very evasive, Mrs. Holley. She told me that Donnelly had come here to see her. She gave me to understand that he was infatuated with her, and was attempting to win your good will, for that reason. Further questioning made it plain that she knows nothing at all about the man. She doesn't know his first name, for instance, or his address. She 'can't remember' where or when she met him. She then told me the same story about Darby. That if he had come here at any time—which she didn't admit—it was to see her." He paused. "How long have you known Donnelly, Mrs. Holley?"

"Oh, not long. He's—just an acquaintance."

"How did you make his acquaintance, Mrs. Holley?"

"Well, I *think* some life-insurance agent introduced him."

"Do you know what Donnelly's occupation is, Mrs. Holley?"

"No," she said. "No, I don't."

"He was arrested five times in connection with bootlegging and rumrunning, during prohibition. At present, the O.P.A. is interested in him. There's good reason to believe that he's active in the black market, particularly in meat."

"But he hasn't done anything really—criminal, has he? I mean, robbery, or——?"

"Mrs. Holley," said Levy, "your attitude is surprising. If you don't consider black market activity, in wartime, a criminal offense——"

"I *do*!" she said, quickly. "Of course I do!"

"Mrs. Holley," said Levy, "I shall have to ask you what you and Donnelly removed from the boathouse this afternoon."

She sat very still. She did not realize that she was holding her breath until it burst out in a faint gasp.

"An engine," she said. "An outboard motor."

"That's what your daughter told me," he said. "When I asked her where you were, she told me you'd driven Donnelly to the station, taking with you an outboard motor. I made an opportunity to visit the boathouse, and the engine is still there."

"There were two."

"Did the landlord give you an inventory of the contents of the boathouse, Mrs. Holley?"

"Yes. Yes, I think so. But I don't exactly remember where it is. I can *find* it, of course, later on . . ."

"Why did you put the engine in a chest, Mrs. Holley?"

"Well, I always like to put things in boxes . . ."

The end of the tether, she said to herself. You go as far as you can, and then the rope is stretched tight and you can't go on.

"Where did you take this chest, Mrs. Holley?"

"Well, we were going to take it to a boat yard, but we ran out of gas, and I came home by train."

"Where did you leave Donnelly?"

"In the country. In a lane."

"What part of the country?"

"I don't know exactly."

"What station did you take the train from?"

"It was—I think it was called West Whitehills."

"When is Donnelly going to return your car, Mrs. Holley?"

"Well, very soon, I guess."

"I'll have to question Donnelly, Mrs. Holley. Will you give me his address, please?"

"I haven't got it."

"How do you communicate with Donnelly, Mrs. Holley?"

"Well, I don't."

"Has any member of your family his address?"

"No. I'm sorry."

"Mrs. Holley, I suggest that you and Donnelly removed evidence pertaining to Darby's death."

"No! Really we didn't. I promise you we didn't."

You get to the end of the tether, but nothing happens. The rope doesn't break; it doesn't choke you to death.

"I can't accept your story about this engine, Mrs. Holley. You've given me no satisfactory explanation for the presence of your market list under Darby's body. Neither you nor your daughter has given me any plausible explanation for Darby's presence in your boathouse. I'll have to ask you to come with me to the District Attorney's office."

"Well, but—when?"

"Immediately."

"But it's almost dinnertime!"

"I'm sorry."

"But—when would I get back? I mean, what time shall I tell Sibyl to put dinner on?"

"I don't know, Mrs. Holley."

"An hour?"

"It would be better not to count on that, Mrs. Holley."

"You mean . . . ? You don't mean—they'd keep me?"

"That's a possibility, Mrs. Holley."

"You mean—arrest me?"

"I think it's a possibility that the District Attorney may consider it advisable to hold you for further questioning."

"Hold me? In prison?"

"It's a possibility, Mrs. Holley."

"I can't," she said, flatly. "I can't possibly just walk out of the house like this, and go to prison. You don't realize . . . I've got my children and my father . . . Perhaps you didn't know that my husband's overseas, in the Navy?"

"Yes. I knew that, Mrs. Holley."

"Then don't you see . . . ? Don't you see what it would do to them all? I *can't* . . . Don't you see? They can't—just sit down to dinner . . ."

She rose; she clasped her hands, to keep from seizing his sleeve.

"Please!" she said. "You understand human nature. You *know* I didn't kill Ted Darby. You don't want to bring such disgrace and misery—to all of us——"

"Mrs. Holley," he said, "you've been consorting with a known criminal——"

"'Consorting'?" she repeated, looking into his face.

"That's the usual expression," he said, returning her look steadily.

He thinks we're lovers, she told herself. Everyone will think so. The police will find out about that lunch. About everything.

But nobody knows anything about Nagle; maybe they never will. Maybe if I tell the truth about Ted Darby now, it will be the end. Only I've got to warn Father.

"Lieutenant Levy," she said. "Let me have until tomorrow morning. I beg of you."

"It's not possible, Mrs. Holley."

"I'm—so tired," she said. "I can't put things very clearly. If I can just have a good night's sleep, then tomorrow I'll—tell you."

"Tell me what, Mrs. Holley?"

"About Ted Darby," she said.

"You admit that you know the circumstances of his death?"

"Please," she said, "please just let me have until tomorrow morning."

"That's impossible, Mrs. Holley."

"It has to be that way," she said.

Because I won't let them spring it on Father, she thought. It'll be hard enough for him, no matter how careful I am about telling him. He doesn't even know that the man he met in the boathouse was the horrible Ted Darby he read about in the newspapers. He'll——

"Mrs. Holley," said Levy, "I don't think you understand your position. It's extremely serious. You've admitted that you have knowledge of Darby's murder——"

"It wasn't a murder."

"Of Darby's death. By admitting this knowledge, Mrs. Holley, you've rendered yourself liable to arrest."

"Look!" she said, with desperate earnestness. "Lieutenant, let's just talk, like—people. You *know* I'm not a murderess. I should have told you the whole thing before, but I had a reason—it seemed to me a good reason. I'll tell you everything tomorrow morning. As early as you like."

"Why not now?"

"I need a good night's sleep. I'm—really, I'm so tired . . ."

He moved away, his hands clasped behind his back.

"Mrs. Holley," he said, after a moment, "I'll postpone questioning you any further until tomorrow, if you'll get Donnelly here tonight."

Chapter Twenty

SHE WALKED over to the window, and she was startled to see how it looked out there in the world; everything bathed in a clear lemon light; the coarse grass looked yellow, the leaves on the young trees were a translucent green, and trembling strangely in the strange light.

He's gone now, she told herself. He's on the train, going to Montreal.

But in her mind she could see him only in the lane, as she had left him, tall and neat, his right arm hanging useless by his side. And that's the bargain, she thought. I'm to sell him out. I'm to get him here, and hand him over to the police.

There were footsteps overhead; a door closed. Father, she thought. I suppose Bee's upstairs, too. And David? It's nearly time for dinner.

"Mrs. Holley?"

Levy's tone was courteous and patient; too patient. It's ridiculous for him to wait like this, she thought, with a sudden anger, when he could make me give him an answer.

"I don't know where Mr. Donnelly is," she said, evenly.

"Then I'm afraid we'll have to be getting along, Mrs. Holley."

"You can let me have my dinner, can't you?"

"I'm afraid not."

She turned to face him. The room was growing shadowy, and that made him look very pale, his hair very black.

"I didn't think *you'd* behave like this," she said.

He said nothing.

"Why don't you find Mr. Donnelly for yourself?" she demanded. "If you're so anxious to see him."

"I've tried. But the New York police have lost track of him, temporarily. They'll trace him, of course, but I'd like to see him now."

"You'll arrest him, won't you?"

"I want to question him, Mrs. Holley. If his answers are satisfactory, he'll have no further trouble."

He's been arrested five times, Lucia thought. And they never could convict him. He knows how to look after himself. And they won't ask him about Nagle. Why should they? Nobody can know yet that anything's happened to Nagle. The rest of it isn't dangerous for him. Lieutenant Levy will only ask him about Ted Darby, and he can easily clear himself. He must have an alibi for that evening; certainly he wasn't here.

And about the chest? He'll certainly have got rid of that, long ago. And nobody can possibly know about Nagle yet. No. Martin will say what I said. That it was an engine. He'll be able to answer all Lieutenant Levy's questions—much better than I can. He's been arrested five times, and they couldn't hold him. *He* knows how to look after himself.

She heard the screen door in the kitchen bang, and David's voice, loud and hearty.

"Hello, Sibyl! What's with dinner?"

"Lieutenant Levy's talking to your mother just now," Sibyl answered, in her gentle voice.

"Aha!" said David, pleased. "He's a smart cooky. I bet he cracks this case. Any coke in the icebox, Sibyl?"

"No, Master David. Can't get any."

"Well . . ." said David. "Maybe I'll mix up a chocolate malted."

"Spoil your appetite!"

"It never does," said David.

"I'll mix it for you," said Sibyl.

All the little sounds were strikingly clear to Lucia. That was the bowl being set down on the kitchen cabinet; here was the egg beater clattering, and catching, and starting again. David, she thought, would be sitting on the edge of the kitchen table, happy to be home.

I can't spoil this for David. For all of them. I *will not* go off now, just at dinnertime, to the District Attorney's office. And maybe not come back tonight—not for days. And let them hear—let everyone hear—that I consorted with a known criminal . . .

I'd do anything, to keep that from happening.

He would keep it from happening, if he came. He'd know how to answer Lieutenant Levy, and the District Attorney. He'd know how to help me out of this, if he came. He'd put that first.

"Mrs. Holley, I'll have to have your decision," said Levy.

The egg beater had stopped; she heard the oven door open and shut.

"Yes . . ." she said, and went out of the room, along the hall to the kitchen.

"Hello, David, dear!" she said. "Sibyl, will you come into the sitting room for a moment, please?"

"Sibyl's going to be grilled, is she?" asked David. "Well, watch your step, Sibyl!"

Sibyl smiled at him softly, and followed Lucia back to the sitting room.

"Sibyl," said Lucia, "do you happen to know Mr. Donnelly's telephone number?"

Sibyl looked at her; their eyes met. If she said no, that would be fate.

"Yes, ma'am," said Sibyl.

"You might call him now," said Levy. "Say that Mrs. Holley would like him to come out this evening, as early as possible. Don't mention me."

"No, sir," said Sibyl.

The telephone was on a little table in the hall, just outside the sitting-room door; they could both see her as she sat down on the chair and dialed. Her face looked composed and sorrowful, with her eyes lowered. She's dialing a wrong number, Lucia thought. She likes Martin, and she knows this is a trap for him.

"Hello?" said Sibyl. "May I speak to Mr. Donnelly, please? . . . You expect him in soon? Well, will you please tell him Sibyl says will he please come out to see her this evening, soon as he can? Thank you, sir."

"He's not home, ma'am," she said, rising. "But I left a message."

"With whom?" asked Levy.

"Don't know who it was, sir."

"You might give me the number, please," said Levy, and Sibyl repeated a number which he wrote down in a notebook.

It's a wrong number, Lucia thought. Sibyl wouldn't do this to Martin.

Anyhow, he's gone now. He's on the train now, going to Montreal. He's not coming here. He's gone.

"Thanks," said Levy, putting the little book back into his pocket. "Then I'll see you tomorrow, Mrs. Holley. Good night!"

"Good night!" Lucia answered.

As soon as the door had closed after him, Lucia hurried to the kitchen, almost breathless with impatience to hear what Sibyl would have to say.

"Sibyl . . . ?"

"Yes, ma'am?"

Their eyes met, and Sibyl's were unfathomable, dark, sorrowful and steady.

"Sibyl . . . Do you think he'll come?"

"Left the message, ma'am."

But did you, really? Lucia thought. Or did you just pretend to? You like him. Would you really get him out here—for a policeman?

She stood looking at Sibyl, and she could not ask her that question.

Anyhow, he's gone. He's on the train to Montreal.

"Shall I ring now, ma'am?"

"I suppose so," said Lucia.

She thought that Sibyl enjoyed sounding the gongs in the hall, a series of four strung on a red silk cord; an old thing, that had belonged to Lucia's mother. David and Bee had loved the chimes in their childhood; it was a part of their family life; they had brought it along as a matter of course.

The setting sun made a gold dazzle on the glass of the front door, but the brilliance did not reach Sibyl; she stood in shadow, with the little padded wooden stick in her hand. She struck the lowest and deepest gong, and went on, up to the fourth, then down, then up once more; the notes hummed through the house. And it was like a charm; old Mr. Harper at once came out of his room, then David opened his door; before they had reached the hall, Bee was coming down the stairs.

I want Tom here! Lucia said to herself, in passionate rebellion. I want them all here, all safe. It was an impious wish, a rebellion against heaven, against life itself. She knew that. But she would try, she would fight, to turn away the tide from her doorstep.

She felt that she could do anything. She could sit at the table, she could even eat a little. That was because she had set a limit to her ordeal.

At nine o'clock, she told herself, I'll say I'm tired, and I'll go upstairs. And I'll take one of his pills and go to sleep.

Bee and David were "queer"; she noticed that at once. They were unusually silent; they were disapproving of her. Let them. They would get over it. Her father talked, and she responded, soothed by his kindly vagueness. He had never disapproved of her. If he had noticed any of her strange goings-on lately, or if anyone were to tell him of still stranger goings-on, he would dismiss it all. She was his daughter; she was the irreproachable wife and mother, the wise and prudent housekeeper. The worst he would ever admit against her was, that perhaps she had been somewhat lacking in judgment.

But her husband and her children did not consider her beyond criticism. She belonged to them; whatever she did affected them; their pride, their good name in the world lay in her hands. They would give her love, protection, even a sort of homage, but in return for that she must be what they wanted and needed her to be.

They all went into the sitting room after dinner. Bee sat down at the desk to write a letter; David took up a science magazine; old Mr. Harper proposed a game of cribbage. It was only a little after eight, but Lucia could not keep to her self-imposed limit of nine o'clock.

"Father," she said, "if you don't mind, I think I'll just write to Tom, and then go to bed."

"Very good idea!" he said. "Have you anything to read, m'dear? I have this book from the lending library, very amusing; light touch. This family in a cathedral town in England——"

"I'm sure I'd like it, Father, but I don't think I'll read anything tonight. I think I'll go right to sleep. Good night, Father. Good night, children."

David rose, and kissed her cheek; it was a stern kiss, but at least he accepted her.

"Good night, Mother," said Bee, not even raising her head from her writing.

You're unkind, Lucia thought. But that's because it's much, much harder for you than it is for David. He just thinks I'm being silly and trying, but you feel that there's something more, something dreadful, and you're frightened. I'm sorry . . .

It was necessary to write Tom's letter quickly, while she

could. Her room was tranquil in the lamplight; a soft salt wind blew in at the open windows.

Dear Tom.

It was as if something stirred behind a curtain.

Dear Tom. The weather. Dear Tom. Oh, Tom, *come alive*! Be real. Let me remember how you were, let me see you. Let me feel something about you. Anything. You mustn't, you can't be this far away, so that you're not real.

But there was no feeling in her, for anyone. She was in a hurry to get to sleep, that was all. Folded in the back of the writing tablet she found an old letter to Tom that had not seemed good enough to send. She copied it, almost without change. There were little domestic details; there was a reminder of a day they had spent together at Jones Beach, long ago, when the children were little. It had been a special day, specially happy, but it evoked no feeling in her now. That young, happy Tom and Lucia were no more than bright little dolls.

She addressed the envelope and stood it up against Tom's picture, where every night an envelope stood. She had wrapped the yellow capsules in a paper handkerchief and put them into a bureau drawer. She took one out now, and swallowed it with a glass of water. I don't even know what it is, she thought. I don't know what it will do to me.

Only it would do her no harm. She was not afraid of anything from his hands. She undressed, and bathed, hurrying, for fear sleep would suddenly overcome her. I might fall down, she thought; I might fall asleep just anywhere, and in the morning, they'd find me on the floor. How long will it last, I wonder? So that they'll have trouble waking me up in the morning?

It worried her to think of that, of being drugged and "queer" in the morning. Especially when I've got to tell Father about Ted, she thought. But nothing really mattered except getting through this night, sleeping through it, utterly unconscious. There's nothing to stay awake for, she thought. It's out of my hands now. I let Sibyl give that message. But he won't come. He's on his way to Montreal now.

She got into bed and lay there, propped up on two pillows, the lamp still lighted. She took up a book, but that was no good. What's the matter with that pill? she thought, impatiently. Why doesn't it start? I'll give it twenty minutes more, and then, if nothing's happened, I'll take another.

She closed her eyes, and a face was forming before her; she watched it anxiously. It was a familiar face, bony, wearing pince-nez, and a simpering smile. Now, who's that? she thought. I ought to know. Why, yes; it's Miss Priest, our English teacher. But didn't I hear from someone that she'd died? Well, has she come to give me a message?

"Miss Priest?" she asked, apologetically.

No answer. Lucia sighed, and put the pillows down flat; she stretched out her legs, relaxing. Miss Priest, she thought, trying to remember something. About school, was it? I don't care whether I actually sleep or not, she thought, as long as I can relax like this. And not worry.

Sibyl's voice was hissing in her ear.

"I'm asleep!" Lucia said, angrily. "Let me alone!"

Hiss, hiss, hiss. Misss-ess Holley.

"Let me alone, Sibyl."

"Mrs. Holley, he's here, ma'am. Got to hurry."

Holley. Here. Hurry. Hiss, hiss, hiss.

Sibyl laid a cold, wet washcloth across her forehead, drew it across her eyes.

"Again!" Lucia said.

She opened her eyes and sat up.

"Got to hurry, ma'am. He's here."

"I can't hurry, Sibyl. I took a pill. I was asleep."

"I'll help you, ma'am."

This was a dreadful way to feel, so leaden, so confused. And so indifferent. She sat in a chair while Sibyl put on her shoes and stockings and pinned up her hair.

"What time is it, Sibyl?" she asked.

"Nearly two o'clock, ma'am."

Lucia began to cry a little.

"I didn't get to sleep until after nine," she said. "I haven't had—enough sleep."

"You can go back to sleep later, ma'am."

The dimly lit hall frightened her; she held back, in dread that one of those closed doors would open. But Sibyl took her hand and led her to the stairs; she went down carefully, on wooden feet, still holding Sibyl's hand. They went through the dark kitchen and out onto the back porch, and it was black as pitch there.

"It's raining!" she whispered.

"Just a little bit, ma'am," Sibyl whispered back. "Got to be very quiet now, ma'am."

There was a man moving along the drive; Lucia saw the dull gleam of his raincoat as he passed within a few feet of them.

"Now!" Sibyl whispered.

They went, half running, across the grass, to the boathouse. Sibyl opened the door and they entered, and it was pitch-dark in there, and there was a cold, musty smell.

"This way, ma'am," Sibyl said.

She opened the door that led to a little pantry without a window, and the light from the unshaded bulb that hung from the ceiling was dazzling. He was there.

"It was kind of you to come," he said, with formality.

This was not a dream, and she was not leaden and drowsy now. He was most immaculately neat, in his dark suit and dark tie, his arm in a black sling; he was not blurred now, but sharp and clear. He was completely a stranger to her, and she was cold with fear at the sight of him.

This brilliant little room without a window was a trap, that she had got him into. And now she was shut up in it with him. This was the meeting that she had dreaded more than anything in the world.

"I wouldn't have bothered you," he said, "only my arm is broke on me."

"Broken?" she cried.

"Broken," he repeated, apologetically. "If it wasn't for that, I'd have mailed you the things, with a bit of a note, to explain. Only the way it is, I cannot write."

"Have you had your arm set?"

"That'll come later. Look, will you, what's on the shelf?"

"You can't go on like this! It must hurt you—horribly."

"I don't think of it," he said. "Don't worry. It'll be cared for, later. Look, now, what's on the shelf."

But she kept her eyes upon his face, that had so strangely gay a look.

"Look, now!" he said. "Here's your girl's letters, every last one of them."

He picked up from the drainboard a little bundle of envelopes in an elastic band.

"You'll have no more worry about them," he said. "And here . . . Won't you look? Here's your jewels." He smiled a little. "They're not so grand as I'd been thinking."

"Martin . . ." she said.

The dam was giving way, the great wave was mounting, to engulf her.

"Martin," she said, "your arm is broken. Martin, you must get away, quick."

"There's no great hurry."

"There is! There is! There's a policeman——"

"He is just patrolling. I saw him before, and I kept out of his way while I knocked on the kitchen window and Sibyl came out."

"Martin . . . I'll take you in the rowboat—farther down the shore. Hurry! You must hurry! The policeman might come here."

"He wouldn't be bothering with me."

"But that's what he's here for! I'll take you in the rowboat. I'll get you away, somehow."

"The cop's not looking for me."

"But, Martin! Lieutenant Levy knows about the message——"

"What message?"

He doesn't know, she thought. And if he finds out . . .

"What message was it?" he repeated. "I want the truth of it."

He was looking at her, in a narrow, thoughtful way, as if he were making up his mind. She could not speak; she could not turn her eyes away from him.

"You sent me a message?" he said. "What was it?"

He waited a moment.

"So that's the way of it?" he said. "You turned me in."

"Martin . . ." she said.

He gave a long sigh.

"Ah, well . . ." he said. "That's what poor Nagle meant, y'know."

Chapter Twenty-one

S HE COULD not understand the words; only the tone, that had in it no trace of bitterness or reproach.

"You could not help it," he said. "Levy got after you, did he?"

"It was only about Ted Darby," she said. "He doesn't know about anything else. He only thinks we took something away—evidence—about Ted. Nothing else. Nothing—that could really hurt you. I wouldn't—you know I wouldn't . . . Never about—the other. Never!"

"My poor girl," he said, "you couldn't help yourself at all. That's what Nagle meant, y'know. A woman like yourself will always have to be thinking of her family and her good name first."

"No. Not about—the other. I'd never give you away. Never!"

"Sure, I believe you," he said.

"You don't. I can see that you don't. You think——"

"Look, now! Would I forget the way you helped me get him out, in that chest? Would I forget the courage you had, and the spirit, answering your girl as quick as a flash? You've been good to me."

"No," she said. "I haven't."

"Well, I'm satisfied," he said, with a flicker of that strange gaiety. "Sit down now, will you not? There's a few things——"

"No! You've got to get away now—this instant—in the rowboat."

"You will have to listen, my poor girl," he said, "for my mind is made up."

"You must go!" she said.

"There's no chair in it," he said, glancing around the pantry. "Well, I'll be quick. There's no one ever need know Nagle was in the chest, and the chest itself is burned to ashes. You've only to say you don't know what I had in the chest at all, or where I took it."

"Where is Nagle?"

"It's better you don't know that. Anyhow, he is far from here, and there's nobody knows he was ever in the boathouse but the two of us, and Sibyl. Your car's in the garage by the station. I sent a young boy with it. There's nothing to tie you with Nagle."

"And what about *you*? What are *you* going to do?"

"I can't get away with it," he said, "if the cops are looking for me here."

"You can! I'll take you in the rowboat."

"No," he said, "I can't get away with it. And well I knew it, from the start."

"Martin, even if they did catch you tonight, they'd only ask you questions about Darby. They don't know about Nagle."

He took out a pack of cigarettes and shook one into his hand.

"Will you give me a light, please?" he asked. "It is hard——"

"Aren't you *going*?"

"A few drags . . ." he said, apologetically. "It is a comfort."

She struck a match and held it out for him.

"Martin," she said, "you're not being—sensible. You *can* get away. If I take you in the rowboat——"

"I'll not go in the boat with you," he said.

"Then go by the road. We'll watch, Sibyl and I, until the policeman's on the other side of the house, and then you can get away."

"Sure!" he said, absently, drawing on the cigarette.

"Martin!" she cried. "You've got something in your mind! Something silly."

"A life for a life," he said. "That's the way of it."

"It doesn't have to be—unless you just give up. Martin, aren't you man enough to fight for your life?"

"There are things you can't fight," he said. "Carlie and I, we were friends for near twenty years. It never came into his head I'd do that to him. Surprised, he looked, like——"

"Stop! Don't talk like that! You——" She stopped for a moment, appalled by the look on his face, the blankness. "Don't be a fool! Pull yourself together. You've got to fight for your life."

"And what kind of life would it be at all, with never a moment's peace, day or night? I'd never lay my head on my pillow that I wouldn't see Carlie——"

"Shut up!" she said, furiously. "You did it for me."

"That was the same as doing it for myself," he said. "There is no merit in that."

"Snap out of it! You can get away—if you'll stop being such a dope."

He was looking down at her with a smile.

"Stop that smiling!" she said. "There's nothing to smile about. For God's *sake*, will you pull yourself together and *think*?"

"I will," he said, readily.

"And you'll go to Montreal?"

"I will try."

"Don't say that. Don't think that way. Say you will go to Montreal."

"I will," he said.

"I don't trust you! You've got something in your mind. You think that because I sent—because I had to send that message—you think it's fate, or something."

"It is not fate I believe in," he said.

She was silent, in a furious effort to find the right words, to reach him, to rouse him.

"Martin," she said, "you've managed so well, up to now. You've burned the chest; you've—managed everything. You won't go to pieces now, when the worst of it's all over?"

"Oh, I won't," he said. "Don't you be worrying, dear."

"Martin, you don't—you can't believe—what Nagle said . . . ?"

"I do not," he said.

She was leaning against the drainboard, supporting herself with one outstretched hand. He laid his hand over it.

"Good-by now," he said.

"Martin . . ."

But he had opened the door and gone into the dark room beyond. She moved after him, groping, lost in the blackness. The front door closed softly.

"Sibyl?" she called, sharply.

"Yes, ma'am?"

"We ought to——"

Ought to do what? She made her way across the room and

opened the door. It was lighter out there, and she saw Donnelly moving quickly across the grass, going toward the highway. Then a flashlight swung in a half circle, and she shrank back against the house.

Now there would be a shout. Now there would be a shot.

The flashlight swung again, and she had a glimpse of stunted bushes that seemed to slide along the beam of light. The water lapped softly against the boathouse; the rain made a whispering sound.

"Now, ma'am?" said Sibyl, close to her ear.

It was a dreadful thing, to cross that dark, open space. The flashlight would catch them, and they would be paralyzed by it; they would stand frozen.

It was a dreadful thing to go up the stairs. A door would open, a voice would call to her.

"I'll help you get to bed, ma'am."

"No, thank you, Sibyl. No, thank you."

Her own lamplit room was not safe. Someone could knock; someone could open the door. She undressed in frantic haste, and threw all her damp clothes into the closet; she put on her pajamas and lay down on the bed.

She lay very still, waiting for the shot to ring out, for the sound of footsteps running up the stairs.

Chapter Twenty-two

SHE WAKED in a gray twilight, and looked at her watch. It was half-past four. That's too early, she said to herself, and frowned, worried by the words. What was it about "too early"? Something important. Too early . . .

Come as early as you like tomorrow morning, she had told Levy, and this was tomorrow morning. I'll have to talk to Father first, she thought, but not just yet. I can sleep a little longer.

She had a dream, about Sibyl. Sibyl was living in a little shack, by the edge of a swamp, and the sheriff and his men were coming to get her husband. But that was all right, because she knew it was only a dream. The swamp was a dream swamp, a jungle of tall, dark trees festooned with strange white moss that rustled like paper. The sheriff and his men had brought bloodhounds with them, and they went into the jungle-swamp, splashing through water. She could not see them now, but the hounds began to bay, and it froze her blood.

She heard a high, squealing whistle. That's a bazooka gun! she thought. Oh, Tom, be careful! Now she knew that it was Tom in the gloomy swamp, hunted by dogs, and his leg was broken. She tried to run to him, and she could not stir; she tried to call to him, and her voice was strangled. Some gasping little sound came, and waked her.

There was the same gray twilight in the room, and the house was very quiet. But it was after seven, by her watch. I'll have to talk to Father, she thought, and got up. A sick dizziness came rushing up, spinning round and round, from her feet into her head; she fell back on the bed, and the bed rose from the floor and spun, in a great swoop.

When that stopped, she was afraid to move, for fear it would start again. She still felt sick, and too tired, too weak to lift her head. I can't talk to Father, she thought. I can't get up. They'll have to let me alone for a little while, until this goes away.

There was a knock at the door, and Sibyl came in with a tray. She set the tray down, and came over to the bed; she helped

743

Lucia to lie back against the pillows; she drew the sheet neatly up over her chest.

"Thought you'd like some breakfast, ma'am."

"Sibyl . . . Have you heard anything?"

"No, ma'am."

"Did you look in the newspapers?"

"Yes, ma'am. There's nothing."

"Sibyl, I'd like to rest for a while."

Sibyl poured her a cup of coffee.

"If you'll just tell the others that I'm tired, and that I'd like to rest until lunchtime . . . If you'll just see that no one disturbs me, Sibyl . . ."

"I'll tell them, ma'am," said Sibyl, with no spark of hope.

"Can't you see to that for me?" Lucia demanded, ready to cry.

"I'll tell them, ma'am. That's all I can do," said Sibyl.

There was nothing sympathetic in her tone; her face was completely inexpressive. Tears were running down Lucia's cheeks as she drank her coffee. Sibyl's absolutely heartless, she told herself. She could see that I got a little peace and quiet, if she wanted.

The coffee made her feel better. No, she thought, Sibyl's not heartless. She's a realist, that's all. She knows you have to do things. I'll lie here until Lieutenant Levy comes. Then he can wait downstairs until I've talked to Father. He can just wait. Do him good.

She drank two cups of coffee, and lit a cigarette. But it was curiously bitter, and she put it out. I really don't feel at all well, she thought. I think I'm on the verge of a breakdown. What, exactly, was a breakdown? Aunt Agnes had a nervous breakdown. Lots of people do. Maybe this was it, this bodily weakness and weariness, this refusal of the mind to think or to feel. This is how sick animals feel, she thought. When Tom's collie was sick, he always wagged his tail when Tom spoke to him. I used to think he hated to do it. Toward the end, he didn't even open his eyes; just gave one little thump with his tail. Because he felt he had to, on Tom's account. I always thought he didn't like Tom to pat his head and say, "Good old scout, aren't you? Aren't you, Max? Good old scout, aren't you?" Enough to drive you crazy, when you're dying.

She lay with her eyes closed, and thought about dogs, and then about cats. People don't make such exorbitant demands upon cats, she thought. Nobody expects them to grin and pant and wag their tails and be overjoyed every time anyone speaks to them. No . . . People feel rather flattered if they can make a cat purr.

Birds . . . she thought. Why should everyone think that a skylark was so full of rapture? I think birds are frightfully fussy and worried. People say "nervous as a cat." I think "nervous as a bird" would be much better. When you think of birds, hopping around, and chirping, and looking for food all the time . . . They push each other, too. I've seen them. They're rude, birds are.

There was a knock at the door, and she began to cry.

"Come in!" she called, drying her eyes roughly on the sheet.

It was David. He stood in the doorway, slight, too slight, in slacks and a blue shirt, and he was not smiling.

"I hear you're not feeling so fine," he said. "What's the trouble?"

"I'm tired, that's all," said Lucia.

"Well, I hadn't noticed you'd been doing such a heck of a lot lately," he said.

"Everyone gets tired, sometimes," said Lucia, nettled by this tone. "And, after all, I'm not fifteen, David."

"You look funny," he said. "I think we'd better get a doctor."

"No!" said Lucia. "I'm not going to have a doctor. All I need is a little rest."

"Well, I think you look funny," said David.

She fought against her anger; she reasoned with herself. It's always like this, she thought. Even Tom is sort of furious if I get sick. What have you been *doing* with yourself, to get a cold like this?

"I'll be all right, David, after a little rest," she said.

"Well . . ." said David, "I don't want to bother you, but there's one thing I'd like to ask you. What's happened to our car?"

"It's in the garage by the station."

"Well, I hope it is," said David.

"I *know* it is," said Lucia.

"Well, I hope so," said David.

Lucia closed her eyes, so that she need not see his irritating face.

"Mother?" he said, and when she did not answer: "*Mother?*" he said, in a different tone, in a panic.

"Oh, what *is* it, David?"

"Well, when you closed your eyes . . . I thought maybe you felt faint, or something."

She remembered him, when he was a little boy, shaking her by the shoulder, waking her out of a sound sleep, crying "Mother!" in that same tone. "What *is* it, David?" she had asked.

She remembered how he had looked, thin and wiry in his striped pajamas, his black hair ruffled. "I thought you were dead," he had said.

"I'm sorry I worried you, dear," she said. "Don't worry any more. I'll just rest for a while, and then I'll be perfectly all right."

She smiled at him, and his face relaxed.

"Okay!" he said. "Want anything from the village, Mother? Any medicine, or anything?"

"No, thank you, dear. But ask Sibyl what she wants."

It's going to be dreadful for David, she thought, when the story comes out. He wanted his mother to be not only conventional, and beyond measure respectable, but practically invisible. He had been disturbed even by her going out in the motorboat earlier than was the custom for mothers. How would it be when he learned what she was doing with the boat? And if he learned about Donnelly?

He had gone out of the room now, reassured about her health, but he left her miserably agitated, all the vague calmness gone. Now Bee will come, she thought. Bee was frightened yesterday. I know how she felt. When I was seventeen, if my mother had gone driving off with a strange man, leaving a guest she'd invited to tea, coming back so much later, and smelling of whisky . . . I'd have thought it was the end of the world. And I didn't explain anything to her.

Explain? *Explain?* But did I really do that? Did I help to put Nagle into that chest?

Oh, the chest is the worst! Far the worst! I drove the car, and I never even thought about the chest. He was there, in the chest, and I wasn't even sorry for him. Suppose he wasn't really dead? O God!

Sweat came out on her forehead. How do I know he was dead—when we put him——?

There was a knock at the door.

"May I come in, m'dear?"

"Oh, come in, Father!"

"Resting, eh?"

"Yes, I am, Father."

"Very good idea. Keeping house, in times like these—great strain. You need a rest, now and then."

"Well . . ."

"There's one thing, m'dear," he said, standing beside the bed. "I don't want to disturb your rest, but I dare say you can solve the mystery with one word."

"What mystery, Father?"

"Thing is," he said, lowering his voice, "I had a bottle of Scotch, in the sideboard. Hadn't even opened it. Well, dashed if it hasn't disappeared!"

"You've got another bottle, haven't you, Father?"

"Oh, yes. Yes. Plenty. But that's not the point, m'dear. I put that bottle in the sideboard myself, day before yesterday. And it's gone. I don't like to ask Sibyl about it. Colored people are sensitive—and you can't blame them. Shouldn't like her to imagine I was accusing her."

"She wouldn't think that, Father. She knows how we feel about her."

But Sibyl did take his whisky! she thought, remembering. And I drank out of the bottle. And Nagle . . .

"It occurred to me . . ." he said. "D'you think Bee might have offered drinks to some of her friends?"

"She'd never *touch* your whisky without asking you, Father. And she doesn't drink whisky. Only a little glass of sherry, once in a great while. Bee isn't like that, Father."

"No, no. Naturally. Don't worry. Rest. Enjoy yourself. Don't worry about anything."

He laid his hand on her forehead.

"Headache?" he asked. "Any aches or pains, m'dear? The great thing is, if there's anything starting, to nip it in the bud."

She looked up at him, into his steady blue eyes that had never looked at her except with affection and trust, and tears rose in her own.

"I'm—just tired . . ." she said, very unsteadily.

"Come, come!" he said, in alarm. "That's not like you, m'dear. Nerves . . ."

She forced a smile; she could feel how stiff and forced a smile it was, but it satisfied him.

"That's better!" he said. "I'm going to write to Tom today. Going to tell him how you keep the flag flying, eh?"

When he had gone, she cried . . . She wanted to cry wildly and violently, but only a few slow tears ran down her face. Why doesn't Bee come? she thought. I want Bee to come.

She was asleep when Sibyl brought her lunch tray.

"Is Miss Bee home?" she asked.

"Yes, ma'am. Went down to the village with Master David, and they came back in the car."

"Sibyl . . . Haven't you heard anything?"

"They brought back an evening paper, ma'am. It's in that."

"What is it? Did they get him?"

"I'll bring you the paper, ma'am, soon as they start their lunch."

"Tell me."

"I'll bring you the paper, ma'am."

She waited, waited, waited, not even looking at the tray.

"Can't you eat anything, ma'am?"

"No. Let me see, Sibyl."

SLAYER CONFESSES UNSUSPECTED CRIME
QUESTIONED IN DARBY CASE, SUSPECT
ADMITS FEUD MURDER

Early this morning, the Horton County police got not only a full account of the accidental slaying of Ted Darby on the 17th, but also the surprise confession of a murder wholly unsuspected by them.

At 3 A.M. a police car picked up Martin Donnelly, 42, who gave his residence as the Hotel De Vrees, New York City, and took him to headquarters for questioning in regard to the Darby case.

Darby Death Accidental

In a statement to press representatives, Lieutenant Levy, of the Horton County police said that Donnelly's account of Darby's death tallied with medical reports and other factors. The two men had, according to Donnelly's account, engaged in a quarrel, on the private pier of one of the Glendale Beach palatial estates, which Donnelly was unable to identify. In the course of the quarrel, Donnelly stated that he had pushed Darby off the pier, and had then gone back to his car, in which he had slept until morning.

Alarmed then by Darby's continued absence, Donnelly stated that he returned to the pier, where he found Darby's body impaled on an anchor in a motorboat. He ran the boat over to Simm's Island, four miles or so offshore, and concealed the body in a marsh.

Confession a Surprise

"We were wholly unprepared," Lieutenant Levy told press representatives, "for the confession which followed. Donnelly stated, voluntarily, that on the previous day he had strangled and killed Anton Karl Nagle, 57, believed by New York police to have been an associate of Donnelly's in black market activities.

Following Donnelly's directions, police found Nagle's body in a lake . . .

"Sibyl!" cried Lucia.

But Sibyl had gone, and she was alone.

Martin, you fool! You wicked, wicked fool! You can't get out of this. And you don't want to. You wanted to be arrested. You wanted to confess. You want to die—in the electric chair.

Well, I won't let you. I'll tell Lieutenant Levy the truth about Ted Darby.

That won't do any good. Ted Darby doesn't matter now. It's Nagle. He did that for me. Martin, you fool! You fool, to choose that dreadful death. You didn't trust me. You thought I'd give you away. Again.

I've got to talk to him. I've got to see him. And I never can. Never, never again. But it can't——

"Lieutenant Levy is here, ma'am," said Sibyl. "Shall I bring him up?"

"No, no! He can't come up here. No. Ask him to wait. I'll be down in a moment. No . . . Ask my father to come here, please."

"Mr. Harper's stepped out, ma'am."

This is too much. This is too much, Lucia thought. She got up, and tried to dress in haste, but her hands trembled so, her heart beat so fast. What dress? she thought, opening the closet door.

She took down the brown dress, and hung it up again. She took down a clean pink cotton dress, and that was not right. O God, I've got to hurry! What dress? She picked out two others, and laid them on a chair, and they were not right. O God, what shall I do? I've got to find the right dress . . .

There was a gray flannel skirt in the closet, with the hem half unripped. That was the right thing. With shaking hands she opened her preposterous sewing basket, a jumble of thread, darning silk, shoulder pads, bits of ribbon. She threaded a big darning needle with gray silk, and stitched up the hem, so badly that it was in puckers. She put on the skirt, and a white blouse, and forgetting to glance in the mirror, she went out of the room and down the stairs. She thought she heard Mrs. Lloyd's voice, but that was impossible.

She stopped in the hall outside the sitting room, and it was Mrs. Lloyd in there, sitting on the edge of a chair. She was stylish today, in a high black hat from which a cyclamen veil floated, and she was just drawing off a cyclamen glove. But Lieutenant Levy was not there.

He's in the dining room, Lucia thought, and was moving away when Bee called to her.

"Mother!"

"I'm sorry . . ." Lucia said. "I'm sorry, but I've got to see Lieutenant Levy."

"He's gone, Mother. Mother, Mrs. Lloyd is here."

"I know. But——"

Bee crossed the room and took her mother's hand.

"Come and sit down, Mother."

It was inhuman of Bee to ask her to sit down and talk to

Mrs. Lloyd. She hung back, like a rebellious child, but Bee drew her forward.

"I'm afraid *I* drove Lieutenant Levy away," said Mrs. Lloyd.

"Oh, no!" said Bee. "He said it wasn't anything important. He just stopped by, to tell Mother that the Darby case was closed."

"I've been to a meeting of the hospital committee," Mrs. Lloyd said, "and everyone was talking about this case. The Donnelly man was absolutely desperate. He fought off the police like a tiger, for hours, and they had to shoot him in the leg before he'd give in. Mrs. Ewing heard the shots."

"I'm afraid Mrs. Ewing's mistaken," said Bee. "Mr. Donnelly didn't even try to get away."

"But these gunmen always seem to defy the police, don't they?"

"Mr. Donnelly isn't a gunman," said Bee. "You see, we know him."

"You *know* him?" said Mrs. Lloyd, fascinated.

"Yes. And we liked him, Grandpa, and David and me, and Mother . . ."

"Then weren't you appalled, when you found out what he'd done?"

"No," Bee said, rising. She sat down on the arm of the sofa beside Lucia, and laid her hand on her mother's shoulder. "We're just terribly sorry."

Her hand lay heavy on her mother's shoulder.

"He had lots of nice qualities," she said. "Only, the war makes people do—queer, horrible things." Her voice was a little unsteady now. "Especially middle-aged people."

"Oh, do you think so?" Mrs. Lloyd asked, a little surprised.

"Yes!" Bee said, vehemently. "It's psychological. Middle-aged people feel—sort of left out. As if everything was finished for them. They get a sort of craving for adventure . . ."

It was not Donnelly she was defending; it was her mother. She had tried to understand Lucia's bewildering and frightening behavior; she was trying now to present it as the foolish, but pitiable, last fling of a middle-aged woman. Lucia glanced up at her, and their eyes met.

"Mother," Bee said. "I'm sorry you felt so tired, but I thought I wouldn't bother you."

She had forgotten Mrs. Lloyd, so important in her scheme

of life. All she wanted now was, that Lucia should know she understood, that she loved her.

"I'll look after the housekeeping for a while," she said. "And you can take things easy, Mother."

Be easy . . .

"Excuse me, ladies!" said Mr. Harper. "But the young fellow from the gas company wants to see the contract, Lucia."

"What contract, Father?"

"He says the owner of the house has a contract for maintenance. He must have left it with you, m'dear."

"I don't remember seeing it, Father."

"Well . . ." he said, indulgent and resigned, "if you can't find the contract, m'dear, we'll have to pay, and pay through the nose, for these repairs to the icebox." He smiled at Mrs. Lloyd. "I'm afraid you ladies don't take contracts very seriously," he said.

"I'm frightful about losing things," said Mrs. Lloyd.

This is my life, Lucia thought. The things I dreaded aren't going to happen, the shame, the disgrace. I don't know whether Lieutenant Levy believes Martin's story about Ted Darby, but anyhow he's going to accept it. Nothing's going to happen to me.

This is my life, going on just the same. I haven't hurt the children, or Tom, or Father. I haven't shocked people like Mrs. Lloyd. The man is here to fix the icebox, at last. This is how I'll go on.

And all that had happened to her would be, must be, pushed down, out of sight; the details of daily living would come like falling leaves to cover it. I don't really know what's happened to me, she thought, in wonder. I haven't taken time to think about it.

Maybe I never will. Or maybe, when I'm old, and have plenty of time and quiet . . .

Sibyl came in, with tea and cinnamon toast. The butter on the toast was margarine, colored yellow; the cinnamon was artificial. Lucia had read the label on the little tin with an unreasonable interest; she remembered some of it now. Imitation cinnamon. Cinnamic aldehyde. Eugenol. Oil of cassia, quite a lot of other things, too.

But nobody knows the difference, she thought. Only Sibyl and me.

BIOGRAPHICAL NOTES

NOTE ON THE TEXTS

NOTES

Biographical Notes

VERA CASPARY Born Vera Louise Caspary on November 13, 1899, in Chicago, Illinois, the youngest child of Paul Caspary, a buyer for a department store, and Julia Cohen Caspary. Caspary's birth was a surprise to the family, as her mother, over forty with three grown children, had hidden the pregnancy. She graduated high school in 1917 and enrolled in a six-month business college course, after which she worked as a stenographer and as an advertising copywriter. Created the "Sergei Marinoff School of Classic Dancing," a mail-order dance course, and wrote articles for publications such as *Finger Print Magazine* and the New York-based *Dance Lovers Magazine.* Turned down a raise from fifty to seventy-five dollars a week to work on her first novel in 1922. Her father died two years later, by which time Caspary was fully supporting her mother with her writing. Moved to Greenwich Village in New York as *Dance Lovers Magazine*'s new editor; eventually left to finish her first novel, *Ladies & Gents* (1929). Published novel *The White Girl* (1929) about a black woman who passes for white and *Music in the Street* (1930), set in a working girls' home, inspired by Caspary living under an assumed name at a similar home. Moved back to Chicago and cowrote the play *Blind Mice* (1931) with Winifred Lenihan, which became the basis for the film *Working Girls.* Moved back to New York and published the novel *Working Girls* (1932), a roman à clef about her own family. Nearly broke, Caspary wrote a forty-page original story for Paramount for $2,000, which allowed her to move to Hollywood for the first time. Joined the Communist Party as "Lucy Sheridan," but later claimed she never fully believed in the cause and confined her activities to fund-raising and hosting meetings. Visited Russia in April 1939 to "see how people lived" and (until blocked by paperwork delays) nearly married an Austrian Jew to get him to the United States. Back in America, Caspary attempted to resign from the Communist Party, agreed to "temporary leave of absence," and returned to Hollywood. Wrote *Laura* in 1941, finishing it in October. The story was serialized in *Collier's* over seven issues, October–November 1942, and published by Houghton Mifflin in 1943. Wrote dramatization of *Laura* in 1942 with George Sklar, eventually mounted in London and in New York (the latter production starring Miriam Hopkins) while waiting for meaningful work from Office of War Information. Tried to join the army but was turned down. Met future husband, the Austrian film producer Isadore "Igee" Goldsmith, but his British citizenship re-quired him to return to England; they were separated for thirteen months. Sold film rights to *Laura* to Twentieth Century-Fox; it was filmed in 1944, with Otto Preminger as director and a cast including Gene Tierney, Dana Andrews, and Clifton Webb. Novel *Bedelia* (1945) was first published as a serial by *Good Housekeeping* and in book form by Houghton Mifflin. Devised a scheme to see Igee in England by cabling him that he could have the film rights to *Bedelia* for a British production, if she could be brought over to write the screenplay. Made deal with British Ministry of Information to write articles about wartime England for American newspapers and maga-zines. Arrived in England in January 1945, but left London once the war ended. In Hollywood, Caspary adapted John Klempner's *Letters to Five Wives*, eventually filmed by Joseph L. Mankiewicz as *A Letter to Three Wives* (1949). Published the novel *Stranger Than Truth* (1946) and the novella *The Murder in the Stork Club* (1946). Married Gold-smith in 1948. Formed short-lived Gloria Films production company, eventually tied up in United Artists bankruptcy in 1950. Published the novel *The Weeping and the Laughter* (1950). Learning she had been added to the "gray list" for Communist Party links, left country to avoid naming names. Shuttled between Hollywood and Europe until the House Un-American Activities Committee lost interest, and screen-writing jobs returned, starting with *Les Girls* (1957). Published novels *Thelma* (1952); *False Face* (1954); *The Husband* (1957); *Evvie* (1960), loosely based on Caspary's 1920s career girl days; and *Bachelor in Para-dise* (1961), based on a film treatment. Goldsmith died of cancer in Vermont in 1964. Caspary returned to New York and published novels *A Chosen Sparrow* (1964), *The Man Who Loved His Wife* (1966), *The Rosecrest Cell* (1967), *Final Portrait* (1971), *Ruth* (1972), *The Dreamers* (1975), *Elizabeth X* (1978), as well as her autobiography, *The Secrets of Grown-Ups* (1979). Died of a stroke at St. Vincent's Hospital in New York City on June 13, 1987.

HELEN EUSTIS Born Helen White Eustis II on December 31, 1916, in Cincinnati, Ohio, daughter of Harold Clayton Eustis, a socially prominent stockbroker, and Bessie Langdon Eustis. Mother died on October 18, 1918. Father married Mabel Ethel Wood Pogue, who had a son from a previous marriage, Samuel Pogue, born in 1919 after his father's death. Eustis attended Smith College in Massachusetts, where she won a creative writing award; graduated in 1938 with a bachelor's degree in English literature. Married Alfred Young Fisher, a professor of English at Smith previously married to writer M.F.K. Fisher. They had a son, Adam Eustis (Genkaku) Fisher. Pursued graduate work in literature at Columbia University but did not finish her degree.

Divorced Fisher and married Martin Harris, a press photographer; marriage ended in divorce. Father died of a self-inflicted gunshot wound at the Netherland Plaza Hotel in Cincinnati, Ohio, on December 3, 1945, after wife had filed for divorce. Eustis briefly worked as a copywriter. Published debut novel *The Horizontal Man* (1946), loosely based on her experiences at Smith College; it won the Edgar Award for Best First Novel the following year. Story "An American Home" (1947) won an O. Henry Prize and was included in the collection *The Captains and the Kings Depart, and Other Stories* (1949). Published children's book *Mr. Death and the Redheaded Woman* (1954), which had first appeared in the February 11, 1950, issue of *The Saturday Evening Post*; short stories "The Private Ghost of Benjamin Kell" (*Cosmopolitan*, 1952) and "Good-by To Oedipus" (*Harper's Monthly*, 1953); and novel *The Fool Killer* (1954), a Civil War thriller echoing classic boys' tales. *The Fool Killer* was adapted into the film of the same name, starring Anthony Perkins, in 1965. Translated several books from French, including works by Christiane Rochefort (*Cats Don't Care For Money*, 1965), Edmonde Charles-Roux (*To Forget Palermo*, 1968), Georges Simenon (*When I Was Old*, 1971), Didier Decoin (*Laurence: A Love Story*, 1971), Michel Salomon (*Prague Notebook: The Strangled Revolution*, 1971), and Romain Gary (*The Enchanters*, 1975). Published the short story "A Winter's Tale" (1986) in *Ellery Queen's Mystery Magazine*. Died in New York on January 11, 2015.

DOROTHY B. HUGHES Born Dorothy Belle Flanagan on August 10, 1904, in Kansas City, Missouri, the oldest child of Frank S. Flanagan and Calla Belle Callahan Flanagan. Knew she wanted to be a writer at the age of six, when she first learned how to read. Graduated from the University of Missouri in 1924 with a major in journalism, did graduate work at the University of New Mexico, and also attended Columbia University. Worked as a journalist in Missouri, New York, and New Mexico. Married Levi Allan Hughes Jr. in 1932. They had two daughters, Helen and Susan, and a son, Antony. Published a book of poems, *Dark Certainty* (1931), which won the Yale Series of Younger Poets competition, and *Pueblo On the Mesa* (1939), a history of the first fifty years of the University of New Mexico. Her first novel, *The So Blue Marble* (1940), began a streak in which Hughes published eleven novels in seven years: suspense novels *The Cross-Eyed Bear* (1940), *The Bamboo Blonde* (1941), *The Fallen Sparrow* (1942), *The Blackbirder* (1943), *The Delicate Ape* (1944), *Dread Journey* (1945), *Ride the Pink Horse* (1946), *The Scarlet Imperial* (1946), and *In a Lonely Place* (1947), as well as *Johnnie* (1944), a non-crime novel. A number of Hughes's novels were adapted as Hollywood films: *The Fallen Sparrow* (1943, directed by Richard Wallace and starring John

Garfield), *Ride the Pink Horse* (1947, directed by and starring Robert
Montgomery), and *In a Lonely Place* (1950, directed by Nicholas Ray
and starring Humphrey Bogart and Gloria Grahame). Moved to Los
Angeles in 1944. Reviewed mysteries for the *Albuquerque Tribune*,
the *Los Angeles Times*, and the *New York Herald-Tribune* beginning in
1940. Published non-crime novel *The Big Barbecue* (1949), as well as
suspense novels *The Candy Kid* (1950) and *The Davidian Report*
(1952). Published short stories "The Homecoming" (1946), "You
Killed Miranda" (1958), and "The Black & White Blues" (1959). Returned to Santa Fe, New Mexico, after the death of her mother in 1961.
Published her final novel, *The Expendable Man* (1963), later explaining
she had stopped writing novels in order to care for her dying mother as
well as to support her children and grandchildren. Continued to review
new crime fiction for the *Los Angeles Times*. Published the short stories
"Danger at Deerfawn" (1964) and "Everybody Needs a Mink" (1965).
Named Grand Master of the Mystery Writers of America in 1978. Published *Erle Stanley Gardner: The Case of the Real Perry Mason* (1978),
which won her an Edgar Award for best critical/biographical work in
1979. Died in Ashland, Oregon, on May 6, 1993.

ELISABETH SANXAY HOLDING Born Elisabeth Sanxay on
June 18, 1889, in Brooklyn, New York. Attended Miss Whitcomb's
School for Ladies and other finishing schools throughout her childhood. Married George Holding, a British diplomat, in 1913, traveling
widely throughout Latin America and the Caribbean. Had two
daughters, Skeffington and Antonia. Lived for many years in Bermuda, where husband was a government official. Published six romantic novels, including *Invincible Minnie* (1920), *Angelica* (1921),
Rosaleen Among the Artists (1921), and *The Unlit Lamp* (1922), as
well as many short stories and novellas. Turned to suspense fiction
after the 1929 stock market crash, starting with *Miasma* (1929). Published an additional seventeen detective novels: *Dark Power* (1930),
The Death Wish (1934), *The Unfinished Crime* (1935), *The Strange
Crime in Bermuda* (1937), *The Obstinate Murderer* (1938), *The Girl
Who Had To Die* (1940), *Who's Afraid?* (1940), *Speak of the Devil*
(1941), *Kill Joy* (1942), *Lady Killer* (1942), *The Old Battle Ax* (1943),
Net of Cobwebs (1945), *The Innocent Mrs. Duff* (1946), *The Blank Wall*
(1947), *Too Many Bottles* (1951), *The Virgin Huntress* (1951), and
Widow's Mite (1953). *The Blank Wall* was adapted into the films *The
Reckless Moment* (1949), directed by Max Ophüls and starring Joan
Bennett and James Mason, and *The Deep End* (2001), directed by
Scott McGehee and David Siegel and starring Tilda Swinton. Moved
back to New York in the late 1940s upon George Holding's retire-
ment from government work. Died in the Bronx on February 7, 1955.

Note on the Texts

This volume contains four crime novels written by American women in the 1940s: *Laura* by Vera Caspary (1943), *The Horizontal Man* by Helen Eustis (1946), *In a Lonely Place* by Dorothy B. Hughes (1947), and *The Blank Wall* by Elisabeth Sanxay Holding (1947).

Laura appeared in *Collier's* magazine as a seven-part serial, October–November 1942, as "Ring Twice for Laura." It was published in book form by Houghton Mifflin in 1943. In 1944 an English edition was published by Eyre & Spottiswoode. The text printed here is taken from the first American edition.

The Horizontal Man was published in New York by Harper & Brothers in 1946. An English edition was published in London by Hamish Hamilton in 1947. The text printed here is taken from the first American edition.

In a Lonely Place was published in New York by Duell, Sloan & Pearce in 1947. An English edition was published in 1950 by Nicholson and Watson. The text printed here is taken from the first American edition.

The Blank Wall appeared in an abridged form in *The Ladies' Home Journal* in October 1947, and was published in New York by Simon & Schuster the same year. The text of *The Blank Wall* printed here is taken from the first edition.

This volume presents the text of the original printings chosen for inclusion here, but it does not attempt to reproduce non-textual features of their typographic design. The texts are presented without change, except for the correction of typographical errors. Spelling, punctuation, and capitalization are often expressive features and are not altered, even when inconsistent or regular. The following is a list of typographical errors corrected, cited by page and line number: 29.26, lacquerred; 81.12, sound."; 100.28, possibilities."; 106.10, Faithful; 116.20, "You're; 138.27, He not; 161.23, warnings.; 161.40, weakness.; 173.15, place . . ."; 237.21, psychiatrist is; 264.11–12, vintage) the; 269.1, brisky; 271.29, sort.; 310.8, "oughn't; 322.29, is; 378.4, on an; 390.9, Alexander,; 418.10, see; 420.16, to a a; 459.37, she pictures; 473.13, Cashmere burberry,; 481.7, as flicker; 554.25, whomever; 637.3, Sibyl.; 639.23, courteously,; 640.36, the way.

Notes

In the notes below, the reference numbers denote page and line of this volume (the line count includes headings). No note is made for material included in standard desk-reference books. Biblical quotations are keyed to the King James Version. Quotations from Shakespeare are keyed to *The Riverside Shakespeare*, ed. G. Blakemore Evans (Boston: Houghton Mifflin, 1974). For more biographical information than is contained in the Chronology, see Sarah Weinman, ed., *Troubled Daughters, Twisted Wives: Stories from the Trailblazers of Domestic Suspense* (New York: Penguin Books, 2013); Jeffrey Marks, *Atomic Renaissance: Women Mystery Writers in the 1940s and 1950s* (Delphi Books, 2003); Vera Caspary, *The Secrets of Grown-Ups* (New York: McGraw-Hill, 1979); John Connolly and Declan Burke, *Books to Die For* (New York: Atria/Emily Bestler Books, 2012); David Bordwell, "Murder Culture: Adventures in 1940s Suspense" (2013), davidbordwell.net/essays/murder.php.

LAURA

6.1   Cassius . . . lean and hungry look] See *Julius Caesar*, I.ii.194.

6.31   Haviland] Porcelain manufacturer in Limoges, France, established by the American David Haviland in the 1840s.

8.30   Saranac] The Adirondack Cottage Sanatorium, a center for the treatment of tuberculosis, was established in 1885 in Saranac Lake, New York.

9.10–11   Thackeray . . . offensive creature."] The novelist William Makepeace Thackeray (1811–1863) wrote in *The Book of Snobs* (1848): "James I was a Scotch Snob, than which the world contains no more offensive creature."

9.21   Gibbon] Edward Gibbon (1737–1794), author of *The History of the Decline and Fall of the Roman Empire*, which was published in six volumes from 1776 to 1788.

9.26   Prescott and Motley] The American historians William H. Prescott (1796–1859), author of *History of the Conquest of Mexico* (1843) and *History of the Conquest of Peru* (1847), and John Lothrop Motley (1814–1877), author of *The Rise of the Dutch Republic* (1856).

9.27   Josephus' *History of the Jews*] *Antiquities of the Jews* by the Jewish historian Josephus (c. 37–c. 100 C.E.).

9.29   *pour le sport*] French: for the fun of it.

9.40 Apollo Belvedere] Ancient marble sculpture unearthed in Italy in the fifteenth century and subsequently praised as a model of aesthetic beauty.

12.34 Bambi] Deer fawn who is the protagonist of Felix Salten's novel, published in 1928. Walt Disney's animated feature was released in August 1942.

15.23–24 "Concealment . . . damask cheek."] See *Twelfth Night*, II.iv. 111–112.

16.8–9 President . . . devotee of mystery stories] Franklin D. Roosevelt's fondness for mystery stories was well-known. The novel *The President's Mystery Story* (1935), cowritten by a group of writers including S. S. Van Dine and Fulton Oursler, was based on a premise suggested by Roosevelt in conversation; it was subsequently filmed as *The President's Mystery* (1936).

16.36 *Time, You Thief*] See Leigh Hunt, "Jenny Kiss'd Me" (1838), line 3.

17.1 Dalí] Artist Salvador Dalí (1904–1989).

17.21 Biedermeier] European furniture style associated with the period 1815–48.

19.32 *Odontoglossum grande*] Synonym for *Rossioglossum grande*, the Latin name for the Central American tiger orchid.

23.6 Sargent] American painter John Singer Sargent (1856–1925).

24.12 Bernhardt] French actress Sarah Bernhardt (1844–1923).

33.1 Cookie Lavagetto] Harry Arthur "Cookie" Lavagetto (1912–1990), third baseman, manager, and coach, playing for the Brooklyn Dodgers at the time.

33.17 Eugene Speicher] American realist painter (1883–1962).

34.30 *Gulliver*] *Gulliver's Travels* (1726) by Jonathan Swift.

38.2 Ethelbert Nevin] American pianist and composer (1862–1901).

38.4 *Finlandia*] Orchestral and choral work (1899) by Jean Sibelius (1865–1957).

38.4–5 *Toccata and Fugue*] *Toccata and Fugue in D Minor* (1833), organ work commonly attributed to Johann Sebastian Bach (1685–1750).

48.37 Mickey Rooney] Movie actor and entertainer (1920–2014).

54.9 *Lachrymae Christi*] Latin for "Tears of Christ"; Neapolitan wine produced on the slopes of Mount Vesuvius.

54.23–24 Noël Coward wrote an unforgettable line] See *Private Lives* (1930), Act I: "Strange how potent cheap music is."

54.32–33 Bach . . . a Benny Goodman record] *Bach Goes to Town: A Fugue in Swing Tempo*, composed by Alec Templeton, was released by Benny Goodman and His Orchestra in 1938.

56.26–31 So I smile . . . Tamara] From "Smoke Gets in Your Eyes" (1933), song by Jerome Kern and Otto Harbach from the musical *Roberta*; in the Broadway production it was sung by Tamara Drasin.

57.10 Max Gordon] Broadway producer (1892–1978).

57.12 Alice Duer Miller] American writer and poet (1874–1942), best known for her verse novel *The White Cliffs* (1940).

58.3–5 Nature must blush . . . "This was a man!"] See *Julius Caesar*, V.v.74–75: "So mix'd in him that Nature might stand up / And say to all the world, 'This was a man!'"

58.32 Sir Walter and Sir James] Novelist and poet Walter Scott (1771–1832) and playwright James M. Barrie (1860–1937).

60.32 O Henry story] The short stories of O. Henry, born William Sydney Porter (1862–1910), were known for their reliance on coincidence and twist endings.

61.6–7 Charles Boyer and Margaret Sullavan] The costars of the tragic love story *Back Street* (1941).

61.38 *February, Which Alone*] From a variant of the traditional rhyme: "All the rest have thirty-one, / Save February which, alone, / Has twenty-eight and one day more / We add to it one year in four."

67.23 Jefferson Market] The Jefferson Market Courthouse in Greenwich Village was built in 1876, and by the 1920s was used primarily for the trials of female criminal defendants. The Women's Detention Center was constructed adjacent to it in 1929. The courthouse closed in 1945.

74.14 Robert Ingersoll] American lawyer and defender of agnosticism (1833–1899).

74.22 Frank Merriwell] Character created by Gilbert Patten (1866–1945) under the pseudonym Burt L. Standish. Merriwell's adventures, which became the model for American juvenile sports fiction, were the basis for a popular radio serial in 1934 and a series of films starting in 1936.

106.9–10 Elwell and Dot King and Starr Faithfull] The reference is to a trio of cases covered intensely by the press. Joseph Bowne Elwell (1874–1920), an affluent bridge writer and tutor, was murdered on June 11, 1920, in his locked house; the case remains unsolved, and it inspired S. S. Van Dine's *The Benson Murder Case* (1926), which introduced detective Philo Vance. Dorothy "Dot" King, a showgirl, was murdered in 1923; while there was a prime suspect, the murder was never officially solved. The body of Starr Faithfull (1906–1931) washed up in Long Beach, New York; her life and death became the basis of John O'Hara's novel *BUtterfield 8* (1934) and other works of fiction.

109.15–16 Josiah Wedgwood] English potter (1730–1795) who founded the Wedgwood company.

149.19–20   Sylvia Sidney] Actress (1910–1999) who was noted for her roles in films involving urban crime and social issues, including *City Streets* (1931), *Street Scene* (1931), *Ladies of the Big House* (1931), and *Dead End* (1937).

155.13   Lizzie Borden] Borden (1860–1927) was tried and acquitted for the ax murders of her father and stepmother on August 4, 1892, in Fall River, Massachusetts.

165.8   Lucretia] According to legend, she was the wife of the Roman consul Collatinus and was raped by the son of the Etruscan king Lucius Tarquinius Superbus and subsequently committed suicide; reaction to her death precipitated the overthrow of the Roman monarchy.

173.29   Ebbetts Field] Stadium on Flatbush Avenue in Brooklyn where the Brooklyn Dodgers played; it opened in 1913 and was demolished in 1960.

175.20   Ruth Snyder] Snyder (1895–1928) was convicted, along with her lover Judd Gray, of murdering her husband Albert Snyder in Queens Village, New York, in 1927. Snyder and Gray were executed at Sing Sing.

183.16   'The Porches of Thy Father's Ear.'] See *Hamlet*, I.v.63–64: "And in the porches of my ears did pour / The leprous distilment."

THE HORIZONTAL MAN

187.3–6   *Let us honor . . . the horizontal one.*] The lines are dedicated to Christopher Isherwood in W. H. Auden's *Poems* (1930).

188.1   JONAH] Johanna De Witt, a friend of Eustis and author of the children's book *The Littlest Reindeer* (1946).

206.4–7   *Oh God . . . eternal home.*] Hymn (1719) by Isaac Watts.

207.19–20   *Once more the liberal year . . . gems or gold*] The lyrics of this hymn are taken from John Greenleaf Whittier's "Occasional Poems for an Autumn Festival" (1859).

216.35   *sometimes I . . . ni-i-ights*—] From "Stardust," composed by Hoagy Carmichael as an instrumental in 1927; lyrics added by Mitchell Parish in 1929.

237.36–37   *The Criminal, the Judge and the Public* by Alexander and Staub] The study by Franz Alexander and Hugo Staub appeared in German in 1929 and in English translation in 1931.

240.4–5   *The Round Earth's Corners*] See John Donne, *Holy Sonnets* 7, lines 1–4: "At the round earth's imagined corners, blow / Your trumpets, Angels, and arise, arise / From death, you numberless infinities / Of souls, and to your scattered bodies go . . ."

240.6   *Where No Man Pursueth*] See Proverbs 28:1: "The wicked flee when no man pursueth: but the righteous are bold as a lion."

240.10   "Where there is no vision the people perish,"] See Proverbs 29:18.

241.27   As to Pluto, Persephone, who ate pomegranate seed.] In Greek my-
thology, Persephone, daughter of Demeter and Zeus, was abducted by Hades;
as a consequence of having eaten six pomegranate seeds while in the underworld, she was obliged to remain there for six months of every year.

260.3–4   Lohengrin . . . swan] In Richard Wagner's opera *Lohengrin*
(1850), the hero arrives in a boat drawn by a swan to come to the defense of
Elsa of Brabant, who stands accused of murder.

261.16   Lincoln Steffens] American muckraking journalist (1866–1936), author of *The Shame of the Cities* (1904) and *The Autobiography of Lincoln Steffens* (1931).

261.37   Hercule Poirot] Belgian detective featured in a long series of novels
by Agatha Christie, beginning with *The Mysterious Affair at Styles* (1920).

262.1   Elsa Maxwell] Gossip columnist and hostess (1883–1963).

265.6   *Timor Mortis Conturbat Me*] Latin: The fear of death disturbs me.
The phrase, from the Roman Catholic office for the dead, appears in many
medieval works and is the refrain of William Dunbar's fifteenth-century poem
"Lament for the Makars," mourning the death of Dunbar's poetic contem-
poraries.

265.28–29   as dead as an old T. S. Eliot geranium] See Eliot's "Rhapsody on
a Windy Night": "Midnight shakes the memory / As a madman shakes a dead
geranium."

282.30   Kafka-esque] This appears to be one of the earliest literary usages of
this adjective.

285.36   Lombroso] Cesare Lombroso (1835–1909), an Italian criminologist
who attributed criminal behavior to hereditary causes.

294.28   Orphan Annie] The comic strip *Little Orphan Annie*, created by
Harold Gray (1894–1968), became the basis for a highly successful radio program, 1930–42.

310.15–16   sob sister] Journalist, primarily female, employed to write sentimental stories.

310.37   Caspar Milquetoast] Comic strip character created by H. T. Webster
(1885–1952) for his cartoon series *The Timid Soul*; the term "milquetoast" became a byword for "weak and ineffectual."

311.8   Frank Buck] Animal collector and motion picture actor and producer
(1884–1950), author of *Bring 'Em Back Alive* (1930) and *Wild Cargo* (1932).

313.20   *transition*] Literary journal, 1927–38, founded in Paris by Eugene
Jolas and his wife Maria McDonald. It published segments of James Joyce's
Finnegans Wake under the title *Work in Progress*.

313.32   New York edition of James] Henry James (1843–1916) prepared editions of his works, under the title *The Novels and Tales of Henry James*, which were published (1907–9) in twenty-four volumes by Harper & Brothers in New York and Methuen & Company in London. James revised the included works, sometimes heavily, and added prefaces in which he discussed them in detail.

314.3–4 Milly Theale . . . *The Sacred Fount*] Milly Theale, incurably ill heiress in Henry James's *The Wings of the Dove* (1902); *The Sacred Fount* (1901), James's novella in which an unnamed protagonist attempts to discern the secret lives of those around him through their outward behavior.

314.7–10 *Amazing grace . . . but now I see.*] First stanza of the hymn "Amazing Grace" (1779) by John Newton.

316.26–27 white rabbit in *Alice*] In Lewis Carroll's *Alice's Adventures in Wonderland* (1865).

316.35–36 "If it were done . . . done quickly."] See *Macbeth*, I.vii.1–2.

344.1 Venusberg] In German poetry, mythical mountain containing the court of Venus; the opening scene of Wagner's opera *Tannhäuser* (1845) takes place there.

344.2–3 "The whore that sitteth on the waters!"] See Revelation 17:1: "And there came one of the seven angels which had the seven vials, and talked with me, saying unto me, Come hither; I will shew unto thee the judgment of the great whore that sitteth upon many waters."

357.24 a passage in *Madame Bovary*] See Gustave Flaubert's *Madame Bovary* (1868), chapter 3: "The daylight that came in by the chimney made velvet of the soot at the back of the fireplace, and touched with blue the cold cinders. Between the window and the hearth Emma was sewing; she wore no fichu; he could see small drops of perspiration on her bare shoulders."

365.26 *Memento mori*] Latin: Remember that you will die.

367.4 *The Tropic of Cancer*] Henry Miller's *Tropic of Cancer*, published in Paris in 1934, was banned in the United States until 1961, when its publication by Grove Press led ultimately to a 1964 judgment by the U.S. Supreme Court that the novel was not obscene.

383.20 Prince Mishkin] Morally pure protagonist of Fyodor Dostoyevsky's *The Idiot* (1868–69).

384.17–18 Miss Beauchamp, Doris Fischer] Celebrated cases of multiple personality. "Christine Beauchamp" was the pseudonym of a woman studied by neurologist Morton Prince, as recounted in his book *The Dissociation of a Personality: A Biographical Study in Abnormal Psychology* (1906); "Doris Fischer" was studied by Walter Prince beginning in 1909, and the case was reported at length in the Proceedings of the Society for Psychical Research.

392.13   Botticelli countenance] Thin and finely featured like women painted by Sandro Botticelli (1445–1510).

IN A LONELY PLACE

394.3–6   "It's in a lonesome place . . . evening of the day."] See J. M. Synge's one-act play *In the Shadow of the Glen* (1903).

401.40–402.1   O'Keeffe and Rivera] Artists Georgia O'Keeffe (1887–1986) and Diego Rivera (1886–1957).

412.33–34   Kirby, Weinstock, and Pearson] Rollin Kirby (1875–1952), Pulitzer Prize–winning editorial cartoonist; Matt Weinstock (1903–1970), columnist for three Los Angeles daily newspapers, including the *Times*; Drew Pearson (1897–1969), author of the syndicated column "Washington Merry-Go-Round," who also had a program on NBC Radio called *Drew Pearson Comments*.

433.9   Junior G-Man] The 1936 radio program *Junior G-Men*, hosted by former FBI investigator Melvin Purvis (1903–1960), which led to the formation of "Junior G-Men" boys' clubs throughout the United States.

433.21–22   Chandler or Hammett or Gardner] Crime writers Raymond Chandler (1888–1959), Dashiell Hammett (1894–1961), Erle Stanley Gardner (1889–1970). Hughes's biography of Gardner, published in 1978, won an Edgar Award.

433.23–24   Queen and Carr] Crime writers Ellery Queen (joint pseudonym of Fredric Dannay, 1905–1982, and Manfred Bennington Lee, 1905–1971) and John Dickson Carr (1906–1977).

453.9   *To sleep, perchance to dream*] See *Hamlet*, III.i.64.

461.4   Jack the Ripper] British serial killer whose identity is still unknown; he murdered five women in London's East End in 1888.

499.31   Ciro's] West Hollywood nightclub on the Sunset Strip, 1940–57.

505.1   Simon's] Drive-in restaurant that opened in 1935 on Wilshire Boulevard and Fairfax Avenue, with other locations elsewhere in Los Angeles.

531.39–40   The Savoy . . . Romanoff's] The Savoy, nightclub in Inglewood, California; Romanoff's, Beverly Hills restaurant that operated from 1941 to 1962, located at 362 Rodeo Drive.

532.3   the Derby or Sheetz] The Brown Derby, restaurant on Hollywood and Vine, 1926–85; Albert Sheetz, restaurateur and candymaker, operated a number of establishments in the Los Angeles area from the 1920s to 1940s, among them Sheetz's Hollywood Restaurant on 5575 Santa Monica Boulevard.

549.34–35   *she didn't even, say she was leavin'*] From "Somebody Stole My Gal" (1918), song by Leo Wood.

THE BLANK WALL

587.16   V-mail] Short for Victory Mail, a system used during World War II by which letters to military personnel were written on standardized sheets, censored, and transported in microfilm form.

640.28   Stern's] Department store chain with flagship store on 42nd street, 1867–2001.

648.1–2   *Life With Father*] Play (1939) by Howard Lindsay and Russel Crouse, the longest-running play in Broadway history; it was filmed in 1947, directed by Michael Curtiz and starring William Powell and Irene Dunne.

654.14   'A policeman's lot is not a happy one,'] See the Sergeant's Song from W. S. Gilbert and Arthur Sullivan's *The Pirates of Penzance* (1879), Act Two: "When constabulary duty's to be done, to be done, / A policeman's lot is not a happy one."

657.27   red points] A reference to the wartime rationing system relying on red stamps for meat and dairy products.

687.22   'Oh, pilot, 'tis a fearful night,'] Title and first line of a poem (1842) by Thomas D'Arcy McGee: "Oh, pilot, 'tis a fearful night, / There's horror in the sky, / And o'er the wave-crests, sparkling white, / The troubled petrels cry!"

*This book is set in 10 point ITC Galliard Pro, a
face designed for digital composition by Matthew Carter
and based on the sixteenth-century face Granjon. The paper
is acid-free lightweight opaque and meets the requirements
for permanence of the American National Standards Institute.
The binding material is Brillianta, a woven rayon cloth made
by Van Heek–Scholco Textielfabrieken, Holland.
Composition by Dedicated Book Services. Printing and
binding by Edwards Brothers Malloy, Ann Arbor.
Designed by Bruce Campbell.*

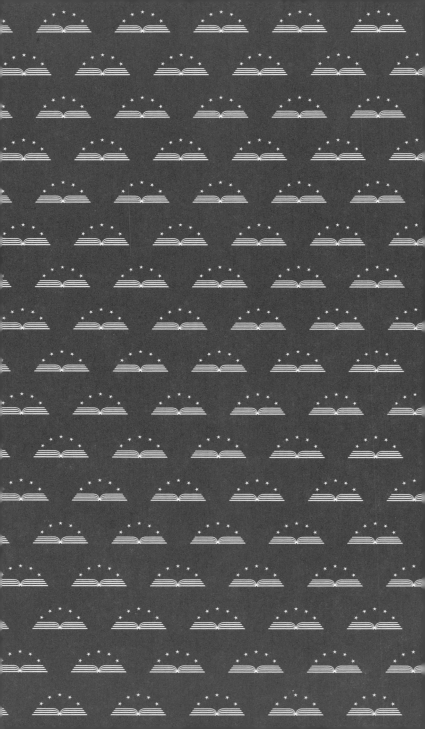